Endgame

WRITTEN BY COLIN GEE

The Seventh book in the 'Red Gambit' series.
20th August 1946 to 19th August 1947.

1

ISBN-10: 1539309290

ISBN-13: 978-1539309291

If I might take the opportunity to explain copyright in the simplest terms. It means that those of you who decide to violate my rights by posting this and others of my books on websites that permit downloading of copyrighted materials, are not only breaking the law, but also depriving me of money.

You may not see that as an issue, but I spend a lot of my limited funds to travel and research, just to make sure I get things as right as I can.

I ask you sincerely, please do not break the copyright, and permit me to profit properly from the labours I have undertaken.

Thank you.

Series Dedication

The Red Gambit series of books is dedicated to my grandfather, the boss-fellah, Jack 'Chalky' White, Chief Petty Officer [Engine Room] RN, my de facto father until his untimely death from cancer in 1983, and a man who, along with many millions of others, participated in the epic of history that we know as World War Two.

Their efforts and sacrifices made it possible for us to read of it, in freedom, today.

Thank you, for everything.

Foreword by author Colin Gee

If you have already read the first six books in this series, then what follows will serve as a small reminder of what went before.

If this is your first toe dipped in the waters of 'Red Gambit', then I can only advise you to read the previous books when you can.

In the interim, this is mainly for you.

After the end of the German War, the leaders of the Soviet Union found sufficient cause to distrust their former Allies, to the point of launching an assault on Western Europe. Those causes and the decision-making behind the full scale attack lie within 'Opening Moves', as do the battles of the first week, commencing on 6th August 1945.

After that initial week, the Soviets continued to grind away at the Western Allies, trading lives and materiel for ground, whilst reducing the combat efficiency of Allied units from the Baltic to the Alps.

In 'Breakthrough', the Red Army inflicts defeat after defeat upon their enemy, but at growing cost to themselves.

The attrition is awful.

Matters come to a head in 'Stalemate' as circumstances force Marshall Zhukov to focus attacks on specific zones. The resulting battles bring death and horror on an unprecedented scale, neither Army coming away unscathed or unscarred.

In the Pacific, the Soviet Union has courted the Empire of Japan, and has provided unusual support in its struggle against the Chinese. That support has faded and, despite small-scale Soviet intervention, the writing is on the wall.

'Impasse' brought a swing, perhaps imperceptible at first, with the initiative lost by the Red Army, but difficult to pick up for the Allies.

The Red Air Force is almost spent, and Allied air power starts to make its superiority felt across the spectrum of operations.

The war takes on a bestial nature, as both sides visit excesses on each other.

Allied planning deals a deadly blow to the Soviet Baltic forces, in the air, on the sea, and on the ground. However, their own ground assaults are met with stiff resistance, and peter out as General Winter spreads his frosty fingers across the continent, bringing with him the coldest weather in living memory.

'Sacrifice' sees the Allied nations embark on their recovery, assaults pushing back the weakening red Army, for whom supply has become the pivotal issue.

Its soldiers are undernourished, its tanks lack enough fuel, and its guns are often without shells.

Soviet air power is a matter of memory, and the Allies have mastery of the skies.

In 'Initiative', we see a resurgence in Allied military power, offset by a decline in the Soviet ability to wage war to its fullest extent, as supply issues and the general debilitation of their force comes into greater play.

None the less, the Red Army performs some real heroics and inflicts some heinous losses on the Allied soldiery.

The Japanese Army in China suffers defeat after defeat and ceases to function.

The US uses the atomic bomb on targets in Japan, and the Mikado announces Japan's surrender before the Empire has made its full contribution to Project Raduga.

However, Japanese military and scientific fanatics continue to support the project, and slowly the necessary assets are put in place.

Politically, the call to use the bombs on the USSR rises with the return home of more dead sons and husbands from the battlefields of Europe.

Stalin and his closest advisors still cling to the options offered by Project Raduga and its offshoots, but are presented with the unpalatable truth that the Red Army is on the verge of defeat in Europe.

The Soviet leadership agrees to use Sweden as a go-between to broker a peace deal, insisting that the Swedes present it all as their idea.

However, Allied intelligence learns that the Soviets initiated the talks, and use their strong position to get more of what they want.

On one battlefield, a rogue element within the Soviet military employs Tabun nerve agent, which nearly brings about a cataclysmic response from the Allies.

However, a Soviet apology draws both sides back to discussions and a ceasefire is agreed.

Initiative ends with a clandestine agreement between a resurgent Germany and a disillusioned Poland, an agreement that appears to threaten the progress towards a final peace settlement between the combatants.

5

In the six previous books, the reader has journeyed from June 1945, all the way to August 1946. The combat and intrigue has focussed in Europe, but men have also died in the Pacific, over and under the cold waters of the Atlantic, and on the shores of small islands in Greenland or the Atlantic-washed sands of the Kalahari Desert.

In Endgame, the series heads towards its conclusion, bringing together many of the main characters into focal points where their destiny, and the destiny of the world, is decided.

The task of doing that and bringing Red Gambit to a conclusion has proved too large for one book, so there will be one more to come.

As I did the research for this alternate history series, I often wondered why it was that we, west and east, did not come to blows once more.

We must all give thanks it did not all go badly wrong in that hot summer of 1945, and that the events described in the Red Gambit series did not come to pass.

My profound thanks to all those who have contributed in whatever way to this project, as every little piece of help brought me closer to my goal.

[For additional information, progress reports, orders of battle, discussion, freebies, and interaction with the author please find time to visit and register at one of the following-
www.redgambitseries.com, www.redgambitseries.co.uk, www.redgambitseries.eu
Also, feel free to join Facebook Group 'Red Gambit'.]
Thank you.

I have received a great deal of assistance in researching, translating, advice, and support during the years that this project has so far run.

In no particular order, I would like to record my thanks to all of the following for their contributions. Gary Wild, Jan Wild, Jason Litchfield, Peter Kellie, Jim Crail, Craig Dressman, Mario Wildenauer, Loren Weaver, Pat Walsh, Keith Lange, Philippe Vanhauwermeiren, Elena Schuster, Stilla Fendt, Luitpold Krieger, Mark Lambert, Simon Haines, Carl Jones, Greg Winton, Greg Percival, Robert Prideaux, Tyler Weaver, Giselle Janiszewski, Ella Murray, James Hanebury, Renata Loveridge, Jeffrey Durnford, Brian Proctor, Steve Bailey, Paul Dryden, Steve Riordan, Bruce Towers, Gary Banner, Victoria Coling, Alexandra Coling, Heather Coling, Isabel Pierce Ward, Hany Hamouda, Ahmed Al-Obeidi, Sharon Shmueli, Danute Bartkiene, and finally BW-UK Gaming Clan.

It is with sadness that I must record the passing of Luitpold Krieger, who succumbed to cancer after a hard fight.

One name is missing on the request of the party involved, who perversely has given me more help and guidance in this project than most, but whose desire to remain in the background on all things means I have to observe his wish not to name him.

None the less, to you, my oldest friend, thank you.

Wikipedia is a wonderful thing and I have used it as my first port of call for much of the research for the series. Use it and support it.

My thanks to the US Army Center of Military History and Franklin D Roosevelt Presidential Library websites for providing the out of copyright images.

Thanks also go to the owners of www.thesubmarinesailor.com, from which site I obtained some of my quotes.

I have also liberally accessed the site www.combinedfleet.com, from where much of my Japanese naval information is sourced.

All map work is original, save for the Château outline, which derives from a public domain handout.

Particular thanks go to Steen Ammentorp, who is responsible for the wonderful www.generals.dk site, which is a superb place to visit in search of details on generals of all nations. The site has proven invaluable in compiling many of the biographies dealing with the senior officers found in these books.

If I have missed anyone or any agency I apologise and promise to rectify the omission at the earliest opportunity.

Author's note.

The correlation between the Allied and Soviet forces is difficult to assess for a number of reasons.

Neither side could claim that their units were all at full strength, and information on the relevant strengths over the period this book is set in is limited as far as the Allies are concerned and relatively non-existent for the Soviet forces.

I have had to use some licence regarding force strengths and I hope that the critics will not be too harsh with me if I get things wrong in that regard. A Soviet Rifle Division could vary in strength from the size of two thousand men to be as high as nine thousand men, and in some special cases could be even more.

Indeed, the very names used do not help the reader to understand unless they are already knowledgeable.

A prime example is the Corps. For the British and US forces, a Corps was a collection of Divisions and Brigades directly subservient to an Army. A Soviet Corps, such as the 2nd Guards Tank Corps, bore no relation to a unit such as British XXX Corps. The 2nd G.T.C. was a Tank Division by another name and this difference in 'naming' continues to the Soviet Army, which was more akin to the Allied Corps.

The Army Group was mirrored by the Soviet Front.

Going down from the Corps, the differences continue, where a Russian rifle division should probably be more looked at as the equivalent of a US Infantry regiment or British Infantry Brigade, although this was not always the case. The decision to leave the correct nomenclature in place was made early on. In that, I felt that those who already possess knowledge would not become disillusioned, and that those who were new to the concept could acquire knowledge that would stand them in good stead when reading factual accounts of WW2.

There are also some difficulties encountered with ranks. Some readers may feel that a certain battle would have been left in the command of a more senior rank, and the reverse case where seniors seem to have few forces under their authority. Casualties will have played their part but, particularly in the Soviet Army, seniority and rank was a complicated affair, sometimes with Colonels in charge of Divisions larger than those commanded by a General. It is easier for me to attach a chart to give the reader a rough guide of how the ranks equate.

Also, please remember, that by now attrition has downsized units in all armies.

Fig # 1[rev] – Table of comparative ranks.

	SOVIET UNION	WAFFEN-SS	WEHRMACHT	
1	KA - SOLDIER	SCHUTZE	SCHUTZE	1
2	YEFREYTOR	STURMMANN	GEFREITER	2
3	MLADSHIY SERZHANT	ROTTENFUHRER	OBERGEFREITER	3
4	SERZHANT	UNTERSCHARFUHRER	UNTEROFFIZIER	4
5	STARSHIY SERZHANT	OBERSCHARFUHRER	FELDWEBEL	5
6	STARSHINA	STURMSCHARFUHRER	STABSFELDWEBEL	6
7	MLADSHIY LEYTENANT	UNTERSTURMFUHRER	LEUTNANT	7
8	LEYTENANT	OBERSTURMFUHRER	OBERLEUTNANT	8
9	STARSHIY LEYTENANT			9
10	KAPITAN	HAUPTSTURMFUHRER	HAUPTMANN	10
11	MAYOR	STURMBANNFUHRER	MAJOR	11
12	PODPOLKOVNIK	OBERSTURMBANNFUHRER	OBERSTLEUTNANT	12
13	POLKOVNIK	STANDARTENFUHRER	OBERST	13
14	GENERAL-MAYOR	BRIGADEFUHRER	GENERALMAJOR	14
15	GENERAL-LEYTENANT	GRUPPENFUHRER	GENERALLEUTNANT	15
16	GENERAL-POLKOVNIK	OBERGRUPPENFUHRER	GENERAL DER INFANTERIE*	16
17	GENERAL-ARMII	OBERSTGRUPPENFUHRER	GENERALOBERST	17
18	MARSHALL		GENERALFELDMARSCHALL	18
			*OR ARTILLERY, PANZERTRUPPEN ETC	

	UNITED STATES	UK/COMMONWEALTH	FRANCE	
1	PRIVATE	PRIVATE	SOLDAT DEUXIEME CLASSE	1
2	PRIVATE 1ST CLASS	LANCE-CORPORAL	CAPORAL	2
3	CORPORAL	CORPORAL	CAPORAL-CHEF	3
4	SERGEANT	SERGEANT	SERGENT-CHEF	4
5	SERGEANT 1ST CLASS	C.S.M.	ADJUDANT-CHEF	5
6	SERGEANT-MAJOR [WO-CWO]	R.S.M.	MAJOR	6
7	2ND LIEUTENANT	2ND LIEUTENANT	SOUS-LIEUTENANT	7
8	1ST LIEUTENANT	LIEUTENANT	LIEUTENANT	8
9				9
10	CAPTAIN	CAPTAIN	CAPITAINE	10
11	MAJOR	MAJOR	COMMANDANT 1	11
12	LIEUTENANT-COLONEL	LIEUTENANT-COLONEL	LIEUTENANT-COLONEL 2	12
13	COLONEL	COLONEL	COLONEL 3	13
14	BRIGADIER GENERAL	BRIGADIER	GENERAL DE BRIGADE	14
15	MAJOR GENERAL	MAJOR GENERAL	GENERAL DE DIVISION	15
16	LIEUTENANT GENERAL	LIEUTENANT GENERAL	GENERAL DE CORPS D'ARMEE	16
17	GENERAL	GENERAL	GENERAL DE ARMEE	17
18	GENERAL OF THE ARMY	FIELD-MARSHALL	MARECHAL DE FRANCE	18
	1 CAPITAINE de CORVETTE	2 CAPITAINE de FREGATE	3 CAPITAINE de VAISSEAU	

ROUGH GUIDE TO THE RANKS OF COMBATANT NATIONS.

Fig # 1a - List of Military map icons.

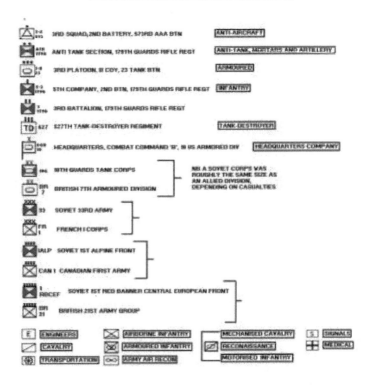

3RD SQUAD, 2ND BATTERY, 573RD AAA BTN — ANTI-AIRCRAFT

ANTI TANK SECTION, 179TH GUARDS RIFLE REGT — ANTI-TANK, MORTARS AND ARTILLERY

3RD PLATOON, B COY, 23 TANK BTN — ARMOURED

5TH COMPANY, 2ND BTN, 179TH GUARDS RIFLE REGT — INFANTRY

3RD BATTALION, 179TH GUARDS RIFLE REGT

527TH TANK-DESTROYER REGIMENT — TANK-DESTROYER

HEADQUARTERS, COMBAT COMMAND 'B', 9I US ARMORED DIV — HEADQUARTERS COMPANY

9TH GUARDS TANK CORPS

BRITISH 7TH ARMOURED DIVISION

NB: A SOVIET CORPS WAS ROUGHLY THE SAME SIZE AS AN ALLIED DIVISION, DEPENDING ON CASUALTIES

SOVIET 33RD ARMY

FRENCH I CORPS

SOVIET 1ST ALPINE FRONT

CANADIAN FIRST ARMY

SOVIET 1ST RED BANNER CENTRAL EUROPEAN FRONT

BRITISH 21ST ARMY GROUP

E ENGINEERS
CAVALRY
TRANSPORTATION

AIRBORNE INFANTRY
ARMOURED INFANTRY
ARMY AIR RECCE

MECHANISED CAVALRY
RECONNAISSANCE
MOTORISED INFANTRY

S SIGNALS
MEDICAL

Book Dedication

I do not know their names, or in what capacity they all serve, but I do know that they are there and are constantly vigilant.

I also know that if it were not for them, then all our lives would be affected more openly by world events and the actions of a few lunatics.

The war on terror continues without break, day in, day out, and sometimes we lose.

In honesty, I think we all know that some will get through; to be successful all the time is impossible.

Some home grown fanatic will not be spotted in time, or a group will manage to slip through the net, and outrages will be visited upon us, all in the name of something or other that has motivated some imbecile to take innocent lives.

However, I have no doubt at all that the efforts of those I cannot name have prevented many outrages and will continue to do so.

So, I take this opportunity to go on the record and address those who protect us from the evils of terrorism, fanaticism, and the brutality of the warped mind.

No matter what your agency or your contribution, I thank you all.

May I remind the reader that his book is written primarily in English, not American English. Therefore, please expect the unashamed use of 'U', such as in honour and armoured, unless I am using the American version to remain true to a character or situation.

By example, I will write the 11th Armoured Division and the 11th US Armored Division, as each is correct in national context.

Where using dialogue, the character uses the correct rank, such as Mayor, instead of Major for the Soviet dialogue, or Maior for the German dialogue.

Otherwise, in non-dialogue circumstances, all ranks and units will be in English.

List of chapters and sections.

15

23

Fig # 223 - List of important locations within Endgame.

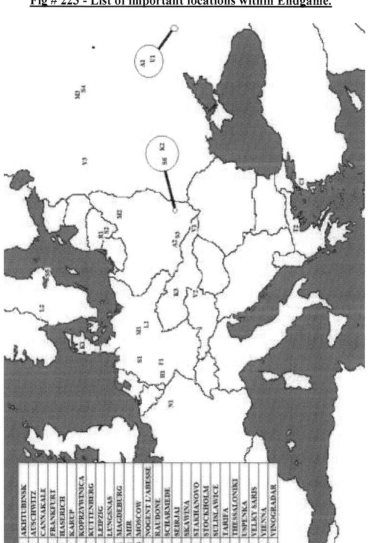

A1	ARCHT-UBINSK
A3	AUSCHWITZ
C1	CANNAKALE
F1	FRANKFURT
R1	HASERICH
K1	KARUP
K2	KOPRZYWNICA
K3	KUTTENBERG
L1	LEIPZIG
L2	LUNGSNAS
M1	MAGDEBURG
M2	MIR
M3	MOSCOW
N1	NOGENT L'ABESSE
R1	RAUDONE
S1	SCHARMEDE
S2	SEIRJAI
S3	SIGAWINA
S4	STAKHANOVO
S5	STOCKHOLM
S6	SULISLAWICE
T1	TARIFA
T2	THESSALONIKI
U1	USPENKA
V1	VELKY SARIS
V2	VIENNA
V3	VINOGRADAR

25

Never was anything great achieved without danger.

Niccolo Machiavelli

Chapter 172 - THE STRAIGHTS

1509 hrs, Monday, 19th August 1946, Chateau de Versailles, France.

Kenneth Strong, Chief of Military Intelligence to NATO, stood as his visitor was ushered in.

"General Gehlen. Good afternoon. Tea?"

The head of the Germany's Military Intelligence Section shook his head.

"I'm afraid not, General Strong. I've only a little time. This is an unofficial call, as I told your aide... I must not be missed."

In itself a curious statement, and one that piqued Strong's interest.

"Well, that's got my attention. I'm all ears, General."

No words came by way of explanation.

Instead, Gehlen extracted a set of pictures from a grey folder and set them out on the desk.

"What am I looking at, General?"

"The Soviet Union's May Day parade this year. I can only apologise, but I did not have sight of these pictures until yesterday, otherwise I would have brought them to you much earlier."

Strong was puzzled.

"But we had a briefing document through, with pictures your agents took on the day... didn't we?"

Gehlen sat back in his seat and shrugged.

"Yes, you did. These were not considered of sufficient quality to have been included in the original submission, neither did they appear to contain anything not covered elsewhere in the original briefing documents."

"But they obviously do, or you wouldn't be here, eh?"

"What do you see, General Strong?"

"Big bloody tanks... big bloody bombs... and some..."

"The bombs, Herr General."

Strong concentrated.

"Big blighters, like I said. I assume the technical people have run up some numbers?"

"I suspect not, as I regret that there were no pictures of these bombs in the original submission, Herr General. Otherwise, I would have been in your office many weeks ago."

Strong screwed his eyes up, trying to make a deeper appreciation of the grainy photographs.

"Allow me to show you another photograph set, Herr General."

Four more pictures were laid out, photos of excellent quality, precise and defined, showing a large bomb.

"Hmm... I'll warrant that these weren't taken in Moscow in May."

"You are correct, Herr General. They were taken at the Karup air base in Denmark on 12th December."

Gehlen left it all hanging in the air and waited for Strong to put it all together.

"They look the same... admittedly these Moscow ones are a trifle fuzzy, but I think... and clearly you think... they're the same, or at least born of the same bitch."

The German intelligence officer could only nod.

NATO's Intelligence Chief had a bell ringing in the back of his brain.

"Karup?"

He had been thinking more of the photos than of Gehlen's words, but the name suddenly shouted loudly enough to be heard, despite his concentration.

Strong searched his mind and found the answer in a second.

"Bloody hell! Karup!"

"You understand the problem, Herr General."

"Karup. Where the special unit is based."

"Yes."

"But the special unit has only recently formed there..."

"Yes... but..."

"But the advance units have been there for ages."

"Yes, Herr General. The base was adapted in anticipation last year."

Strong returned to the two sets of photos.

He knew no weapon had been deployed to Europe as yet... and wondered if the intelligence officer opposite him knew too.

Examining the Red Square photos again, the British officer posed the only question that really mattered.

"So what the merry hell are these?"

"The Karup unit started using weapons called Pumpkin bombs, which have the same size and ballistic characteristics... so I am told."

Which roughly meant, German Intelligence has someone within the unit who supplied that very information.

"A B-29 bomber went missing in December last year... the 13th to be precise. Nothing overly remarkable, save the regrettable loss of life involved. It was on a Pumpkin test-bombing mission in the southern Baltic. I think we now know where it went."

"It came down in Russia?"

"It most certainly would seem so, Herr General, for I suspect these items paraded in Moscow are copies of the exact same Pumpkin bomb shown in the photos from Karup."

The two locked eyes and the possibilities flowed silently back and forth.

Strong gave voice to their fears.

"Copies..."

Gehlen played his silent game, allowing Strong to finish his own bombshell thought.

"Or are they something more?"

Gehlen stood.

"That, General Strong, is something our agencies need to find out very, very quickly."

0101 hrs, Tuesday, 20th August 1946, two kilometres northwest of Ksar es Seghir, Morocco.

"Hai."

The distant voice half-whispered a response in a strained tone, such was the tension throughout the submarine.

Adding an extra knot of speed gave Commander Nanbu Nobukiyo more opportunity to control his passage, the strong current having dragged the huge submarine a little closer to the Moroccan shore than intended.

"Up periscope."

The gentle hiss caused by the extending tube was the loudest sound in the submarine, and drew more than one tense crewman's attention.

Nobukiyo aimed the periscope at the lights of the Spanish town of Tarifa.

He found the flashing navigation light that marked the promontory.

"Jinyo... bearing one...mark."

28

First officer Jinyo made a note of the bearing and checked the ship's clock.

The periscope swivelled nearly ninety degrees towards the Moroccan village of Eddalya, a normally sleepy place that tonight was decidedly wide-awake.

The illuminations were courtesy of two men who were handsomely paid to light a beacon of celebration on the seashore, ostensibly to hail the formation of the Moroccan Democratic Party for Independence but, in actuality, to provide a navigational point of reference for the passage of some vessels of interest to the Soviet Union.

I-401, Nobukiyo's craft, was second in line, the procession of four vessels led by I-1, with I-14 bring up the tail, sandwiching the two huge Sen-Tokus.

Nobukiyo easily found the fiery beacon.

"Bearing two... mark."

Jinyo moved to the navigation table and handed the two bearings and times to the navigation officer.

Within seconds, the map showed two intersecting pencil lines, marking I-401's present position.

"As it should be, Commander."

"Time to turn?"

Jinyo checked the navigator's work.

"Three minutes, Commander."

"Up periscope."

After ninety seconds, Nobukiyo repeated the process of getting bearings.

He took another quick sweep round and saw nothing that troubled him.

"Down periscope."

"We've drifted south, commander."

"Increase speed by two knots...recalculate."

The two senior officers exchanged looks as the navigator worked confidently with his map and slide rule.

"Jinyo... depth is approximately three hundred and sixty metres here, yes?"

"Yes, Commander."

The navigator interrupted.

"Fifty seconds to turn, Commander."

Nobukiyo grunted by way of reply.

The clock slowly made its way to the appropriate point.

"Lieutenant Dosan. New heading?"

The navigator never looked up from his table.

"Zero-eight-eight, Commander."

"Come to starboard. Steer course zero-eight-eight. Make our depth one hundred and thirty metres."

The orders were repeated, and the huge submarine turned and dropped further into the waters where the Atlantic and Mediterranean mixed.

Nobukiyo thought about the other submarines breaking through the straight at the same time, and of yet others ships, vital to the plan, many miles behind them.

Still out in the Atlantic were the support ships I-353 and the Bogata Maru, the latter now returned to the original German look as the German freighter 'Bogata', although Japanese crew managed her, and the submarine tender modifications were retained.

Bogata had been anchored on the protected east side of the island of Deserta Grande, one of the Madeira Islands.

Beneath her keel, I-353 lay on the bottom by day, surfacing by night, waiting until other arrangements could be brought to fruition.

A boring but vital duty, broken by excursions to a small hidden base ashore for those not required to act as a skeleton crew to dive and resurface the boat.

Close behind them were the Nachi Maru and Tsukushi Maru, two submarine tenders under Allied orders, and laden with returning prisoners of war and modest wares for trade, were ready to do their part when needed.

The Hikawa Maru 2, a hospital ship, also carried Allied servicemen being repatriated, as well as other things more crucial to Operation Niji.

Nobukiyo snatched himself from his musings and put his mind firmly back on the mission in hand.

Commander Nobukiyo took up his seat and closed his eyes, displaying no nerves about the venture they were now engaged in.

After all, many German U-Boats had successfully done the same journey into the Mediterranean, and in times when the Allies were much more aware.

Now that peace, such as it was, ruled the world, the passage would be that much easier.

Nobukiyo certainly hoped so, for the Black Sea was still a very long way away, even with the Turks turning a convenient blind eye.

Perhaps, by the time it came for them to exit the Mediterranean and seek the freedom of the Atlantic once more, things might be different, but they would climb that mountain when it was there in front of them.

Until then, there was one small fact that constantly niggled away in the back of his mind, a fact he did not care to share with any of his crew.

It announced itself once more, and he felt a chill run down his spine.

As he conned his submarine into the blue waters of the Mediterranean Sea, his mind battled to put the fact back where it belonged.

He failed, and his processes suddenly all locked on to the one inescapable fact.

Once in the Mediterranean, no U-Boat had ever made it out.

However, that had been in time of war, whereas an uneasy peace had descended across Europe.

In Gibraltar, the peace was taken very much to heart, as the war had rarely visited itself upon them.

The arrival of two Japanese ships full of POWs and the sick caused a modest ripple across the Rock, but nothing more than that.

The patrols between Europe and Africa were still conducted, but everyone from admiral to the meanest civilian knew that the enemy had no navy to speak of and there were no conceivable threats against which they had to guard.

Which attitude greatly helped the 'inconceivable threats' slip quietly through into the waters of the Mediterranean, on their way to a secret place on the shores of the Black Sea.

0737 hrs, Friday 23rd August 1946, House of Madame Fleriot, La Vigie, Nogent L'Abbesse, near Reims, France.

"Meant to show this to you the other day, darling. Slipped my mind."

She sat up in bed, allowing the covers to spill from her magnificent breasts.

"What am I looking at exactly?"

"A message for me that came from my godmother in the Mosel. Willi Bittrich gave it to me."

"So what does it mean, Chérie?"

"Well, I can progress some of the way towards answering that, my darling. It's from my cousin David... we used to write messages to each other all the time. All we did was simply reverse everything."

31

"But it was sent to your godmother."

"Schildkröte... it was my name for him... means turtle. I assume he simply sent it to somewhere that he knew would get it to me."

Anne-Marie looked again and recited the message back to front.

"235U92-92KR36/141BA56-USPENKA"

"Exactly right, darling."

"So what does it mean?"

"Your guess is as good as mine to be honest."

She rose from the bed and stretched her lithe body, the slightest hints of their lovemaking vaguely apparently until she swathed herself in the silk robe.

"The thing is... David died during the last war... I mean that I was told he died in 1942. Nothing more than that."

"And yet it seems he didn't, Chérie?"

"No. I'll ask around and see what I can discover. Until then that jumble of letters and numbers will remain a mystery. All except Uspenka, of course."

"Why 'of course'? What is it?"

"It's a place in Russia, not far from Kremenchug. I fought around there back in the old days of '43."

She lit a cigarette and tossed Knocke the pack, followed by the lighter.

"So, why would a dead cousin send you a note now about a place you fought over in in 1943?"

The smoke caught Knocke's throat and his reply was cut off in a bout of coughing.

"A mystery worthy of Maigret or Sherlock Holmes, Chérie."

She rose and moved towards the slipper bath, intent on making herself presentable before breakfast and her fiancée journeyed back to the Corps later that day.

Knocke sprang from the bed and swept her up in a bout of laughter and female giggling that ended in yet another consummation of their engagement, this time on the impeccable rosewood chaise-longues.

Madame Fleriot was late out of bed that morning, as were the girls, so, unusually, Ernst and Anne-Marie found themselves breakfasting alone, all save for Jerome, who fussed over the happy couple as always.

He topped off their coffees and removed himself to prepare more food for those who were clearly stirring in the rooms above.

The note sat on the table in front of the Deux agent, her natural curiosity and stubbornness driving her to extract more information from the text.

Frau Hallmann,
Hauptstrasse,
Haserich,
Mosel,
Germany.
AKNEPSU-65AB141/63RK29-29U532
Für-EAK
Schildkröte.

"The message is for you... not for your godmother... why for you?"

"Something I alone could understand?"

"Clearly yes... in as much as you understood it's reversed text... and his childhood nickname... but you don't understand it."

Knocke shrugged and selected a generous slice of cheese.

Anne-Marie declined the offer of a piece for herself and carried on analysing the problem.

"So, it's for you... because you understood the code... such as it was... and signed so that you alone would know who it came from... that's important... he needed not to be identified by anyone else. And yet he was, in your words, a simple shopkeeper... although you think perhaps he was more... maybe this is proof that he certainly was?"

Knocke waved his knife to emphasise his words.

"Yes, indeed, Cherie. That much seems obvious. But what is the point on sending me something... specifically to me... if I actually can't read what he's written?"

Her reproaching look made Knocke realise that he was waving a knife at a woman who had a certain set of deadly skills, and who didn't appreciate such gestures, even from the man who would be her husband.

"Pardon, darling. Just getting carried away."

By way of forgiveness, she fluttered her eyelashes in a very un-de Valois like way, bringing a giggle for Knocke.

33

"Well, Cherie… that's also obvious, isn't it?"

The sound of running feet across the landing warned them that the girls were descending on the bedroom of Madame Fleriot, which meant that their discussion would soon be cut short.

Jerome bustled in with more plates of cheese, meat, and bread and the two waited until he was gone again.

"I think that he sent it to you so you could give it to someone else. Someone connected with you. Someone military?"

"Who I know, rather than me? Use my military connections... I can see that clearly. Right, then we both know who to show it to. I'll stop off at his office on the way to Camerone, eh?"

She nodded as the door burst open as Greta and Magda escorted Armande Fleriot to the breakfast table, ending their discussions.

1104 hrs, Monday, 26th August 1946, French Military Headquarters in Bavaria, Altes Schloss Eremitage, Bayreuth, Germany.

"Welcome, Ernst, welcome."

De Walle and Knocke embraced as De Walle was accustomed to, and Knocke was gradually becoming less embarrassed about.

"How's Anne-Marie?"

"Well, thank you. Apparently finishing up ordering the wedding dress before she returns."

"Again, thank you for the honour you do me, Ernst."

"Anne-Marie had no one else in mind, Georges… and thank you for agreeing to participate anyway."

"My pleasure. Anyway, down to business. You know you will be moving forward again soon?"

"I never doubted it, once they'd sorted out the demarcation lines between us and the German Republican forces. Seems to be as difficult to get agreement as it is with the Russians up in Sweden."

De Walle grinned, not totally in humour.

"There's an element of truth in that it seems. My sources tell me that there are often some strange sticking points. None the less, we're all going in the right direction. So, what can I do for you?"

Knocke pulled out his wallet and sought the coded message.

"And there was me thinking you were going to offer me a bribe."

They shared a laugh, Knocke rising to get a drink as De Walle read the message.

"Now... you have my full attention, Ernst. What am I holding?"

"That message was sent to me, via my godmother. It was sent by a dead man, my cousin, so it would appear he isn't dead after all."

"So what does it mean, and why do you show it to me?"

"That is the question. I know part of what it means, but not all. I'm showing it to you so that you can use your contacts to see what you can find out about its message. Reverse it... a simple childhood code. The name Uspenka stands out. I fought there in the war. Nasty place. But what the numbers and letters mean, I haven't got an idea... which is where you come in, Georges."

De Walle produced a pen and made a precise copy of the note before returning it to Knocke and accepting his coffee.

"What's your cousin's name? Maybe I can find out about him too?"

"Steyn, David Steyn. He was... or even still maybe is... a shopkeeper in Königsberg. Actually, the most intelligent shopkeeper you ever might meet. Ex-Kriegsmarine engineer submariner from 1918. I always felt that there was something else in his life... something government... official and decidedly secret...but I never asked... didn't want to put him in a position."

"Quite understand, Ernst... Kriegsmarine engineer... hmm... worth checking that angle too..."

De Walle made a few more notes and tucked the paper in his tunic pocket.

"I'll see what I can find out, Ernst. Now... how's the nerves?"

Knocke scoffed in such a way as to confirm his increasing unease with the approaching wedding day announcement.

"None at all and neither should there be!"

"And neither should there be, as you say. Many a man would jump at the chance to wed such an intelligent and loyal beauty."

"The pistol under the pillow takes a bit of getting used to though."

"All joking to one side, Ernst, she is one of my best."

35

That De Walle said 'is' rather than 'was' still hurt, as Knocke had tried so hard to get Anne-Marie to retire and put together a family home.

De Walle understood.

"She's a free spirit, Ernst… one that has attached herself to you… but you can never cage her… you do know that?"

Knocke shrugged and moved to get the coffee pot.

"Yes, I know. One of her many charms, Georges."

They clinked mugs in a silent toast to Anne-Marie de Valois, soon to be Knocke.

Even peace may be purchased at too high a price.

Benjamin Franklin

Chapter 173 - THE PEACETIME

August 1946

The World descended into peace and there was a period of wondrous nothingness, almost as if the armies and civilians collectively exhaled in relief and decided to take a moment's rest before starting on the path that would return the planet to something approaching normality... or whatever normal would be after two huge conflicts over eight bloody and horrible years.

The mechanics of the Soviet withdrawal were decided upon, and the two combatant sides liaised at national and local level, in an effort to ensure that there was no incident that could bring the two sides back to aggression and death.

This often meant that combat officers who had pitted their wits against each other found themselves sharing cigarettes and coffee whilst poring over maps, working together to ensure that no more of their young men would die.

Occasionally there were problems, as happened in the area of the Legion Corps D'Assaut, where not-so-old memories made liaisons more difficult.

There were also the other sort of problems, those decidedly inevitable errors of judgement that touched lives on both sides.

On Saturday 24th August, a Soviet-manned Curtiss O-52 Owl made the mistake of straying over the Allied lines and was chopped from the sky by DRL FW-190s.

Two days later, an Estonian fishing vessel broke the exclusion zone off the north coast of Poland, bringing interception by the patrolling Żuraw, a Polish minesweeper. The crew were imprisoned and subsequently revealed to be Soviet naval personnel.

The most serious incident of the month occurred over the approaches to Berlin, when two Arado-234 jet reconnaissance aircraft were bounced and knocked from the sky by Soviet-manned ME-262s from 2nd Guards Special Red Banner Order of Suvorov Fighter Aviation Regiment, one of which was piloted by Djorov's 2IC, Oligrevin.

Aggressive aerial patrolling followed, and a LaGG-5 was shot down for threatening a repeat of the German's recon operation, which was undertaking the agreed monitoring of Soviet withdrawals around Bad Lauterberg.

Night drew the posturing and dying to a close and, although both sides flew night fighters in large numbers over the area, no further encounters of note occurred and by morning the situation had returned to an uneasy calm.

The most significant events of August 1946 went completely unnoticed by the Allies, or at least, one was noticed but not comprehended and one was noticed only by those who had been bribed not to notice.

2003 hrs, Tuesday, 27th August 1946, Thessaloniki, Greece.

The two vessels from another ocean, the Tsukushi Maru and Nachi Maru, dropped anchor as directed by the pilot, a devoted clandestine member of the Greek Communist Party, the KKE, who was privy to the needs of the operation, as far as he needed to be of course.

Lights burned brightly as their small cargoes of rubber and other exotic far-eastern goods started the final stage of their journey into the warehouses ashore.

The British naval officer supervising the arrival and unloading had already been briefed on the nature of the two vessels, and quickly checked to ensure that all the paperwork was in order before returning to the pilot's craft for the short trip back to his billet and the waiting local beauty who had finally succumbed to his advances and then some, her eager sexual compliance done at the suggestion of her KKE uncle, in order to make him less inclined to nose too deeply.

Part of the logistical planning of Raduga required avoiding putting all the eggs in one basket so, when the unloading lights disappeared with the last stevedores and night fully embraced the anchorage, four small boats put out to shore, carrying silent figures with the papers of Chinese government officials with official business ahead in Bulgaria.

Which was true, except for a few minor details... in that not one was Chinese, neither was any of them government officials in the truest sense of the word, and that their only business with Bulgaria was to get through it as quickly as was humanly possible.

The ex-military members of the group had taken steps to appear less military, mainly by growing hair or going unshaven.

In the main, they were educated and highly qualified men from Unit 8604, formerly the Epidemic Prevention and Water

38

Purification Department of the Japanese Southern China Area Army, the cover title for the unit's real and deadly purpose; that of biological warfare research.

The scientists that accompanied them more often than not had no military bearing whatsoever and solely shared the group's fanatical concept of service to the Emperor, which fanaticism drove the eighty-seven men to continue with their part in Project Raduga.

At 0300 precisely, other members of the KKE created the noisy and spectacular diversion in Kalachori that drew Greek and British eyes away from the anchorage and allowed two small vessels to pick up their human and paper cargo, and land them unobserved.

By the time that the fire had been bought under control and the 'revellers' rounded up for questioning, the 'Chinese' were safely secreted within an NKVD safe house on Agias Sofias, ready to move on to their destination, when the circumstances allowed.

1951 hrs, Saturday, 31st August 1946, Çanakkale Naval Fortified Command Building, Çanakkale, Turkey.

Turkish Naval ranks

Koramiral - Vice-Admiral
Deniz Albayı - Captain
Deniz Yarbayı - Commander
Deniz Yüzbaşısı - Lieutenant
Deniz Üsteğmeni - Lieutenant j.g.

Vice-Admiral Cevdet Tezeren replaced the receiver with barely concealed satisfaction, the report from his trusted aide confirming that everything was in place for the 'arrangement' to work.

He had placed himself in the CNFC building for one reason only, and that was the man who commanded the team that constantly watched the comings and goings of traffic on and under the important strip of water known locally as the Çanakkale Boğazi, or as it was more widely known, the Dardanelles.

Other fortified command officers had understood the high-powered documentation bearing his signature, but he expected issues with the CNFC duty officer, Captain Aydan Mimaroğlu, who had a reputation as an independent thinker, which was decidedly not what Tezeren needed that night.

The admiral composed himself and started the short walk from the office of the CNFC commander, which officer had found himself unexpectedly called to Ankara for a conference on the Çanakkale Boğazi's security measures.

He nodded to the two expressionless men who were his personal aides, or as most people understood, his enforcers.

The three set off in step, heading towards the command facility.

The smartly turned out guards challenged the party and were quickly satisfied with Tezeren's credentials, allowing him entry.

He waved Mimaroğlu back into his seat with a friendly dismissive gesture, but employed the man's formal rank when he spoke.

"Well, Deniz Albayi Mimaroğlu, anything from our special guests yet?"

"No, Koramiral. Not a twitch as yet… and as you say, other stations will not be reporting the transit."

Tezeren detected the questioning tone… almost defiant…

He immediately congratulated himself for his decision to locate at Çannakale.

A hand was raised at one post towards the front of the large room, attracting one of Mimaroğlu's staff to move quickly to the station and take both verbal and written reports.

The junior grade lieutenant moved forward to the officer overseeing the plotting board that was scrupulously maintained to show the location of each and every vessel in the waters under the watchful eyes of CNFC, as well as those other commands along the whole length of the Dardanelles.

The report changed hands as the young officer passed the information on verbally to both the commander and the plotting officer.

Commander Nadir took the written message in hand and watched as the plotter recorded a new contact entering the western approaches of the seaway.

When the plotter had finished, he turned to ensure Mimaroğlu had noted the arrival, and received a nod by way of confirmation.

He handed the written report up to the waiting hand.

The Admiral loaded his çibuk with his special concoction of Yenice and Burley tobaccos and sucked lightly on the stem to draw the flame into the pipe's cup.

Satisfied, he puffed away, doing his absolute best to appear nonchalant and unworried about what started to develop on the CNFC situation map.

He and Mimaroğlu watched silently as more markers appeared, bringing a total of four detections to the plot.

"Koramiral? Four transitions in total?"

"Yes, Albayi Mimaroğlu. Four. Please contact your shore batteries and lighting units to confirm the orders."

"Sir... four... what is Command's purpose in allowi..."

"Now, Mimaroğlu, now. The General Staff will not accept any errors from either of us, so be quick about it."

The Captain could not escape the feeling that he was being railroaded into something, but his inkling could not overcome direct orders, so he summoned a waiting lieutenant.

"Yüzbaşısı Reis, contact all gun and searchlight batteries, patrol vessels, and torpedo stations... confirm order 592, issued at 1700 today. Require positive confirmation of receipt and understanding."

Senior Lieutenant Reis moved quickly having already heard the order, as his waiting position well within earshot of the two senior men.

"What is that?"

Tezeren extended his pipe stem towards the errant plot.

"What the hell's that?"

Mimaroğlu was already checking the information in front of him, paperwork that recorded the vessels expected to traverse his area of responsibility for forty-eight hours to come.

Whatever it was did not appear on his sheet.

"Reis! Contact that vessel immediately! Find out who the idiot is and tell him... no... order him to heave to...I want him on the shore track by Eceabat as soon as possible."

"Sir!"

"So, Albayi?"

"Koramiral, there is no record of anything traversing east to west until tomorrow morning at approximately 0800 hrs, when the Gayret is due to make passage through our area on her way from Gölcük to Izmir."

"So who is it?"

Reis stepped forward.

"Sir, there is no response from the vessel in question."

"Try every radio channel known to Allah! They must be listening, even if they're struck dumb..."

Mimaroğlu suddenly felt something wash over his brain, a something that could mean disaster for him and his men.

There was no time for niceties.

41

"Someone... anyone... find the original notification from Fleet Headquarters about the passage of the Gayret... find it now!"

It was the 'struck dumb' thought that had prompted the memory, of a routine order amongst many routine orders that spoke of the Gayret's passage under strict radio and radar blackout.

It took less than a minute for the full original order to be located, and less than thirty seconds for the error to be revealed.

'0800...2000...'

'Oruspu! 8am... 8pm... which fucking idiot...'

Setting aside that someone would pay for the simple and stupid error, Mimaroğlu acted immediately.

"Yüzbaşısı Reis, contact all searchlight batteries... have them standby to illuminate the channel on my command!"

"What the fuck do you think you're doing, Albayi?"

"Sir, the vessel is the Gayret and it's under strict radio and radar shutdown, conducting a night navigation exercise through the strai..."

"Then order her to heave to. You have the authority!"

"It won't respond to us even if it's listening, Sir. Our friends are sailing in a narrow waterway, straight at a large vessel coming the other way... neither group will be using lights... neither group is using navigational radar. It's a recipe for disaster and I'm going to avoid it by acting right now."

"What are you proposing, man?"

"I'm going to light the whole place up so they can't fail to see each other."

"But secrecy is key to..."

"With the greatest of respect, Koramiral, if they collide your secrecy is shot and we'll all have blood on our hands, not to say a diplomatic incident with our neighbours!"

Tezeren turned to examine the plot.

The Turkish Navy's Gayret, once called the Oribi, an 'O' class destroyer of His Majesty's Royal Navy, was already executing the port turn that would bring her down towards Çannakale.

The four other vessels were four kilometres from Kilitbahir.

"Yarbayi Nadir, to me!"

Commander Nadir sprang forward quickly.

Mimaroğlu explained the situation and his plan.

"Understood, Sir."

"Excellent."

The Captain took a last look at the plot and made his decision.

"Albayi Mimaroğlu, I must protes..."

He cut the Admiral's remonstration short.

"Now. Get the searchlight batteries illuminated immediately. Priority is to pick out the vessels and keep them in their beams. We must give each vessel plenty of opportunity to see the other. Order the shore batteries to stand by to put a shot across the bows of any vessel that appears to be a danger... emphasis considerably across the bows... two hundred metres at least... we don't want any accidents."

Mimaroğlu had once been a submariner, so wanted distance to avoid any issues with shockwaves and torpedo tube doors.

"I'll take a small signal party aloft and issue any further orders via the command line."

Tezeren went to protest again but action overtook him.

Beckoning three men to him, the captain was already heading to the stairwell and the open-air command position on the roof of the CNFC building.

The cool breeze that greeted the men as they sprang up three stairs at a time paled into insignificance as night became day.

The searchlight batteries arraigned along the banks of the Dardanelles illuminated and sought out the vessels that were bearing down on each other.

Both Tezeren and Mimaroğlu sought out the group of submarines first.

"Oruspu! What in the name of..."

Mimaroğlu drew in every detail of the partially submerged vessels that were moving across his field of vision, left to right in line astern.

His binoculars picked out the Bulgarian flag on the lead vessel, a large submarine of a type unfamiliar to him.

His submariner's brain examined the revealed features as his inquisitive brain screamed to look back at the second one again.

He controlled himself before moving slightly to the left and taking in the immense shape that was second in line.

"Oruspu! What in the name of... what is that?"

Tezeren slipped in beside the incredulous man.

"Now you understand why the need for secrecy was paramount, Mimaroğlu. The Gayret is manoeuvring to come in closer

43

to land, and the lead Bulgarian seems to have moved over. Kill the lights immediately!"

The Captain remained silent as he took in the incredible proportions of the huge Bulgarian submarine.

His professional eye recorded detail after detail, some familiar, some merely posing questions to which he had no response.

"I must make sure they have both heeded the other, Koramiral… it's huge, Koramiral. Never seen its like."

Tezeren went with the pre-arranged explanation.

"They're experimental submarines from the Rijeka shipyards, built by the Yugos for their Bulgarian friends. Present circumstances have forced them to make passage to the Black Sea. Our government has exacted a heavy price for our compliance and tolerance of their passage. Now kill the lights, Mimaroğlu!"

The Captain judged that there was now no risk, and he grabbed the telephone and issued the order.

Within seconds the searchlights started going out, which created an artificial darkness as their eyes attempted to readjust to the normal night light.

Tezeren stuck the dead pipe back in his mouth and lit it up again, weighing up his options and deciding that the agreed plan would be sufficient for his needs.

"A secret passage would have been better, but we have prevented disaster, so our political masters will understand, I'm sure."

He slapped the younger man on the shoulder.

"You did very well, Aydan, very well. I'll ensure that your part is known. But now we must ensure that any wagging tongues are encouraged to silence."

Inside, Tezeren was seething, both with Mimaroğlu and with whichever goat-shagging clown had fucked up with the time on the messages, carefully ignoring the fact that he should probably have been aware of the Gayret's secret schedule himself.

Aydan Mimaroğlu took a final look at the submarines making passage before returning to the command centre to issue the orders his Admiral required.

Koramiral Tezeren took his leave to rendezvous with a boat sent ashore by and containing the puzzled commander of the Gayret, intent on ensuring that no official report would be made of the evening's events.

The CNFC building returned to something approaching normal and Mimaroğlu accepted iced water and some oranges.

As he peeled the fruit, his eyes would not stray from the rough sketches he had made and the estimates he had pencilled in on the dimensions of the two huge submarines.

'Well over one hundred metres in length... well over... '

'Huge conning tower extended structure behind it... '

'Ramp... '

The image was actually remarkably accurate, but very few would have ever recognised it as an I-400 class Sen-Toku submarine of the Imperial Japanese Navy.

Submariners are a special brotherhood. Either all come to the surface or no one does. On a submarine, the phrase all for one and one for all is not just a slogan, but a reality.

Rudolf Golosov, Vice Admiral, Russian Navy.

Chapter 174 – ZA ENSHINBUNRIKI

September 1946

The Swedes maintained the Camp Vár facility at Lungsnäs so that both sides had a meeting place to bring concerns.

Permanent missions were established on the steadily expanding site, and often the different groups were seen to relax together when the business of representing their own national interests had been discharged.

As ever, the intelligence agencies increased their clandestine presence, each hoping to find some piece of information to give their side advantage in the ongoing negotiations.

In capital cities across the globe, some pieces of snatched conversations were refined into hard intelligence and presented to heads of state by intelligence chiefs, keen to give their country the edge.

On the frontlines, the business of relocation carried on, improved by a lowering of tension across the board, and a lack of any clashes or incidents of note.

1822 hrs, Sunday, 1st September 1946, Mimaroğlu's private residence, Dumlupinar Cd, Suluca, Turkey.

Adding some iced water to the fig raki, Mimaroğlu passed one glass to his friend before relaxing back into his rattan chair to enjoy the light sea breeze blowing up the Dardanelles from the Mediterranean.

Commander Mohammed Nadir cleared his mouth of cheese and olives.

"Very decent of the Koramiral."

They clinked glasses and savoured the exceptional quality raki, enjoying the unusual distinctive taste.

"Now that's special. Never had any before… very nice."

Mimaroğlu nodded as he added some cheese to the mix.

"I wish I knew what that was all about, Maymun."

46

The two had been friends for as long as they could remember, so the informality of Nadir's school nickname flowed easily from his commander's lips.

"Well, at least you saw the things. I've only got your words and that sketch to go on."

Feeling hot, Nadir pulled out his handkerchief and mopped the sudden rivulets of sweat from his brow.

"I will send it to old Öz. He'll have an idea about them."

Feeling hot suddenly, Mimaroğlu grabbed for the small towel and plunged his face into it.

His stomach contents flooded his mouth and spilled into the towel.

"Aydan? Aydan?"

Nadir leant across to put his hand on his friend's shoulder but never got there as he vomited across the small table.

He collapsed onto the tiled verandah, grabbing his stomach as he added more vomit to the growing puddle.

Mimaroğlu dropped onto his knees alongside him, groaning with pain.

By now, both were dry retching, there being no more stomach contents to bring up.

Struggling for breath, Nadir managed to speak.

"Bad cheese..."

He retched again and fell into a coughing fit that brought forth excruciating pain.

Mimaroğlu understood the situation with clarity, despite the pain and shortness of breath.

"Tezeren... that bastard... he's poisoned us..."

Both men wheezed as their respiration became more difficult.

Mimaroğlu, coughing and retching, strained and defecated in his robe.

In a small fishing boat roughly a kilometre from the shore, a pair of eyes examined the scene with satisfaction.

The owner lowered the binoculars and nodded to the man by his side, who jumped up on deck and instructed that the sail be set.

Ashore, two heavily built men saw the signal and moved towards Mimaroğlu's residence.

By the time they worked their way around to the rear, the two naval officers were both dead.

Following their instructions precisely, they removed the glasses and bottle, and replaced the latter with less tainted fare.

One disappeared inside the house and washed up the glasses, replacing them on the table and adding a good measure of the second bottle's contents.

The fig raki given to Mimaroğlu by a grateful Tezeren contained a lethal reduction of Oleander and was not to be left to be found by any investigators.

Walking away from the death scene, the senior man went to empty the bottle but realised that the road was becoming busy so retained it until the pair were some distance away.

Checking around him, the NKVD agent tossed the bottle over the edge of the hill towards the rocks below.

Twenty minutes later, Tezeren's staff car drove along.

On the outskirts of Lapseki, at the junction of Bursa Çannakale Yolu and Gulpempe Sk, he noted the yellow-clad woman peddling her street foods.

'Yellow. Excellent.'

The simple colour code told him all he needed to know, so the rest of his journey to Naval Headquarters was free from the worries that had been plaguing him since the searchlights highlighted the submarines the previous evening.

The sole outstanding problem had been Mimaroğlu and his well-known independence of thought.

Tezeren mentally checked off his list and satisfied himself that the lid had been put on the problem. The woman's yellow garb indicated success in the mission the Russians had insisted upon; in truth, it was a course of action that Tezeren had hardly resisted.

By the time he dozed off, the four submarines of the Imperial Japanese Navy had sunk to the seabed off the coast of the island of Kinaliada, ready for the renewed night to cover their move through the tighter Bosphorus channel at Istanbul, and on into the Black Sea.

The sketch of the submarines had blown off the table and lay in the bushes next to Mimaroglu's patio, unseen by the NKVD clean-up party, or the police who attended the scene of the two unfortunate deaths.

0952 hrs, Monday, 2nd September 1946, Headquarters, NATO Forces in Europe, Frankfurt, Germany.

"Thank you for seeing me at such short notice, General Strong."

"Your message seemed to imply urgency, General Gehlen. Please sit. No secrecy issues, unlike your last visit? Tea?"

48

"Thank you, but no thank you. None at all either, as I'm here on official business anyway. Meeting with our French colleagues at midday. I'll get straight down to business. I've further information about the pumpkin bombs from the May Day parade."

"You have my full attention."

"My sources tell me that the original bomb was photographed, but not recovered. A submarine found the wreck of the B-29 on an island near Sweden. I'll try and get the location if I can."

Strong scribbled a note to that effect.

"I've lost two agents getting this information, including the one who took the Moscow photographs."

"I'm very sorry to hear that, General Gehlen. Very sorry indeed."

"My prime source is lying low for now... safe... I sincerely hope anyway."

"I hope your agent remains undiscovered."

"Thank you. I hope this is worth the cost. I've established that the bombs were fakes... copies built from the photographs their submariners took, nothing more. Their insides are now high-explosive in nature... in the bombs recently manufactured for real I mean... these were simply wooden mock-ups of the photographed device."

"That's wonderful news."

Gehlen slid a folder across the crowded desk.

"It is and it isn't, General Strong."

Strong read the document carefully.

"Stakhanovo?"

"We've known about it for some time. Testing of experimental aircraft... that type of thing. It's a site we don't reconnoitre in any way... lost too many aircraft trying... although I recently managed to get an asset in place."

"And they have B-29s there... and loading pits of the same style as Karup?"

"Indeed, General Strong. They also are preparing to receive a new Soviet aircraft, a virtual copy of the Amerikan B-29... the Tupolev 4."

"So they're developing a strategic bombing capability."

"You didn't really expect them not to, did you?"

"No, of course not, General Gehlen."

"But there is more... information that raises sinister possibilities, General Strong."

Strong sipped his tea.

"Go on, General."

"My agent communicated that there are two personnel from a special department on site, liaising with the base commander and the regimental technical branch."

"I'm not going to like this, am I?"

"I'm not sure you will, Herr General, especially if you know what the Ministry for Middle Machinery is, that is?"

"One moment, General Gehlen."

Strong picked up the phone and issued an instruction.

Within moments, the requested folder was in his hand.

He apprised himself of the contents, which took surprisingly little time.

Handing over the folder, he picked up his tea once more, summarising in between sips.

"Seems we know of its existence through a couple of mentions in their signals traffic... before they changed their codes regularly... damn effective that has been too I might add... anyway, we've assumed it's some agricultural department... no more than tha..."

Gehlen's look made him stop in mid-flow.

"You know different though. Don't you?"

"Yes, General, I'm think I do. Acquiring this information cost me another long-standing and excellent agent, and cost her considerably more than that from what I expect. None the less, whilst I know little of what the Ministry for Middle Machinery is concerned with, I'm now aware who's in charge of it."

Strong finished his tea and set the cup and saucer down with a gentleness that belied his anticipation.

"Malenkov."

"Malenkov?"

That meant a number of things, the first of which was that the Ministry for Middle Machinery was now something they needed to know about very quickly, for Malenkov had fingers in a number of pies, one of which they knew was to do with aircraft production, and one of which they had suspected, ever since a report had placed him in a one to one meeting with Kurchatov... the atomic scientist.

1230 hrs, Monday, 2nd September 1946, Headquarters, NATO Forces in Europe, Frankfurt, Germany.

The monthly exchange between German Military Intelligence and the Bureau Central de Renseignements et D'Action had run its normal course.

De Walle had encouraged him to remain behind when the others left the room.

They slipped naturally into German as their preferred language for private discussion.

"How may I be of assistance, General De Walle?"

"A mutual acquaintance received a mysterious note a while back. I wondered if your agency could shed any light on its contents, or provide me with some background on the originator of it?"

"Most certainly I can try, Herr General."

A copy of the copy of Anne-Marie's note changed hands and De Walle watched closely for any reaction from the man whom he had only recently started to trust.

"Uspenka clearly. That's in Russia... near Luhansk if memory serves. We had some suspicions about underground works there. I had one of my people check it all out. Came to nothing."

He lowered the paper to the desk.

"The rest means nothing to me. I'll show it to some people. We'll see what comes up. This name?"

"David Steyn, cousin to Ernst Knocke."

"Ah, the famous tank general... still in the French Legion from what I heard. Declined to return to serve his Fatherland."

"Yes, he remained true to his word... something I, for one, am truly grateful for."

"Steyn? A Jew?"

"I believe so. I'm sure you knew that not all the SS were rabid anti-Semites."

"Just most."

De Walle conceded the statement with a typically Gallic shrug.

"On that subject, Knocke seems to think that his cousin was supposed to have died in Belzec, along with his uncle Jakob, a medical doctor."

"And you think this is important?"

"I'm unsure to be honest. But Knocke seems to suspect that Steyn was more than the simple shopkeeper he appeared to be... an ex-Kriegsmarine engineer who may have other skills... official contacts possibly... perhaps even a clandestine life... don't know.... but I do know you're better placed to discover the truth of the matter."

"May I?"

"But of course."

Gehlen responded by marking a couple of extra notes on the message and then pocketed the paperwork.

"Leave it with me, Herr General. Now, I must go and see Vietinghoff before I travel on."

"Thank you, Herr General. My regards to your family."

2100 hrs, Saturday, 7th September 1946, Vinogradar Young Communists Sailing Club, Black Sea, USSR.

The pilot boats had made contact and the mammoth voyage was nearly complete.

On the stroke of 2100 hrs, the hydraulic doors that separated the Black Sea from the secret facility started their slow journey, permitting a soft red light to play upon the gentle swell outside.

Inside the facility, six sets of red lights pulsated, hidden from any view save the eyes aboard the vessels carefully approaching the entrance.

The order of arrival was decided by the Japanese themselves, and the pilot boat flashed its lights towards the red cavern, silently communicating which vessel was first in line.

Inside the facility, the red lights extinguished until solely one set was illuminated, along with a matching green set, the two colours marking the hospitable darkness of the welcoming mooring bay into which the AM class I-1 would slide.

The sea doors themselves were marked by an array of low power red and green lights arranged in the same pattern as the mooring bays, with red to port and green to starboard.

The arrival took eight minutes precisely; longer than the five and a half minutes achieved by the practiced crews of J-51 Soviet Initsiativa and J-54 Soviet Vozmezdiye... or Initiative and Retribution as official circles knew them... or Jana and Velika as those who manned them affectionately called the two type-XXI submarines.

Next came one of the real leviathans, the I-402 displaying the shielded blue light on her conning tower, which meant that she was the one that carried the all-important hardware upon which the later stages of Raduga so heavily depended.

402 took eleven minutes to berth, the turn into her resting place proving tighter than imagined when the plans were altered to accommodate the immense Sen-Tokus.

The transport was already in place to accept the precious machinery, the berth normally occupied by 'Jana' filled by a sturdy new diesel engine powered barge that would take the delicate instruments from Vinogradar on the journey across the Black sea, into the Volga, to their final destination at Akhtubinsk and Camp 1001.

There was another similar dilapidated-looking barge in a vacant bay adjacent to 401.

Fig # 224 - Important locations in Southern USSR.

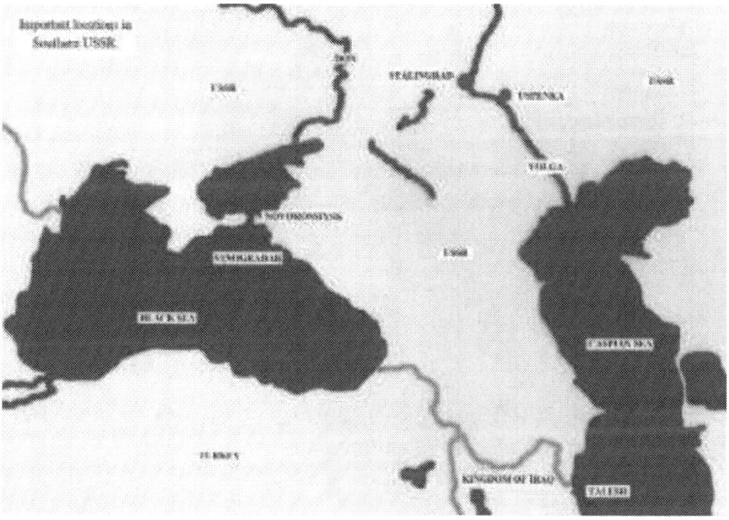

The barges were carefully constructed to look like anything but a modern piece of seagoing transport, the maskirovka so good that the Japanese conning tower crews wondered why such tramp-like vessels were moored within the secret facility.

The Soviet scientist thronged the bays, waiting to have first sight of the machines that promised so much.

The plans had already been with them for months, and copies had been made. However, results had been poor by comparison with the Japanese claims, so the Soviets were anxious to see the technical differences between their own attempts and the ones that were about to be unloaded from the hangar on I-402.

The arrival of I-401 was almost a non-event for most of the people present, although it carried some equally important substances, paperwork, and personnel.

Last into the base was I-14.

Her stern almost clipped the doorframe but the Captain skilfully applied some extra revolutions to avoid contact and the AM class submarine moored perfectly.

Thirty-nine minutes after they had opened, the hydraulic doors shut tight, allowing the working lights to be turned on and the work of unloading all the vessels to begin.

Each submarine had its official party ready to greet the important naval officers and scientists who came ashore.

Admiral Oktyabrskiy waited patiently as the shore party worked with the deck crew of I-401, noting the ragged honour party form on the giant submarine's deck. Normally a stickler for such matters, he was conscious of how long the submarine had been at sea and the incredible journey it had undertaken.

'Hardly surprising, given their achievement!'

Three Japanese officers, rigged in their best uniforms, emerged on deck and inspected the honour party with what could only be similar acceptance and understanding, as not one of the line of submariners would normally pass muster on the first morning at training school.

The naval officer saluted the deck officer before the three turned to salute the national flag that had magically appeared.

Ceremony over, they moved to the gangway and set foot on dry land.

All three were clearly unsteady on their feet, the oldest of them, Yamaoka, even grabbed for a support.

Oktyabrskiy threw up a salute, which received salutes and bows in return.

"From the General Secretary and people of the Soviet Union, may I welcome you and your men, and congratulate you on your amazing achievement."

Yamaoka, still unsteady, moved forward, bowed again, and offered his hand.

"Taishō Oktyabrskiy… Shōshō Yamaoka. Thank you for your most generous welcome. If I might introduce my officers?"

Yamaoka turned to his left.

"Shōsa Nanbu Nobukiyo, captain of the I-401 and senior naval officer on the mission."

Nobukiyo bowed as Oktyabrskiy extended his hand.

He retracted it and went to bow as Nobukiyo went to accept the handshake.

Both men got into synch and shook hands.

Yamaoka turned to the other officer.

"Surgeon General, Chūjō Shiro Ishii, former director of the Epidemic Prevention and Water Purification Department of the Kwantung Army."

There was no repeat of previous embarrassing exchange.

54

"Gentlemen, there's no time to lose. I've work parties ready to start moving the equipment and files from your vessel. I appreciate your men will be weary. I have arranged rest and food in the mess hall for all..."

Oktyabrskiy ground to a halt as he realised that the naval officer wanted to speak.

"Taishō Oktyabrskiy, with the deepest respect, but my men wish to finish the mission and I request that they be included in the work parties to transfer all matters of our responsibility to Russian soil."

The admiral could only grin.

"But of course, Comrade Nobukiyo. Perhaps your men could hand over to my men on the dock? We have practiced loading, so we will load into the barges and lorries. Is that acceptable to you and your men?"

"Hai!"

Nobukiyo bowed to the Soviet admiral, and then to his own mission commander.

Turning to the waiting deck officer, he shouted the agreed command.

"Daii Jinyo!"

Lieutenant Jinyo sprang to attention.

"Ima, Jinyo, ima!"

The deck became an instant mass of bodies, some of the honour group sprinting to their work parties as other groups brought crates and other articles from within the hull.

Oktyabrskiy observed for a little while, and then turned to watch the activities on the other submarines, particularly the large blue crates being gently shifted out of the I-402's huge hangar.

Yamaoka saw the Russian's interest pique.

"Ah, Taisho Oktyabrskiy, in many ways they are the prize, eh?"

"I wasn't sure. So... they're the machines on which the programme depends?"

"Hai. Enshinbunriki."

Whilst the Black Sea fleet had an all-important part to play in the whole operation, Oktyabrskiy wasn't briefed on all specifics, but he was certainly aware of the emphasis on careful handling and transport regarding fifty-four specific crates that would be contained in blue packing, and how vital the contents were to all things Raduga.

The two men looked at each other hoping for more but neither had the language skills for the job.

"Kapitan?"

A Captain Third rank stepped forward, Oktyabrskiy's Japanese specialist.

"Enshinbunriki."

"Arigatō, Shōshō."

The Captain bowed and turned to his commander.

"Sir, the contents are Enshinbunriki... centrifuges."

Oktyabrskiy looked like he understood but actually didn't have the faintest idea what a centrifuge was... but he knew a man who might.

But for now, he contented himself with watching the hive of activity that had transformed the base into an anthill.

0109 hrs, Sunday, 8th September 1946, Vinogradar Young Communists Sailing Club, Black Sea, USSR.

The scientists and some of the smaller items had long gone, whisked away to their rendezvous with cars or aircraft, depending on the movement schedule that covered absolutely everything from man to file.

When the Soviet personnel had stopped for a break, the Japanese commanders had permitted their men a ten-minute cessation for refreshments and other comforts before driving them back to work once more.

All the blue crates were loaded on the barge in the berth adjacent to I-402, and the skipper of that craft was anxiously waiting the opening of the doors, as he had to get the precious load under cover in the camouflaged dock in Novorossiysk before the prying eyes of the Allied air forces came snooping.

Next to I-401, the last items were being secreted and covered with waterproofing, all under the watchful eyes of Yoshio Nishina, the former director of the Riken Institute and head of His Imperial Majesty's Nuclear Weapon research programme, and Soviet scientist Igor Tamm, head of theory at the Lebedev Institute, the senior man present from the Soviet Atomic Weapons project.

The two men compared their ledgers and were satisfied.

Beside them, a Soviet naval officer waited patiently.

"Da?"

Tamm's voice queried the final check box.

"Hai."

Nishina punctuated his response with signing the checklist.

Tamm followed suit and turned to the lieutenant.

"Comrade Leytenant. Inventory complete. You may proceed."

"Thank you, Comrade Academician."

The young officer turned and gave a gesture to the base commander, who in turn gave the command that started a low-level klaxon sounding, indicating that the lights were about to be extinguished prior to the base doors opening.

Thirty seconds quickly passed and the lights disappeared to be replaced by the low red lights.

The doors remained closed as numerous eyes became accustomed to the new light.

As per procedure, the base commander waited for reports on activity at sea.

Soviet vessels off shore and the base stations that probed the seas and skies of the Black Sea all reported in to Naval Command at Novorossiysk, and it was from there that the all-clear came.

Again, the low-level klaxon sounded, this time ten times in succession, indicating that the base was about to open itself up to the sea.

The vast majority of the workers, both Russian and Japanese, had taken themselves off to consume the food and drinks laid on for them, so they missed the departure of the two barges and the closure of the huge doors.

Admiral Oktyabrskiy found Nobukiyo enjoying fresh coffee and fine tobacco… American.

"We liberated many nice things from the Capitalist's storehouses. No reason why we shouldn't enjoy them, eh, Comrade Captain?"

The interpreter's words drew a smile and a courteous nod from the submarine's commander.

"Please walk with me. You may enjoy what is about to happen."

The two strode off to the viewing stand at the end of the empty bay next to I-401.

The facility's clocks clicked round to 0130.

A strange low moaning sound made itself known, initiated by an order from the base commander.

The jury-rigged speakers directed their sound not into the air but into the water in the two recently vacated bays.

No submariner could fail to understand what was about to happen as the water in the bays churned and bubbled.

The two XXI submarines rose to the surface almost perfectly together.

Nobukiyo was impressed, not just with the sleek and beautiful lines of the submarine he focussed on, but also with the depth of water in the base that permitted such a concealment.

"Twenty-seven metres."

Oktyabrskiy answered the Japanese officer's unspoken question, but still Nobukiyo questioned the interpreter's words.

"The submarine itself is twelve metres high… we allowed fifteen… the draught of the barge was four metres at full load… there was no risk."

Nobukiyo nodded his understanding and turned back to watch as the crew started to emerge from their confinement.

Oktyabrskiy sipped his coffee and felt a chill travel the length of his spine.

In front of him sat two of each of the AM class, a pair of the huge Sen-Tokus, and both of his advanced type XXIs.

Whilst he was not briefed in on the mission that lay ahead of his command, the admiral sensed that the six submarines secreted in the facility were to be employed on a mission that would change the nature of warfare forever.

In that, he was in every sense correct.

Common sense is not so common.

Voltaire

Chapter 175 - THE SHIELD

1522 hrs, Friday, 13th September 1946, Panemunė, Route 146, the Šilinė - Pauliai road, Lithuania.

Her eyes narrowed as the man she had positioned to warn of any approaching traffic whistled from his position in the treetops.

She looked up and saw six fingers, the lookout's way of telling her that the approaching convoy was of six vehicles.

He also held up a dirty palm, which indicated that there were no armoured vehicles involved, an enemy that the Lithuanian partisan group tried to avoid at all costs.

Normally led by the 45-year-old Antanas Pyragius, today it was the young Janina Mikenas in command, a position which she had earned by right.

Pyragius lay recovering from wounds he had sustained during a raid outside Ariogala a fortnight beforehand.

The partisan group, known throughout their native land as 'The Shield of St. Michael', were experienced and competent and, most importantly in the majority of Lithuanian's opinion, lucky.

Many such national resistance groups had been liquidated by the dreaded NKVD, but the Shield had survived all such close encounters.

Mikenas checked her group's dispositions as best she could, the warning whistle having already made the men and women melt into the undergrowth with weapons held tight and ready.

Her eyes returned to the road and immediately the lead Soviet vehicle, a staff car, came into view, rounding the bend and starting on the gradual slope that led to the junction of Routes 1710 and 146.

Mikenas' eyes instinctively flicked back to the road, seeking out any tell-tale marks that might give away the mines, but there were none.

Behind the staff car came five lorries of different lineages but all marked with the insignia of the NKVD.

'Bastards!'

The hated NKVD, responsible for deporting most of her family and murdering her brother Romek, and probably younger brother Maxim too.

Fig # 225 - Areas around the Neman River, Lithuania.

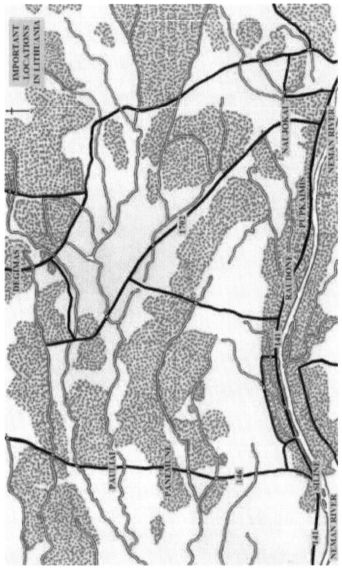

Janina Mikenas smiled an unsmiling smile similar to a cobra about to strike.

The staff car slowly moved past the waiting partisans, at which time luck deserted the Shields.

Unbelievably, it missed the five mines and drove on its unsuspecting way, unaware of the reprieve.

The first lorry found two at the same time and all hell broke loose.

The reprieve for the occupants of the staff car proved to be purely temporary as one of the partisans' two DP light machine-guns was positioned to flay the length of the road and the gunner was experienced enough to concentrate on the staff car first.

The NKVD Major commanding the convoy lost his head, literally.

His second in command lost his metaphorically, and ran screaming from the car covered in the spray of grey-red detritus from his former commander's brain.

The two soldiers in the front had no chance as the DP's bullets carved them up.

The fleeing 2IC ran into a tree in his panic, knocking himself out in the process.

Up and down the small convoy, the partisans poured fire into the rear of the covered lorries and their cabs, and were rewarded with shrieks and screams as bullets struck home into defenceless flesh.

One of Mikenas' partisans had run a string of mines out behind the convoy, but not one vehicle made an effort to escape.

Two slipped back down the gentle slope, coming to rest against one lorry that stayed put, its dead driver having applied the handbrake before failing in an attempt to grab for his rifle.

Yet another ran back and angled itself into the modest ditch where flames lazily started to consume it, burning from the engine compartment backwards.

Janina Mikenas wasn't sure but she felt that not one shot had been returned from the convoy, which in itself started warning bells ringing in her head.

Acting on impulse, she stepped out onto the road, waving her hands above her head. One by one, her partisans responded to her command and the firing died away.

The sound of guns firing was replaced by the sounds of men and women in extremis.

61

The experienced guerrillas made their move. Some crept forward leaving others to watch over them in case of any resistance, while yet others formed at the head and rear of the shattered convoy, ready to repulse any new arrivals.

Voices were raised, voices seeking mercy... or help... voices speaking Lithuanian.

'Oh Jesus and Maria!'

Janina understood immediately.

"Oh Jesus and Maria! Help them!"

The convoy had been transporting prisoners.

Reaching the rear of the nearest truck, she threw open the cover and was greeted by a veritable charnel house.

The two NKVD guards caused her no upset, but the sight of the bodies of her countrymen and women gripped her heart like a vice.

'Oh God, what have I done?'

A hand waved weakly from the pile, and she hoisted herself inside to take hold of it and burrow deep for the still-living owner.

The young man died before she could pull him clear.

There was no one else in the vehicle who needed anything more than his or her own small plot of Lithuania and the ministrations of a priest.

All along the shattered convoy, Janina could hear the groans of wounded combined with the wails of her own men and women, who so wished they could undo the work of the last few minutes.

The burning lorry yielded up two survivors. A third died in the act of being dragged clear.

One of her best men, Jurgis Lukša, was screaming his wrath whilst also crying like a child, all at the same time as two of his group pulled him away from the awful sight in the third lorry.

Janina's second in command ran up to her, his face as white as a sheet.

"His sons... he killed his own sons... fucking hell... we all have... Mother of God, Janina..." his voice trailed away as his tears came.

The information had been that the NKVD were shifting police records back to Soviet soil, records that were better off destroyed as far as the partisans were concerned.

Janina worked through the shock and pain of what had come to pass, and tried to reason what had happened.

Despite her youth, she managed to overcome the grief and work out what had happened... or at least what she feared had happened.

"Get ready to move! If you find anyone alive, bring them with us. We set fire to everything. Two minutes! Two minutes!"

The already burning lorry was beacon enough to anyone closing in on them, so Janina had no compunction about ordering everything else to be burnt with it.

"And our people?"

"Burn them all."

Some lifeless forms were pulled from the third truck; the sons.

Jurgis Lukša and his cousin took one each and moved to the main group, both men clearly in the extremes of grief.

Someone, a woman, scrabbled free from the second lorry and was assisted down by two partisans. Her unsteady feet gave way and she was picked up and put over one of the men's shoulders.

A man and a woman were pulled out of the last vehicle, both wounded and disoriented, but capable of walking.

In total, eight Lithuanian prisoners survived the ambush.

Two of the NKVD guards were found alive and dispatched with knives and without mercy.

The whistling burrowed into Janina's conscious thoughts and she looked up.

The hand signals said it all.

They had been tricked.

Eight vehicles in total, three of them armoured.

'Shit!'

Karelis, the woman in charge at the rear of the column, finished her work and looked up the road to Janina, seeking guidance.

Mikenas cupped her hands and shouted at the lookout.

"How far?"

The tree dweller looked to confirm his figures.

His hands did the talking.

'One and a half.'

"Move! Move now!"

Karelis understood the gestures and ordered her group away as the tree dweller descended more in a controlled fall than by a proper descent.

The prime escape route was to the southeast, over a small watercourse and into a temporary hiding place, hidden by fallen leaves and the boughs of a dense wood.

It was two kilometres distant, and now the party were encumbered by the wounded and the dead.

"Move!"

Mikenas fell in with the rear group, jogging alongside Audra Karelis.

The older woman understood the younger's pain.

"Shit happens, Janina. We weren't to know... clearly we were set up. Another thing that the devils will pay for."

Mikenas nodded, knowing the words to be fair, and knowing that they wouldn't help.

"I left a present for the communist bastards."

They dropped into cover both sides of the narrow path and watched to the rear as the final members of the group moved through.

Something surrendered noisily to the fires on the road and the rising smoke became thicker.

A number of shots rang out as the two young men who lead the pursuers away did their best to attract the undivided attention of the NKVD unit.

"Mines?"

"Of course. I had my people put some in the road, just in case... plus we didn't want to carry the shitty things another metre, did we?"

Janina smiled as Karelis rose up and started to move on.

No sooner had they moved than one of the mines found a suitable weight on top of it and exploded.

A second explosion followed in quick succession.

"Just bits of the first one. We couldn't be... can't be that lucky!"

Janina Mikenas laughed as they ran.

'No, we won't be.'

But they were.

The two decoys returned to the hidden resting point almost five hours to the minute after the group had run from the ambush site.

Their news was encouraging but, none the less, Janina decided to keep the group hidden until dawn, if only to give the casualties more time to gather some strength.

There was something about two of the women that made her senses light up, a something she didn't understand, but a something that was very real.

So much so that, under her orders, Karelis kept an eye on them at all times.

Janina Mikenas had spent some time with Lukša and consoled him as best she could, which was nowhere near enough to console the distraught father.

Her rounds took her amongst all her people, for the enormity of what they had done was now visiting every mind and bringing its own brand of torture.

Another of the ex-prisoners died but it seemed likely that the rest would survive.

The partisan leader moved amongst them, asking names and places of origin, offering encouragement but always falling short of apologising.

The examination of what had happened and how the partisan group had clearly been fed false information would come later, along with the recriminations.

For now, Janina returned with a piece of bread and sat next to Karelis.

"So?"

"I'm sure you're right. They're different... always aware... they miss nothing."

That left a big question hanging unspoken in the silence.

'Agents... but ours or theirs?'

Janina studied the pair, immediately understanding what Karelis meant.

'Can we afford to risk it? Why not kill them both now?'

There was a presence to the two women, one that screamed that they were more than they seemed.

She immediately noticed that they watched different areas, maintaining a surveillance that had no overlap, no wasted areas.

"I'll talk to them... but keep watching."

'It is decided. What they say now will determine their fate.'

Grabbing a flask, she stood and wandered over to where the pair were leant up against a tree trunk,

Both women swivelled their heads as one. The thinner-faced blonde accepted the flask and passed it to the other woman, who drank heartily.

"So... who are you two?"

Clearly the pair had discussed the matter already, as the answer flowed quickly.

"My friend is Polish, I'm Lithuanian. We're both Allied agents captured by the Russians."

Janina Mikenas held up her hand to interrupt.

"Your accent isn't natural. You speak the language well though."

"I grew up in London, but my parents were both from Kaunus."

"And you?"

"Lublin."

"OK, so what's your names and who do you really work for?"

The two women had decided that the partisans were genuine, and represented their best chance of being safe, so had elected to tell the truth.

"I'm Renata Luistikaite"

"Karin Greim."

Janina indicated the two obvious bumps but kept her thoughts to herself.

'Sending pregnant women would be a masterstroke of course!'

Greim responded to the unspoken question.

"Women in prison get raped."

"How long?"

"We were taken at the end of March... the rapes started straight away... minimum of five months."

"Sorry."

"It happens."

Renata Luistikaite drew a quick line under the matter.

"We're both SOE... British intelligence agents. We were based in Torun but got arrested before the landings were due. Been in prison ever since."

"They tortured you, of course."

"Of course."

'Convincing... such marks would need to be convincing.'

"And?"

"And we told them everything they wanted to know... eventually."

The women's distorted hands told part of the story of what they had been through, the presence of burns and bruises on their faces, arms, and legs, and the bulging bellies filled in the gaps.

Greim also bore the angry scar of a head wound that would always remind her of the nearness of her brush with death in the Torun bar.

"And how would I be able to confirm that you are who you say you are?"

"Do you have a radio?"

"Maybe."

'And now we get to it...'

There was no maybe. The Shields had a number of radios available to them, all of which could be used to contact the Allies.

A sudden hissing sound stopped the three in mid-conversation.

The hissing died away to be replaced by nothing.

... just silence...

... but a silence full of approaching malice and terror.

The silence was replaced by birdsong and engine sounds.

One of the lookouts dropped next to his leader.

"One armoured car and a lorry stopped up the lane. The soldiers are out and on foot, the armoured car is following them up. Two hundred metres and coming our way."

"How many?"

"Maybe twenty."

"Straight at us?"

"Not quite, but if they move a few metres to one side they'll fall on top of us."

It took but a moment.

"Pass the word. Total silence. We stay... but everyone's to be ready."

The sound of the armoured car's engine growling in low gear started to invade everyone's senses, almost like the approach of predatory tiger in search of a fine meal.

Janina checked that Karelis was still watching the two women and, in her concentration, was startled by the voice next to her ear.

"We can fight. Give us weapons."

It was Greim who had spoken, and in that second Janina saw the eyes of a killer pleading for the means to kill.

"No. I think not. Maybe when we know who you are. For now, just shut up and pray."

'For the moment, I'll stay my hand.'

A low moan caught everyone's attention, but the wounded man's sounds were quickly silenced by a dirty hand.

Janina was at the wrong end of the site, and had no idea how close the NKVD soldiers came to finding the group, but she sensed and saw relaxation in the stiff bodies, and then realised that the sounds of the engine were now fading.

Still, the partisan group remained in hiding for another fifteen minutes, holding its collective breath until Janina decided it was safe to move.

"Pick everything up. We move immediately."

She turned her attention back to the two women.

"You two walk?"

They nodded and rose to their feet.

"Good. We'll soon see if your stories are true. If not, I promise you an interesting time."

The threat was left hanging.

"Audra, these are your responsibility."

The 'Shield of St Michael' moved off towards safety.

Throughout the Baltic States, special units of NKVD troops used a variety of tactics to lure partisans into the open, with a great deal of success.

Many groups were wiped out completely, and the vast majority were badly damaged and driven underground to lick their wounds.

'The Shield of St Michael' was one of the very lucky ones that managed to disengage without being brought to heel, and compounded its luck with moving rapidly into an area that had just been declared as 'partisan-free' following the total destruction of the resident resistance fighters group, mainly because it had been infiltrated by turncoats.

The patrols in their new area were few and Mikenas decided to try and establish some sort of contact with the Allies before exposing her group again.

2017 hrs, Sunday, 15th September 1946, Mir Castle, Mir, USSR.

It was the first time they had been together for a very long time and it was not going well.

They sat in silence, eating their way through a very average meal, drinking a very average wine, the best fare that the senior officer's guest centre could find in austere times.

Uniforms were rare in the restaurant, most visitors preferring to relax in civilian clothing and leave behind the pressures of military life.

Those who didn't know her by sight simply assumed that the beautiful woman was merely the trophy wife of the thin officer who sat opposite her, whereas it was she who was there by right, and he who was her guest,

Yuri Nazarbayev was a changed man; gaunt and lacking the humour and compassion that had marked him aside from other suitors when he had pursued the woman of his dreams.

Tatiana Nazarbayeva played with her food, the newfound coolness between them so stark and clear that she found so little in common with the man who had fathered her children.

They had made love, or as she felt, rutted their way through a sexual act that carried no great meaning and was simply an animal release, which had never their manner.

Yuri had made officer rank of his own accord, although there were rumblings from those jealous or simply being provocative, that he secured his position through the support of his GRU wife.

Whether the possibility of it or the suggestion of it contributed to the wall he seemed to have constructed was unknown to Tatiana.

The wall was very real, and had been built slowly since she had revealed the events at the dacha in Moscow.

In truth, she had even built a version for herself, perhaps as some sort of coping mechanism.

Whatever was happening, there was something solid and inexorable between them, an obstruction that neither he nor she tried to surmount, and one that neither seemed inclined to overcome.

During their walk around the castle that afternoon, they had hardly spoken a dozen words and the distant atmosphere was tangible.

After dinner, they adjourned to the bar and drank heavily, probably as much to avoid the need to talk as any need for drink.

They staggered to their first floor bedroom and simply collapsed on the bed without ceremony or exchange.

Yuri Nazarbayev woke alone, a simple note informing him of his wife's early recall to duty.

It was a lie and he knew it, but was relieved that it saved him the awful and strained goodbye he had anticipated.

Beria chuckled as he read.

A recent report from his main man in the 3rd Guards Mechanised Corps had recorded great success, as NKVD lackeys goaded the newly fledged Lieutenant with stories of his wife's affair in Moscow, constructing rumours about her sexual proclivities, as well as spreading reports about her involvement in his promotion.

The latest report, hotly arrived from Mir Castle, amused him greatly as it was quite clear that he had driven a huge wedge between the woman and her husband.

He laughed again, this time loud enough that it could be heard by his secretary through closed doors.

It was not a pleasant laugh.

'Fuck with me and pay the fucking price, bitch!'

1054 hrs, Saturday, 21st September 1946, the Kremlin, Moscow, USSR.

As was her new habit, Nazarbayeva arrived ahead of schedule to get through the security in good time.

The metal detectors had been augmented with searches beforehand, and more intimate pat-downs afterwards.

Today the time plan had gone to pot, as the political governor of Ukraine set the alarms ringing.

Errors were frequent and the man pleaded his innocence, stating he had simply forgotten that there was a clip of pistol ammunition in his greatcoat pocket.

Beria's deputy, Lieutenant General Kaganovich just happened to be passing and stepped forward.

"Now, now, Comrade Commissar... you should know better than that."

The guard commander was about to summon an arrest detail, as per standard procedure.

He was waved to stand down by Kaganovich.

"I'll deal with this, Kapitan."

He extended his hand in a way that dared his authority to be challenged.

"Have your men escort the Commissar to my office immediately. I'll return them to you when I have completed my interrogation."

The Ukrainian Governor did not complain and went with the two guards.

"Log this in your report, Comrade Kapitan. I'll deal with this and lodge my own report with your commander."

70

Not waiting for an answer, Kaganovich strode off in the wake of the 'prisoner' and escort, catching up with them on the threshold of his personal domain.

"You two remain here and guard this entrance. You, Comrade Commissar, come with me and prepare to justify your actions."

The guards shut the door and set themselves at an alert position, fully aware of the seriousness of their orders.

1104 hrs, Saturday, 21st September 1946, Lieutenant General Kaganovich's office, the Kremlin, Moscow, USSR.

Keeping their voices low, the two men embraced each other and kissed in the traditional Russian fashion.

"So, that gives us twenty minutes?"

"More if we need, Comrade."

"So, let us be quick, Ilya Borisevich."

"Tea, Nikita Sergeyevich?"

"Thank you."

And as Kaganovich poured, Nikita Sergeyevich Khrushchev delivered his information.

1108 hrs, Saturday, 21st September 1946, the Kremlin, Moscow, USSR.

"Finally! Welcome Comrade Mayor General. We heard there was some trouble with security… that rogue Khrushchev apparently?"

Whilst it was clear that Stalin and Beria were well informed, the statement was put more like a question, encouraging a further response.

"Yes, Comrade General Secretary. Fortunately Comrade Leytenant General Kaganovich was passing and he stepped in quickly to prevent any problems."

The General Secretary moved on effortlessly.

"So, what's the latest news you bring us?"

"Almost the same as the last time I briefed you, Comrade General Secretary. None of GRU's assets have detected any sign of double-dealing by the Allies. Everything is being done according to the schedules devised by the Camp Vár delegations. Our Air Force reports no more incidents, and that our own reconnaissance missions have not been impeded. I'm assuming that you'll have seen the same reports I have, Comrade General Secretary?"

"You may assume that, Comrade Nazarbayeva."

"So... the only military incidents of note were the collision between the two vessels in the Baltic and the death of some of their troops on a booby-trap, neither of which have posed a problem to our negotiators in Sweden, who have issued guarantees that have been adopted by Red Banner Forces HQ."

"Guarantees? Specifically?"

"Booby traps, Comrade General Secretary. There will be no more booby traps."

The report from Sweden had actually been a little inaccurate, as the Allied delegation had been extremely vocal, angry, and threatening about the deaths of eleven Canadian soldiers, something that Beria knew and Nazarbayeva did not.

As always, the smallest victory brought a light to Beria's eyes.

"So, Comrade Nazarbayeva, what have you discovered?"

Beria emphasised 'have' in the manner of a teacher to an under-performing student, something not wasted on either her or Stalin.

"They continue to improve their technology. New vehicles and weapons are appearing, although the older equipment appears to be being improved or is being recycled to the other... err... lesser nations."

Beria piped up as Nazarbayeva took a breath.

"As you recall, Comrade General Secretary, the NKVD report indicated that many of the Amerikanski tanks were being allocated to the Dutch, Spanish, and French. We also found that a considerable number of the British Comet tanks had been given to the treacherous Poles."

Nazarbayeva understood well enough that Beria was harping but was unconcerned as she knew that she held a few nuggets of her own.

Continuing without realising that he was not getting a rise out of the woman, Beria added more information to overshadow the GRU report.

"NKVD assets have identified a new tank division being assembled in America, comprising assets removed from their Pacific forces and newly-trained personnel. My agents have also confirmed that it will be bound for Europe to replace a number of divisions, who will return to their homeland."

This was not news to Stalin and he all but ignored Beria's words, instead silently encouraging the GRU officer to continue.

"Comrade General Secretary, I can confirm that the new division is called the 17th Tank, and that is slated to replace the 2nd, 3rd, and 4th Tank Divisions who are already out of the line and transferring their equipment to the French and Spanish. The new division is also already forming on European soil."

She checked her notes before continuing, not fully understanding that she had just scored a major point on Beria, who was now silently seething.

"A GRU asset in Antwerp has confirmed that the new dock facilities are operational, and have seen the passage of a large number of weapons and vehicles in the last two weeks..."

Stalin and Beria both said nothing, but their looks were sufficient to give her a moment's pause.

"I investigated the matter, Comrade General Secretary. Apparently, my agent's house was occupied by some enemy troops and so communicating was a problem, hence the delay."

A nod drew a line under the matter.

"It has been difficult to establish exactly what the types of vehicles were. My agent was familiar with the M-46 Pershing II and Super Pershing types, and reported that these were not of either of those vehicles, but much larger and heavier. My intelligence interpretation section have concluded that the new influx of in excess of ninety vehicles, based upon the best description my agent could supply, are almost certainly either or both of the rumoured super heavy tanks, the M-29 Chamberlain or M-30 Hancock."

Again Beria steamed as Stalin shot him a piercing look, surrounded by a mocking smile, as both men knew that the recent NKVD report had all but committed itself to stating that the M-29 and M-30 were drawing board warriors, and no imminent threat to the balance of power.

"We must thank the GRU for being so efficient whilst your own service is crippled by the Allied codebreaking efforts, eh Lavrentiy?"

The contemptuous tone was apparent to both Beria and Nazarbayeva, and the NKVD Marshal blushed noticeably.

At least his own force had discovered that the damned Allied codebreakers were reading NKVD codes. Had the GRU discovered it, the humiliation would have been total.

"Indeed, Comrade Secretary. Our communications have been badly hurt by this discovery... but better my men found out about the problem than the damned Allies discovered our inner secrets."

Stalin had pressed Beria for a long time over whether any aspect of Raduga could be compromised.

He had staked his reputation on that not being the case, and no one 'in the know' thought it was simply his reputation that rested on him being absolutely correct.

Stalin moved on.

"So, Comrade General... what's your view of these new arrivals... combined with the reports from Southern France, Portugal, and Italy?"

As usual, Nazarbayeva had an opinion and ventured it immediately.

"I see nothing really hostile here, Comrade General Secretary. If my department and the NKVD are correct, we are actually seeing a large reduction in Amerikanski forces, certainly in terms of numbers. I suspect that we'll see more and more units returning to their various homelands in the near future. Only one Brazilian unit remains... the Spanish have returned four full divisions to the Pyrenees for conversion training to Amerikanski equipment, and two more divisions have returned to Spain as garrison troops."

She took a sip of the water and continued.

"Yes, we are seeing some increases in their order of battle. The Dutch, Belgians, French, and Danes have all put extra forces into the field, armed with equipment handed over by units already back in their homelands. Of course, the Germans are increasing the most, but we know that this is being encouraged to permit more Amerikanski, British, and Commonwealth forces to return home."

"And yet there's something that holds you back from making full assurances... some gap in your information maybe.... or some female intuition we are not yet informed of?"

"You are correct, Comrade General Secretary. There's something that concerns me greatly in all this."

It was Stalin's turn to take a drink, and he sipped his tea deliberately slowly as he took in the woman's face.

"Is it the reorganisation of the Red Army?"

"No, Comrade General Secretary. The reasons for that are sound and will profit the Motherland greatly. No, it's something else entirely."

"Proceed, Comrade General."

"Whilst the manpower of the enemy forces in Europe and the Pacific has reduced, we see a focussing of his existing eastern manpower, specifically concentrating in China, Manchuria, and Korea... the garrison of Japan apart."

"And that poses a threat... this we know, Comrade Nazarbayeva."

Beria's interruption drew no response as the GRU officer simply continued as if his words had not been spoken.

"Our forces in the east were reduced by the needs of the west, dangerously so... this we can now see and have acknowledged... a risk that the GKO considered acceptable at the time. Again, across the borders of China and the east, the enemy seemingly displays no hostile intent, and continues to scale down his manpower... but there is the issue that causes me concern. We have an imbalance of forces in Persia and the Pacific, one that is greatest in the east."

The anticipated interruption didn't come and the uncomfortable vacuum drew her into its embrace.

"It's a question of quality... across the board... the Allies have made technological advances and these are now in place across the battlefield and above it."

"Our own tanks... the IS-III, IV, and VII... the T-54 maybe... now seem to be equalled or even bettered by new arrivals."

She counted points off on her fingers as she recited the concerns one by one.

"Super Pershing... Pershing II... Chamberlain... Hancock... Centurion... Black Panther... and that's just in tanks."

She consulted her notes before continuing.

"They have new bombers... the B-29 used in the Pacific now arrives in numbers, and the improved B-50 version has started to trickle across the ocean."

"Their new fighters...the Amerikanski's Shooting Star and Thunderjet fill over half the US fighter regiments... and the damned Skyraider aircraft that hurt our ground forces so badly has increased from ten regiments to twenty-seven at least... at least... and the Amerikanski are producing enough to let the Royal Air Force and Luftwaffe have some of their own. That tells us a lot, of course. The British have the new Lancaster, and their own jet fighters have trebled in numbers since the ceasefire."

"Even the new British piston engine aircraft are extremely formidable opponents, as we discovered near Estonia."

Nazarbayeva referred to an incident involving the new RAF twin-engine fighter, the Hornet, three of which ran rings around a full regiment of the latest La-9 fighters.

No shots had been fired but the De Havilland aircraft had appeared to be superior to the latest Lavochkin across the board, as the reports of the humiliated regimental commander and his pilots indicated.

'And yet your report made no mention of these issues, Comrade Beria!'

Her thoughts transferred to action, and Nazarbayeva indicated Beria with a gesture that she didn't mean to be dismissive.

"The NKVD commission on our own technological advancements appears to lean towards some exaggeration, and has some glaring omissions."

Beria jumped to his feet but was cut off by Stalin's raised hand.

"Quite rightly, you need to justify that statement quickly, Comrade Nazarbayeva. The NKVD report was most thorough and was signed off by Comrade Marshal Beria himself."

The eyes of the man in question blazed in fury.

"I meant no disrespect, Comrade Marshal. I apologise. What I meant was that the findings of the commission tended towards the upbeat to avoid discouraging results, which is understandable in these times of positivity and hope for the future."

"So… what exactly do you think has been misreported… or presented to us in too positive a fashion?"

"Comrade General Secretary. Our tanks were at a great disadvantage towards the end of the war. We saw increased losses in tank versus tank combat, apparently due to some new type of shell, something both the NKVD and ourselves have yet to fully confirm and identify, although NKVD has made some inroads by identifying the name 'HESH'."

She nodded to Beria in mid-sentence, as an acknowledgement of his office's work, not as a weak attempt to curry favour, which was how the NKVD head interpreted it.

"From survivor's descriptions, the new shell seems to break open our tank's own armour and send it around like shrapnel. We have not yet developed a defence, and yet the NKVD report avoids the issue and speaks only of the up armouring of existing tank types, and more spaced armour to combat their hollow-charge weaponry."

"We know of the powertrain improvements made to the IS-III, and they have maximised the reliability of the vehicle, its previous weak point. This is reported in the NKVD report, as well as the new installations being made in the latest T-54 production vehicles. Yet no mention is made of the problems that remain with the IS-IV and the proposal that was made to discontinue its production in favour of more reliable and mobile vehicles."

Stalin struck a match as he examined Beria's reaction to the woman's words...

The reaction was quite plain.

'...*traitorous accusations! You bitch!*'

"The IS-VII is spoken of in great detail. The first experimental vehicle has proven to be more than was hoped, but it may not see service in numbers for at least another year, probably more... and yet it forms nearly two pages of the report all by itself."

She displayed the two pages in question.

"Two pages for what will probably be no more than forty vehicles by this time next year."

She opened the folder in another pre-marked place and moved neatly to the inventory of aircraft, where glaring omissions were apparent to anyone, regardless of the upbeat nature of the NKVD commission's report.

"Our current aircraft are almost universally outclassed by the later marks of their existing inventory and most of new aircraft of the enemy. Even our ex-German equipment, what little we can still run, appear to offer a difficult match for the latest jet fighters of our enemy. And what do we propose now? Copies of German, Japanese, and Allied aircraft that perform in an inferior fashion, most of the time because our best fuels are unavailable or our re-engineering of their engines is unsatisfactory. These matters are hidden away quite thoroughly, whilst the performance of our own new aircraft... well..."

She turned to a page of the NKVD report and quoted.

"The new Lavochkin-9 is a superior piston-engine fighter at least the equal of the standard aircraft of the enemy in speed, firepower, and performance. And yet... no mention of the encounter with the enemy over the Baltic in which it proved decidedly second best, Comrade General Secretary."

The report was tossed to the table like a matador's cape, and the bull in Beria prepared to gore his opponent.

"Clearly, the La-9 is superior to all our propeller aircraft, but its opponents are changing, and it's already outclassed by the enemy jets fighters and, as we know, some of their latest propeller craft too."

The human bull scraped at the ground, preparing its 'charge'.

"The MiG-9 continues to have problems, and no matter of revision by our engineers is having an effect. The I-250 development is a total disaster and is wasting precious assets that we could do better preserving for other projects. Our efforts, both the NKVD and my own agency, have failed to procure all the information and specifications needed to produce consistently reliable jet propulsion units, and our own engine development programme is under-performing."

Nazarbayeva did not have the word 'shambles' in her vocabulary, which would have been perfect to describe the Soviet Union's own efforts to get a decent home-designed and engineered jet engine into an airframe.

"OKB MiG is failing with its efforts on Allied copies, and the Lyul'ka Bureau's TR-1 engine is presently under-performing in every department... except fuel consumption!"

"How do you know that, woman?"

Beria cracked.

"How can you claim that, eh? My department's report has access to all levels of information, plus our own intelligence. How can you claim such rubbish, eh?"

Stalin relaxed back in his seat, content to let the two contest matters in front of him.

"Because, Comrade Marshal, I too have access to many levels of information... such as academician's gossip around the canteen table... such as engineering reports from the maintenance units at regimental level... or encounter reports filed by our own pilots and crews... peacetime encounters for sure, but none the less enlightening."

"Such claims require evidence, Comrade Nazarbayeva."

"I have prepared it, Comrade General Secretary."

Two healthy-sized documents appeared from her briefcase and made their way into the eager hands of the two senior men, eager for different reasons.

Both Beria and Stalin were absorbed by the documents, so Nazarbayeva decided to produce three teas from the ornate samovar set against the wall to one side of the great man's desk.

Stalin accepted his drink without words, so intent was he on consuming the information in Nazarbayeva's paperwork.

"Really? Unguarded comments as evidence of our jet's problems, Comrade General?"

"Comrade General Secretary, I understand your reservation, but the names of those involved speaks of the importance of their words."

Stalin re-examined the document, seeking out the information he had clearly not comprehended.

'Arkhip Lyulka... jet engine designer... Mikhail Vasilyevich Khrunichev, the Minister for Aviation?'

"The Minister for Aviation?"

"Yes, Comrade General Secretary. He submitted a report on the state of the TR-1, but it seems not to be reflected in the NKVD's assessment."

"Comrade Marshal?"

Beria sought a moment's pause and resorted to polishing his glasses.

"Comrade General Secretary. No report was received from Comrade Leytenant General Khrunichev regarding the TR-1, at least not when the commission was undertaking its assessments."

"Did Comrades Lyulka and Khrunichev contribute at all?"

Both Beria and Nazarbayeva checked the list of names in appendix four, and both failed to find either man's name present.

Nazarbayeva stayed silent, leaving Beria to announce his own failure.

"No, Comrade General Secretary."

"No, Lavrentiy?"

Stalin tossed his copy of the NKVD report across the table towards his henchman, and followed it with the GRU assessment.

"I want your commission to crawl back into this mess and produce a report that tells the GKO... tells me... exactly what the situation is. Can your department manage that... or shall I task the GRU to do it for me, eh Lavrentiy? Eh?"

Beria considered dignified silence was a suitable response and simply nodded, unsure which of the two creatures present he detested the most.

Stalin decided to push the matter further, increasing Beria's feelings of resentment and humiliation, both of which made bad bedfellows to his more common traits of cunning, scheming, and violent resolution.

"Perhaps you should start immediately, Comrade Marshal?"

The gesture towards the door was made dismissively, as Stalin intended, in order to reinforce his unhappiness with Beria.

Nazarbayeva nodded to the NKVD commander with as blank a face as she could manage, but he still managed to see some sort of triumph, some celebration, some satisfaction in her eyes.

His dismissal did not sit well, neither did his interpretation of the woman's face, and the man who left the room silently vowed revenge upon those he left behind.

"Thank you for your report, Comrade Nazarbayeva."

"It was necessary to ensure you and the GKO were not misled, Comrade General Secretary."

Stalin nodded and stood up but waved the woman back into her seat when she started to respond.

"Comrade Beria is efficient, but he sometimes can be guilty of telling us what we want to hear. I shall always rely on you to present the truth, no matter what form it may take."

"In his defence, he has many duties, Comrade General Secretary, so he must rely on those under him to produce efficient and truthful reports."

Stalin chuckled.

"Don't we all, Comrade... don't we all..."

He considered some new thought for a moment and then almost imperceptibly nodded to himself as the decision was silently made.

"I shall create a new commission, one drawn from not just the NKVD, for the purpose of overseeing and appreciating our technical challenges, progress, and comparisons with the Allied forces."

He returned to his seat and drained the last of his tea.

"I'll speak to Polkovnik General Kuznetsov and have him appoint someone from the GRU immediately. Whoever it is, make sure you feed your information directly to them. That way you may make yourself less of an enemy to Comrade Beria."

Nazarbayeva opened her mouth to protest but was cut short by a wagging finger.

"Oh yes, Tatiana Sergievna Nazarbayeva, he considers you his enemy... and today's display has made that more clear in his mind. You humiliated him..."

The hand stopped her objection in an instant.

"I know... I know... you serve the Rodina and the Party to the best of your ability, but what he saw today was a GRU officer tell him he was wrong and make play of it in front of his boss. Don't stop telling me the truth... ever... but be more wary, Comrade. That's my advice on the matter. Now, I've a meeting to chair."

He stood and fished in the top drawer of his desk as Nazarbayeva came to attention, ready to take her leave.

"Comrade, you serve the Rodina and Party to the absolute best of your ability. I commend you for it, Leytenant General Nazarbayeva."

The words penetrated her brain instantly and she saluted smartly.

"Thank you, Comrade General Secretary."

He handed over the insignia of a Lieutenant General with a smile that conveyed real warmth.

"I look forward to your next report, Comrade General."

1253 hrs, Saturday, 21st September 1946, the Kremlin, Moscow, USSR.

The door opened to admit a calmer Beria.

Stalin decided on a reconciliatory approach.

"Don't blame the woman, Lavrentiy. She means well and has the Motherland as her priority. Look to those who misinformed you, eh?"

Beria sat heavily, his morning exertions having unusually tired him.

"Yes, Comrade General Secretary. I've already addressed that matter, and the new Commission is already assembled. There will be no repeat of that shambles. I'll not let that bitch make a fool of me like that again."

Stalin chuckled.

"Of course, you mean that you'll not let a commission falsely report to myself and the GKO again."

Beria looked at his master and was unable to mask the genuine anger still burning inside.

Stalin placed the pen on the desk and steepled his fingers.

"Sometimes I really do wish that you and she could be rolled into one... then I would have the best of both your worlds."

Far from helping the situation, the General Secretary's words fanned the flames even further, which he realised without Beria uttering a word.

"Right then. Before I eat, the matter of the money. Where are you with that?"

Beria took the opportunity to gain some of his self-esteem back by falling back on a project in which he was totally confident.

"The counterfeit currency is too bulky to dispatch via normal channels, and if we did do so, it would arrived in small quantities. My advisors say that, for maximum effect, it all needs to be put into the system as quickly as possible, not fed in over a period of time."

Beria produced a simple document.

"Five hundred million pounds of currency occupies a huge space, and getting it to where it would cause the most damage is an extremely difficult exercise in logistics. This is the NKVD proposal, draft only at the moment. I'm sure the mechanics of it can be sorted out, so the main issue of note would be the Irish."

Stalin dropped the document onto the table.

"Quickly... I'm hungry... explain this master plan to this poor peasant."

"Simple, Comrade General Secretary. The biggest problem is transport. That can be overcome with your backing. We can order the Navy to detach submarines for our purpose. They'll take the currency to our contacts in the IRA. In turn, the Irish will move the counterfeit notes into England and flood the system. The chaos will be immense and the damage to their financial structure catastrophic."

"How does that work, Lavrentiy?"

"In a number of ways, so my financial advisors tell me. Confidence in the currency will waver and plummet. Inflation will rise critically for their economy. Money, good or counterfeit, will take on less value. Simply put, it will throw them completely off track and, if you bear in mind how they bankrupted themselves for the German War and the recent fighting, their house will come falling down around their ears in short order."

"So, for the risk of a submarine or two, we can take that drunken shit Churchill and his pack out of the equation for the foreseeable future?"

"Yes, Comrade General Secretary, although it hinges on the Irish being able to perform some simple tasks."

"How long before you find out if they can do what we need?"

"I already have my staff in Dublin working on the matter."

"Excellent. Once that's resolved, you may present this plan to the GKO."

Stalin's lunch was simple, but he enjoyed it with a relish he hadn't felt for some months.

Of all those in the army close to the commander none is more intimate than the secret agent; of all rewards none more liberal than those given to secret agents; of all matters none is more confidential than those relating to secret operations.

Sun Tzu

CHAPTER 176 - THE USPENKA?

1537 hrs, Monday, 23rd September 1946, US Fleet Activities Sasebo, Nagasaki, Japan.

The task of sifting through the documentation was not easy, for more than one reason.

Admittedly, Yoshiro Takeo had it easier than many, for he needed no interpreter, either for spoken or written Japanese.

After all, he was Japanese, or at least that was how he was viewed by those around him.

Yoshiro Takeo had been born in Waikoloa, Hawaii on 1st January 1922, and considered himself an American through and through.

His elder brother fought with the Nisei warriors in Europe, but Yoshiro had been denied combat, and was instead sent to Naval Intelligence, where his keen mind and language skills were put to great use.

With the surrender of the Empire of Japan, he found himself back in the land of his ancestors, his skills employed in sifting through mountains of official paperwork and intelligence reports in order to record and log all aspects of the Imperial Navy's war.

Which brought him to the records in front of him.

He sipped gently at his tea, savouring the flavour as he focussed his mind on the figures in front of him.

He didn't bother asking for a second opinion; confidence in his own ability was never lacking.

In simple terms, many tons of steel had been delivered to Sasebo and some of the records that recorded their disposal had survived the Allied bombing campaign.

Enough to indicate considerable allocation to two special projects that commenced in April and October 1943, neither of which, at first sight, attracted any other mention in any of the remaining dockyard records.

He had caught that first sniff of something, the 'Mongoto' as he called them, a week previously but it was not until this morning that other information had come to light.

Whilst the Japanese Naval records had generally suffered from the attentions of the Allied air forces, the dockyard armaments distribution and allocation administration had somehow avoided any losses, meaning full records were available.

It was a portion of these that sat in front of him now and, try as he might, he could not tally a number of weapons with the stated receiving vessels and remaining stock, less those marked as destroyed in air raids.

Six Type 96 triple AA mounts were simply unaccounted for, as well as two 140mm 11th Year gun mounts.

The 140mm 50-caliber was a standard naval weapon, issued to surface vessels.

It had taken Takeo a moment to realise that the notations seemed to indicate a 40-caliber weapon.

What had piqued Takeo's interest further was the casual remark of his submariner friend, Baumer.

He did a little research to confirm Baumer's observation and quickly established that the 40-calibre 11th Year guns were indeed almost exclusively mounted on the IJN's big submarines.

He had found Baumer back at his desk that lunchtime and questioned him on the larger IJN submarines, specifically the huge AM class that were Baumer's special area of reference.

Initially, the former submariner rained on Takeo's parade.

Type 96 mounts for submarines had a different make-up, with large amounts of stainless steel to help resist corrosion.

Plus the AMs had two triple mounts and a single mount of Type 96s.

There were traces of two single mounts that could possibly be involved, having been tasked for an abandoned submarine project but not installed. Pencil notations recorded both as '特型潜水艦', which he translated into 'Special Type, Submarine.'

They were both of the modified stainless steel variety, which supported their probable use in submarines.

"So that means the numbers don't add up basically, Marvin."

Baumer could only agree and he seized the moment.

"Yep. Anyway, now that you've barked up the wrong tree, gimme a hand with this lot, will ya?"

The matter of the guns was side-lined in favour of translating dockyard records on Sasebo's abandoned AM submarine projects.

At that moment, the guns in question were mounted on submarines thousands of miles away in a secret base on the Black Sea.

The very existence of the two Sen-Tokus still remained a secret.

1203 hrs, Wednesday, 2nd October 1946, Dankerode, Germany.

Guderian allowed the binoculars to fall slowly away from his face, which also allowed the smile that creased his weathered features to become apparent to those present.

The exercises had gone superbly well, each force growing in confidence in their own skills, and in those of the men around them.

With the exception of one mistake on road selection by a tank company commander, the week had gone far better than any of the generals or staff could have anticipated.

So much so that Guderian had decided that this would be the last one he would watch, and he promised himself a few days of peace and quiet in Schwangau, his new home.

Something drew his eye and the binoculars flew to his face.

"Mein Gott! Herrlich! Herrlich!"

He looked at the man standing away to the left and exchanged a nodded professional courtesy.

Guderian could not contain himself.

"Tell me. How did that happen?"

He looked at the scene of 'Red' team tanks appearing from nowhere, exactly where they shouldn't be for the 'Green' team.

He could imagine the umpires trying to sort out the mayhem of who was dead, and also the indignation of the massacred 'Green' soldiers who were no slouches at the art of war themselves.

He continued to watch as the German green force was 'butchered' in front of him.

"Incredible, General... I didn't see a thing before they were all over the grenadiers."

"Those men learnt the art of camouflage from the very best, Herr Feldmarschal."

Guderian conceded the point and offered his hand to the Polish general.

"Well done, General... very well done. Please make sure that your commander meets the German force commander and briefs him personally on how his force was dismantled."

Zygmunt Berling saluted and, grinning from ear to ear, rushed off to radio Wojciech Bewziuk, commander of the 1st Division, in order celebrate the success of their efforts and pass on

Guderian's request. He also, wisely, advised caution in Bewziuk's dealings with their new German allies, who would undoubtedly be sore about being handed their collective arse by their traditional enemy.

As it happened, the commander of the newly formed panzer-grenadiere division was a professional who understood he had been bested and was keen to learn the lessons so it would not happen again.

Across a range of such sites in Northern Germany, the two armies trained and exercised together, and developed an understanding and comradeship that cut across much of their nation's history of enmity.

Much… but not all.

1601 hrs, Thursday, 3rd October 1946, the Lighthouse Tavern, Barnatra, County Mayo, Éire.

"God bless all here."

The two men shook their jackets, sending rainwater in all directions, but there were no complaints or shouts of annoyance.

Everyone in the pub knew who they were.

It didn't pay to get yourself noticed unnecessarily.

At the far end of the long bar, adjacent to the roaring fire, two other men rose from their table, preparing to welcome the visitors, who moved towards them briskly, as much as to close on the source of warmth as to commence business.

Two other men slipped into the bar, but stayed distant… watching… alert.

Outside, four others endured the rain, maintaining a perimeter within which the two senior IRA leaders could operate.

Brian O'Scanlon and Stephen Wood took the empty chairs as they exchanged handshakes with the two waiting men.

"I'm guessing that you're O'Farrell?"

"That I am, Mister Wood."

"So that makes you Lieutenant Ulianov?"

"Indeed so, Comrade Wood."

Shandruk extended his hand.

The secret base at Glenlara had proved like a gas light to a moth for both the IRA and the Soviet Navy, and both had returned to the facility, albeit the former not necessarily as they thought, and the latter only once.

The Soviets had deposited a team of four men once they had successfully made contact with the local IRA, in the shape of the

86

G2 agent, O'Farrell, who had stepped into the void left by the death of Reynolds.

Eager to get over the loss of so many men in the accidental explosion at Glenlara, which was how the IRA leadership understood the deaths of most of the Mayo brigade's personnel had occurred, they found a man who was known to them already organising affairs, and had no hesitation in keeping him in place.

Thomas Ryan O'Farrell was the commander of the new Mayo Brigade. He was also Irish G-2's most valuable asset in the fight against the very organisation he was a part of.

The Soviet naval group had long since been replaced by men from the OSS Ukrainian unit, and everything ran on a day-to-day basis solely for the benefit of Allied intelligence, and against the Soviets and IRA.

"So, down to business, O'Farrell. No problems with your set up on the coast there?"

"Not now, Mister Wood. The accident made one hell of a mess and we basically started from scratch. Still turn up a bit of a body now and again. Poor bastards. Don't hardly see the Gardaí much at all. We've a man on the inside anyhow, so they'll be no surprises from those cocks. The fucking Brits have been very accommodating in providing materials when we've strayed across the border. Most problems we get is from the occasional flight over by their fucking flying boat things. Mind you, some of the locals turn up now and again, looking for a son or a brother. Nothing we can do save tell 'em a little and assure 'em that their boy died for the cause. Apart from that, we're top."

"Good, good. We've something brewing that'll need you to be extra sharp for a time... not yet mind. For the future, but Brian and I are here to smooth the path and see if there's anything you need."

"Such as like what, Mister Wood?"

"Our Russian friends have a plan that'll put the shit up the English. The Council's on board with it. Your part'll be simple as chips, son. Receive two deliveries and store 'em safely. We'll arrange for pick-up as soon as possible after, and that's that."

"Guns? Explosives? Men?"

"Well, our friends intend to sweeten the deal a little with some weapons and explosives, and they'll be a share of the guns for you and your boys of course, but the important load will be sealed wooden crates. The contents don't need to concern you. Council business."

"No problem with me, so long as I can have some of the explosives for a jaunt across the border."

It was a statement, not a request, and both the senior IRA men understood it to be such. What more impressed them was that the man simply accepted the situation with the crates.

Independently, the two senior men wondered if O'Farrell was a serious contender for promotion to become a bigger player in the future of the cause.

O'Scanlon slid a piece of paper across the table to Ulianov.

"Your bosses gave us those dates. Make sure you monitor the channels. Our Russian friends are aware of the perils of using radio, so it'll be kept to the minimum. When you get the message, reply...", he pointed to the Cyrillic text, "Padanets... three times only, one minute apart."

Shandruk/Ulianov took the proffered paper and slipped it into his jacket pocket in one easy movement.

"We've one specific request. Our friends want to know about the fuel cells, whatever the fuck that means. They want to know they're intact. Yes? Can I tell 'em yes?"

Shandruk/Ulianov thought on his feet and at lightning speed.

"My men are checking them as we sit here, Comrade Wood. After the storm yesterday... routine check couldn't be done... plus we had flying boat flyovers. I'll ensure the answer is radioed to..."

"No!"

His snappy voice drew gazes from those who had been trying hard to avert their eyes.

"Sorry, Lieutenant. No, avoid the radio as per your last orders.

"You, O'Farrell... you let us know by the normal route when the state of the fuel is known and, for that matter, when you've taken delivery. Expect two visits in total. The first rendezvous will bring further information. Clear?"

"No, but it'll do. One thing. What sort of delivery, boss? Fishing boat?"

"Fuck me but I'd forget my bloody head, so I would. Submarine."

"OK."

Again, both men were impressed as to how the new man took things so easily in his stride.

"Now, the weapons and explosive. Get it hidden... probably in more than one place, but that's your business. Get it listed

88

and a copy of that list to us sharpish. No fucking gung-ho operations, laddie. We'll allocate the resources… but you'll get enough to have some fun with the bastards over there."

All four men reached for their whiskey glasses simultaneously, and they clinked together.

Wood spoke a toast.

"Ní síocháin go Saoirse!"

Irish whiskey lubricated dry throats.

The four rose and shook hands.

"You're doing well, young Thomas. The council has its eye on you, so it does. Keep it up."

The two turned on their heels and walked from the bar, followed by the two IRA soldiers who had watched over them.

O'Farrell and Shandruk sat back down, as leaving straight after the others would have been poor tradecraft.

Not that the watchers would have been waiting for them, of course.

G2's men and women had other fish to fry, namely developing a list of people visited by O'Scanlon, Deputy Commander of the Northern Forces and, more importantly in so many ways, Stephen Wood, the IRA's Chief of Staff.

O'Farrell and Shandruk used the time to try and work out where the fuel might be stored and how the hell they had missed it in the first place.

1412 hrs, Saturday, 5th October 1946, Lieutenant General Kaganovich's office, the Kremlin, Moscow, USSR.

"Welcome, welcome, Comrade, and very many congratulations on your promotion. Well deserved, of course."

Nazarbayeva took a seat and accepted the plaudits with good grace.

"I understand a few people have their own issues with it, but to hell with them, I say. A drink in celebration… as equals!"

Despite her insincere protestations, Kaganovich produced a bottle and two glasses and, just as quickly filled both, seemingly in one graceful movement.

"Your health and your success. Congratulations, Comrade!"

The vodka disappeared just as quickly as it had arrived.

"Apparently, you made Comrade Beria look a fool during your last briefing?"

"It was not my intention, Comrade, but the report he presented was flawed and incomplete, so I had no choice but to reveal it for what it was. Our leadership must know the true situation."

No matter how often he spoke with the woman, he could never quite understand how politically naive she was, or how little she understood the precariousness of her position, especially in her dealings with his boss... or for that matter, his boss's boss.

"And what's the true situation as you see it, Comrade?"

"We're technologically inferior to our enemies across the range of arms, except submarines, and that's only thanks to the German boats. Our efforts to narrow the gap are being hampered by shortages of the necessary minerals, fuels, and by the same blight that affected our Germanski enemies. Too many projects, too many people working separately, using valuable and finite resources, when one project could push ahead and succeed."

"Give me an example, Comrade."

"We selected the SKS and AK-47 to replace the Mosin rifle and the range of submachine-guns, and they have proceeded at great speed... successfully so. An example of success in giving our troops the best. And yet, our tank bureaus seem to be trying to produce a nest of vehicles, all with different characteristics, each consuming resources that defeat the overall objective. We have the T-54 tank, which seems wholly effective and the equal to most of the enemy tanks, and yet we continue to dabble with new designs in the same class... designs that seem to offer no great improvement. We have seven... seven different groups working on a range of bigger and heavier vehicles, instead of concentrating on the T-54 and improving it, like we did with the T-34 and IS series. The IS-III has been improved without huge modification, and is now more than capable on the modern battlefield. That is a success. The Germans failed to understand this simple concept and poured resources down blind alleys to satisfy their leader's whims. It seems to me that now we too seem to have lost the art of keeping things simple, Comrade General."

Kaganovich, having been subjected to what amounted to a speech by the exercised GRU officer, could only grin at her candour and clear exasperation.

"Do you always speak so freely, Comrade Nazarbayeva?"

"Comrade General, I try to speak honestly, for the sake of the Rodina."

He refilled the glasses and offered a toast, hoping that the woman would heed his words for what they were.

"To all those who serve the Rodina as best they can, regardless of the consequences to themselves."

They drank the toast.

"Regardless of the consequences, Comrade General?"

"As I said, Comrade Nazarbayeva, you made Marshal Beria look a fool, at least as far as he was concerned. He's a... err... unforgiving man. At the moment, he's very busy now trying to make up for his mistakes but I advise you make your peace with him as soon as possible."

He checked his watch and rose to his feet.

"Unfortunately, I've an appointment elsewhere now, otherwise I'd offer you more vodka, Comrade. Was there anything else?"

Nazarbayeva shook her head.

"Nothing that cannot keep, comrade. Your man keeps me supplied with the information I need... thank you."

"Excellent. Now, I must go I'm afraid."

"Thank you for coming, Comrade Marshal."

"Is it what you suspect?"

"I don't know myself. Haven't watched it. One of my aides learned of its existence and managed to appropriate it. She quietly arranged for a copy to be made and the original is back in place, hopefully not having been missed. We're going to watch the copy."

"I'm not comfortable with this at all, but if it's what you suspect, it might be of great use to us, eh?"

"Indeed, Comrade Marshal."

The knock on and opening of the door were as one, and Senior Lieutenant Laberova entered, snapped to attention, and saluted the senior officers.

"Well, Ludmilla. Is it the same person in the film?"

"Without any doubt, Comrade Leytenant General. I got a good look when the General walked past me. One and the same."

"Thank you. When you're ready then."

The two men turned to the blank wall of the staff recreation room as Laberova locked the door, turned out the lights, and started the projector.

A bedroom sprang into view, one that seem modestly appointed but none the less clearly in a building of some importance.

Two oil lamps burned brightly, but the focus was on a large naked man and a woman lying on the bed, a woman they both knew.

Nazarbayeva.

"And who the fuck is **that** bastard?"

Kaganovich had absolutely no idea, which surprised him greatly.

Neither man could recognise the immensely endowed man, but the voices of the men who commented on the apparition as he took his pleasure were at first vaguely familiar, and then unmistakeable.

"Sarkisov and Nadaraia. Blyad!"

Kaganovich hummed an agreement, partially horrified, but partially stimulated by the unfolding degradation of the GRU officer.

"Those two NKVD bastards, Sarkisov and Nadaraia. Beria likely ordered this then."

Kaganovich, General of NKVD, understood the Army Marshal's indignation on behalf of a woman they had come to respect.

Although not enough to stop them from incorporating the unsuspecting and politically inept woman in their own grubby plans.

They watched as the woman was violated and violated again.

"You hear that, Comrade General. They're taking still pictures too. I take it you know where this was taken?"

"NKVD dacha. It's used quite often for certain delicate tasks, mainly with visiting foreigners."

"Wait… wait… rewind! Turn the volume up."

Laberova did as instructed.

"…can be edited out later, Comrade Marshal."

"Comrade Marshal he said! Beria… he was there…watching this… this act he ordered… he was there!"

"So it would seem, Comrade Marshal. Continue, Leytenant."

The rape went on.

"…Dzerzhinsky Street for him after Stranov has had his way…"

They both heard that loud and clear.

"Stranov."

"Whoever he may be, Comrade Marshal. Now I have a name, it won't take me long to find out everything we need to know."

The Marshal stood swiftly.

"I've had enough of watching this. It's suitable for our purposes, but I pity the poor woman for her ordeal. There'll be a day of reckoning for these bastards, I'll see to that personally."

"Actually, I don't think you will, Comrade Marshal. Our political thinker has an idea on how best we can use this to our advantage."

"Explain."

"Thank you, Leytenant. That will be all."

Laberova unlocked the door and left. The key was turned in an instant and Kaganovich passed on Khrushchev's idea in hushed tones.

"I don't like it…. not at all… in fact… it stinks."

"I agree, Comrade Marshal, but despite that it would seem to offer us everything we need in one foul swoop."

It did, without a doubt.

But at a huge cost.

"We'll talk on this some more. In any case, we'd be nowhere near using this yet."

"I agree, comrade Marshal. Now… at least you've seen it. Let's get you out of here and back into the real world without anyone seeing you. Where do you go now?"

"I have a meeting with Vladimir Konstantinovich. He is eager, I'll give him that. Always felt he was lacking in commitment but, judging by the note I received, his doubts have gone. Any reason I should know about?"

"None at all. I'll put some men on it, Comrade Marshal."

Kaganovich knew only too well why Vladimir Gorbachev was now straining at his master's leash, but the Marshal didn't need to know, and he had sworn Gorbachev to secrecy, not that the recently promoted commander of military training for the Moscow Military District would wave the folder proving that his niece had become one of Beria's night time sexual victims under the Marshal's nose.

Whilst it might have been true, the folder was carefully constructed to ensure that the commander of military training for the Moscow Military District, a man who was responsible for over one hundred thousand men, was fully with them when it changed from planning and talk to action.

Lieutenant General Vladimir Konstantinovich Gorbachev, incensed by the evidence set before him, had sworn loyalty to the coup and extracted the promise that he and he alone, would be responsible for avenging his family, a promise that Kaganovich had no problem honouring and no intention of facilitating, unless it suited him personally and aided him in his quest for command of the NKVD… or more.

Nazarbayeva waited as two NKVD officers were ushered to their waiting transport.

Her meeting with Malenkov had gone well, but she couldn't help but think he was hiding something, a something she could not fathom, either for what it was or for why it should be hidden from her.

Her own vehicle moved forward and was then stopped in favour of another, which quickly drove into prime position at the bottom of the steps.

She almost missed the arrival of the senior officer, but managed to hide her surprise behind a smart salute.

"Good afternoon, Comrade Marshal."

The man returned the salute, accompanying it with a genuine smile, for Nazarbayeva was universally popular with the men who commanded the soldiers of the Motherland.

"Are you returning to Headquarters, ahh... I see... Comrade Leytenant General? A promotion?"

"Yes, Comrade Marshal. And yes, Vnukovo flight at 1710."

"Congratulations and that is excellent. Me too. We'll travel together. Come in my car. I've got a lot to ask you before we return."

The driver doubled round to the rear door and opened it, permitting the Marshal and GRU officer to enter.

At the entrance to the square, two smart guards came to attention and saluted the exiting vehicle as Vasilevsky and Nazarbayeva quickly descended into an earnest conversation on European intelligence matters.

0755 hrs, Saturday, 12th October 1946, Headquarters, NATO Forces in Europe, Frankfurt, Germany.

Gehlen was ushered into the office by Strong's aide, and his demeanour told the general everything he needed to know about the nature of the meeting ahead.

The normally reserved German intelligence officer was clearly agitated beyond words.

"Coffee?"

Gehlen nodded as he rummaged in his briefcase.

"Maitland. Coffee for General Gehlen. Tea for myself. Thank you."

"Sir."

The door closed and Strong eyed his visitor.

"So, General Gehlen. Middle Machinery?"

"Indeed, General Strong."

94

The paperwork passed from hand to hand.

"Uspenka? Enlighten me."

"There is, so typically Russian, more than one place of that name."

He stood and walked over to the wall map.

"May I?"

"Be my guest, general."

Gehlen picked up the pins and stuck them in the map, one at a time.

"Uspenka... near Luhansk in the Ukraine."

"Uspenka, southwest of Donetz... here."

"Uspenka on the Dneipr River, just southeast of Kremenchug."

"Another here... near Akhtubinsk."

"One here, south of Yelets."

The knocking preceded the arrival of the drinks and Gehlen took a moment to check his notes. He waited until they were alone again before continuing.

"One here, southwest of Novosibirsk."

"Uspenka... north of Odessa... about here."

"Kazakhstan."

"Uspenka... halfway between Kursk and Kiev."

"Another one just the other side... east of Kursk, and another southeast of Kursk."

Strong got the idea.

"To be honest, general, there's probably more that we have yet to discover."

Strong joined Gehlen at the map and handed him his coffee.

"The proverbial needle in a haystack."

"I do not understand, General."

"Apologies. So one of these, or maybe one we have yet to find, contains something relevant to the Ministry of Middle Machinery?"

"And the intelligence doesn't narrow the field at all?"

"No, General. The source was a travel document. It was a hand notation on the official documentation. Best guess from my agent is that was made by someone on Malenkov's staff."

They drank in silence as their eyes flitted from pin to pin.

"Novosibirsk?"

"That is logical, General Strong. Industrial relocation took so much of their war industry there. We would expect to find such things there. Better to hide something in such a place."

95

"Indeed."

"The others are not all familiar to me. This one has a large camp close by at Akhtubinsk. Perhaps I can get one of my Red Cross agents near the place."

"Or I one of mine."

"Or both."

Strong tapped the map.

"This one near Luhansk. We had suspicions about it some time back. From memory, I think we thought it had some underground facility. Turned out to simply be mining. Perhaps we should take another look."

Gehlen nodded.

"General Strong, it makes sense to me that any secret facility would be more likely some considerable distance away, either well-hidden or, as we say with Novosibirsk, hidden in plain sight."

Strong understood the point.

"Kazakhstan or Novosibirsk then?"

"If the Russian stays true to form, then one of those two would be my choice, General Strong."

"So… who do we have? I can ask the Poles. They've a few people in the strangest of places. We need to review our interrogations of Soviet prisoners, in case there is something relevant that we've missed… now we have the name."

"Of course. I may have someone I can use in Novosibirsk. Difficult communications naturally. Very difficult indeed. I'll try and get in touch."

"Excellent. Now, I'm thinking we keep this close to the chest for now… until we get something firm. Agreed?"

"Agreed, General Strong."

They resumed their seats and finished the drinks, during which Strong sensed there was something else on the German's mind.

"I have a meeting at 0830… do I need to cancel it, Reinhard?"

Gehlen was taken aback that Strong should use his name, which was the precise reason the British Intelligence officer had used it.

"Just something that is concerning me, General."

Strong sensed that it was more than concern but decided on a soft pedal approach.

"If you wish to share, then it will stay in this room. If not, perhaps I can help in other ways?"

Gehlen picked up his cup, not remembering he had already finished his drink.

"Another?"

"No, thank you, General Strong."

He decided to share his concerns, a mark of how much he trusted the Englishman.

"Does the name Rudolf Diels mean anything to you, General?"

"Not immediately, but I assume it should."

"Diels was a protégé of Göring... a former head of Prussia's Department 1A..."

"The Gestapo?"

"Yes, the Geheime Staatspolizei."

"Yes, I remember now... wasn't he implicated in the assassination plot against Adolf?"

"Implicated yes... but he was not involved. Diels fell short of being a committed Nazi in many ways... but not all."

"Meaning what, Reinhard?"

"Meaning he was considered to be not ruthless enough in his prosecution of Nazi ideals."

"OK, so where does he fit in with your clear concerns?"

"He has an office in the government building. For what purpose I'm unclear, but I believe he has an intelligence brief."

"But you're th... oh."

"I'm excluded from many matters now, more than ever before. I give information but receive little on what is going on."

"And what is going on?"

Strong had caught the tone in Gehlen's voice and understood that the issue was not simply one of Diels' presence.

"Speer is working to a plan. I am sure of this. To what end, I'm unclear but I can tell you this. It involves the Poles. I have never known so many secret exchanges between us and our old enemy. Exchanges from which I am excluded... totally. I receive nothing. My agents in place have all been moved on or silenced in other ways. My top agent in the Polish government met with a fatal riding accident only a month ago. My best man in the Oberkommando was close to Guderian. He's now attached to our embassy in London!"

"Bloody hell."

"No accident... all of these moves or losses are no accident at all. I seem to serve no purpose in the upper circles any more. Whenever I'm in a meeting, I feel like the fifth cock at a four whore party."

Strong stifled his laugh, understanding that the unusual outburst was simply Gehlen letting off steam, built up under the pressure of the obvious exclusions.

"What do you want of me, Reinhard?"

"Do you have anyone in our government who might be able to establish what the hell is going on?"

That was both a huge admission from the Abwehr chief, and a considerable declaration of his own impotence.

"I'll do all I can to find out for you, Reinhard."

"Thank you, Kenneth. Thank you so very much."

History is a lesson for the future based the resolutions of the past.

Marion J. Crisp.

Chapter 177 - THE CRATES

"Son of a bitch!"

Bradley looked on with a straight face, determining to say nothing and immediately failing.

"Amphibious operations were once your speciality, Ike."

Eisenhower shot his friend a murderous look.

"Seem to remember that I sent **you** into the water. You fancy a repeat, Brad?

"No, Sir, no way, no how."

Eisenhower's fury had been put on, for the most part anyway, and he selected another tee and placed a ball on it.

"One more word out of you and I may fill the liaison vacancy in Finland with some well-known Missourian who just happens to look just like you. Kapische?"

"You wouldn't dare!"

The two laughed and then fell silent as Ike addressed the ball.

The whoosh and crisp click of the club indicated a drive straight down the fairway, and not, as previously, the dreaded tell-tale of a pulled stroke that was condemned to fall into the nearby lake.

"Nice work for an old guy."

The drive had been ruler straight and would have graced a professional tournament.

"Three years older, that's all I am... technically two and a half years. Desist, General!"

They laughed as they strolled forward enjoying the warm October sun, their casual relationship on the course as different as chalk to cheese to their formal military relationship.

"101st and 17th Airbornes have been relieved by 82nd finally, Ike. Few stopovers, mainly officers to help ease the new boys in some, but the Eagles are pretty much all on the way back home."

"God knows they earned it, Brad."

"Sure did. How's the 17th Armored settling in? There's a lot of anxious officers ringing my staff every day."

99

Bradley was looking at his ball as he walked forward, and judged a wedge to be most appropriate.

"Well, from the last report, there's next to nothing left to do. Divisional command is up at the front, getting familiar with their area of responsibility and tapping into the neighbours. Best guess is Wednesday, Ike."

"Outstanding. That'll make a lot of boys very happy. The armored boys all wanna be home for Christmas. Also, it'll reduce our logistics some."

Bradley went to address his ball but stopped himself, instead leaning back on the club as a support.

"Tell you something though, Ike. It's not just the refugees who are causing us logistical problems, although that particular nightmare doesn't go get any better. It's the Germans. Krauts are chewing up a lot of supplies. Seems like they have a live-fire drill, manoeuvre exercise, or some sort of complicated training almost every day."

"They're efficient and want to keep up their skills obviously. You know Guderian, Brad."

"Yeah, I know, Ike... but them and the Poles are almost living for it. One of my staff discovered they're working side by side constantly, living and training in the field for days on end."

"Yeah, I heard summat about that. Old enemies seem to have suddenly found some common ground, eh?"

"You mean a common enemy doth unite?"

"Something like that. You gonna hit that damn thing or am I going to die of old age?"

"Well, now that you mention age..."

"As you were, General!"

They laughed easily.

"Seriously though, those boys are certainly going to be well-prepared and fighting fit if things start up again... heaven forbid!"

"Amen to that, Brad. Like I said, they're a warrior people, and if they're ready and willing if the whole mess starts up again, then I, for one, will be grateful of their skills. Now... any chance, General?"

"Move on, old timer."

Eisenhower walked on a little way and turned just in time to see Bradley perform a beautiful chip.

Both pairs of eyes followed the ball up and down.

"Go on! Yes... yes... go on... hallelujah!"

"You gotta be kidding me!"

100

cup.
Bradley trotted past on his way to retrieve the ball from the cup.

"Make way, old timer... it's a young man's game, you know."

Eisenhower chuckled as he lined up his own riposte.

"I reckon it'd be wise to start learning Finnish, General Bradley. Soon as I get back, I'm cutting your orders!"

Bradley's reply was lost in the click of Eisenhower's own chip to the green and the exasperation that immediately followed it flying well past the cup.

"Son of a bitch!"

1312 hrs, Tuesday, 22nd October 1946, Stakhanovo Airfield, USSR.

Sacha Istomin heaved a sigh of relief.

Out of his left-hand windows he watched as the fire crews extinguished the fire in the port outboard engine, whilst his co-pilot watched the same process being conducted on the starboard outboard engine.

"Navigator to pilot. Crew all out. I'm the last one aboard. Leaving now."

Istomin had ordered his men out as soon as the aircraft came to a halt, and they had obliged at record speed, as no one likes to be in a burning aircraft at any time.

"Come on, Leonid! Let's get the fuck out of here! Raus, raus!"

Bolkovsky, the experienced co-pilot permitted himself to be chivvied along by the commander of 901st Independent Special Aviation Regiment, the Red Air Force's special operations bomber squadron.

Both men dropped onto the foamy tarmac one after the other.

Two firefighters dashed forward and pulled the men clear in dramatic fashion, clearly keen to demonstrate their professionalism to the regimental commander.

Istomin was much more interested in the damage to his aircraft, and the damage to future missions that went hand in hand with further problems with the huge bomber.

As if to taunt him, the wreckage of one of his American aircraft lay in direct line of sight, his eyes flicking from the ruined port outer to the charred wreckage of the 'General H.H. Arnold Special', one of the three B-29s with which he had started the 901st.

101

The accident had claimed six of his men, as well as writing off the valuable aircraft.

The other aircraft of the original group was 'Ding Hao', which along with the recovered pieces of another B-29, 'Cait Paomat', which had been salvaged from a crash site in the Sikhote-Alin mountain range, had contributed knowledge to the Soviet Union's aircraft designers.

They then faithfully reverse-engineered the aircraft and subsequently placed in the Red Air Force's hands the new Tu-4, a virtually identical copy of the B-29, but one that didn't suffer from engine problems quite like the R-3350 Wright Cyclones did, but was slightly inferior in speed performance and with considerably less range and bomb load, for reasons no one quite understood. This was offset by greater reliability in the engines, a higher ceiling, and much greater firepower in its defensive armament.

Istomin turned to examine the starboard engine and took time to look beyond where, lined up on the far side of the airfield, were eleven of the brand new Tupolev aircraft, all under his command.

His train of thought was interrupted by Pranic, the base engineering officer, who seemingly prepared to deliver his normal 'how the fuck was he supposed to keep the fucking Amerikanski bombers flying with no spare parts' monologue.

"Comrade Polkovnik. I'm glad you are safe."

"Thank you, Comrade Mayor of Engineering, although I seem to be giving you back a badly wounded bird."

Pranic, unusually, waved his hand dismissively at the smoking aircraft.

"Provided the surfaces and mounts are undamaged, the engines won't be a problem, Comrade Polkovnik."

Bolkovsky and Istomin both looked in astonishment at the dour officer, who normally only had death to look forward to.

Pranic understood their expressions and smiled warmly.

"Comrades, our friends in the NKVD have been successful in obtaining some replacement engines... apparently from China. I have seven such engines en route... all new, still in their shipping crates. Should be here in four hours."

Istomin slapped the man on the shoulder and laughed in triumph.

"Excellent, Comrade Mayor of Engineering. I hope to be ready for a test flight by 1400 tomorrow."

The smile departed from Ivan Pranic's face and he returned to his normal self.

"I'll report to you on my findings as soon as it's cooled down enough to examine, Comrade Polkovnik."

"Excellent, excellent. I'll be in the mess sampling some vodka with my valiant co-pilot. Keep me informed, Comrade."

The group parted with salutes typical of air force personnel the world over.

A small GAZ jeep slipped alongside the two pilots. They dropped into it with practised ease, and sped off towards the distant buildings.

2103 hrs, Tuesday, 29th October 1946, Vinogradar Young Communists Sailing Club, Black Sea, USSR.

Nobukiyo clicked the stopwatch and grunted with satisfaction.

He said nothing and simply showed the watch to the Soviet officer alongside him.

They shared a smile.

"Congratulations, Comrade Commander. The best time yet."

Nobukiyo had been mercilessly drilling his hangar and deck crews for over a month, devising new routines, improving on existing practices, all with the target of ensuring that his beloved submarine was exposed on the surface for as little time as possible.

Recently promoted to Captain First Rank, a decision made by the High Command once they discovered Nobukiyo's status, Mikhail Kalinin was extremely satisfied that, when... *more like if...* the mission was given the go ahead, the Japanese submariners were more than up to the task.

"So, are you calling a halt for tonight, Comrade Commander?"

Nobukiyo grinned without a hint of mercy and compassion.

"One more time, I think."

Kalinin had expected no less.

"FUTATABI, JINYO!"

The shout carried across the secret base, loud enough to be heard by the furthest sailor, and the collective groan of men who had hoped for respite was equally loud.

Officers and NCOs chivvied their sections into order and the task of extracting and erecting a V-2 on the Sen-Toku's deck began once more.

1100 hrs, Wednesday, 30th October, 1946, Camp Steel, on the Meer van Echternach, Luxembourg.

Camp Rose had long gone, the lack of casualties meaning that the hospital, so long an excellent cover for the goings-on at Camp Steel, no longer embraced and protected the secret base.

The previous commander had created a small 'supply depot' to explain the presence of armed soldiers in the woods, but the tarpaulins merely covered empty crates and oil drums, the whole 'depot' nothing but a charade for the benefit of the nosier locals.

Zebra Company were presently responsible for manning the gate and general camp security, and were therefore first to discover that the times were changing.

The previous CO had been invalided out, having broken both femurs and shattered his pelvis in a failed practice jump, his partially-opened parachute doing enough to spare his life, but virtually ending it in the same act, as the idea of being in a wheelchair for the rest of his life was as close to death as Colonel Steel could be and still draw breath.

The new CO arrived unannounced in the middle of an inspection by Zebra Company's Executive Officer, accompanied by one of the unit's senior NCOs.

"Well that's just swell! OK, boys... fall in... fall in...", the first lieutenant encouraged the guard detail into some sort of order whilst his sidekick moved to the gate to back up the young corporal who was in charge.

"Steady on there, Buck. This looks like a man who knows his business."

The corporal grunted in reply and waited as the jeep slowly came to a halt in front of the pole barrier.

He grunted again as he checked that the .30cal was manned and trained on the jeep by two business-like soldiers.

Rosenberg eased his Thompson a little and resisted the temptation to accompany Buck Polson to the jeep.

He sensed Hässler arrive by his side.

"So this is the new boss... looks like a vet. Catch his name yet?"

"Nope. Figured I'd go by the book and let Buck handle it."

"Good call."

The corporal stepped back from the jeep and saluted, the officer in question sending one back in smart but brief fashion.

He stepped out of the jeep and straightened himself and his uniform out.

The full colonel bore ribbons that indicated he was no desk soldier, and had spent a lot of time at the sharp end with a gun in his hand.

Both Hässler and Rosenberg examined the minutiae of his awards before they realised that the details were becoming clearer, for no other reason than the colonel was moving towards them.

They both saluted.

"Sir, First Lieutenant Hässler, Executive Officer, Zebra Company, on guard post inspection, Sir."

"Sir, First Sergeant Rosenberg, Zebra Company, on guard post inspection, Sir."

"Thank you. Is everything in order?"

"Sir, yes sir."

The stereo effect of their replies brought a smile to the senior officer's face.

He had sought a new command and always been turned down for reasons that no one in authority satisfactorily explained. He had been given this opportunity solely because his predecessor had nearly killed himself in training.

It was great to be back amongst proper soldiers.

As the two men wore solely rank markings, he had no idea that the NCO in front of him was the holder of a DSC and Silver Star plus change, and that the officer held the same honours.

But he did know that they were veteran soldiers, and he felt home again.

For their part, any officer who sported the evidence of a Bronze Star, two Silver Stars, and two DSCs was clearly a competent man with experience of being in harm's way. He was also airborne, which also counted for a lot.

The Colonel turned to the Corporal of the guard.

"Please inform the camp duty officer that I've arrived..."

He swivelled back to the two friends in an easy movement.

"... and if you two've finished your inspection, you could walk me round the perimeter of the camp."

"Sir, yes sir."

And so it was that Colonel Marion Crisp assumed command of Group Steel.

A command that would provide him with his finest and most tragic hours.

"Allow me to show you to the Comrade Polkovnik's room, Comrade Marshal."

The senior nurse stepped aside as the doctor led Marshal Bagramyan and his entourage into the monastery.

Along the way, Bagramyan was feted and saluted, made the subject of squeals of joy and adoration, and offered many a disfigured hand to shake. He had always been popular, and Lyskovsky was not normally on the agenda for Army Marshals to visit, probably because of the horrors it held.

"This is his room, Comrade Marshal. Would you lik…"

"Thank you, Comrade Polkovnik. You may return to your patients."

The flustered doctor saluted and went on his way, upset that he was not going to be privy to whatever had brought Bagramyan to the door of that particular man.

Behind him he heard authoritative knocking, such as might be made by an extremely senior rank on a door that would normally have been opened for him.

From within came a gruff invitation and Bagramyan strode in to find the object of his visit standing in front of a full length mirror, fiddling with his tunic buttons.

The fiddling stopped immediately, to be replaced by a twitchy nervousness as the Colonel of Tanks tried to decide whether he was dressed to salute, should throw himself on the floor in a position of supplication, or simply stand erect and see what happened next.

"Polkovnik Yarishlov?"

"Yes, Comrade Marshal. Polkovnik Arkady Arkadyevich Yarishlov, 1st Guards Rifle Division."

Yarishlov went for the salute and was delighted that the normal pains associated with moving his arm in the officer's tunic were less than normal, and without his normal lunchtime pain killers too.

Bagramyan had seen a picture of the man in his file, and had also been warned that the burning tank had made certain 'alterations' to his appearance, but even then the foreshortened nose, curled lips, and hairless head, sans eyebrows et al, gave him a moment of horror.

Bagramyan moved forward and extended his hand, something that caught Arkady off guard.

The Marshal's grip was firm and caused him a little discomfort, but Yarishlov kept his face straight, declining to show any reaction.

"How may I assist the Comrade Marshal?"

Yarishlov resumed the attention position and was amazed that Bagramyan moved forward, pulled a chair out from under the modest table, and expected Yarishlov to sit on it.

"Please, Comrade Yarishlov. Sit."

One of Bagramyan's aides appeared with a slightly plusher chair for his commander.

The two suddenly found themselves alone.

"So, Comrade Yarishlov, how are your wounds now? I understand that you've made excellent progress."

"Thank you, Sir. I confess, from the position they expected to what I have now, then I have come much further than the experts or myself anticipated. There's further to go, of course, but I would welcome the opportunity to serve the Rodina once more."

"Indeed, the battlefield calls you back, so I hear."

"Yes, Comrade Marshal. I'm not designed for clean sheets and comfortable beds."

"Ah, the call of the field. Muck and mud and the comradeship of men under arms."

They shared the laugh of professionals who understood each other completely.

The door opened and coffee arrived on cue.

Bagramyan waited until they were alone again.

"Now, any decent officer would have something to sweeten this with."

Yarishlov understood and retrieved a copy of Lermantov's 'A Hero of our Time' from the window sill.

The pages had been hollowed out and held contraband.

He 'sweetened' both mugs with cognac.

"I believe that you have bombarded command with all sorts of requests these last few weeks?"

"I've sent a number of requests seeking an assignment, Comrade Marshal."

"And so far have nothing in return."

"No, Comrade Marshal."

"No."

Bagramyan sipped his scalding hot coffee and grimaced as Yarishlov took a deeper draught of his.

"I am advised that you could profit from a few specialist physiotherapy sessions at the Academy for Medical Science in Moscow."

"Comrade Marshal, with respect, I get physiotherapy here, and the view is better."

Bagramyan laughed and slapped his leg.

"Very true. The Academy is not the prettiest of buildings, neither does it have such magnificent countryside, Comrade Yarishlov. But it'll do you good and hasten your return to fitness."

Yarishlov had made all the arguments before, successfully, but he sensed he was about to have a card played that he could not counter.

Rank.

He was correct.

"Well, you will attend and that's that, Comrade Yarishlov."

Bagramyan drained the last of his coffee and gestured towards Lermantov's tome.

Yarishlov poured an ample measure and the Marshal waxed lyrical over the fine cognac.

"That's bloody good… by the mother, that's very bloody good."

"Apparently so… it's Prunier cognac, Comrade Marshal."

"Really? How in the name of the steppes did you get hold of that in here?"

Yarishlov considered his answer quickly and decided to take refuge in the truth.

"I have an extremely resourceful Praporschik who keeps me well provisioned, Comrade Marshal."

Bagramyan drained the glass and savoured the contents, allowing the warming liquid to evaporate and warm inside his mouth.

Both men enjoyed the silence brought on by the fine cognac.

Bagramyan ended it with a reluctant final swallow.

"Well, tell your Praporschik that he's transferred to my personal staff with promotion if he can guarantee a supply of this fine cognac."

He stood, declining the offer of a refill.

"Can't sit down for too long. Spent hours in the car getting here. Anyway, Comrade Polkovnik. While you're in Moscow, you'll attach yourself to the personal staff of the Commander of Military Training, Moscow Military District. I'm told he needs someone with tank experience."

Bagramyan shouted towards the door.

"Vlassev!"

The door opened and one of the Marshal's aides entered on cue.

"Orders."

The Major produced a set of papers immediately.

"These are your orders for joining, travel documents, and everything that will permit you to reach Moscow and obtain a suitable billet. Also there are details of your therapy schedule the Academy, which I expect you to honour. Are we clear, Comrade Yarishlov?"

"Yes, Comrade Marshal."

"Now, let's get you properly dressed. Mayor?"

The Major went to the door and retrieved an officer's tunic from a pair of hands that magically appeared.

"I believe you'll find this correct."

Bagramyan's aide passed over the tunic of a Major General of Tank troops.

"Congratulations, Comrade Mayor General Yarishlov."

The Major helped Arkady out of his tunic and into the new one.

He could not help but shoot a look in the mirror as the Major transferred the honorifics across to the new tunic, carefully avoiding wounding the burned man further.

"I read the after-action reports from Naugard. You and Deniken performed magnificently, Comrade Yarishlov. Your promotion is well-deserved, Comrade."

"Thank you, Comrade Marshal."

The Major stood back and allowed Bagramyan to examine the newly fledged general.

"Excellent. Now that's what I call a soldier. Again, congratulations, Comrade Yarishlov. You've given so much to Mother Russia. Now, your orders allow for you to remain here for another four days. I have ordered a car to pick you up at midday on the 5th. Good luck with your new assignment. Now, whilst I am here I shall visit some more of our Motherland's brave soldiers. Take care, Comrade Mayor General."

With only time to offer a salute, Yarishlov found himself alone with his reflection, the reflection of a man who now had a mission.

A man who, in his own eyes, was once more a useful soldier for his country.

He freshened his own glass with a modest Prunier and raised it to the reflection.

"Well, God bless 'em but you've to admire their bleedin' sense of humour if nowt else, Bill."

O'Farrell's second in command's grin was immediately illuminated by the lightning.

"Fucking All Hallows' Eve. Jesus, Mary, and Joseph, what a night!"

Around them the wind and rain of an Atlantic Storm threw itself against the rocky bastion of the north Éire shore.

"You think they'll still come, boss?"

"You tell me. Stubborn fuckers from what I can see. Anyways, we ain't got a choice but stand here getting fucking soaked, have we?"

The whole base had been ready to receive the Soviet submarine since 2200, the earliest time scheduled.

"This shite has gotta slow the sub up for sure. Go and get yourself dry for a while, Bill. Relieve me at one. Now fuck off before I think better of it."

No sooner had William Parsons left his side than a shadowy figure appeared in front of him.

It quickly materialised into a hobbling Soviet Naval Lieutenant in wet weather gear.

"Ah... Leftenant Vlad. Top of the morning to you."

They had long since agreed that no matter what, the cover name would be used.

"Leg playing you up now, is it?"

"Just a little. No sign of it yet."

"It'll be along directly, don't you worry yourself. The Sovs won't let a little thing like an Atlantic gale stop them."

And yet the sea remained stubbornly empty.

'Vlad' pulled his hood around him and struck his lighter, the light illuminating his bearded face even as the wind struggled to destroy the flame before its work was done.

"Least we know those bloody fuel cells won't disappear in all of this. Your man Lach... stroke of brilliance to think of it, otherwise we'd never have found the bastard things. Wish we'd had more time to practice with the fuelling procedure. That could give us away if we're not careful."

'Vlad', better known as Shandruk, emerged from under his hood with two lit cigarettes.

"Here."

110

With cupped hands, the two smoked quietly.

"I've thought about that problem. I think we're fine. How can a small monitoring team be expected to know how to run the equipment? Plus, the sub'll bring the expertise with it... err... won't it?"

"Maybe you're right. We'll know soon enough, so we will."

Bill Parsons had stood his watch and was back in the dry before something broke the surface of the roiling sea off Glenlara.

It was 0401 when one of Shandruk's men spotted the veiled signal lamp flashing the coded two-letter message.

Word spread quickly and soon everyone was ready.

The submarine had surfaced some considerable distance off shore, so took its time drawing in to the anchorage point.

Shandruk was the first to identify it.

"One of the German boats... type twenty-one. Intelligence said the Northern Fleet had got hold of at least one. Seems it's here. Something to inform our masters of later, eh?"

"Yep. Right... let's get this done as quick as possible and get the bastards on their way."

The Soviet crew were nothing if not efficient, and the cargo flowed freely out of every orifice in the submarine.

The choke point was the boats used to bring the crates ashore.

There were five hundred and six of them and the supply overwhelmed the space on the rowboats that O'Farrell's 'IRA' men had on hand.

Two inflatables were deployed from the type XXI, and they helped ease the burden, but the whole process took far too long, and dawn started to show its coat tails before the last crate left the submarine's deck.

Some of the sub's crew had come ashore to help secrete the cargo in the store that had been hastily constructed, and the mad scramble to get back to the submarine ended in tragedy.

One seaman slipped as he tried to get back into a boat, pulling another into the water with him.

The swell of a wave pushed the boat sideways and both were crushed between it and the cliff face near the bottom of the loading ramp.

O'Farrell's men swept them up and onto the ramp.

The young Soviet naval officer in the party swiftly decided that they should stay and be tended on shore, so the boat pushed off two men light.

The two injured men were carried off to the dormitory and the local doctor sent for, or at least that was what the Ukrainian Lach told the submarine officer would happen.

The two were simply placed on camp beds whilst all eyes observed the submarine's departure.

"Didn't even want the fucking fuel after all, Vlad."

"Suits me just fine… just fine."

The XXI had turned out to sea and was slowly sinking beneath the waves.

"Said he'd be back by the end of the month with the rest."

"Maybe, maybe not. Right. Take it you'll deal with our unwanted guests and then meet me in the store. I've to see what's in the crates."

"Give me five minutes."

Four minutes later, the two bodies were already dragged outside ready for weighting and sinking, and Shandruk was in the store stood next to a speechless O'Farrell.

"I'm not fucking dreaming, am I? That is what it looks like?"

"Yes. Koorva! It is. Pizdets!"

"I'm not going open any more. I've done five… all the same…fuck!"

"All the same?"

"Yep… five hundred and six crates… all the fucking same… Jesus, Joseph, and Mary… it's incredible, man!"

"The men mustn't know."

"Oh too fucking right they mustn't. We'd have a fucking mutiny on our hands. Everything'd be in flitters, so it would. Mixed guards, two of yours, two of mine, twenty-four hours... not in the room but outside... you'll need to bring some more men over. You got the uniforms available?"

"I have the uniforms. I'll organise it as soon as that sub clears the area."

They both stopped and looked at the contents of the crate one last time.

"Jesus."

"Koorva"

O'Farrell tapped the lid back in place again and they both left, locking the door behind them, the modest padlock now feeling wholly inappropriate as a guard to the contents of the store.

The two most powerful warriors are patience and time.

Leo Tolstoy

CHAPTER 178 - LE BOUDIN

1501 hrs, Friday, 1st November 1946, Karup Air Base, Denmark.

Colonel Banner listened intently, or that was how it seemed anyway.

The Air Commodore finally dropped the volume to a level just below a scream and completed his lengthy diatribe on low-flying B-29s and their effect upon his ground attack squadron's exercises that morning.

The sound in Banner's ear stopped so he correctly concluded that the RAF officer had too.

"I agree, Air-Commodore, but I'll not sanction the three crews involved because they were acting under my direct orders."

The rant started up all over again and Banner's face quickly flicked from an 'imminent heated response' look back to the previous one he had mastered so well during the initial roasting: that of feigned attentiveness.

"Again, Sir, I can only state that I gave my men detailed orders, which they appear to have followed to the letter. I might also add that there was no filing of an exercise by any of squadrons in and around that area, those under your direct command or any others, as required by an order for Air Officer commanding Denmark.

He had checked up on that immediately the original angry phone call had been terminated.

"Colonel, there is no such order in being and I don't have to pander to you bloody Yanks if I want to run exercises for my chaps. I run the ground attack squadrons in Denmark, and I don't expect to find bloody great lumbering bombers running about in my airspace at one hundred feet off the deck. I nearly lost two aircraft, man! I want your men's guts for garters... do I make myself clear?"

That Wing Commander Cheshire RAF was stood in the room made no difference to the irate officer. He had the whole fiasco tabbed as an American foul up.

"I understand you, Air-Commodore, but again I cannot permit my men to be criticised as they were acting under my orders."

114

"Well, I don't know what sort of useless bunch you have here, or what type of squadron you are, but I assure you that I outrank you... both of you... and I will have my way. I'll have your head as well if you insist in this 'under my orders' approach. Now produce your men or I'll go over your bloody head and there'll be hell to pay for insubordination and refusal to obey my direct orders too!"

Despite his best efforts, the other less compliant Banner surfaced.

"Easy now, before you blow yourself a valve, Commodore. I understand that you outrank me, but you ain't the top dog in the pound by any means. My orders come from those that crow from the top of the dung heap. Here," he fished a single page document out of the bottom drawer, one that he'd been put in place for moments such as this, "Wind your goddamn neck in, read that, and get off my base pronto, fella!"

The signatures on the document alone let the Air Commodore know he was in a no-win situation.

"Now, as a courtesy to my British Allies, I'll forget this happened, and forget that your officers failed to file full flight plans and communicate any warnings on aerial activity conducted within my squadron's practice area, as per the order of August 1st last."

He placed the appropriate order in the man's hand, completing his deflation.

The paperwork was returned and the Wing Commander's brain started to work on a protest.

Banner jumped straight in.

"Listen, Commodore, we gotta work together here. You fucked up, simple as that..."

The RAF officer went purple and opened his mouth, only to find Banner's pointed finger inches from his face.

"Easy, fella. You fucked up... it happens... no need to get twisted outta shape. It's our secret. Just make sure you file as required in future, and we'll say no more about it."

The RAF officer spun on his heel without exchanging any further words and flounced from the room, muttering words like 'insubordination', 'mutiny', and 'treason'.

The door slammed so hard the plaster cracked around the frame.

"Jeez but he has a burr up his arse, Leonard."

Cheshire could only agree.

The officer in question was well known as a first-class ass, but Cheshire was unused to such displays between ranking officers, regardless of the lack of merit in one or other's position.

115

None the less, he was getting used to Banner's way, and now found that he liked the less formal way he went about his business, at least in the environment of the special unit at Karup.

"Never liked the chap personally."

"I can understand why, fella. Now, can you wheel their sorry asses in here and then we can go and have our game as planned."

Cheshire opened the door warily, checking for impending collapse, and ordered the waiting pilots into the squadron commander's office.

Banner sat behind the desk, looking far less friendly than he had a moment beforehand.

"Right. Start talking, and make it a goddamn work of art, cos I've a chewing out to pass on, which you might've heard me getting. My ass is sore and I need victims to assuage my pain...so... what in the name of Hades were you doing flying my birds in vic-formation at one-zero-zero feet in the ground attack zone? That's one-zero-zero feet which my math tells me is four-zero-zero goddamned feet below mission parameters."

The senior man, a Captain, spoke up as had been agreed.

"Colonel, you told us to fly formation and spend the last hour flying out of the norm stuff... get a handle on our birds in every way we can. We just wanted to get a head start on next weeks' itinerary. You did say out of the norm stuff, Sir."

"Did I say that, Captain?"

"Yes Sir, Colonel. You sure did. So we flew deck-level... we figured you'd get us on it at some time, in fact it is in the training schedule... so we thought ahead."

The other five men nodded their agreement.

Banner' face would have been at home in a witches hearing in Medieval England, or in the court of Torquemada.

"Really? You thought ahead?

"And it's in the training schedule?"

"Yes, Sir... err... not yet...err... next week, Colonel."

"No... not yet... next week... and I told you out of the norm stuff, did I?"

"Yes, Colonel, Sir. We all heard it, didn't we boys?"

The rumbles of agreement disappeared under Banner's close scrutiny.

He stood sharply, causing his assembled victims to rock backwards like a wave of hot air had hit them in the faces.

"Well then I guess you were acting under orders, just like I told our gallant RAF ally. Now, get your goddamned faces out of my sight before I start to chew on your sorry asses, and don't move outside the agreed flight parameters again. Move!"

The six men almost competed to be first out of the door.

Banner lit a cigar and puffed away the last of his annoyance.

"Can't fault their keenness, Leonard... not at all. They've taken to all the training... despite the fact that we don't want to do the mission... not ever!"

"I certainly don't, Colonel, but train for it we must, eh?"

"Amen to that, old boy."

Banner choked at the end of his impersonation, the rich cigar smoke catching his throat.

"You really should give them up, Colonel."

"All in good time... say... when I'm ninety or so."

They shared a laugh.

"So, next week we start a fortnight of low flying exercises, and then pack to practice drops until December, when Jasper practice bombs will arrive. Have you picked your crews for Jasper yet, Colonel?"

Banner laughed out loud.

"Natural selection has just taken place, Wing Commander. And you?"

The three crews involved in today's near miss would be the US crews designated to learn the art of dropping the Jasper, Barnes-Wallis' latest creation.

"Excellent. I've picked three good sets of lads. All of which have some sort of Tall Boy experience, which should stand them in good stead."

Cheshire had the advantage on Banner, as he had been in 617 Squadron, one of the RAF's super heavy bomb trained units.

However, even he was chastened by the thought of dropping a Jasper.

A new concept, Barnes Wallis had designed a super penetrating bomb similar to the Grand Slam and Tall Boy weapons, only Jasper had a much greater sting.

An atomic sting.

Cheshire picked up his racquet and made a practice stroke.

"Now, if you will, Colonel. I need the money."

Two hours later, Cheshire struck the winning backhand volley and was one English pound richer.

The man froze in the middle of the road.

'I hear something... a vehicle... fuck, fuck, fuck... hide... hide quickly...Adonai preserve me...'

"If I thought for one moment that you were deliberately driving into the potholes, I'd have you transferred to the Russian Front!"

"Beg your pardon, Oberführer, but we're on the Russian Front already."

Jorgensen, accompanying Knocke on his return trip to the division, failed to stifle a laugh.

"I meant further forward, you stupid ass! Like bloody Moscow"

They shared a roar of laughter, which was punctuated by a violent thump as the Krupp's back wheel found a pothole.

"Right, that's it. Pull over, Hässelbach... quickly... before I soil myself. We'll speak more on this matter once I'm two litres lighter."

The Krupp came to a swift halt and Knocke alighted, already fumbling with his flies.

Jorgensen decided to take the opportunity and soon both men were unburdening themselves with audible sighs of relief.

Sergent-Chef Hässelbach got out of the vehicle and stood to one side, ST-44 held ready, just in case, for Czechoslovakia was a dangerous place, even to the new liberators.

Alert as he was, he was unprepared for the sudden shouts from his two officers.

The appearance of a pistol in Jorgensen's hand caused him to bring the ST-44 up to his shoulder and ready himself for whatever threat was about to visit itself upon them.

Knocke emerged from the bushes with a ragged man, half dragging, half assisting the man up the gentle slope to the road.

Jorgensen relaxed as the emaciated man, wrapped in what looked like rough sacks, was clearly no threat. The return of his pistol to its holster signalled a reduction of tension in the group, although Hässelbach decided to retain his weapon in hand for now as he surveyed the area around them, just in case.

"Some water, Hässelbach."

The NCO looked sheepishly at his commander.

"Oh really? What do you have then?"

The water bottle arrived in Knocke's hands, and he swiftly smelt the contents.

"What in the name of Brunhilda's knickers is that?"

"Some sort of Slivovitz, Oberführer. A fruit drink."

Knocke ignored the attempt at humour and extended the bottle to the desperately thin man.

"Here... drink... slowly... a sip."

The man warily took the bottle, his senses sharpened by months on the run from the authorities, and confused by the clash of French uniform and German medals.

Jorgensen rummaged in his pack and took out a salami and some bread.

"Here, Oberführer. I daresay the man can use some food to soak the fruit juice up."

The food stayed in Knocke's hands for the briefest of moments before it was scooped up and forced between cracked and bleeding lips.

"Who are you? Czech? Pole? German?"

There was something about the rags under the sacking that suggested some organisation... some official group...

"Czech... Bohemien..."

The man spoke in German, or as best he could through a rapidly moving mass of bread and sausage.

"Sudeten?"

"Ja."

"We're German soldiers here."

The man said nothing, but was clearly still weighing up how to proceed.

Knocke played the matter softly.

"We were in the German Army but now fight with the French Foreign Legion against the communists."

"Army?"

"Yes," Knocke replied semi-truthfully.

"He called you Oberführer. That's not army."

Knocke inclined his head by way of contrition.

"In one sense, perhaps not. We were soldiers of the Waffen-SS. And you?"

"I'm a Jew."

"You are safe wi..."

119

The rags under the sacks suddenly metamorphosed into something that jolted Knocke's mind.

"...from a camp?"

"Ja. Theresienstadt, Herr Offizier."

"And you escaped when?"

"I don't know, Herr Offizier. The SS went, the Russian came. Nothing changed."

He stopped only to cram more of the food in his mouth.

Knocke accepted the cigarette offered by his procurement specialist and waited for the rest of the story.

"The Russian was about to leave and started killing again."

The food induced a heavy belch.

"I ran... weeks ago... maybe months... I've been running ever since."

"What's your name?"

"Mandl... Ahron Mandl. I was... am... a journalist"

The man was staring with pure hunger at the cigarette pack in Hässelbach's hand.

"Well, you're safe now, Ahron Mandl, journalist."

Hässelbach placed a lit cigarette in Mandl's hand and the three watched as he alternated between chomping on the bundle of food in one hand, and dragging on the cigarette in the other.

Conscious of the darkening skies, Knocke made a decision.

"Why don't you come with us, Mandl? We can have you looked at by our doctor, and you get to sleep in clean sheets for the first time in quite a while I expect."

With less reluctance than had been expected, the emaciated form of Ahron Mandl, former Sonderkommando at Theresienstadt, slid into the Krupp.

Ten minutes later the vehicle made a hurried stop as Mandl summoned up the whole contents of his stomach, his system having rebelled against such comparatively fine fare.

He then proceeded to snore his way through the journey back to Camerone's headquarters.

0237 hrs, Saturday, 2nd November 1946, a field, two kilometres southeast of Baltrušaičiai, Lithuania.

The signal pots had been lit at 0230 as had been arranged, coinciding with the sound of aero engines in the night.

The partisan group were facing out, ringing the drop zone, securing it in case the NKVD were prowling in the night.

Only Mikenas and the heavily pregnant Luistikaite were looking towards the illuminated space.

Normally, Luistikaite would not have been there, but SOE had insisted that one of theirs was present when the 'packages' arrived. After all, this was the first insertion into Lithuania since the 'peace' had been agreed, and the British were rightly nervous.

Mikenas had progressed to operational command of 'the Shield', as Pyragius, the de facto commander, fought a continuing battle against the infections in his old wounds, despite Greim's radio message and the subsequent air-dropping of medical supplies.

Suspicions had long departed, and both Greim and Luistikaite were full and unequivocal members of the group.

The latter pointed into the air.

"Here's the first."

Mikenas couldn't see anything, and marvelled, not for the first time, at the night vision of her comrade.

"Where?"

She looked down Renata's arm and immediately spotted the round parachute. It seemed to be descending at considerably above what she thought would be safe for the man dangling underneath.

He slammed into the ground and rolled as he had been trained to do.

"Damn and blast it!"

A second pair of feet came into view and the next man came to ground in a similar fashion some fifty metres further away.

Mikenas watched as five men touched down, all within her field of vision.

'These men know what they're doing for sure!'

"Round them up, Sarnt!"

"Sah, You heard the Major. Speed your arses up, lads!"

The men were battling to organise their parachutes into a portable bundle.

The Major moved towards the double light, which marked the direction they would leave the drop zone, as well as where he would encounter the reception committee.

He didn't get there before an urgent voice reached his ears.

"One missing, Sah."

"Who?"

"Just checking, sah... Joy... it's Joy, sah."

"Damn and blast. Move them to the exit point, Sarnt."

Bottomley decided to discuss the missing man with the partisan leader, rather than go off half-cocked.

121

He was surprised to discover that Mikenas was a woman, but didn't let it show, greeting her and Luistikaite with a handshake.

"Bottomley, Major, SAS. We've lost a man somewhere. Do you have sufficient men to look for him?"

Renata translated his comments, but he understood the nod without any problems, and recognised Mikenas' authority as she barked out orders to some of the partisans, who quickly moved off.

Cookson brought up the rest of the party and they took a knee, just as one of the partisans extinguished one of the twin fires, a signal to the circling aircraft that it could come in lower and deposit its other cargo in the centre of the ring.

The details had been sorted out previously, and another group of partisans were ready to rush out onto the drop zone and recover the canisters containing all sorts of items with which to hurt the enemy, as well as a few items to make life easier for the Lithuanian freedom fighters.

The good news and the bad news arrived together.

The SAS soldiers watched as the canisters were dragged past them, and as the body of Lance-Corporal Kevin Joy was carefully laid out near Bottomley.

His radio pack, such as it was, was placed next to him.

Cookson, one of the SAS's rare Lithuanian speakers, translated for the benefit of his boys.

"They found him outside the zone. Chute had only partially opened. Bounced off a tree. Probably broke his back. Fuck and abhorrence."

He looked around, anticipating Bottomley's orders.

"Tappers, Choc… you bring Smiler along, nice and gentle like. OK?"

Corporal Tappett and Trooper Cadbury said nothing but moved off ready to pick up the gruesome burden.

"I'll grab the radio. Boozy, you're point. Suprasti?"

"Lay off the bleedin' Lithuanian, Sarnt. I'm Polish."

"All the same to me, now move yer narrow ass up front and wait 'til I give the signal."

Trooper Bouzyk took up position, ready to lead the small SAS group off.

Cookson dropped down beside Bottomley.

122

"I've got the lads organised for when you're ready, Sah."

"Excellent, Sarnt. Shame about Smiler. Radio's u/s."

"I'll bring it along with me. Can't leave it here and it may be useful for spares."

"Indeed."

They both looked at a modest exchange between three partisans.

"Fuck me, she's up the duff and then some!"

"She's one of ours, Sarnt. Anyway, looks like we're ready for the off."

Mikenas nodded and made a gesture to her group, all of whom rose and moved off in the direction she pointed.

"Righty ho, Sarnt. Let's move."

Within two minutes the large field was silent and dark, clear of beacons, canisters, and personnel.

The only possible tell-tale of their presence was next to a large Birch tree, where a studious eye could possibly find an indentation in the ground that was roughly the same size as a man.

1417 hrs, Sunday, 3rd November 1946, Urakami First Hospital, Nagasaki, Japan.

Ordinarily, Takeo would be on a day off but his section chief had asked him, although it had seemed more like an order, to replace a man who was sick.

The explanation was fair, so Takeo agreed, especially as the interrogation was in Nagasaki itself.

The subject, an IJN Lieutenant Commander, had only recently come to the attention of the authorities as he had been incarcerated in a civilian hospital following a bombing raid on Nagasaki towards the end of the war.

Too ill to move and close to death, it had been decided to get as much information from the man before he went to his ancestors, hence the dispatching of two men across the city on a Sunday.

The questioning was supposed to be undertaken by Royston Waynes, a USN lieutenant, with Takeo translating both question and answers.

Both men took notes, a procedure to ensure that everything was recorded although, by his own admission, the lieutenant's Japanese was barely up to the basic of communication.

The dying man, transferred to the Sasebo dockyard following the sinking of his old ship, had a good memory of events and, under direction from the new Japanese authorities, cooperated fully.

The whole interrogation was easy, almost dreary in its simplicity.

Until the moment that Takeo did a double-take on one answer.

Without seeking permission, he spoke over his superior.

"Kagesawa-san, surely you mean 'Special Type, Submarine?'"

Kagesawa shook his head, bringing on pain and a bout of coughing.

"No. It is as I say."

Waynes kept his mouth shut and gave Takeo his head.

The Hawaiian quickly scribbled in Japanese and showed it to the man, who examined it with his good eye.

'特型潜水艦'

"As I said, special type submarine. One of the big ones built in secret."

"Big ones built in secret?"

"Yes, Takeo-san. There were a number being built, but two only went to sea. That's who the guns were for. I oversaw delivery personally."

Takeo raised a hand to silence the questions about to spring from his companion's lips and pressed Kagesawa further.

"So, Kagesawa-san, that notation meant that the equipment was not of a special type for submarines, but actually meant for use on the special type submarines?"

"Hai."

"Why special?"

"They have two hulls."

"What?"

The coughing started and Kagesawa used his good hand to dab at the blood spots on his lips.

"Two hulls, Takeo-san. They're very big."

"Do you want some water, Kagesawa-san?"

"No, arigato."

"Then please go on."

"Just that. They're very big... long... wide... more guns... more hangar space... nearly one hundred and fifty men..."

"Hangar space... like the AMs?"

"Much more. Room for three aircraft, Takeo-san."

"Three aircraft?"

"Hai."

The two Americans exchanged looks.

"What happened to them, Kagesawa-san?"

"They both left for Kannonzaki at the same time. 4th June. Left during the night. I remember they'd gone that morning."

"4th June. Are you sure of that date?"

"Yes, Takeo-san. It's my birthday."

"Kannonzaki. Are you sure?"

"Yes, Takeo-san. A faulty part on one of the Type 36s had to be replaced. I redirected it to a base code that I recognised as Kannonzaki... plus that was where the secret base had been constructed, so it made sense."

Both men scribbled furiously.

"Anything else you can tell us about these Special Type Submarines?"

"Not really. I supplied the weapons. One 11th Year, three triple mounts, and a single mount Type 36 for each. I did ask some of the officers about their mission, but Rear-Admiral Sasaki Hankyu made it clear it was not for me to know."

"He was there in person?"

"Yes, Takeo-san, often. Throughout the fitting out, Rear-Admiral Hankyu was a regular visitor to the yard overseeing his special project."

"And you don't know where they were going after Kannonzaki?"

"No, Takeo-san. I heard rumours that a number of dignitaries would be going board before they sailed... extra comforts were installed for them... I do know that the vessels were fully provisioned, which was a rarity in those times of course."

Kagesawa suddenly started a bout of coughing which immediately became a serious problem, as blood foamed at his lips and nostrils.

A nurse bustled over from her duty station and tended to the wounded man.

"You should go now."

In the way of nurses the world over, her words were an instruction, not a request.

The two US officers stood and took their leave.

The bout of coughing got worse and a doctor joined the throng around the bedside.

"Arigato, Kagesawa-san."

Outside the hospital, Takeo did all the talking.

"Lootenant, we gotta get back to base immediately, cos unless I'm very much mistaken, the Combined Fleet still has two huge submarines out there somewhere … cloaked in secrecy… unaccounted for… and carrying some important people."

He skim read the last page again before folding them and slipping them into his breast pocket.

'Special type submarines…chikushō!'

By 1800 hrs, Waynes and Takeo had assembled the evidence to take before their section chief; evidence that two huge submarines had been assembled and sent to sea with next to no history of their existence, probably carrying some important personnel, and were most likely still at large.

The section chief had disappeared for the day so the two excited men set everything aside ready for an early morning presentation.

Waynes couldn't sleep and took to examining the contents of a bottle of bourbon.

Takeo couldn't sleep either, but went to bed anyway.

As he fell into a fitful sleep and Sunday became Monday, a life ended in Urakami First Hospital, as Kaigun-shōsa Daisuke Kagesawa slipped from this world into the embrace of his ancestors.

1200 hrs, Monday, 4th November 1946, Former SS-Artillerieschule Beneschau, Beneschau, Czechoslovakia.

The group had congregated on the verandah of the commandant's house at the former SS Artillery School, where they had exchanged news and smoked cigarettes together.

Just prior to the start of their meeting, two of the brand new Sabre jet fighters had swept overhead, creating a favourable impression on the ground troops below.

Rumour had it that they had many teething problems but, to the men on the ground, they were pretty birds and friendly air was always welcome.

"It's time, messieurs. The Général awaits you."

Cigarettes were hastily thrown and uniforms tugged into place before the senior officers of the Legion Corps D'Assaut filed into the room set aside for their critical meeting with De Lattre.

It fell to the French general to break the bad news, even though it was in many ways not news at all.

"Simply put, the Corps can no longer sustain itself, even with the new influx of vetted personnel. You've lost too many men to the German Army. I'm here to offer all German personnel an honourable release so you can return to your own army, with the grateful thanks of France."

Even though they all knew it was coming, it was still a shock.

Many of the officers present were old Legion or French, or both, and they also knew that their futures hung in the balance. Some eyes swivelled to Bittrich, the most senior German legionnaire, but most focussed on the man in the centre of the room.

None the less, it was Bittrich that spoke first.

"For myself, I'll return to the Wehrmacht as soon as is convenient. I have been offered a position in the new German Legion, which will carry forward the élan and spirit of this legion and the force from which many of us came."

A silent dismay fell upon the listeners who had hoped beyond hope that the Corps could stay intact, in some way or other.

One or two German officers spoke their agreement with Bittrich's decision, but everyone, De Lattre included, understood that one man of great importance had yet to speak.

"So, who else will take up the offer and return to Germany?"

De Lattre asked to try and provoke a response from Knocke, the clear focus of attention.

A few more men raised their hands in response, a total of eleven men signalling their wish to depart.

But Knocke's hands stayed firmly in his lap.

"And who will stay and serve La Legion?"

There were no hands raised, even though only a few had thus far indicated their choice.

Knocke rose slowly and, as was his habit, tugged his tunic into place.

"Legionnaires... for that is what you all are... the choice is simple. Return and join our new army and serve Germany, or remain here and serve France. For my part, this is an easy choice. I gave my word to serve, so serve I will. All of us here served before, different masters in different times, but with the same common enemy as the men we fight alongside now. We wore our uniforms with pride, and served alongside our comrades through good and bad times."

He looked around the room, seeking the more junior men in particular.

"And now we are here, consistent to our word, serving with our comrades, old... and new... and have the same spirit... the same élan... the same incredible togetherness that drove our men to the gates of Moscow, and helped them endure the unendurable."

He pointed out well-known faces... Haefali... St.Clair... Beveren... Desmarais... Durand.

"These men are my comrades as every German serving in the Corps is my comrade. In honour, I cannot go back on my word, neither can I desert my comrades. I will remain as a legionnaire."

Knocke retook his seat in silence.

"Thank you, Général Knocke."

The tension slipped away in an instant and De Lattre dropped in behind the small desk, on which sat four different scenarios, depending on what went on from this point forward.

But that was for tomorrow.

"So, messieurs, I must ask again. Whomever wishes to return to the German Army may do so with honour. This is a big decision for all of us, so please, consider it overnight. I have officers who will be visiting all units throughout the afternoon and evening to inform the men and offer them the same choice."

The compassion evaporated from De Lattre's voice in an instant.

"Those who wish to depart should report to their parade grounds at 1100hrs tomorrow, where they'll be required to sign release papers, receive back pay, and will be required to hand over relevant equipment. Any insignia may be retained as a mark of our gratitude for your service."

"Senior commanders will report back here at 1300 tomorrow with the revised personnel levels of their units, at which time we'll work out what sort of force we have to command."

He rose to his feet, as did the rest of the room.

"For those of you that decide to return to your own army, I can only understand, and thank you for your gallant service. For those of you that decide to stay... thank you. Honneur et Fidélité, mon braves. Dismissed."

[Beneschau is modern-day Benešov.]

"General Gehlen, a pleasure... and a surprise."

"General De Walle. I felt it correct not to announce or parade my arrival. What I have to discuss is delicate."

The Belgian indicated the silent man who took up position at the doorway.

"My man, Strauch... here to guarantee my safety in this increasingly dangerous time."

They gravitated towards a pair of comfortable seats that seemed somehow out of place in the stark barracks building.

Ever the professional, Gehlen got straight down to business.

"I've made no progress on your note, except to discover that there are a number more Uspenkas in the Soviet Union. The rest of the message means absolutely nothing to anyone."

De Walle's look of disappointment was writ large on his face.

"However, yesterday evening I received the information I've been waiting for... or rather... information arrived... revealing and worrying information."

He removed a file from his inner coat pocket and handed it over.

"I've spoken to no one of its contents."

The file, written in German, with excerpts of documents in Polish and Russian, had been heavily censored, something that disappointed the Belgian intelligence officer.

Again, Gehlen understood his thoughts.

"The files mainly came pre-censored. It was necessary for me to censor three pieces in the main file. I am sorry. The translations of the Polish and Russian documents are in the back of the file."

"Thank you."

De Walle read the main file with incredulity, and then examined the translations, which did nothing to drop his level of astonishment.

He looked up at Gehlen, who extended a hand holding a cigarette case.

"Thank you. Astonishing."

"I have to ask, General. Are we free to speak openly?"

"Yes."

"Good. So, in brief, we have discovered from these files that the Steyns, both David and Jakob, were falsely listed as dead. You were correct, by the way. Belzec records simply do not exist, except for the one we found, a record that was most secret... a record associated with something known as the Uranprojekt."

He left the word hanging for De Walle to consume.

"Scheisse!"

The Belgian knew nothing specific about the Uranprojekt, simply its purpose.

Which was to produce nuclear weapons for Nazi Germany.

"It seems both men were associated with the Uranprojekt, by working in a Geheime Auergesellschaft experimental facility in Konitz, Pomerania."

He fished out a photoreconnaissance set that covered the area, taken by Allied aircraft over the space of two years from 1943.

"Nothing there. That's how secret it was. It's simply not there. I'll have my men check the area out, but it's simply not listed on the official documentation of known facilities of either the Reich or the Soviets."

Gehlen extracted another document from his pocket.

"This document does not exist and cannot be referred to at this time. That may change, but for now its contents must remain strictly between us, Georges."

"As you wish, Reinhard."

The highly secret list of which German scientist and intelligentsia had been acquired by the Soviet 'Osoaviakhim Project' made for interesting reading in its own right.

"This is more comprehensive than the official list."

"I have my orders, although sometimes I don't understand them... but I felt that I would share this with you... on the basis of it remaining between us."

Both the Steyns were listed as being removed to the USSR by officers of 'Osoaviakhim'.

Of greater interest in so many ways was the heading under which they were placed.

'Nuclear research and weapons section - VNIIEF.'

"VNIIEF...Merde."

The VNIIEF, the acronym for the All-Union Scientific Research Institute of Experimental Physics, was a flag for any intelligence officer, although so little was known about its abilities and progress.

"I think you'll agree that this information makes the understanding of Knocke's message all the more important."

"I agree, Reinhard... but if I'm not supposed to know about it, how would I know whom to ask?"

"Have you heard of Farm Hall?"

"No."

"It's in England... a place called Godmanchester... it's where a number of German scientists were kept and interrogated after the last war."

"Damn... yes... I've heard of it, yes."

De Walle offered up his pack, which Gehlen declined.

The Belgian lit a cigarette, all the while concentrating heavily on the espionage goldmine to which he was slowly becoming privy.

"One of my agents was within that process... an interpreter and interrogator... he became friends with a number of those imprisoned there."

"And that enduring friendship will enable him to speak to them... quietly... without anything official."

"I think that would be wise, Georges."

"Good... but again I see this... err... reluctance to do things officially... which I simply don't understand. What is the problem, Reinhard?"

"I'm being excluded from matters within my own sphere. My men are either being moved from their positions to where they can no longer keep me informed or, in some cases, being removed in accidents."

"Mon Dieu."

"Do you have anyone in a position who might be able to help me understand what is going on within my own government?"

Coming from Germany's spymaster, that was a huge confession of his own weakened position.

De Walle weighed his answer carefully, just in case it was a play by the German. Trust only goes so far in the espionage game.

"I will carefully find out, Reinhard."

"Thank you. But remember this name. Diels. Don't trust him... ever. Now, I will go. As soon as I get anything on the note from my man, I'll come and see you personally."

They rose and shook hands.

"And I'll let you know if I can find out anything about what is going on in Germany."

Strauch opened the door and checked around before allowing the two senior men to leave.

1050 hrs, Tuesday, 5th November 1946, Headquarters of Camerone Division, Kuttenberg, Bohemia, Czechoslovakia.

The door opened and the morning sunshine flooded the room.

131

"Good morning, mon Général."

"Good morning, Colonel Haefali. Are the men assembling on the field?"

"Yes, they are, Sir."

Camerone's base area didn't have a defined parade square, but a vast and level grass field served just as well, and it was here that Knocke had dictated that those who wished to leave Camerone should assemble.

"Your car is ready, Sir."

Knocke rose and opened the curtains, completing the illumination of the room, something he had not allowed until the moment of truth was upon him, preferring the relative darkness to insulate him against what was to come.

The previous afternoon and evening he had travelled through his units and spoken with the men, shaking hands, accepting a cigarette or a coffee, and discussing the concerns that were brought on by the French offer of a return.

As men sought his view, he focussed on each man in turn, advising that they should do what was right and honourable for themselves.

When pressed, as he always was, he confirmed his intent to remain in the Legion but each time he advised that the enquirer should look to his own needs and desires and not be influenced by others.

He declined to enquire as to their thoughts, and always stopped men who pledged their loyalty to him, constantly reminding his soldiers that their loyalty was owed to no one man.

This morning he had elected to dress in his preferred formal uniform of a dark blue French tunic, blue waist sash, black trousers, German combat boots, and gaiters.

As was the case for all men in the Legion Corps, the blue and red divisional armband graced his left sleeve and rank markings were carried on the collar.

The whole uniform was replete with the medals awarded a courageous man, as ever, the Mérite over the top of the Knight's Cross.

Carrying his black officer's kepi under his arm, Knocke strode out of the room.

"Come on then, Albrecht. Let's see what we have left."

Haefali kept his own counsel on that, for he had just come from the field and knew what lay in store for his commander.

132

The Kfz 71, Knocke's recently acquired Krupp vehicle, made the short trip to the parade field in quick time, although the sight of men drawn up in parade order around the area could not be avoided from distance.

With a heavy heart, Knocke understood that the vast majority of Camerone was on the field in front of him; nearly five thousand men, give or take those on leave, in sickbay, or on important duties elsewhere.

They would all be given their opportunity later.

But for now…

"Mein Gott, Albrecht."

Haefali shook his head.

"As you say, mon Général."

The Krupp drove through a gap in the ranks and onto the centre of the field, where eighteen men were drawn up in three lines of six.

Knocke was taken aback, and then immediately understood, a faint reaction that Haefali noticed, which finally allowed him to smile.

"Yes, mon Général. Eighteen… just eighteen."

The Krupp came to a halt and Haefali stepped out first.

"Parade… Parade… atten… tion!"

Thousands of feet stamped into the attention position.

Haefali swept a magnificent salute in his commander's direction, which was returned in kind by a still shocked Knocke.

"These men wish to leave and rejoin the German Army, mon Général."

Knocke nodded and moved forward, speaking to the eighteen men as a group, but not so the parade could hear.

"Your decision is honourable, Kameraden. Report to the duty officer's hut, where you can complete the administration. There will be transport arranged to take you to the nearest German army facility. Thank you for your service… and for your comradeship. I wish you all well. You are dismissed."

Haefali stepped in.

"Section…right turn."

"By the front, double… march!"

Knocke threw up a salute as the men marched off, rather than dismiss into an aimless walk in front of their former commander.

133

Knocke and Haefali watched them depart, silently, one wondering what would happen next, one knowing only too well.

"Mon Général, if you will indulge me please?"

Knocke could only nod.

Haefali strode forward, giving himself some space from his commander.

His voice lifted across the massed ranks.

"Parade... parade... Général salute... present... arms!"

In the way that martial sights can bring the full range of emotions, the sight and sound of five thousand men offering their tribute to Knocke left a lump in his throat.

But not as big a lump as came next.

"Parade... parade... attention!"

The clash of hands and weapons was almost gunshot perfect.

"Parade... parade... on my command... now!"

Five thousand throats gave voice to thirteen words.

"Mon Général! Legio patria nostra. Honneur et Fidélité! Nous sommes à vos ordres!"

Knocke sprang onto the Krupp and stood on the back, and offered his own tribute to the men who had decided to follow him.

Saluting in all directions, he tried as best he could to keep moisture from his eyes, but failed.

'What men these are... what wonderful men...'

"Parade... parade... left... turn!"

The men turned as ordered and drumbeats rose from a previously unseen group of musicians.

"Parade... parade... by the front... march!"

The drum marked the slow steady beat of the Legion march.

The first echelon started to move off the field but Haefali had not finished with them yet.

"Parade... parade... Le Boudin!"

The classic legion marching song sprang from five thousand lips, and Knocke's joy was complete, his pride at the men under his command never greater than this moment.

...Tiens, voilà du boudin, voilà du boudin, voilà du boudin
Pour les Alsaciens, les Suisses et les Lorrains.
Pour les Belges y en a plus.
Pour les Belges y en a plus.
Ce sont des tireurs au cul.
Pour les Belges y en a plus.
Pour les Belges y en a plus.

Ce sont des tireurs au cul...

Knocke shook Haefali's hand

"Thank you, Albrecht. That was well done... very well done indeed."

"Not my idea, mon General. A deputation came to me in the late hours. The men were very insistent. They worked it out themselves and just wanted you to understand that they'll follow you to the gates of hell... and through if necessary."

They shook hands slowly and with meaning.

"The trust and comradeship of men... it's a wonderful thing, Albrecht... a privilege that men give to their commanders... but it's also a huge burden... as you already know. At least Camerone is safe... let's hope that the other units have been equally fortunate."

Unfortunately for the Legion Corps, the number of returnees in the other formations was far greater

De Lattre's subsequent meeting with the Corps hierarchy quickly established that a reorganisation was necessary, a reorganisation that meant that the Corps D'Assaut was greatly reduced.

To add insult to injury, the reduction was accompanied by orders that requisitioned some of the French-built Panthers, reducing the Corps even further, although a subsequent delivery of brand-new Schwarzpanthers and Schwarzjagdpanthers was made direct from German factories as part of an agreement between the two nations.

They were remarkable weapons of war, but simply not enough.

In order to bolster the weakened Corps materiel, men on 'leave' were dispatched to all corners of Allied Europe in search of anything that could be used, should the battle be rejoined.

Camerone was the only formation of any size but more resembled a reinforced brigade in reality, until Tannenberg was absorbed into its ranks.

The other legion units were formed into small all-arms brigades that came under the control of the Alma Division.

Both units came under the command of the Legion Corps D'Assaut, to which Lavalle was appointed as commander.

The 1er Division D'Infanterie became part of the Corps by De Lattre's direct intervention, thus bringing all Legion units in Europe under one unified command.

135

There is some good in the worst of us and some evil in the best of us.
When we discover this, we are less prone to hate our enemies.

Martin Luther King Jr.

Chapter 179 - THE REUNION

1148 hrs, Thursday, 7th November 1946. Headquarters of Camerone Division, Kuttenberg, Bohemia, Czechoslovakia.

Ahron Mandl accepted Knocke's outstretched hand.

"Thank you, Herr Knocke, thank you."

"I wish you luck on your journey home, Herr Mandl."

Knocke turned and picked up the bottle provided by Hässelbach.

"For you, courtesy of my supplies officer."

"Again, thank you, Herr Knocke. I wonder if I could ask a favour before I go?"

"Of course."

"Could you please take this letter for me? I'm sure the army system will be more effective than anything civilian authorities have developed. I've started another which I'll send by different means... or maybe from home."

Knocke accepted the letter and made a cursory examination of the address.

"Your father?"

"Son... my father... well...he is gone... this is for my son."

"I understand. Biarritz though?"

"He was a child when we placed him with friends... to avoid the inevitable... you understand."

"A wise precaution, Herr Mandl."

Knocke slipped into a more formal mode.

"The transport officer has orders to take you to Prag. These are rail orders for you as far as Carlsbad. This is a safe passage order signed by myself. I regret, the journey from Carlsbad to your home is one I cannot guarantee."

"Pechöfen's not so far. I'm used to walking... and am stronger now, thanks to your doctors... and you, of course."

"Best of luck to you, and I hope you find your son."

"Thank you, Herr Knocke."

[Carlsbad, Kuttenberg, Pechöfen, and Prag are modern-day Karlovy Vary, Kutná Hora, Smolné Pece, and Prague respectively.]

1150 hrs, Sunday, 10th November 1946, office of the Commander [Special Projects], Moscow Military District Mechanised Units Directorate, Arbat District. Moscow, USSR.

The secretary looked him up and down with something approaching disdain.

"Your orders."

She held out an imperious hand that Kriks filled with his documentation.

"Ah, Praporschik Kriks."

The woman almost melted and became a different and decidedly more receptive person before his eyes.

From harridan to courtesan in an instant.

"The General instructed that you were to be shown in straight away, Comrade Kriks."

She rose from behind the desk and moved to the ornately carved door, knocking and opening it all in one easy movement.

"Comrade General, Praporschik Kriks is here."

She beckoned the bewildered NCO forward and into the General's office.

Kriks had been plucked from his position in the 1st Guards Rifle Division and summoned to whatever he had just been summoned to without a say in the matter, and he was mystified and angry in equal measure.

Both feelings evaporated in an instant.

"Thank you, Comrade Leytenant. That will be all... and please see that we are not disturbed."

"Yes, sir."

She closed the door as the office suddenly exploded into laughter and the sounds of friends reunited.

The telephone rang.

"Mayor General Yarishlov's office... I'm afraid the General cannot be disturbed at the moment, Comrade Polkovnik... he left precise instructions... certainly... most certainly... I'll make sure of it, Comrade Polkovnik."

She replaced the receiver and settled back into her seat, prepared to defend the privacy of her commander against all comers.

A patrol of Czech police were summoned to the forest on the southern outskirts of Meziroli, where children playing had discovered a body.

Those children that remained were quickly chivvied away by the younger officer, as the senior took in the scene and started making notes.

It was quickly apparent that they were dealing with a murder, or more likely an execution, given the fact that the man had been hung from a tree and carried a placard stuck in the bindings that would have prevented him from struggling as he was trussed and hoisted up off the forest floor.

His partner returned and wordlessly the sergeant indicated the line holding the corpse aloft.

It was quickly cut and the senior took the weight and lowered the emaciated corpse to the leafy earth.

"There's nothing to him, Svoboda. No weight at all."

"Not surprising is it, sergeant?"

"No... I suppose not."

He pulled the placard out of bindings, although the single word had been easy enough to read, even when six foot or so above the ground.

'Jüden.'

Sergeant Kolar fished in the dead man's pockets, pulling out documents, some of which had official military markings.

He sat down on a nearby fallen bough and lit a cigarette to help him concentrate.

"French Army travel documents."

"Shall I get the..."

"Do nothing for the moment, Svoboda."

Annoyed at being interrupted, Kolar snapped at his partner, and quickly held up an apologetic hand.

"Just sit for a moment, man."

He continued rummaging through the documents.

"Letter here... Biarritz eh?"

"That's in France."

"Thank you so fucking much, encyclopaedia man. I'm not a total fucking peasant."

"Sorry."

"Safe conduct note... bollocks... definitely something to do with the military then... that Legion uni... ah, now I understand."

He chuckled knowingly.

"Old habits die hard, Svoboda."

"How do you mean, Sergeant?"

"That Legion bunch are all ex-SS hard nuts. A Jew'd be a red rag to them. But they've played it safe, giving him lovely paperwork so they could say 'wasn't us Mister American, we now love the Jews'."

"Really, Sergeant?"

"Damned fucking right, and we're having fuck all to do with it as far as those legion bastards are concerned. Go get the spade."

"Eh?"

"Go get the spade, We'll bury him."

"What?"

"You need a bloody picture? We report this in and Lieutenant Marek'll have the military all over us, including those SS bastards. Bring nothing but a fucking world of hurt down on our heads."

"OK... but..."

"But nothing. We report back and say that we're satisfied that there was a body but that family must have come and claimed it. Clear suicide from the children's description and crime scene. That bastard Marek's due to transfer in two weeks, at which time I'm back in charge. We'll have another look at it then. Meantime, I'll send the papers off to this address in Biarritz... which is... apparently... in fucking France... with a note stating the facts, or actually nothing like the fucking facts... and when the army and Marek have fucked off, I'll send a note with the results of our proper investigation."

"Err... I don't understand."

"That's why I'm a fucking sergeant and you'll be the one digging, Svoboda my son."

He flicked his cigarette off to one side and shivered involuntarily, the temperature drop suddenly finding its way into his consciousness.

"Military authority is going to be removed, all good and well, and the area will again become civil police jurisdiction... my jurisdiction... I'll then reconsider the investigation... and keep the bloody SS and the rest out of it. Quick paperwork exercise and the job's done, just in case the kids get mouthy. Clear?"

"Yes, Sergeant. I understand."

"Excellent. Now... go and get the fucking spade and let's get Mister Mandl in the ground."

[Meziroli is modern day Sittmesgrün.]

1533 hrs, Thursday, 14th November 1946, Vnukovo Airfield, Moscow, USSR.

The band waited expectantly as the unfamiliar aircraft rolled slowly into its allotted position, the waiting dignitaries shuffling uncomfortably in the driving rain.

As the engines were switched off and their throaty roar stopped rivalling the noise of the impressive wind and rain, the C-54 Skymaster's door opened.

A version of the Stars and Stripes greeted the ears of the first man down the stairs who was, unfortunately for the Soviet protocol officer, British.

Lieutenant General Brian Gwynne Horrocks KCB, KBE, DSO, MC led the delegation that had come to Moscow to establish military protocols for the new frontline to be.

The Swedish camp was a diplomatic mission primarily and both sides had agreed a different venue should be selected for the purely military exchanges, and the Soviets had suggested the first visit be to Moscow, much to the surprise of the Allies.

Future exchanges would take place in NATOFE Headquarters in Frankfurt, or back in the Soviet capital, close to where the senior military men controlled the nascent peace.

Malinin stepped forward and saluted the senior British man, thankful that the band had at least recognised the protocol error enough to stop playing.

They shook hands and Malinin was shocked as Horrocks spoke in excellent Russian.

"Marshall Malinin, thank you for the welcome, and congratulations on your recent promotion. Perhaps we should wait for the formal introductions until we are somewhere dry?"

"Agreed, Comrade General Horrocks. My car."

Malinin indicated a large black staff car and ushered his visitor towards it.

The rest of the Allied deputation paired up with their Soviet counterparts and were directed towards a large coach with comradely gestures and declarations of friendship, all save for the two German officers, for whom there was at best reserve, and at worst a blank face that hid both memories and feelings.

The final Allied officer to board, a British colonel, had some difficulty in getting his leg up to the high step, but refused the offered hands, preferring to overcome by himself.

His counterpart, a procurement Colonel from the Ministry of Armaments, spoke reasonable English.

140

"So, Comrade Colonel. You are stiff from big flight, eh?"

"Something like that, Colonel."

"Oleg Panteleimonevich Laranin, once being of 2nd Guards Rifle Division, since I got this."

He indicated the scar adjacent to his left eye, a wound that had clearly claimed his sight.

Laranin stuck out his hand and it was accepted.

"John Ramsey, once of His Majesty's Black Watch, until I lost these."

He rapped a quick pattern on his two wooden legs.

"Ah, I understanding. So, we both are on the heap now, eh?"

"Seems so, Colonel."

'You speak for yourself, Colonel. I'm not on the 'heap' by a long bloody way!'

Ramsey looked around him and suddenly realised why the light was strange.

The coach windows were all painted grey, obscuring the view.

He pretended to drop off, whilst debating with himself whether the obscuration was to stop the Allied officers seeing out, or the Soviet population seeing in.

0900 hrs, Monday, 18th November 1946, the Georgievsky Hall, Grand Kremlin Palace, Moscow.

Horrocks and his party had been invited to a presentation ceremony at the Kremlin and had accepted, but not without some serious thought.

After all, those being honoured were men and women who had fought against the Allied forces.

Two senior members of the delegation requested to be excused, but the rest attended to witness the ceremony in the magnificent vaulted hall, its ornate stone and gold leaf a throwback to an older, less austere age.

The Allied party had a very prominent position at the front of the right aisle, which would enable them to see the General Secretary up close... close but yet so far.

Since the events surrounding the attempted assassination, something the Allies had generally been unaware of until a Soviet aide let the details slip the day before, security had been tightened up, and more armed personnel added to the force inside the hall, something that inadvertently lent more power to the whole occasion.

141

The entire room rose as the members of the GKO assembled, followed by Stalin, who took the central position in front of the carefully selected audience.

The Kremlin band struck up the national anthem, and the assembly set about singing it with great vigour, save for the members of the Allied party who remained tight lipped but respectfully silent.

As always, the incredible harmonics of the great hall massively added to the patriotic fervour of the anthem.

An immaculately dressed and bemedalled NKVD colonel stepped forward to a small lectern, prepared to read each of those to be presented in turn, complete with a small resume of their career and reasons behind their award.

The recipients would be individually marched up in parade fashion, their steps echoing off the walls, despite the carpet on which they marched to protect the ornate floor.

As ever, the presentation was carefully stage managed, but this time there was a difference, in that the last man to receive an award was unable to properly march, something that had prevented him from being the first to receive his medal, the normal protocol for one of his rank, given the high honour he was to receive.

The flow of brave soldiers ended, each presentation having been marked by the hanging of a medal and kisses from Stalin.

The last man had been granted a seat at the back of the hall and he rose from it on cue and marched forward as best he could.

What was unusual about this presentation was the growing soft but audible gasps from those assembled as they caught sight of the horrendously wounded man.

The gasps rumbled throughout the hall, causing those at the front to turn and witness the apparition of a horrendously burned man painfully trying to bring as much military bearing as possible to his procession.

He came to the mark and assumed a position of attention.

The NKVD colonel's voice rose over the hubbub.

"Mayor General of Tank Troops Arkady Arkadyevich Yarishlov to receive his second award of Hero of the Soviet Union..."

The rest of the words were lost on Ramsey as he looked closely for some indication that the figure to his left was indeed the man he had met twice before, although he only remembered the once.

Yarishlov's eyes remained focused straight ahead as he listened to the story of his service and the reasons behind his new award.

The words hardly scratched the surface of what he and his men had achieved in Pomerania all those months previously.

On cue, he walked forward as Stalin took the Hero Award from a red cushion.

The medal was set in place but Stalin, briefed on the likely effect on the burned officer beforehand, did not hug and kiss the apparition in front of him, for which Yarishlov was grateful for more than one reason.

Instead, Stalin offered his hand and whispered words of congratulations in the tank officer's ear, his own sensibilities unusually outraged by the hideous injuries inflicted on a son of Russia.

The curled lips, lack of facial hair, reduced nose, and absence of anything that could really be called ears, all set on a skull covered with tightly stretched pink and white skin, created an impression of horror and pain in unimaginable quantities.

Stalin stepped back and clapped his hands in genuine admiration.

The applause outshone all previous efforts, ringing around inside the building, the sympathy in their hearts lending strength to their hands.

Yarishlov saluted and turned right to march towards the exit but checked himself... in spite of himself...

One of the visiting Allied delegation stepped forward and turned, came to full attention and offered an immaculate salute.

Yarishlov recognized the British colonel immediately and his joy doubled in an instant.

He returned the salute, ignoring the pain in his arm.

Stalin beckoned an aide over but the man was unable to answer his question so he tackled the new recipient of the Hero Award.

"Mayor General Yarishlov. Do you know this man?"

"I most certainly do, Comrade General Secretary. He and I once shared friendly words, and later fought each other in a terrible battle. He's a real soldier... and a friend."

The British officer moved forward, indifferent to the hands that tightened on weapons as the guards sensed a threat to their leader.

Yarishlov was aware of the sudden risks to his friend, and moved forward as quickly as he could, extending his gloved hand to a man he had last seen in pieces and near death on a bloody mound at Barnstorf.

"Colonel Yarishlov. Fate has brought us together again in the most unexpected of places."

"Major Ramsey. Indeed it has."

With studied care, the two men gently, and for Ramsey unexpectedly, embraced, momentarily indifferent to the surroundings and the wide-mouthed dignitaries that wondered about the story behind the friendly reunion.

The ceremony closed and the two men were summoned to a meeting with the Premier of the Soviet Union.

Over tea and cigarettes, at Stalin's direction, Yarishlov and Ramsey related the story of their meeting and the battle in and around Barnstorf.

Ramsey also contributed the story of the receipt of Yarishlov's note, and the Victoria Cross that resulted.

As a result of the meeting, Ramsey found himself in a privileged position, with special dispensation authorised by Stalin himself that allowed him to move around the Moscow area, albeit with plenty of 'official' company, including opportunities to spend time with Yarishlov, both in and out of his official duties.

It was an incredible opportunity for an old soldier who was, unknown to Horrocks, more than that stated on his official attribution.

Ramsey had long since found useful employment as a clandestine member of MI6, reporting to others in London at the behest of his mentor, Sir Stuart Menzies.

0901 hrs, Wednesday, 20th November 1946, twelve nautical miles due south of Sumba Point, Suðuroy, Faroe Islands.

They had closed up to actions station in record time.

"Sparks, make to Admiralty, in contact with confirmed submarine target. Give our position. Will engage if no satisfactory response. ROE of 18th last will be applied. End."

The captain swivelled to his second in command.

"Check again, Number One, and be bloody quick about it."

Whilst the man was away confirming Admiralty communications with the chart room and wireless department, Commander Hamilton Ffoulkes RN ran the present rules of engagement through his brain.

"Sonar, report."

"Skipper, target is at five hundred. Speed... six knots... zero degrees, changing depth but not deviating. Think he's coming shallower."

"Roger, Sonar. All ahead slow."

The telegraph clanged, sending the order for speed reduction to the engineers below.

Number One returned.

"Skipper, this is a weapons-free zone. Officially, Danish Navy, but their subs are Baltic based. There're no subs reported in this area from any of our Allies."

Ffoulkes grunted.

"Our orders are crystal clear then. Latest ROE will apply. Do you agree, Jimmy?"

"Absolutely, Skipper."

The Captain turned to the Gunnery Officer.

"Have 'A' and 'B' turrets prepare. Fire one round each, two hundred yards either side of the target. On my command. Standby depth charge. Standby Spike. Standby sonar."

As the two offensive groups readied themselves to attack and the sonar crews removed their headsets, the Gunnery Officer chivvied his crews through the speaker set and was quickly able to report 'guns ready'

"Shoot."

Both forward 4.5" guns fired simultaneously, and the sea erupted four hundred yards apart.

Such explosions often wrecked the chances of redetection for some time, such was the effect on the hunter's apparatus, so Ffoulkes waited patiently.

His patience ran out after two minutes.

"Sonar?"

"Nothing yet, Skipper. Wait one…"

Petty Officer Coots was an efficient man, and Ffoulkes knew he was working the problem as best he could.

The roiled water was still doing its obstructive work, but Ffoulkes was anxious to detect some sort of reaction, preferably the reaction of a friendly submarine that realised its error rather than that of an angry enemy.

"No change detected, Skipper. Still got the after-effects' troubling us, but my bet is he hasn't deviated one little bit."

"Depth?"

"Wait one… looks like he's steadied out at one hundred feet, Skipper. That's a guess at the moment."

Standing orders for an Allied submarine were to surface in such circumstances. The submariners would recognise that their would-be assailant was a friendly, rise to the surface and communicate with whoever it was that had found them out, with no more than rapped knuckles and red faces to show for the encounter.

"Not rising? Definitely not rising?"

"Steady at depth one hundred, Skipper."

"Roger, Sonar."

Ffoulkes dropped into his command position and the Number One drew close, anxious to understand how HMS Charity would now prosecute the contact, if at all.

"Skipper?"

"Jimmy, ROE is simple... we attack. They haven't responded as they should. Has to be an enemy. Agreed?"

"Absolutely, Skipper."

"Quartermaster, increase speed to two-thirds, steer hard a-port."

The quartermaster repeated the order back but Ffoulkes had already moved onto other matters.

"Jimmy, make sure the depth charge crews are ready, but I intend to fire Spike when we've lined back up on the blighter. If no luck, we'll put a pattern down on him when we come back. Clear?"

"Roger, Skipper."

"I'll get her lined up on the blighter for a stern run."

With the ship at action stations, there would be no delay to any order Ffoulkes issued, but giving his crew a heads up would not go amiss.

"Ship's tannoy."

The bosun's whistle died away to be replaced with Ffoulkes' clipped tones.

"Do you hear there? Do you hear there? Submarine contact has not responded to our warning. We'll be attacking an underwater target considered a hostile submarine with our hedgehog and depth charges. All gun crews stand ready for surface action if whatever it is comes up. End."

He handed the tannoy back to the bosun and moved to the front of the bridge.

HMS Charity was gently swinging back onto the same course as the submarine, which the Number One had just confirmed with the Sonar division.

"Sparks, make to Admiralty, am engaging confirmed submarine target. Give our position. End."

"All lined up, Skipper. Range to target twelve hundred yards, dead ahead. Steering course 220."

"Roger, Number One. All ahead, one third, steer 220."

HMS Charity bled off speed slowly, all the time gaining on her target.

"Sonar?"

"Skipper, constant bearing on 220. Range eight hundred. Depth one hundred, speed six knots."

"Number One."

146

He beckoned the Lieutenant over for a whispered conversation.

"Any doubts, Jimmy?"

"Skipper, we've gone by the book. There are no friendlies in the area. He hasn't responded as he should. Seems to me it's not one of ours, but he's trying to play it very steady. I reckon he feels that by doing nothing, we'll think he's one of ours."

"My thoughts exactly, Jimmy."

Ffoulkes shot a quick look at the sea.

"Sonar?"

"Skipper, constant bearing on 220. Range six hundred. Depth one hundred, speed six and a half knots."

"Roger, Sonar. Constant reports."

He dropped his head close to his Number One for a final time.

"We attack."

"Aye aye, Skipper."

The two men moved to different areas of the bridge.

Coots' voice provided a monotone commentary on the sea ahead, counting down the yards.

The Hedgehog's range was two hundred and fifty yards, and the gap was rapidly closing.

"Standby on Spike."

And then the moment was on him.

"Standby on Spike...Shoot! Standby, Sonar!"

The hedgehog mount started to spit its deadly little charges into the air, twenty-four deadly Torpex bombs dispatched in just under twelve seconds, held on target by the recently updated gyro-stabilised mount. The new mounting ensured that they all landed as aimed, creating a deadly circle of splashes ahead of HMS Charity.

The bombs sank at about twenty feet a second, and Ffoulkes, along with everyone else on the bridge, started counting off.

'One...'

'Two...'

'Three...'

'Fou...'

KABOOM!

"Fuck a rat!"

"Silence on the bridge!"

The chastised rating's face was split from ear to ear, despite the fact that he would be on report later.

A total of four explosions had split the water, the last three almost simultaneous but decidedly separate from the first.

"I make that four solid hits, Skipper."

No binoculars were needed to see the large bubbles of air disturbing the surface, added to by the sweet smell of diesel that now accompanied other detritus to the surface.

There were two bodies, both naked as the day their mothers brought them into the world.

There were the standard artefacts that escape from a smashed submarine hull; clothing, bottles, paper, wood...

"Jimmy, get a boat away smartish and pick up what you can. I shall stand off and make another sweep, just in case."

"Aye aye, Skipper."

The Number One disappeared to organise a boat party.

"Sparks, make to Admiralty, as per ROE 18th last, underwater target engaged and sunk, repeat confirmed sunk. Give time and our position. Wreckage and body recovery underway. End."

The knock on his cabin door was more than insistent.

It was urgent beyond measure and full of portent.

"Enter."

"Skipper."

"Number one? Christ but you look like you've spent a night with a Pompey whore and plenty of money in your skyrocket!"

"Skipper..."

The man's face was ashen and he was clearly disturbed.

"Go on, man. Spit it out!"

"Nothing recognisable at all. No tattoos on the bodies to help. Both are with the surgeon being examined."

"Dammit! Nothing in the paperwork at all?"

"Nothing that would make you think it was a Soviet submarine we just sent to the bottom, Skipper."

There was something there that made Ffoulkes pose his question very carefully.

"Anything to make us think it was something else entirely, Jimmy?"

"Yes, Skipper."

An icy hand gripped Ffoulkes' vitals, and he understood what it was that had his Number One so agitated.

"What?"

The Lieutenant placed a sodden English five-pound note in front of his Captain.

"Souvenir. Means nothing.

"Ordinarily I'd agree with you, Skipper."

"Ordinarily you'd agr… go on."

The Jimmy emptied a duffel bag onto the floor, wet five pound notes creating a growing pile until he could shake no more free.

"Fucking hell… oh fucking hell…"

"Skipper, there's more."

"What?"

"We recovered three sealed boxes from the wreckage, Skipper. I've the Master-at Arms guarding them now. By my estimate they each contain five hundred."

"Five hundred?"

"Five hundred thousand, Skipper, We've over one and a half million pounds of currency recovered from that boat."

"Fucking hell!"

"Maybe it wasn't a Russki after all. Skipper."

"Fucking hell!"

The voice tube erupted next to Ffoulkes ear.

"Captain."

He listened intently.

"I'll be on the bridge immediately, Nav. Thank you."

He replaced the pipe.

"That was the Nav. Apparently another five crates have surfaced on the port bow."

"Fucking hell, Skipper!"

"Language, Number One."

The two senior men made their way to the bridge, with Ffoulkes already composing an 'Admiralty: Most Secret' message in his mind.

By the time he and the Jimmy arrived on the bridge, the Nav reported a total of eleven crates bobbing on the surface of an increasingly agitated sea.

1102 hrs, Friday, 22nd November 1946, Downing Street, England.

Winston Churchill listened impassively as Dalziel started into the briefing on recent events in Eire and the Atlantic.

Given the sensitive nature of the content, there were only two other pairs of ears present to absorb the incredible story.

The CIGS and the First Sea Lord, respectively Lord Alanbrooke and Sir Andrew Cunningham, Baron Cunningham of Hyndhope, were simple spectators as the story of huge quantities of counterfeit cash, the IRA, and Soviet submarines played out before them.

Dalziel's delivery was impeccable and full, so there were no interruptions until it came to the maths, when Churchill, still incredulous, sought a check on his calculations.

"So, Sir Roger, you seem to be saying that the efforts of our intelligence agencies have prevented the Communists from dumping about two hundred and sixty million pounds of counterfeit currency into our system?"

"At least, Prime Minister. We think more… much more."

"Because you think they took half in the first run?"

"Possibly, Prime Minister. Submarine officers I have chatted to could see no reason to overload their vessel if they intended to make two runs… which we know they did from what the first visiting officer said to Éire's G2 agent."

"Go on."

"Considered opinion was that, if the Soviet sub and naval commanders had anything to do with it, the load would have been split half for each trip, Prime Minister."

"Yes, yes. That would make sense. I can see that."

Churchill turned to Somerville and received a nod in agreement.

"There is more, Prime Minister."

The cigar glowed as Churchill drew deeply on it, sending out a virtual smoke screen between him and his briefing officer.

"In the monitoring of discussions between senior German prisoners of war in Austria, parts of a whispered conversation were recorded. One of those speaking was Ernst Kaltenbrunner. The recording was of poor quality, but some of the words were identifiable.

He consulted the document to refresh his mind.

"…Sachsenhausen… the concentration camp near Berlin."

"…the British money…"

"… Bernard… "

Dalziel looked up.

"Which we now know should be Bernhard, Operation Bernhard, Prime Minister."

Churchill nodded his understanding but said nothing, so Dalziel continued.

"…safely hidden…"

"…lake…"

The naval officer finished lifting the words from the transcript of the recording.

"Subsequent rumours pointed us all towards lakes in the Alpine Redoubt."

"Even though Kaltenbrunner mentioned Sachsenhausen, we had no idea what went on at the camp, over and above the normal horrors, until August, when we were fed information by a former member of the Polish 2nd Infantry Division. He even showed us some British five pound notes he had liberated at the time."

"One inmate of Sachsenhausen… an Adolf Burger, made a report to the Czech Central Bank… he's a Czech national and a Jew, so he considered that appropriate. He spoke of millions of pounds worth of counterfeit currency, not just our own, a lot of American dollars too, Sir. All produced by inmates of the Sachsenhausen Camp. He also supplied us with the name 'Bernhard' and linked it directly to the counterfeit money. "

Dalziel produced one final piece of paper.

"This is an American report from April '45, which mentions a young local girl, Ida Weisenbacher, who claimed to have seen SS soldiers putting items into Lake Toplitz in February."

He handed over a copy to each of the listeners.

"The report had little credence over and above any other report at the time. There were constant reports from people trying to ingratiate themselves with the new occupiers, and Weisenbacher's was no different."

Churchill looked up from the paper, examining the Rear-Admiral over the top of his glasses.

"But it was different I assume?"

"Yes, Prime Minister, in as much as it was true. Kaltenbrunner was a frequent visitor to the area in happier times, and she named him as one of the men she saw dumping items in the water."

No one gave voice to the thought that such a piece of information should never have been buried or ignored.

Dalziel continued.

"When the Soviets took over the area, it appears that she told her story to someone else, which resulted in the lake being investigated. We only found this out when the area was reoccupied. Fraulein Weisenbacher has disappeared, but some of the local population spoke of Soviet activity that resulted in the removal of many objects from the lake, roughly around the end of June, beginning of July."

Dalziel brought the pile of paperwork together neatly, ensuring all the edges were perfectly aligned as he delivered the final piece of information.

"We are aware that NKVD Colonel General Serov was in the area at the time. He was the man charged with recovering the German uranium oxide and other sensitive items."

"Good lord. We seem to have escaped a disaster by the skin of our teeth, Sir Roger. Damnedly well done to all involved... Damnedly well done. And the money is where now?"

"What was recovered from the sea is now safely within the Naval arsenal at Scapa Flow, under increased guard."

Somerville eased himself on his seat.

"Prime Minister. That was under my orders. My inclination was to burn the bloody lot of them, but I assumed Bank of England would want a look at the damn things."

"Quite right too, Sir James. I'll get Hugh Dalton on it immediately. I'll have him liaise directly with you."

"Splendid, Sir."

"Thank you again, Sir Roger. I won't forget this, I can assure you."

Churchill stubbed his cigar out with a celebratory flourish and stood, cueing the others in to do likewise.

"One last thing, Sir Roger."

"Sir?"

"The dollars. Where are they?"

"Haven't the foggiest idea, Sir. No intelligence on them whatsoever."

"Best we give our cousins a warning then."

"Yes, Prime Minister."

Dictators, unlike Democrats, depend on a small coterie to sustain their power. These backers, generally drawn from the military, the senior civil service, and family or clan members, have a synergistic relationship with their dictator. The dictator delivers opportunities for them to become rich, and they protect him from being overthrown.

Bruce Bueno de Mesquita.

Chapter 180 - THE SCHEMERS

1107 hrs, Saturday, 30th November 1946, 2nd Grenadier Guards Maintenance Section, Kolberg, Poland.

The gathering at the maintenance section was graced by nearly all the senior officers from 2nd Grenadier Guards, including its commander, Lieutenant Colonel Cecil Keith.

'C' Squadron's commander was absent, still looking for the missing items whose absence had drawn so much unwanted attention upon the maintenance section.

2nd Lieutenant Charles, recently returned from his officer training, was under the spotlight from the moment Keith and his entourage had arrived.

"Is this your signature, Lieutenant?"

"No, Sir."

Pansy Flowers handed another document over to his commander, who turned to Corporal Wild.

"Is this your signature, Corporal?"

Making a play of checking closely, Wild shook his head.

"So neither of you signed for these acceptance forms, so neither of you are responsible for this missing vehicle or the other one."

They wisely stayed silent.

Keith's attention turned to Flowers, the WO2 in charge of all matters paperwork within the maintenance section.

"So, Flowers, what have you got to say for yourself? 27th November these vehicles were signed out. The 27th, man!"

"Colonel, Sir, I can't say. I wasn't here when the vehicles were signed out. Either of them. I've just got back from a spot of leave in Rostock, Sir. It was Lieutenant Charles' enquiry that prompted my checks on the paperwork, as I noticed both vehicles had gone. I'd noticed their absence previously, but assumed they'd been picked

153

up... err... by the right parties. Sergeant Ferris was responsible for signing the two vehicles out. He's just in from England, so he wouldn't know either Lieutenant Charles or CSM Head by sight."

The Colonel interrupted.

"So where is Ferris now?"

"Sir, he's out with the redcaps trying to spot those responsible for... err... removing the vehicles."

Godfrey Pike, B Squadron's commander, piped up."

"Sir, I was with Peter Carington when he interviewed Ferris. He provided a good description of all four men. Procedures were followed. The sergeant's not to blame as Peter and I see it."

Pike was never slow in stating his opinion.

"After all, I mean, who on earth steals tanks and transporters?"

Keith, whose battalion was light two Centurion Mk IIIs, two Diamond T M-19 tank transporters, and their M-9 trailers, controlled his anger.

"Well quite clearly someone does, Pike!"

He swallowed and forced himself to calm down.

"Right. We'll sort out the whys and wherefores of this bloody mess later. For now, I want parties out searching for the vehicles first and foremost. Find them, we find the swine who did this, and heaven help them if I get my bloody hands on the sods. I'll have their guts for garters."

He turned to Charles and Wild, wagging an admonishing finger.

"And if I find out that you lot have anything to do with this, I can guarantee you an extremely unpleasant time before your courts-martial!"

He leant forward.

"Are we clear, Lieutenant... Sergeant?"

"Yes, Sir!"

"Right... get out there and find your bloody tank!"

Keith strode from the office with the rest streaming in his wake, almost running in an attempt to keep up.

Charles and Wild remained at attention long after it was necessary.

Flowers, also at parade attention, broke the silence.

"Fucking hell. He's not a happy puppy, is he?"

Charles relaxed and moved closer to Flowers.

"For that matter, Sarnt-Major... neither am I. That's my bloody tank that some bastard is gallivanting 'round the Polish countryside with and, quite bloody frankly, I'm not fucking happy! If

154

I find that your man Ferris has anything to do with this, then I will visit myself upon you... mates or no fucking mates. Understand, Pansy?"

"No need for that, Andy... no need at all..."

"There better not be, old son, or I'll have a set of garters of my own. Are we clear?"

"Crystal."

"Excellent. You hear anything, I wanna hear it before the echo's died away or else."

"I can do that."

"Good. Now, we're off, and woe betide anyone who is involved in this fucking abhorrence!"

"Right, Laz. Before some other busybody works out that we don't have a tank, get the boys rounded up, organise a jeep, and we'll go off on a jaunt and find Lady Godiva smartish. Can't have gone far, and unless I miss my mark, we should start with either the Coldstreams or the Irish... and I'm betting that our dear friend Cuthbert le Lièvre from His Majesty's Coldstream Guards has a hand in this... you mark my words, Laz."

"I hear you, boss. Never forgiven us for the kipper wheeze."

In the German War, le Lièvre and Charles had a run in over a shared route, where the Coldstreams were off course and on the wrong road.

The Channel Islander had crossed their paths a few times since, one of which had resulted in bad feeling and, by way of a reprisal, Lazarus Wild introducing two fish into the exhaust system of le Lièvre's tank.

Such things never go unrevenged, and it was Charles' hunch that the Coldstreamer had a hand in recent events.

1311 hrs, Sunday, 1st December 1946, Pardubice, Czechoslovakia.

The meeting was jovial, even though none of the visitors were getting what they wanted.

Not that they had expected to, given the shortages.

New vehicles had been allocated from France, from American sources, and even from Germany, the latter for reasons that were not wholly clear to the Legionnaires of Camerone and Alma, but they were not about to refuse.

Over the weeks, the foraging parties had turned up with some surprises, some of which were cherished additions to the order of battle, others received less warmly, depending on their state or nature.

All in all, the reforming units of the Legion Corps D'Assaut received a reasonable boost from official and unofficial sources.

Uhlmann was just into his questioning on the mechanical state of three Felix vehicles from his regiment when items from a clearly unofficial source arrived in clouds of diesel smoke and much rattling of chains.

The four officers looked up from their table and, collectively, their jaws dropped.

Fiedler, the workshop's commander, immediate thoughts turned to where he could get the spares from.

Felix Jorgensen thought nothing of them particularly, as they clearly weren't going to be for his anti-tank unit.

Uhlmann admired their lines and appreciated the fact that he was looking at something that was probably extremely potent on the modern battlefield.

"They'll do, whatever they are, Walter."

Fiedler shook his head in mock sternness.

"No can do, Obersturmbannführer. You don't get heavy tanks. You know that."

"Looks like a medium to me."

"Not my decision but, whatever it is, I'm thinking it'll go to the heavy tank company no matter what. They're light on vehicles and these will do nicely. Not my decision, Obersturmbannführer."

Rolf knew he was right, but wanted to have a look at these new vehicles close up.

He moved off, and the other followed out of curiosity.

The young officer in charge of the two transporter vehicles saw Uhlmann's approach and jumped down, saluting impeccably.

"Beg to report, Obersturmbannführer, Untersturmführer Jung, 3rd Kompagnie, 1st Chars D'Assaut reporting. We've returned, following the successful discharge of our orders, with new vehicles for the division."

Uhlmann smiled at his own young officer, whom he knew well without the introduction.

"Well then, Heinz... what do we have here eh? No, first tell me how you came by them?"

156

Jung gestured to the man in command of the second transport, who alighted from the tank transporter.

"Now I understand! You've been led astray by that old rogue!"

Their relationship was well known, so no one was at all surprised when salutes were hasty and comradely hugs and slaps were long and clearly heartfelt.

"What have you done, Johan, eh?"

Braun, smiling from ear to ear, merely shrugged.

"I followed the express orders of my superior officer, Sir."

Jung, now surrounded by more men from the foraging party, stood up to the senior NCO.

"Sir, I beg to report that I was persuaded to steal from our allies, on the basis of information gleaned from some drunken British guardsmen. I would not have done so without immense pressure from the Sturmscharführer, and would advise that he is arrested immediately."

Uhlmann slapped Jung on the shoulder.

"Well spoken. I've often thought of doing that myself!"

"Well, think again, the pair of you. I was just discharging my orders... orders... as it happens... written by you, Obersturmbannführer."

"Damn. You escape again."

The laughter was universal and the whole group were relaxed.

Cigarettes went round before Uhlmann posed the question.

"So, what have you got here?"

"These are the very latest British tanks. The opportunity to take this was too good to pass on. They're Centurion tanks. 84mm gun that can use the new ammo. We've picked up some of that as well. No spares for the engine, but we can work on that. I've had a play inside and it seems pretty good. Stabilised gun system, all sorts of lovely toys. I'm assuming you'll let me have it as my own tank. Seeing as I know all the bad things about you?"

Everyone laughed except Fiedler, who was quick to interject.

"No, Sturmscharführer. As I was explaining when you drove in, these will be slated for the Schwere Panzer Kompagnie, you can be assured of it."

Braun prepared to challenge but Uhlmann waved him down.

"That's the way of it, Johann. However, I can say I've set aside a turbine Schwarzpanther just for you to ride in, if that helps?"

157

Braun weighed it up and figured he had done all right.

Not that it mattered of course.

Uhlmann climbed onto the trailer.

"Come on then. You going to show me around this beast?"

"Of course."

"What's this?"

"Ah. It's a naked woman."

"No it isn't. Even I can see that!"

"Lady Godiva rode through her home town naked. That's what it says."

"I prefer pictures. Anyway, show me."

The two heaved themselves up and dropped into the turret of what had, until recently, been Charles' Centurion tank.

1312 hrs, Sunday, 1st December 1946, Dai Ichi Life Insurance Building, Tokyo, Japan.

Far East Command, more commonly referred to as FECOM, had been in being for a little over two months.

Its commander, Douglas MacArthur, did not feel valued, despite the huge 'empire' over which he held sway.

His command of the Pacific War that ultimately laid low the Empire of Japan had been constantly overshadowed by the German War, and subsequently the war against the Soviet Union, in which Japan played a minor part... or at least that was how the papers so often played it, despite his own large set piece battles on land, at sea, and in the air.

The great crusade against the evil Empire had been the focus of American rage following Pearl Harbor, slipping to sharing newspaper inches with Northern Europe, Italy, and the other places from where fascism had been driven.

The focus swung wholly back to him after the German capitulation, and he enjoyed the media spotlight upon his generalship at Okinawa, even though the fighting dragged on and on, way past the deadline he set and reset, and on into August.

When the acts of surrender on Okinawa were accepted, MacArthur had taken centre stage, but events in Europe always overtook him, and he was singularly hacked off with it all.

Set against the background of a disgruntled C-in-C, the staff of FECOM worked hard to do everything well and give MacArthur little to find fault with.

158

His relentless need to have invasion plans for Siberia updated drew constant groans from the men and women under his command, but they set to it

MacArthur's first idea had to be to name the projected Siberian invasion after the commander of the last US forces to set foot there, the American Expeditionary Force Siberia, which landed in August 1918.

His advisors quickly advised, and he quickly understood that Operation Graves, named for Major General William S. Graves, should be consigned to the waste bin as wholly inappropriate.

It was subsequently replaced with the more upbeat 'Operation Tiger'.

The sister operation, designed to explode out of China to numerous points west and north, was known as 'Operation Cougar'

The staff of FECOM kept both constantly updated, integrating new units into the plans, removing those who returned stateside, upgrading expectations when new equipment arrived, or downgrading when some other theatre required an asset they had marked down for use.

Today, MacArthur was taking lunch with two of his senior men, Admiral John H. Towers, the C-in-C Pacific Fleet, and Lieutenant General Ennis C Whitehead, C-in-C PACUSA, the unified command group for the US Air forces in the Pacific.

As usual, lunch did not obstruct military business, although it was taken at a slower and more relaxed pace.

MacArthur slipped a piece of beef into his mouth and used the redundant fork to point at the folder sat alongside the naval officer.

"That the latest Tiger updates on the carrier force problem, John?"

Clearing his mouth, Admiral Towers spoke as he loaded another forkful.

"No, Sir, that it isn't. The temporary loss of Task Force 58 is a bitch, that's for sure, but if Tiger becomes a reality tomorrow, we can still run an effective prosecution of the existing plan. Just need to shuffle the assets some."

Again the fork selected the folder.

"So what's that you're dragging along? Mess accounts?"

They chuckled together, the 'Top Secret' markings clearly marking the contents as anything but.

"No, Sir. Something better examined without the plates and cutlery getting in the way."

MacArthur nodded his understanding.

"Fair enough, John. Wanna bring us up to speed as far as you can while we eat?"

Towers took a refreshing sip of wine to clear his mouth before outlining the contents of the intelligence folder.

MacArthur and Whitehead had both finished their main courses before Towers took another bite from his.

Going as far as he could without resorting to opening the folder, Towers returned to the contents of his dinner plate, leaving the two others to pose questions.

Whitehead got in first.

"So, in summary, we may or may not have one or two special nip subs still at large. It's possible that they sank one of their own off Kannonzaki, but that's not confirmed. We know a submarine was sunk by aircraft from the Oriskany, thirty miles off Kholmsk on Sakhalin, which somehow we appear to know was one of the big AM class subs?"

"Yep. Sorry... should have explained. When it was sunk it briefly broached and our aviators took a photo. Intelligence has confirmed it as one of the AMs."

"Which leaves two of them unaccounted for."

"Yep, but possibly not, as we have the reports from the Hibiki's attack near Kannonzaki, carried out on an extremely large underwater target. Could be they sunk whatever it was, and it was an AM, or something else entirely."

The two men permitted Towers to finish his lunch before they posed more questions.

Dessert was waved off as the Admiral opened the folder and showed them the modest evidence that Naval Intelligence had built up, evidence of the presence of some underwater leviathans built in secret.

"Special Type Submarine?"

"Yes, Sir. There was some confusion early on about that name, but that's the designation officially used by the Combined Fleet, from what we can establish."

"And they're bigger than the AMs?"

"From the evidence we have, they're twin hulled monsters, with a hangar that can take three seaplanes. Probably the Seiran type they designed for such subs."

He pulled the transcript of a conversation that took place in a Nagasaki hospital.

"We have a Japanese naval officer who confirms the armament installed, talks of rumours that dignitaries went aboard before two of these subs sailed from Sasebo on the June 10th."

160

"June 10th? Where did they sail to and where are the bastards?"

"That, Ennis, is the problem. We don't know. My staff are unanimous. These are a problem, and I agree. So much secrecy involved, even now. The nip Admiral in charge is saying absolutely nothing. We're still working on him but he simply won't even acknowledge their existence. We need to find out. Two of my boys has come up with a theory, and... well..."

He fished in the folder for the submission from a Lieutenant Waynes and Lieutenant j.g. Takeo and passed it to MacArthur.

The silence of concentration fell over the table, sufficient to discourage the waiting steward from approaching with coffee.

After a while, MacArthur passed the document to Whitehead, beckoned the coffee forward, and started to load his favourite pipe.

Both men watched as the Air Force man read the 'theory' in front of him.

"Shit."

MacArthur nodded.

"Your opinion on that, John?"

"Sir, I'm not sold, but I'm not rubbishing it either. They make a good case for it. Lotta stuff has to be surmised, coincidences...but it's not impossible, that's for sure."

Whitehead tapped the paper with the tip of his finger as MacArthur lit up.

"So their time line works out?"

"Sure does."

"This suggestion of a special task force of five submarines?"

"Dockyard gossip, nothing more. Some slight evidence in signal evidence from Sixth Fleet correspondence that was not fully destroyed."

"And their suggestion about the missing stocks from Okunoshima fits obviously... the Hibiki attack... the Oriskany attack which sunk an AM... if this was a five boat force...well..."

"Force 731? You gotta be shitting me. They're reaching too far."

Towers shrugged.

"I thought so, but you can see it's possible. Key personnel from Units 731 and 516 are missing from Manchuria. We believed the Commies didn't have them, but that's being re-evaluated right now, in the light of a report from Kharbarovsk. A review of photo recce

161

information is also being undertaken as we speak, particularly from around a place called Sovetskaya Gavan."

Another piece of paper was produced.

"A Chinese agent in Kharbarovsk reports seeing Japanese personnel accompanying a heavily guarded convoy that was loading aboard a special NKVD train on 23rd June. Again, that fits in the possible timeline."

Yet more evidence was laid out.

"We had a report of some strange Soviet ships hiding there under a temporary shelter around 21st June, which fits in with my men's time line."

"Ships?"

"That's all we know. Our informant was at distance apparently."

MacArthur's pipe was smoking heavily and he waved his hand through the air to clear his view.

"One moment."

He beckoned to his aide, Francisco Salveron, and whispered in his ear.

The Filipino Sergeant disappeared and reappeared almost in the same moment, and handed MacArthur the file he had asked for.

"Thank you, Francisco."

MacArthur opened the file and took out the top sheet, handing it to the naval officer.

"List of academics and such presently missing without trace."

Towers scanned the list, beside which was the area of expertise of each individual.

"Holy crap!"

'... Riken Institute... Scientific and Research Group...Weapons Research Group... Institute of Chemical and Physical Research... Imperial Institute of Sacred Knowledge...Kyoto University Special Research Projects Team...'

"Sir, this list seems to be a who's who of their top researchers."

"Sure is, John."

Towers passed it across to Whitehead who whistled as he took in the specialities involved.

"I can tell you both, in strictest confidence, that the names on that list have drawn attention from some very important folk."

MacArthur sipped his coffee and accepted the list back, which he swiftly returned to the file.

Whitehead asked the question.

162

"Such as, Sir?"

"Hoover, Secretary Stimson, the President… even had one of Leslie Groves' men on the horn."

"Groves? Leslie Groves? Oh fuck."

Whilst General Leslie R. Groves was not well-known, the three men sat round the dining table were sufficiently high up the food chain to know who he was, and which project he was involved with.

'Manhattan'

"Oh fuck indeed, Ennis."

MacArthur beckoned the steward forward, and their coffee was refreshed before he continued.

"So… it now all takes on a more sinister aspect and bumps this way up the list of priorities. Let me be clear on that. Finding these subs is now our number one job. Raise the level of alert… let the boys know what we're looking for. There's no room for territorial disputes, inter-service rivalries, or pissing competitions. Understood, gentlemen?"

"Yes, Sir."

"Make sure Europe gets to see this information too, ok?"

He took a deep draught of the hot coffee and relaxed back into the dining chair.

"Ok, John. So, based on what we know, where could these bastards be holding up?"

"In short, Sir, by now… with enough supplies…anywhere on the planet where there's enough water to put under their keel."

When the two senior officers departed, MacArthur spent an uncomfortable hour on the phone with the interested parties, all of whom were extremely unhappy to find a possible link between the existence of two huge Japanese submarines and the disappearance of much of the Empire's biological and nuclear research talent.

Unhappy was an understatement, and huge amounts of the Allied resources were suddenly directed to finding the submarines in question, and discovering the purpose of their existence, as well as locating the scientists and engineers that could possess secrets too dreadful to contemplate.

Reconnaissance flights trebled throughout the whole Pacific, and naval ships that had relaxed into a pseudo peacetime routine suddenly found themselves back to old ways, searching the silent waters for signs of a lurking enemy.

Key areas like Ulithi, Tokyo Bay, Pearl Harbor, San Francisco, and the Panama Canal were suddenly under full war footing, and thousands of men who had hoped to return to their homes found themselves once more guarding against a very real threat.

All of which was wasted effort.

1902 hrs, Monday, 2nd December 1946, Vinogradar Young Communists Sailing Club, Black Sea, USSR.

"I can't sanction that, Comrade Commander. We simply cannot permit the submarines to venture into the open sea ahead of time. There's too much risk involved."

Commander Nobukiyo's language skills had developed immensely, so no translation was needed.

"I regret, Admiral, I must ask for higher authority to sanction this mission. There is little point in keeping the Sen-Tokus secret from the enemy if my men have forgotten what it is like to be at sea when the time comes."

Nobukiyo turned towards the massive submarines and gestured at each in turn.

"These wonderful machines of war are as nothing without the men that drive them, and those men have grown stale as sailors whilst they have developed their skills as engineers and missile handlers, Admiral Oktyabrskiy. I simply must insist that we be given some sea time."

"I can only agree, Comrade Admiral. All our men have been bottled up without anything but static diving exercises for months. We must get our subs wet out there, or there will be errors made. If nothing else, we need to practice with the 'Sheptat' in open water."

Kalinin referred to the 'Whisper' underwater acoustic communications system recently installed on their submarines, drawings of which had been copied from the US Navy blueprints of 'Gertrude' by agents of GRU [East].

The Admiral was not a submariner by trade, but he was a navy man through and through, and understood precisely why the Japanese officer was so insistent.

He also had strict orders from people who were extremely unlikely to bend, regardless of how good an argument might be. They had their orders from other people, who were not known for their tolerance.

164

None the less, he had to try.

"I'll pass on your request immediately, together with my endorsement. If it's possible to get you some sea time, I'll get it."

Oktyabrskiy saluted and left the two submariners to complete the day's programme.

Commander Nobukiyo, much to his embarrassment, arrived last.

"Thank you for coming at such short notice, Comrades."

It was rapidly approaching midnight and both Kalinin and Nobukiyo had been in their quarters inside the bunker, although Kalinin had not yet gone to bed, hence his swifter arrival.

"Comrades, I can report that your request has been granted. You're to be permitted to conduct sea exercises that can commence no sooner than one hour after sunset, and conclude no later than one and a half hours before dawn. We're to coordinate with all commands to ensure there are no errors and no unwanted visits from Allied snoopers. I'll take care of all that, as well as arranging for distractions for those with terminal curiosity."

Kalinin punched his fist into his other hand in celebration, whilst Nobukiyo bowed and bowed.

"Thank you, Comrade Admiral, thank you, thank you."

Oktyabrskiy interrupted the Japanese's display.

"I have permission for four excursions over the next month, no more. Present me with an operational plan and any other requirements for a date no sooner than 10th December by 1600 tomorrow. I confess, I'm no less surprised than both of you are. Now, get some sleep. There'll be no relaxation in training, despite the extra work you two now have. Good night, Comrades."

0839 hrs, Wednesday, 4th December 1946, NATO Forces in Europe Headquarters, Frankfurt, Germany.

"Morning, Sir."

"Morning, Walter."

Ready for his meeting with the Mexican air force officers at 0900, Eisenhower had already had breakfast and was well into his fifth cigarette of the day.

"Sir, we've had this come in from the Pacific, and it coincides with communications from both Secretary Stimson and General Marshall."

Eisenhower received the report in silence.

After a moment, he looked up at Bedell-Smith.

"You read this, Walter?"

"Skimmed it as I walked it round to you, Sir."

Eisenhower resumed his reading and stayed silent until he had finished.

"Wow. That's worrying. Those two related?"

He indicated the messages from Stimson and Marshall.

"Yes indeed, Sir. Both giving you some specific instructions and expectations."

He handed them over and Eisenhower was taken aback by the size of both messages.

"Précis them for me."

He skim read as Bedell-Smith did just that.

"Basically, you've got orders. Every effort to find these submarines and the people they carry. Some specific measures are detailed... navy and air force tasks in the main. Quite clearly the folks back home are worried, Ike."

Eisenhower looked at the clock and found he still had enough time.

"OK. Specifics of what they expect?"

"Well, Sir. Eastern and Western seaboards are on full alert now. Canal's locked down. We've got to do the same across the board. And then we search everywhere... pretty much the whole of our side of the Atlantic, the Med, anywhere with water."

"Have they got intel that says it's our threat?"

"No, Sir, but both orders are quite specific. Consider everywhere at risk."

"At risk from what?"

"That's the part I'm not getting, Ike. Just subs and people are mentioned. General Marshall will be visiting here. He's coming via London, so he's obviously briefing Churchill in person. Must be pretty sensitive stuff. Anyway, I'm going to speak with a couple of guys in Washington, see if I can get the information firmed up some."

"OK, Walter."

Eisenhower rose and consumed the last of his coffee.

"Get the staff on this straightaway. Pull in all the heads of service for a meeting at... 1300hrs. Get that lot to George Tedder... have him briefed in immediately. Heads up to all commands, be vague for the moment. Have a plan ready for implementation that can be discussed at that meeting."

"Yes, Sir."

"Right, I'm off to chat with our Allies. Get that plan sorted and find out what the heck this is all about please."

"Yes, Sir."

"Oh and Walter...anything happening in Berlin?"

Eisenhower referred to the Soviet enclave that remained after the Red Army's withdrawal, one that was now surrounded by the Allies and supplied solely by an air corridor that was designated for Soviet use.

"It's settled down now, Sir. They've fortified their ground but nothing that looks aggressive."

"Thank you, Walter... and keep me informed."

By some strange twist of fate, as the 1300 meeting was being briefed about the new orders and being shocked by the use of words like biological and atomic, scientists at the underground facility in Camp 1001 turned on the last of the fifty-four high capacity Japanese centrifuges, bringing the process of enriching uranium to its peak.

1058 hrs, Friday, 6th December 1946, the Kremlin, Moscow, USSR.

Stalin had greeted the news with great joy.

"Finally! How long?"

"The academics are unable to say with certainty, Comrade General Secretary."

Academician Kurchatov remained silent, reinforcing Minister Malenkov's words.

Stalin clapped his hands together, the sound almost shot-like, causing more than one person present to jump.

"But, nonetheless, this will greatly assist us in producing a weapon... and producing one sooner than we could have ever expected, yes?"

Both Kurchatov and Malenkov nodded.

"Most certainly, Comrade General Secretary. Whilst I cannot give you a definite date on its availability, we're most certainly

167

talking months. There's much more to do... engineering, delivery systems, the minutiae of technological progress, but the new arrivals from Japan have brought with them much research, and it's all helping reduce the time."

Beria looked on, his eyes gleaming with triumph, as his NKVD had overseen the project to bring men, equipment, and research papers to the Motherland.

Stalin acknowledges his security boss with a rare smile.

"This pleases me greatly, Comrades. Keep advancing... keep Raduga on track... and keep me informed of all progress. Thank you."

Kurchatov and Malenkov took their cue and left.

Nazarbayeva stood as soon as the door opened, but quickly realised it had only opened to allow two men to exit the room, not to encourage her forward.

She nodded to Kurchatov and Malenkov, who quickly went on their way.

Eight minutes later, she was admitted to give her own report to the General Secretary.

Her brief was interrupted by a report from Vasilevsky, stating that the Red Army would be installed in its final withdrawal positions by 1800 hrs that day.

1300 hrs, Friday, 6th December 1946, Lieutenant General Kaganovich's office, the Kremlin, Moscow, USSR.

"And what did they say to that, Comrade Nazarbayeva?"

"Unconcerned. I was surprised at that. Such an increase in Allied activity seems to me to be unprecedented. Specifically the flying hours. Immense rise in reconnaissance flights. But they didn't seem to worry about it at all, Comrade."

"Maybe because it's all sea area concentrated. No increase of note in activities on land in Europe... or in China I can also tell you."

"I understand, but we've picked up a lot of twitches in their intelligence services. Questions being asked... questions about our former allies."

"Yes, we've noticed that too. I suspect Comrade Beria had already informed them of that. Didn't worry them either, did it?"

"Not at all, Comrade. To be honest. I've never seen the General Secretary in such a fine mood. It was almost as if nothing could be said to dampen his day. His reaction to the news of the final withdrawal was non-existent... the idea of giving up hard-won ground has constantly exercised him since we started the process, and yet nothing."

"Perhaps he got some good news, eh?"

"Comrade Malenkov and Academician Kurchatov saw him just before me. Can't have been them, as we all know our programme is behind time, hence the abandonment of Raduga."

Kaganovich stuffed his mouth with beetroot and ham for no other reason than to buy himself a moment's thinking time.

"Can I share a confidence with you, Comrade Nazarbayeva?"

"But of course, Comrade Kaganovich."

"The atomic research part of our programme has recently been lifted by some assistance from other sources and is now in advance of schedule."

"How is that possible? There's been no such information given to the GRU. The last report, dated early November if I recall... the Ministry of Middle Machinery made it quite clear. We're behind in all but a few of the development stages."

"You're correct, comrade. It did."

What he was about to do was also in advance of schedule, but he reasoned he would have more to lose if he didn't use the opportunity the woman had presented.

He went over to his filing cabinet, unlocked it, and removed a box file.

"November 4th if my memory serves me."

He immediately produced a copy of the document she had already seen.

He then covered it with another document dated 4th November.

One she had not previously seen.

"That is the real report from Middle Machinery, Comrade."

"Real report? What do you mean, Comrade?"

"GRU is not included in certain matters any more. I'm not clear why, but there seems to be a trust issue, Tatiana."

He used her name to help soften the blow, not for her, but for his own purposes. He needed to concentrate on what he was saying.

"Your men were withdrawn, remember?"

"Yes, I remember there was a freshening of staff within the projects, men out, men in, an exercise suggested by…"

"Suggested by Comrade Beria."

"Yes."

"Your personnel are all loyal to the NKVD. Their reports to you are coordinated to coincide with the official reports of Middle Machinery. Beria engineered the whole thing to remove you from the process… with the compliance… no, agreement of the General Secretary."

Something lit off in her brain.

"That's why Malenkov was strange during our last meeting."

Kaganovich leant forward and lowered his voice.

"Perhaps there is also another reason, Comrade Nazarbayeva."

It was a statement, but despite her lack of political awareness it was one she understood immediately.

"Beria wants me excluded so I can be blamed if there's some disaster. He'll prepare evidence of my ineptness… by the Motherland… my own agents within the projects will supply the evidence that I knew of problems and did nothing."

"Always possible, Tatiana. As I said before, he has you in his sights for more than one reason. But I suspect Malenkov had another reason for being less than honest with you."

They held eye contact and Nazarbayeva immediately understood what that 'other reason; was.

"Raduga. I'm going to be blamed for the failure of Raduga?"

"On the contrary, Comrade Nazarbayeva. Raduga is not a wholly dead project."

"What?"

"Raduga is still underway and progressing ahead of schedule."

"My agents left the project when it was abandoned…"

"Your agents left Raduga when it was time for you to be taken out of the circle. The two men you relied on were, in any case, Beria's men first and foremost."

Nazarbayeva fell silent, absorbing the totality of what she had just learned, leaving Kaganovich with ample opportunity to enjoy more food.

Leaning across the desk, Nazarbayeva selected some biscuits and settled back in her chair.

170

"If Raduga is still running, at least in part, then why am I excluded? It's the single most important project our nation has embarked on. To exclude the GRU is a huge risk."

Kaganovich chuckled, the sound clearly without humour, resembling the laugh of a teacher faced with a particularly stupid pupil.

Even though he knew his room was free of any recording devices or bugs, he dropped his voice to a barely audible whisper, drawing the woman forward.

"Oh, Tatiana. The GRU isn't excluded... you're excluded. Raduga carries risk with it from start to execution. I believe that my boss and Comrade Stalin have set you up... in case Raduga fails... or in case Raduga is successful."

The enormity of that took a few moments to sink in.

He spoke again, keeping his voice low.

"If Raduga fails at home because of whatever circumstances, I fear that evidence will come to hand of your complicity in some events that led to failure. If Raduga is executed and conditions become unfavourable, then I also believe that you will be sacrificed as the sufficiently senior element that acted independently."

Nazarbayeva said the first thing that popped into her head.

"Is that why he promoted me yet again?"

Kaganovich shrugged.

"That I cannot say... but the head of a lieutenant general sits nicer on the pole than that of a lower rank, Comrade."

With unexpected humour, Nazarbayeva laughed and replied.

"Then perhaps I should expect my Marshal's stars by the New Year."

'Do you not understand your predicament, woman?'

"Nothing will happen yet."

"What do you advise, Comrade?"

"I have your back for now, Comrade Nazarbayeva. I can give you warning in good time. There are some people, good friends close to me... I will discuss the matter in general terms... no names mentioned... *'no names needed, they already know you well, Tatiana'*... see what they think."

He leant back and stretched his arms and legs.

"To be honest, I believe this'll be more about the fallout from any successful prosecution of Operation Raduga. The new advances have made failure unlikely. That makes it easier for us to monitor."

171

"Us, Comrade Kaganovich. Why us? Who is us?"

"Well, you and I for a start, plus friends who have the Motherland's best interests at heart."

She looked him in the eye with greater understanding than ever before.

"Friends... friends whose greater loyalty is to Mother Russia than any of her overseers, you mean?"

His position suddenly became extremely uncomfortable and he dithered over his response, which was not wasted on the suddenly razor-sharp GRU officer.

He took the plunge, trusting to his judgement, or at least the partial plunge that he felt would convince Nazarbayeva of his commitment to Mother Russia.

"Friends who, with me, work to find those who would threaten Mother Russia from within, those whose efforts do nothing but harm her, and those who seek only personal advancement and glory over the needs of the Rodina."

She nodded firmly.

"As do we all, Comrade Kaganovich."

"Indeed, Comrade Nazarbayeva."

'Depending on your definition of threatening, harm, and glory, of course, Tatiana.'

"That's why I took this uniform, Tatiana, and I mean to do my duty without fear or favour."

'Depending on your definition of duty, Tatiana.'

"I agree. In any case, that's my duty and purpose as a soldier, Comrade Kaganovich."

"I'll watch over you, Tatiana. But you must also watch yourself. Observe without being seen to observe. Understand without being seen to fully comprehend. To acquire knowledge without being seen to acquire it... they're the skills of a Chekist!"

She laughed with him.

"So, may I expect information from you... to keep me informed of Raduga and such things from which I'm excluded?"

"Yes, but only face to face in this office. There'll be no paperwork trail for any nosey bastard to follow, and you'll also make no written record of anything we have or will discuss. I must insist on that, Tatiana."

"Of course, Comrade Kaganovich."

"Good... now we have run over our time. We shall say we were discussing the new aerial activity by the damned capitalists if asked. Until next time, Comrade Leytenant General."

His formality marked the end of the meeting.

As usual, they shook hands and spared each other the military courtesies.

"Until the 20th, Comrade Leytenant General Kaganovich."

2120 hrs, Friday, 6th December 1946, Lieutenant General Kaganovich's Dacha, Moscow, USSR.

Khrushchev stamped the snow from his feet before entering.

They hugged like old friends, which they certainly were.

"Sorry I'm late, Ilya. An accident on the way here. Some damn fool crashed into tree. Are we all here?"

Taking Khrushchev's coat, he nodded by way of reply and gestured the civilian towards the roaring fire, around which three other men sat.

They rose as one to embrace the new arrival.

"Vladimir, you've lost weight. I can get my arms round you, you old rogue."

"Can't say the same for you, Nikita! The Party life clearly puts meat on a man's bones!"

They play sparred as friends do, before Vladimir Konstantinovich Gorbachev, commander of the Moscow Military District, resumed his seat, leaving the way clear for Khrushchev to hug the next in line.

"Vassily!"

They kissed each other's cheeks and slapped shoulders and backs so hard that it made the onlookers wince, but neither man seemed fazed.

"Vassily Karlovich. By the great whore, you look well comrade. Very well!"

"The climate in the south is good for these old bones. What more can I say... Sochi agrees with me."

Attention turned to the other man in the room, for whom Khrushchev had a warm but less frantic greeting.

"Comrade Marshal, welcome, welcome."

"Comrade Khrushchev, to you too."

He grinned and turned to Kaganovich.

"Right, where's the fucking vodka, Ilya. I'm frozen to the core."

The three drinkers raised their vodka glasses alongside the tea cup of the non-drinker and toasted themselves and the Rodina.

"Na Zdorovie!"

173

Searing liquid hit throats and the glasses were emptied in record time.

Khrushchev took the lead, as he always seemed to do.

"So, why exactly have we all been summoned here ahead of our normal time, Ilya?"

"Nazarbayeva."

"What has our darling GRU officer been up to now?"

He told them, holding back only a couple of small details.

"You're fucking joking of course... you seriously didn't say that, did you, Ilya?"

"Yes, I did. I felt it was right... to have told a lie then might have undermined me in the future... the future when I need... we need her to believe me... follow my lead... my direction... according to our plan."

Gorbachev spoke quickly, keen to get in before Khrushchev went off on one of his tirades.

"I can see the sense in that, Ilya... but did you have to go so far?"

Kaganovich held out his hands in a supplicatory manner.

"It seemed right, Vladimir. The moment was then... and I can say that she gave off all the right signals as we spoke... and when we parted. I have her followed of course... she's in her normal Moscow routine."

Khrushchev was beaten to the draw by a second man.

"I wasn't there. I'm prepared to trust your judgement... but at the slightest sign of any problems, she's to be killed immediately."

The normally mild-mannered Gurundov drew shocked looks from most of those present.

"Calm yourself, Vassily Karlovich! That will not be necessary!"

"I hope it won't be, Ilya. But there can be no risk to this group whatsoever."

That drew unanimous nods.

Khrushchev got in before anyone else could speak.

"Personally, I think it's regrettable that these matters were brought in ahead of schedule... but I understand why it happened."

Which, by Khrushchev standards, was extremely tame language.

"Comrades," they turned to the senior military man present, "There'll be no need to worry about her. I'm convinced of the woman's loyalty to the Motherland, and she will see no disloyalty from any of us, or our men. All she'll see is those committed to the Rodina. This... err... conversation... we can turn this to our

174

advantage in some way. Her relationship with Ilya will be better... yet more entrenched. I agree with Ilya's view that to have avoided telling the truth could have undermined our future plans. Let's just bring her more and more under our control. Keep her informed... facts... not necessarily all but certainly nothing concocted... leave out the names of those who we have in our sights... play down their complicity until we are ready... ready to clean the whole house of vermin. She'll play her part. We know how that'll be achieved, so I say let it all run."

The assembled plotters grunted their agreement.

"Fine... but I agree with Vassily. Make sure we keep someone on her constantly, someone with specific orders if she steers off the road. Can we all agree on that?"

All eyes turned back to the Marshal.

"It won't be necessary... but for your collective peace of mind, I'll agree."

"Yes. Excellent. Ilya, another glass of your peasant piss!"

A thought occurred to Kaganovich.

"Oh, and on that subject, I'm told that our woman is acquiring a regular thirst. I also noted it. Not a problem yet, but it may need watching."

Fig # 226 - Reorganised Legion Corps D'Assaut, December 1946.

	DIRECTLY ATTACHED UNITS	4e R.A.C.E.	1e B.A.S.	1er Battaillon Chars Legers	7th Régiment de Tirailleurs Algériens	1e D.C.A. [AA]	
CAMERONE DIVISION	1e Régiment Chars D'Assaut	1e Régiment de marche	5e Régiment de marche	1er Régiment Étranger de Cavalerie	1er Régiment Artillerie	1e Battaillon de Genie	1e Régiment Blindé
ALMA DIVISION	2e Régiment Chars D'Assaut	3e Régiment de marche	7e Régiment de marche	4e Battaillon Étranger de Cavalerie	3e Régiment Artillerie	3e Battaillon de Genie	2e Régiment Blindé

1000 hrs, Monday, 9th December 1946, office of General Strong, NATO Headquarters, Frankfurt, Germany.

"Thank you for coming, General Gehlen."

"Thank you, General Strong."

They both sat as the ordered coffee and biscuits was placed on the exquisite rosewood table before them.

Relaxing into the comfortable chairs, Gehlen looked like a cat on a hot tin roof.

175

"I take it you have gathered nothing new on our problem, General?"

"Nothing at all, General Strong. Yesterday I discovered how it was that my agents were being moved out of their positions. One of my own staff was supplying information, Ludwig Schneider, a long-serving and trusted man. He's now out of the way."

Strong raised an enquiring eyebrow but managed to say nothing, resisting the opportunity to further enlighten his intelligence colleague.

"Oh no, he doesn't know about my meetings with you on the matter… and neither have I killed him. I have trusted men asking him a long list of questions. They've all the time they require to get me the answers I need."

"Well, good luck with that. My own news is less stark but as important."

He took a healthy draught of his coffee before setting the cup down on the saucer with studied care.

"Diels. I believe he's running a security operation within the hierarchy of the German Republic. I believe you've just set that in stone."

He took up his cup again but paused, knowing he could not leave that just hanging there and replaced it, rising quickly and picking up a file from his desk.

Thumbing through the surveillance reports, he selected the appropriate one and passed it to the mystified Gehlen.

"Verdamnt!"

"Quite."

"On Thursday… Schneider met with Diels on Thursday? May I use your phone please, General Strong?"

"Of course."

Gehlen quickly got a line to his headquarters and his bark guaranteed that he was quickly through to the required extension.

The initial part of the conversation was brief, and heavily featured the words 'Pyramide', 'Donnerstag', and 'Schwein'.

Strong noted the word Pyramide, as it was the agreed name for Diels, to be used at all times when not in private conversation.

There was an impatient pause, during which Gehlen was twitching and unable to stand still.

"Ja? Gut… gut… danke."

He nodded at Strong and completed the call with a flourish.

Returning to his coffee, he sat down with an air of triumph.

"Just using Diels' name was enough. Schneider is being debriefed at the moment... he knows he's in big trouble and has agreed to tell us all he knows."

"Still, I don't think we've enough yet to go and trouble our masters with."

He caught Gehlen's look and immediately realised what he had said.

"My apologies, Reinhard. It must be very difficult for you."

Strong refilled the cups by way of apology.

"So, we wait on what Schneider has to say for himself then?"

"Yes, General Strong."

"Any progress on Uspenka?"

Gehlen lied smoothly.

"No. Nothing. I assume you have nothing to tell either?"

"I think that puts it rather well."

Auschwitz speaks against even a right to self-determination that is enjoyed by all other peoples because one of the preconditions for the horror, besides other, older urges, was a strong and united Germany.

Gunter Grass

Chapter 181 - THE ABOMINATION

1439 hrs, Friday, 20th December 1946, Auschwitz-Birkenau, Poland.

The Major of Engineers saluted briskly, clearly showing his displeasure with the task allotted to his battalion.

The man was steeped in the all-pervasive odour of death.

"Comrade Leytenant General. Our mission is complete. Comrade Polkovnik Ursov has carried out a final inspection of the main site and directs me to inform you that all locations have been prepared and dressed as directed."

NKVD General Oleg Yegorov, sent from Moscow to specifically manage the task, grunted his satisfaction, his eyes still taking in the horrors that had been created under his instructions.

He corrected the thought.

'Comrade Beria's instructions.'

Yegorov considered the moment and decided that all that could be done had been done.

"Very well, Comrade Mayor. Our work here is completed. Inform Polkovnik Ursov that I'll meet him at the main entrance shortly, but that he may start withdrawing his units."

The Major saluted and strode away, keen to be away from the man who had brought them to this place and handed them the very worst of tasks.

"Leytenant."

The aide hovered nearby and responded immediately.

"I'm going to the main camp. Send a message to Moscow headquarters. Mission complete."

"Yes, Comrade Leytenant General."

0820 hrs, Tuesday, 24th December 1946, Orzesche, Poland.

Knocke had experienced what was, for him, a lie in.

178

He followed that with a large breakfast and had stuffed himself on a sausage, egg, and fried potato breakfast that could have, in his opinion, sustained a platoon in the field for a fortnight.

Two of the senior men from Camerone noisily stowed away the hot food with him, food that had been prepared by the headquarters cook from ingredients 'liberated' by Caporal-Chef Ett, a man who would, according to SS and now legion legend, find a crate of beer and a bottle opener on the moon.

Between him and Hässelbach, the senior officers of Camerone wanted for little.

Camerone had come to its present positions in Silesia six days previously, and the division was still shaking out the last few details of its deployment, although many metres of defensive positions had been dug and comfortable bunkers had sprung out of the ground in record time.

Uhlmann had arrived early, the morning ahead mapped out for him and Emmercy to deliver their ideas on the new structure of the tank and marching regiments respectively.

The European scavengers had been filtering back with various pieces of equipment, and the French factories had supplied a healthy number of new Panther Felix vehicles.

Fiedler had been correct, in that the two Centurions were not destined for Uhlmann's armoured regiment, but instead bolstered the small number of heavy tanks in the Corps' heavy tank battalion.

The recently promoted Commandant Jorgensen already had his force sorted, the supply of SPAT vehicles having dried up to nothing, although his unit boasted a good number of old Jagdpanthers and new Schwarzjagdpanther, plus the two remaining Einhorns.

St. Clair, commanding Alma, the other division in the Corps, had similar problems, especially as Camerone seemed to always manage to get in ahead of his units when it came to new kit or scrounged equipment.

Knocke had barely started sorting out the new order of battle before the meeting was interrupted.

Lutz entered clasping a radio message sheet, his face relaying the fact that the day would not go as planned and things were about to change.

"Message from Corps Headquarters, Oberführer. Marked most urgent."

"Thank you, Lutz."

The men around the table tensed as Knocke read and reread the message… order.

He held out his hand and gestured at the table.

179

"Map please."

Emmercy took one from the other table and quickly laid it out.

"Hmm."

"Sir?"

Knocke passed the order to Uhlmann, and he and Emmercy gathered together to read it as their commander drew a mental line on the map.

"Scheisse!"

"Merde!"

Camerone had spent some days preparing its present final positions opposite the Soviet final withdrawal line, only to find out that it wasn't the final withdrawal line, and that they now had to move forward again.

At that time, they were not to know that it was a renegotiation of the position initiated by the Soviets, who considered their foothold on the west bank of the Vistula a problem, at least a problem in that area.

Of course, there was a trade-off elsewhere.

Both officers looked over the map to where Knocke was beating a discontented rhythm with his fingers.

"Przeciszów... we're ordered up to Przeciszów. Apparently an oversight... up to the Vistula... and then the Skawa just east of Przeciszów. That's where we're supposed to have been all along."

"That's why we haven't seen or heard a sound from the bastards since we've been here."

Emmercy could only reiterate his previous observation on the matter.

"Merde!"

The three men understood just how much effort their men had put into creating excellent defensive positions, which were, to all intents and purposes, now useless.

"Twenty-six kilometres."

Knocke said it to no one but the map, his mind working the problem quickly.

"Right. I'll send Bach's troopers ahead immediately. Haefali is closest so he can put two battalions on the road immediately. The rest of his unit can bring up the bits and pieces. Rolf, get your ready Kompagnie in line behind Bach's column. I'll get a platoon of pionieres in case you meet up with any presents from our Socialist colleagues.

"I've been there before, Général."

180

"Where exactly?"

Knocke's tone was unusually strained.

Emmercy indicated his former haunts.

"I used to come here carp fishing in happier times. Lovely carp around there, General. I went with friends from Munich, which is how I learnt your atrocious language."

"Instead of catching fish."

Emmercy grinned at Uhlmann's retort, but Knocke was already factoring in the new information.

"Right, Pierre. I want you up there as soon as possible. Move your headquarters up with the first column. Advise Rolf, who will be group commander. I'll worry about the left flank. Alma has the right… I'll speak with General St.Clair to coordinate our moves."

"I want the first men on the road in twenty minutes, Klar?"

They responded positively, knowing they had no choice.

"Leave orders not to dismantle our present positions. We'll build new, and these will do for breaks from the line and training exercises. Klar?"

Knocke seemed to gather himself before delivering his final instruction.

"Unless militarily necessary, there will be no investigations of any facilities on the route of march. There'll be time for that later."

He considered everything and decided the rest could wait.

"Right then, Kameraden. Let's get the division on the move."

The senior men quit the room at speed and Lutz appeared in their stead, anticipating orders.

Instead he received none as Knocke seemed preoccupied by something on the map.

"Sir?"

"Lutz? Something else?"

"No, Oberführer. I was awaiting your orders."

"Yes, indeed."

He rattled off his instructions to the various units under his command, halfway through which Haefali arrived, clearly armed with the new knowledge.

Knocke continued as he passed the new orders to the commander of 5ᵉ RDM, who immediately tried to marry the words to the map.

"Right, Lutz. Please get them off immediately and make sure the headquarters duty officer knows we'll be moving tomorrow… by 0800 at the latest."

181

"Zu befehl, Oberführer."

"Albrecht."

"Mon Général."

"As you see, we've wasted our efforts here."

"Soldier's lot, mon Général. Dig holes... move on... dig more holes."

"Yes, slightly more than digging a few holes of course, but you're right, Albrecht."

Knocke fell silent as he examined the map, and Haefali felt an undercurrent of something he didn't recognise from the German legionnaire.

"Anything I should know, mon Général?"

"There is certainly something you'll discover, Albrecht."

He tapped the map, some distance away from their final destination.

Haefali took in the map and the name and failed to appreciate its significance.

He questioned Knocke with his eyes, silently seeking further knowledge.

"When your forces swept through Germany in the previous war, you came across some places... awful places... places where murder was done in the name of the German people."

"Dachau... Belsen... Mauthausen..."

"Yes... to name but a few, Albrecht. A stain on my country and something that haunts me and, I suspect always will. I fought for that regime... the regime that brought such abominable places into being."

"And you... pardon... the SS are forever associated with them, of course."

"Yes. I did not know of Dachau other than its beginnings before the war. I'd heard of Belsen and Mauthausen and understood them to be other than what we now know they are... but this is different."

Knocke sat down heavily.

Haefali drew a glass of water and placed in front of his divisional commander.

"Sir?"

"We're going to somewhere that I believe to have been hell on earth. I found out about it... heard gossip... that sort of thing... refused to believe it... but I now know it's there... and that everything I was told was true."

"Where, mon Général?"

He drew a pencil circle round the name.

182

The map was an ex-Wehrmacht map, so the names reflected their German history.

"I did nothing, Albrecht. Ignored it all."

Haefali looked at the map closely and saw a name associated with rumours since before the world had stopped fighting in May 1945.

They were just rumours, although those troops that had liberated Dachau, Belsen, Mauthausen, Ohrdruf, and a hundred other places would vouch that rumours of that kind had a habit of becoming reality.

This rumour had turned out to have an appalling individual reality all of its own.

Auschwitz.

With an awful irony, the ex-SS units of the Foreign Legion would now drive through the very worst of the Nazi concentration camps on their way to their new positions.

1454 hrs, Tuesday, 24th December 1946, Villa Speer, Schloss-Wolfsbrunnenweg, Heidelberg, Germany.

"Deutschland!"

Four voices shared the toast.

The glasses were drained and smashed, as tradition dictated, the fireplace suddenly glistening with sparkling fragments.

"Now, I am conscious that you all have some distance to go, but I felt it very necessary to confirm our decision on a certain matter before we enjoy our celebrations with our families. My apologies that we were interrupted previously."

One of the family's children had burst in excitedly, halting their discussion at the moment of decision.

Which had thrown out their timings, meaning that two of the three visitors were now overstaying their allotted time.

Rudolf Diels wasn't married or greatly endowed with family that accepted his presence without rancour, so Christmas was decidedly not a family affair. However, he had decided which of his current string of women he would spend Christmas with, and he was keen to get back to her bed in Aschaffenburg with as little delay as possible.

In a 1944 air raid, Horst Pflug-Hartnung's family had been placed well beyond the reach of man, so Christmas meant much less to him than many others. His inclusion in the Speer family celebrations was gratifying, and he had dared not refuse, although he wished to be somewhere quiet... and alone.

183

Von Vietinghoff had family in Mainz, and wished to get on the road, although not at the expense of having input on the main subject of the day's discussions.

Speer moved closer to the standing men and lowered his voice.

"Can I confirm that we're agreed on direct action to remove our concerns?"

Each man spoke, each one in the affirmative.

"For both cases?"

Again, they agreed.

"Staggered. They must not be too close together, for fear of arousing suspicion."

Pflug-Hartnung spoke in his normal flowing fashion.

"That will not be a problem, Kanzler, and there'll be no link to us in any way as it will be done simply and effectively. I already have method in mind. Do you wish to know?"

All three listening shook their heads, sharing mutters about leaving the details to the intelligence officer.

Speer clapped his hands with joy, wringing together as the burdens of state were suddenly lifted and he could now enjoy Christmas in all its glory.

"Excellent, Kameraden. Then I need detain you no further. A very merry Christmas to you and your families. Let me see you out."

"May I use your phone, Kanzler?"

"Of course, Horst. Be my guest."

Speer enjoyed his intended humour and left Pflug-Hartnung to make two telephone calls, calls that were seeming innocuous but that activated men intent on murder.

We know that a man can read Goethe or Rilke in the evening, that he can play Bach and Schubert, and go to his day's work at Auschwitz in the morning.

George Steiner

1535 hrs, Wednesday, 25th December 1946, Auschwitz-Birkenau, Poland.

As Camerone had advanced, many units passed by Auschwitz-I, the camp inside the village.

Shocking reports started to filter back.

As word spread, more and more of Camerone's leadership found time to come and see for themselves, Knocke's order to avoid all installations somehow forgotten in the growing consternation that affected every unit within the division.

Based around the pre-war billet of a Polish cavalry battalion, Auschwitz-I was 'tidier' than previously imagined, in as much as it was not in ruins and had not been trashed by the local populace, although the twin additions of gallows and a small gas chamber were stark reminders as to its recent grisly purpose.

It was an organised place, properly laid out, and could, without the knowledge of what it had been, have easily returned to its military configuration or something similarly ordinary, with very little effort.

The sign above the main entrance now almost seemed to taunt those who walked under it, and many wondered if it had provided any comfort or hope of normalcy for those who had been herded underneath it during the camp's operational years.

'Arbeit macht frei.'

'Work sets you free.'

Inside the compound, evidence was easily found as to its recent purpose, from the execution yard, its bullet holes almost shouting out about the lives taken on a sadistic whim after mock trials,

185

to the small but efficient gas chamber, complete with ovens for immediate destruction of their victims.

The minute standing cells for up to four prisoners, where simple incarceration so often ended in death.

The piles of belongings, of suitcases, personal effects, shoes... so many shoes... the utter tragedy of a huge number of artificial limbs, removed from Jews, Gypsies, and others, many of whom had almost certainly sustained their loss in German uniform during the Great War.

The human hair... bag after bag of it removed from the living and the dead, to be used by the German war industry.

The Soviet engineers, under NKVD orders, had dressed the entire site in much the way that the Red Army had found it in 1945, but with the addition of signs, some placed on the bodies of the dead, others simply nailed on doors and walls.

'THIS IS WHAT YOUR GERMAN FRIENDS ARE CAPABLE OF'
'GERMANS DID THIS. THE SAME GERMANS YOU NOW FIGHT WITH'
'THE SS ARE RESPONSIBLE FOR THIS'
'LEGION = SS = MURDERERS'
'SS BASTARDS'

The messages were everywhere, different texts expressing the same basic sentiment, intended to undermine the bonds between the legionnaires and their ex-SS comrades.

The piles of bodies, exhumed for the purpose, added weight to the accusations.

Lynched decomposing men and women hung from every high point, most with a placard that marked the reason for their death at the hands of the SS camp guards.

'Jude'
'Roma'
'Homosexuelle'

And yet, Auschwitz I had been, and was now, the lesser evil in so many ways.

For some reason, only one or two units were routed past Auschwitz-II Birkenau, the real killing machine in the Nazi's extermination programme, and they did not stop to investigate the silent lines of barbed wire and huts, as orders drove them further on towards the Vistula.

186

Perhaps their eyes did not see or perhaps their brains failed to acknowledge that such barbarity was possible in a civilised world.

Christmas Day arrived and saw most of Camerone in place and celebrating as best a soldier can in the cold of a Polish winter.

Some officers went back, keen to discover the secrets of the huge second camp; others merely got caught up in the boredom of the day and were swept along in the steady stream of legionnaires that went to see what all the fuss was about.

That attitude did not survive first contact with the sights on offer, and very soon tension and anger ruled.

The Soviets had excelled themselves.

Piles of exhumed bodies, again announced with placards, sat around the site.

Ashes, unmistakably awful in origin, were piled high next to the destroyed gas chambers or lined the entranceways into the huge camp.

Medical specimens, clearly human, were laid out along the sleepers of the rail line, containing anything from dissected livers to whole foetuses.

Everywhere there were pictures... ones that had been taken by correspondents attached to the 322nd Rifle Division when it stumbled across the awfulness that was Auschwitz on 27th January 1945.

Wherever the eye looked, the awfulness and sheer barbarity of purpose was evident.

It shook hardened men to the very core.

The messages intended to divide the Camerone Division were everywhere, both written and visual.

And divide they did.

A veritable chasm opened up between the German and other legionnaires present, one that was punctuated by oaths and disbelief, by suspicion and hate.

Haefali, the senior officer present, did the only thing he could do, and dispatched a message to his commander.

Knocke stepped out of the Kfz 71, already sensing the pain in the men around him.

He saluted the large group of officers that had gathered around the gates of what had once been known as Auschwitz II.

Birkenau.

A place that had clearly once been the closest thing to hell on earth.

Intelligence reports had stated that during the Soviet occupation Auschwitz I had been used as a hospital, whereas Birkenau had been an NKVD prison camp, whose conditions were as bad as could be, probably no different to what it had been under Nazi rule but without the death chambers operating day and night.

Intelligence also stated, and the evidence before their own eyes would confirm, that the local population had ravaged the area, seeking firewood from the huts and disturbing the mass graves in the search for artefacts and gold teeth amongst the human wreckage.

The Soviets themselves had looted much of the I.G Farben machinery from the Buna Werke at Monowitz, known as Auschwitz-III.

Knocke had read the report before, and refreshed himself on its contents as he drove to the camp, but was still unprepared for the desolation that awaited him.

The Soviet 'dressing' was very apparent, and he took in the signs, immediately understanding their purpose and the challenge that now faced him.

He noticed that the group had split into two defined sections; German and French legion officers separated as never before, separated by the place... the sights... the stories... association... the allocation of blame... anger...

He understood why the message from Haefali had urgently requested him to come to this place on Christmas Day.

His very division, perhaps the Corps D'Assaut itself, was at stake, as clearly these men, probably over eighty of his leaders, were visibly distraught and angered by the vision that had greeted them.

"Gentlemen, Merry Christmas to you all... although such a greeting seems so very out of place in a place such as this. Come."

He boldly strode forward and swept through the divide between the two groups, deliberately leading them through the central arch under which the railway had carried its hundreds of thousands of victims during the Nazi Holocaust.

The narrow way through the piled ashes brought them back in close proximity, but the absence of comradeship between the two groups was extremely noticeable.

Tensions rose.

The party walked on, past the medical specimens, each lighting gantry with its own special sort of horror dangling by a neck, the walk swiftly allowing the men to move apart into two distinct groups, until finally Knocke came to a halt at the central point between the infamous entrance and the distant ruins of what had once been the chambers where men, women, and children were destroyed by the regime for which many of those present had fought.

Knocke had walked the extra distance so that he could compose himself, and prepare for one of the most important messages he had ever delivered.

He stopped, turned, performed the trademark pulling down of his jacket, and gathered his men around him in a semi-circle.

Albrecht Haefali had gravitated to his right side but Knocke felt a coldness between them like never before.

"So, here we are... in this place... this... this abomination."

All around them were huts, some complete, others no more than a brick chimney rising from a bed of blackened timbers.

To their right, the railway lines, side by side.

As far as the eye could see there were bodies, placards, and the detritus of man's unspeakable inhumanity, as prepared on the orders of Beria.

Unwittingly, Knocke had gathered his men in the area where much of the selection process had taken place; where a simple push in one direction or the other spelt either a life of servitude and miserable living conditions or immediate death in the chambers.

"Perhaps it is fate that brings us here... perhaps it's something else entirely. I wish we were somewhere else because for me, as a German, this place will forever tarnish my country, long after the last holders of its experiences and memories are gone from this earth."

He looked around, seeing pain and contempt, depending on which group he looked at.

"Our unit has been based on comradeship forged in the most desperate of circumstances... that of combat. Now, in front of my eyes, I see men... comrades all... who have trusted each other with their lives broken apart by the sights of this place... the understanding of what happened here... and our association wit..."

There was a rumble from the German officers.

"Yes... our association with this place and others like it."

He addressed the Germans directly.

"We are associated with it, Kameraden, in the first place for no other reason than we wore the same insignia as those who oversaw this place. We cannot hide from that!"

Knocke dropped his voice down to a normal one and continued.

189

"I'll not speak for you... none of you. I'll just speak for me."

He turned his back on the group and swept his hands across the from left to right, from kitchen block, past dormitories, gas chambers, more dormitories until he dropped his hand back to his side.

'Oh my god... I never imagined this to be... never thought... it could never be possible...'

Knocke had prepared himself to heal the wounds caused by the awfulness of their surroundings and the uniforms he and his men once wore. He had simply not expected to find that he had wounds of his own that would need attention before he could address those of his men.

"I knew of this."

He turned back and saw genuine horror and disappointment on the faces of all of his men; French and German alike.

"No... not what it was... not what it did... but I was aware of its existence. I admit, I heard some rumours of its purpose, rumours I dismissed as propaganda by our enemies... set to cause discord... set to fire their armies and civilians to greater efforts against us."

He grabbed his jaw and wiped his hand slowly across his face.

"Rumours... Mein Gott!"

He closed his eyes and held back tears.

Tears for those comrades who had died in defence of the cause that was capable of visiting such horrors upon fellow human beings.

Tears for those who had perished in the frenzy of Nazi idealism.

"How could I even have begun to believe them... at that time... eh? How could I ever have conceived that such monstrousness was actually being perpetrated?"

He picked at the corner of his eyes where moisture had started to form.

"What do you feel here?"

No one answered and he hadn't expected them to.

"I feel nothing, save what is already in me. There's nothing here to feel. It is almost as if this awful place has surrendered every single bit of emotion possible, leaving a nothingness that defies description. Can you feel that nothingness, Kameraden?"

The silence remained unbroken, but each man could understand what Knocke meant.

190

There was a vacuum in Birkenau; a space, an absence unlike any other in their experience.

It was tangible.

"God has deserted this place."

It was Haefali who had spoken.

Knocke opened out his hands in acknowledgement of the statement.

"In truth, I know nothing of God any more, Albrecht. He deserted me and mine many years ago. There'll be some who speak of him here... but perhaps he has no place here... or perhaps he should always have a place here... I don't know."

There were a few rumbles of agreement from the gathering, mainly from the French side.

"I really don't know any more. This place is beyond my wildest imagination... that my fellow man... my countrymen even... could bring this place into being."

He considered his next statement carefully.

"This place was brought into being by sane minds. Qualified minds designed its machinery, professional minds devised its systems of work, skilled minds oversaw construction of its buildings, and railway lines... medical minds... there's a thing, isn't it?... Scheisse!... medical minds that we've always treasured as exceptionally intelligent... compassionate... caring... such men devised and conducted such vileness upon fellow human beings as to be unimaginable... right here... in this awful... so very awful place!"

The silence was oppressive as he settled himself to speak further.

"I don't know how that happened. Maybe each of them in turn thought 'I'm just doing my job'. Maybe they didn't understand what they were actually part of, although those who designed the ovens cannot have that excuse... nor can a number of the other responsible parties."

Knocke wiped his hand across his face once more.

"And then there are those who ran the camp, enforced its rules and practices, who were responsible for the day to day operation of something that we now suspect destroyed nearly a million people."

He touched his Knight's Cross gently.

"I once wore my old uniform with pride. The people that oversaw this horror wore the same uniform."

Again the German officers railed at his comments, forcing him to stop and hold his hands up for quiet.

"Yes, kameraden... they did. That's what the world sees, that what's the world knows, so therefore it's true."

191

He looked at the French officers very deliberately.

"I am SS... was SS... this you all know. As far as I'm concerned, I fought an honourable war... as hard as I could... with every weapon at my disposal."

Again he turned around, displaying his back, inviting those behind him to look at what he was seeing.

"Those who were stationed here were obeying their orders, but we all know that some orders simply shouldn't be obeyed."

He wished he had the intelligence folder to use, simply as a prop to focus their attention, but it was still in the staff car.

He produced his pistol instead.

Brandishing the Walther P38, he suddenly realised their faces had taken on a collectively horrified expression.

Knocke was suddenly carried away with the moment, and the pistol became more than a prop to his words.

"Do as you are ordered or I'll shoot you!"

He pointed the gun at Haefali and spoke deliberately.

"Herd those prisoners into the chambers or I'll shoot you. Someone else will do your job anyway."

The pistol moved to Oscar Durand.

"Choose those who'll live and those who will die. Someone else will do your job anyway."

The next target was Ettiene Truffaux, a highly decorated French Major from Haefali's regiment.

"Pour the gas canister into the chamber or I'll shoot you. Someone else'll do it anyway."

The gun moved quickly to Felix Bach, ex-Totenkopf Division.

"Execute those prisoners or I'll shoot you. Someone else will do it anyway."

Knocke took a purposeful step closer.

"Execute those prisoners or I'll shoot you and you'll have died for nothing more than principle."

The barrel of his weapon was now almost in Bach's face.

"Execute them or die! I'll shoot you where you stand, you bastard! Execute them or die!"

"Sir... Ernst!"

Haefali's hand gently took hold of Knocke's arm and brought the weapon slowly downwards, allowing him to get a hold of himself, his attempt to reflect what might have happened having taken hold of him to such an extent that he had forgotten his surroundings.

He holstered his weapon carefully and grabbed Bach by the shoulder.

"My apologies, Felix. I really don't know what came over me."

The tears were streaming down Bach's face, his lip faintly twitching, which many put down to the fact that he had until recently had a close up view of the business end of a Walther pistol.

Knocke held out his hands in supplication.

"Apologies, kameraden."

He shook his head.

"I've no excuse… it **is** no excuse, I think."

He changed direction quickly.

"It is no excuse… not for me."

He patted Haefali's shoulder by way of a thank you for his intervention, and moved around his officers, both French and German, as he spoke.

"I would like to think that I possess enough moral courage… enough honour… enough human decency… that were I placed in the situation of being given one of those orders, I would refuse it… and accept the consequences."

He stopped at Durand and patted his back.

"I think we all would, wouldn't we, Oscar?"

"Oui, mon Général."

Moving on, Knocke found himself by Truffaux and he extended his hand, tentatively grasping the man's arm, being none too familiar with the new arrival.

"We'd all like to think we would act with courage and decency if it came to it, wouldn't we, Commandant Truffaux?"

"Most certainly, mon Général."

"But each man will only know his resolve when the moment comes."

He returned to the front of his men and deliberately placed his hands on his hips.

"I would like to think that I'd have the courage to stand by my principles and say no… even though not doing so wouldn't spare a life… just extend it by a few seconds and deprive me of mine…"

He shook his head.

"…but I don't know."

Knocke knew his words were going home.

"It may be that I'd have acted as these men here did… sorry, some of these men, for I have no doubt that sadistic and cruel men were in the majority that ruled here."

"Had I been transferred here, might I now stand accused as the likes of Hoess, who was in command of this camp, stands accused."

"What I do know is quite simple really… and remember I'd heard rumours of this place, so I stand more guilty than those who knew nothing of the camps and their sinister purpose."

He relaxed his posture and scratched his thinning hair.

"Yes, I'm guilty of wearing the same uniform as those who commanded here. I'm guilty of ignoring the signs, the rumours of the existence of places such as this. I'm guilty of being a soldier who fought for the regime that brought this into being. I'm guilty of being a German!"

He addressed the German contingent directly.

"Yes, I'm guilty of wearing the same uniform, which to me always meant membership of an elite force of soldiers who had no equals in combat."

"Yes, I ignored the rumours, but how could I have anticipated that this was all happening?"

He caught himself up in a thought process and inadvertently spoke aloud.

"Should I have anticipated this?"

Knocke realised he had voiced his thoughts but set the moment aside and continued.

"Yes, I'm guilty of being a soldier, but I fought for my country, as any man who loves it would do."

He nodded, more to himself than any of his audience.

"Yes, I'm guilty of being a German and that more than anything is what will haunt me now. For now being me is not about what I have done or achieved any more… it's about my country and how it has been stained by the actions of those who were entrusted with its safekeeping… and who abused it and the world so badly."

"This will not define me… I'll not let it define me. Nor will it define who I was, nor will it define those brave men who died wearing the same uniforms as the rabble who ran this camp."

"You all knew of the camps before this… when we came together to form the Corps… to form Camerone… and we forged a wonderful spirit, which is now risked by being here… and the Russian has been clever but… perhaps… correct in some way… for we can now understand more of the horrors of this place. By recreating it in an attempt to divide us, they have shown all of us the very pits of human existence… something we'll always remember… and that will always affect the way our lives go forward from this day."

More than one man in the two groups had a tear roll down his cheek.

"But I understand, kameraden. Being here makes everything less distant. There is a reality in this nothingness that will stay with all of us for as long as we live."

He gestured towards the Frenchmen with genuine affection.

"You're the same men you were before this day dawned."

He swept his arm across the German officers.

"They're the same men as well. Some of you owe some of them your lives... and the reverse is true, is it not?"

There was mumbled agreement from many a mouth.

"They're not responsible for this, no more than any of you are responsible for the capitulation of France and the rise of Vichy."

That hurt a few of the listeners.

"You all know that some things have happened during our time together that are regrettable. We all remember poor old Vernais and what happened afterwards. Our kameraden at La Petit Pierre and the price the communists paid for their behaviour? What our American friends did at Hattmatt, eh? But we understand and condone those things, even though we were involved."

He pointed at the gates, drawing everyone into turning around to examine the long brick structure.

"We were not involved in that... any of it... none of us."

He waited until they had all turned back to face him before coming to the end of his words.

"Kameraden, what we are now involved in... responsible for... committed to... is ensuring that the horrors of this place are never repeated, no matter what. We, as legionnaires, are committed to that task, and together we will keep Auschwitz, Birkenau, and a hundred other awful places as memories, ensuring they are lessons learned, not models for the future."

"The man opposite you is the same man he was yesterday. He's your comrade and he'll die for you as you would for him. Such men should not stand apart. They should stand together."

He studied the two groups.

"So... stand together."

Gradually, some movement started, and it was Durand who first extended his hand to Johannes Braun, with whom he had the best of relationships.

The rest followed suit and the rifts that had suddenly appeared faded, although not totally and some wounds might always remain, for Auschwitz-Birkenau was a place that would not fade in the memory of those who saw what it had to offer.

195

"We're not responsible for this... but we must accept responsibility for it in a wider sense. Would that none of it had ever happened... but it cannot be undone. So we must all accept responsibility for what we can achieve in this place's memory, for the memories of all those who died and suffered, and for guiding the future."

His words had a keen edge and found the men's hearts.

"Atten-shun!"

They sprang to the attention as Knocke about turned and offered the silent ground a formal salute, followed by the assembled officers and NCOs.

He moved back round to face his officers.

"Now, we must attend to the unfortunates here. First thing tomorrow... volunteers only... and make sure your men understand the enormity of the task ahead."

He gave them a magnificent salute.

"Dis-miss!"

Knocke came to his senses, still stood in the selection area of Auschwitz-II, Birkenau.

His mind had become so wrapped up in itself that he had failed to recognise the departure of his officers.

All but one of his officers.

"Felix?"

"Oberführer."

"Why are you still here? It's Christmas. You should be celebrating."

"You're right."

"I know I am, Now, say hello to your boys from me and..."

"No, you're right. I should have said no."

"Should have?"

"Yes. I should have."

"You were here?"

"No, not here. Not here!"

"Where were you, Felix?"

"Majdanek, near Lublin. When I was wounded. I spent four months there waiting for my call up to Bad Tolz."

Knocke had heard of Majdanek in much the same way as he had heard his present location; rumour, gossip, and the hushed whispers of men who knew they should speak no further.

196

"I did what I was ordered, no more, no less, but I did it... and I should have said no."

"Mein Gott."

"As you said, God has no part in these fucking places, Oberführer."

He sobbed without tears.

"I was a coward."

"No more than most would be, faced with choices like that."

"No, you were right... there was only one choice."

"You say that now, but at the time..."

"At the time I did what I was ordered, which is no fucking excuse... you said so yourself in so many words, Oberführer."

"Felix, I..."

"No. I'm guilty... guilty of Majdanek, this place, all the awful places..."

"No, Felix, yo..."

"Enough, Oberführer. Our French comrades were right. We're guilty and should be punished."

"Stop this at once!"

The movement and the shot blended into one, and blood and brains splattered Knocke from waist to head.

Haefali appeared, running for all he was worth, followed by a few others who had been congregating on the other side of the entrance building.

Remarkably, Bach was not dead, despite the huge hole in his head, although his hold on life would not last much longer.

Knocke cradled the dying man, holding him close and whispering words of comfort, unsure if they could be heard or comprehended.

By the time Haefali arrived, gun in hand, Bach had joined the thousands upon thousands of other souls that had travelled from Auschwitz to wherever their God took them.

The new arrivals either spread out to find whoever had fired the shot or instinctively understood what had happened.

Knocke slid out from under the body and laid Bach gently to rest.

"He had blood on his hands, Albrecht. He told me that he served at a camp such as this. I fear my words brought him to this. I'm so sorry."

Standing, Knocke was conscious of the spray of Bach's vitals that covered him.

Haefali offered a handkerchief, which he gratefully accepted.

"We all have blood on our hands, Albrecht... the SS, Wehrmacht, the German people... Germany itself. When von Papen committed us once more to the fight against the spread of communism, he spoke quite clearly about atonement for our crimes."

"I remember that speech, Ernst."

"As do I. I wrote a bit of it down, but I never fully understood what he meant until today."

Knocke fished in his tunic pocket and brought out his notebook as Haefali stood the circle of men down, ordering four to remove the body of their comrade.

He thumbed through the worn pages until he found what he sought.

He then read aloud, alternating between looking at the text and watching as Bach's body was tended to.

"Crimes have been committed and those crimes must be atoned for by those responsible. There can be no other way. Regardless of whether you pulled the trigger, drove the tank, or stayed at home enduring the bombs, the German people have a collective responsibility to make amends for these excesses, to fully atone for our national actions before we can move forward as a nation without the burdens of our past."

Having put the notebook back in its place, Knocke came to attention and saluted the corpse as it was carried away. Those not carrying Bach followed suit.

Within a minute Knocke and Haefali were alone in the gathering gloom of a winter's evening, surrounded by the quiet of the ruined camp, accompanied only by the gentle whistle of the growing wind, and the smell of blood freshly spilt upon a ground already enriched by the blood of thousands.

Haefali broke the silence.

"Your words have done much, but I fear it'll take much more for things to become whole again."

Knocke took out his cigarette pack and checked himself, returning them to his pocket having thought better of the idea. It was somehow disrespectful in his eyes.

"I believe you're right, Albrecht. For my part and, I suspect, for a number of my men, we may never be whole again."

Haefali nodded, trying to put himself in the ex-SS officer's position, and not liking what he imagined.

"Being here... in this awful place and armed with the knowledge of what went on here... overseen by my countrymen...

actioned by members of the SS... well... it makes me want to stand in defence of everything that is weak, victimised...whatever... just be a soldier and stand up for what is right... not just my own country as a soldier... or for France as a legionnaire... but for all... for anyone and everyone... to make sure this fucking abomination can never ever happen again!"

Haefali extended his hand and gently placed it upon the shoulder of a man he had come to admire but who, at this time, was tarnished by association with the horrors around him.

"Auschwitz is not your fault, Ernst... I think we all know that... but it was the SS who ran this death camp... you and your men may not have served here, but it's your collective responsibility, that's clear... so it's also your responsibility to atone for it."

Knocke extended his hand, patted the Legion officer's side, and walked forward before turning around and facing Haefali.

"You're absolutely right, Albrecht. But the Gods of War have denied me the opportunity to soldier, now that peace has descended on Europe. So I'll have to find another way... another means by which I can do my utmost to make up for this... and to say sorry to all those who perished here."

The Camerone commander came to full attention and saluted his friend, who returned the honour smartly.

Knocke then turned and offered another salute to the darkness of the ruined gas chambers.

As his hand remained steady at the peak of his kepi, he spoke a few words, words that would remain with Haefali until his dying day.

"For my soldiers, my people, and my country, I offer this apology and promise. This will never happen again whilst I draw breath. On my honour, I swear it!"

The two men held the salute for what seemed like an eternity, both making other silent promises that were for them to honour in their own way, before returning to the entrance, walking perfectly in step, to start repairing the damage to their beloved Legion.

It is such a secret place, the land of tears.

Antoine de Saint-Exupery

Chapter 182 - THE ELIMINATIONS

1107 hrs, Monday 30th December 1946, Marktplatz, Oberursel, Germany.

"That's him."

"Ja."

"We just do it. Nothing fancy. There's no kripos or soldiers that I can see... in fact... the only uniform I can see is that fat bastard on the junction... and he won't catch us when we run. So... straight up... you watch, I'll do it. OK?"

"Ja."

"Do you ever say more than one fucking word at a time, Klaus?"

"Nein."

"Fucking comedian."

"Ja."

Despite the fact that the two were about to take a man's life in public, they had no qualms about it and were relaxed enough to go through an exchange they had done many times before.

They strolled casually out of their concealment and ate up the distance between them and their mark in slow confident steps.

Their mark was drinking coffee outside a small establishment that claimed to provide the best coffee in the town, which was true, mainly because it had a special link with nearby US army units, which kept it properly supplied.

The target brought his cup to his lips and brought his head upright, intent on finishing his drink, but instead bringing the approaching pair to his attention.

All his senses lit off in a moment, and he instinctively knew that they were coming for him.

As they instinctively knew they had been seen and recognised for what they were.

'Where is Strauch?'

Three hands grabbed for weapons and found them.

"Die, you Nazi bastard!"

Shots mingled with screams as the three men sent bullets flying at each other.

200

The screams of the frightened were boosted by those of the injured, as confused people ran in all directions and some got in the way of bullets intended for others.

None the less, some of those shots fired found the targets for which they were intended, and the firing ended as abruptly as it had started.

Klaus would never utter another word, his face ruined by a single shot that struck the bridge of his nose and shredded the brain beyond.

His accomplice was coughing out the last of his moments as his lungs filled with blood, both having taken a round.

A woman who had run across the field of fire lay in soft repose, almost sleeping, except for the fact that she had no throat.

The café waiter was screaming in pain as his shattered elbow refused to stop moving.

A woman in the café suffered the double indignity of taking a bullet in her shoulder and being drenched in shattered glass, her screams less for the excruciating pain of her broken bone than for the clear sensation of broken glass ruining her eyes.

The fat policeman arrived, gun in hand, with nothing to shoot at but everything to bring under control.

He was helped by a local doctor who had sprinted from his practice with his bag in hand and started tending to those who were injured, some of whose injuries were simply sustained by falling over in the rush to escape.

The policeman started to make notes on what he saw and grabbed a journalist who arrived with a camera, allowing him close to the scene if he would take pictures for his report.

The camera fired its blinding flashes through the increasingly grey morning light, recording the bodies and the scene as directed by the policeman, who hadn't always been old and fat.

More policemen and Kripos arrived, securing the whole scene.

The two assassins were quickly identified as communist sympathisers, known to the police, men who had served in the German Army but who resurfaced after the end of the war.

The identity of the third man was not known, he being devoid of any formal identification, which in itself was extremely unusual.

It was not until his photograph appeared in the newspapers that his name became known.

Reinhard Gehlen.

January 1947.

1947 started with either a fizzle or a burst of energy, depending on the people concerned.

Those in the Allied intelligence community were exercised by the murder of Gehlen, possibly by men who could likely be working under Soviet instructions.

That made the community both nervous and vigilant, and made the Germans bay for blood of any kind, but mainly that which lay in abundance to the East.

At home in the USA, the political situation had died to a murmur, occasionally rising to a shout as Truman refused to return industry to a peacetime footing, reasonably citing recent events from 1945.

The casualty count dropped to a trickle, mainly accidents on the road and in the air, or those caused by the intensive training that was the hallmark of the Allied peace... this time.

Elsewhere, the arrival of 1947 caused little fuss as the lines were now set and tensions, at least politically between the Western Allies and the USSR, and militarily across the board, were at an extremely and tolerably low point.

Above all it was the cold that calmed the situation throughout Europe. Although not as bad as the previous year, winter made itself felt and, even though late in arriving, bared its fangs to all comers.

0912 hrs, Thursday, 2nd January 1947, Dai Ichi Life Insurance Building, Tokyo, Japan.

"Morning, Lieutenant. Where's the goddamned fire?"

"Good morning, Sir. Admiral Towers' apologies, but he's asked us to bring this to you immediately. He's busy with other matters at the moment."

MacArthur raised an eyebrow, drawing a response.

"He also felt that we were the best people to present this information to you at this time. This has been our baby from the start, Sir. You'll understand, Sir."

Waynes sorted out his folder, placing a copy of a most secret briefing in front of the General, whilst Takeo laid out a series of grainy and indistinct photographs next to some copies of Japanese documents, complete with translations.

MacArthur's morning agenda had been shattered on the insistence of Towers, and he sure as hell hoped it wasn't a fool's errand.

"OK. What am I looking at here?"

"Sir, Admiral Towers has filled me in on what you already know, so I'll cover what we have now learnt."

He pointed at the documents.

"These are manifests which have just come to light. One of our investigative parties on the island of Okunoshima, where the Japanese had a poison gas facility."

He pushed one under MacArthur's nose.

"Dated June 6th last year, this is a receipt for three tons of compound seven and four tons of compound ten, signed illegibly, but reported as correctly stowed and secured, responsibility handed over to Special Weapons Detachment officer, Combined Fleet special type submarine 402."

"Special Weapons officer?"

"Sir, we believe that, given the nature of the facility giving up the items to be stowed, that compounds seven and ten are destructive gases."

"Logical. Submarine 402?"

"Yes, Sir."

Waynes promoted two grainy pictures to the front of the pile.

"These only came to us yesterday, Sir. They were taken by an agent in the Soviet Union on June 20th last year. I believe Admiral Towers mentioned Sovetskaya Gavan?"

MacArthur gave the naval lieutenant a look that sort of said '*do you know how much shit I hear in a day, son*' but held his piece and simply nodded, especially as, for some reason, he suddenly remembered the conversation.

"Soviet boats undercover or something?"

"Yes, Sir... except they're not. See here."

The two images showed something, but MacArthur wasn't totally sure what it was.

"Here is a picture we've doctored some. Drawn in the lines to emphasise the submarines."

The third picture did just that.

"Big sons-a-bitches."

"Yes, Sir. For scale, that is an AM class submarine. They come in at about three seventy-five feet in length. This one is probably a little over four hundred feet."

"How does that compare to ours?"

"For perspective, one of our Gatos would be a little over three hundred feet long, Sir."

"Big sons of bitches."

"Beam wise, they're big. Both types. One of ours sits about twenty-seven foot. Best guess by some experienced interpreters is that the biggest sub is slightly larger than the AM. They come in at about thirty-nine... which means the big sub is probably forty."

"And the photos show three su..."

"No Sir!... apologies... no, sir... here... one... two ... three... four... four submarines... two AMs and two Special type."

MacArthur continued, airing his thoughts.

"There were five, and we pretty much know that one of our carriers put one down hard... and here we have the remaining four holed up in commie land... under cover... is this where you start talking about 731 and 516 again?"

"Yes, Sir. That remains a serious possibility, although we cannot confirm or deny it for now."

"So do we know anything more about these things... what they're capable of?"

Yes, Sir. We know that the Special types can accommodate three aircraft each. That's confirmed. What isn't confirmed is their range. We have interrogation evidence from a civilian designer which we are having corroborated by our own technical engineering people right now. One moment please, Sir."

Waynes consulted his notes and MacArthur took the opportunity to fire up his pipe, a signal that transferred to his orderly, who magically appeared with coffee.

"Yes, Sir. Our own data on the AMs is sound, and supported with evidence gained from Japanese naval records. They can theoretically sail for twenty-four thousand miles without refuelling. Our Gatos will do something over fourteen thousand."

MacArthur puffed away without a care in the world, although his insides were churning.

"From what we can glean, the Special Types will go forty thousand miles."

"Forty thousand?"

"So it seems sir. We have discovered a paper from Admiral Yamamoto on the subject of large raiding submarines, in which he gives the specification that the new submarines must be able to sail to any point on the planet and return without refuelling."

"Good god."

"There is a part of Yamamoto's specification that Admiral Towers wanted me to make sure you understood, Sir. That is that the

Special Submarines should be capable of making three journeys from Japan to the western seaboard of the United States without needing more fuel."

"Good Lord! So Admiral Towers thinks that they are going to do something to us on the west coast?"

"Actually no, Sir. But he's presently looking at the possibilities, and stepping up our defensive measures at all points east of Midway. That's why he can't be here, Sir."

"Why doesn't he think the West Coast is threatened?"

"If they've split up, then it is, Sir. Admiral Towers can't take the chance that they haven't, but an interesting piece in the puzzle fell into place at six this morning."

The lighter clicked again and rich smoke flowed around the room.

Waynes produced another set of photos and laid them out over the pictures of the Sen-Tokus.

MacArthur understood exactly what he was looking at, but asked the question anyway.

"What am I looking at here, Lieutenant?"

"Sir, these items were recovered from the ocean on Christmas Day... by the frigate, HMSAS Transvaal. They were in a weighted bag. According to the report, the find was purely accidental."

He placed the written report from the commander of the Transvaal in front of the general."

"Sir, the Transvaal was searching for recently identified U-Boat supply points, with orders to recover anything of importance and nullify the contents, leaving no risk to civilians. This was found during their Christmas Day lay over at one of those sites."

The pictures showed a Japanese naval rank marking, a leather wallet, the contents of which had not survived the ministrations of saltwater, a silver neck chain, and a uniform cap.

"The bag itself had suffered. However, the rank insignia are clearly those of an IJN ensign. The wallet is no help, except that it has a wooden button, which might make it recent... the nips moved to wooden buttons as resources failed... the chain is nothing special... but it's the cap that gave us what we needed, Sir."

The rate of puffing increased.

"Ensign Kisokada I... we have him on record, Sir."

Waynes produced his final copy with a flourish and placed in front of MacArthur, to whom the Japanese writing was nothing but gibberish, but for whom the English language notation meant everything.

He read the simple words aloud.

"Kisokada, Ito... passed... 4/62... assignment 6th Fleet... STS... STS..."

MacArthur caught sight of a heavily marked section of the original document.

"What's this, Lieutenant?"

"That is the most interesting part of all, Sir. Our best guess is that the clerk noted down his duty station and then erased it and inserted STS."

"What did it say?"

"Our best guess is 4-0-1, which is probably the I-401."

"I-401?"

"Yes, Sir. It should be noted that the official Combined Fleet records do not show an I-401, even in the planning stage."

"Alternatives? What else could it be?"

"None that we can imagine, Sir. No surface vessel could have made it to South Africa. Had to be a submarine that this Kisokada came from, Sir."

MacArthur rose up, pipe in mouth, coffee in hand, and walked briskly to the map that had priority place on the wall.

He dropped onto his haunches and used the stem of his pipe to trace the route from Imperial Japan to the east coast of Africa.

"So, what's Admiral Towers' think about their plans... what the nips are up to... what's got them so interested in Africa... what's around there...?"

MacArthur looked for anything that jumped out at him.

The other officer Lieutenant j.g Takeo, spoke rapidly.

"Sir, I'm sorry. Did you not see the map work? The items were found at the mouth of the Ondusengo River, where intelligence had placed a U-Boat supply dump."

Takeo, being nearest the map, dropped down alongside the general and pointed.

"That would be here, Sir... in South-West Africa... on the Atlantic coast."

"What?"

The two stood up in response to Waynes' cough as he stood ready with the map he had placed before MacArthur very early on in the briefing.

"Admiral Towers is making sure the West Coast stateside is prepared, but sure as eggs is eggs, whatever the Japs are planning is not within our area, Sir."

"Hold on one cotton-picking minute, sailor. Are you telling me that the Nip navy had submarines, probably four big submarines, at large in the Atlantic since... when?"

"Probably since late July, early August, Sir."

"Goddamnit!"

The pipe started to chug as General MacArthur worked the possibilities.

"Anywhere in the world, you say?"

"Yes, Sir."

"Goddamnit!"

He headed back to the desk, followed by the two junior officers.

MacArthur's mind was working overtime.

"We know that some of the Nips are quite happy to fight on... but that's mainly those who haven't heard of the surrender... or who disbelieve it."

He rummaged through the evidence on his desk, here and there examining a piece more closely.

"This is organised. Slipped out of Japan... in convoy probably... to the Russians... then they sail into the Atlantic..."

"There are people working on the possibilities right now, Sir."

"So, lieutenants... where could they be by now?"

The two men exchanged looks and Waynes took the lead.

"Anywhere on the planet, Sir."

That piece of information, along with the rest of the intelligence brief, arrived with General Eisenhower later that evening, as a priority message from Washington.

A pleasant but extremely cold Thursday was suddenly transformed into a boiling maelstrom as department after department was brought in, all with a view to answering a number of questions that were foremost in the mind of the head of NATO's European forces.

All of a sudden, the world seemed to be less safe.

1054 hrs, Saturday, 4th January 1947, the Apostles Simon and Jude Thaddaeus Church, Skawina, Poland.

This was not the first time that he had been in a church in recent weeks.

The last time he had slipped into Wawel Cathedral in Krakow and lit a candle in memory of those who had perished in the camp.

His mind wandered to that visit, and the events of Christmas Day.

Lavalle leant closer to his friend and whispered, startling him from his reverie.

"You know, your sergent... Hässelbach... he's got a book running on when she'll arrive. Celestin's the official time keeper apparently."

Knocke raised an eyebrow and looked at the French officer at the end of the row of benches, eyes glued to a pocket watch, before returning to fix the gaze of his commander, Lavalle.

He mercilessly interrogated the Frenchmen with his eyes, the slightest of grins revealing his amusement.

"Yes, ok...a small wager...but at least I said she'd be on time... none of this late nonsense... unlike some."

He eyed Haefali and Uhlmann, who seemed to be constantly checking their watches.

Knocke followed his line of sight and received smiles in return.

"So, whilst I'm embarking on the most important of events, you and your officers are trying to make money out of the proceedings?"

"C'est la guerre, mon ami."

They both snorted loudly, the sound almost echoing around the inside of the old church.

Outside, the white walled building blended seamlessly with the recent heavy snowfall, despite the efforts of teams of legionnaires, who laboured long and hard to remove as much of the blizzard's product as possible.

The same men now formed a guard of honour, waiting for the arrival of the woman who was to marry their commander.

Knocke looked at his two daughters, sat either side of Madame Fleriot and being fussed over by old Jerome, their attendance made possible only by the direct intervention of De Lattre, who sat prominently in the second row of the bride's side, the empty spaces around him emphasising his importance.

208

The number of his officers looking at watches became apparent, and Knocke realised that Hässelbach had been very very busy indeed.

The smile on his face spread, for he knew that Lavalle's bet was safe.

At 1100 to the second, the doors opened and the choir started to sing, as Anne-Marie de Valois, on the arm of Georges de Walle, proceeded steadily down the aisle.

More than one eye greedily took in her beauty and form.

Despite the unrevealing nature of the dress, the fact that Anne-Marie was a woman in her prime was evident for all to see.

Knocke risked a look in all directions, seeing disappointed faces checking and rechecking their watches.

He returned his eyes to the vision of beauty that was approaching and, not for the first time, thanked fate for bringing this woman to him, and for giving him the greatest gift; her love.

The ceremony was brief but elegant, with De Walle giving away the bride and Lavalle acting as best man.

It seemed like only a few moments later that they were married and walking back down the aisle, arm in arm, surrounded by friends and comrades, all armed with the broadest of smiles.

Ernst-August and Anne-Marie Knocke stepped out into the cold to be illuminated by the brightest of winter suns and greeted by the smartest detachment of legionnaires in parade dress, who immediately gave a general's salute at the order of Capitaine Durand, who had slipped out of the church unobserved.

At Durand's invitation, the newly-weds inspected his formed detachment, something that seemed odd to the civilians watching, but that was fully understood by the military observers.

Photographers plied their trade, and friends and comrades closed in or dispersed, depending on who was summoned.

After a long delay, the bride and groom mounted the carriage that would take them to the reception at the Sports Club in the old Falcon Palace.

1155 hrs, Saturday, 4th January 1947, Pałacyk Sokół [Falcon Palace], Park Miejski, Skawina, Poland.

The food was amazing, considering all the privations that visited themselves on Europe.

Over two hundred people were crammed into the main rooms of the Falcon Palace.

209

It had been agreed that lots would be drawn amongst the legionnaires and the lucky men, three from every unit under Knocke's command, plied their commander and his new wife with soldier's gifts from their different units, given to the man and woman out of true love, comradeship, and respect.

Although not a draw winner, Haefali had arranged for one legionnaire to attend, albeit briefly.

Offering the newly-weds a gift of two hand-carved wooden candlesticks was Yitzhak Rubenstein, the old legionnaire who had helped Knocke and Haefali bring peace to the dead Soviet paratroopers in the courtyard of the Chateau so long ago.

Rubenstein and Knocke shared a handshake, and for a few seconds as they clasped hands, they shared a silent memory.

"Thank you, Yitzhak. They will be treasured."

The old legionnaire slipped away without further ceremony.

Knocke was refreshed that the recent events had not lain too hard on his soldiers, and that this wedding seemed to have brought them back closer together.

He could only laugh when daughter Greta proudly announced that she was the official mascot of the 1er RdM, a position granted to her by the three men from Emmercy's unit.

The top table was set with its back towards large French windows that allowed the winter sun in and provided a superb white backdrop to the wedding party.

The hall was graced by many displays of material flowers worked with evergreen foliage, the most impressive of which were set in front of the feet of the main table; two large ceramic pots, hand painted with local scenes, which contained the finest and tallest of the handmade displays.

Waiting staff from the local population walked out with glasses already primed with champagne, or as close as they could get in war-torn Poland, and started to distribute the contents of their trays amongst the well-wishers.

The waiter bringing the drinks to the top table seemed to be the clumsiest of all the Poles, and certainly the oldest, but he had given his time freely and was apparently in charge of the volunteers.

With studied care, he set a glass down in front of each person...

Lavalle...
Greta...bridesmaid
Armande Fleriot...
Magda...bridesmaid

210

De Lattre...

Sabine de Rochechouart, maid of honour and Anne-Marie's long-time friend.

Ernst...

Anne-Marie...

De Walle...

Plummer...

Clementine Plummer, his wife...

Haefali...

Each in turn received a glass.

The old man set down the tray to place out the last two glasses and coughed, extinguishing two of the candles with the gust of air, and then contrived to knock the last glass onto the floor.

The shattering of glass drew a few looks, but nothing was particularly out of the ordinary, so all minds returned to the task of celebrating.

All except one, a trained mind that understood something simply wasn't correct but couldn't identify what.

Madame Fleriot had quickly engaged with General De Lattre, and the two became involved in deep conversation for most of the reception, or up until the glasses started rattling to quieten people down, ready for the speeches.

De Walle rose to his feet, the act accompanied by a few growls from officers, keen to bring the group to order.

The old man bent down next to the large floral decoration, and picked up the pieces of glass with studied care.

The redness in his face marked embarrassment to those who gave him a second look, but not to the eyes that bored into him as he moved up and down from floor to table.

The old man finished picking up pieces, relit the candles, and moved away.

De Walle stood to give his speech, as the new Frau Knocke rose to shout a warning.

"Stop!"

The room fell into instant silence, marked only by the sounds of breathing and a single set of footsteps.

"Stop him!"

From those on the top table, Haefali was the nearest, so he and two legionnaires grabbed at the old man who grimly tried to push them away with his tray full of broken glass.

Another legion officer grabbed the tray, allowing the two legionnaires to hold the man.

All eyes then swivelled to Anne-Marie who pointed at the floral display.

"The display!"

He had been clever, but not clever enough.

The candle smoke had masked the slight smell of burning associated with a pencil fuse.

The glass had been the perfect distraction, and provided him with a reason to get down on the floor next to the floral decoration.

Without a second thought, Plummer, now the nearest, moved round the table and looked into the display, his face reflecting his horror even as his mouth started to work.

"Get out now!"

The room galvanised and the reactions of the soldiers took over, most grabbing someone less aware.

Plummer grabbed the charge and ran for the French windows.

He half kicked, half-shouldered open the double doors and ran, mentally counting off ten large bounds before he threw the device as far as he could.

It exploded two seconds after bouncing for a second time, transforming an old wooden cart into something much less recognisable, but infinitely more deadly.

Inside the building, the explosive shock wave showered the occupants with glass moving at high speed.

There were many injuries.

Knocke's two daughters had been swept up in strong arms and shielded from the blast, Greta by the body of Lavalle, who simply turned his back on the blast as he hurried her away in the opposite direction, and Magda, who was pushed to the floor and lain on by Armande Fleriot, whose still sharp reactions betrayed her murky past.

Both Lavalle and Madame Fleriot were cut by glass, but nothing that was serious, at least not when compared to others.

De Lattre escaped without injury, as did Knocke, although his dress tunic was cut in three places by flying glass.

Anne-Marie received her injury when her face collided with a rapidly moving chair and her eye closed up within seconds.

Clementine Plummer's back was bloodied from head to foot from many glass and wood splinters that had opened up her flesh and turned her yellow dress red. The wounds were numerous but none was severe.

More serious were the wounds sustained by Georges de Walle.

The indomitable Belgian lay on the floor hissing his pain through clenched teeth, a portion of the door framing deeply embedded in his inner thigh, a wound from which blood copiously flowed.

A piece of glass had laid his cheek open, exposing his upper teeth, before it moved on a surgically removed the top of his left ear, both wounds providing more free-flowing exits for his vital fluids.

The smallest but the most dangerous of wounds was a piece of glass that protruded from his neck, so close to the vital jugular that Anne-Marie never even thought about dressing the wound.

It did not bleed overly but undoubtedly had the capacity to kill.

"Gently, Georges… gently now."

She took hold of the wounded man and relaxed him against an upturned chair.

As she worked she asked a question of her new husband.

"Ernst… is she dead?"

She ripped up her lilac and white dress, to provide a tourniquet for the leg wound and then a wad for the facial wound.

"Yes."

"Then come and help me here."

Knocke moved away from the body of Sabine de Rochechouart, her life taken by a piece of the cart that had smashed into her chest and destroyed her heart.

Holding up De Walle's leg for his wife to work on, Knocke watched her deftly slip a tourniquet above the wound and tighten, bringing more sounds of pain from the Belgian.

All around them, other people were attending to those injured and identifying those beyond hope.

Haefali, his broken arm quite obvious from distance, assisted with the attempt to save the life of the man who had initiated the bomb, a battle that would ultimately be lost.

He had been thrown forward and smashed his neck into the edge of a table, which heavy impact had destroyed much of the soft tissue, the swelling now cutting off his airway.

One of the legionnaires lay still, his cause of death not immediately apparent, but none the less very dead.

Elsewhere in the room, there were three more dead, and a score more injured enough to need more than a plaster or a bandage.

Outside, the bomb and wooden splinters had claimed twelve lives.

Four Poles, seven legionnaires... and Benoit Plummer.

1602 hrs, Sunday, 5th January 1947, Pałacyk Sokół [Falcon Palace], Park Miejski, Skawina, Poland.

The medics had quickly decided that moving De Walle any distance was not a good idea so, adopting a practical approach, they had set up a medical facility within the part of the Falcon Palace unaffected by the bomb blast.

There were a total of eight in-patients and a regular procession of wounded returning for change of dressings and other medical interventions.

Local Polish medical personnel supplemented the Legion staff, and together provided the very best of care.

The Knockes had just left the palace having visited their friend who, despite being in considerable pain was, according to the doctors, going to survive the injuries.

The neck wound had come close to ending his life but the doctor, a man who had plied his trade on the steppes and in the bocage, had skilfully extricated the sliver from de Walle's neck, all the time marvelling at how close it had actually come to the main vein without actually causing the slightest hint of damage.

There was a hint of infection, and the thigh wound was causing the Deux commander considerable pain, but he grinned and grimaced his way through the Knocke's visit.

A nurse had come in to administer some pain relief but had retreated to allow the three to say their goodbyes.

Both Ernst and Anne-Marie nodded to her when they left.

"Time for some medication, General Waller."

De Walle tried to move himself up the bed but pain shot through his damaged limb.

"Let me help get you comfortable."

The Polish nurse caught hold of his left arm and pulled upwards, virtually dragging the Belgian up the bed, splitting one stitched wound on his shoulder.

"So sorry, General. I didn't know that was there."

De Walle nodded his acceptance of her explanation, although he was surprised at the roughness of her approach.

"Haven't seen you before."

'...or have I... you do look familiar come to think of it...'

"I'm just in from Krakow to help out. Only for a few days. Sorry again, General."

"There's a few more stitches here and there, It's all in my notes... err... nurse?"

"Radzinski... Urszula Radzinski."

"Georges de Walle... I would get up but..."

Radzinski interrupted, ignoring his attempted gallantry.

"Now, some pain relief that'll help you relax."

She took a syringe from a kidney dish and filled it with studied care from a glass vial.

"Just 15 mills of morphine to make things go away, General."

The needle went home and Georges felt an immediate wave of relaxation wash over him, dulling the pain in his thigh and neck almost instantly.

The nurse made a record in the notes, although her signature bore no resemblance to anything intelligible or pronounceable.

'Ah... no more pain...'

He relaxed into the wave of relief that washed over him but suddenly a part of his brain went on full alert.

'Mallman... Irma Mallman... Abwe...'

Taking his wrist, Radzinski checked his pulse and waited until the full effects of the narcotic overtook her patient.

De Walle lapsed into a deep sleep.

Removing three more vials from her pocket, Radzinski quickly filled the syringe and injected three further doses of morphine into his veins, a total of 60 mgs dose of the effective barbiturate.

An effective and intentionally fatal dose.

Busying herself elsewhere in the room, Radzinski watched as De Walle's breathing became less pronounced and he went into respiratory failure.

There was no struggle, no fight to prevent an untimely end, just a nothingness that she observed come to an end as the chest rose for the final time.

'Sehr gut.'
And in a moment, Radzinski was gone forever.

1631 hrs, Sunday, 5th January 1947, Szczęście Farm, Ul. Łanowa, Skawina, Poland.

"Here's to Georges!"
Anne-Marie raised her glass and they both drank a toast to their friend.
"Close... he's a lucky man, darling."
"Yes, so it seems."
"As are you, Darling. How's your eye?"
"Sore."
They relaxed into silence as they grappled with the information that they had been made aware of prior to visiting the makeshift hospital.
"A Jew."
"Yes, a Jew. Which makes it all clear, I suppose, Cherie."
Anne-Marie could understand the motivation for a Jew to kill ex-SS, Germans, anyone who could be faintly connected with the death camps.
That the bomb had not claimed such a life was ironic to say the least, although one of the legionnaires slain outside the palace was German, but had always been a legionnaire, even through the German war.
"They'll be able to trace him by his number... if records permit."
The arm tattoo had betrayed both him and his likely motivation in short order.
"We've lost more friends, Cherie. Will it ever stop?"
The statement was about as un-Anne-Marie-like Knocke had ever heard.
Then he remembered.
A woman carrying a child has other influences on her deportment; ones that involve protecting and nurturing the life in her belly and evaluating the world she will be bringing it in to.
"Our child is fine?"
"Yes, Cherie. All's well in here."
She made great play of rubbing her hands over a belly that still had to make show of her condition.
"Anyway, I'll make us dinner. Will you get some more wood please, Ernst?"
"Of course."

216

They kissed like young lovers and went about their chores.

Anne-Marie busied herself in the large kitchen of the farmhouse that the Legion had refurbished for their few days of peace, but still heard the flick of a lighter as her husband took his simple pleasures outside before bringing in the wood for the fire.

She also heard the sound of a vehicle approaching and shouts of consternation from the armed legionnaires who stood watch over their commander and his new wife.

Having been uncharacteristically unarmed during the wedding, she now had a weapon close to hand, so she grabbed it and moved quickly to the front door, only to see the recently splinted Haefali and two of his men in agitated conversation with Knocke.

Whatever she was watching, Anne-Marie realised that something was very wrong, and she tensed instinctively, scanning around her, ready to act in a second.

All of a sudden the scene in front of her changed to one of calm resignation?... almost solemn?... almost...?

'Georges?'

Knocke slapped Haefali's shoulder softly and turned to his wife.

No words were needed.

She could see it writ large cross his face... across Haefali's face... in their eyes... and in the way they walked.

"No!"

Ernst held out his arms as he approached her and she fell into them, sobbing inconsolably.

The guard legionnaires watched in awe as the iron maiden came apart in her grief, and then joined her in their own way when they were told of De Walle's death.

He had not been a legionnaire, but he was a popular man who had stood his ground alongside them during some difficult times.

"Come inside, Albrecht. Join us."

Anne-Marie composed herself and led the two men inside, where they sat down and learned of what had happened, and drank to the memory of her mentor and friend.

"He was found dead on the doctor's round."

Anne-Marie took a good sip of the schnapps.

"When we left he was in pain, but there was no clue... we had no idea that he could just...well... go."

217

"He had some morphine before the end so…"

"Yes, we saw the nurse. She postponed giving it because we were there. So we left quickly to let him have his medication without delay."

Knocke stood by the fire, making a study of positioning the latest logs just so, simply to cover his feelings of loss.

Whilst the sudden void inside surprised him, having known the irascible Belgian for under two years, he accepted it for what it was, as he had come to genuinely like the man, and to value his presence and friendship.

He listened in on the conversation as he jiggled the final piece of wood into place.

"The doctor assures me he felt no pain… that he simply drifted off."

"But why? The same damn doctor said he would be fine… possibly hobble a bit, but that he would survive."

Haefali shrugged.

"I don't know, Anne-Marie, really I don't. Except I've seen it before. Men who seemed to recover from wounds, but who simply just died when all seemed well. It happens."

Knocke joined in.

"Yes, it does, and we should always be prepared for it. This time we dared to hope."

He reached for the schnapps bottle and filled each glass in turn.

"So my darling… Albrecht… let us drink to our comrades and friends."

He raised the glass in turn as he named those who had perished on their wedding day, and that very afternoon.

They acknowledged in turn and, when Georges de Walle's name was mentioned, drained each glass to the bottom.

"I'll speak to the nurse when I get a chance. See what more she can tell us."

Knocke acknowledged his wife's words and sat down in one of the comfy chairs, rather more heavily than he intended, a sign of both the mental strain and his physical tiredness.

He had been on the go virtually every hour since the bomb had exploded. Visiting the wounded, writing letters to the relations of those who died, or in the case of the Polish casualties, visiting the next of kin in their humble homes.

The others gravitated towards seats surrounding the fire, which drew their eyes as they sat in silence, reflecting on the weekend's events.

Haefali refilled their glasses and sat down again, aware he was sat with a newly married couple on their honeymoon whilst being aware that he was there without intrusion, sharing their grief and silence like the friend he was.

Knocke shifted in his seat and laughed softly.

"Ernst?"

"I was just thinking, Albrecht. If this is the peace, what would the war be like?"

"Noisier."

They smiled and clinked their glasses in salute.

Knocke raised his to his wife, whilst she exchanged toasts with the Swiss.

She sipped the fiery liquid carefully as she recalled a quote from Aristophanes.

Anne-Marie decided to share and held her glass out for a final toast.

"A quote I just remembered, from Aristophanes, the Greek poet."

She had their full attention.

"Our lost friends are not dead, but gone before, advanced a stage or two upon that road, which we must travel in the steps they trod."

She let the words settle in their minds before raising her glass high.

"To our friends who've gone before."

Three voices joined in unison.

"To our friends who've gone before!"

Triumphant science and technology are only at the threshold of man's command over sources of energy so stupendous that, if used for military purposes, they can wipe out our entire civilization.

Cordell Hull

Chapter 183 - THE TEST

1202 hrs, Monday, 6th January 1947, the Black Sea, 80 kilometres southwest of Sochi, USSR.

"Do you want to abandon the test, Commander?"

"No. We continue... we must continue."

Nobukiyo and Kalinin watched as the badly injured seaman was taken below, his shattered and mangled arms flopping around uncontrollably as the medical crew attempted to get him out of the way of the deck crew.

Using a megaphone, Nobukiyo shouted his orders.

"Restore the equipment to stowage... prepare to run the test again in ten minutes. Lieutenant Jinyo, have that man replaced immediately."

"Hai!"

"And get it right this time!"

"Hai!"

The Japanese officer turned back to his guest.

"They were doing well... no blame attached for that I think."

"I agree, Commander. Freak wave... your men were not at fault. In fact, they were performing excellently."

Nobukiyo nodded his acceptance of the compliment.

"If I might make a suggestion, Commander?"

"Of course."

"Double the sea watch. Two pairs of eyes on each quarter might have seen that coming."

"Yes, I agree. I already gave the order when you were watching the events on deck."

That he had given it in Japanese meant that Kalinin had not realised that the man had made the small but important adjustment.

"Of course. I should have fully expected you to do so, Commander. You know your business. My apologies."

Nobukiyo bowed slightly, acknowledging the compliment.

However, the delay would mean that they would only get one more attempt at the practice session before the air cover that guaranteed their anonymity had to return to base.

Tea was brought to the bridge and the two men drank in silence, each in turn taking in the sights of a crew working efficiently in preparation for testing their main reason for being.

Nobukiyo checked his watch and leant towards the voice tube.

"Captain, control room. Standby to initiate missile deployment drill. Standby... initiate."

A strange squawking sound emerged from the open conning tower hatch and men spilled out from the hull hatches, accompanied by harangues of encouragement from their divisional officers.

The main hangar door was swinging open by the time that Kalinin shifted his gaze from the bloody red patch that marked where the unfortunate sailor had become pinned under the blast plates during the previous drill.

Initially, they had been welded in place with the intention of being external for the entire mission, but the effect upon performance and an unexpected increase in transit noise levels had changed all that.

So now the heavy blast plates had to be manhandled from the hangar to the bow of the submarine, far enough away as to not affect any of the hatches, or the seals to the main hangar door, not to mention the crew on the bridge.

Three working parties of twelve men, one party to each plate, two runs each to position six plates in all, mounted in place with special bolts that could have their heads struck off to recover the plates, as so far, each test firing, albeit on land, had resulted in the bolts welding to the plates.

The two senior officers observed the plates being dropped into place one by one, in a pre-designated order.

Nobukiyo had a stopwatch running and held it out to his Russian counterpart.

It was eighty seconds over the best time achieved in the dock, something that would earn the handling crews special praise later, regardless of what came next.

The whistles blew and the handling party moved quickly back and across, permitting the second group to run the V-2 and firing pedestal out of the hangar, rear end first.

221

Some of the plate handlers then reinforced the missile crew, lending their weight to the run down the catapult tracks, now set up for the rocket trolley.

A senior NCO handled the braking mechanism, and important part of the modifications. To send the V-2 off the end of the track would probably be terminal for the missile and submarine, as the new procedures meant that the rockets were pre-fuelled before being loaded into the hangars, a situation considered undesirable but unavoidable.

The trolley came to a halt and the deck clamps were put in place.

'116 seconds.'

To overcome the increased weight when raising to vertical, the engineers had developed a simple but effective multi-support that extended in the correct ratios, maintaining fourteen separate support points with the missile during the operation to bring the V-2 to the vertical.

This was electrically driven and offered a smooth ride all the way.

The huge rocket achieved its final position swiftly, and the deck crew reduced in number, the final group off deck removing the rails to permit the hangar door to be closed.

"Firing sequence, standby."

'118 seconds.'

Kalinin nodded his pleasure at the time, their best estimate having placed the total time needed at four minutes minimum over the steady environment of the sub's base.

The final 'go' signal came from the missile position itself, given by the senior deck officer once he was happy that the missile was erected properly and all was as it should be.

The white flag meant Nobukiyo could give the order. He acknowledged the signal and the remaining missile crew dropped down hatches, leaving the erect missile as the deck's sole occupant.

"Firing sequence, commence on my order."

The two men exchanged satisfied looks before Nobukiyo leant forward and spoke the word that set history in motion.

"Commence!"

Kalinin first, followed by the lookouts, then the submarine's commander, dropped down the conning tower, Nobukiyo having sealed the hatch as he descended.

Kalinin was immediately glued to the intercom, where Jinyo's calm voice relayed all he saw through the thick glass inspection hatch that had been installed in the hangar door.

At sea, the vulnerable glass would be protected by watertight metal pressure covers both inside and out, but for missile launching the viewing port was exposed.

Nobukiyo busied himself with obtaining radar reports, as the Sen-Toku was now on the surface with no eyes to watch over her, save those of the radar operator and the Red Air force that presently, albeit temporarily, owned the Black Sea's sky.

During the non-firing drills, Kalinin had come to understand a few words of Japanese, so he was able to follow the countdown.

'Nana.'

'Rok.'

"Go."

"San."

"Ni."

"Ichi."

The submarine shook tangibly as the rocket engine started forcing the missile off the deck.

The trim of the submarine altered in an instant, but the crew were ready, earning the diving officer a pat on the shoulder from his captain.

Jinyo's voice confirmed that the V-2 had left the deck successfully and Nobukiyo wasted no time in ordering his recovery operation commenced.

The intention on the mission was to dump the raising frame into the sea, but it had been decided to recover it, repair it, and re-use it, given the complexity of its construction.

Therefore, Nobukiyo didn't worry about the additional time taken to clear the deck, other than the normal concerns of a submariner on the surface.

The frame and plates were recovered once seawater had been applied liberally, the red-hot protective plates having taken the full blast from the V-2's rocket motor.

Even then they remained hot to the touch, and the plate handlers welcomed the heat-resistant gloves they had been issued with.

Including recovering the missile-raising frame, the whole operation took two minutes twenty-three seconds over the best practice time, an overrun that was less acceptable than that experienced during the raising operation.

None the less, I-401 disappeared beneath the waves less than seven minutes after firing the first missile ever fired from a submarine at sea.

It was an achievement that the IJN and Soviet Navy did not intend to publicise.

The V-2 rose from the sea surface, leaving a smoke plume in its wake.

A Soviet hospital ship, the Lvov, a vessel of the Black Sea Fleet and currently employed outside its intended purpose, used a modified version of the German's Leitstrahl Beam guidance system to bring the V-2 onto its target, the Neva, an ex-Spanish refugee ship that was another anonymous vessel, although this time one well past its prime and considered expendable.

The swell made things difficult and it was no surprise that the rocket came down some distance from the target.

The missile, filled with an equal weight of concrete instead of its normal payload of explosives, arrowed into the sea at such speed that it was invisible.

It smashed into the water at just under one thousand eight hundred miles an hour.

A Beriev Be-4 reconnaissance aircraft observing the target area reported that the V-2 splash was observed two and a half kilometres from the expendable old ship, a huge distance when aiming at such a target...

...but within acceptable bounds when aiming at a city.

Those wars are unjust that are undertaken without provocation. For only a war waged for revenge or defence can be just.

Marcus Tullius Cicero

Chapter 184 - THE PROVOCATION

1357 hrs, Thursday, 9th January 1947, Justizzentrum, temporary government building #3, Magdeburg, Germany.

"Thank you, Zimmerman. Coffee in my office please, and see that we're not disturbed."

"Yes, Sir."

The old man wandered off with the remains of the dessert course and ordered up the coffee immediately, which he quickly delivered to the private office of his boss.

The two men were suddenly alone.

"So, your report is excellent news. Our problems have been removed."

"Yes indeed, and although it didn't all go to plan, the team on the ground in Poland adapted and achieved the goal… and more to the point did it without arousing suspicion."

The senior man flicked to the page in the report that had caught his eye.

"The tattoo… a master-stroke I must say."

"Thank you, Sir."

"Seems to have thrown the investigation down a one-track road to a dead-end. You were unfortunate not to get the prime target with the bomb, but I agree that your team adapted well in getting to him quickly."

He flipped the folder shut and pushed across the desk.

"So, that's an end to the matter, yes?"

The junior man shifted uncomfortably as he replied.

"Sir, you know I can't promise that but, as far as we're concerned, they were the only two who had started to put together the situation. They're both removed, and there's no suggestion that anyone else knows. However, we'll remain vigilant."

"I would hope so, Vögel"

They sipped their coffee in silence.

"So, I can report to higher authority that the problem has been efficiently removed and there is no threat to our plans?"

"Within the limitations I've stated, yes, Sir."

"Excellent."

The senior man pushed the file across the table and Vögel swept it up as if it was contraband.

"This will now be destroyed, Sir. I'll see to it personally."

"No trace?"

"None at all, Sir."

"Excellent. Well done. Now, I've a call to place."

"Thank you, Sir."

The call was connected and Pflug-Hartnung passed on news of the success, selecting his words to represent the completion of some low-level intelligence mission in Norway, whereas he was in fact reporting the successful assassination of both Gehlen and De Walle.

Rudolf Diels replaced the receiver with unconcealed joy and made his report.

"Pflug-Hartnung has done well. Good news, Diels, well done. Now we can progress without having to look over our shoulders all the time."

"Jawohl, Herr Kanzler."

Oberfeldwebel Martens checked again.

He checked again.

He checked a final time and picked up the telephone.

'Trauenfeld.'

"Herr Hauptmann, Martens here. There's a problem with the latest repositioning maps."

'What sort of problem, Oberfeldwebel.'

"There's some border lines that simply don't work, Sir. I think it's an issue that could lead to some problems. Can I come up, Sir?"

'I'm with the Maior right now... moment...'

Clearly Hauptmann Trauenfeld had put his hand over the receiver to speak to his commanding officer.

The conversation was brief and Trauenfeld was back in seconds.

'Come up now, Oberfeldwebel. The Maior would like to see what you have.'

The phone clicked before Martens could reply.

Picking up the two maps and his notes, he moved quickly up the stairs to the second floor office.

1234 hrs, Saturday, 11th January 1947, over the demarcation line, Maków Mazowiecki, Poland.

"Yaguar-krasny-odin. I see them. Maintain formation. Let them pass with no interference. Stay with our big cousin. Out."

Djorov settled his hands on the control stick, relaxing his grip, as he kept an eye on the approaching enemy aircraft.

His flight of five MiG-9s had already taken station above and behind the single reconnaissance aircraft that was their charge for this mission.

It was an unusual beast, one of the first Soviet copies of the incomplete Junkers-287 jet bombers captured in April 1945.

The strange sweep of the wings never failed to impress the veteran ace despite the EF-131s, as they were designated or Trident as the crews called them, having trained at the special Stakhnovo airbase.

Colonel Djorov could have sent someone else on the mission, but he had been back at his squadron for four weeks, and the stiffness of a desk needed to be flown out of his legs.

The approaching enemy were clearly moving at high speed as they started to quickly loom large.

Six enemy aircraft whooshed past, engines roaring, two over the top of the fighter group and four through the gap between the Trident and its protective force, perilously close to the single reconnaissance aircraft.

Their jet wakes created difficulties for the Trident's pilot and he struggled to keep his charge stable in the roiled air.

"Yaguar-krasny-odin to flight, close on our cousin. We'll tolerate no repeats of that. Out."

The five Soviet jets dropped some height, something that fighter pilots the world over rarely conceded during combat, but in these circumstances, Djorov considered the Trident would appreciate the closer company.

He was correct, and the three crew on board the Trident breathed easier as the MiGs came closer, leaving no gap through which the DRL fighters could pass.

The six ME-262s swept round in a tight circle and drove hard across the front of the Soviet formation, cutting aggressively close to the nose of the four-engine bomber.

"Yaguar-Krasny-Odin to Karusel', over."

"Go ahead, Yaguar-krasny-odin."

Djorov sought a positional check from the ground control radar station in their sector, which was satisfactorily within shared airspace.

Which then meant that the DRL aircraft were also within the shared zone, and perfectly within their rights to demonstrate against aircraft seemingly heading to cross the line from an acceptable presence into an unacceptable intrusion.

Which was, in essence, part of the mission.

To poke but not provoke.

What happened next nearly brought the sides to blows once more, as each blamed the other for the air battle over Maków Mazowiecki.

'191'

Johannes Steinhoff totted up a kill for the first time since 'peace' had descended on Europe, his 30mm Mk 108 cannon flaying one of the Soviet MiGs into strips of scrap.

Behind him, five more 262s of the 200th ZBV Jagdgeschwader set about the now maneuvering Soviet fighter group.

Three MiGs were down in under a minute, the aircraft well matched for speed, but with surprise on their side, the DRL aces had little trouble in putting shells on target.

His pilots broke into two groups, one of four, and a pair that he ordered to take down the strange forward swept winged aircraft, after having taken pictures for his intelligence officer back at base.

He led the four plane element after the surviving MiGs, who were desperately trying to get back to cover their charge.

Steinhoff tried a short burst, for no other reason that reminding the enemy pilot he was there and distracting him from the purpose of protection.

The ruse worked, and the MiG broke right, away from his preferred route, leaving only one Soviet fighter committed to protecting the eccentric aircraft.

Steinhoff turned back onto course, followed by his wingman, just in time to see one of his aircraft smoke and fall away from its position behind the Trident.

The swept wing bomber had a modest defensive armament of two 12,7mm machine-guns, but they were enough to wreck the starboard engine of Oberleutnant Schmidt's Schwalbe.

The 262 slowed and fell to one side, allowing the Soviet gunner another opportunity.

More bullets struck home, in both metal and flesh, and the fighter dropped away with an unconscious man at the controls, both coming to a final resting place in the ice-cold water of Lake Narew.

The other 262 pilot made sure his camera with its evidence was safely secured before gaining on the manoeuvring Trident and steadily feeding a stream of 30mm shells into the delicate airframe.

The aircraft simply came apart under the hammer blows, permitting time for one man to escape and take to a parachute.

Screamed warnings alerted the victor to his danger and the ace threw his 262 around the sky in some impressive combat manoeuvrings.

However, on his tail was an expert who had survived the harshest of tests, and the surviving Soviet fighter fired a burst that simply smashed apart the wing at the base, allowing the damaged structure to fold over the canopy and entangle itself with the engine on the other wing.

The strange sight, almost like a piece of origami, fell from the sky in an ungainly fashion.

Djorov spared a seconds look at his victim, whereas the German pilots who left their radios on receive heard him scream all the way to the ground, fully conscious and unwounded but simply unable to escape from his cockpit, enclosed as it was in bent metal.

Steinhoff cursed his thoughts of relief when the aircraft struck the ground and the pathetic screams stopped.

The MiG was diving and building up an incredible speed, causing Steinhoff to weigh up the pros and cons of pursuit.

He decided to return to base and officially report the encounter to NATO headquarters, and unofficially inform the strange intelligence officer that his clandestine mission had been successfully accomplished.

By 1330 hrs, because the combat had clearly taken place over Allied territory, the entire German Army was given an order to go on full alert.

The Polish forces received a similar order twelve minutes later.

Eisenhower begrudgingly gave the same order at 1421 hrs and Europe moved closer to a renewed war.

The initial reports from Karusel control were reinforced by the swift verbal report of regimental commander Djorov, and the fact that the Allied aggression had clearly taken place over Soviet territory was considered sufficient cause to bring the Red Army to a state of full readiness from the Baltic to the Adriatic.

By 1430 hrs on 11th January 1947, the world stood on the brink of war once more.

1501 hrs, Saturday, 11th January 1947, Camp Vár conference facility, Lungsnäs, Sweden.

"Gentlemen please!"

The shout was loud enough to cut over and through the angry conversation that had grown to the level of a football crowd's baying.

"Gentlemen, please… seat yourselves and let us resolve this matter with no more blood spilt and your countries still at peace. Please… be seated."

Östen Undén, on the site by the purest of chance, calmed the assembled politicos and soldiery enough to promote discussion.

"Now, whilst you have been shouting threats at each other, my staff have spotted the problem and it's not the fault of your air forces. I repeat, no one in the sky over Maków Mazowiecki is at fault. It's an error in our own processes here that has triggered this unfortunate event."

He nodded to his aide who had quickly prepared the basic information to tell the assembled negotiators how a simple cartography error had brought the two sides into conflict once more.

The short of it was a simple misdrawing of the line on the Soviet version, something that had been missed by the Swedish cartographers as well as both sides, who possessed a copy of each version.

Given that the 'two frontline' process was intended to keep ground forces apart, two versions were needed each time the Soviets conceded ground and the Allies moved forward, thus ensuring the armies did not come into contact and reducing the chance of any unfortunate incidents.

The ground lines had been accurately drawn, but the overlapping air limits, overlain to permit peaceful monitoring of the territory five miles either side of the front line, had been slightly misdrawn around Maków Mazowiecki, which meant that both sides

230

were correct in believing that the combat took place in air space either belonging to them or permitted for their use, and that the other side were the aggressors... depending which map you read.

Despite the Swedish assurances, the two sides took a further two hours to agree the facts were as Undén's aide had presented, and that they would immediately advise a cooling off and scaled reduction in readiness over the next three days, suspending all relocations and stipulating no flights beyond land forces boundaries until all air boundaries had been double-checked by both sides.

A session that had started with hands on holsters eventually broke up at 1900 prompt, allowing the two sides to experience a calm dinner and evening in their various camps.

In the various headquarters across the continent, the men who would have shouldered the responsibility for a renewed combat all heaved a collective sigh of relief.

Almost all anyway.

2013 hrs, Saturday, 11th January 1947, the Kremlin, Moscow, USSR.

"Thank you for your report, Comrade Nazarbayeva."

He listened to her closing words, his mind already moved on to other matters.

"Yes, thank you, Comrade. I'm as relieved as you. Good bye."

He replaced the receiver and picked up his pipe, lighting it thoughtfully and enjoying the first few puffs in contented silence.

"The woman confirmed everything you said, Lavrentiy. A simple error... for which we must be thankful."

"Indeed, Comrade General Secretary. It's too soon, far too soon."

"However, this report from Oktyabrskiy is wonderful news, is it not?"

Beria played his cards carefully, as usual.

"It's one exercise only, and their first attempt ended in abject failure it seems. However, the Navy's pleased with it. I'll be happier when they've repeated the exercise so we know it's not a fluke."

As usual, Beria's verbal dance was not wasted on Stalin, but he was too buoyed by the avoidance of a premature return to war to be too concerned at his henchman's lack of enthusiasm.

The pipe went out and he thought better of reloading it, instead extracting a cigarette from the pack on his desk.

"None the less, I want those responsible for this close call dealt with appropriately. Some examples made publically for the benefit of the Allies will further reduce tensions. Now we're committed to our course, we can't afford to fight ahead of time."

"I agree, Comrade General Secretary."

"Even with this good news."

The dictator held up the report on the Black Sea tests.

"Even with that news, such as it is, Comrade General Secretary."

Stalin smiled in seeming acceptance of Beria's restated position.

'One day I'll wipe that smug look off your face, you Chekist fuck.'

Beria smiled back.

'One day I'll be sitting in your fucking chair, you Georgian peasant.'

Externally, there was harmony and agreement.

"So, how goes the infiltration of the German intelligence network and government?"

Beria sipped his tea before slipping his glasses off and polishing them.

Which standard behaviour meant that Stalin had his answer before Beria uttered a word.

1357 hrs, Sunday, 12th January 1947, Friedrich-Ebert-Strasse, temporary government building #1, Magdeburg, Germany.

"Well, it was worth a try, Feldmarschal."

Guderian shrugged rather than restate the objections that had preceded the operation, objections that were still as sound now as they were then.

To him, the Republic had escaped a possible crisis, whereas to the politicians who had seized the moment, Germany had tried but failed to exploit the mistake that they alone had spotted.

The DRL Oberfeldwebel who had first noticed the overlapping air zones was now enjoying an extended leave with his fiancée, who was extremely impressed with the officer's uniform that her husband-to-be sported, as a newly fledged Leutnant.

On return he would be assigned to a safe post on the Swiss border, with a spectacular officer's quarter made available for the couple, courtesy of a grateful nation, which might also wish to see him tucked out of the way where no questions could be asked.

232

Those above him in the chain of command also found themselves moved to higher and better things.

The map issue had come to the attention of the high command on Thursday evening.

Guderian chose to ignore it, but one of his staff knew one of Diels' staff and so the information moved even further up the chain.

The opportunity was considered too good to miss, and the DRL's elite squadron was briefed on how to best play their part at provoking the Soviets.

The sudden exercising of a great portion of the German and Polish armies had been surprise for Eisenhower and his staff, but von Vietinghoff had assured them it was a scheduled affair and would only be run to test the ability to move forward against a Soviet strike, consuming relatively few resources.

The German and Polish commanders on the ground cursed the new and 'most immediate' orders, and sent their men forward from nice warm positions into the cold snowy European Friday.

They were now back in their normal positions, wondering why so many men and vehicles had moved up and back at such short notice, and without the normal monitoring from headquarters personnel, who were seemingly always eager to berate a commander for his lack of efficiency, or failure to observe a timetable.

It had been two days of holding breath for the few men in the know, and now they were breathing again, despite the failure of the effort.

"Unless another opportunity presents itself, we'll stick to our plan."

"Kanzler, there'll be no repeat of this border issue, I'm sure of that. The Swedes for one won't permit it. Their credibility has suffered, at least in their eyes."

"Quite right too. Perhaps there may be some advantage we can gain there, considering our loss, eh?"

"Possibly, Kanzler, but I daresay the Russians are thinking the same thing."

"Good point, Feldmarschal."

Speer rose from behind his modest desk and moved to shake Guderian's hand.

"Until Monday then, Feldmarschal. I'll have the latest production projection on new armour and the gas-turbine engines then, and I suspect they'll make good reading for you and your staff. I've no doubt that the Reich has provided for your needs."

"I hope so, Kanzler. Until then."

He came to attention, saluted Speer, turned on his heel, and was gone before Speer could muster a quip on the way Guderian had seemingly started to give a Nazi salute and moved quickly into a formal military one.

The door closed behind him.

Another opened after Speer had tapped gently on it, signalling the all-clear, allowing two men to resume their former places around his desk.

"Well, I assume you heard most of that, gentlemen?"

They nodded.

"For my part, I can understand why you did what you did, and I have no problems with your decision. The venture failed, but it was worth the effort, Albert."

"Thank you for your gracious words, Karl."

Karl Renner sat back having said his piece, and not having totally meant all he said, but it didn't pay to provoke over a situation that had since passed.

Władysław Raczkiewicz, President of Poland had already discussed his discontent with Renner, but followed the same course of open acceptance.

"Is there anything else you need to know about yesterday's events?"

"No, thank you, Herr Kanzler. You've made everything clear."

"Thank you, Herr Präsident. So, we fall back on our agreed agenda. Our tracks have been covered and our loyal allies suspect nothing. We'll continue as before then."

He picked up the phone.

"Sperrman. We're ready to eat. Good... good."

He replaced the receiver and stood enthusiastically.

"Gentlemen, our lunch awaits... venison and chicken."

The three enjoyed an excellent meal and kept their darker thoughts to themselves.

*I have learned to hate all traitors, and there is no disease that I spit
on more than treachery.*

Aeschylus

Chapter 185 - THE GERMANS?

1157 hrs, Wednesday, 15th January 1947, Army Training Ground, south of Allentsteig, Austria.

The battalion of tanks had certainly looked impressive from the start.

General Pierce, commander of the expanded 16th US Armored Division, had seen the new beasts of war close up, but this was the first time he had seen an entire battalion arraigned, and he confessed his excitement to his CoS, Edwin Greiner.

"Damn but if that ain't the finest sight I've seen for many a while, Ed."

Greiner could only agree, his binoculars taking in the details of the lines of brand new M-29 Chamberlains that constituted the 5th US Tank Battalion.

The Chamberlain sported a 105mm main gun, good armour protection and excellent speed for a tank of its nearly sixty-five tons.

To one side sat the light tank company, its seventeen M24 Chaffee tanks dwarfed by their larger brothers. Behind them sat the six 105mm howitzer equipped M4 Shermans, the only tanks that had been with the 16th since they first arrived in Europe, albeit two were replacements for vehicles lost in battle.

Before the two senior men in the division drove off to inspect the arraigned battalion, the plan was for them to observe a shoot designed to bring the whole of the 396th Field Artillery onto the field, deploy, and fire a concentrated barrage in support of a fictitious infantry attack.

The battalion would then redeploy, in line with the new aptly named 'shoot and scoot' policy, designed to keep artillery alive in the face of improvements in counter-battery fire.

The artillery officer waited patiently for his cue.

Pierce dropped his binoculars, still marvelling at the power under his command and switched his attention to Barksdale Hammlett Jnr, the Divisional Artillery commander.

"You may proceed, Colonel."

The radio was in Hammlett's hand and the order given before Pierce could draw a breath.

From behind the northern woods came a roar of revving engines and very quickly the SP guns of the 396th charged into view, almost competing for the front position.

The senior officers watched with experienced eyes, understanding the subtle openings in the massed group as the different fire groups altered course.

Eighteen M-41 SP 155mm guns led the way, side by side with battery commander vehicles, and leading the ammunition train.

Behind them came Hammlett's ace; a unit of five M-40 GMCs he had managed to retain and that were over and above the normal complement for an motorised artillery battalion.

For this exercise, M19 SPAA vehicles shook out on the flanks, occupying positions to screen the assembled artillery from any possible air attack.

Pierce always had high expectations of Hammlett and his men, but the exercise exceeded them, the guns putting rounds in the air in record time.

An eight round shoot was planned and it was over in the blink of an eye, the whole battalion suddenly up and moving like a spooked herd of buffalo.

"Goddamnit if that wasn't impressive, Barksdale. Very impressive indeed."

"Thank you, Sir."

Greiner couldn't help himself.

"Well, let's just make sure you put rounds on target before we start writing weekend passes eh, Colonel?"

"Do you have doubts, Colonel?"

Greiner had the scent immediately.

"What do you suggest, Barksdale?"

"I've got fifty that says we put 90% in the target area. What you got, Colonel?"

"I'll cover that. I can't lose, can I? I've either got an incompetent artillery commander but I'm fifty bucks up, or we're on the ball, and the commies will get theirs. Win, win."

Pierce grinned.

"My money's on the arty. You want some?"

"I'll cover that bet, Sir."

Ninety percent was not unheard of, but to deploy so rapidly and make an accurate shoot, even with some prior knowledge of the telemetry involved, would be extremely impressive.

When the results of the shoot were in, Greiner was extremely impressed, as well as being a hundred dollars down.

Ninety-three percent of the shells landed within the designated zone, and there were weekend passes a plenty.

Unfortunately for Pierce, or more accurately, unfortunately for Acting Lieutenant Colonel Ewing of the 5th Tank Battalion, the artillery shoot was the highlight of the day.

Whilst the battalion achieved all of its objectives during the exercise on the old Austrian army training ground, it did it with an increasingly fewer number of vehicles, as mechanical casualties rose, along with Pierce's blood pressure.

On the final exercise, one of the Chamberlains caught fire and became a total loss when it exploded, killing two men from the battalion maintenance company.

The General showed his harder side when dealing with Ewing, who was quickly advised that the whole thing would be re-run the next day and, as Pierce so eloquently put it, *'the whole goddamned battalion better be on the final parade or you'll be driving the shit wagon for the rest of your career.'*

The repeated exercise saw two more Chamberlain breakdowns, but the efforts of the maintenance company saw them on the final parade and Ewing was saved from any further indignities.

Pierce's report was forward to Corps HQ, and the 16th was rated combat ready.

1103 hrs, Saturday, 18th January 1947, the Viennese enclave, Austria.

Part of the negotiations over territory had resolved that Vienna would remain within Soviet hands until the wishes of the people of Czechoslovakia were fully known.

Hungary, pressured by an increasingly angry Tito, chose to remain within the Soviet sphere of influence, which meant that a small isthmus in the Soviet line could easily be maintained, a situation that most of the Allies were content with, except for the obvious noisy objections of German and Austrian contingents.

The Soviets were still in place long after the expected handover should have occurred, mainly because of the political situation in the Czech homeland, where the country seemed to be divided on an east-west basis, the eastern segment being more inclined to remain within the Soviet lines.

One of the easiest parts of the realignment of front lines had been from Bratislava southwards, where the Hungarian army took over much of the responsibility, bolstered by a few units of Tolbukhin's Front, until the political boundaries met and Yugoslavian forces sat defending their homeland.

From the Soviet point of view, this released many units to return to Byelorussia and the Ukraine, or even to be transferred east or to the southern borders of Iraq.

The sole exception was Vienna, which remained occupied by the Red Army's 4th Guards Army, one of Chuikov's old formations, which was set in place in and around the Austrian capital; a powerful force placed to send the clear message that the Red Army would leave when it was good and ready.

Speer and Renner brought as much pressure to bear as they could, but the simple truth was that nothing would happen until the Czech question was resolved.

For their part, the Czech government was caught between two waves of strongly held feelings, and failed to bring about any useful decisions.

So Vienna remained a Soviet enclave, and Renner continued to cry foul to anyone and everyone who would listen.

"All quiet then, Al."

"You betcha, Lukas. Far too cold for any shit. They know it… we know it… anyway, here's hoping the Czechs pull their fingers out soon so we can spend the rest of this winter in warm houses in Vienna."

"Somehow, I doubt it'll be over by then. The Czechs seem to be in a right SNAFU."

"You can but hope, Lukas."

"Guess the neighbours ain't got any fuel, eh?"

The Soviet troops were exercising vigorously the best part of eight hundred yards away.

"Fitness or keeping warm. Gotta be keeping warm. Only a complete lunatic would be out in this cold."

Gesualdo kept a straight face and looked square at the man by his side, who had struggled through the snowfall from the battalion CP.

"Yep. No arguments from me on that score."

"Fuck off, Captain."

"Rank has gone to your head I see. Used to be that you were a nice guy."

"I'm still a nice guy... just not to you. Anyway, like I said... only a lunatic would be out in this cold if a warm bunker was available."

"Best we make sure we bring some along when we occupy their house then, Lukas."

"Yep."

They both dropped their binoculars at the same time, looking like performing artists with the precision of their movement.

Major Lukas Barkmann tapped out a cigarette and lit up.

"Yeah... well anyway... I'm here to see your updated planning, should we have to go and kick their asses along a'ways."

"Let's get back in the warm then, but there's little change, except for some new fire missions based the latest aerial intel."

"The Colonel wants it all just so, and he's still got the hots for you after that punch up with the Brits."

Barkmann referred to a mass brawl that involved B Company and a bunch of British soldiers from the Queen's Own Cameron Highlanders that wrecked a fashionable establishment in Linz.

"You're top of his shit list, Captain Gesualdo, and I suspect it's as much for getting your asses whooped by men in skirts as for the brawl itself."

Al Gesualdo bristled.

"We did **not** get our asses whipped. There were a goddamned sight more of the lunatics than we could handle for sure, but we stood our ground."

"Not how he sees it, Captain."

"Well, the Colone..."

The bullet clipped the top of Barkmann's helmet long before the sound of the shot reached Allied ears.

Raised voices indicated that the officers and NCOs of Baker Company were rousting their men into the trenches, ready to deal with whatever threat had declared itself.

Barkmann checked his helmet and ran an enquiring finger along the new silver line.

"This a regular occurrence, Al?"

He knew it wasn't, but fell back on understated bravado to mask his nervousness at the close call he had just experienced, which Gesualdo identified for what it was.

"Hell no. First time, otherwise I'd not let the both of us stand up there watching them exercising. I ain't that stupid! I'd have just left you standing there and hope to get a promotion."

Barkmann threw a mock punch at his friend.

"You bastard! My report to the Colonel'll reflect your insubordination."

"Do your worst. Anyway, I'm gonna do the rounds, See you back at my bunker shortly. You'll report the action?"

"Roger that, Al, and yep, I'll get straight on the horn."

Whilst Gesualdo went round his troops, keeping heads down, assessing the situation, Barkmann sat alone in the modest bunker, holding his hands out over the stove that kept winter at bay.

Hands that were, despite his best efforts, trembling uncontrollably.

0942 hrs, Monday, 20th January 1947, Dai Ichi Life Insurance Building, Tokyo, Japan.

The USN officer was halted in mid flow as MacArthur failed to understand a term.

"Let me stop you right there, Commander."

"Sir?"

"What in the name of the Lord is a centrifuge?"

"Might I answer that, Sir?"

"Please do, General Groves."

"Sir, in layman's terms, it's a machine that spins at incredibly high speed, permitting the separation of different grades of the same element. In my line of work, that might be uranium 235 from uranium 238, the former being used for nuclear fission, such as in the bombs."

"Just like a spinning top, you mean?"

"Sort of, Sir, but spinning at an incredibly high rate."

"So what makes these so special?"

"They spin at the highest possible rate, Sir."

"Such as? Five thousand rpm? Six thousand rpm?"

"Sir, you must understand that it's difficult to say for sure. We haven't examined an actual machine, but the drawings and figures discovered in Nishina's office have been analysed and... well... I'm assured that the projections are a rate of fifty-eight thousand revolutions per minute, with a factor of plus or minus three thousand."

"Incredible. Almost a thousand revolutions a second."

"Yes Sir, it is, and yes, almost."

"How many of these things would they need to make material for a bomb?"

"That depends on how long they are run and how many are run at the same time."

"OK. How many do they have?"

"None that we've found."

"Then that's good news surely? Isn't it?"

MacArthur saw Groves' face and decided it simply wasn't good news at all.

"Sir, our intelligence agencies have ascertained that these centrifuges have been constructed... we've found some parts... evidence of delivery... we even have an engineer who assisted in installing the array."

"Array?"

"Yes... sorry, Sir... that's the term for a line-up of these machines."

"How many then?"

"Sir, we found a single building, previously unknown to us. It was empty, but contained the mountings for fifty-four devices."

"Fifty-four... which I assume is enough?"

"More than enough, Sir."

"OK. Thank you... Commander?"

"Sir. What we know is limited, but what we suspect is grave indeed."

MacArthur relit his pipe as he was assailed by words that meant nothing but trouble.

"Our best guess, based on the available intelligence, is that the centrifuges were loaded into one or both of the Special type submarines and removed from Japan, possibly to the Soviet Union, and if so, probably by way of Sovetskaya Gavan, or a location on the Soviet mainland as yet unknown."

"And then they went on this huge voyage to nowhere?"

"Given the belief that the submarines made it to the Southern Atlantic, that could mean they are anywhere, but it makes sense that they were being taken to somewhere Soviet controlled, or at least, not controlled by us."

"But if they've dropped the damn things off already, why the big voyage?"

"That's the issue that's exercising us, Sir. Maybe they haven't dropped them off and it was purely a collection of other equipment... and of personnel... and they're now on their way to wherever."

241

"Does Naval Intelligence have any other suggestions on the identity of 'wherever', Commander?"

"It would be speculation only, but the FBI and other assets have turned their attention to South America, the west coast of Africa... and Sweden."

"Sweden? Why on earth Sweden?"

"Just some noises that were apparently heard in the capital. Nothing specific. But the British are checking them out now, Sir."

Beria would have been delighted to know that his distractions had all been noticed and were taking focus away from the actual area the Allies should have concerned themselves with.

"And this briefing is being given to Eisenhower in Europe, and to the President, yes?"

"The President already had his briefing, Sir. It was he who directed the FBI to investigate in support of the intelligence agencies."

"One thing, General Groves. If these things have been operating since they disappeared, would they be producing the right sort of uranium by now?"

"Yes."

"Enough for a bomb?"

"Yes, more than one."

"Damn."

"That's why finding these machines is now priority, Sir."

"And once they're found?"

"We destroy them, no matter where they may be."

"And risk war again?"

"I think the President might say that it's better to risk a war now when we hold all the cards, rather than have one later where we may well face a stacked deck."

"Damn. Keep me informed."

1021 hrs, Monday, 20th January 1947, NATO Headquarters, Frankfurt, Germany.

Eisenhower's briefing had just finished and he was left to contemplate the incredible news with Walter Bedell-Smith, Kenneth Strong, and Omar Bradley for company.

The four leaders sat silently drinking coffee, trying to grasp the enormity of what they had been told.

It was Bradley that broke the silence.

"So, stop me when I go wrong... even if they do develop a device they ain't got anything to deliver it with. No rocket, no bomber of note, nothing."

"General Bradley," Kenneth Strong interjected, "I believe what was said was that we know of no such delivery system, not that they don't have one."

"Yeah, sorry. You're right. Either way, we've no idea where these things are spinning or how much of this U-235 stuff they're kicking out."

Eisenhower stubbed out his cigarette and waved a finger at no one in particular.

"I tell you one thing. I don't buy the South America - Africa thing. Neither do I buy Sweden. Wherever they are, the whole goddamned shebang has to be close at home, where the commies can keep it tight and protected. It has to be in Russia... somewhere in Russia. Heck, we don't know for sure that the stuff went in the subs, do we? Could well be that they unloaded everything on the Pacific coast and it all went inland by rail."

Strong spoke quickly, cutting Bedell-Smith off with a look of apology.

"Sir, I tend to lean towards the view, given the air raids that had pummelled the eastern seaboard of the USSR and the severe destruction of their rail network, that transport by submarine, even though it would take longer, was probably viewed as safer and more secret. We already know of five rail crashes that have occurred due to poor repair work. The Japanese were certainly and recently on the west coast of Africa. The evidence for that is quite clear on that, but I tend to agree that if these centrifuges are anywhere, they're on mainland Russia."

Eisenhower lit another cigarette and formulated his decision.

"Right. Sir Kenneth, you'll head up a group that has one task. Find out where these machines are. Hand off your normal duties to your deputy. I don't see any need for this to be quiet, do you? There's no orders to that effect, so be open and thorough."

"Yes, Sir."

"Suborn anyone you need, on my authority. One mission. Find them, and damn quick."

Strong nodded.

"Walter, get orders cut to our reconnaissance troops. I want new photos of everything, and all the old photos looked at again. I'll speak with Sir Stewart and Sam Rossiter... have them liaise with Sir Kenneth directly... but keep me in the loop."

Strong nodded again, spilling a drop of tea on his immaculate uniform.

243

"Find this equipment and find it fast, gentlemen. Spare no effort."

The meeting dissolved quickly, leaving Eisenhower alone with Strong, who had surprisingly remained behind, something that alarmed him greatly.

"I take it you have something else of concern... something you don't want to share at the moment?"

"Indeed, Sir."

Strong slipped a sheet of paper out of his briefcase and placed it in front of the NATO commander in chief.

"What am I looking at exactly?"

"Bear with me please, Sir. That's the original submission on German production of vehicles of all types, covering November last. I've pulled this page from the report. It deals with tank production, Sir."

"I've seen our report, so these figures are not news, Sir Kenneth."

Ike didn't mean it to sound terse, but it did.

"Beg pardon, Sir, but you will have seen these figures, but not the actual ones."

He produced another sheet and placed it next to the first.

Eisenhower didn't need a translator to notice the differences.

"Schwarzpanther production is different. Administrative issue?"

"Could be, Sir. I don't think so. The Germans keep pretty good records."

He leant forward and pointed a finger at the two clashing figure.

"According to their submission to us, they produced sixty-five of the new Panther type, twelve with the gas-turbine engine, yet their other figures show ninety-two, of which thirty are the enhanced engine type. That's not administrative error in my view... that's a deliberate change, Sir."

"Why?"

"That I don't know, Sir."

"Anything sinister in it, Sir Kenneth?"

"I really don't know, Sir."

"I'll ask Vietinghoff. I'm seeing him later."

"I'd strongly advise against doing that for the moment, Sir. There's something else."

He directed Eisenhower's attention to items simply missing from the report submitted to NATO.

Ike absorbed the German words and numerals, an all too familiar word.

'Panzer'.

He sought their repetition on the NATO report, but they were not to be found.

"Five Panzer VIIs... Panzer VII... refresh my mind please, Sir Kenneth."

"Sir, as far as we're aware the VII was an abandoned project from back in 42-43. There is no such tank."

"And yet they have five?"

"So it would seem, and it would also seem important to conceal their existence from us... for reasons I cannot advise you on, Sir."

"Again I must ask you, Sir Kenneth. Is there any sinister intent here? Could it simply be our ally wishing to produce a new weapon and surprise us with it at some time in the future?"

"Yes, it certainly could, Sir."

Eisenhower narrowed his eyes.

"But?"

"But..."

"But combined with the possible tampering with the submission, and the keenness of the new relationship with the Poles, you advise caution and further investigation, Sir Kenneth?"

"Quite."

He lit a cigarette and spent a few seconds looking at the two contradictory documents.

"Find out what this is about... let's have a look at their reports and see if we can turn up anything else. I'd rather not be looking over my shoulder at Allies if anything goes wrong, so please get this wrapped up soon, Sir Kenneth."

"Yes, Sir... and in the meantime... General von Vietinghoff?"

"OK, in the meantime I'll say nothing about it to anyone, especially our German allies."

"Thank you. I'll get on it right away, Sir."

Strong left the room, leaving Eisenhower more ill at ease than he had felt since pen was put to paper in Sweden all those months previously.

He sat back to consume a cigarette and order his thoughts, a process that was interrupted by an urgent knock and the entry of Colonel Hood.

'Surely the day can't get worse?'

The day got worse.

245

Civil war had erupted in Czechoslovakia.

1313 hrs, Wednesday, 22nd January 1947, Dankerode, Germany.

The combined assault had gone like clockwork, the Polish armoured infantry sweeping in past the suppressing tanks of the newly reformed 11th Panzer Division, 'Der Geist Division' as it had been known in WW2.

The two units coordinated brilliantly and Guderian could barely conceal his joy at how the assault was conducted.

Right up to the moment that the exploitation force, comprising a company of re-engined Schwarzpanthers from the 1st Deutsch Legion Panzer Brigaden, accompanied by some their own integral panzer-grenadieres, ruined everything.

One by one the gas turbine engine Panthers fell out of line as faults declared themselves, leaving only three runners to accompany the tracked Kätzchen vehicles loaded with heavily armed infantrymen.

What had been a joyous experience of military expertise turned sour quickly, and the commander of the II Deutsches Mechanisierte Korps [Legion] was quickly put in the spotlight.

"What in the name of the Fatherland's going on there, Willi?"

He gave the Generalleutnant no chance to reply.

"The whole unit's spread across the field... not by the umpires but by clear failures in maintenance!"

Again, the commander of II DMK[L] had no opportunity to offer a view or defence, as Guderian was on a roll.

"I want that piece of piggery investigated and the report on my desk first thing in the morning!"

"Jawohl, Herr Feldmarschal."

"If that had been a proper advance the grenadiers'd have been ripped to pieces because your tanks couldn't move forward without breaking down. What the hell are your maintenance units playing at, man?"

"The new gas-turbines still have teething problems, Herr Feldmarschal. We thought we'd sorted the cut-out issue... clearly not."

Guderian took another look across the exercise area, now littered with broken-down tanks and APCs unsure of what to do next.

He beckoned the general off to one side.

246

"Look, Willi. We simply can't have fucks ups like this. You know... you **know** what we hope to achieve in the future, and we'll need all our forces at their peak. You and your men were given the new Panthers because of your pedigree. Sort this... sort this now. Either these new engines are fit for purpose and we can look at the tactical advantages they offer, or we discard them and remain with the proven Maybachs. It's that simple, Willi."

"Jawohl, Herr Feldmarschal."

"I want that report tomorrow, and I want to know if we can fix these tanks in the field, or if they have to go back. If they go back, they can go to hell for all I care. I'll get you standard Schwarzpanthers as replacements and we'll let the engineers and designers sort it out at leisure."

"I'll oversee it personally, Herr Feldmarschal."

"Good. Now, I can't afford for a top unit like yours to be less than fully ready, so, with or without the new Panthers, you will have your Korps combat-ready by 18th February. Klar?"

"Alles klar, Herr Feldmarschal."

"Gut."

The two men saluted in turn and Guderian moved off to his vehicle and left the exercise ground in the possession of the seething commander of the II Deutsches Mechanisierte Korps [Legion].

He moved to the signals section, where the operators and overseers studiously avoided his gaze.

"Get me Maior Bauer immediately."

The operator worked the radio and the commander of the workshop unit labouring on the plain in front of him was soon responding.

"Ringelblume-six, Sonnenblume-six. I'm coming down to the exercise area and I'll expect a report as soon as I arrive. Over and out."

Bittrich tossed the handset back to the waiting operator.

"Inform all units 'exercise over'. Return all units to laager. Senior Officers meeting at 1800 hrs."

"Jawohl, Herr Generalleut... nant?"

Bittrich was already heading for his staff car.

1602 hrs, Wednesday, 22nd January 1947, NATO Headquarters, Frankfurt, Germany.

"Welcome back, Brigadier General."

Eisenhower was genuinely pleased to see his USMC spymaster returned from stateside leave.

247

"Thank you, Sir. Pleased to be back."

"I hate it when you lie to me, Sam."

Rossiter conceded with a shrug.

"You got me, Sir."

"Did you attend to the other matters?"

"I did indeed, Sir. The training schedule for Europe-bound USMC units has been adapted. Took some persuasion, but your letter helped."

The statement concealed many hours of USMC officers refusing to change certain aspects of training and falling back on their proven record in the Pacific, countered by Rossiter's insistence on increased attention to aspects that were more prevalent in Europe than in the Pacific theatre, namely cold weather training, anti-tank work, tank/infantry cooperation, and increased close-combat input.

Rossiter considered it indicative of the nature of the US Marine that the appeal for more hand-to-hand combat training was heeded immediately and with relish.

After all, he was a marine himself and the aggressive attitude only left a marine when he was put in the ground and, even then according to folklore, God and the Devil always trembled when worldly battle released some of the Corps upon them.

Ike checked his watch and realised he was fast approaching the time of his next briefing.

"Anything else of note... official note I mean."

"Went to some Navy missile tests at Chincoteague, plus spent a few days with the USAAF weapons testing unit at Alamogordo. You'll be shortly getting some interesting new weapons it seems."

"Another way of killing the enemy is always welcome."

Eisenhower made his statement evenly and Rossiter could not understand if it was humour or sorrow that he detected.

"Anyway, enough of that. What did you do for yourself, Sam? I take it you had some 'me' time."

"Sure did, Sir. Had a little time out at San Pedro with my buddy Howard and his damn plane. Man's obsessed but, that aside, he sure knows how to relax, and his girlfriend Jean is an angel... leastways I think she is."

Eisenhower raised an enquiring eyebrow.

"Well, it's a matter of public record stateside. She wants to be an actress...but loves the lifestyle Howie offers... but won't commit as she thinks it'll clash with her career. As for Howie... well he's pretty certainly in love with her. It's public knowledge that he's considering marriage to the woman... ... it's complicated, Sir."

248

"Oh. Well. I'd love to meet the great man one day."

"I'm sure that can be arranged, Sir."

"Thank you, Sam. Now, I must be on my way."

"Have a good day, Sir."

Rossiter threw up a smart salute.

"You too, Sam."

The briefing on the Czech situation had been informative, and the general situation seemed to have calmed down considerably, in as much as there now seemed to be active fighting in only five places.

The Czechs and the Slovaks had started shooting at each other as political ideals struggled for supremacy, the communists and the democratic nationalists fell out, creating a maelstrom of uncertainty set right in the middle of Europe, a maelstrom that affected the positions of both recent belligerents.

The USSR still refused to remove its forces from Vienna, citing the fluid situation in Czechoslovakia as the main reason, and the Red Army displayed increasing numbers along the Czech border, enough to properly police and monitor events according to their negotiators in Sweden, more than enough to move forward and occupy the eastern end of the ravaged country according to their counterparts at Camp Vár.

Both sides immediately agreed to halt all movement of their forces within the old national boundaries of the beleaguered state.

Both sides agreed to allow the Czechs to resolve their differences without direct military intervention or supply, and both sides agreed to actively bring both sides to the negotiating table at Camp Vár and honour any deal reached by the two factions struggling to achieve power in the region.

Both sides carefully avoided placing other restrictions, which enabled supplies to be moved in from all borders, destined for the faction of choice, supplies that often pushed the boundaries of what was and wasn't military.

A Curtiss O-52 Owl supplied under lend-lease, reconnoitring the fighting had a close run-in with a USAAF Thunderbolt, so close that it lost two feet of its port wingtip, provoking an angry confrontation over the Swedish negotiating table.

An accidental mortaring of a Soviet position by Slovaks brought about a swift and terminal battlefield response from the Red Army unit attacked, which drew nothing but a murmur of understanding and agreement from the Allied side of the table.

What tested the military and politicians of both sides was finding accredited parties to bring to the negotiating table in Sweden, and the absence of suitable candidates ensured that the fighting continued.

The briefing officer retired, leaving the handful of senior commanders to chew over the details.

"So not even the fresh snowfalls are calming them down, Sir."

"Which is surprising, Brad."

They both turned to the dapper Frenchman who had raised his finger to speak.

"We continue to have Czech units present themselves to us seeking anything from munitions to food."

De Lattre accepted another coffee from Simpson, who had got the role of drinks officer, as he was junior rank in the room.

"Thank you, General. It is difficult for us, especially when we have men who wear Allied uniforms seeking our help. My men do what they can to help."

French and American forces were responsible for the Czech sector, and within de Lattre's area were the soldiers of the Czech forces that had fought through occupied Europe, side by side with the men who now stood aloof and unsupporting.

At least… that was the official policy.

De Lattre knew that items outside the agreed assistance limits had changed hands, up to and including vehicles, and he had done nothing to prevent it then or in the future.

For him the situation in the Czech lands was a simple struggle between good and evil, and he intended to make sure that evil did not triumph.

"I'm out of it obviously, all save some air assets that I've lent to our Gallic allies."

De Lattre raised his mug in a modest toast to McCreery's words.

The reconnaissance squadron had been a welcome supplement to his own air assets.

The group settled into silence marked with the occasional sound of slurping.

Eisenhower moved to the desk and fished out another new packet of cigarettes.

"Well, one thing's for sure, there's no advantage for us to exploit here. The weather's bad, the Soviets are tucked up nice and warm in their bunkers, so all we can do is sit this out and hope the two parties negotiate it to a stop quickly."

Stalin rubbed his hands in glee.

"Well, one thing's for sure, we can turn these events to our advantage. The cold weather means the soft Allies will be tucked up in their beds so, apart from their nosey aircraft, we should be able to act in support of our Slovakian comrades and help them gain the advantage."

"I agree, Comrade General Secretary. More agents should soon be embedded with the Slovakian military forces and reports will soon come back as to how we can best assist in ensuring an appropriate victory."

Stalin sucked on his bottom lip, a sign of frustration more and more frequent as progress on another matter was not forthcoming. He voiced his frustration for the umpteenth time.

"If only Raduga were more advanced, then we could exploit this situation even more… perhaps…"

"I understand, Comrade General Secretary. My sources inform me that there's no great progress since our last official briefing, although the centrifuge basing issues have all been resolved and performance levels are now considerably above expectations."

"That's good news indeed, Lavrentiy. Why have I not been informed before?"

"I rather suspect that the project director doesn't yet know himself, Comrade Secretary General. I refer to information only recently arrived with me."

Stalin laughed heartily, reverting to the peasant he once had been and, occasionally, was proud to let escape.

"Well done, Lavrentiy. Now, if you can magic some nuclear devices for the Motherland then perhaps we can move forward with our plans."

Beria joined his leader in a rare moment of humour.

"I can work miracles but magic is beyond me, Comrade General Secretary."

"Anything else?"

"Yes, a matter on which I am still unclear. It seems that the German intelligence officer Gehlen has been killed. According to GRU reports, by communist agents no less."

"Did you order such a thing?"

"No, Comrade General Secretary, and neither did the GRU."

"Why hasn't the woman informed us of this officially?"

Beria looked wholly smug.

"I rather suspect that the woman doesn't yet know herself, Comrade Secretary General. The information has only just arrived with me."

Stalin pondered that for a moment.

"So if not us, who... or was it some random personal event?"

"I am having this investigated as we speak, Comrade General Secretary. It comes at the same time as the death of a senior French intelligence officer, one who was known to have close relations with Gehlen."

"Connected?"

Beria waited until Stalin had got his pipe going again.

"Wholly different ends. One shot down in the street... a messy affair... no refinement. The Frenchman was part of a wedding party that was bombed."

Stalin raised an eyebrow.

"The wedding was attended by a number of the French legion... the bastard SS soldiers who fight for France. Apparently the perpetrator was a former inmate of one of the Nazi death camps. At first, sight a simple act of revenge."

"But?"

"But it may not be. The Frenchman was not killed immediately, but died subsequently in hospital."

"Go on."

"He was expected to make a recovery and his injuries, although serious, were not considered life-threatening. There's also the matter of a nurse who cannot be traced, something baffling the authorities."

Beria's memory failed him for once and he consulted one of his reports.

"Urszula Radzinski. She offered to assist at the makeshift hospital as she was in the area visiting from Krakow."

"Very good, Lavrentiy, but is this going anywhere?"

"There is no Urszula Radzinski... at least not now. She was liquidated during our occupation for acts of resistance."

Stalin puffed deeply, his eyes clear indicators of the processes going on within.

"So you think the two are connected. You think that someone took out two Allied intelligence officers. For what purpose?"

"That's the problem, Comrade General Secretary. I don't know. Neither do I know whom, assuming the killings were orchestrated by the same hand. When I do find out, I'll be closer to knowing the why."

"And the woman?"

"Nothing comes from her except that I've just told you. She's drawing a blank."

A knock echoed around the room and Stalin's irritation was aroused momentarily, until Kaganovich, Beria's deputy, hurried into the room.

...Four and a quarter hours previously...

In his assessment of Nazarbayeva's efforts, Beria was wholly mistaken, for the GRU had acted quite swiftly on both matters, once they had become known.

That Gehlen had been the victim of the street shooting had only just come to light, but De Walle was known to Nazarbayeva and she had taken a keen interest in events, directing some important assets to gather information.

Which was why she had taken delivery of an artist's drawing of Urszula Radzinski, drawn from the memories of hard-worked medical staff in the Falcon Palace.

She recognised the face... or thought she did.

GRU files arrived at her direction, and she and the staff worked through them one by one, trying to marry up the artist's drawing with photographs or descriptions of suspected agents on file.

Two possible matches were brought to her and quickly rejected, the suspicion more based on hope than substance.

Food and drink were organised and the afternoon grew long as file after file received close examination.

At 1605, an excited junior lieutenant sought Rufin's attention.

Within a minute, the young woman stood next to Rufin in front of Nazarbayeva's desk, holding a report from the SD section.

"Relax, Mladshy Leytenant... what is your name?"

"Rikardova, Comrade Leytenant General... Hana Rikardova."

"So, what do you have for me?"

The young woman held out the file in a trembling hand, her excitement working with her awe at being in her commander's presence.

"Comrade Leytenant General. I have shown this file to Mayor Rufin and he thinks this is who you seek, Sir."

Nazarbayeva nodded as she pushed her empty bottle and glass to one side and started to consume the numerous details on the jacket, particularly the numerous identities attached to the agent meticulously recorded inside.

Friese, Gelda.

Frontstrom, Elsabeth.

Grüber, Agneth.

Hoffmann, Lene.

Mallman, Irma.

Obermann, Hiltrude.

Vögel, Imke.

Von Fahlon, Viktoria

'A busy woman indeed.'

She set the file pictures to one side. Neither was of great quality but the likeness was undeniable and yet unconfirmable...

'... and yet it is her, I swear it...'

The words leapt out into her mind and were soaked up as a sponge consumes water.

She read aloud as she went, cherry picking the crucial sections.

"A member of the Ausland-Sicherheitsdienst Amt-E... which governed SS espionage in Eastern Europe if I remember rightly."

Rufin nodded, the smile set firm on his face.

'He's confident this is the one... we'll see...'

"Never directly linked to any known SD operations... however... this photograph comes from Oslo... ah, the famous Eddie Chapman..."

The photograph had come from their penetration of British Intelligence, as had a number of such photos, taken by the notorious double agent Chapman whilst he was in Oslo training other German agents.

"SD... and yet the Oslo operation was purely an Abwehr affair... interesting..."

She read on.

"Possibly involved in the assassination of Party leader in..."

She sat upright.

"Possibly involved the assassination of party leader in Bialystok. Believed to have infiltrated the underground cell... poisoned."

"Possibly involved in the assassination of..."

The list went on.

Nazarbayeva went to the first photograph, one of a much younger... err... woman.

'What's her real name?'

The one under which the main documents were filed as Mallman, so she went with that.

"A young Mallman."

She flipped the photo and read the inscription.

'3rd May 1920, Philipps-Universität Marburg.'

Turning it back again, Nazarbayeva took in the pretty face and the surroundings, assuming that the crowd were gathered in front of one of the university buildings.

She looked, her eyes wide open, desperate to take in every single point of the photograph.

An urgent knock was answered with a gesture and Rufin obliged by opening the door.

"Mudaks!"

Polkovnik Orlov walked in as the expletive exploded from her mouth.

The young lieutenant recoiled from the violent outburst.

Nazarbayeva held up a calming hand.

"Comrade Rikardova, please bring me the file on Rudolf Diels immediately. Abwehr officer."

Relieved to be leaving a room full of senior officers, Hana Rikardova almost ran to the records centre.

As she departed, Nazarbayeva handed to innocuous picture to Orlov.

"Irma Mallman... picture taken in 1920 at a university in Germany... in the background there... you see?"

The name had already been spoken, so it was easy for Orlov, and then Rufin, to identify the figure raising a glass.

"Diels."

Rikardova returned in record time and the folder of the new head of the Abwehr was quickly examined.

"Make sure this picture is copied and added to this file with cross-referencing on these documents, Comrade Mladshy Leytenant."

"At once, Comrade Leytenant General."

Again the young officer scurried off, leaving the three to ponder their find.

"Either of you think I'm wrong when I suggest that Diels and Mallman know each other very well, and that she was in the SD as a snooper for the Abwehr, as well as clearly being a competent field agent for the SD's assassination missions?"

They were with her so far.

"We have Gehlen murdered by apparently communist elements, but neither GRU nor the NKVD ordered the attack... so Beria says anyway... an attack that now places Diels at the head of the Abwehr. The same Diels who we can tie to Mallman, a woman with a background in poisoning, who is seen in the same location as a senior member of French Intelligence, who mysteriously dies when expected to recover..."

They both waited, although something was burning the fingers of Orlov's right hand, he decided not to interrupt the moment.

"Fuck coincidence. They're connected. I can smell it. Somehow, they're connected."

"Comrade Leytenant General, if I may?"

Orlov extended his hand and two reports arrived in Nazarbayeva's possession.

"The first is a report and pictures from an agent with the German police force. A man with an eye for detail and an excellent memory."

"What does it say?"

"The two men were indeed known communist sympathisers, although they were not GRU... and NKVD deny ownership as well. The fact that they were apparently known as such I find strange, for they were not apprehended... not even once according to our agent."

256

"Strange indeed, Comrade Orlov. Mayor, perhaps someth…"

A bottle slid easily out of Rufin's trouser pocket.

"Carry on."

"Immediately after the murder, a local photographer was allowed to take pictures. He took many… this one in particular caught the eye of our man."

"What am I looking at?"

Clearly the body of Gehlen was the object of the photographer's attention but Nazarbayeva understood it was not the focus of Orlov's thought processes.

"There… behind the wounded waiter and the man with the bag… in the hat…"

"None the wiser, Comrade."

"That's Vögel."

"What? Hans Vögel?"

"I'm positive, Comrade Leytenant General."

"Vögel… who works under Pflug-Hartnung… who reports to… mudaks!"

She threw the fiery vodka straight down her throat and held out the glass for a refill.

"They've cleaned house… or it's a power struggle that has ended badly for Gehlen."

"Or not, Sir… the second report may shed some light on matters… but I now understand that it raises more questions… worrying questions."

Nazarbayeva opened the file and took in every word of the Abwehr internal memorandum.

'Jochen Strauch assigned as bodyguard… reports meeting between Gehlen and De Walle… overheard the name 'Diels'… and De Walle promise to investigate matters in Germany…'

She placed the paperwork carefully on the desk and drained the refilled glass.

"That's it. They **are** tied together. It's not a house cleaning operation… Gehlen and Walle suspected something was going on in Germany… and they were silenced because of it."

Orlov tilted his glass in acknowledgement of her words and drained it in one.

"The German bastards are up to something!"

In minutes, Orlov and Rufin were on their way through the headquarters, redirecting staff from one set of files to another, trying to focus on what was happening in Germany that was so secret and important that two senior intelligence officers had been murdered to protect it.

Nazarbayeva completed her notes and sought an urgent connection to Moscow.

The connection was denied to her, although the clerk informed her that the General Secretary would call her back as soon as possible.

Taking what she could get, Nazarbayeva made another connection.

It was swiftly done.

"Comrade Leytenant General Kaganovich, Nazarbayeva here... yes well, thank you... but I need to quickly inform you of something. I think it's vital that the General Secretary knows as quickly as possible."

At the other end of the line, the deputy head of the NKVD made his own notes, pausing occasionally to ask a question, or confirm a point.

"Thank you, Comrade Nazarbayeva."

The connection was broken.

'Blyad!'

1312 hrs, Sunday, 26th January 1947, the Black Sea, 82 kilometres southwest of Sochi, USSR.

The Neva had once known as the 'SS-Essequibo', a ship on which thousands of Spanish had fled their homeland in search of sanctuary in the communist heartland.

The rocket arrived unseen, its speed defeating the eye.

Its arrival meant destruction for the old ship, which simply disintegrated as the missile struck her amidships.

The submarine missile system was now fully operational.

Man is the only animal that deals in that atrocity of atrocities; War. He's the only one that gathers his brethren about him and goes forth in cold blood and calm pulse to exterminate his kind. He's the only animal that, for sordid wages, will march out and help to slaughter strangers of his own species who have done him no harm, and with whom he has no quarrel. And in the intervals between campaigns he washes the blood off his hands and works for 'the universal brotherhood of man'... with his mouth.

Mark Twain

CHAPTER 186 - THE DRUMS

February 1947

Whilst the temperatures remained appallingly low, the forecasters reassured worried political and military minds that the winter would not be a repeat of the previous disastrous year.

Some projected that a relative normality would return by mid-March; some said sooner, some later.

Whilst the winter remained, agreements were reached on suspending the realignment of the front lines, again inspiring the Austrians to great protest as their capital remained in Soviet hands.

The cold weather did not prevent the two factions in Czechoslovakia from killing each other, and the situation continued to cause concern to both sides of the European No Man's Land, despite the slow but steady progress around the negotiating table in Camp Vár.

There were flare-ups in Ukraine and in the Baltic States, and even a clash between the pugnacious Australians and Soviet forces on the southern border, one that resulted in six Soviet dead and a standoff that lasted for nearly forty-eight hours.

That the standoff clearly took place in Allied territory was denied by the Soviets, even after a member of the Swedish military delegation visited the area and confirmed that the Red Army unit was over five hundred metres inside the Allied zone.

The most serious losses were sustained by the US Navy in the Northern Pacific, although not as a result of any Soviet interference.

USS Lake Champlain CV-39, an Essex class aircraft carrier, fell victim to a series of happenings that eventually required she be torpedoed by her escorts.

A returning Grumman Bearcat started events rolling by crashing onto the deck and cartwheeling into the tower.

The fire spread quickly, aided by the fuel load of the aircraft that had only just taken off and aborted its mission due to engine issues.

Secondary explosions apparently hindered the damage control teams, and subsequently negated much of their efforts when some of the fire-fighting mains were lost.

Internal explosions continued to ravage the carrier, preventing any close-in efforts to assist in firefighting from the supporting vessels.

An attempt by the light cruiser USS Tucson CL-98 to get water onto the burning Champlain ended when seventeen of her firefighting team were killed as the carrier side opened up in a huge explosion.

Tucson laid off to recover and the decision was made to abandon ship.

Six hundred and seven departed souls remained on board the stricken vessel as torpedoes from USS Rupertus DD-851 opened the hull to the ocean, and Lake Champlain slipped beneath the surface.

1651 hrs, Saturday, 1st February 1947, Dankerode, Germany.

The 11th Panzer Division performance was more than Guderian could have hoped for, given the events just over a week before hand.

None of the new turbine Panthers broke down, thanks to field modifications by the divisional werkstatt units, modifications which were even now being factory fitted and rolled out through other similarly equipped units.

II Deutsches Mechanisierte Korps [Legion] was the main unit on display, having the assault role, but the 11th had been assigned a wide sweeping advance, which Guderian observed from the BV-141 reconnaissance aircraft lazily flying over the mock battlefield.

The Poles performed magnificently but were outmanoeuvred, initially by a superbly unexpected oblique shift in the legion line of advance that cut between two of the Polish prime defensive units as they tried to relocate.

Secondly, the cooperation between the grenadiers and panzer elements was absolutely top notch, and Guderian could only watch in unfeigned horror as the Poles suddenly found themselves being rolled up from the middle out.

260

The final nail in the coffin was the speedy and accurate move by the 11th, who arrived in the rear of the Polish defences as they were attempting to reform for a third time.

Guderian had absolutely no doubt that the defending Polish formations would have been utterly destroyed has the exercise been the real thing.

He decided to be extremely gentle with the Polish contingent, whose sole error of note had been to not coordinate the withdrawal of two units.

Umpires on the field had decided that the day belonged to the German Republic, but that the victory would still have been bloodily achieved.

After debriefing and congratulating the senior officers involved, including a buoyant Bittrich, Guderian returned to his temporary headquarters and made a phone call.

"Good evening, Feldmarschal."

"And to you, Herr Kanzler."

"Do you have good news for me this evening?"

"Yes indeed, Herr Kanzler. I have managed to locate a copy signed by Remarque himself. I thought you'd want to know, in case you were still looking."

Speer could not conceal his glee and tried hard to remember the precise words he should use.

"That's marvellous. Danke, danke, danke, Feldmarschal. When do you think I could have it by?"

"Well, it's not yet in my possession, Herr Kanzler, but I should think I'll be able to get my hands on it and pass it to you by Monday week... the tenth I think."

"So soon! Excellent. That's really excellent news. Thank you. I bid you good night, Feldmarschal."

"And to you, Herr Kanzler."

Speer replaced the handset with studied care, his smile broad and unforced.

"So... you'll gather that was Guderian."

"I did, Herr Kanzler. Good news I assume?"

"Absolutely, Rudolf. The teething problems with the new engines have definitely been sorted and the final units are now combat-ready. He states that our forces will be able to respond to our requirements by 10th February."

Diels have suspected it to be so, but the confirmation drove him to shout.

"Great news!"

"Yes. Now we must look to ensuring our planning is perfect, and that we gather as much useful information as possible."

"Of course, Herr Kanzler, of course."

Speer allowed himself a moment of pause to calm his inner thoughts, during which he poured two cognacs for himself and Diels.

"And our Allies still suspect nothing?"

Diels raised his glass.

"What is there to suspect, Herr Kanzler? Our forces are just ensuring they're operationally ready and prepared for any eventuality. We're simply being the efficient and organised military that our Allies know us to be. To our forces."

Speer considered the toast and decided to up the ante.

"No, I think we'll drink to something greater. To our resurgent fatherland... to Deutschland!"

"Deutschland!"

1801 hrs, Monday, 3rd February 1947, Office of the Deputy Commander of Armoured Forces Training, Moscow Military District. Moscow, USSR.

"Please sit, old friend."

Yarishlov ushered Ramsey towards a seat by the roaring fire and moved towards the sideboard, where he poured two good measures of Dalwhinnie single malt, a case of which had been appropriated and passed on by the very man who was about to consume some.

"Na Zdorovie!"

They sampled the delights of the superb whisky in a silence broken only by the crack and spit of logs on the fire.

Yarishlov spoke first.

"So, your time here has been coming to a end, John."

"Yes. We're scaling down now that the main work is done. I must say I won't miss the bloody weather here."

"Me too."

"Oh? So you have some news eh?"

"Yes, I have. I have been transferred... somewhere being warmer in summer."

"Is this good or bad, Arkady?"

"Good for sure. I hating all this politics shit. I've new job training qualified tankers in battle practices. No more 'this is how you being in a tank, this is how you firing the gun'… perfect for me, John."

"Dare I ask where?"

"It's not secret facility but you will be understand if I, with regret, say nothing, except perhaps that it is near the Volga."

"I regret my knowledge of your country lets me down at this point. The Volga's quite long, but I'm assuming down south if it's warmer?"

"Another?"

Ramsey held up his glass for a freshener.

"Yes, down south. No more or I'll have the NKVD arrest you for a spy. Let us be happy but I will get to be proper soldier again."

The glass returned and they clinked them together.

"To your new post, Arkady. I hope it'll bring you joy."

"To your return home to your wife and family, John."

They drained the scotch easily.

"Now, we must leave for the goodbye reception. We'll talk more in my car."

The two friends had long since agreed that their conversations would not be the subject of reports to superiors, as were the official expectations for all such encounters between the different military groups.

That both actually did was suspected, and both men understood that the other was a patriot first, a friend second.

In the car, Yarishlov explained that he expected that the new assignment to the tank training unit would be a backwater, and that his career would stagnate, but he balanced that against the joy of being with proper soldiers again, as well as being able to pass on the lessons learned in more desperate times.

His wounds meant he would never lead men again in the field, so the new post was a golden opportunity, despite the modest nature of the facility.

That was something that Ramsey could wholly understand.

Although both his new jobs offered stimulation, there was nothing like the challenge of commanding men in the field.

The reception was a jolly affair, its highlight being Horrocks' rendition of Stanley Holloway's 'Battle of Hastings' monologue in Russian, complete with a more than reasonable attempt at Holloway's accent and style, which both confused and amused his audience.

Their hosts completed the evening with a drunken 'Kalinka' that extended well beyond the normal time and reduced in volume as more and more performers fell by the way side, succumbing to the excesses of the evening.

At 0800 the following morning, the new delegation took its place at the table, and the old group were in the air, nursing headaches and pleasant memories.

With the exception of Ramsey, who could think only of his friend.

Partly emotionally, as a man who has bonded with a fellow warrior and is then parted can be; parted probably forever, by circumstances beyond their control.

Partly professionally, as a man who sensed rather than knew that something was not as it seemed, and that a Major-General of Tanks with Yarishlov's pedigree simply did not get side-lined in such a fashion, and that his friend had to be destined for something more important than command of a training camp.

He would have been surprised to learn that he was wrong on all counts, although the fortunes of war would later conspire to make him right in the most extreme and bloody way.

1329 hrs, Wednesday, 5th February 1947, Raudonė, Lithuania.

'The Shield of St. Michael' had relocated after the births of four healthy baby girls.

Karen Greim had borne her daughter first, almost nine months to the day that she was incarcerated.

Next had been one of the Shield's fighters, who brought twin girls into an uncertain world.

The move had been delayed even as the group had prepared to move off, as Renata Luistikaite completed the cycle with another girl.

Now, the newborns were crèched with some of the older women and, Renata aside, their mothers were back in the fighting line.

'The Shield' had returned to a previous haunt, one from their time opposing the Soviet advance into their country in 1944, a spot that had remained undiscovered and offered them the advantages of fresh water and dense cover, combined with existing structures that needed little attention to make them warm and habitable.

The dense forest surrounding Raudonė, Route 141, and the Neman River offered them sanctuary, peace, and a chance to warm their bones.

Pyragius had returned to full health and Mikenas had resumed her position as his second.

Their conversation with Bottomley, through Cookson, was rudely interrupted by the appearance of Audra Karelis.

Beckoning Pyragius to one side, she softly passed on her information, accompanying it with gestures to add weight to her words.

The leader simply nodded and returned to the main discussion.

"We may have an opportunity. One of our scouts spotted some communists working on the riverbank at Pupkaimis. It would appear they are renewing a small jetty and creating moorings."

Cookson finished translating.

"Boats?"

Pyragius grinned, understanding that the Englishman had grasped the situation.

"Barges."

He fingered the map, indicating a place on the river that was not too far from where they presently stood.

"Two kilometres... no more, Sah."

"Ask our friend why the Russians would use barges."

Janina Mikenas answered the question.

Cookson smiled his way through the translation.

"A little less noticeable possibly? Easier to shift larger and heavier loads, plus, as she says, it's more difficult for the Shield to mine a river."

Bottomley smiled at the woman.

"So, the scouts think they're planning to sit into the bank at Pupkaimis."

Antanas Pyragius nodded, which reply Bottomley understood perfectly.

He also understood that Pyragius was a cautious man, and the fact that he had just moved his group to the area for recuperation and rest would probably mean that the Russian river convoy would probably go on its way unmolested.

The balance of that was the need for food and medical supplies, both of which had been reduced over recent weeks.

It took little time to decide that the convoy offered an opportunity that could not be ignored, but that caution dictated that they would steal their needs, rather than attack and destroy it.

Pyragius stressed his decision meant that no risks would be taken that could reveal their presence nearby, and any hint of confrontation then the raiding group would simply melt into the snowy night as if they were never there.

The plan would have to be constructed at the moorings, but the principles were established.

Previous convoys had consisted of barges towed by a lead boat, with another tethered to the rearmost barge to enable control.

When moored, they tended to be separated and tied up individually, which would assist in their chosen target 'accidentally' floating off downstream.

They would not be greedy and there were orders to make sure that, before sinking the barge, sufficient supplies were left to create the illusion that it was an accident and nothing was missing.

The best laid plans.....

2259 hrs, Wednesday, 5th February 1947, the Neman River, four hundred metres south of Pupkaimis, Lithuania.

They had taken up an overwatch position during the last of the daylight hours and had been able to watch the last of the barges being secured.

What was immediately apparent was the level of security.

Previous such convoys had sported no more than ten men, but the latest arrival was accompanied by a full platoon of what were clearly alert NKVD troopers.

Pyragius, ever cautious, sent out scouts again, and reports quickly came back about more Russians nearby.

A mechanised platoon in vehicles no one recognised had concealed themselves in the woods just north of Route 141.

Word also reached the Shield that a large force of mechanised infantry had billeted themselves in Pupkaimis for the night.

They had already hidden from a third group of mechanised infantry that had moved westwards towards Raudonė itself.

Bouzyk had sketched the new vehicles as best he could, snatching glances they drove past the concealed SAS unit. The presence of three T-70 light tanks further reinforced the suspicion that the river convoy was more than the norm.

Pyragius held a council of war and nearly called off the operation but the group's doctor, along to identify certain medicines, convinced him that the needs outweighed the risks.

The decision made, Pyragius made the signal and a group of 'civilians' approached the Soviet encampment, bringing with them music and alcohol and, more importantly to the NKVD platoon guarding the barges, women.

A simple hand signal initiated the mission, and the Lithuanian partisan leader watched as the two inflatables slid into the icy water, each manned by two SAS soldiers in Soviet NKVD uniforms.

Those at rest amongst the Soviet platoon were very much at ease, the unexpected arrival of such simple pleasures enough to keep their minds off their charges.

The dozen men who walked the perimeter were kept focussed by their officer, a man who had neither time for wine and song, or women for that matter.

But the night was dark and his efforts were not totally rewarded as patrolling guards spent less time near the cold water and more gravitating towards the sounds of pleasure emanating from around their vehicles.

The target had been chosen before the dinghies had slipped into the Neman, and the four SAS men silently and inexorably homed in on it.

There were three defined 'bays' into which the twelve barges had been pulled, one of them slightly irregular, which had dictated that the fourth barge had not been moored as the others, but instead lay side on to the bank and still in the flowing stream of the river.

What they had not counted on was the blizzard that had started as they had put their paddles in the water.

The heavy snow obscured a great deal; the ability to see was reduced to next to nothing in an instant and the noise of it was sufficient to mask the gentle sound of paddles moving water and override much of the noisy revelry from the other bank.

Members of 'The Shield' were spread out along the opposite bank, covering with instructions not to fire unless given a direct order.

There was a covering group a hundred metres away, concealed to the west and on the same bank as the convoy was moored, ready to react as Janina dictated. They were supported by the rest of the SAS contingent under Bottomley.

For now, the members of 'The Shield' lay low and held their collective breath.

Cookson motioned to the other dinghy and Corporal Tappett mirrored his actions, both men sitting up to tie a holding line in place before grasping the side of the barge and levering themselves upwards, knives at the ready.

The two NCOs swiftly moved around the small craft, but found no sentries.

Cookson nodded to Tappett who took station by the bow mooring line, where there was also a small gangplank.

His job was twofold.

Firstly to provide security as the rest of the small team deployed and secondly, when the time was right, to undo the mooring line.

Cookson moved amongst the cargo, seeing the tell-tale signs of foodstuffs and medical supplies.

'Fucking jackpot!'

He slipped up to the river-side of the barge and signalled with a shielded red lens torch, which sign was only just recognisable to the waiting partisans through the heavy snow.

Bouzyk and Cadbury were gestured aboard.

They tugged on the small lines secured to the back of the dinghies, signalling the bank that both were now unmanned

Bouzyk took station at the rear mooring and all eyes focussed on Cookson.

He pumped his fist and the lines went slack, undone, not cut.

Cadbury was at the bow and used his paddle to gently steer their barge away from contact with its companion.

The Neman then played its part, applying a gentle force to the barge, which started to move downstream.

All eyes switched back to the moorings, waiting for any sign of alarm.

But there was none.

Careful not to disturb the tarpaulins too much, Cookson was joined by Cadbury and some of the crates were shifted to one side, ready for when they could unload some of their prize into the dinghies or, hopefully, into waiting hands on the bank.

Downriver, Audra Karelis' group was entrusted with a vital task; that of 'catching' the barge.

With one party on the southern bank and one in a small rowing boat, lines were ready to throw out to the SAS soldiers, who in turn would secure them to the barge.

The other end would already be secured to the southern side

Pyragius hoped the barge would be nearer the southern bank, but took no chances, posting another force on the northern side with lines at the ready, just in case.

The barge, fickle and uncooperative, moved into the centre of the river, and remained almost central between the banks as it slowly approached the point where Karelis' line parties waited.

The river narrowed to about two hundred metres at that point, but even so, the rowers poured with sweat as they juggled to get their small craft near enough to get lines aboard the barge.

They managed… just… and Tappett swiftly wound the line around the bollard, carefully trying to get his fingers out of the way in case the line went taut.

It did, and he didn't.

Little and fourth finger disappeared between the metal bollard and the line and were immediately crushed.

Tappett added more pain to the mix as he bit his tongue in an effort to control himself.

Bouzyk heard the muffled gasp and reacted with incredible speed.

He grabbed the line and pulled it away from the bollard, allowing a moment's separation that allowed Tappett to pull his ruined hand out.

The Polish SAS soldier pulled out a bandage and wound it around the hand, leaving the trigger and third fingers exposed.

The two exchanged no words and Bouzyk slipped back to his position, missing Tappett's nod of gratitude.

By now the barge was nearly at the bank and shapes materialised through the snow, quickly resolving into waiting partisans.

With the hand injury, Tappett's contribution to shifting some of the load was greatly reduced, and he quickly swapped with Cookson and became the lookout.

It was Cookson who first spotted that not all was as it seemed.

"What the bleeding hell is that?"

Said to no one in particular, it drew both Cadbury and Bouzyk to the gap he had just created.

No one could supply the answer, but the metal drum carried more than enough warning markings indicating a horrible death that none of the three doubted it was something special, and very, very deadly.

Cookson risked a quick look with his red muffled torch and saw that inside the stack of supplies there were ten, possibly twelve such metal drums.

Knowing Bottomley was on the other side of the river, the decision fell to the SAS sergeant, and he swiftly processed the details.

"We need one... but fucking carefully does it, boys. Slow and steady."

Slow and steady became less likely as the night was riven with sounds of automatic weapons, away up river for sure, but still close enough to impart urgency to the recovery process.

The partisans beckoned for more supplies but Cookson stood firm.

"No! We only take a little. They must think it's lost, not stolen."

Pyragius arrived and stepped in to the discussion.

"The man is right, my children. We have enough now... we must leav..."

"No, Boss. We can't yet. We have to take one of these. It's important."

"What is it?"

"Haven't got a clue. Metal drum filled with something very nasty."

"How big?"

"Hundred litres."

"We can't carry that. Come on. Let's sink the barge and be on our way before whatever that is up there comes down here."

Pyragius slapped one of his men on the shoulder, encouraging him to pick up one of the boxes with him.

"Come on, my children, let's get our booty home."

"I'm not talking about carrying it... the dinghy will take it. We'll float it away and hide it for now. I need one of your men... just for a few moments."

The partisan leader calculated the stolen supplies and the hands available.

"Norkus... help them and then follow on. Stay safe."

He slapped the man on the back and turned back to Cookson.

"Then you're on your own. See you back at the camp. Let's move!"

The whole partisan unit disappeared into the night in an instant, leaving the three SAS men to move the drum as Norkus pulled the barge in tighter to one of the dinghies.

"Parbuckle."

Cookson gave the order and slipped up to the stern where Tappett was watching the east for any signs of what had caused the burst of fire.

"How's it going, Tappers?"

"Nowt, Sarnt. Nowt at all. Firing stopped a'while back. Now nothing."

"And yer hand?"

"I'll have to wank with the left forra while, but I can still fire a gun if that's what yer asking."

"Keep sharp. We'll sink the fuckers shortly. We're using the dinghies…"

Tappett went to comment but he barely drew breath.

"I'll explain later. We're going out by dinghy, and we're taking something nasty with us. Be ready on my shout, Tappers."

"OK, Sarnt."

Cookson slithered back to the waiting pair and saw that the drum was ready to lower.

A parbuckle was a simple use of a line to lower a round object, and the process was quickly initiated, the two men slinging the heavy barrel with relative ease, thanks to the looped line.

The drum sat in the dinghy quite snugly and Cookson dropped gently off the barge onto it, recovering the line from his two men, and using the ends to secure the barrel as best he could.

"Front and back… we'll tie the other alongside it… it'll take all of us."

Bouzyk and Cadbury understood and waited patiently as the two dinghies were secured together.

"Norkus. Throw them the line now. Thank you."

The partisan undid the securing line and threw accurately. With a simple salute, he disappeared into the snow.

The barge moved along, again under the influence of the flowing river.

Cookson pulled himself back aboard the vessel and hissed at Tappett, who moved back to the bow.

271

"Choc, you babysit the bloody thing. Tappers, you get yourself in and comfy. For fuck's sake be careful of whatever that is. Boozy and I'll spring the boards. Cast off if you think you're in bother, but I'd rather not go for a dip. Move."

Whilst the two men slipped over the side and onto the 'raft', Bouzyk and Cookson dropped into the bottom of the barge and sought the best way to sink the barge 'accidentally'.

The drain plug was an obvious target but allowed surprisingly little water in, so they sought other methods, each of which seemed terminally noisy in the circumstances.

A crowbar helped with one of the more rotten members, but the water stubbornly refused to flow through the weakened timbers.

"Fuck it."

Cookson reached around and pulled out his pistol, a CZ-27, onto which he attached a silencer.

Four shots created a weakness that Bouzyk quickly exploited, disguising the bullet holes.

Water burst in through the damaged hull.

"That's the fucking boy, Boozy. Over the side with you."

The water level grew steadily and it was obvious that the barge was doomed.

However, the removal of some crates had made the load less balanced and the barge quickly assumed a lean, one that worked against Cookson's attempts to climb out of the hold.

As the angle grew worse, part of the load shifted and the barge rolled, allowing the water over the side and into the hold to complete the job.

It sank.

The SAS team had cast off so that the barge didn't carry them down, but kept a loose hold on the sinking vessel to help get Cookson off.

The sergeant scrabbled up to the edge of the barge, now the only dry part, and rolled over towards the dinghies.

In a moment of petulance, the sinking vessel lurched and opened a gap roughly the size of an SAS NCO, through which Cookson dropped into the freezing cold water of the Neman River.

Rough hands grabbed at the floundering man and brought him upright at the side of the dinghy.

"Fucking hell. Me bollocks have done a runner!"

Laughing softly, Boozy and Choc pulled their leader into the dinghy, the belch of air from the barge signifying the exchange as the river gave up Cookson and claimed the barge.

The NCO's teeth were already chattering as his soaked body as exposed to the wind that now drove the snow even harder.

The snow burst into a whiter light.

"Flare!"

It was stating the obvious but Bouzyk said it anyway.

More flares rose and the firing started up again, this time closer and decidedly more threatening.

The tell-tale chatter of an MG-42 declared that the north bank group had run into trouble.

The plan had allowed for them to remain in overwatch whilst the barge was looted, and Cookson calculated that they should have already moved off, but the evidence of their continued presence was unequivocal.

"Paddle into the left bank!"

Cookson led my example and his small oar bit into the water.

He explained in between strokes.

"Tappers, keep a sharp lookout on the left. There's a stream… saw it on the map… drops off the main river… we get into there…"

He stopped as he pondered whether or not the contents of the drum were heavier or lighter than water.

"We either sink the bastard, or hide it. Whatever the fuck… we get outta here sharpish. You got me?"

The heavy breathing men muttered something that Sergeant Cookson took for understanding.

"On the left, Sarnt!"

'Shit… too close…'

"Paddle like fuck, boys!"

Despite their efforts, it seemed that they had missed the entrance to the small stream, until Cookson threw himself into the icy waters once more and made the short distance to the bank.

He caught the thrown line and quickly tied it to a tree.

Together with the renewed efforts of the two and a half oarsmen, his efforts on the line overcame the flow of the river and the 'raft' was pulled back up and into the stream.

Cookson moved quickly along the bank, pulling his men and the barrel after him.

He rounded a sharp left turn in the stream and neatly fell into a concealed hollow, the heavy splash bringing cries of enquiry from his men.

Cookson waved his hand to show he was fine, and quickly reasoned his present bathing area would be perfect for hiding the

273

barrel, if not in the stream then under the vegetation and snow that had obscured the water.

He could feel himself turning blue so moved appropriately.

"Move… get 'em undone and I'll pull the plug on it."

As Bouzyk and Cadbury undid the ties, Cookson decided to deflate the boat and leave it under the barrel. They only had two and waste was abhorrent to him.

He waited to see if the barrel floated and breathed a mighty sigh when it dropped below the water and settled on the bottom.

Dropping his head beneath the water, his hands ran around the barrel, discovering that it was prevented from rolling by a large piece of wood stuck in the bed.

He quickly pulled the line tight around the barrel, made some knot, something his trainers would probably have lost sleep over, and secured the other end to the base of a small shrub, making sure as best he could that it couldn't be seen in a casual inspection.

The dinghy had moved a little away, despite the efforts of the paddlers, and Cookson found himself having to swim a few strokes to get back to it, where he was quickly hauled aboard.

"Who the hell do you think you are? Bleeding Esther Williams?"

"Not now, Choc… in fact, not ever… I'm sodding frozen!"

Tappett started rubbing his sergeant's body violently.

"You need to get moving…. Get out of these clothes, Sarnt. Otherwise…"

"Otherwise fuck all, Tappers."

The firing had taken on the proportions of a full-scale battle, and Cookson had other priorities.

"Move it… Viking power!"

It was an old joke from an operation they had undertaken in Norway.

The paddles bit into the water at double the pace, and the remaining dinghy carried the four weary men away from whatever was happening.

Cookson wasn't sure. But he had a feeling that the small stream joined back up with the main river again, and he was delighted to be proved right as the dinghy once again came under the influence of the faster flowing main watercourse.

His original plan had been to move overland back to the river, dinghy in hand, but his luck had held and even the Neman lent a hand, grabbing hold of the four men's craft and pushing it inexorably towards the north bank.

"You throw ok, Tapper?"

274

"I'll do, Sarnt."

"Stand ready."

If the partisans had not all disappeared, there should be a two man party on the riverbank, marking the spot where there was a track to take them north of Route 141 and back towards their base.

Again, lady fortune smiled and the snow parted sufficiently for the two female partisans to be spotted.

Tappett threw the line and the two women pulled it in vigorously, almost spilling the corporal from his perch.

The dinghy bumped against the bank and the four men were out and on firm ground in under three seconds.

Bouzyk took the hauling line and pulled the dinghy onto the grass, where he opened the valve to collapse the inflatable.

The firing seemed to have followed them and their expert eyes started to pick out muzzle bursts amongst the snowflakes.

"Move out. Up and over the road pronto."

He grabbed part of the dinghy and he and Boozy ran side by side, pressing on various parts in an effort to exhaust all the air.

There as a sound like an angry wasp, and another, as bullets fired at someone else came close.

An explosion illuminated the road to the east, and moving figures became apparent.

"That's our lot for sure."

Cookson dropped into cover by the roadside, the very core of him chilled beyond description.

His strength started to ebb at a greater speed.

"C'mon Sarnt. We gotta get you into the dry and warm."

Tappett took a closer look and made a decision.

He used sign language to cajole one of the women to part with her spare blanket.

Cookson seemed almost drunk as he flopped around whilst Tappett wrestled with the soaking camouflaged jacket.

He got it off and the dry blanket around his commander's shoulders after some effort, during which he knew he had not done his damaged fingers any favours.

"Boozy, Choc... grab the Sarnt. He's fucked up bad. We need to get him out of here damn fast or he's a goner."

A scream close by made them all grab for their weapons again, all but the now unconscious Cookson.

Out of the snow came two partisans, supporting a third who was leaking vital blood from a number of important places.

Tappett stepped up and motioned the party to the side.

He examined the woman and quickly established that she was beyond help.

The bigger of the two men picked up the body and slung it over his shoulder.

'The Shield' did not abandon its own.

More figures moved back down the road and dropped into positions in and around the SAS group.

Bottomley arrived with the rest of his men and the partisan rearguard and immediately took command.

"What's up with the Sarnt?"

"Hypothermia, boss. Went in the water a coupla times."

"Right. Get yourselves away sharpish. Janina, send some of your people with them please."

Mikenas snapped her fingers at a group of four who almost swept the three SAS men up as they moved away.

More bullets zipped through the air around them, and the MG-42 spat back, scoring hits from the sounds of distress that greeted the controlled bursts.

Bottomley beckoned Mikenas to one side.

"We'll take the main party off the road here. We need a group to fall back up the road... continue to lead them on... for at least ten minutes."

Janina Mikenas understood, and also understood what the order might entail for the distraction group.

"Audra!"

Karelis flopped beside her leader, fresh blood flowing from a nasty gash in her cheek.

"You alright, Audra?"

"Scratch. Fell as I got out of the boat. Nothing to it."

Mikenas gave Karelis her instructions, hugged the older woman, and sent her friend and six men to their deaths.

The main group moved away quickly, the rearmost partisans doing everything they could to disguise the traces of movement, mainly with little success.

The return route had been chosen because there were some exposed rock surfaces that would help mask the direction the partisans took, but for now they relied on the distraction provided by Karelis' party.

The firing seemed to be getting further away, and the rearmost men sent a message forward reinforcing the view that the subterfuge had worked.

Keen to take advantage of the 'victory' earned by the sacrifice, Mikenas and Bottomley drove the force on to greater efforts.

The events of that night were slowly pieced together by both sides, who arrived at very different conclusions.

From the Soviet viewpoint, the local villagers had distracted the NKVD guards with their drink, food, and flesh, to permit the Lithuanian partisans to mount an attack.

That the commander of the convoy had arrived on the scene before they were in position and ordered the execution of the villagers had thrown the partisan's plan completely out, which meant that the guarding troopers were able to protect their charges and inflict a significant defeat on 'The Shield', counting fifty-nine dead partisans, whilst sustaining twenty-one dead and an equal number of wounded themselves.

Despite extensive questioning, the old woman and sole surviving man they had captured gave up no significant information, even when roasted alive and skinned.

The report concluded that the loss of one barge was caused by nothing more sinister than an accidental uncoupling of the mooring line.

Most of the load had been recovered, a few cases of food and medical supplies having been washed away.

A nearby Soviet engineer unit was seconded to help with the recovery of some of the barge's load, and the report initially indicated that ten of the twelve drums were recovered.

An addendum later reported that one of the missing drums was found at the engineer unit's base, surrounded by dead and dying men.

Volunteers dug a communal grave for the seventy men who died and the corpses were first incinerated before being buried deep and NKVD clear-up teams dealt with the survivors.

One drum was left unaccounted for, and special diving teams were to be flown in to help locate it.

What really happened was different in many ways.

The partisans received word that Audra Karelis and one other had been taken alive, and then accounts arrived of their screams and suffering, before one final message told of their refusal to bend and death under the torturer's blade.

Partisan stocks of food and medical supplies had received a welcome boost, but less than had been hoped, for which Cookson was eyed with some annoyance.

The SAS had lost no one, but Tappett and Cookson were casualties, whereas the partisans brought home only five wounded, but left fourteen of their brothers and sisters lying in the snow.

The villagers of Pupkaimis accounted for the rest of the bodies in the Soviet report, a total that was added to subsequently, when the surviving villagers were herded into the Neman to die.

The losses had been severe for 'The Shield', particularly those of Karelis and Lukša, and even the prospect of some important item falling into their hands failed to raise the collective morale.

Some days later, the story of the Soviet engineer unit reached Pyragius' ears, and the barrel took on an almost sinister significance.

Without prompting from Bottomley, the partisan leader understood that the clearly dangerous contents of the barrel were suddenly extremely important, and plans were laid to recover it.

0900 hrs, Friday, 7th February 1947, Semipalatinsk-21, Kazakh SSR

At 1500, scientists and engineers at the new secret complex successfully created a 'rainbow'.

It was an extremely small device, but it proved that they could make a device that would work.

The Soviet Union entered the Atomic age.

The scientists and engineers spread throughout the Soviet Union now had a three-week deadline to satisfy their immediate orders and produce four Izdeliye 500 mini-bombs, exact copies of the moderate yield device that had ravaged the Kazakh countryside, and somewhat longer to satisfy an order for eight Izdeliye 501s, their best effort to copy the US atomic device, based upon their direct knowledge of the Pumpkin bombs.

1759 hrs, Sunday, 9th February 1947, the Neman River, four kilometres west of Pupkaimis, Lithuania.

Cookson dropped into the freezing cold water and immediately found the drum.

The line was still as he had placed it and recovery proved easier than expected.

Inflating the dinghy was swiftly achieved and within ten minutes the barrel was safely in the inflatable and being towed across the Neman to rendezvous with a horse drawn sledge, whilst Cookson, this time properly equipped, exchanged his sodden clothing for warm and dry replacements.

With the barrel safely hidden underneath a load of hay, the old crone guided the bag of bones that could once have been a horse towards the selected hiding place, a small weather-beaten barn just south of Bartiškiai.

Once there, the barrel was hidden in a specially prepared pit, but not before Bouzyk had recorded all the details in a sketch.

At Bottomley's insistence, a Westland Lysander was dispatched to pick up the vital information.

It didn't make it, for reasons that would never be known.

Two nights later, another aircraft made the attempt and it arrived safely, dropped off some morphine, and took the sketch and other intelligence materials back with it, its wheels on the cleared field for less than two minutes.

Whilst the Lithuanian group knew the barrel contained something nasty, they had absolutely no idea of the hurricane they had just unleashed upon the Allied intelligence agencies.

So they went about the business of christening the four new arrivals whilst the world changed around them.

The discovery of truth is prevented more effectively, not by the false appearance things present and which mislead into error, not directly by weakness of the reasoning powers, but by preconceived opinion, by prejudice.

Arthur Schopenhauer

CHAPTER 187 - THE BITCH

1515 hrs, Tuesday 11th February 1947, Chihkiang Air Force Base, China.

Lieutenant General Ennis C Whitehead, C-in-C PACUSA, the unified command group for the US Air forces in the Pacific, watched through the two-way mirror as one of his Colonels went back over the startling information one more time.

His scheduled visit to the headquarters of the 14th US Air Force had coincided with the delivery of the unkempt man sat opposite the neatly turned out USAAF colonel.

Normally he would not have dirtied his hands in such matters, but the Chinese military personnel who brought the prisoner were wholly insistent that a most senior officer should speak with their charge, a man who claimed to be a Japanese officer in possession of important information.

His claim had saved his life, for most Japanese who fell into the hands of their archenemies lived but a few brief heartbeats more.

Yukio Kikutei had been precise in his words, his English impeccable, as befitted a man who had attended Cambridge University.

The information he delivered, all kept in his head, chilled every listener to the very core.

Kikutei, or to give him his full dues, Major the Count Yukio Kikutei, was a former officer of Unit-731 and, as personal aide and confidante of its second commander, Lieutenant General Masaji Kitano, was privy to every little grubby secret and despicable act attributable to the inappropriately named 'Epidemic Prevention and Water Purification Department' of the Kwantung Army.

"So what's so goddamned important that you wake me up like that, Walter?"

"Sir, if you'll grant me a moment please."

Eisenhower took his place at the front of the hastily arranged chairs and took alternate swigs and puffs, clearly extremely unhappy at being rousted out on what was rostered as a day off for him.

Bradley, in Frankfurt to enjoy a relaxing day's golf with his commander in chief, looked glummer than usual as he clattered through one of the doorways, almost tripping on the recently installed carpet where it terminated in a metal strip.

"Where's the goddamned fire, Walter? Morning, Sir."

Eisenhower indicated the chair next to him and Bedell-Smith found himself under the glaring eyes of two unhappy men as he gathered the last elements of his briefing.

Eisenhower had, in his half-asleep state, approved Bedell-Smith's request that every two star and above in the headquarters be pulled in for the briefing, and pretty soon senior officers of all shapes, sizes, and nationalities drifted in.

Von Vietinghoff walked in with precise movements looking like he had just spent hours on his uniform and grooming, causing Ike and Bradley to share a look of exasperation, given their own delicate states.

Eisenhower spotted Patton amongst a group at the back and decided to let it ride, not wishing to cause a scene by ordering the General without portfolio from the room, or more accurately, not feeling up to the confrontation.

It had been a long night and the lack of sleep was taking its toll.

Colonel Hood, looking as tired as Ike felt, slipped in through one of the side doors and passed Bedell-Smith a piece of paper.

The briefing could commence.

Some of the language used was difficult for the translators to get right, and they had several attempts at some of the names used.

281

Okunoshima.

Sovetskaya Gavan.

Lewisite.

Mustard Gas.

Bubonic Plague.

Anthrax.

Cholera.

That the Japanese had released fleas carrying the plague in China and in the initial stages of the new war was already known, but the full extent of the activities of facilities like Units 100, 516, 731, and 1644 were suddenly laid bare before them, as the recently discovered information was revealed in all its horrible glory.

The listening officers started to shift more uneasily as the evidence that much of the Japanese research, and probably considerable amounts of the product of it, had been willingly handed to the Soviet forces.

Hand in hand came the suspicions about the Sen-Tokus, and the possible progress of a Soviet nuclear arms programme.

Again the translators were challenged by the briefing.

Centrifuge was not a common word in Portuguese, Spanish, or any of the other languages being whispered around the room.

All in all, it was a lot for the listeners to take in.

Whilst the briefing was eye opening, most of the assembled officers understood it was also as much about what was not known, and the glaring holes in Allied understanding became more and more apparent when Bedell-Smith took questions.

There were a lot fewer answers than questions, and the feeling of concern mounted the more times Bedell-Smith conceded a hole in Allied understanding.

Eisenhower eventually stood and held his hands out to calm the growing volume of discontent.

"Gentlemen, please! The purpose of the briefing is clear. Share what we know and highlight what we don't know. We keep all of this under wraps, but now you all know what the issues are, and will be on the lookout for any clue... any piece of information that may help us in finding out exactly what is going on... and there is something going on, and that something may threaten our future more than it's been threatened before."

The throng had fallen silent.

Eisenhower moved to the pedestal, ceded to him by his CoS.

"Gentlemen, like most of you, I was unprepared for this briefing. I anticipated one later this morning, but it was brought forward, given the nature of the new information received this morning. Some of this stuff we knew already, but the totality of it all is such that I feel I must act."

He exchanged a look with Bedell-Smith, who understood what his commander was about to say.

"The political masters will have their say in the matter, but I'm in charge of the Allied Forces in Europe, and I'm now ordering an increase in our readiness state. All absences will be reduced to an absolute minimum and units will be kept at fully operational levels, effective immediately."

That meant a lot of people were going to be extremely unhappy.

"I want all commands to furnish this headquarters with complete readiness reports before 1500 today."

He looked at Tedder and Cunningham who were sat together nodded.

"Naval and air patrols will be increased across the board. We're not going to be taken by surprise by anything. New rules of engagement will be issued as soon as possible, but anything that crosses a line is to be taken down immediately. If the Soviets have these... these... terror weapons, then we'll take no chances whatsoever. Remember what happened at Hofbieber. An unauthorised use, which explanation we've accepted, but none the less some of our communist opponents have already demonstrated their willingness to use such awful weapons and they'll not get a chance to again... not on my watch!"

He swivelled to speak to his CoS.

"Anything to add, Walter?"

"No, Sir."

Turning back, Eisenhower lifted his voice to ensure that the passion of his words carried to those at the furthest corners of the room.

"Gentlemen, we've no real proof that the Soviet Union is intending to attack us, but then... neither did we before December 7th 1941, not until the nips bombers came out of the morning and caught us with our trousers round our ankles. It must not... no... it will not happen again!"

The rumble of voices told Ike that he was fully understood.

"Remain vigilant, make sure your G-2s are all over everything that could possibly give us a clue to intentions... miss nothing... spare nobody... report anything at all suspicious to headquarters as per normal but also separately to the group under General Strong. I want nothing going astray here. I'm depending on each and every one of you. Good luck, gentlemen."

Chairs scraped as, to a man, the room came to its feet and returned the salute.

In short order, the room was clear, all save Ike and his CoS.

"Anything else came in I should know about?"

"No, Sir. The additional information from the Pacific arrived in the early hours. I considered it prudent to integrate it with the intended briefing and give it all in one go, rather than roust you from your bed, Sir."

"Thank you for that, Walter. I wish I was still there now… head under the blankets… not knowing what I now know."

"Amen to that, Sir."

An orderly brought in coffee and both officers sat in silence, drinking in the hot liquid and the atmosphere now percolating throughout the headquarters building.

An atmosphere that spoke of danger; of fear, and of urgency.

The world had moved closer to renewed war with a few well-chosen words, but Eisenhower had no other choice.

"Right, Walter. I guess I'd better let the President know that we may be back in a shooting war in the near future."

"Level shot, play it up, or play it down, Sir?"

"He'll have the same intel we have. He'll see it all from a political angle. Me… I see it as a soldier. I'll just tell it how it is."

Ike affected an official voice.

"Mr President, the world just got a whole lot more complicated."

Bedell-Smith angled his mug in acknowledgement at the black humour.

"I understand, General."

Others in the Oval Office were listening in on the conversation, and by their body language they clearly did not understand why the armies of Europe were suddenly standing to along the No Man's Land between the West and East.

"I'll take that under advisement, General. Politically, we'll probably raise the matter directly in Sweden in the first instance. I'll think on it some more, take some input from trusted sources, but I think your suggestion has merit."

Stimson's reaction was plain, but as to whether it was fuelled by exasperation at the Soviet's probable duplicity, or at Eisenhower's suggested responses was unclear.

"General, let me interrupt you there. I will not make a decision in haste. I understand why you have increased your readiness levels and taken the other precautions, That's laudable and, I repeat, I've no problem with it whatsoever. But let me be abundantly clear here. I will not, repeat not, undertake or sanction any act that could place us in the role of aggressor, and I will not act precipitously."

Truman nodded at Eisenhower's response.

"Good. I'm glad you can understand that. Now, General, your job is to make sure we are ready for another shooting war at the same time as you do everything you can to make sure we don't get into one. My job here is exactly the same. How best to do that, I'll decide directly and keep you informed, but I do suspect that political pressure may reap benefits, combined with your suggestions."

Truman wound up the conversation.

"Yes, thank you, General."

The other members of the 'audience' relaxed their postures and gently placed their listening pieces on the desk.

"Indeed, General. Let us pray that is the case, for now and for generations to come. Good day to you."

Replacing the receiver, Truman knotted his fingers together and flexed his hands.

"Well, to be blunt, I can see that we're not all carried by the strength of General Eisenhower's words."

Stimson looked up from the sofa.

"Again? We're going to go through it all again?"

"I do hope not, Henry. By God, I do hope not, and that's why we mus... excuse me, gentlemen"

The telephone rang, causing the President to stop.

"Hello... yes, well, put him through."

He placed a hand over the mouthpiece and successfully mimed the word 'Winston', causing a renewed rush for the listening pieces.

"Good afternoon to you, Prime Minister. What can I do for..."

Truman grimaced as he was cut short by his friend's interruption.

"Yes... yes... I've just finished speaking with him just now, I expect he'll be calling you directly, Winsto..."

285

Stimson arrived in time to hear the piece of information that had not been available at the time of the early morning NATO briefing.

"Say that again please, Winston."

Collectively, the US Administration's highest officials drew breath in a gasp.

"On February 26th you say. How did you come by this information, Winston?"

Churchill explained in the briefest way, knowing that the full information was already being disseminated to Allied intelligence agencies across the globe, albeit in a controlled and very top-secret way.

HMS Vivid, a British 'V' class submarine on silent patrol within the Black Sea, had trailed a number of large enemy submarines over a period of two days.

'A large enemy submarine was known to have surfaced in the Black Sea, and erected and fired a missile of a type similar to the German V-2 weapon. Periscope camera shots had been failures due to some water-seal malfunction, but the experienced submarine captain had not recognised the type of submarine involved, and had discontinued his periscope monitoring due to the numerous enemy aircraft that were overflying the area.'

Because of the extremely dangerous and secret nature of its mission, the vessel had not been able to report what they had heard and observed until back at their base station in Greece.

That report had been communicated to Churchill at the same time as Eisenhower was rousing his officers at Frankfurt.

Forrestal mouthed two words as Churchill was winding up his summary.

'Delivery system?'

Truman paled at the whispered question.

"Thank you for letting me know, Winston. You'll know what Eisenhower has done. He has some other proposals which we need to discuss, but I think I need to expand on this new information before that."

He nodded vigorously at the man in an office thousands of miles away.

"Yes... that would be fine. Should give us both enough time to understand more about this new development."

The same two words that Forrestal had introduced floated across from England and into the Oval Office.

"That is a possibility, Winston. Let us pray we are wrong. I'll call you this evening. Yes... yes... and please pass on my best regards to the King. Thank you. Goodbye."

This time Truman placed the telephone back in the receiver with all the gentleness of a chimpanzee with a new hammering set.

Without humour, he addressed Stimson directly.

"So, what do you think of Eisenhower's other ideas now, Henry?"

Stimson snorted.

"I still don't like them Mister President, but the need for them has become clearer than it was. In time, we'll praise General Eisenhower for his foresight. For now, perhaps we should simply pray that the world has not become what we now think it has, and work as hard as we can to prevent any renewed hostilities."

"Amen to that, Hen..."

"Not that it'll do any good, Mister President."

"What?

"It seems inevitable that war will return, clad in all its old horrors and resplendently garbed in the new weapons of death and destruction."

They all remained silent to allow Stimson to continue.

"We know... we've used atomic weapons, so we understand that they will destroy all of us if we come to further use, for there will be no control, no limit on their use once both sides throw that at each other. That German fellow, Brecht... he wrote something that aptly describes the situation we find ourselves in, and no matter what we do will we avoid what is to come."

Stimson flopped into a chair like a man exhausted by life.

"I saw a Brecht play whilst I was visiting Chicago last fall... Louis Schaffer ran a small production to test its stage viability. The Resistible Rise of Arturo U it is called. It's an allegorical work, set in Chicago itself and substituting a Capone character for Hitler. I remember one line from it... it struck me clear as a bell, Mister President."

He wet his lips as he summoned the quote from the recesses of his memory and burned the words on their minds with his gentle but powerful delivery.

"Do not rejoice in his defeat, you men, for though the world stood up and stopped the bastard, the bitch that bore him is on heat again."

Truman smiled at his weary warhorse.

"Let us pray that you're mistaken, Henry, and plan for you being right. So, Gentlemen... what responses do we make?"

287

Speer nodded, barely able to contain his excitement and pleasure.

"We must, of course, cooperate fully with any requests from NATO command. Our forces will respond immediately, Feldmarschal."

Speer stood and walked quickly around the desk, quickly pouring and handling two coffees, one for himself, and one for his military supremo.

"So, are we capable, militarily speaking?"

"If matters go as we foresee, then yes, we are capable, Herr Kanzler. However, matters rarely go as foreseen. We will deal with eventualities, provided our Allies remain steadfast."

"And from what we learn today, they have every reason to remain steadfast. Do we have any ideas about these weapons?"

Guderian took a sip and answered with a snort that came too close to dismissive for Speer's liking.

"Ha! Not that I know, Herr Kanzler. A question better put to your new master of the dark arts, I think."

It was well known that Guderian and Diels were not friends, and on the few occasions that professional requirements had placed them together, it was clear that the Feldmarschal had nothing but disdain for the Abwehr chief.

"A fair point, Feldmarschal. I'll speak to him shortly. We can use this increase in alert to mask some of our own activities, can we not?"

"Most certainly, Herr Kanzler. I'll move some units openly, rather than hide their redeployment as exercises. The Luftwaffe will step up their work of course."

"Excellent, excellent. We have an opportunity here, Feldmarschal. Stand ready to act immediately if it develops into what we need."

"Zu befehl, Herr Kanzler."

1847 hrs, Tuesday, 18th February 1947, 733 15th St NW, Washington DC, USA.

The sound of their lovemaking penetrated through the walls, carrying to the ears of fellow residents above, below, and to the side of her bedroom.

Normally, their liaisons took place somewhere clandestine, secrecy being vital for maintaining his political position, and her rank in local society.

However, today it was different.

Her call had driven him from his office into her arms, the sheer desperate need for his attention made totally clear by the explicit note that had been delivered to his office that afternoon.

Now, here he was, driving himself into the vitals of the woman who was his lover, confidante, and friend.

They had been lovemaking for nearly an hour and he had enjoyed every part of her body with equal vigour, but now he was nearing the moment of climax.

As he drove into her from behind she rose up, pushing herself onto him, appearing to hasten her own orgasm.

He came.

She came.

It was noisy and intense.

The two fell back onto the sheets panting with exhaustion, sweaty, sticky, and worn out from their intense physical acts.

"Damn but that was something, darling. Unbelievable, really unbelievable."

Olivia von Sandow rolled over and clutched the sweaty old body by her side, kissing her lover on the shoulder.

"Darling Humphrey... what a lion you are. I've never been so well fucked in my life, darling."

While her lips said one thing, her mind was working out how to end the evening quickly and pass on the information she had teased out of him during their marathon sex session.

As she had fellated him, he unburdened himself about his day... and the latest stupid panic by the boys in Europe... and the Jap chemical stuff... and their subs.

When she rode him like a rodeo bull, she taunted him about the matter, and he revealed the Soviet missile test and what it probably meant.

As he had sodomized her, he had clearly felt empowered, dominating her, taking her like a Viking rapist, and had been easily enticed into more indiscretions.

The revelation that atomic weapons were being released to the European theatre almost caught her out, but she continued to moan in time with his violent thrusts.

Her orgasm had been as fake as her love.

'Emergency... what could be more of an emergency than this?'

She kissed Senator Humphrey Forbes another time, before slipping out of bed and heading into the bathroom.

Outside, a watching German Intelligence agent noted the opening of the bathroom curtains to a certain position and understood the message immediately.

'She wants me to recall her.'

It was not until both windows were cracked open as well that he realised the emergency code accompanied the first signal.

He moved quickly, leaving his car door unlocked, and was quickly in the phone booth, spilling coins into the slot and dialling her number.

In the apartment, Olivia deliberately stayed in the bathroom, shouting at her love to take a message, which meant that Humphrey Forbes answered the phone

"Deputy cultural attaché von Sandow please."

"I'm afraid she's otherwise engaged at the moment. May I take a message?"

"Certainly. She is to report to the Embassy immediately. Thank you. Who am I speaking to, please?"

"I'm a friend... Randall..."

Caught on the hop, he used his middle name.

"Thank you, Randall. Immediately though please. It's a serious matter. I cannot say of course... state business."

"Of course. I'll see she gets the message immediately."

He replaced the receiver as the stunningly attractive woman, now partially dressed, exited the bathroom.

"Who was it, darling?"

"The embassy. They need you back there right now. Some sort of emergency. He couldn't say what it was... hush hush stuff, darling."

"Damn. I was looking forward to dinner and another round of fucking, darling Humphrey."

"Another time, Olivia. Duty calls eh?"

They both dressed and left the apartment, after Olivia von Sandow had declined his offer of a lift and called a cab.

In truth, Humphrey Forbes was slightly relieved, for he doubted he had the stamina for another sex session with the insatiable brunette.

His car took him home to his family.

In the taxi on the way to the German Embassy, von Sandow relayed all she had learned to her NKVD contact.

Replacing the phone, having verbally trounced his secretary for interrupting the briefing, Stalin replied to Beria's summary of the European situation.

"Excellent. We may have an opportunity here. Slow down any further withdrawals until we can assess the situation."

'Brrring...Brrring...'

Stalin answered the phone again, not attempting to hide his irritation at the interruption, the second in as many minutes.

"What is it now?"

Beria took the moment to stretch his legs.

"Yes. Very well. Put her through."

Stalin spoke softly, almost hiding the receiver in his collar.

"It's the woman, Nazarbayeva. Maybe she can add to what you are saying, eh?"

Beria shrugged a shrug that managed to convey both his doubts and his dislike of the woman.

"Comrade Nazarbayeva, what is it that disturbs my undisturbable meeting?"

Stalin's face remained the same as he heard nothing that Beria hadn't already imparted.

He closed his eyes and listened, appearing to almost daydream as the woman told her story.

"Yes, I'm aware of that. Comrade Marshal Beria was just briefing me in on these new developments."

The dictator's face changed, something Beria picked up on instantly.

"When?"

The thunderclap of Stalin's hand slapping the desk made his crony jump.

"Tell me this is a fucking joke, Comrade General!"

By his expression, it clearly wasn't.

"Confirm all this information immediately. Take the first flight available to Moscow and present the full information to the GKO at once. Contact my secretary. I'll ensure you have priority. Good day to you, Comrade Nazarbayeva."

Stalin held onto the handset and stared at it with unforced malevolence.

"Fuck."

He threw it onto the table as if to throw away the words it had just delivered to his ear.

"The GRU confirm your intelligence on the enemies' readiness increase, Lavrentiy. She also stated that the enemy has recovered information from our former allies, information that has led them to believe that there are rogue Japanese submarines still at large... and that significant items from their nuclear, biological, and chemical research products were sent to us."

Beria grimaced.

Moments beforehand he had assured his leader that such information was still secret.

"And the British saw the rocket test in the Black Sea... our fucking sea... where our Navy assured us no enemy vessel would roam. They had a submarine that was trailing our special force. It witnessed everything, so it seems."

Beria kept his mouth firmly shut.

"So, far from our plan being wholly secret, if the woman's right, then the bastards suspect what we have and how we're going to attack them with it."

The room fell into strained silence, broken by an unexpected rumble of laughter from the General Secretary.

"She's put one over on you again, Lavrentiy."

Beria had already worked that one out, but was surprised that Stalin had time for humour as Raduga stood on the precipice of discovery.

"We both serve Mother Russia and the Party, Comrade General Secretary."

Stalin laughed again.

"And you also serve another master of course, Lavrentiy. Yourself."

Beria knew he was being 'teased' but bit on the dangled bait in any case.

"I do all I can to serve the Rodina, the Party, and you, Comrade General Secretary. Yes, I am ambitious. Ambition is a good thing when properly channelled... you've said so yourself."

"Whereas Nazarbayeva serves only the Motherland and the Party... without ambition..."

"Perhaps that's her weakness, Comrade General Secretary."

Stalin stood and took a final large drag on his cigarette.

"Weakness or not, she doesn't play the political games

He made great play of crushing the ember out of the last vestiges of the cigarette and deposited the pieces in the full ashtray.

"Whereas you do. You see yourself as sat in my chair one day, Lavrentiy. Ambition can also be a bad thing if pursued too vigorously."

The report from Olivia von Sandow was waiting on Beria's desk when he returned.

Nazarbayeva was airborne less than two hours after her conversation with Stalin.

Given the information she had uncovered, she spent her time pondering the central issue.

Not the issue that they had possibly been discovered, or that the Allies were gearing up for conflict again...

...but the inescapable fact that not part but all of Raduga was still running, and that she was excluded from all parts of the operation. She had hoped that Kaganovich had been wrong, but clearly he was anything but.

Her aircraft landed at Vnukovo Airfield without her having arrived at an acceptable conclusion.

Finally, the powers that be had agreed to Bottomley's pleas and sent an aircraft.

The Lysander was down in the corner of the grassy field, having skilfully landed on the modestly sized cleared area.

A small handling party were manoeuvring the dangerous barrel into a safe position inside the fuselage.

Bottomley had decided that Cookson should accompany the material, partially because the man was still suffering from his ordeal, and partially because he wanted someone to ride with the barrel and ensure its safety.

That Cookson would also be able to provide first-hand information was also a bonus.

The plane had brought in a replacement NCO, and he now stood next to the SAS officer, observing the slower than normal turnaround.

"Six minutes. Hope you boys are normally better at their jobs than that, Sir."

Bottomley kept his mouth shut, his opinion of the new man already nose-diving.

At the end of the strip, the figures moved away from the little plane and the engine note rose, driving it down the greeny-white line and into the freezing night sky.

Bottomley nodded and saluted the hand waving from the observer's seat.

'Good luck, Cookie.'

On arrival at the Danish airfield, Cookson was met by a number of medical personnel equal to a number of imposing men of high rank, and a group of agitated civilians.

The medical personnel had his health in as their priority, whereas the latter two groups sought precise answers to pressing questions.

2357 hrs, Friday, 28th February 1947, Europe.

Group Captain Stagg had waited up to see what he had predicted come to pass, and it did, almost to the minute that February moved into March.

The cold night felt warmer, not greatly, but enough to detect for a man who was waiting for such a change.

"We were right. We were bloody well right."

With only a statue of some well-endowed but unknown ancient female deity for company, it was a one-sided conversation.

"It's going to thaw... and thaw quickly. We were right."

He got no argument from his companion.

Stagg, often maligned when his predictions in the inexact field he had chosen went wrong, celebrated his success with closed eyes and a smile.

He patted the statue on the shoulder.

"Nice chatting with you, old girl."

He returned to the weather centre as the reports of the weather change came rolling in.

Winter had come, and now it was going.

Which, Stagg conceded, was not necessarily a good thing.

It is easier to lead men to combat, stirring up their passion, than to restrain them and direct them toward the patient labours of peace.

Andre Gide

CHAPTER 188 - THE RUMBLES

March 1947, Europe

As March moved slowly forward, the snows across Europe melted, and melted fast, and the Czech infighting increased in tempo.

The thaw brought its own problems as roads became impassable and rivers became so swollen as to carry away some of the temporary bridges that proliferated throughout the continent.

Army engineers from all contingents on both sides of No Man's Land laboured to keep open roads, lay new airfields, and replace washed away rail tracks, all to keep the vittles of war flowing.

Refugees started moving again, less than before, many thousands having perished in the extreme cold, mainly from combinations of disease, exposure, and starvation.

The decomposing bodies presented yet another problem, and Army grave registration units found much work in towns, hamlets, and villages across the continent.

Military courts were kept busy, as men who had expected to go home on leave, or even be released from service, found themselves denied such privileges and rebelled against the decision.

Discipline became an issue that started to erode efficiency in some, but not all, units.

The Air Forces came close to violent confrontation on a number of occasions, particularly over the Baltic Sea and the Viennese enclave.

On land, there was one brief exchange between the Polish and Soviet forces near Lubawa, Poland.

The resultant seven dead and wounded forced angry exchanges over the table at Camp Vár, but the issue was swiftly resolved when the Polish commander on the ground admitted fault in a meeting with his Soviet counterpart, defusing tensions locally which eventually spread up the chain of command to the negotiators in the Swedish facility.

It was at sea that the major confrontations came.

0300 hrs, Saturday, 1st March 1947, Vinogradar Young Communists Sailing Club, Black Sea, USSR.

The base's lights had been gradually extinguished until only a handful of red bulbs contributed their modest illumination to the grand cavern that contained the submarines.

At 0300 hrs precisely, the great doors unlocked and silently moved into the open position.

At 0302, I-14 started to extract herself from the secret facility and make her way into the open waters of the Black Sea.

By 0340 the entire group of six submarines were out and the doors were already closing.

Raduga had commenced.

0201 hrs, Sunday, 2nd March 1947, the Baltic Sea, thirty kilometres due south of Rønne, Bornholm.

The sonar rating leant forward and screwed his eyes up, trying to isolate as much information as possible and allow him to concentrate on his earpieces and the 'something' he thought he had heard.

The frigate had stopped engines nearly forty minutes beforehand, a standard listening tactic for their passive detection apparatus.

HMS Loch Tralaig, pennant K655, was a frigate with a difference.

Launched on 12th February 1945 and commissioned the following July, she entered into a world where conflict existed solely in distant climes.

Intended for anti-submarine work, she was fitted with the latest technology the Royal Navy could supply, from the devilishly effective Squid ASW mortars, of which she boasted two, to the very latest versions of the best radars and sonars available.

She was destined for the Pacific, and journeyed across the Atlantic to the eastern seaboard of the USA as soon as her sea trials were complete and her crew judged ready.

The Portsmouth-based vessel docked in Portsmouth, Maine, where she was to be fitted with a new version of the WW1 US towed sonar array 'Electric Eel' as a reciprocal arrangement for British release of an improved 'High Tea' sonar system to the USN.

At the time her hull again tasted the cold waters of the Western Atlantic, she was the most deadly anti-submarine platform in the world.

Her reign was cut short by a crippling accident, which saw a fire on board cause two welding cylinders, acetylene and oxygen, to blow up.

The violent explosions and subsequent fierce fire wiped out much of the bridge, charthouse, and forward accommodation, as well as severely damaging the squid launchers and damaging their wiring system.

Seventeen crewmembers died and another twenty-seven were badly injured.

The errors that had permitted a small fire to ignite the two cylinders resulted in an unspoken sanction of the petty officer who had commanded the welding detail, and his posthumous recommendation for the George Medal was quietly brushed under the table.

However, three others of the ship's crew received the award and the report on the firefighting operations undertaken became a standard on how to fight a ship fire, as well as a permanent testament to the bravery and skill of her damage control teams.

HMS Loch Tralaig never made it to the Pacific, as she was repaired in the States and did not put to sea again until two weeks after the Japanese surrender.

Assigned to work with HMS Dolphin, the shore establishment based at Fort Blockhouse in Gosport, Hampshire, Loch Tralaig conducted mock attacks on submarines as part of their ongoing training programme.

HMS Dolphin was the main RN submarine training establishment, and Loch Tralaig put many a new submariner through the wringer, as she won her encounters with monotonous regularity.

Despite her obvious effectiveness, work in the USA and at home on similar vessels was slow, and there were only five such ASW frigates in existence when the world went hot again.

The Admiralty removed her from training duties and, along with one of her peers, HMS Loch Veyatie, she was assigned to the Baltic, operating along the north German and Polish coasts, all the way to the border with Swedish waters.

At 0202 hrs, the equipment, the training, and the expertise gained in hundreds of simulated detections, came together in deadly fashion.

0202 hrs, Sunday, 2nd March 1947, the Baltic Sea, thirty kilometres due south of Rønne, Bornholm.

"Eel contact... quite distant... bearing unknown... working on that, Chief... has the feel of a sub."

"Ok lad. Anyone else got a sniff?"

No one acknowledged his enquiry, which meant that they had nothing, but it served to focus the other operators on the possibility that there was something to find.

Chief Petty Officer Roland patted the young operator on the shoulder and waited patiently.

The advanced Electric Eel system was revolutionary and required experienced and skilled operators to understand its information.

Detecting a submarine was made considerably easier with it, but understanding where the submarine was in relation to the parent vessel needed men with the skills that Thresh possessed to make it a truly effective piece of anti-submarine equipment.

Despite his youth, Thresh was the best Eel operator on the ship, and probably in His Majesty's Navy.

Roland leant back and activated the phone to the bridge.

"Bridge, Sonar. Active Eel contact. No bearing at present. We're working on that... Thresh is on the set... he feels it's a sub. No other contacts, Skipper."

"Thank you, Chief."

Commander Robert Taggert RN, his full name of Robert William Forbes Mac An Tsagairt being used solely on the official paperwork of the desk-bound navy, was a legend amongst the sub hunters of the Atlantic.

One of Walker's prodigies, he had cut his teeth with the hunter-killer sub group aboard HMS Woodpecker, which was torpedoed and subsequently sank whilst being towed back to Liverpool.

As the vessel was not sunk immediately, survivors leave was not granted, and Taggert found himself shipping out with the group's next sally.

He eventually rose to command of his own vessel and was responsible, in whole or part, for the sinking of nine U-Boats.

Taggert had been the perfect choice as captain of the Loch Tralaig and he moulded his crew into a machine that oozed efficiency.

HMS Loch Tralaig was a happy ship, and it showed in its performance.

Roland waited, holding his tongue, as Thresh worked on isolating the various receivers on the towed sonar. The other systems still didn't have a sniff of whatever it was, so the contact was probably some distance away.

On the bridge, Taggert was sending messages to all parts of the ship, keeping his men informed, and at the same time reminding them of the need for silence.

He also ordered the radio shack to inform the ace up his sleeve.

In the sonar house, things started to happen.

"Chief."

Roland bent forward to view the display that carried the information Thresh had developed.

The sonar sensor cable was three miles long, and Thresh had concentrated on the sensors twenty-six to twenty-eight. There were only thirty-two, each one hundred and fifty yards apart, starting four hundred and eighty yards away from the ship's stern.

Using his equipment, Thresh used volume levels to gauge the proximity of the contact... he thought of it as a definite submarine... and his experience allowed him to work out the position with uncanny accuracy.

The system worked when it was quiet and the sea was calm, otherwise surface and water noise destroyed much of its capabilities, but Thresh was notorious for getting the most from the least.

In this case, his information was based on solid knowledge.

"Chief, I've a definite submarine contact ... bearing 160 to 165 at no more than four thousand two hundred, closest possible range three thousand nine hundred. Best guess is 160 at four thousand. I'm not sure but it seems almost on the surface."

"Keep working, lad."

Roland leant back for the telephone but hesitated, sensing Thresh had more to say.

"Go on, lad, Spit it out now."

"Chief, I think it's one of those twenty-ones. We've got some of those, don't we?"

"Aye we do, lad. The skipper'll sort it all out. No worries."

There was more.

"It's snorkelling. I'll put ten bob on it, Chief."

Roland had been impoverished a few times by Thresh's uncanny abilities and refused to take the bet.

"Bridge, Sonar... update on contact, now classed as definite submarine. Thresh thinks it's snorkelling."

He reeled off the information, and updated the bearing and other details at Taggert's request.

"Right, Chief. I'm going to alert Snowy, but I'll need an up-to-date set of figures to give them. Rework it, Chief."

"Aye aye, Skipper."

He replaced the phone.

"You heard the skipper. Start from scratch, lad."

Topsides, the crew closed up on the searchlight and, on receipt of the order, illuminated, and sent their invisible infrared beam down a bearing of 160.

"Sonar, bridge, report target details."

"Bridge, sonar, target steady at 160, probably making six knots, range decreasing, now approximately three thousand four hundred and closing. Over."

The First Lieutenant arrived on the bridge with the Radio Officer in close attendance.

"The bastard's coming right at us, Number One."

"Righty-ho, Skipper. I've confirmation from the Admiralty. Definitely no friendly submarines in our patrol area. No Swedish vessels have been registered either. Rules of engagement apply."

Taggert had sought confirmation, even though his current information gave no Allied submarine anywhere west of the Danish islands.

No self-respecting submarine captain would be snorkelling as he stalked an enemy contact, but that simply didn't matter.

It was in the wrong bit of sea.

"Rules of engagement permit us to open fire. An unidentified, but not friendly, submarine is now closing on us. Concur, Number One?"

"Absolutely, Skipper."

"Sparks, radio Snowy-two-two. Standby to initiate attack. Target data to follow shortly. "

"Roger, Skipper."

"Sonar, bridge. Report target details."

"Bridge, Sonar... target holding on 159 at six knots, range three thousand, closing. Over."

"Number One..."

Taggert need say no more as his First Lieutenant was already on the phone to the searchlight position, relaying the slight change of angle.

"Bridge, radio. Inform Snowy-two-two that he may attack. Target is illuminated... presently on bearing 159, closing, and probably snorkelling."

"Aye aye, Skipper."

"Number one, reel the eel."

The crew were already standing by to recover the electric eel array, the first five hundred yards of which was the easiest and required no special handling.

After that the sensors started coming aboard and, despite the redesign, they were still easily damaged.

Leaving them trailing in the ocean in the presence of explosions was guaranteed to wreck them, so the procedure was to recover prior to any attack, as spares were scarce.

It also meant that Loch Tralaig lost contact on her passive systems.

Taggert accepted that this time, especially as whatever it was seemed calm and unworried.

Ears attuned to the sounds of the sea suddenly wrestled with a new sound as the growl of engines rose.

Snowy-two-two flew on a course almost perfectly perpendicular to the bearing of the submarine, and at a height that seemed no more than a few feet above the waves.

The RAF Lancaster MR-3, a coastal command conversion of the successful heavy bomber, guided in by the infra-red line that Loch Tralaig used to show where the submarine was, suddenly illuminated its own searchlight, a powerful Leigh Light, which bathed the waves ahead with roughly twenty million candelas of penetrating light.

The nacelle mounting the light was slung under the rear belly of the giant aircraft and, to the watching seamen, gave the Lancaster a deadly halo.

Aboard the coastal command aircraft, the snorkel was clearly marked by the small wake it left as its parent submarine moved gently ahead, although it suddenly disappeared, which the crew assumed meant they had been detected.

Behind them, HMS Loch Tralaig, its work done, came about and cleared the immediate danger zone whilst readying the Squid launchers, should Snowy-two-two's attack fail.

Inside the Lancaster, the order was given and two objects detached themselves.

The two Fido acoustic torpedoes were newly modified versions, whose attack patterns could be pre-programmed just before launch from within the aircraft, and these two were told to go to active

302

sonar search from the moment they entered the water, and to look straight ahead.

Both the Fido torpedoes also had improved engines that offered nearly twenty knots, which was roughly three times the speed that the submarine was achieving, and more than enough to chase her down, if they acquired her.

The Lancaster pulled up and turned away to port, leaving both submarine and frigate behind her.

It would not put any more Fidos in the water unless specifically authorised by the commander on the surface, for the acoustic torpedo tended to be indifferent to the nationality of any metal it detected.

Both found the lump of metal they had been fired at and both struck within a second of each other.

Aboard HMS Loch Tralaig, headphones had already been removed to avoid ruptured eardrums. With the successful hits, they were replaced and the listeners bore witness to the death of whatever it was that threatened them.

Commander Taggert accepted the confirmation with little elation. His brother and his wife's cousin had both died in submarines in the last show, so he had an understanding of the terrible death that awaited the men who sailed beneath the waves, but it didn't stop him sinking them, just from overly celebrating the end result.

Throughout the ship there were whoops of joy as the result was announced over the ship's tannoy, immediately followed by an order to maintain silent routine.

Snowy-two-two rose back up into the night, her patrol not yet finished.

"Number One, reposition us to the east and trail the eel again. We'll make a sweep at daylight for any survivors. Not risking ourselves now."

There were no further contacts and the Lancaster was back at her Dutch base by the time that HMS Loch Tralaig returned to the area of the kill.

The sea was covered with the detritus expected after the sinking of a submarine.

Paper.

Cork.

Oil.

Lifejackets.

Wood.

Bodies.

The presence of smashed corpses in Soviet naval uniform relieved the last vestiges of doubt.

The whaler was deployed and Loch Tralaig moved away again, leaving the small boat, commanded by one of the Sub-Lieutenants, to sweep through the remains of a Soviet submarine and her crew.

No one was more surprised than Taggert when the cutter signalled for pick up and confirmed it had two survivors recovered.

The two men had somehow survived the night by finding enough wreckage to keep themselves out of the water. They were also equipped with some sort of dry suits, a subject on which they would be questioned when they were suitably recovered.

Both were placed in the sick bay, with a fierce looking Leading-Seaman armed with a trusty Webley pistol positioned to act as gaoler.

HMS Loch Tralaig was due back in her temporary patrol base at Gedser two days later, so the Admiralty were informed by radio of the two survivors.

The other items recovered were kept ready to be handed to naval intelligence as soon as HMS Loch Tralaig docked at the small Danish port.

By the time that Commander Taggert had brought his vessel alongside at Gedser, a lot of things had changed.

Naval Intelligence had become aware that the Soviets were trying to contact something called 'Karusel'', broadcasting on the Baltic Fleet frequencies that had become associated with their submarine units, which analysts considered final confirmation of the identity of their target.

Concern had grown that a Type XXI submarine had been constructed and put to sea without Allied knowledge, which caused a wave of reviews of everything from photoreconnaissance evidence to reports from human resources on the ground.

Of greater concern to the Admiral overseeing operations in the Baltic were the reports of problems amongst the crew of his best ASW platform.

HMS Loch Tralaig docked ahead of schedule and the quay was immediately cordoned off and secured by business-like Royal Marines with orders not to let anyone on the ship, and especially not off the ship.

An initial party of four medical personnel, suitably attired, boarded the frigate and found a medieval scene acted out on every deck.

Even as they walked up the gangplank, a party from Porton Down landed on the Gedser Landevej, the straight road having been closed and isolated by security detachments provided by the Danish Army.

Aboard Loch Tralaig, the dead were already set aside and placed in the meat locker where their temperature was kept low.

Both Russians, the Sub-lieutenant and two of his boat crew, the ship's surgeon, and one sick bay attendant had joined them only a few hours previously.

The rest of the whaler crew were extremely ill, presenting with a range of symptoms, from sickness and diarrhoea, respiratory problems and vomiting blood; some also presented with black lesions on the skin.

The newly arrived personnel took command, and organised the care of the five men directly affected, although three other members of the crew had reported sick that morning.

It was not until the personnel from Porton Down arrived that suspicions were raised.

One of the men, dispatched on a gut reaction by Admiral Parry, head of Naval Intelligence, understood precisely what he was looking at and HMS Loch Tralaig became a quarantine area.

By the time the information had reached England, another seven men were sick, and one more had joined the men in the freezer.

1122 hrs, Monday, 3rd March 1947, NATO Headquarters, Frankfurt, Germany.

"Good morning, General."

"Brad, thanks for coming so quickly. You know these gentlemen. Grab a coffee and take a chair."

Omar Bradley had been in the air before the message came, causing him to divert to Frankfurt and be part of an urgent meeting of NATO top brass.

"OK, Colonel. You may proceed."

Hood nodded to Eisenhower and, with Anne-Marie Foster's assistance, outlined the general events in the Baltic over the previous thirty hours.

"Admiral."

305

Hood ceded the floor to Rear-Admiral Dalziel, now second in the pecking order at British Naval Intelligence, and the man chosen to impart the bad news.

"Thank you, Colonel. I should hasten to add that the Captain in command of the operation followed the rules of engagement to the letter. It has since been confirmed that this was a Soviet submarine, most probably of the excellent XXI type designed by the Germans in the last show."

He nodded at von Vietinghoff who remained impassive.

"The frigate vectored in a Coastal Command aircraft, which successfully launched torpedoes that hit and sank the enemy submarine."

He turned to the map and selected the red marker point.

"Here, some twenty miles due south of Rønne on Bornholm."

He allowed them a moment to orient themselves before forging ahead.

"Quite correctly, the captain did not immediately search for survivors but swept the locale for signs of any other threats. He subsequently returned some hours later and dropped a small boat to investigate the floating wreckage. Major, if you please."

Foster illuminated the projector and the small group were shown photographs taken from the whaler, ones that showed the dead as well as the two recovered alive, and a plethora of other items that were fished from the water.

"Both these two survivors subsequently died, which would normally be reasonable to expect, given the fact that they were immersed in icy water and left unrecovered for many hours. Major, thank you."

Anne-Marie Foster removed the photographs and placed them carefully back in the top-secret folder, extracting the next set, ready for her cue.

"Loch Tralaig continued on her patrol, again quote normal, but reported on a strange illness that affected some of her crew. These were originally, without exception, members of the whale boat crew who had rescued the two Soviet submariners."

He again turned to the map and drew their attention to Gedser.

"The ship returned to her temporary patrol base earlier than planned as a number of fatalities occurred amongst her crew. These included the ship's surgeon, his senior rating, a rating assigned as security, and two of the whaleboat crew. Major."

Foster switched on the projector and some of the assembled senior officers almost recoiled from the graphic images that assailed them.

"On docking, the ship was quarantined immediately, and medical personnel went aboard. They were unable to identify the nature of the affliction. Admiral Parry, given the nature of some of our recent intelligence, took the step of ordering a party from Porton Down to the area, and it was they that identified the disease in questi... sir?"

"Porton Down? Don't know the place."

Dalziel did a mental check on the questioner and reasoned he would be cleared for such knowledge.

"General, Porton Down is a British facility that deals with research into counter-measures against special weapons."

"Special weapons?"

"Such as the Tabun used against us, or the plague the Japanese let loose on the Chinese and your naval facilities."

"Thanks, Admiral."

"One of the scientists that went to Gedser had previous experience in one particular field of research, and swiftly identified the nature of the infection."

He had already decided not to mention the goings-on at Gruinard Island.

'On going goings-on.'

He laughed to himself at the thought.

"Gentlemen, to date, nine men have died and another five are grievously ill. The cause of death has been identified as Anthrax."

A number of voices gave vent to a mixture of shock and anger.

"Anthrax?"

"Yes, Anthrax. All the sufferers showed what I am told are classic signs of exposure to the disease. The black lesions and abscesses we saw in the photographs are typical of Anthrax, especially if it has entered the skin through sites where there were already lacerations or scratches. It's also possible to spread through contact with bodily fluids and possibly from inhaling any fluids produced by a patient coughing."

Everyman sat around the table had made the connection to the intelligence assessments regarding the Japanese research and the sudden appearance of Anthrax in the Baltic.

"I should say that there is some disagreement amongst the scientists on this, and there's still much work to be done, but it's felt by many that this is a new, virulent, and particularly resilient strain of the infection. You will recall that such an infection was included within the possible items researched by the Japanese biological units."

The murmurs clearly confirmed that they did.

"At this time, more tests are being carried out. The Loch Tralaig is in quarantine, which does affect our anti-submarine capability but the Admiralty is taking steps to cover this vital area with another Loch class ship, which has already received orders to relocate."

Naval problems were naval problems to most present, and therefore of little consequence.

"As soon as Porton Down has any further information, I will ensure it's presented to you. I should also say that intelligence reached us from special units with the partisans in Lithuania... intelligence that confirms that Soviet NKVD units transported a large number of drums of hazardous material... as much as one hundred and fifty drums of it, roughly one hundred litres per drum. The drums appear to have been specially weighted so as to sink, not float as I'm assured they would do normally. We're unsure if that is significant."

Eisenhower stood and stopped the barrage of questions in their infancy.

"Gentlemen, quite clearly we simply don't know enough at the moment, but I think I can summarise matters quite simply."

They quietened down quickly and Ike delivered the bottom line.

"The Soviet Union appears to have attempted to transport a biological weapon into our lines but, thanks to the Royal Navy, failed. We have no idea if this was the first or only attempt to do so. At this time we remain at peace, but we cannot ignore this new threat... this unusual and deadly menace."

He moved across to the map and examined it quickly.

"From where the sub was sunk, they could be accessing Denmark or Germany directly, or maybe they even intended to go beyond... Holland... the North Sea... England?"

The muttering stopped when he turned back to face them.

"One thing's for sure. Things just got a whole lot more complicated again. After the enemy use of a nerve agent, certain stocks were released for our use, should it be felt prudent to use them. I immediately dismissed it, as I felt it was more dangerous to use when set against the advantages it gained. Progress on some protective clothing was made, but only recently did it see a genuine leap, and that was when we discovered the information from Japan. Basically, we don't have enough good protection in country if this thing gets outta hand."

He put his hands on his hips and set his jaw.

"The best protection we have is to be vigilant... as it always is of course. I don't like this at all. Everything points to the Soviets thinking about attacking, and yet they comply, in the main, with the terms agreed at Camp Vár. Our intelligence agencies can find little of substance on their intentions... which helps us not one goddamned bit!"

He slapped a hand on his thigh to emphasise his point.

"So I'm going to need to develop a plan, so now's the time to ante up if you've any ideas."

The discussion was energetic to say the least, and covered anything from pre-emptive air strikes to first use of the chemical stocks recently dispatched from the US.

The matter of informing the Soviets about the submarine and what they knew was heavily discussed, and the intelligence view of not doing so won the day.

Subsequently, the political view agreed.

The nature of the submarine's contents would also be kept secret amongst the Allies, limited to those in the room, and certain others cleared for such grave matters.

By the end of the meeting, the senior officers went back to their respective headquarters and let their men know that, yet again, the game had been ramped up by events and that the stakes were getting higher and higher.

Once the main group had left, Eisenhower waited until the equipment had been stowed away before ordering the staff out, leaving him, Bradley, and McCreery alone with the intelligence officer.

Ike tackled Dalziel on the one burning question that had been avoided by those who were in the know.

"Sir Roger, is there any possibility that this submarine was one of those missing from the Japanese navy?"

Dalziel nodded in acknowledgement that Eisenhower and the others had resisted asking in front of those who were not cleared for such matters.

"Sir, that's a question that is presently troubling us. From what I know, the sonar operator aboard Loch Tralaig is a genius who recognised the sub as a Type XXI or derivative; he's steadfast in that belief and is backed up by his watch officer, despite continuing questioning. The uniform means nothing of course, as Soviet seamen could be aboard a Japanese submarine for a number of reasons... plainly, none of them good."

Bradley made a sound like a labouring water buffalo, outlining his annoyance and feeling of helplessness with one all-encompassing display.

"We share your discontent, General Bradley. If it's a Soviet manned Type XXI then we can probably look at the possibility that items came overland from the East, as we understood. If it's a Japanese submarine, then we'll have failed to prevent it entering the Baltic, which suggests it has a capability for hiding that has defeated our systems. That, in itself, is of major concern, without the possible cargo they carried from the Empire."

...Twenty-two minutes earlier, seven miles north-northeast of Ceuta, North Africa.

"Well, I suppose their lordships know what they're doing... but damn and blast it, Jimmy... damn and blast it!"

"Quite, Skipper."

"The men may mutiny, you know."

Lieutenant-Commander Hamilton-Hewitt RNR made the comment only partially in jest.

"You'll soothe their troubled minds, Skipper."

The order to relocate had arrived at the worst possible moment.

The following day they were to be relieved on station and allowed some time ashore in Tangiers, where much was anticipated by way of female company and alcoholic entertainment.

"Still, nothing for it. Clueless!"

The navigator came running, his name no reflection on his skills or the esteem in which he was held.

"Set a course for Brest... that's Brittany to you Cambridge types. We'll refuel there before proceeding on to our destination."

"Might I be so bold as to ask, Skipper?"

"Somewhere a lot colder, Clueless... bloody Baltic... based out of Rostock. So... frauleins and pils instead of the pleasures of the North African souks for us. Quick as you can, Clueless."

"Aye, aye, Skipper."

Within a few minutes, HMS Loch Tarbert, pennant number K-431, one of the excellent ASW frigates with the electric eel, infrared searchlights, and Squid launchers, left her station at Gibraltar and headed north to replace Loch Tralaig.

1618 hrs, Tuesday, 4th March 1947, Lindingö, Sweden.

Colonel Keranin of the GRU had overseen the delivery personally, although his hands never once touched the information itself.

Once dispatched from Moscow, the thin folder was left within its disguise, not to be viewed until it was delivered to its ultimate destination.

The deliverymen knocked on the door three times before a sleepy looking man answered and signed for the package.

Outwardly, the sleepy man maintained his confused appearance, but the arrival of the unexpected package, sent by an art dealer in Stockholm, brought him immediately to a peak of awareness.

The package was from his Soviet masters.

To Lingström, the painting itself was of average quality, although he liked the subject matter; a pair of striking horses at the gallop.

He eased the back plate off and removed the envelope, replacing the wooden plate before exploring the material.

Lingström read the contents three times before picking up the telephone and arranging an urgent dinner meeting.

After that, he made another call making further arrangements for later in the evening.

He then copied the envelope details onto another one that was intact and untarnished, slipping both into his briefcase before he changed into his uniform.

1903 hrs, Tuesday, 4th March 1947, Den Gyldene Freden Österlånggatan 51, Stockholm, Sweden.

The two men sat down together and perused the menu in silence, even though both already knew what they would order, as they were regulars in the establishment.

As usual, the restaurant staff accommodated Lingström's telephone booking; such customers always got preferential treatment, such was the clout of his rank and position.

He retained his briefcase but allowed the greatcoat and cap to be taken away with due reverence.

When Tørget arrived as his dinner companion, the headwaiter almost went into an apoplectic fit, fawning constantly over both of the senior officers and ensuring his staff were chased back and forth until the two were settled with everything their hearts could desire.

They engaged in small talk throughout the splendid dinner, dropping to hushed whispers when eager-to-please staff drew near to top up a glass or to seek any further needs.

The dessert course over, Tørget excused himself and, picking up his briefcase, disappeared off to the gentleman's facility.

There was nothing unusual in that, given that briefcases were never left unattended.

After a few minutes, Tørget returned to the table and slid the briefcase back between the two seats.

The two men finished off their coffees and rose to go their separate ways.

Only an attentive eye would have considered the possibility that Lingström picked up the briefcase that had accompanied Tørget to the cloakroom.

The junior man paid for dinner and offered the waiter his normal five-krona tip, in which came his report confirming receipt of the envelope and its intended delivery later that evening.

The two intelligence officers shook hands and went their separate ways, the whole evening being solely about the exchange of information that had happened in the men's lavatory of Den Gyldene Freden.

2130 hrs, Tuesday, 4th March 1947, Riksplan, Stockholm, Sweden.

"Mister Fenton, thank you for coming."

"Lieutenant Colonel."

They shook hands and walked together.

"How could I refuse such an indistinct invitation?"

"My apologies, but my master required that I pass this on to you as soon as practicable."

"So what is it that old Tørget wants me to have?"

Lingström laughed.

"I serve a different master tonight, Mister Fenton."

Ernest Fenton, MI-5's man in Sweden, frowned and his senses lit off.

The silence was only broken by the feet crunching on the chilled gravel path.

"This comes straight from Moscow... at the orders of General Nazarbayeva herself."

"What?"

"What can I say, Mister Fenton. I've played on both sides of the road for some time now."

"What? I mean... Christ's sake, man. You mean to tell me you're a double agent? Whose side are you really on?"

Whilst he took the proffered envelope, Fenton kept his gaze firmly on the Swedish officer and his concentration on his right hand and the Walther PPK concealed in his pocket.

"I'm a Swede first and last. I'm Tørget's man through and through, so don't worry about that. By the way, my colonel asks that you do not reveal this to anyone. I'm only telling you so that you have some idea of the worth and authenticity of this information."

Fenton processed the request and nodded.

"The Russians think I'm their top man in the Baltic. I feed them enough old news to keep that place in their hearts."

He tapped the envelope.

"That has come to me direct from the GRU headquarters."

"Have you looked at it?"

"Certainly not. My orders were very specific."

"Ok. Is there anything else?"

"Not tonight, Mister Fenton."

The envelope disappeared into a large inside pocket and the two went their separate ways without shaking hands.

Nazarbayeva's plan of using the Gehlen/De Walle information to cause discord between the Allies took a step forward.

2159 hrs, Tuesday, 4th March 1947, Headquarters, Swedish Military Intelligence, Stockholm.

Tørget accepted the developed photographs eagerly, the roll of shots he had taken in Den Gyldene Freden having been developed in record time, with two of each print now sat before him.

His mouth hung slightly open at the enormity of what was being suggested in the documents the Russians were so eager to pass on to the Allies, but he knew some of it was certainly at least founded on some fact from his own understanding of matters.

But the suggestion that German Intelligence was somehow responsible for murdering two senior Allied spymasters was simply to huge to form an opinion on without much more thought and investigation.

He read it all again, drinking in every morsel in the photographs.

'Vögel... Diels... Mallman...de Walle... Gehlen...'

There were holes of course… gaps in the intelligence… the meaning and intentions of it all were clearly open to interpretation, anything from a coup inside the German government to something far more sinister.

But he kept returning to the murder of de Walle.

Why de Walle?

He couldn't answer the question, despite his best efforts, and couldn't supply the Swedish Prime Minister with an answer when he briefed him in person just before midnight.

Fenton and the envelope were on an aircraft bound for London as Monday became Tuesday, the importance of the information ensuring that the BOAC Mosquito flew straight to the capital rather than its normal base at RAF Leuchars.

The protestations of the two crewmen were swiftly overcome with gentle words that assured them of horrible foreign postings were they not to comply with their instructions.

By the end of 2nd March, suspicious intelligence eyes were silently and relentlessly focussed on their German allies and, despite efforts to be normal, a fog of distrust settled across the continent amongst those in the know.

Which was exactly what Nazarbayeva had hoped for when she suggested sending the file to their enemy.

Stalin and, reluctantly Beria, had both agreed that there was nothing to lose and everything to gain.

They were wrong on both counts.

Things are not always what they seem; the first appearance deceives many; the intelligence of a few perceives what has been carefully hidden."

Phaedrus

Chapter 189 - THE SUSPICIONS

0151 hrs, Wednesday, 5th March 1947, Çanakkale Naval Fortified Command Building, Çanakkale, Turkey.

Koramiral Cevdet Tezeren had ensured that much of the channel was monitored by either his own men, or not being monitored at all.

According to the Soviet request, the submarine force had already started its journey through the Dardanelles, and very shortly he would telephone his stations for reports before a casual meeting with his NKVD contact to receive his payment.

He could but hope that this phase was not as fraught as the mission that had earlier brought them safely through the Bosphorus, when army launches from 11th Infantry Division of Bosphorus Area Fortified Command had somehow found themselves in the midst of traffic.

Two had been rundown by the Greek freighter Makeconia, leading a column of civilian vessels moving through the narrow waters, concealing darker purposed vessels that moved beneath them.

One of the launches managed to get off some flares, bathing the whole channel in light for far longer than Tezeren cared for.

But the matter had been resolved, despite the loss of seven Turkish soldiers' lives.

The army commander locally had exceeded his orders by running a night time exercise in the shipping lane, and the survivors had been recovered by Makeconia and her consorts.

The schedule allowed for a few days in the Sea of Marmara, which permitted the army to fete the captains of the rescuing vessels.

He picked up the telephone and made the first of his calls.

The procession of ships had taken nearly three hours, which had passed too slowly for Tezeren's taste.

The final report had arrived just before four o'clock and he had taken it even as he stood to make his way home.

He drove himself for once, for no other reason than ease of meeting with an NKVD officer on a road out of Kepez.

Teoman Schiller had waited a long time, not knowing precisely when his man would appear, but the naval staff car ground into sight and pulled over by the stand of olive trees in which the NKVD agent had had taken up residence since about two in the morning.

"Good morning, Koramiral. I trust all went as planned?"

"Not quite… but the vessels are out and safely into the sea beyond. I should ask for double. It has been a very stressful few days, I can tell you."

"My commander understands this and he hopes that the Bosphorus situation is now resolved?"

"Yes. I've managed to make it go away."

"Excellent. My commander has included something extra for your efforts on our behalf."

"Very kind."

"He also asked me to give you a special gift and asked me to assure you that it's quite safe. I assume you know what he means by that, Koramiral?"

Tezeren looked at the bottle of superior Fig Raki and laughed.

"I understand fully. Thank you."

The Admiral swept up the modest canvas bag that contained enough Turkish Liras to ensure a comfortable and happy life ahead, plus the bottle of Raki.

Back in his luxury villa on the Mediterranean coast near Kumburan, Tezeren decided that he would examine the bottle over early morning coffee.

There were no tell-tale marks of tampering but, despite that, he broke the seal and poured its contents into the ground around an apricot tree, musing that it might become a popular move if the apricots take on board any of the flavour…

'… and none of the poison if the dogs put any in!'

He poured another coffee and enjoyed the early morning view of an awakening world.

Screwing up his eyes he could even imagine the faint smoky marks of the 'Soviet' surface group disappearing over the horizon.

Twisting his neck from side to side, Tezeren tried to ease the stiffness from his joints, and used his hand to manipulate a jaw that suddenly felt heavy and leaden.

He had talked to every command post along the Dardanelles that very night, so he was not in the least bit surprised.

His odalik... he liked to use the old term... brought forward another jug of hot sweet coffee but he declined, feeling that the pool was more for him.

As was usual, Tezeren simply removed his clothes and handed them to his attendant, squeezing her breasts as he did.

She was more than a maid, a symbol and throwback to an older age, when concubines were more common and humans could be owned by another.

Her face remained passive as he cupped and squeezed her ample flesh, his ownership and subjugation of her demonstrated as total.

Tezeren simply fell into the pool and felt the coolness of it immediately alleviate his aches and pains.

But only for a moment.

His stomach started to cramp and swimming became difficult.

"Sidika!"

The odalik was stood by the side of the pool.

"Sidika... help me... I can't swim..."

He dropped beneath the water and tried to fight his way back up to the surface.

His feet touched the bottom and he found the strength to thrust upwards and gasped in the warm air.

"Help me, woman."

He spluttered and drank in some pool water.

The combination of the look on her face and his present predicament combined into one horrible thought.

"You fucking bitch!"

He went under again as his arms and legs started to seize up and spasm.

Once more he came to the surface, trying hard to draw air into his lungs but finding the action more difficult than he could ever remember.

317

"Help me, Sidika…. Help… me!"

"Just shut up and die, you fat fuck."

"Bitc…"

His efforts to stay afloat floundered as pain wracked his muscles and his stomach convulsed.

One last time he came up, to witness Sidika holding the coffee pot and, when she saw him break the surface, pouring its contents into the earth around the Apricot tree.

Her smile was the last thing Tezeren saw.

Sidika summoned the police and within an hour the villa was crawling with constabulary and high-ranking naval officers.

Her story clearly tallied with the evidence and, given Tezeren's well-known proclivities, was swiftly accepted as the truth in the matter.

The admiral had taken coffee and gone swimming, only to suffer some sort of arrest whilst in the pool. His loyal odalik was in the kitchen but heard his cries for help and, on dashing to the poolside, plunged in to pull out the distressed man, only to fail in her attempts.

Given the size of the two, no one doubted that she had tried hard but had been destined to fail.

The villa was cordoned off and guards were placed to keep away prying eyes, but Sidika was permitted to stay, although the circumstances of her residence prevented her from signalling her NKVD controller on the success of her mission.

But in any case, Schiller already knew.

1212 hrs, Wednesday, 5th March 1947, Headquarters of the Red Banner Forces of Soviet Europe, Brest Litovsk, USSR.

"Very careless of them… but very interesting."

Nazarbayeva looked up from her lunch and silently quizzed Orlov.

"A snippet from our man at Baltic Naval Headquarters, Comrade General. They've lost a submarine."

He handed the report over, careful not to smear any butter from his own meal on it.

Tatiana was less successful and ending up wiping a little residue away before she read the brief message.

Her foot was aching so she eased her boot as she read and felt immediate relief.

"Failure to report... Soviet submarine J-57... two days overdue... two days? I thought they went weeks without checking in."

"Well, yes, Comrade General. Maybe a special training mission trying something new, so they needed closer contact?"

He had lost his commander's attention already, but he knew the look and waited patiently for the torrent of orders that would probably come next.

"Have the records of messages regarding the sinkings of our submarines in the Baltic in the last twelve months brought in straight away please."

Orlov disappeared to issue the orders and to organise something that would meet with his General's approval.

Rufin arrived with his normal liquid stash, only to find that Nazarbayeva not only got in first, but her supply was considerably larger.

Slipping his bottle back into his trouser pocket, he poured two measures each before the reports arrived; there were quite a few, each one marking the loss of scores of Mother Russia's sons.

But Tatiana Nazarbayeva wasn't interested in the contents, simply the circulation list.

"No... no... no... no... ," she looked at each list in turn and saw the omission.

"Not there."

She put the entire glass of vodka down her throat and held it out for another refill, which Rufin supplied, despite Orlov's raised eyebrow.

"There is a standard circulation list on these reports, each marking a submarine overdue. It's a standard procedure obviously. They're all the same on these reports... see?"

She dropped the files on the table in turn, each with the 'overdue' report foremost.

The circulation lists were identical.

"Now, J-57."

"The same, Comr... ah, I see."

Rufin read the difference aloud.

"Nine-two-two-six... what's that?"

Nazarbayeva knocked back her fourth vodka and slid the empty glass towards the broached bottle, but this time Orlov's eyebrow won over Rufin's habit and the glasses stayed empty.

She leant forward and grabbed a pencil and paper.

"I haven't got the faintest idea to be honest."

Drawing him towards the paper, the pencil danced and words formed under it as she talked innocently.

'There was a special project I was part of. It was called Raduga.'

"Perhaps it's a new agency? A casualty bureau of some sort?"

'I'm told that the project was cancelled. It involved the deployment and use...'

"I have seen such number groups before... special routings."

'... of biological, chemical, nerve agents, and atomic weapons on the Allies. I know it wasn't cancelled.'

"Of course, this could simply be a typist's error, Comrades."

'This is not the number group for Raduga...'

"Unlikely it's of any significance now I think of it. These reports can go back, thank you."

'... but they are not used lightly. This sub's loss is significant and I need to know why."

"Straight away, Comrade General."

Orlov opened the door as the scribbled notes were screwed up and a match made ready.

"Leytenant Rikardova, return these files to records immediately."

The woman and files virtually flew out of the door, which was quickly shut to prevent the smell of burning paper reaching the noses of those in the main office.

"I need to fly to Moscow tomorrow. I'll ask Comrade Admiral Kuznetsov whilst I'm there. For now, see what you can find out through Baltic command, Comrade Mayor."

Rufin saluted and left.

Orlov heard the chink of glass on glass and realised that his boss was fuelling her increasing habit once again.

Nazarbayeva had noticed his attempts to prevent her drinking.

"Don't be an old woman, Bogdan Vasilyevich."

"I would be remiss in my duty if I do nothing, Comrade Leytenant General."

She laughed.

"Your duty is discharged. Thank you... now join me for another before I go off duty... contact General Poliakov and regretfully inform him that our chess game is cancelled this evening… and please have the offices swept again this afternoon."

As she lay fully clothed on her bed snoring her way through a few hours' sleep, the technical section carried out another close inspection of her offices.

At six p.m. she returned to discover that there were two items of note that had been placed in the office since the last inspection, some forty-eight hours previously.

They had been left in position and were clearly marked with signs.

This was standard practice, in case the tables could be turned on the listeners.

One was a standard NKVD type listening device.

The other, more worryingly, wasn't.

2054 hrs, Thursday, 6th March 1947, the Kremlin Grand Park, Moscow, USSR.

"Comrade Leytenant General! What a surprise! I thought you had returned to the front."

"Comrade Polkovnik General. My heartiest congratulations on your well-deserved promotion."

The two senior officers embraced and Nazarbayeva invited the deputy head of the NKVD to sit with her.

His security detail eyed the woman and the major accompanying her with a mixture of disdain and wariness, until Kaganovich gestured them to one side, clearly relaxed and unworried.

They tensed for a moment as the woman fished in the pocket of her thick overcoat, only relaxing when the two officers took turns in consuming some of the contents of the flask that had materialised in her hand.

The two engaged in small talk, or so it seemed.

"We're safe to talk here, Tatiana. What worries you so much that you drag me out in the cold evening, eh?"

"The submarine we seem to have lost."

"What submarine?"

"J-57 is overdue in the Baltic… or should I say 'Sovetskaya Vynoslivost' has not contacted base."

"Careful, Tatiana Sergievna."

"Why do I need to be careful, Ilya Borisevich. I serve the Motherland. What's happening here?"

"A submarine has failed to report i…"

"That's not what I mean and you know it."

321

Her outburst drew every eye and Kaganovich laughed and slapped her on the shoulder, which immediately relaxed the watchers.

"So what do you mean?"

"Nine-two-two-six."

Kaganovich laughed again and pulled her to him as if hugging an amusing close friend.

His laugh trailed away and he whispered in her ear before releasing and sitting back.

"Not your business, Tatiana. Drop it."

The flask appeared again and Kaganovich took a generous swig before passing it back.

"That keeps the chills at bay."

"Indeed, Ilya Borisevich. But I need... I want an answer. There's something going on that I'm being excluded from. Something clearly important enough to warrant a four number code. The last such was issued to Raduga. Is this the code group for the new Raduga?"

His face said all, even in the low and subtle lighting in the park.

"It's all still running, isn't it? Every fucking bit of it... not just research... but everything... plus more besides I expect?"

He stayed silent.

"Raduga is still running, every part of it, despite the peace... you told me so and I now know it... you know this... you also know it wasn't just the atomic advances... for fuck's sake, Comrade... are they fucking ma..."

She stopped in mid-sentence as her mind threw something into the mix.

"The submarine... I remember part of Raduga involved using biological weapons against the rear line and civilians in Germany... submarine delivered diseases to be introduced into water supplies. That's J-57, isn't it? J-57 was carrying bio... they're taking us to war again, aren't they? Raduga was a response option, not an attack."

Kaganovich noticed the unease amongst his guards and waved them into relaxation with casual gestures.

"I cannot say, for I too am excluded from many things, Tatiana. As I told you, I do know that Raduga's progress continues, but its concept has changed... whether it is for war or for the future protection of the Motherland is unclear to me."

"What could be clearer than one of our submarines transporting biological material... or worse... to Allied territories?"

"We don't know that, Tatiana Sergievna. I'm trying to find out."

"And what if the Allies know?"

"How could they know? If the submarine's sunk, then it lies at the bottom of the Baltic, together with whatever it carried."

"And were you going to tell me any of this, eh?"

"In honesty, no. I wouldn't have involved you, Comrade."

"Well now I'm involved. I can only see one way forward."

"Tread lightly, Tatiana Sergievna."

"I will ask."

"That may not be wise, Comrade."

"It's very wise, Comrade, regardless of how I am answered, I will know the truth with the question alone."

"You may well place yourself on dangerous ground."

"We all serve the Motherland, Comrade."

"That we do, but in different ways and guided by different ideals."

Nazarbayeva frowned sufficiently for it to be noticed by those watching.

"Enough for now, Comrade Leytenant General."

Kaganovich clearly signalled an end to the familiarity and stood, stamping his feet as a signal to his men that he was preparing to move off.

"I advise caution. Comrade Nazarbayeva. Above all, be careful."

They hugged and went their separate ways.

Rufin closed up on Nazarbayeva's shoulder and asked the burning question.

"Yes is the short answer, Comrade. There's something going on and I mean to get to the bottom of it tomorrow morning."

Blowing into his cold hands, he floated the obvious riposte.

"And how will you do that, Comrade General?"

"I'll ask Stalin himself."

2143 hrs, Thursday, 6th March 1947, Colonel General Kaganovich's office, the Kremlin, Moscow, USSR.

The Marshal collapsed heavily into the third chair by the roaring fire.

"Na Zdorovie!"

The three men raised their glasses and drank.

"So, why am I summoned here at this stupid hour, Comrade?"

"I met with Nazarbayeva as planned. She has discovered about nine-two-two-six from a routing on the naval communications."

"She was bound to find out sooner or later... I wish it had been later of course."

The other man in the room held out his glass for a refill before speaking.

"What's she planning to do, Comrade Kaganovich?"

"In front of me, she worked out that Raduga's probably running as an offensive mission prior to renewed conflict, and that it's likely the missing submarine was undertaking one of the planned missions to deliver certain... err... items to the German mainland."

"And?"

Khrushchev was not renowned for his patience.

"She intends to ask the General Secretary tomorrow."

Both the other men protested immediately and Kaganovich found himself holding out his hands as if to protect himself from their words.

"Comrades, please. I could do nothing. We know her quality and steel... it is to be expected that we cannot control it, simply try to channel it. My question is simple. Are we ready?"

He and Khrushchev looked directly at the Marshal.

"No... we're not ready."

"Fuck... so if it blows up tomorrow we'll have wasted all our good work... all will have been for nothing."

"True, Comrade Khrushchev, but we'll live to fight another day. However, there's another possibility here."

They both leaned forward, better to catch the Marshal's words.

"There may be opportunity here for us... the General Secretary may do all we need done for us. It may simply require a light push for our new keystone to be put in place. It all depends on what's said when she asks."

Khrushchev nodded vigorously.

"Yes, yes... I can see that... but if we're not ready then..."

"I didn't say we couldn't be ready soon, Comrade. Not tomorrow for certain, but all could be in place by Sunday, although there will be holes in the scenarios we have discussed."

Kaganovich chimed in.

"Yes, but we'd have to act if she inadvertently started something."

"Yes, we would, so... I think we really do need to make sure she doesn't."

Again, the Marshal became the focus of attention.

"I have an idea."

They listened as the Marshal outlined his plan to prevent Nazarbayeva acting precipitously, and agreed wholeheartedly with the proposal.

They left separately.

Khrushchev first, the Marshal second, and finally Kaganovich, who locked up his office and went to his apartment greatly troubled by the events that had been and those that might well still come to pass.

0403 hrs, Friday, 7th March 1947, senior officer's guest bedroom, the Kremlin Armoury, Moscow, USSR.

The knocking disturbed Nazarbayeva eventually and she grabbed enough clothing to protect her modesty before allowing entry.

A Kremlin Guard Captain reluctantly delivered his report.

"Comrade Leytenant General. I've been ordered to wake you immediately. My apologies but there's a report from your headquarters. There's been a severe fire and several of your staff have been injured. We've woken your officer, Mayor Rufin, and he'll be trying to get more information."

She processed the facts slowly, inadvertently giving the Guard an eyeful of an ample breast before acknowledging and ordering him to arrange for a car and contact the transport office for the first flight home.

In the car on the way to Vnukovo, Rufin gave her the additional information he had gleaned.

An accidental fire had started in the records office. Two members of her staff had been inside at the time and they were both confirmed as dead. Seven others had been badly burned trying to prevent further destruction to the records, even though most were backed up by other copies at a secondary location.

Orlov had taken charge but GRU [West] was badly hurt by the incident.

Rufin and she were on the aircraft back to Brest Litovsk before her mind started to ponder other possibilities.

Such as… *non-accidental fires…*

Such as… *distractions that took her away from Moscow…*

325

Such as... *now not being able to confront Stalin...*

Such as... *what was Kaganovich's part in matters?...*

Such as... *was she being played for a fool?...*

"I wonder why they woke you before me?"

"Comrade General?"

"The Guards woke you before me, so I was told. They didn't wake me until you ordered it."

"I didn't order you woken up, Comrade General. The officer that woke me said you were being informed at the same time."

"Hmm."

"And it wasn't a Guards officer that woke me. He was regular army... a signals podpolkovnik."

"Obviously a misunderstanding, Comrade Mayor."

Rufin nodded and went back to trying to catch up on his lost sleep, despite the buffeting that the aircraft was taking.

Nazarbayeva simply closed her eyes, knowing that sleep would not come as her mind worked over all the events of the last twenty-four hours.

1005 hrs, Friday, 7th March 1947, House of Madame Fleriot, La Vigie, Nogent L'Abbesse, near Reims, France.

Anne-Marie Knocke was now unmistakably with child, her pronounced bump so large as to draw comments from visiting Legionnaires and Deux agents as to the likelihood of twins, or even more.

She had sought permission to return to Nogent L'Abbesse to have her child, something that her husband had suggested in the first place.

If he could, Knocke intended to be there, but for now he remained with the division in Poland.

A number of boxes of De Walle's personal papers had been delivered to La Vigie, as the Belgian had no family and had declared Anne-Marie Knocke, née de Valois, his sole heir.

It had taken her some time to pluck up the enthusiasm to start sorting through the boxes, but she had eventually set to the task.

This was her third morning, and probably her last, as the mountain had gradually been reduced, most of the items being set aside for subsequent disposal in a brazier that the gardener had already prepared.

There was little of note worth keeping.

She decided to hang on to De Walle's personal assessment of the members of the Colloque for a number of reasons, not the least

326

of which was the astute assessment of the man she now called husband.

Some communications regarding Molyneux made her laugh, the more so as she could imagine her old friend and mentor saying them aloud and with undisguised passion.

A transcript jotted down from memory detailing a relaxed conversation with the Soviet paratrooper, General Ivan Alekseevich Makarenko, reminded her of a brave man who had decided to do something about a corrupt system.

An unpaid bill for Bossong's Wine Shop in Selestat was set aside to be paid.

She would ensure his bill was honoured.

De Walle had left a considerable sum to her and the forthcoming child, as well as bequeathing a wonderful lakeside property in Pierre-Percée.

Jerome knocked and entered in one easy movement, a silver tray brimming with the makings of morning coffee and some sweet bites that his employer, Madame Fleriot, had insisted Anne-Marie ate to keep her strength up.

The elderly butler closed the door behind him without saying a word and Madame Knocke returned to her meanderings.

As she leant forward to pick up the delicate cup, her eyes caught and processed two words that intrigued her.

'Herr Furt.'

It was Georges' special name for the German spymaster, Gehlen, who had been born in Erfurt. The play on words had always amused the affable Belgian.

She pulled the contents out of the envelope and raised the cup to her lips.

It never made contact as words spilled out of the pieces of paper and into her brain, words that would have made no sense some months beforehand but now drew her attention like a vulture to a ripened corpse.

"Uspenka… Steyn… General Strong… Uranprojekt?"

That one she hadn't heard about, nor the words 'Geheime Auergesellschaft, or Konitz.'

She continued reading… *Osoaviakhim… VNIIEF… Godmanchester…* and whilst not understanding the words, she understood enough to know that Gehlen and De Walle had discovered something important and were working…

"Merde!"

The thought spurred her to swear openly.

327

"They're both dead... both dead... Gehlen assassinat... Merde! Both assassinated! The bomb was meant for Georges. He survived and then... the nurse no one found!"

She reached for the telephone and sought a connection, her heart and mind racing each other and making her head feel light.

A tinny voice answered.

"Commandant Vincennes."

"Bonjour, Henri, it's Anne-Marie."

"Bonjour! How are you?"

"I'm fine, thank you. I was just wondering if you could send me a file I was working on, I forgot to finish it. I'm staying with my Aunt... you recall where I hope?"

He sat up straight in an instant, the words sending a small chill into his heart.

"Mais oui."

Vincennes fished for the emergency card relating to Anne-Marie de Valois.

"The file number's 1225. Easy enough to find. If you could send it as soon as possible, 1830 at the latest, that would be lovely. Natalie sends her regards, by the way. Thank you, Henri."

"But of course, send her mine in return please...and now I must go. Work calls. Bon chance."

The telephone went dead and Anne-Marie leant back into her chair.

In the office of Commandant Vincennes all hell broke loose as the information she had passed required an immediate response.

He double checked the coded communications against the emergency card and came up with the same results.

'1225...Unable to communicate as unsecure.'

'1830... in possession of vital information.'

'Natalie... immediate danger.'

Within ten minutes, three Deux agents were mobilised from the Reims office with orders to pick up Madame Knocke and to follow her orders.

As she waited for them to arrive, Anne-Marie considered her options and decided that she would go straight to the top.

By 1052, the SDECE Citroen was speeding eastwards towards Frankfurt.

The heavily pregnant woman was ushered in and Strong rose to his feet, inviting her to sit.

"Madame Knocke, my apologies for the delay. Can I get you anything?"

"No thank you, Général Strong."

He resumed his seat and leant forward on his elbows.

"So, how may I be of assistance to the SDECE?"

"General Strong, until recently I was aide and bodyguard to Georges de Walle."

"A great loss... a great man... he'll be missed. Such a tragic end."

"His end was not as it seemed."

"Oh?"

"I have reason to believe he was killed in the hospital after surviving the bomb attempt on his life."

"On his lif... hang on... the bomb was aimed at the SS officers, was it not?"

"That's what we thought, but I suspect it wasn't so."

"And what makes you think that, Madame?"

She produced a leaf of papers and worked through them one by one, placing each in front of him in turn.

His reaction to some of the words she hadn't understood was noticeable.

Anne-Marie finished working through the documents.

"One moment please."

Strong rose and picked up a decanter, offering the woman a glass, which was declined.

He sat down with a fine measure of single malt and considered the evidence.

"This is to remain between us, Madame Knocke."

"Of course, mon Général."

"Much of what you have spoken of here is connected to the Soviet Union's atomic weapons programme. VNIIEF and Uranprojekt for instance. That obviously makes any intelligence associated with it of extreme interest to me."

He leant forward, inviting Anne-Marie closer.

"I do know there were some other concerns that Gehlen and de Walle had been keeping an eye on. Matters with the Germans and some game playing in higher circles."

329

Quite deliberately, Strong stopped short of mentioning the Soviet information.

"I'll give that some more thought of course, but for now I would like to keep this information. I'll have a copy made for you immediately, but I'd like to run some of it past someone who might have a different perspective."

"That's fine, mon Général. I came to you first… given your position. I have yet to report this fully to my own superiors…"

The fact that the superior to whom she normally reported was named in the papers struck her in an instant, and brought a tear to her eye.

Strong understood, and also grasped the struggle inside the normally ice cold woman as she tried to keep her emotions in check.

"Thank you for bringing this to me, Madame Knocke. I understand that it must have been a difficult decision for you. I'll have you shown to a room where you can rest until the copies have been completed. Can I get you anything at all?"

"Nothing, thank you, mon Général."

He rose and showed her to the door.

She staggered slightly and he instinctively reached out to offer her support.

"When is the baby due, Madame?"

"We think about a month's time, mon Général."

"The very best of luck to you both, and I hope all goes well, Madame. I'm going to ask the doctor to come and have a look at you, just to be on the safe side"

It was a mark of how tired she felt that there was no resistance.

They shook hands and Anne-Marie was escorted to a waiting area whilst Strong organised the copying of the paperwork.

A number of staff introduced themselves to Madame Knocke as she sat waiting, more often than commenting on her state and wishing her well.

A bouquet had been hastily arranged and was hand delivered to Anne-Marie by Strong's secretary.

The doctor arrived and gave her a check-up and, with the normal advisories about rest and proper eating, left without a fuss.

The original paperwork arrived in the hands of one of Strong's staff, complete with a letter from the head of NATO intelligence to the head of the French SDECE, expressing thanks for the woman agent's actions and deportment.

2032 hrs, Friday, 7th March 1947, Imperial College, London, England.

"Penney."

The professor always worked late, so Strong had expected him to answer his call.

"Good evening, Bill, Kenneth here, Sorry to bother you so late."

"Not at all, old chap. How are you keeping? Brita well?"

"In the pink, so she says, Bill. Eleanor still on the scene?"

Penney's first wife, Adele, had died in 1944, but his friends were delighted when he started to take a shine to a new woman.

"Yes, indeed, Kenneth... not that I have much time for those sort of shenanigans."

"Yes, well, Bill... I'm going to steal a little more of your time soon enough. I'll be sending a courier to you with some documents that you need to take a look at. Don't want to cause too much of a stir at the moment, and there are the normal security implications as ever, plus some interesting new ones."

"Mum's the word then, Kenneth."

"Quite, Bill. Especially as I think your time at Tube Alloys might help you in understanding them."

The conversation took a different turn when the code name of the British and Canadian atomic research project was mentioned.

"Right, Kenneth. I'm with you."

"Good, Bill. I'll have one of our chaps stay with you for a while. Hope you understand."

"As you wish, Kenneth. I've an appointment at Balliol tomorrow, but I'm spending the weekend at home. I'll be back at East Hendred by teatime, I should warrant. Have your chap come round. I'll find him a bed for the night, maybe a spot of breakfast, Suit you?"

"Perfect. I'll have the stuff flown to Benson and my man will pick them up from there... be with you, say... five?"

"Five should be perfect. If I'm not home, William'll let him in and tend to his needs."

"Splendid. Now, I need to get things organised. Have a good evening, Bill."

"You too, old friend."

Sir Kenneth immediately sought another line.

"Ah Major. I have a package for immediate pick-up. Destination Benson. I need one of your men to pick up and deliver. Sensitive stuff... Yes, thank you, Major."

He inserted the paperwork that Anne-Marie Knocke had given him, addressed it to the country's leading mathematical physicist, and handed it to the courier who presented himself shortly afterwards.

'Interesting.'

Major von der Hartenstein-Gräbler of the Abwehr, liaison officer on Strong's staff, went on his way, already forming a report in his mind.

Being at a loose end he had assisted the new British 2nd Lieutenant with overseeing the copying, which had granted him enough opportunity to read some vital pieces concerning his own Government and Allied suspicions.

He also recognised Anne-Marie from her file photograph.

His previous reports on liaisons between Strong and the two intelligence officers, Gehlen and de Walle, had already caused some consternation, and he didn't doubt that he was at least partially responsible for their untimely deaths.

But he was Diels' man, so it didn't particularly matter, even though Gehlen had mentored him and recommended him for the position in Strong's department.

Now the French bitch was in the mix too, and he expected that his report might promote a similar reaction.

Shame, as the woman was a beauty, had tits to die for, and was clearly good in bed.

His report arrived in Magdeburg the following day.

He had grossly underestimated the effect it would have.

The most shocking fact about war is that its victims and its instruments are individual human beings, and that these individual beings are condemned, by the monstrous conventions of politics, to murder or be murdered in quarrels not their own.

Aldous Huxley

CHAPTER 190 - THE UNCONCEIVABLE

Fig # 227 - Demarcation lines in Europe as of 15th March 1947

Speer sat impassively, occasionally looking at his closest advisors, who sat similarly silent, still absorbing the latest news.

Diels rustled the paper of his notes deliberately, trying to provoke some sort of response from those present... unsuccessfully.

He felt it necessary to fill the void.

"At this time, the matter is being kept to Strong himself... and obviously the woman who brought him the information. Herr Kanzler, I feel I must advise that we take immediate action here. That action must be total. Nip this in the bud now and we guarantee the safety of our plans. There are too many dangers here"

Guderian thumped the Marshal's baton into his gloved hand.

"Dangers! Of course there are dangers... we knew that when we embarked on our plans. But what you imply goes well beyond that... that... level that is acceptable."

He turned to Speer.

"Surely we cannot take this risk, Herr Kanzler?"

Speer shrugged in slow motion, considering his response.

"I'm not sure that we can afford not to, Feldmarschal."

He looked at Pflug-Hartnung for support and found it in an acquiescent nod.

Adolf Schärf considered his words very carefully.

"I think the risks are great, no matter what happens from this point... but surely we've come too far to risk our enterprise on inactivity?"

Guderian gave vent to a scornful sound.

"The trap is to feel that we have to do something. The difficult decision is to do nothing. Action is always easier to decide upon."

Karl Koller, head of the DRL, made a quiet but firm contribution.

"I agree, Herr Feldmarschal."

The two nodded at each other, already knowing which way the dice would be cast.

"And you, Wilhelm. What do you think?"

Wilhelm Hoegner, Prime Minister of Bavaria, had already decided where his support lay.

"I say we do it. Too much has been invested already for our plans to be destroyed by inactivity, Herr Kanzler."

The scarcely veiled barb drew silent scowls from both military men.

Speer decided to defuse that particular tension immediately.

"The Feldmarschal is correct in what he says. The difficult decision is to do nothing, and I'd have no problem making that decision..."

...those assembled held their collective breath...

"... were it the right decision, which I believe it isn't."

He focussed on Diels.

"This can be done by way of accidents or other events... nothing to tie us to it in any way... nothing even remotely... given the way we now seem to be under suspicion for other recent matters?"

"I'll put my best man on it and it will be done without any link to us. No mistakes, Herr Kanzler. We'll eradicate these risks immediately."

Speer made great play of considering the choices, even though he had already made his.

"So be it, Kameraden. We'll move quickly and remove the threats. It will be done so that we cannot be blamed or even associated in any way with events. It's limited but necessary action. When can it be done?"

Diels looked at Pflug-Hartnung, prompting his man to answer.

"The order will be passed to our man. It'll be up to him to get this done as quickly as possible, Herr Kanzler. My orders will state that operational secrecy is paramount. I expect that will cause some delay, but not too much. He's an expert at what he does and he won't let us down. It will be done as you direct, Herr Kanzler."

Speer nodded.

"Good. That's all, Kameraden. I wish you all good day. Thank you. Diels, a moment of your time, please."

The military men saluted and the civilians nodded before shuffling out.

The two men were alone.

Speer hammered his hand on the desk.

"You better get this right this time, Rudolf. No fuck ups, no mistakes... we can't afford to show our hand too early or the whole fucking thing may come tumbling down around our heads."

"You can rest assured, Herr..."

"That's what you said last time... and now we've paperwork flying around that links us to the deaths of Gehlen and that French asshole! You fuck this up, Rudolf, and I'll make sure you have

335

an interesting last few days of your life. Do we understand each other?"

"Yes, Herr Kanzler."

"Now go and get it done... just let me know the moment success is reported."

"Yes, Herr Kanzler."

Once they had left the room, Speer turned back to reading the latest reports regarding strains in Berlin, where the Soviet-held area lay surrounded by Allied zones, and where tensions were clearly mounting.

Sat in her quarters with a bottle of Slivovitz for company, Nazarbayeva pondered the decision to send the information to the Allies, and wondered how it had been received.

Slipping out of her clothes, she took a healthy swig of the fiery fruit brandy and collapsed on the bed.

Refilling her glass, she laughed to herself, half expecting the information to be seen as nothing but an attempt to drive a wedge between the new Allies, but something told her that existing natural suspicion would simply be fed by the latest information.

In any case, it was all quite true and had been presented without embellishment or addition.

The door opened and General of Artillery Poliakov slipped in to the room.

The phone rang and Nazarbayeva took a scheduled report from her office as Poliakov slid himself inside her and started to grunt with pleasure.

Halfway through, she finished on the phone and started to properly enjoy herself, rising rhythmically up to meet his thrusts, the extreme pain as he brutally squeezed her breasts and dug in his nails almost cleansing her of the mental agony and anger she had felt since her sexual encounter in the Moscow dacha.

Her husband was lost to her so she sought other solaces, and hated herself each time, her needs and wants only temporarily satisfied by the sexual encounters with the passionless Poliakov, and each time her growing guilt burgeoned

When she was alone again, she went through the same old ritual of hating herself, crying, despair, and pledging herself again to Yuri, her husband.

Her other self mocked her, for her husband had no need for a wife who has no respect for him or herself, for a woman who would sleep with a common soldier in a dacha in Moscow.

At the end, as ever, Tatiana Nazarbayeva sought solace and answers in a bottle.

As ever, she fell asleep before either came.

1359 hrs, Sunday, 9th March 1947, Opera Square, Frankfurt, Germany.

"Zwei... mit frites und mayo. Danke."

There were a number of street vendors plying their trade but 'Ludwig's' had the reputation as having the very best bratwurst in Frankfurt, and his stall was always busy.

He busied himself selecting the bratwurst and repositioning them on the small grill.

What he was actually doing was sending a message to the British officer who stood waiting patiently for his order; a bratwurst in this place or that meant different things.

He placed the last bratwurst in the position signifying 'all clear' and then hastily put the order together as the queue started to multiply.

"Danke."

"Bitte."

The officer handed over a five-dollar bill and received his change before hurrying away, already stuffing fries and sausage into his mouth.

'Ludwig' served through into the afternoon and as usual was out of stock before four o'clock arrived.

He pushed his barrow past the ravaged old opera house and along Hochstrasse, before turning right at Börsenstrasse and pulling the double doors of his modest premises closed behind him.

He had made the usual checks and, satisfied that he had not been followed, he lifted the cash tin and climbed the stairs to the small flat.

He came back down after stowing the cash tin and went through his cleaning routine, leaving the trolley ready for tomorrow's labours, all save a fresh supply of foodstuffs.

Back upstairs he made himself coffee and removed the note that had accompanied the five-dollar bill.

He didn't look at it; it wasn't his business. He simply inserted it into the spine of a hymnbook.

337

'Ludwig' savoured the coffee and then took a gentle stroll to his normal place of worship.

Inside St. Katharinenkirche, he took in the evening's service with his normal piety, singing and praying with vigour.

Pausing to chat with the pastor, simply to suggest a hymn choice for the following week's service, 'Ludwig' returned to his spartan lodgings, his work complete.

When the congregation had departed, the pastor closed up and went straight to the pew that had been occupied by his contact and retrieved the hymnal that had been left in plain sight.

The message went on another journey.

1127 hrs, Monday 10th March 1947, Justizzentrum, temporary government building #3, Magdeburg, Germany.

Its destination was a desk in the Justizzentrum, one belonging to Horst Pflug-Hartnung.

In his hands he held the information requested and he grunted at its completeness.

Without taking his eyes from it, he lifted the receiver and spoke briefly to his secretary, summoning one of his officers.

Eight minutes later, Vögel was admitted to the room.

"Ah Vögel. We have the information. Here."

Pflug-Hartnung slid the original paper across the desk and it was immediately swept up by the Abwehr's premier hatchet man.

The piercingly intense eyes drank in every detail, assigning each piece of the itinerary a marking of 'no', 'yes', or 'maybe'.

There were many no's… two maybes… and two yesses.

"Your thoughts, Vögel?"

"Two opportunities, Sir. Friday looks best to me. More time to plan and get organised."

"Really? I would have thought Wednesday would have been better."

Vögel re-examined the itinerary.

"Understand what you mean, Sir. But I think not. Too many people about… too many armed personnel who would be alert. Friday will be best."

"And the other two named?"

"Not known to me, Sir. If they're not known to you either, I can suggest we don't need to worry."

"A fair point. I'll leave it up to you, Vögel, but…"

He leant forward to emphasise his point.

"... it's absolutely essential that we're not associated with this in any way. There must be no comeback against us whatsoever... do I make myself clear, Maior?"

"Yes, Herr Generalmaior. It shall be so."

"An aircraft. I assume you mean to use a bomb?"

"I may well do, Sir, but with some subtlety of course. Aircraft crash all the time. This one will simply carry someone important."

"Advise me when you are ready to proceed. I'll obtain the necessary authorisation. We need codewords..."

"If I might suggest, Sir?"

"Please. Go on."

Vögel, ever conscious of gaining favour with his masters, selected words of meaning to his superior, who was formerly of the Kriegsmarine.

"For stopping the mission, Falklands."

Pflug-Hartnung stared at his man.

"For holding the mission, Jutland."

He understood where his man was going and completed the trio of code words.

"And for proceed, Coronel?"

"Yes indeed, Herr Generalmaior."

"Excellent. And the other matter?"

"Much easier, Sir. A simple robbery. There'll be a small delay as nature takes her course, but it'll be done without problems."

"Excellent, Vögel. Get them done efficiently and I think I can find you a different office."

"Thank you, Sir."

Promotion was only a small part of Vögel's motivation, but he accepted the offer with good grace.

He left the room without another word as Pflug-Hartnung consider the choice of code words.

Victory, followed by defeat, followed by a draw.

Named for naval engagements, the Falklands was a decisive defeat for the Imperial Navy, and Jutland had been a bloody draw.

Coronel had been a glorious win.

It had come first, the 1st November 1914 if his memory served, but Von Spee and his armoured cruisers, having smashed the British at Coronel, paid the ultimate price just over a month later when, on 8th December, they were destroyed at the Falklands, with only Dresden and Seydlitz surviving.

There was a delicious irony in the selection that was not wasted on him, an old sailor from the Kaiser's navy

The Dresden had later been cornered and sunk by British warships, acting in violation of Chilean national waters.

The captain had tried to preserve his vessel by sending a negotiator to the British, a man Pflug-Hartnung had known and admired.

That man was Wilhelm Canaris, former head of the Abwehr, then an Oberleutnant zur See.

The same Wilhelm Canaris who was rumoured, during his numerous trips to Spain, to have met Allied contemporaries such as Stuart Menzies of MI-6, William Donovan of the OSS, and Kenneth Strong, then Deputy Intelligence chief for the Allied Armies in Europe.

He mentally doffed his hat to his old friend and wondered if he would support the present course of action.

'Not a hope. You were always too much of an idealist, Wilhelm. An honourable man for sure, but not capable of sacrificing for the common good, or for the glory of the Fatherland. Now's the time for strong and decisive men to act... and act we will.'

Horst Gustav Friedrich von Pflug-Hartnung stood and tidied his desk, ill at ease with his final thoughts.

'All that's needed after that is a sieg heil'

The phone rang, dragging him back into the real world.

2204 hrs, Monday, 10th March 1947, the Straits of Gibraltar.

It was an unusually busy night for the officers and men of the vessels monitoring the route from the Mediterranean into the Atlantic, or vice versa.

Usually they could expect no more than ten vessels at one time, something that peace now permitted, and also travelling at night with full lights on, something that would probably have brought instant death in the bloody days of 39 to 45.

This night there were, not including naval vessels, some thirty-one vessels in or approaching the Straits.

It was still a peaceful night, although death was abroad and riding the waves, by design, not by accident.

The Bogata, a German freighter, fired a distress flare and the radio crackled into life with warnings of broken steering.

The monitoring station ashore passed word to the Straits controller, who had already noted the flares and heard the distress messages.

340

Seemingly oblivious to the out-of-control freighter was the hospital ship, Hikawa Maru 2, a well-known sight in Gibraltan waters, constantly plying back and forth between Africa and Europe with refugees and casualties.

The radio howled more warnings, as the German captain declared he was carrying old submarine munitions.

Ashore, the admiral in charge sent a clear warning to all vessels in the area.

"All stations, all stations. Clear the channel, repeat, clear the channel. Remain as close inshore as possible and clear the area."

The Bogata bore down upon the highly illuminated hospital ship, which seemed to simply accept its fate without an ounce of effort to avoid the collision.

The two vessels came together in a tortured grind of metal that could be heard on two continents.

And then there was a flash.

The sound wave came next, and the pressure wave followed as quickly as it could.

Bogata had exploded.

In fact, there was no Bogata worth the name, simply a twisted something that somehow still floated.

In fact, there was precious little Hikawa Maru either, and what there was wreathed in orange flame.

Fire at sea…

The stricken vessel reportedly carried over two thousand souls, plus any that had survived from the Bogata.

That drove the rescuers forward and the naval vessels descended on the scene like bees round honey.

More explosions came from the Bogata, some sending playful rockets into the night, 105mm semi-armour piercing rockets that would be wholly deadly if they struck an approaching vessel.

Aware of the risks, the Straits admiral ordered fast responding Vosper MTBs to put to sea, to provide some sort of security as the rescue attempt went on.

He followed that with an order for two corvettes to raise steam and get out of the harbour to reinforce the flimsy security ring he was now presented with.

The first reports came in from a French frigate that slowly edged through the packed waters.

"Hundreds dead… hundreds badly burned… water full of dead and injured… more survivors still aboard… fire uncontrollable…"

341

It was the stuff of nightmares, and the Allied sailors braved many perils to do their duty.

Nachi Maru and Tsukushi Maru, both outbound to the Atlantic, radioed in and offered their assistance but the Admiral rightly reasoned that the area was crowded enough and that the continued explosions would pose a major risk to any vessel.

Other merchant vessels offered their help too, but all were declined.

On the outbound side, eight ships ran almost nose to tail as they moved closer to the African shore, as directed by the Straits admiral, safely putting distance between them and the fiery explosive hell that was the Bogata and Hikawa Maru.

That Admiral's fears became a tragic reality as the Royal Hellenic Navy's Apostolis, a Flower-class corvette, came apart in an instant, the flash, the sound, and the shock wave coming in close sequence as before.

Prior to feigning steering issues, Bogata had dropped a few mines overboard, all to help with the confusion if they struck home.

They were supposed to be moored mines, so they had a corroded and severed cable piece attached, all to maintain the illusion of accident should any be discovered.

Apostolic was beyond help and, cut in half by the magnetic mine, she quickly slid under the water, taking all but three of her crew with her.

The remaining naval vessels redoubled their efforts, but also set watches for anything suspicious in the water, and started working with any detection apparatus capable of doing any job underwater.

In short, in a dozen minutes, the Straits of Gibraltar had gone from tranquillity to mayhem.

Which suited the two Japanese surface vessels, both of whom nestled in between other merchant ships, two of which were there by coincidence, and four of which were there by design.

The commander of HMS Fowey, one of His Majesty's Shoreham class sloops, decided he could not presently contribute to the rescue efforts and laid off the scene, returning to his search duties.

In the sonar room, there was only one subject of conversation, and it wasn't the burning wrecks.

"Whatever that is, it ain't natural, Number One."

The First Lieutenant listened in on a repeater headset and could not help but agree.

"Ye gods, White. That sounds like a canteen of cutlery being turned in a butter churn. I grant you... there's some other sounds there too."

The hydrophone operator tried to clean up the sound but failed miserably, as even more incredible noises made themselves known.

"Now that's something going whizzbang... the wrecks for sure... but..."

He concentrated and then had a 'road to Damascus' moment.

"Bearing, White?"

"Bearing one-seven-zero, Sir."

"Bridge, sonar."

"What have you got, Jimmy?"

"Skipper, bearing one-seven-zero. What have you got in sight?"

There was a delay as a number of pairs of binoculars concentrated down the designated bearing.

"I'm guessing you have a bagful of spanners on the hydrophones, yes?"

"Too true, Skipper."

"There's six merchies over there, including both of those bloody Nip ships that you can hear coming from Iceland. Not surprised you can hear World War Four, Jimmy."

"There are some other weird sounds too, Skipper."

"Very possibly, Jimmy. Keep sweeping but I'm going to cut back into the channel now. Looks like our Gallic cousins have pulled off. We may have an opportunity. Come back up as soon as you're satisfied that there's no battlecruisers amongst the merchies."

"Aye, aye, Skipper."

The First Lieutenant replaced the phone and picked up the repeater headset again.

"What do you reckon, Chief?"

"Strange sounds, not like I've heard before. But it's a weird night, Sir. All sorts of harmonics at work out there."

As if to emphasise his point, something else let go on board the sinking Bogata.

"Keep on it for as long as you can, Chief. Good work... good work, White."

"Tell you what, Sir."

"Chief?"

"If you're thinking something like a sub is out there, think again. No self-respecting submariner would be anywhere near one of

343

those merchie rust buckets, and we all know they spook easily. The sound of yonder bonfire party would have sent them off in a tizzy by now."

"You're probably right, Chief. Still, stay on it. "

"Aye, aye, Sir."

He and White did so, but without hearing anything specifically.

Maybe an active sonar search might have found something, but the order was never given.

The six merchant men cleared the area as quickly as the labouring engines allowed, although, had they been closely observed, an experienced eye would have noted near-perfect station keeping.

Their six charges worked to the same strict pattern and speed, all perilously close to their protective vessels, but all confident that they would escape into the open Atlantic and their rendezvous with destiny.

I-1, I-14, I-401, I-402, J-54 Soviet Vozmezdiye, and finally J-51 Soviet Initsiativa had carried out the most dangerous part of their mission.

That men willingly sacrificed their lives to ensure their success was the subject of ceremonies to honour the dead and recognise their selfless acts.

That over fifteen hundred innocent civilians and wounded military personnel also perished was of absolutely no significance whatsoever.

Two nights later the final legacy of their breakthrough visited itself upon the Dutch vessel Macoma, a tanker converted to a MAC ship by adding a flight deck over the top of its hull.

The single mine detonated alongside forward on her port beam and her plates opened up like they were papier-mache.

Tankers died hard and Macoma took two days to go down, despite the best efforts of Portuguese naval ships who responded to her desperate pleas for help.

One of the Greek merchant ships that had formed part of the breakout effort responded, resuming its normal duties to avoid too many questions.

The two Marus and one other vessel, a non-descript Turkish steamer, stayed in relative close company, heading for a rendezvous with old comrades at Deserta Grande in the Portuguese archipelago of Madeira.

Stalin and the rest of the GKO listened in varying stages of concern and genuine horror as the ramping up of Allied military readiness was laid bare by Zhukov, ably supported by Kaganovich and Nazarbayeva.

The simple question posed that the General Secretary posed lay hanging in the air.

"Why?"

Carefully choosing his words, Zhukov took the agreed step and deferred to the two intelligence officers.

Kaganovich followed suit and stuck to the script the three had hastily prepared.

"Comrade General Nazarbayeva is better equipped than I to answer that question. Comrade General Secretary."

"So?"

"Comrades, the NKVD and ourselves have pieced together some information. I stress that this is not yet confirmed, but the GRU sources are normally reliable, and Comrade General Kaganovich vouches for his own agents in this matter."

The two exchanged professional nods.

"It would appear that there's some concern about a submarine that was sunk in the Baltic, one that was broaching declared Allied waters and was sunk, as per their rules of engagement."

"Preposterous... absolutely prepost..."

Stalin's raised hand stopped Nikolai Voznesensky's loud objection in its tracks.

"Let her finish, Nikolai!"

Tatiana waited for an appropriate moment and then continued.

"It's our belief that the Allies are more concerned about what the submarine might have been carrying than the submarine itself."

She looked directly at Admiral Isakov, who avoided her gaze, something that told her all she needed to know.

The men to her left already knew, something they had failed to share with her for reasons known best to themselves.

Bulganin, a member of the very inner circle and privy to all things Raduga, shifted uncomfortably in his chair.

Voznesensky, on the outside of the inner circle, stayed silent and confused.

"We know for a fact that one of the British patrol vessels responsible is presently tied up in Holland and under quarantine. Lots of civilians, who we believe to be scientists, are going back and forth, and extremely tight military security is in place all around the whole area. According to Comrade General Kaganovich's agent, the security faces both ways, which tells us that they're concerned about what's on board that vessel."

Khrushchev, a recent appointee to the GKO, raised his hand to speak.

Stalin saw the gesture and, having brought him into the GKO as a trusted comrade and advisor, gave him his opportunity.

"Comrade?"

"Comrade General Secretary. I think that we must first establish if this was one of our submarines."

'Nicely done, Nikita... not that we don't know of course.'

Stalin declined to ask Isakov outright, as they both knew that it was, but chose to continue the farce for the benefit of those members of the GKO who had been excluded from important decisions and for the naive woman.

"Comrade Nazarbayeva?"

She may not have been the sharpest politically, but Nazarbayeva understood that the simple of question would have been better put to Isakov, and she suddenly realised that she was stood in the middle of some grand game.

"Comrade General Secretary, our sources inform us that survivors wearing Soviet naval uniform were recovered, along with a number of bodies... similarly attired."

Eyes turned to Isakov.

He knew his position was not under threat, but played the cornered fox to perfection.

"One of my submarines has been reported missing. This is common knowledge amongst this circle. It seems that it must have had a navigational problem and strayed into Allied waters, as its orders clearly prohibited coming within fifty nautical miles of the line that has been negotiated. My searches have been in its assigned patrol area, which was some considerable distance away from the Allied maritime exclusion line."

Stalin moved in quickly.

"This we'll discuss at greater length shortly, Comrade Admiral. Now, Comrade Nazarbayeva, what else?"

"If I may finish the submarine issue, Comrade General Secretary, there's some suggestion that the submarine was in Allied waters for aggressive purposes, and was carrying some new weapons."

"Thank you, Comrade. We'll deal with the naval matters later. Now, move on please."

Stalin clearly shut her down on the submarine matter, so she proceeded with the brief on the land situation.

"Tensions are extremely high because of this enhanced military level, particularly around Vienna and our military lines opposite the Germans and Poles. Air forces on both sides are being aggressive, up to the levels of the no-fly areas and, in some cases, broaching it in what we can only assume is deliberate provocations. I must state that this is true of pilots from both sides, Comrade General Secretary."

Stalin again waved a commanding hand, this time directed at Nazarbayeva.

"Comrade Repin?"

Deputy Commander in Chief of the Red Air Force Colonel General Aleksandr Repin, present because his senior had taken ill the day before, shifted under the gaze.

"Comrade General Secretary. Only yesterday I issued further firm instructions on crossing the agreed lines. The reports I have seen state mainly navigational error and nothing more. However, fighter pilots will be fighter pilots."

It was not the wisest answer, which most who heard it understood as he delivered it.

"Idiot! Fighter pilots who do not obey my fucking orders will be dead fighter pilots, Comrade General. There'll be no more toleration of these errors. Make examples. No distinction. We cannot afford to go back to war! Do you understand?"

"Yes, Comrade General Secretary."

"Good, no repeats."

Repin now safely settled in at the top of Stalin's shit list, made himself as small as possible.

"Comrade Nazarbayeva... continue."

"As yet there've been no clashes, but the situation is critical... apologies, Comrade General Secretary... in my opinion, the situation is critical. Our own forces have gone on the highest alert possible under your own instructions. We now have two huge armies poised for action and I truly believe that it'll only take the smallest of matters to start the war all over again."

Stalin suddenly realised that the woman had finished.

"Thank you, Comrade Nazarbayeva. So Comrades, how to defuse these new tensions? We're not ready for any restart in hostilities, but if it does all blow up again we'll make sure they regret starting it."

"Withdraw further back to enlarge the zone between forces?"

Voznesensky vied for top place on Stalin's list.

"Concede yet more ground, Comrade? Yet more ground?"

"No, Comrade General Secretary. We're not yet at the limits of the withdrawal that we've agreed upon. We simply move back now and open the gap, removing the tensions. Surely that will also allay any fears they have about the submarine's intent?"

"Fantastic. My own close comrades are now suggesting we give ground to the enemy ahead of schedule... sending what fucking message, eh?"

"Surely the defusing of tensions serves the Rodina, Comrade General Secretary?"

Stalin opened his mouth but decided to exercise a little more thought.

"Yes, you are right. Nikolai Alekseevich. It would, but we have delayed our withdrawals as much as possible for a good reason, a reason that also serves Mother Russia. We have bought time to repair our bridges and roads, and to ensure that the Red Army is provided with the materials for our safe defence."

He stood and walked around the table to stand behind the Deputy Chairman of the Council of Ministers who also wore the hat of the Minister in charge of Soviet Economic Rejuvenation.

Voznesensky also jumped out of his skin as Stalin placed a hand on his shoulder, one that the man of steel intended to impart friendship, whereas the recipient viewed it as a harbinger of death, an instrument of selection that marked him for the executioner.

"Your idea is reasonable, Comrade..."

Stalin started walking again, each head swivelling in turn as he passed behind them.

"But these are not reasonable times we live in. We must find a more direct way to defuse this... a quicker way... one that guarantees success."

There was a silence that had a special quality to it, as often the silences around the communist's leader table chilled and mentally beat those present.

Malenkov dipped his toe in the cold waters.

"Comrade General Secretary... perhaps we could use Camp Vár?"

Stalin turned slowly, as if the idea had not occurred to him, rather than been part of the dance previously orchestrated.

"Yes... I see your idea."

Khrushchev, who was supposed to have presented the idea but had been unseated by Malenkov's swifter than expected recovery, quickly took up the baton.

"Excellent idea, Comrade Malenkov, and if I might suggest, Comrade General Secretary, we need to move quickly on this matter, so, as we have the very best tools to hand, perhaps we can set them to work straight away?"

"Comrade Khrushchev, please continue."

Stalin sat in his chair and was puffing on a cigarette in no time.

"To mark the seriousness of the situation, we should send only a high-level delegation to specifically conduct negotiations... a delegation so impressive that the Allies cannot fail to understand the sincerity of our words."

Stalin nodded and went further.

"Which would also encourage them to send negotiators of equal worth... I'm assuming you mean military, Comrade Khrushchev?"

Nikita Khrushchev giggled like an old woman and held out a hand, gesturing at some still stood at the end of the table.

"But of course, Comrade General Secretary."

Nazarbayeva, easing her foot in her boot as the pain of standing played havoc with her old wound, suddenly realised that the talking had stopped and she was under scrutiny.

"Who better than they, Comrade General Secretary?"

Zhukov and Kaganovich had been forewarned by Khrushchev, but feigned surprise.

Nazarbayeva had no need for such devices.

"Excellent idea, Nikita Sergeyevich. Anyone else?"

Some words can carry hidden meanings, and Stalin's most certainly said 'I like it and that's that'.

There were no more ideas.

"We'll immediately appeal to the Allies to send a high-ranking military delegation to Sweden to discuss the latest tensions and developments. Make sure they know that Marshal Zhukov will be leading that mission. That should ensure an appropriate level opposite you, Comrade Marshal."

"But Comrade General Secretary, I need to speak with you on an urgent matter."

A number of hearts stood still for a second, for a number of different reasons.

"Speak now, Comrade Nazarbayeva, there is little time."

"I cannot, Comrade General Secretary. I must speak with you privately."

Stalin either misconstrued or simply dismissed the possibility out of hand.

"Then private matters must wait, Comrade Leytenant General."

Again Nazarbayeva's effort to tackle Stalin face to face had failed, again by the efforts of the conspirators.

He turned to Beria.

"You'll take care of the invitation?"

"Yes, Comrade General Secretary. Immediately this meeting concludes.

"Excellent. I want you sat opposite your counterparts by Friday afternoon at the latest. Deal with this matter and reduce tensions along all fronts... land, sea, and air. Admiral?"

Isakov was suddenly focussed.

"You'll brief these officers on the submarine tomorrow morning, and supply everything they require."

"Yes, Comrade General Secretary."

It was not until later that Isakov spoke with Stalin and was told that, in this instance, everything was not necessarily everything.

"Well, I've read it twice and I still don't believe it, Walter."

"It's hot stuff, that's for sure, General."

"Zhukov... haven't seen that man since Berlin... liked him... felt he was straight. You?"

"Same as, General."

They lapsed into the silence of individual thought.

Outside there was a squeal of brakes, a metallic graunch, and then a blizzard of expletives.

Bedell-Smith rose up and went to the window.

"Well that's just swell. George is here and his driver just clipped McCreery's staff car."

Eisenhower choked on his cigarette, the laugh turning quickly to lung wrenching spasm.

"Sorry, Walter. Would that be the brand new Humber that he had sent down here last week?"

Before Bedell-Smith could answer there was another graunch as Patton's driver drove his own vehicles away and parked up.

More expletives followed, shouted in with an Aussie twang, as McCreery's driver took to cursing the 'fucking Yank bastard's' parentage.

A military policeman arrived to sort out the problem, and the Aussies protestations were cut short by authoritative words from the German officer.

Bedell-Smith's attention returned to the matter in hand.

"So, I'm assuming we're going to respond in kind, Sir?"

"You betcha, Walter. Can't afford not to... President Truman's wishes aside... I intend to let them know we'll be there. If it helps ease the storm that's gathering, how could we do otherwise? Also, it'll give us the chance to ask some serious questions. I'll get something organised on that score. Anyway. I'll need to speak to the President but I don't see any objections."

"Anyone in mind?"

"Absolutely, Walter."

"What th... hey, hang on, Sir!"

"Hang on nothing, Walter. You're the man for this. We'll get you some sidekicks with clout, but it'll be your ball to run with. You know all the questions... heck, you even know some of the answers already. Has to be you."

Bedell-Smith couldn't find a reasonable argument against, so capitulated.

"So who are you going to send with me? George?"

Eisenhower laughed without coughing this time.

"Like I'd send George. Jeez, can you imagine? No, I've been given a God sent opportunity to put him somewhere out of harm's way for a while. Our German cousins have asked for him to observe some of their exercises over this weekend, and then to have him attached to their headquarters for a month as an advisor."

Bedell-Smith was relieved.

They had been looking for something to do with George Patton since he had returned to Frankfurt six weeks previously.

Some in high position had suggested 'General - Paperclips' or 'Officer commanding Headquarters car parking', but Ike had come down hard on them, mainly men who hadn't served much in the ETO, reminding them of Patton's previous good service.

"No, I think we'll need a Frenchman, a German, and someone else. Need some balance to proceedings."

"Von Vietinghoff?"

"He's just asked for leave. Family bereavement. Couldn't say no, not really. Would've been the perfect man."

"Anyway, Sir, shall I send the message?"

"Let me speak to the President first."

Truman was wholly enthusiastic and encouraged Eisenhower himself to lead the delegation, something Ike successfully resisted.

Within hours, the Soviets received their reply, as did the Swedes, who would be responsible for hosting both new military delegations at Camp Vár.

1109 hrs, Thursday, 13th March, 1947, House of Madame Fleriot, La Vigie, Nogent L'Abbesse, near Reims, France.

Madame Besoinine answered the urgent knocking on the door, Jerome having been confined to his bed with a nasty chest infection.

A second later she was dead, a knife driven up through her throat and into the brain beyond.

Without words, two men grabbed the still-erect body and lowered it gently to the ground as two others moved quietly into the house beyond.

They split into two teams and swung into their plan, moving through the ground floor with silenced pistols at the ready.

Two pairs of young eyes observed them in silence and moved away quickly, knowing that sooner or later the bad men would come upstairs.

They found refuge in the bedroom of Madame Fleriot, who listened to their report with growing anxiety, although the situation brought back instincts learned in a different time, when Armande Valerie Capucine Fleriot had existed within a murky and dangerous world.

She secreted the girls in her wardrobe and moved across to take a seat at the dressing table, from where she extracted a tool of her former trade.

Anne-Marie was walking around the garden, the exercise helping ease the back pain that plagued her every waking moment.

Her bump had become so much more pronounced in a short period of time, so much so that none of the clothing she had purchased for the later stages of the third trimester were simply not up to the job.

Waddling for all she was worth, Anne-Marie made her way towards the groundsman's lodge and the toilet that she desperately needed.

The stairs creaked, marking the progress of the hunters.

Armande settled herself in relaxed fashion, although the weight in her hand was more than she remembered.

Her bedroom door flew open as a boot pushed it.

The sound of the door striking her mother's ornate rococo chair was quickly followed by two heavy shots.

Armande Fleriot put both on target, and the would-be assassin flew back into the hall with as much grace and life as a popped balloon.

A shape tumbled through the door and she fired again, this time missing.

The second man rolled behind the gold leaf bed end and came up in the firing position, getting off two shots before a single 7.65mm bullet took him on the bridge of the nose and continued its journey into the man's brain.

The first had passed along the side of her head and removed much of her right ear.

It was very messy but of little note.

The second bullet had hit her high in the left chest, throwing her backwards and against the dressing table, breaking her collarbone.

Despite the pain, Armande Fleriot kept her Browning 1922 pistol firmly sighted on the doorway.

In the garden, the unmistakable sound of shots carried to Anne-Marie, and to the two men stalking her.

She disappeared into the groundsman's lodge, cursing herself for not having the wits to have her own weapon to hand.

Alternatives quickly suggested themselves, and she armed herself as best she could

Holding her breath, and without the slightest concern for her dignity, she allowed the hot urine to trickle down her legs as she focussed on the doorway.

A shadow played across the gap and she tensed ready to strike.

The door gently opened outwards, and she sensed the presence without seeing.

It was enough and she trusted her instincts.

The sickle swept out of the doorway, curving back round towards her in its natural arc, and contacted soft yielding flesh.

The scream was cut short as she yanked back on the handle, the high-pitched sound replaced by the gurgling of a severe throat wound on a dying man.

"Merde! Chienne!"

The other man put six shots through the wooden walls, hoping to hit the woman who had mortally wounded his brother.

Anne-Marie grunted and sagged to the ground as two struck her and robbed her of her strength.

The shooter heard her sounds of pain and knew he had hit home.

Moving carefully to the half-open door, he stuck his head round and saw their female target lying on the ground trying hard to stem the flow of blood from her left thigh.

He brought his pistol up and tapped her on the side of the head, hard enough to break the skin, not hard enough to knock her out.

"You fucking bitch. That's my brother lying there."

The man was still dying noisily, but vengeance was all the surviving brother thought of, not that he could do anything with his sibling's gaping throat wound in any case.

"I'm going to kill your fucking baby first, and then I'm going to shoot you to pieces, starting with your face."

Anne-Marie, in pain and with shock starting to take its toll, summoned up the strength to plant a gobbet of spit on the man's chest in a show of defiance.

"Fucking SS whore! You fucking SS…"

He heard and turned in the briefest of moments…

Blood sprayed over Anne-Marie's face and chest, then more that came like a fireman's hose.

354

She never heard the shots that took the life of the man who nearly killed her.

Five bullets entered his body at almost point blank range, entering from as low as his navel to the highest point at his neck, and it was the neck wound that produced the geyser of blood.

The Colt Ace .22 was a practice weapon, one not normally used for the purpose of killing, but at close range, a .22 bullet can do a lot of damage, and five on target would bring a lot of hurt on whatever they hit.

The fourth shot was the one that killed him, clipping the aorta before expending the rest of its low power in the stomach beyond.

He toppled forward and his weight dropped across Anne-Marie's legs, dislocating her right ankle in one swift and excruciatingly painful second.

The damaged aorta let go and the second brother went on his brief, dark journey.

Tears clouded Anne-Marie's eyes as she sought the identity of her saviour.

She dabbed her eyes with her good hand and found a handkerchief pressed into her hand.

"Ami... are you hurt very badly, Ami?"

Anne-Marie's floating brain suddenly focussed.

She carefully took the loaded and cocked gun from her stepdaughter Greta.

"Are there any more of them?"

"No, Ami... there were just four."

"Two in the house?"

"Aunty shot them both. She says they are no longer a concern."

"Good. I'm fine, Cherie. Madame is unhurt? You're both unhurt?"

"Aunty is hurt but she says not bad. Greta is looking after her. I came to find you."

"And you brought your practice pistol, you clever girl."

"I had to do something, Ami."

"You did, Magda."

She kissed her stepdaughter despite the pain that her movements caused.

"Now, find Jerome and ask him to call the doctor and then get me to a phone."

"I don't think Jerome is very well, Ami."

Anne-Marie cursed herself for being so stupid.

355

"Find Madame Besoinine instead."

"She's in the hallway. I don't think she's very well either, Ami."

"Ok, ok, sorry Cherie. Can you ring for the doctor yourself?"

"But of course!"

The indignation on the eleven year old's face was writ large.

Anne-Marie could almost sense the assurance in her eyes.

'If I can shoot a man then a telephone call is easy!'

"Of course you can. I'll wait here. Ring for the doctor and then help your sister with Aunty."

Magda took to her heels, a girl with a mission, leaving Anne-Marie to suffer the pain of her injuries and ponder the events that had nearly snuffed out her life and that of her unborn child.

She kept a tight grip on the practice pistol… just in case.

Some time later, Commandant Vincennes received a call from Anne-Marie Knocke, one that created a maelstrom of activity within the local ranks of the SDECE.

The four bodies were quickly taken away and an investigation started to discover who they were and why they had come to kill.

Each man was clean… in as much as there was nothing to identify, except some cash and smoking materials.

No ID whatsoever.

Each man had a bag, probably to carry away the objects they looted, but the sense of it all was that they were there solely for the purpose of killing.

The prime target was the subject of much speculation, and the pregnant Deux agent was considered top of the list.

1058 hrs, Friday 14th March 1947, Rhein-Main Airbase, Frankfurt, Germany.

The engines simply refused to turn.

"Oh c'mon, fellahs. You gotta be kidding me?"

Nothing now worked….. nothing had worked… and now the smell of burning electrics assaulted the noses of the cockpit crew.

"You smell that, Seb?"

"Uh huh… my electrics have just failed… nope… they're bac… failed again… this mission's a snafu, Major."

"Ain't that the fucking truth? Think we better get the VIPs outta here fast. There's smoke here now."

He gestured at the haze coming up around his feet and from behind the instrument panel.

"Abandon ship… aye aye, cap'n."

"Shut it, you douchebag. Just remember who we've got on board and get them off in such a manner as I'll still have a chance at my bird."

"Aye, aye cap'n."

The co-pilot disappeared to break the bad news to the senior officers in the passenger compartment.

The passengers evacuated and moved back to towards their vehicles, confusing the USAAF base commander and his entourage.

A hasty liaison with one of the senior officers from the crippled aircraft brought a possible conclusion to mind, and the tower was instructed to hold another flight on the runway.

The RAF flight sergeant responded to the pilot's instructions and, once the aircraft had stopped its taxi run, opened the nearside rear cabin door.

The first thing that caught his eye was the ground crew racing back with the steps.

Next were the two staff vehicles that sped up from the direction of the tower, complete with four jeeps as escort.

Behind him, the five senior officers started to pose questions, to which he could only guess at a response.

"Seems we have last minute company, Sir."

"Anyone we know, Sergeant?"

"Can't say yet, Sir… but likely they've some serious clout or we wouldn't have stopped."

Kenneth Strong turned back round and rummaged for some light reading.

Bedell-Smith, sharing Strong's aircraft for the trip to Camp Vár, relaxed into quiet conversation with De Lattre.

Behind them, their staffs chatted or snoozed, depending on what they had been up to the night before.

Anne-Marie Foster extracted a Daphne du Maurier novel and settled down as the two RAF officers returned to their bickering over the performance of the latest American jet fighter, something they called a Sabre.

Strong abandoned attempts to eavesdrop their conversation as they slipped into trade talk, but the two highly decorated fighter

357

aces were clearly impressed with the experimental plane that was doing the European tour.

In the refuelling station cross the airfield, a pair of eyes that had narrowed when the aircraft aborted its taxi became virtual slits as the observer tried to decide what the hell was going on.

His fellow tanker driver slid off to the toilet, citing bad chicken the night before, giving Krankel a chance to use the works' binoculars without having to justify himself.

"Donnerwetter!"

Krankel was a decisive man always, but what had just presented itself to his eyes turned his stomach to ice and impaired his brain function so much that he could hardly manage a coherent thought.

"Scheisse! Scheisse! Scheisse!"

Normally one of the Abwehr's eyes and ears at the airbase, his special mission had drawn on all the old talents learned during his time with the Brandenburgers.

He watched, gripping the binoculars so tightly that he expected them to break under the pressure, although he could not prevent himself from risking it.

The new arrivals and their baggage virtually flew up the steps, which were then quickly wheeled away as the door was shut.

The RAF C-54 Skymaster trundled into position and then leapt down the runway, clawing into the air on its way to the talks in Sweden.

"Clerk's Office."

"Vögel, Krankel, we…"

"This is an unsecured line, you fool."

"Shut the fuck up and listen."

He gripped the phone like it was the neck of this idiot agent.

"This better be worth it, Krankel."

The words spilled into his ear as the excited Krankel told his story.

"Scheisse!"

"What do I do… I mean… what do we do, eh?"

"Leave it with me. Now… get off the phone and go and do what you do."

He broke the connection and was out of his office door before the sound of his chair scraping the floor had died away.

Normally, Vögel would saunter to his chief's office.

Today he made it in under two minutes, and almost battered down the door as he ran through it only half-opened.

"What is the meaning of this, man?"

The out-of-breath Vögel stumbled through his words as he eyed the other man in the room.

"Urgent... need to talk to you... alone, Herr General... urgent... but for your ears only."

Horst Pflug-Hartnung looked apologetically at his companion.

Von Vietinghoff stood and clicked his heels without rancour.

"I'll be outside, Horst."

The door closed before Pflug-Hartnung went for Vögel.

"What the fuck do you think you're doing, man? "

"Shut up and listen... Sir!"

The conversation was brief and by the end of it Pflug-Hartnung's mind was trying to deal with a frenzy of thoughts.

"I've no secure line to talk to the Kanzler... that damn bomb broke the cables and they're being fixed as we speak."

Dropped on the old city of Magdeburg on the night of 16th January 1945, the unexploded one thousand pounder finally honoured its mission and did an excellent job at destroying much of the locale, including the covertly laid special telephone system that allowed secret conversations to flow between the Republican government's hierarchy.

"So... make a decision, Sir. We've very little time."

"We'll show our hand if we warn them... we can't... the Kanzler's main concern was preserving our secrecy."

"Then make the decision... Sir."

"Get Vietinghoff back in here now!"

Vögel opened the door and summoned von Vietinghoff in a manner that would have normally earned him a severe rebuke, but the canny general knew better than to bark at a time that he should be listening.

He listened, astounded, shocked, and for once in his life unsure of how he should proceed... would proceed if it were his decision.

Von Vietinghoff realised that Pflug-Hartnung had stopped, and that both men's eyes were on him.

Officially on bereavement leave, he had dropped in to speak to Pflug-Hartnung about a delicate personal matter, only to suddenly find himself at the centre of a big decision.

"The Kanzler must be informed immediately."

"Not possible Heinrich. That bomb… it wrecked the secure lines."

"Verdamnt. You, man. How would you stop it?"

Vögel had already thought that through.

"Too late to send an aircraft up. Radio… only way, Herr General."

"Which would compromise our secrecy."

"Yes."

"So the choice is non-existent. We have no choice. The game will run its course, and we must be ready."

"Your meaning, Heinrich?"

"My meaning is simple, my friend. We have a problem here… or we may have an opportunity."

Pflug-Hartnung understood the meaning, and the gravity of von Vietinghoff's words.

"You mean Undenkbar? Now?"

"We've been waiting for the moment, and maybe this is that moment. This awful opportunity that's been thrust into our hands by fate may be just what we need to make our plans come perfectly together. We would never have considered it, but it may be just what we needed."

Silence greeted his words, the sort of silence that held neither acquiescence nor disagreement, simply fear.

"Vögel is it?"

"Yes, Herr General."

"Are we involved in this in any way that's traceable?"

"No, Herr General."

"Then let us prepare ourselves. The dice are cast."

…Nine minutes and forty-seven seconds earlier…

Kenneth Strong had leapt to attention but had quickly been told to sit down by the flight sergeant in charge, who fussed over his and the newly arrived passengers' seatbelts as the C-54 gathered speed.

"Sorry, Sir Kenneth. Needs must. Our aircraft had a technical problem."

"No problem, Sir, Glad the RAF could oblige. Are you going to Sweden too then?"

360

The Skymaster's wheels left the ground and the sound of the undercarriage's retraction made a few people jump.

Strong's confusion was reasonable, given that his journey to Sweden had been planned over a week ago and he had already had Bedell-Smith join him since the Soviet approach.

"No... well, yes and no actually. Can I smoke?"

The flight sergeant decided it was not within his purview to deny the NATO commander his cigarette.

"Certainly, Sir."

Eisenhower lit up and drew in the satisfying smoke as Bradley explained about the problems with the USAAF C-118 Liftmaster.

"But, if I might ask, what are you two doing here, General Bradley?"

Bradley sat back into his seat looking suitably coy.

Eisenhower puffed out a long stream of smoke.

"Golf."

"Golf?"

"Well, Sir Kenneth... not just golf obviously. The President asked me to stay available for this Camp Vár meeting and someone who shall remain nameless", ... Bradley tried hard to look innocent...."Decided that he was heading up to Denmark to play some golf at Aalborg... the whole course has been cleared of snow apparently... so I figured I'd kill two birds with one stone and head up to be closer to Sweden, and wipe the smug look off this one's face with a few rounds."

Strong knew about their shared passion and could imagine the conversation between the two friends.

"Well, yes, I understand that, Sir, but... err... is it wise?"

"I felt I should remain at NATO but the President wanted me up near where the action is. After all, in his newly-considered view, Zhukov is the top dog and warrants my presence."

He lit another cigarette.

"I argued against having both Walter and myself in Sweden at a time of heightened tension... we agreed on Denmark... Aalborg has a prime headquarters facility and... by some happy chance, an excellent gold course that has been cleared of snow and is ready to play."

"Sounds perfect to me, Sir."

Bradley added a sotto-voce comment

"Until he gets on the tee when it'll all go wrong for him."

Eisenhower, as he was supposed to do, heard the sleight.

"Dream on, General Bradley… I've seen you play remember!"

The group descended into laughter as the aircraft rose steadily to cruising height.

1103 hrs, Friday, 14th March 1947, Imperial College, London, England.

"I need to speak to Sir Kenneth immediately."

Professor William Penney was as agitated as could be, and the secretary's inability to connect him was too much to bear.

"Now… I must speak to him now… it's a matter of vital importance, man!"

Military secretaries, unthreatened by rank, can be the most stubborn creatures on the planet and Penney was getting nowhere fast.

"Well where is he, man? I need to get hold of him right now."

Again, the brick wall was insurmountable.

"Can you get a message to him… I mean straight away… it's absolutely vital that I speak to him?"

The brick wall appeared a little more responsive and Penney gave his details.

"No, no… I can't say. Just please tell him it's about the documents he asked me to look through. I missed something, and he needs to know about it."

He looked at his companion and shrugged.

"Thank you."

He looked at the silent handset with unconcealed disdain.

"Blasted man… bloody blasted man!"

The air force officer held his peace.

"Leonard, can you pull any strings at all?"

Group Captain Cheshire took a steady breath.

"Not likely that I can get hold of him if you can't, Bill."

The two were friends from Tinian, when they both flew in 'Big Stink' for the third bombing mission to Yokosuka.

Cheshire, home for a spot of leave at La Court in Petersfield, had dropped in on his friend for luncheon, and walked into a blizzard of invective from the academician.

Penney finished threatening the telephone with silent words and replaced the receiver.

"I say… have you still got your clearance, Leonard?"

He hadn't told Bill Penney about his latest assignment.

"Yes, still on the inside working on some special projects for the Air Force. All hush hush of course."

"Quite. I wonder if you could pass the information on for me... just in case I can't get hold of Sir Kenneth?"

"Delighted to, Bill. To whom?"

The question flummoxed Penney.

"Who do you see from the programme?"

Cheshire thought about his answer very carefully and made a decision.

"I see Leslie Groves occasionally."

"Excellent... is he still expanding at the waist?"

Cheshire merely shrugged.

"No matter... yes. Perfect. Show it to Groves. Someone in authority needs to know."

Cheshire could hide his curiosity no longer.

"Know what exactly, Bill... I am cleared for these things."

It was Penney's turn to weight up the pros and cons.

He rummaged in the second folder and brought out a piece of paper that was almost clear, except for one typed line of text.

"I'll give you this folder. But this is what I missed first time round. Simply put, it had folded in the bottom of the envelope and I missed it. What do you think eh?"

"Well, I know what I think... but where did it come from?"

"Apparently from some scientists working for the Russians."

"Good Lord!"

Just in case, Cheshire read it again, this time aloud.

"235U92-92KR36/141BA56-USPENKA"

"Quite."

"How old is this... do we know?"

"Haven't the foggiest, Leonard."

"235U92... Uranium 235 with 92 protons... Krypton... Barium... they're ahead of where we had them, aren't they?"

"Well Leonard, depending on the age of this information, they might already have it."

"Which is why..."

"...why you need to get it known fast. I agree."

The two exchanged insider looks that were full of concern.

"And Uspenka is?"

"Ah, that was the easy part. I just looked at a map. It's in Russia but the trouble is... there's more than one."

It was an unsecured line, so the message was not what it would seem to any listener.

"Say that again, Horst?"

"Kanzler, I repeat, there will be no Nibelungen at the Berlin Opera House this year."

"That's preposterous, man! How can this have happened?"

"Kanzler, it's important just to accept it's happened and to make other arrangements."

"Are you sure? Are you really sure?"

"Yes, Herr Kanzler. There's no Nibelungen... no other choice. You must make other arrangements."

"Mein Gott, Horst."

"I wish it was otherwise, Herr Kanzler, but I could not ensure the production went ahead."

"Thank you for letting me know. I'll make alternative arrangements immediately. Thank you, Horst."

"Herr Kanzler."

Speer sat staring at the silent handset, the shock of the message washing back and forth from his brain to his very soul.

He clicked the cradle twice and requested another line.

"Guderian."

"Feldmarschal, Kanzler Speer. I have to inform you that there will be no Nibelungen at the Berlin Opera House this year."

"What?"

"There it is. Unfortunate, but we must make other arrangements."

"How? Why?... I mean..."

"It's just the way it is, Herr Feldmarschal. Horst just contacted me with the news."

"And you have accepted this, Herr Kanzler?"

"I've no choice, Herr Feldmarschal."

"So, do we go to the alternative immediately?"

"We'll do it at the first rescheduled performance."

"The first?"

"Yes, the first."

"Zu befehl, Herr Kanzler. If you'll excuse me then."

"Good luck, Herr Feldmarschal."

Speer replaced the receiver and sat looking at his hands.

They trembled noticeably, the enormity of the course upon which he had set his country just apparent.

364

Although the reasons behind the early activation of Undenkbar were still unclear, he had just ordered Guderian to instigate the plan at the first opportunity, which would be 0200hrs... tomorrow.

Guderian replaced the receiver and composed himself, trying to work out what could have possibly happened to initiate Undenkbar ahead of schedule.

His brain railed against it all, but it also strived to bring order to his thoughts.

'Whatever has started this is immaterial... for later debate... now you must act, Erich!'

He picked up the phone again.

"I want the duty signals officer here now."

Yes, Herr Feldmarschal. General Patton is still waiting in the lobby, Sir."

'Verdamnt... verdamnt... forgot about him...'

"Please give him my apologies and ask him to come in."

Guderian quickly wrote his orders for the Signals Officer, anticipating it would be he who arrived first.

It was instead George Patton, who was unhappy at being kept waiting, especially as the 'Goddamned Krauts' had asked for him specifically.

Guderian rose and shook his contemporary's hand.

"My apologies, Herr General, but there have been some items that simply wouldn't wait. I have one more to complete and then we can travel together to the exercise site."

"Thank you, Fieldmarshal."

Guderian completed the simple but monumental order, complete with the unique distribution code group and finished as the door resounded to an urgent knocking.

"Come!"

The Signals Officer strode in to receive his instructions.

Guderian handed him a sealed envelope.

'Most immediate. Priority.'

The words were bold and unmistakeable.

"Zu befehl, Herr Feldmarschal."

"Danke, Oberst."

The door closed and Guderian felt the burden of the necessities of high command quickly replaced by the doubts and fears that status brought, especially when millions of lives are at stake.

"Now, Herr General. Some coffee, or shall we proceed?"

Patton elected to get out on the road as quickly as possible, and they headed off together to observe the latest exercises near Berlin.

1109 hrs, Friday, 14th March 1947, Christopherusschule, Scharmede, Germany.

The morning playtime was in full swing and the children, mainly those of good German catholic parentage, were deep into their recreations of family scenes with dolls and teddy bears, football matches, or storytelling about what their sister had got up to with her boyfriend the night before.

Adolpha and Roderika Ottwitz were twin sisters and, as teachers at the Catholic School, had pulled playground duty together whilst the other staff had a break from the screaming hordes.

They were sisters in more ways than one, as both had committed to be brides of Christ some years beforehand.

Young Poppelmeyer had earned his third rebuke of the session and would probably be destined for the father's office after any more misbehaviour.

The early morning sun drew their eyes as it burst forth from behind the clouds.

And then something else drew their gaze, something awful… something that had no place in God's world.

The mechanism was quite simple.

The initiating device was a modest but highly efficient altitude barometer that decided that it was now at the pre-set height and sent a current through its wiring to start three processes.

The first burst initiated the destruction of two phials of acid, secured against some vital pipework joints.

The second initiated a timing mechanism that started a countdown to another sequence.

The acid ate through the pipe joints and the internal pressure of the fuel system ensured the destruction was complete.

366

Aviation fuel started to mist into the void and then flowed as a liquid as the joints' failures were completed.

The loss of engine power was quickly noted and the pilots tried to respond.

The second timing sequence fired a small explosive line charge that perforated the skin of the aircraft, allowing fuel vapours to escape.

Five seconds later the white phosphorous charge burst into life providing the fuel with the perfect ignition source.

The resultant explosion partially severed the port wing inboard of engine number two, the airflow, and falling motion of the aircraft completing the job.

The port wing parted company with the rest of the aircraft and, robbed of any ability to fly, the blazing fuselage and remaining wing dropped from the sky, whirling like a sycamore seed, leaving a spiral of smoke and flame as the aviation spirit fuelled a fire that consumed everything in its path.

There were no survivors.

German forces in the area rushed to the burning wreckage and attempted to rescue as many of the children from Christopherusschule as they could, both living and dead.

There were far more of the latter.

The local feuerwehr was overwhelmed and it was only the presence of a German military medical unit that saved the lives of many wounded who had been rescued but would have died uncared for.

Two firefighters were killed when the remains of the main school building collapsed on them, trapping them under wood and rubble to be burned alive when the fuel-fed fire spread further.

The report went out from Scharmede and was quickly passed on, coinciding with those reports from radar stations monitoring air traffic, which had all noted the disappearance of one aircraft.

At Rhein-Main Airbase in Frankfurt, the news of the missing aircraft arrived and was treated with a certain amount of acceptance, as air crashes were still reasonably regular occurrences.

It was not until further details started to arrive that it was realised that a disaster had befallen the Allied community, one that was not totally understood until the association between the personnel listed on the RAF flight were married with the last minute additions.

Eisenhower.

Bedell-Smith.

Bradley.

Strong.

De Lattre.

And others... all dead.

Telephone wires started burning white-hot and NATO lay in disarray.

A small body of determined spirits fired by an unquenchable faith in their mission can alter the course of history.

Mahatma Gandhi.

Chapter 191 - THE CRESCENDO

1307 hrs, Friday, 14th March 1947, Friedrich-Ebert-Strasse, temporary government building #1, Magdeburg, Germany.

"President Truman, Speer here. I must offer my personal sympathies to you and your nation at this time, as well as the sympathies of my nation. This is an awful accident and our cause has lost some great men."

"Thank you, Chancellor Speer. I hope you'll understand that I cannot yet bring myself to speak at length as yet. It's far too soon, and we don't know what has happened here; simply that we have lost some extremely courageous and steadfast souls."

"My forces have secured the crash site tightly, and I've ordered them to defer to your officials in matters relating to the site and any investigation. We shall, of course, assist in any way you wish."

"Thank you again, Chancellor. I've no doubt your assistance will prove invaluable. Clearly this tragedy has struck us hard, and it'll be important to discover its origins, so we can avoid repeating it."

"On the delicate matter of the remains, Mister President, we've placed those bodies recovered, both from the aircraft and on the ground, in a temporary facility in Scharmede. This is also guarded and autopsies are already in progress."

"Chancellor Speer, on that matter I must also express my regret and sympathies. To lose so many young lives is a tragedy of monumental proportions. I believe reports have stated as many as fifty affected?"

"Mister President, I regret to inform you that as of twenty minutes ago, that number was placed at eighty-two confirmed dead, including all members of staff, mainly nuns."

"A tragedy heaped upon a tragedy, Chancellor. Our nations will mourn together."

"Mister President, there's a matter that we, as statesman, must find the strength to discuss, even at this grave hour. The situation is tense and we cannot remain as we are."

"The leadership of NATO?"

"Yes, I'm afraid I see no time for delay, Mister President."

"Such an appointee would have to have the confidence of all, as our dear friend Ike did. That's essential. An immediate replacement doesn't suggest itself, Chancellor."

There was a pause during which Speer willed Truman to continue.

He obliged.

"Do you have anyone in mind, Chancellor?"

"Most certainly not, Herr President. That's a matter for all, but I suspect we would expect that such an appointee would come from your forces. I've no doubt that Feldmarschal Guderian could do the job, but I also don't doubt that it is far too soon for such an appointment from our forces."

"Most likely, I agree, Chancellor. So what do you suggest? I assume you're meaning a temporary appointment?"

"Yes, Mister Truman, I think there's no choice. I believe that you can make a temporary appointment yourself under our existing rules, until such time as a formal discussion can be conducted... and to leave NATO without a leader is courting disaster, particularly at these delicate times..."

"This Swedish meeting?"

"Not just that, Mister President. We have other matters of direct concern at this time, do we not?"

"Yes, indeed we do, Chancellor. My problem here is that the two most likely successors have died along with Eisenhower."

"Perhaps we should seek for the immediate return of Montgomery?"

"That will **not** happen. I'd have a mutiny on my hands."

Speer knew that the suggestion would be enough in itself to agitate the American leader.

"Then it must be someone here... close at hand... and of sufficient worth to command the respect of all nations, Mister President."

The silence multiplied as Speer willed Truman down the right path, and as Truman's brain worked the issue and kept on coming up with the same name.

"Purely temporary, Chancellor. Any appointment I make must be understood as purely temporary to ensure a firm hand on the reins here. We must make sure the other Allies understand that... I'll speak to Prime Minister Churchill immediately I've decided on the appointment."

370

"I'm sure you will do the right thing, Mister President. Again, the sympathies of myself and my nation for your great loss."

"Thank you, Chancellor. May God protect us and guide us in the coming days. Goodbye."

Speer replaced the receiver and slumped as the tension of his deceit left his body.

"And this is just the start!"

The other man said nothing, but understood the huge pressures on his leader.

The Chancellor took a taster from his Ansbach; he had allowed himself a small one, despite the rigours that the following hours would bring.

"I think he's thinking as we would hope, but I couldn't direct. It must be his choice, Rudolf."

"I agree, Herr Kanzler. Shall I continue?"

"Yes, yes do."

"From the report I received it seems that Bedell-Smith simply accompanied Strong as they had a shared destination. Strong we already knew was going to Vár, so he took the opportunity offered."

Speer took another sip and derived satisfaction from the steadying burn in his throat.

"What happened next is still unclear, but something caused Eisenhower and his party to leave their aircraft and get aboard the RAF plane."

"And this list of personnel that were killed when it crashed is complete?"

"Yes, Herr Kanzler. That is the confirmed list of persons on the RAF transport, achieved by combining the original with the stated personnel manifest of the USAAF aircraft, minus the crew of the latter."

"And there was no way of stopping this from happening once we knew Eisenhower was aboard?"

"Yes, there was, Herr Kanzler, but not one that would have done anything but announce our involvement, bringing great harm to the Fatherland and ourselves."

"So our men along the line acted well… in what must have been extremely difficult circumstances."

"I do agree, Herr Kanzler. It would've been easy to panic. They didn't."

"And our men will remove anything remaining of the devices from the plane wreck?"

Diels looked at his watch.

"That will already have been done, Herr Kanzler."

1359 hrs, Friday, 14th March 1947, Friedrich-Ebert-Strasse, temporary government building #1, Magdeburg, Germany.

"Mister President. I had not expected to hear from you again today. How may I be of assistance?"

Speer listened carefully and silently.

There was no need for words, none at all, as his face announced the culmination of their hasty plan.

"Yes, I can do that... and I'll ensure he contacts you as quickly as possible, Mister President... no... I agree... we've no time for niceties... no, the Allies will understand... I'm sure of it... no, indeed, Mister President... yes... yes...yes, I agree. Thank you... and to you, Mister President. Goodbye."

He squeezed the telephone in both hands and held it to his face, eyes closed, almost like a supplicant with a treasured icon of his faith.

"He's done it, but can't get hold of him, so he's asked us to inform him."

"Mein Gott! This is destiny, Herr Kanzler... destiny! So much has gone astray and yet here we stand, with so many things unexpectedly in our favour. This is our moment... our destiny!"

"Perhaps so, Horst... as you say... so much has come together to bring us to this point... so... anyway... give me a moment."

He picked up the telephone again and asked for a connection.

"Kanzler Speer for the Feldmarschal immediately please."

He relaxed, the answerer immediately off to get hold of the German Army's field commander.

Less than a minute later, he heard a gruff voice in his ear.

"Guderian."

"Feldmarschal, are matters in hand for the exercise?"

"Yes, and progressing as expected, Herr Kanzler."

"Excellent... and General Patton is with you still?"

"Yes, Herr Kanzler. We both intend to go forward and observe the night exercise later, but he's still here at the moment."

"Good, please put him on the line."

Clearly Patton actually wasn't there at hand, as Speer could hear orders being shouted.

"Here he is now, Her Kanzler. Any further instructions for me?"

372

"No. None at all. Proceed as planned, Feldmarschal."

"Here is General Patton, Herr Kanzler."

Speer sat up a little straighter, as befitted the gravity of the moment.

"Good afternoon, General Patton."

"Good afternoon, Chancellor. What can I do for you, Sir?"

"Of course, straight to the point. By now you'll know about the tragic circumstances of this day."

"Yes, Sir. I've been informed, Sir."

"I've spoken with your President and tendered our condolences of course, but we've also spoken on other urgent matters."

"Yes, Sir?"

"President Truman has been unable to get through to you so he has asked me to inform you that, effective immediately, you are now temporary Commander of NATO forces in Europe. He asks me that you make your way to Frankfurt and assume command until the member states can appoint a permanent successor... which, I might add, might be some time."

Patton kept his face straight as he was awarded the pinnacle post of his military career.

"Thank you, Chancellor, I understand fully. Now, if you'll excuse me, I've much to do."

"I'm sure you do, General. Good luck to you. Good day."

"Good day to you, Chancellor."

At the field headquarters of Feldmarschal Guderian, Patton handed the telephone receiver back to the waiting signaller and turned to the German commander.

"Well, Fieldmarshal, it seems that duty calls me once again. They've given me command of NATO."

"Congratulations, General."

"Thank you... now, I must get going. I'll be in touch as soon as I've shaken things out."

Within two minutes, he was on the road to Frankfurt.

1601 hrs, Friday 14th March 1947, Camp Vár, Sweden.

Nazarbayeva had travelled back to her headquarters, and then took another flight to Sweden, which was why she was at the negotiating venue, rather than languishing at Vnukovo like her intended companions, whose aircraft steadfastly refused to pass pre-flight checks.

Summoned to one of the grander meeting rooms, she and Rufin found themselves ushered to seating opposite three Allied military men, who stood as she entered.

As had been agreed as standard camp protocol, neither side saluted and they simply took to the comfortable seats.

The Swedish overseer spoke first.

"Good afternoon to you all. It is apparent that the Soviet contingent is incomplete. We understand that this is because of aircraft issues in Moscow?"

Nazarbayeva nodded and shrugged in one easy motion.

"That is so, Mister Erikkson. I came from a different location. My comrades hope to be in the air tomorrow morning, and offer their complete apologies."

"These things happen, General Nazarbayeva. However, new circumstances have apparently made this meeting redundant. General?"

Erikkson looked to the leader of the Allied contingent.

The man appeared to be in some sort of reverie, one from which the second request summoned him.

"General?"

"Apologies. I wish to make a statement on behalf of NATO."

Erikkson had been given an inkling that something was going on, and he knew that the Allies would be stepping away from the negotiating table for the whole day, but the normally efficient Military Intelligence apparatus had not managed to discover what was behind their request.

"Please do, General."

The Allied officer leading the group cleared his throat.

"At approximately 1100 hrs our time, the aircraft carrying General Eisenhower, commander of NATO forces in Europe, appears to have suffered a mid-air structural failure and fire. The aircraft subsequently crashed. There were no survivors. At this time, all negotiations between our forces are to cease as a mark of respect for the General and those others killed in this tragic accident. We hope that you will understand our position and assist us in agreeing to a temporary cessation to permit us to gather our thoughts at this time."

Nazarbayeva was genuinely speechless and exchanged looks with Rufin.

Gathering her wits she spoke with great sincerity.

"This is appalling news, for once Eisenhower was a trusted friend of the Soviet Union. Recently he has been an honourable and capable foe, and I extend the commiserations of the Motherland and

374

her peoples. Of course, we'll suspend our meetings here until such time as we can come back together and proceed, having allowed a proper time for reflection and remembrance. If I or my staff can provide any assistance, please do not hesitate to ask, General."

Lucian Truscott nodded his thanks for the eloquent reply.

"Thank you so much, General Nazarbayeva. Now, if you'll excuse us, there's much to do."

Both sides rose and exchanged respectful nods, the Allied officers trooping out, followed by the Swedish delegation, leaving the Soviets alone.

Dismissing the two other officers, translators for the more exotic languages the Allied contingent sometimes brought to the table, Nazarbayeva sat down heavily and spoke her thoughts.

"Eisenhower dead... and who else, I wonder?"

Rufin couldn't answer that of course, but his mind had been heading down the same line.

"One things for sure, Comrade Leytenant General, Moscow needs to hear about this immediately."

"Yes... yes, you're right. I don't doubt it'll be well received. Despite my words, I'm sure his death will be celebrated in the Rodina."

They both rose and moved off as quickly as possible, seeking out the NKVD colonel who was in charge of the special communications unit.

The news was relayed to Moscow and, as predicted, was seen as something to rejoice over.

At Vnukovo, the three senior men received the news that they were presently not required to go to Camp Vár, and none of them was happy.

They travelled back together, deep in conversation.

"So what will the contact do?"

"Stay silent. He'll stay silent of course."

"No, I suspect he won't. He'll talk."

They both looked at Khrushchev with pained expressions.

"He'll be expecting three... that's what he was told. I'm not listed as being there as yet... I'm the surprise... Now he'll know that two... you two... are delayed. He'll assume she's one of us... he'll talk to her."

"Mudaks!"

"What'll she do...?"

Kaganovich posed the question to himself, as he probably knew the woman better than the others...

'...of course, I know her better than them...now... what the fuck will she do...'

He instinctively knew the answer.

"She'll come and speak to me first."

"Really?"

"Absolutely positive she will. Whom else would she go to? Beria? The Boss? Kuznetsov? Has to be me."

Khrushchev posed a perfectly reasonable question.

"And if that's the case, what do we do if he has revealed matters?"

Zhukov stayed quiet throughout, leaving the two political beasts to sort it out.

Kaganovich's silence drew the bald commissar forward.

"I know exactly what we'll do. Just what we had planned to do... but sooner... we move up the timetable."

"What?"

Kaganovich bristled.

"We're not yet ready. Tell him, comrade, we can't move any quicker."

Zhukov smiled.

"I'm a soldier. Sometimes we have to move when not prepared. It is possible, given the alternatives. I think you're right, Nikita Sergeyevich."

"Ilya Borisevich?"

Kaganovich pondered the pros and cons before committing himself.

"We have no choice, it seems. We'll move the timetable up and if she fucks it up... I'll kill her myself."

2031 hrs, Friday, 14th March 1947, Shared bar, Camp Vár, Sweden.

"May I get you another drink, General?"

Nazarbayeva looked up from the empty glass where her mind had been just a second before, the complications of the day weighing heavily on her thoughts.

She had assumed she was alone in the bar and the voice took her by surprise.

"Yes, thank you, Polkovnik."

"I'm assuming this was vodka?"

"Akvavit please, Polkovnik."

The man moved off awkwardly and returned with two filled glasses.

"Terrible news today eh, General? Even for you, our recent enemy."

"No way for a soldier to die, that's for sure, Polkovnik. To those who died."

They chinked glasses and consumed the contents greedily.

"I've taken the liberty of organising the barman."

He gestured off to the right and soon a full bottle and two new glasses arrived.

"Excellent idea, Polkovnik. Your Russian is excellent."

"Thank you, I've only recently learned the tongue, and it's certainly not yet as polished as your English, General."

She drank the Akvavit as she eased the wounded foot in her boot, all the time consuming the details of the British officer's uniform.

The subtle movement didn't escape Ramsey's eye.

"An old wound, General?"

"I'm only missing a little bit of myself, certainly less than yourself, Polkovnik."

He slapped his false legs with the palm of his hand, like a father lovingly pats his boys.

"Hardly notice nowadays. Wasn't always the case, but I'm still walking around, unlike a lot of my boys."

"Where, if you don't mind me asking, Polkovnik?"

"Barnstorf in Northern Germany."

"I have heard of this battle. Many men died there… and to what real end, eh?"

Ramsey snorted, partially in agreement and partially in disgust.

"As always, we soldiers pay the price the politicians demand for their decisions."

They raised glasses to each other in acknowledgement of a soldier's bond.

Ramsey changed tack.

"I'll bet this county looks magnificent at Christmas time."

A light went off in her head and a phrase simply tumbled out of her mouth.

"Very possibly, Polkovnik, but there is nothing like Christmas in Krakow."

"Except May Day in Moscow, so I'm told, Comrade Leytenant General Nazarbayeva."

'At last!'

He leant across the table and extended his hand.

"Ramsey... John Ramsey... and I bring greetings from Sir Stewart Menzies."

"I had expected General Strong to be here?"

"Unfortunately, he's amongst the dead. It was his aircraft that crashed. The others had hitched a lift on it. Bad luck all round, I'd say."

"Yes... bad luck."

'*Strong too?... who else?... How badly are they really wounded by this?*'

"Fortunately, I've been briefed in and was assigned here to act as Sir Stewart's eyes and ears, and to help Sir Kenneth in any way. I'm told you worked under General Pekunin... another tragic end."

"In many ways, yes, Polkovnik Ramsey."

"You shot him... and yet you're now here..."

"He ordered me to."

"Ordered you to shoot him?"

"Yes. Perhaps Roman was afraid of what he might have revealed had he been taken alive."

Ramsey nodded and left it at that.

"I assume, because you responded to the phrase, that you were included in his plans?"

"I gave you the initiating phrase, didn't I?"

"Indeed you did."

He understood that she avoided the question.

"So, what does General Menzies want with me?"

"To continue the work of your friend and mentor."

"Less riddles, Polkovnik Ramsey, if you please."

"We want to know if you will continue where Pekunin left off, and help us bring about the replacement of your present leadership."

She hurriedly took a draft of the fiery Akvavit to cover her shock and surprise.

Ramsey understood instinctively and spoke again.

"From what I understand, your General was a patriot who understood that Stalin lead your country into another war under false pretences, and was prepared to work with us for the good of all, especially your Motherland. He gave his life for that purpose."

"Pekunin would never betray his country!"

"He didn't... ever. I've seen the file... all the documents relating to him. Above all, he was a Russian patriot who had only the Rodina's best interests at heart. It seems he felt they were best served by ridding the Soviet Union of Stalin's influence."

"Comrade Stalin is our leader. He cannot be replaced. He brought us victory against the German hordes!"

To the barman, who reported directly to Swedish Intelligence, it looked like the two officers were arguing and he tried to edge closer.

He was spotted and sent packing with another order, this time for cold beers. Ramsey figured the lesser alcohol content would help him through the coming conversation, whereas Tatiana was quite happy to feed her habit with the Akvavit.

The conversation level dropped, confounding the barman's efforts to hear anything reportable.

He delivered the beers and grudgingly retreated, the two officers determined to remain silent until he moved away.

"I'll stick with this, thank you, Polkovnik Ramsey. So, what would you have me do?"

"Pekunin was our point of contact. We've been blind and unable to help since he was killed. Plainly, tensions are building again, and there are clearly matters that need answers."

"Such as the lost submarine?"

"Yes, of course, General. That alone has heightened our suspicions about your intentions. Combined with the other items you may have taken from Japan... the missing submarines... it all makes a very volatile mix... one that needs calming down... and the safest way for us to move with confidence is to remove the men who took you to war on such false pretences."

"False pretences? They were sound reasons. Churchill's plan, the acceptance of Germany... the vaunting of the French... Patton's cries for more war... you were going to attack us so we simply acted first."

Since she had read Pekunin's notes, she knew the old man had believed otherwise, but time had made the circumstances less clear and, in so many ways, she wanted to not believe it.

"No, General Nazarbayeva, no we were not... would not. We wanted no more war. Your attack caught us off-guard because we were only thinking of enjoying the new peace."

Nazarbayeva poured herself another measure, which allowed Ramsey time to continue.

"You have lost much in this war, General. Three sons that we know of. Makarenko told us of the futility of your son's death in Alsace, a mission contrived by Stalin as much to punish as to achieve any great success."

She listened, her heart heavy with memories.

"Another son lost in Spain… betrayed by one of the men you now defend… if not both of them."

"And yet another who died whilst in our care, as ordered by your own leadership, a third son lost to you in another man's folly."

Philby had confessed to organising the execution of Ilya Nazarbayev near Shenfield, and it was expected to be a trump card if the female GRU officer still wavered.

She could have enlightened Ramsey further but held her peace.

"I'm a loyal soldier of the Motherland! Sacrifices are inevitable in war!"

"A war that was contrived by your present leaders… for their own purposes… one that has cost the lives of three of your sons so far."

"And Roman signed up to this, did he?"

"Yes, he did. As a patriotic Russian, he understood that there was no choice."

She poured another drink as Ramsey took a large draught of his lager and picked out his cigarettes.

Out of gentlemanly habit, he proffered the pack to the woman and was surprised when she accepted.

"Our file is incomplete, it seems. We didn't know you smoked."

"I didn't. War has a habit of changing people, Polkovnik Ramsey."

"Yes… that's most certainly the harsh truth, Comrade General."

They smoked in silence, enjoying the rich tobacco in combination with the drink of their choosing.

Ramsey had already observed that the alcohol consumption of the woman was remarkable, partially only for its quantity and partially for its seeming lack of effect.

Nazarbayeva finished yet another glass and refilled before speaking again.

"Let us hypothetically proceed as if I were to agree to take up where Roman Pekunin left off. What would that entail, and what would it mean for the Motherland?"

"In the main, he was a go-between. Providing secure communications between two groups with a mutual interest. At times, he was more pro-active, but that was his choice, and we never asked him directly for any military information, and never asked him to betray his country."

"And how does that communication take place?"

Ramsey considered the question.

It had been anticipated, and he was only to proceed if he was convinced the woman was compliant.

He remained to be so convinced.

"That is something we can discuss later, Comrade General."

"Through Sweden then?"

Ramsey held her gaze without moving a muscle, sensing she needed a push in the right direction, and deciding to allow her the information.

"Through Sweden is your preferred route, is it not, General Nazarbayeva?"

She looked at him, now understanding that the Colonel was cleared for much more than a man of his rank would normally know.

None the less, she decided to test him.

"Preferred?"

"Your file was received with some scepticism, but there may be some truth in it."

She filed that comment away as quite important, and wondered it was a slip or an intended statement.

"I used Sweden for that. And you would choose Sweden too?"

"Yes, most definitely. Pekunin used the same route that you employed, and everything eventually got to us. I believe you have his treasured copy of 'The State and the Revolution'?"

She nodded, understanding his meaning fully.

"And within the Soviet Union? Who are my allies there?"

"They'll identify themselves to you. You almost probably already know them."

"The code phrases?"

"Yes indeed, General."

"I've tried a number of times, and yet to find someone who responds."

Ramsey could go no further, as his specific orders prohibited naming any agent or accomplice, come what may.

Obviously the woman had to understand that her two missing delegates were from that camp.

"So, you expect me to communicate with you on behalf of some unknown group which is conspiring with my enemies against the leadership of my country, through Sweden in some way you can't explain. Is that about right?"

Ramsey smiled, accepting the woman's sarcasm.

"Comrade General Nazarbayeva, you must understand that General Pekunin committed himself to this, and was no traitor to the

Rodina. He was a patriotic man, who understood that your country had been brought back to war by the acts of a few evil men, and he was prepared to risk himself to remove those men, as are a few men still in the higher echelons of your government. What we are asking is that you consider replacing him and allow us to assist your own patriots in seizing back the Motherland from the men who are abusing her and her people."

'Unknown group... what the deuce? She answered the phrase!'

She tilted the glass towards him in mock acknowledgement, or so he thought.

"Pretty words, Polkovnik Ramsey. My loyalty is to the Motherland first and foremost, you understand."

She weighed up matters in her mind and decided that her compliance might bring indiscretion from the Englishman, which might enable her to gather sufficient information to denounce the traitors in their midst.

"I will follow the example set by my old friend Pekunin, and trust to his judgement that what I'm doing is not damaging to my country. If it proves otherwise, there'll be hell to pay. You understand?"

Ramsey raised his glass.

"Indeed I do, Comrade Leytenant General Nazarbayeva. Cheers and welcome to the club."

"Na Zdorovie, Polkovnik Ramsey."

The Swedish barman was puzzled, having heard nothing of the conversation, the two officers suddenly clinked glasses and celebrated some sort of deal... joining a club as he thought he had heard.

His report to Tørget carried little of worth apart from those few words. The Swedish spymaster suspected that he knew exactly what that entailed, and decided that Nazarbayeva must now be on board with the operation.

"Now, I would like to ask a question of you, General."

"So soon, Polkovnik Ramsey?"

"It is a matter of some urgency, and I would hope that you can feel free to answer."

"Go on."

"In early February, our intelligence services identified a secret shipment passing through Lithuania. That was subsequently identified as Anthrax."

"A biological weapon?"

"Not weaponised, no. One hundred litre drums, a large number of them."

"Go on."

"Your submarine was in fact sunk by our forces, and men were rescued, all tainted with Anthrax, which we have subsequently discovered as being aboard the submarine in roughly the same numbers as was transported by the NKVD down the River Neman."

Ramsey embellished the truth a little, totally accurately unbeknown to him.

"I know nothing of this, Polkovnik Ramsey... but such an act is not planned by my leadership, of that I am absolutely sure."

Her sincerity was apparent, although he could not read her mind.

'Again, it is confirmed... all of Raduga is still running... the delivery of anthrax into water systems in Northern Germany and Denmark... it is all still running!'

"I can help you no more, Polkovnik Ramsey."

They both stood, each showing physical discomfort in their own individual way.

"General."

"Polkovnik"

They saluted formally and went their separate ways.

Nazarbayeva left the secure signals office, content that her nondescript message to Kaganovich would simply be seen as a normal request for a visit, not an urgent need to bear her soul and commence an anti-revolutionary manhunt within the higher echelons of Soviet government.

At 2200 hrs the Signals Colonel went off duty and knocked on her door, bearing a bottle of vodka and a jar of pickled herrings.

The herrings lay unconsumed, the bottle half empty, as Nazarbayeva took her sexual pleasures well into the night.

0100 hrs Saturday, 15th March 1947, somewhere in Poland.

Guderian watched the night exercise without really seeing anything, his mind so focussed on other events in progress.

In his mind's eye, he could imagine the special groups moving silently towards their targets, each bringing along one, two, or three Russian prisoners, kept healthy and alive until this very evening, soon to be shot dead at the site of each attack and left as undeniable proof of Soviet treachery.

The targets were ones that would help conceal what was about to come; units that had the capacity to interpret that all was not as it seemed.

Guderian had recently finished a telephone with the new NATO commander.

Whilst he understood the man's ego issues, or at least thought he did, he couldn't help but like the man's drive and singularity of purpose.

Since May '45, Patton had preached that they should continue on eastwards and take on the red hordes on their own ground.

The idea of getting him placed in charge of NATO had been the contrivance of a moment of opportunity created by the loss of the leadership in one incident.

That the incident had originated with a German device intended to take down one man was of no consequence in the greater run of things.

Circumstances had provided the Fatherland with an opportunity that none of them could have dreamed of and, whilst he was full of trepidation about the possibility of leading men onto the steppes of Russia once more, he also knew it would be very different this time around.

Guderian took a gentle stroll, enjoying the crisp night air and silence, made more intense by what he knew was to come, and made his way to the intelligence centre.

"Good morning, meine Herren!"

The men gathered around the large table sprang to attention.

"Relax, relax. Is there anything I should know?"

The senior man, Lieutenant General Albert Schnez, pointed Guderian towards the intelligence situation map.

"Herr Feldmarschal, there's some recorded air activity over the British lines near Braunsberg. We understand that night fighters have clashed over our own lines, east of Jata. I suspect that's only because we've asked our airmen to be more vigilant in their policing of our air space tonight."

"And this plot?"

"Ah, that's a Soviet flight that will be inbound to Berlin. An agreed routing of three transports plus two escorts. Nothing out of the ordinary, of course, but…"

"But they'll have to go."

"Yes, Herr Feldmarschal. Our Luftwaffe officers understand this."

He nodded towards the highly decorated air force officer who was already lost in his own intelligence world.

"Gut. Continue, Albert."

"From what we understand, the only two places of concern are Vienna, as always…"

"The usual discontent?"

"So it seems. A few shots, perhaps nothing more than harsh words, but enough to get our American allies hot under the collar. Their radio network is alive with requests to fire… which may suit our purpose, of course."

"Of course. And?"

"And the French, specifically our old friends of the SS. Apparently there was an accidental discharge of a tank weapon at Krzcin, resulting in an enemy casualty. It's being sorted now, but the two forces have gone on alert."

Guderian again wondered if some guiding hand was at work, but decided it was simply fate taking a hand once more.

"Anything from our Abwehr colleagues?"

"Yes, we're getting regular updates, but nothing at all that causes me concern, except for the apparent repositioning of the new Guards Mechanised Army. I've already passed it through to your headquarters. They appear to have been on the move since Thursday."

"Show me."

The map was cleared of pencils, rulers, and hands in order to permit Guderian to see the new situation. He was already aware that the 1st Guards Mechanised Army had moved from its previous position in reserve opposite the junction between the Polish and German armies at Elk, set back in and around the city of Grodno.

"Yes, we factored in their departure… our Polish comrades were more than happy of course… so where are they going do you think?"

"I'm unsure, Herr Feldmarschal, but…"

"But you have a feeling of course?"

"Lvov."

"Enlighten me, Albert."

"If they want a big hard-hitting mobile formation below that there are two other alternatives in the Southern Ukraine and

Bulgaria… plus the railway line they are on… we think they are on goes through Lvov."

Guderian inspected the map, checked the locations of the other new Guards Mechanised Armies, and decided that his CoS was probably correct.

"And this one?"

He pointed at the 3rd Guards Mechanised Army positioned around Leningrad.

"Nothing as yet, but I've requested information from our assets. If they're moving down to reduce the gap then we should be able to work out what's going on."

"But if the 3rd is moving down, that will be the British Army's problem in the first instance."

"Yes, Herr Feldmarschal."

"So, Generalleutnant. I see nothing here to make me worry, and certainly nothing that would obstruct Undenkbar. Agreed?"

"I agree, Herr Feldmarschal."

"Gut. Keep me informed, Albert."

Guderian walked alone out into the morning with his forces now committed to Undenkbar.

Despite the greatcoat, he felt a sudden shiver go down his spine.

The last time he had felt such a shiver was on the morning of 5th December 1941, when he had called off the ground offensive against Moscow, knowing the German Army was spent.

'Calm yourself, man. Now you've other advantages. The great industrial power is with you. There's no defeat ahead, no retreat on the freezing steppe; only victory.'

"Or death!"

He laughed at the sound of his own voice carrying on the rejuvenated wind.

'Or death indeed.'

0158 hrs, Saturday, 15th March 1947, the Elk-Bydgoszcz-Küstrin-Berlin safe air corridor. Northeastern Europe.

"I swear if that fucking Fokker comes close again, I'll put him down."

"Calm yourself, Starshy Leytenant, set an example to this enlisted man."

"It's bad enough that I have to baby sit these lumbering hogs, let alone that I've to put up with your babblings."

"Hang on..."

Braun went all business and fiddled with the radar set.

"There's two barrelling in to come under the transports... directly into the corridor. That's not allowed."

"Steer me in."

Braun delivered the steer and the last He-219A7 in the Soviet Air Force dropped down to play cat and mouse with the harrying German night fighters.

Jurgen Förster, the Soviet Union's top living night fighter ace, formed a superb team with Hans Braun, both of whom were died-in-the-wool committed German communists.

The Heinkel drove in hard, but both men were confident that the enemy aircraft would see the error of their ways and draw off.

They did not, and the situation became even more tense when another two enemy night fighters dropped in astern of the He-219.

"Seems like they're playing to new rules tonight, Oberleutnant."

"One more time and I'll... Mein Gott!"

The world went white as shells hammered into their fuselage, and Förster instinctively flipped the Heinkel into a tight right diving turn.

"What the fuck... Jesus, Jurgen... they got the transports, all three are going down... Scheisse!"

Had Förster been able to look he would have seen that the three Lisonov-2 aircraft had succumbed to Schräge Musik fire, the vertically mounted cannons in the German night fighters ripping open the tender bellies of the transports and dispatching each to a fiery death below.

Tracer bullets flashed past the canopy and Förster improvised into a rolling dive loop that pushed the pair of them back into their seats as the G-forces acted upon them.

"Get on the radio... tell base exactly what's going on here!"

"But I don't have any idea what the fuck's going on here."

Braun flicked the transmit switch and instinctively knew something was wrong.

"Radio's out."

He looked at the screen and shouted a warning.

387

"Target dead ahead... watch out man!"

Förster had but two seconds to react; it was enough.

Six 20mm MG151s put hundreds of bullets into the void and quickly closed down the gap, many smashing into the enemy aircraft, one of the DRL's much vaunted FW Ta-154 Moskito.

It simply came apart and spread itself and burning jet fuel across the night sky.

Their wingman lost the unequal struggle first, and the awful squeals over the open radio told them of the death of their friends.

The old veteran radar operator screamed for his wife and children all the way down as his Heinkel burned around him.

The unsettling noise stopped, either by contact with the ground or by fire spread.

Neither man had time to reflect on the loss of comrades.

They were suddenly in a sky all alone with five enemy jets whilst the ground below sparkled with guns firing.

"Try that fucking radio again!"

Braun fiddled with it and saw it stutter into life.

"Yes! It's wor..."

Six 30mm cannon shells entered the side of the crew compartment, striking everything that was vital.

Braun lived long enough to see his friend's head simply disappear as one shell transited without exploding.

The nose of the aircraft was already coming apart as the last but one shell struck the corner of his radar set and exploded.

The final shell did further ignominy to Braun's flayed carcass and the disintegrating Heinkel prescribed a slow fiery arc as it dropped away to the battleground below.

*The most persistent sound which reverberates through men's history
is the beating of war drums.*

Arthur Koestler

Chapter 192 - THE REENGAGEMENT

0200 hrs, Saturday, 15th March 1947, Europe.

In numerous locations, the special teams had gone to work prior to H-hour, and men had died long before they realised that the war had gone hot again.

At 0200 precisely, artillery shells started to land amongst Allied units and created the first frontline casualties of the renewed ground war.

Officers ordered counter-battery fire, or barrages on suspected concentration points, or strikes on areas where an attacking enemy had to be, and quickly the artillery of both sides were working with gusto.

Aircraft, no longer confined by orders, ranged freely and killed with equal freedom.

Reports flew back to corps and army commands on both sides of the line, with accusations of treachery on every officer's lips.

German and Polish units, already alert and ready to roll for an exercise, suddenly found themselves tasked with moving forward to respond to the obvious and imminent Soviet threat.

In Frankfurt, George Patton was woken from his slumbers to find himself in the position he had always coveted.

Solely in charge of his own war.

He sought information before making his decisions, but he also empowered each and every one of his senior commanders to do everything they could to do the enemy harm.

0200 hrs, Saturday, 15th March 1947, Camerone Headquarters, Staszow, Poland.

Knocke was up even at that late hour, not because of official duties, but because of the anguish brought on by the communication he had received from his wife.

That his daughters were both safe was a blessing.

That the unborn child appeared unharmed by the experience seemed to be a miracle.

He read the section again, where the injuries sustained by his wife and Armande Fleriot were described, seeking something he may have missed; a word indicating matters to be more serious or an unspoken hint of greater harm than directly described.

Ernst-August Knocke could find nothing.

His family had been delivered from harm once again.

At first he thought it was a spring storm, as his solitude was disturbed by a flash-lightened sky.

But only for a moment, as a veteran of the Russian Front knew exactly what was creating the flickering night sky.

"Scheisse!"

He grabbed his tunic and kepi and dashed from his quarters to the command centre, where the duty watch were rapidly being drawn from their shocked state, as telephones and radios burst into life.

The irrepressible Lutz arrived at his shoulder bearing a mug of coffee.

"Here we go again, Oberführer."

The situation board was still blank but the words coming through from the numerous devices told of death and destruction being visited upon the men of Camerone.

"Mon Général, Général St.Clair's headquarters for you."

Knocke moved quickly to the proffered handset.

"Knocke."

He listened intently as his counterpart in Alma told his own story, one that seemed less of an issue, given what was now appearing on the situation board.

"I have no idea at the moment, Celestin…none whatsoever. I do know that I've artillery and mortars incoming on my forward positions, from where I meet up with the German Army north of Czyżów Szlachecki, south to Obrazów."

Hässelbach arrived with a handful of heavily armed legionnaires, the headquarters security immediately beefed up and highly alert.

"No… nothing about ground action as yet… no, I have no orders… yes… you do that. Thank you, Celestin. Bon chance."

He tossed the handset back and swigged the hot coffee as he examined the situation board.

"Nothing on the ground yet?"

"Non, mon Général."

"Has Colonel Uhlmann reported in yet?"

"Oui… there's nothing with his command, except the detachment placed in support of the infantry near Radoszki, which is under fire from heavy artillery. No casualties reported at this time, mon Général."

Colonel D'Estlain, the acting CoS for Camerone, was matter of fact and controlled in his delivery, something his commander greatly appreciated.

"Anything from General Lavalle as yet?"

"No, Sir."

"Alma are trying to contact him whilst we sort out what is happening. Not much happening on their front as yet."

"And us?"

"I need to know what's happening. Is there nothing on the ground at all?"

"Nothing, mon Général."

'Crazy... totally crazy...'

A voice called D'Estlain's name and he sprang to the signaller's side.

"Sir!"

Knocke moved over and received the report straight from the signaller's mouth.

"Sir, our kameraden in the 78th Sturm Division report being under ground attack... tanks and infantry to their front."

The 78th Division was the southernmost unit in the lines of the German Republican Army and butted right up to the French, namely Camerone.

"Details?"

"Sketchy, mon Général. Reports say enemy tanks fighting at Maruszów and Dębno."

Camerone's commander moved to the map, which carried some of the latest information.

"I don't know what we face...and I won't over commit... but we do know we have enemy here so... we will assist our kameraden in the 78th. Have Uhlmann prepare to move his 2nd Battalion up to Czyżów Szlachecki on my order. Issue the same instructions to 5th Regiment and 1st Pionieres. Both reserve battalions, less one company, plus one company of the pionieres. Contact artillery and have them move to support a counter-attack towards the river crossing point at Annopol. I want a blocking force to move up and make sure nothing comes over the river at Piotrowice. Uhlmann will have a secure flank, clear?"

"Oui, mon Général."

"I'm going to speak to Generalmaior Geissler and coordinate. We'll need to stay in close contact with his headquarters throughout."

"Sir! Sir!"

Another operator waved his hand, attracting the duty signals officer as well as D'Estlain.

"1st Regiment reports that their 3rd Battalion at Kobierniki is under artillery fire, Sir."

Knocke leapt back to the map table.

"There's no reports of ground attack, except on our friends of the78th. Now we have another barrage starting, but delayed. Why?"

"Poor planning?"

"Possible... but their artillery are damn good. Something else?"

D'Estlain perused the map.

They both stood back whilst more information was added, and hoped to see something that made sense.

D'Estlain posed himself a question.

"No air activity over us... none..."

"That's strange... but possibly not so. They're outclassed in every department... plus our radars have the technical advantage. Plus, a sky full of artillery shells is not a healthy environment for airplanes."

"True."

A runner moved forward with a message pad and handed it to the Frenchman.

"Merde alors!"

He checked the details off on the map.

"Mon Général. We have a report that the target ranging platoon of 1st Artillerie has been wiped out by some sort of stealth attack. Men dead and equipment destroyed. There are three Soviet bodies in the area."

"That settles that then. Message to all commands. Infiltrators behind our lines. Take appropriate action. Get a warning off to Corps, 78th Division, and Alma immediately. Tell Uhlmann to hold position for now, but be ready to move on my orders."

"Immédiatement, mon Général."

"Oberführer, another report from 1st Regiment."

Knocke read it with growing concern.

'More artillery fire... south of Mściów... this simply doesn't make sense... where's their ground forces... is what's attacking the 78th all they have or is...'

"Mon Général, reports of ground fighting at Podszyn. Sketchy details... trying to get more information for you."

"Quick as you can, Colonel."

He moved over to the main switchboard.

"Get me Corps Headquarters at once."

The man went through the normal routine, and Knocke was seriously impressed with the legionnaire's calm and steady voice and manner.

"Sir?"

He took the offered handset, stretched the cable across to the situation map table and filled Lavalle in on the rapidly unfolding situation.

In turn, Lavalle was able to tell him that the attack was not localised, and that numerous other points along the Allied line had been similarly hit, mainly, it seemed, on joints between national armies.

The British and Polish lines met on the Baltic and on the old Lithuanian border. Both had been attacked.

The junction of German and Polish armies in Northern Poland, and the French and German armies in southeastern Poland.

The Austrian and American hinge south of Vienna had also been heavily bombarded, as had some US positions opposite Vienna itself.

At least six separate points of attack, supported by behind the lines attacks that seemed target radar and AA units in particular.

The possibility that might mean paratroops was obvious, and Allied deployments reflected a response to that threat.

Lavalle understood Knocke's wish to hit back, and agreed a limited counter attack, aimed at relieving the pressure on the 78th and restoring positions back to the Vistula.

Knocke had the order immediately passed to Uhlmann and the infantry, and Camerone went back to war again.

0213 hrs, Saturday, 15th March 1947, Headquarters of the Red Banner Forces of Soviet Europe, Brest Litovsk, USSR.

"In the name of the great whore, shut the fuck up! I'm awake!"

"Comrade Marshal! They've attacked!"

"What? Is this some fucking joke?"

"No, Comrade Marshal. We have numerous reports, from Austria to the Baltic. Enemy artillery fire followed by the movement of ground forces."

"Aircraft?"

"No great incursions as yet, Comrade Marshal, but aircraft on both sides are engaging as we speak."

393

"Have the staff assembled immediately. Go!"

The Lieutenant Colonel almost flew from the room in his haste, leaving Vasilevsky to climb into his uniform as fast as he could.

"Bastards... the fucking bastards... I'll make them pay for this!"

The briefing commenced as soon as the Commander of the Red Banner Forces of Soviet Europe arrived.

It told of an unprovoked attack on six points along the Soviet lines, supported by artillery.

Now there was also evidence of aircraft excursions over Soviet territory, as the first reports of bombing came through.

Contact had been lost with a supply flight and escorts, heading for Berlin, which itself remained strangely quiet.

The Marshal listened impassively, although his anger rose inside.

'We'd stopped, you sons of whores! Retreated! There was peace! PEACE! Why are you doing this, you bastards?'

He suddenly realised that the briefing had stopped and all eyes were looking to him for orders.

"Comrades, we will respond to this unprovoked attack. Order all Army reserves to stand by for movement orders. Air forces on standby for offensive missions, but to conduct defensive and covering missions immediately. We will carry the battle to these treacherous bastards and make them wish they'd stayed at home! Get me information, Comrades, Get me information!"

"Urrah!"

The spontaneous cry leapt from many lips and the staff got down to the task.

Malinin waited for his orders.

"Well Comrade... this is a shitty deal, is it not?"

"Yes, Comrade Marshal. I really thought... well... you know..."

"Didn't we all? Anyway, now we have to manage this and push the capitalist bastards back. I need to speak to STAVKA immediately. Find me some offensive options quickly."

Malinin went about his business with studied calm and efficiency as the telephone rang in Moscow and the leaders of the Soviet Union became aware that they were at war again.

0213 hrs, Saturday, 15th March 1947, NATO's new forward headquarters, Leipzig, Germany.

Colonel Hood knocked urgently on the bedroom door and was immediate hailed to enter.

He did so and found his new commander performing graceful movements with a Model 1913 cavalry sabre, one of the famous Patton swords, named for the man who had designed it.

"General, Sir. You're needed immediately."

"Where's the goddamned fire, Colonel."

"Everywhere, General. The commies have attacked."

Patton stopped his routine in mid-thrust and slipped the weapon back into its scabbard.

"They've attacked, eh?"

"Yes, Sir. From Lithuania to Vienna."

Patton smiled.

"Good."

"Mister President, George Patton here, Sir."

"Good evening, George. Thank you for pulling me from the most boring of meetings."

"Sir, I must report that, as of 0200 European time, the war restarted."

"What?"

"Mister President, as best as we can presently work out, the Soviets started with artillery barrages on selected Polish, German, British, French, and American positions, all of which have caused casualties. I've ordered all forces to full alert and moved units to respond to the tactical situation."

Truman sagged at the knees and tried to find his seat at the Oval office table.

"Is this just a terrible mistake, George?"

"No way, Mister President. Artillery barrages from Lithuania to Austria, all at the same time. Absolutely no chance. This is all by Soviet design."

"I see. What do you need from me, George?"

"Two things, Sir."

"Go on."

"Firstly, send me everything you can. Secondly, I need your orders, Sir."

Truman looked at the faces gathered around the speaker and saw a reflection of his own shock and horror, mixed with a little of something else.

He recognised it for what it was; a mixture of a sense of betrayal, sadness for what was inevitably to come, and a whole lot of anger.

He set his jaw and gave Patton his orders.

"General Patton. The American people and her Allies will provide you with all necessary means to bring this war to a speedy conclusion. Drive them back, all the way back... do not let up until they beg for mercy. Am I clear?"

"Yes, Sir, Mister President, Sir. How far you want 'em back?"

"To Moscow and beyond, General Patton."

"And... Mister President..."

Truman instinctively understood what Patton was about to ask.

"Yes is the answer to that one, General. We **will** use the bomb on the Communists and make them wish they'd never started this whole sorry stinking mess. Now, do what you can immediately and I'll have General Marshal speak with you directly. Good luck and god speed, General Patton."

"Thank you, Mister President."

Truman looked at his closest advisors and saw only steel and resolve.

He put it immediately to the test.

"Right. Henry. I want you to contact Groves, get him up to speed, and tell him I want weapons ready to ship to Europe by next weekend at the latest. Tell him Wednesday... that'll focus him some."

"He's in Europe at the moment, visiting Denmark."

"Then his deputy... put a burr under his saddle instead."

Truman was galvanised into action.

"I'm going to call the Prime Minister, bring him up to date on developments. Sure as heck, Winston'll be fit to burst. Then I'll speak to Speer. Then, I'll address the nation and I will be frank and open. No sense in losing the opportunity to let the Soviets know that they will be visited by a hurricane of their own making."

The laughter was forced, as befitted the seriousness of the occasion.

"Now, gentlemen. Let's get about winning this war!"

0300 hrs, Saturday, 15th March 1947, Europe.

Within an hour of the first shot being fired, ground and air combats were in full swing, as aggressive commanders pushed the limits of their orders and sought out the enemy and night fighters struggled to control the air above the growing battlefield.

A full-blown shooting war was gathering speed an hour after that.

By the time that dawn started to throw its light on the battlefields, thirteen thousand men from both sides had lost their lives in a rejuvenated war that each blamed the other for starting, and both equally pledged full revenge upon the other for their treachery.

In reality, less than two hundred men knew something of what had actually happened, and only forty-three knew exactly who was to blame.

War would end if the dead could return.

Stanley Baldwin

CHAPTER 193 - THE FOUNTAIN

0801 hrs Saturday, 15th March, 1947, the Kremlin, Moscow, USSR.

Stalin listened with a face like fury as the details of the enemy sneak attack were laid out before him and the rest of the GKO, as well as a number of high-up political and military personnel who had gravitated towards the meeting room.

He occasionally took a look at his comrades and understood that he would not need to provoke them to outrage this time; they were all furious, and that fury would clearly be translated into aggression.

Zhukov, plainly lacking sleep and an opportunity to make himself the normal immaculate Soviet Marshal, listed each Allied attack and incursion, complete with the latest reports of air and sea activity, culminating in the sinking of one of their submarines in the Black Sea.

The Marshal's briefing came to an end, but there was an unexpected silence as everyone present deferred to the General Secretary.

He nodded sagely, taking on the role of the village elder listening to some great wrong that had afflicted his fellow villagers, nodding his head very gently as he marshalled his thoughts.

"Iran?"

"Absolutely nothing, Comrade General Secretary."

"Siberia? China?"

"Again nothing, Comrade General Secretary."

"My peasant mind wonders why they might not attack there was well, Comrade Marshal."

"Coordination difficulties possibly? Logistics? Political will? They could simply sit there and do nothing, knowing we have to maintain units to counter the possibility of them attacking us. Pin us in place whilst the real fighting goes on around our western borders, Comrade General Secretary."

The nods around the room demonstrated understanding of the issue.

"So, Comrade Marshal, how do you advise we proceed against the perpetrators of this despicable act of betrayal?"

"We can offer local counter-attacks, but we were simply not prepared for this sort of treachery, Comrade General Secretary. Marshal Vasilevsky and I have already talked about mounting a counter-offensive, but we wish to understand the GKO's will in this matter."

Numerous men exchanged looks with Stalin, looks that spoke of determination and steel.

"Stop them, roll them back, and crush them, Marshal Zhukov!"

"Of course. I must have as many units as possible from the STAVKA reserve, and time to put a proper attack together. We must remember they have unlimited resources, so we must ensure we plan for success, not half measures. That will require some time, Comrades... time which will be bought with the blood of the Russian soldier."

"As ever, Comrade Marshal."

Beria had made the statement, and he drew an expressionless look from Zhukov.

"As ever, Comrade Marshal," Zhukov conceded.

'One day, Chekist... you little shit... one day...'

Stalin lit his pipe and sent a wave of thick smoke over those closest to him.

"Politically, we must act with great firmness. Speak to their minor allies... tell them we were attacked without warning or cause... try and drive a wedge between them all."

He raised a warning finger towards Zhukov.

"We must do nothing to antagonise the neutrals. Sweden, Finland, even the fucking Swiss and that two-faced shit Tito... nothing to make them ally themselves in any way, Clear?"

"Yes, of course, Comrade General Secretary."

Stalin sat back in his chair and looked at two of his comrades.

He raised an enquiring eyebrow and received a small nod of agreement.

"There is more we can, of course. As your leader, I have had to prepare for all eventualities, and I can tell you know that our Motherland has other tools at its disposal in this new fight, tools that will make the whole world tremble."

He stood and addressed the now fully focussed assembly.

"Comrades, with foresight helped by understanding the capacity for duplicity and treachery of these capitalist bastards, your leadership has continued with a special project that will now enable us to strike back at the very heart of our enemies."

He had their undivided attention.

"Project Raduga. It will strike them by land and sea, hurt their soldiers and their civilians, here and in faraway lands."

He puffed on the pipe and decided where he would stop, at what point he would baulk at telling them details to protect security… and disguise the fact that he had intended to bring about another war in any case.

For now, he decided to use their fury at the betrayal.

"Comrades, you'll understand… I cannot say too much… but I'll tell you this. They will die in their tens of thousands, both at home and at the front."

'You want to know how… and you, Comrade, want to know if we have it, don't you?'

He knew the questions they were asking themselves and decided to meet their suspicions… their unspoken questions… head on.

"Yes."

Some looked puzzled.

"Yes, Comrades… the Motherland has the bomb… and we'll use it at the appropriate time."

There was genuine excitement.

"Yes, we have it, but we also have much more."

He put his pipe on the table and moved around to the large map on which Zhukov had pointed out places during his briefing.

"We have much, much more… and we will use it!"

He swept his hand over the map, encompassing everything in one mighty sweeping gesture.

"There is nowhere on this map that is safe for them."

The map went from Portugal and the British Isles on the left, through to Siberia and Japan on the right.

The leader smiled as he had a thought.

Turning back to the excited audience, he pointed over his shoulder.

"Nowhere off the map that's safe for them either."

Even those who were less sharp understood his words.

'Amerika!'

Stalin laughed.

"Yes, Comrades, we will burn them in their beds, be it in New York or San Francisco."

"Urrah!"

They stood as one and applauded, at first the leader, then Zhukov, then themselves.

Only a handful present knew that the rhetoric was little more than simply earnest hopes on claimed technical opportunities translated into promises, and that Raduga would need a lot of luck to experience any successes such as Stalin had just suggested.

The meeting was carried on a wave of emotion, and the USSR was committed to a war the like of which had never been seen before.

All-out conflict with weapons that had the capacity to consume people in their tens and hundreds of thousands.

In the United States of America, the great and powerful of American politics received briefings, either from and in the White House direct, or from those of varying importance sent to bring the information to disbelieving ears, depending on the recipient's place in the food chain.

The incredible act of betrayal brought about by the Soviet Union bore too many parallels to that inflicted upon them in December 1941 for any politician to do anything but throw his or her weight behind a full and deadly prosecution of any renewed war.

The latest 'Day of Infamy' saw the translation of Truman's words to Patton into action, and by the time that Governor Dewey of New York was informed and committed himself to the full prosecution of the renewed violence, the secret movement of L-14 through L-19 and J-3 through J-5 had already started.

Destination... Karup.

1800 hrs, Saturday, 15th March 1947, NATO Headquarters, Leipzig, Germany.

Patton set his jaw and listened with studied severity, hands on his hips in classic pose.

Incredulously, there were no major Soviet incursions, although according to German and Polish reports, the bastards had come close, with disaster only averted at the last moment when forces on exercise moved up and beat the enemy thrusts back.

The British had suffered from artillery and mortar exchanges all along their front line, and in a stiff exchange south of

401

Kalvarija, where the Guards Division had responded by launching a spoiling attack towards the town and come up short in the face of well dug-in anti-tank guns and infantry.

German and Polish forces had responded quickly and had pushed over the Soviet lines in a number of places, creating an opportunity not wasted on the fiery American.

The French had mostly been spared, save for the ex-SS legion units, who had taken a pounding from artillery and mortars without any accompanying ground assault.

A strange report from one of their divisions needed clarification, and Patton moved on, deciding that if the damned SS couldn't find an enemy armored and infantry force reported to be in brigade strength attacking the DRH's 78th Sturm Division, then quite clearly he needed someone to put a burr under the ass of their commander.

"Never happen with my old boys of the Third, goddamn Krauts!'

Around Vienna, the situation was extremely confused.

Austrian reports had the Bundesheer counter-attack and partially break into the designated Soviet corridor into Vienna.

US forces aggressively moved against the Austrian capital and took a bloody nose despite gaining good ground, bringing some infantry units into the city itself.

Who exactly was where was not always clear, but Austrian forces set behind the US lines were already moved up to closely support any further assaults.

He eyed the area around the Yugoslavian lines, and in Italy, with a jaundiced eye.

'I don't trust those motherfuckers one fucking bit!'

The air briefing was music to his ears, with solid reports of kills and targets struck down across the front from the Baltic to the Graz in the south.

"Arthur, we must make sure your boys don't start anything with the Yugos. Make sure of it. No mistakes. Can't afford that critter kicking off down there, ok?"

Tedder had already stressed that to all commands, but knew it wouldn't hurt to say it again.

The navy brought very little to the table.

One enemy submarine sunk in Arctic waters, and a British submarine brought to the surface and severely shaken up during a vigorous attack made by the Norwegian Air Force. Some sorties had been flown off aircraft carriers, but these had netted nothing of note.

Unconfirmed reports had another Soviet submarine down in the Black Sea, but the RAF aircraft responsible had been unable to confirm before being driven away but enemy forces.

Patton strode back to the middle of the briefing area and set himself again.

"Thank you, Brigadier."

The British officer nodded and moved back into the expectant mass of senior personnel, all waiting on orders from the man himself.

"Clearly, the Soviets have made a FUBAR of their attack, almost to the point that you could wonder if they meant to do it at all! Not our problem, but we're sure as hell gonna make the suckers pay big time."

He turned to the situation map and took in the markings and trappings of the manoeuvres of millions of men and thousands of pieces of equipment.

"The President has given me an order and I intend to carry it out without delay."

Patton nodded to himself in acknowledgement of the importance of his decisions, picked up the slender metal baton and flexed it gently between his hands.

"Our German and Polish allies have responded quickly, thanks to their exercises in progress, and their efforts will proceed. In fact… will be enlarged."

Patton's eyes narrowed.

"In general, we'll advance across a broad front… keeping up pressure at as many points as possible but… specifically…"

He flicked the baton to the top of the map.

"I plan to start operations in North Norway within three days, if not sooner. The finer details of that'll be sorted shortly."

The aggressive general was out of the bag.

"The Polish Army on the Baltic will continue to guard the coastline, and will be responsible for moving up the coast in line with the British advance."

McCreery gave Patton his full attention.

"The British forces will keep their right flank hinged on the Poles here," he slapped the map hard, denting the small village of Lazdijai, "With a view to driving forward and occupying Riga as soon as possible."

McCreery understood his task and that the three hundred or so kilometre advance would require extremely careful planning and coordination with his Polish cohorts.

"Meanwhile, the Polish Army will continue their magnificent counter attacks and convert them into main drives, which will focus on Vilnius and Minsk... simultaneously."

He took a look at Guderian and offered a courteous nod.

"Fieldmarshal, your forces have responded superbly and I want you to continue with your assaults towards Bialystok and Lublin at full speed... but your centre should pin the enemy in place... push... but not too hard."

Patton's intention was obvious.

Encirclement.

"The French forces will mount an attack to support the Fieldmarshal's assaults, by threatening Zamosc, and another to threaten an attack north of Lvov... here."

That was a big ask of the reduced French Army, but Patton knew that more units were already marshalling for quick dispatch to the front, and that they were units of better quality than had previously tried and failed against the Red Army.

"US forces will launch a number of attacks from areas in Poland here," he indicated the southern Polish sector, where most of the US Army was either in the front line or camped behind the lines on policing or training, or simply at rest.

'Not that anyone in my goddamned army is resting at the goddamned moment!'

"My objective for the US forces is simple. I intend to take Lvov to protect the northern flank of an advance that will take forces to the shores of the Black Sea. Eliminating Bulgaria, Hungary, and Rumania as threats, and as allies to the Communists. This will have the effect of freeing up considerable assets presently tied down elsewhere."

Patton enjoyed the look on the faces of many of the men present, who quite clearly thought he was asking too much of his forces.

He was asking a lot, but he felt he knew his boys... and no one ever accused George S. Patton of lacking confidence.

"This!"

He again slapped the display, this time precisely on the Austrian capital city.

"We'll take Vienna immediately, with as little damage as possible. A quick sharp blow should be enough to force them to surrender. Austrian forces have already nearly closed up the supply route... so that'll be done as quickly as possible."

He extended a hand to the map, almost tickling the sensitive spot.

"Yugoslavia?"

"Quiet, Sir, but we understand that Tito will be making a very public condemnation of the Soviet aggression. Our sources tell us that there'll be no issues from the Yugoslavs."

"Thank you. In other words, Tito is pissed with Stalin. That's good. We do nothing... I repeat...nothing to bring the Yugoslavs to any other position. None the less, we treat our lines opposite them as active zones. I'm not gonna get caught out. Clear?"

Lieutenant General Morgan, second in command of the Italian theatre, nodded his understanding.

"Right, gentlemen. I want to see some planning by 1100 tomorrow. Ok, then let's get ourselves in the saddle and go and win this goddamned war!"

1800 hrs, Saturday, 15th March 1947, the White House, Washington DC, USA.

"People of the United States of America, I come before you this evening with a heavy heart, to report to you upon events that will bring despair to every soul... heartache to every fibre of your being."

"On December 8th 1941 my predecessor, President Franklin Delano Roosevelt, stood before Congress and told of the Japanese attack upon our country."

"He used some words that all of you will remember."

Truman paused, some thought for effect but in truth it was emotion that seized him.

"He called it 'a day that will live in infamy'."

"Today, I come before you all to report that, for the second time in a generation, we have suffered such an infamous day, no lesser than that visited upon us by the Empire of Japan."

"At two o'clock this morning, European time, the forces of the Soviet Union and her Allies, launched a surprise attack upon the forces of NATO in the free countries of Europe."

Truman paused, even though he suspected that very few listening to his broadcast were unaware of the new ignominy visited upon the world at large.

"I can tell you all that our forces, and those of our Allies, responded quickly and met the aggressors in the field, in the air, and on the high seas, and we have prevented any great advances."

"Indeed, we are already making inroads into the enemies' lines."

"As you will know, following the grievous loss of General Dwight Eisenhower, General George Patton was placed temporarily in command of all forces in NATO, and he has taken charge of the efforts to take the fight to the enemy and punish them for this incredible act of treachery."

He took a quick sip of water and pressed on.

"The gravity of the situation that confronts the world today cannot be underestimated, as the very techniques and weapons of war now available have changed so much since President Roosevelt took us into a righteous war against the Japanese... and against the Axis of evil that threatened the world's freedom."

"These weapons have the capacity to lay waste to land like no other means of war devised before."

"We find ourselves, once again, involved in a war not of our choosing, but one thrust upon us by the decisions of others... others whose motivation is the suppression of rights and freedoms, and the enslavement of nations."

More water.

"I promise each and every one of you that the efforts of this administration, our forces, and those of our Allies, will be focussed on the total and utter defeat of the aggressors, and that we will do so with every means at our disposal."

The glass was drained and Truman signalled for a refill.

"We did not choose this, neither you nor me, but we must now deal resolutely with the challenges to come.

"Often in our lives, we come to a point where we, as nations and as individuals, must choose between alternative ways of life, between how best to deal with the rights and wrongs that life itself throws in our way."

"That choice is often not a free one, for we can be confined by circumstances."

"At this time, I say to you that we have no choices now. There is no other option than to fully prosecute this conflict to its swift and awful end, or we should see our future generations being threatened by the regime that has, once again, visited war upon us all."

"You will know that we possess weapons of a type that can bring destruction on a biblical scale and that, for sound reasons, they were not employed in the recent conflict in Europe."

Even those around him that knew the precise words to come held their collective breath, for the enormity of them would not be wasted on a listening world.

"I take this opportunity to assure you, the people of America, the free peoples of the world, and also, importantly, to the peoples of the Soviet Union and her Allies... we will **not** hold back... we will **not** restrict ourselves... and we **will** avail ourselves of each

406

and every means at our disposal to end this conflict and bring the aggressors to their knees before us, totally defeated."

Truman's voice started to croak towards the end of the statement and he took a sip from the fresh glass.

"We know enough now to understand that nations do not make war."

"It is individuals who bend their people to their own ends, their own ambitions, so I say this particularly to the Soviet people."

"You will suffer for the sins of your leaders because that is the nature of war."

"When this is done and we are at peace again, those leaders will have a day of reckoning, where they will stand accountable for their actions, a day when those who have brought all of us to the pits of hell once more will be tried and judged."

"I ask you all, especially our enemies, to understand that the resolve of this nation is total."

"We are now preparing to obliterate more rapidly and completely every productive enterprise the Soviets and their Allies have above ground in any city. We shall destroy their docks, their factories, and their communications. Let there be no mistake... we shall completely destroy the Soviet Union's power to make war and I urge the Soviet people to heed our warning and remove themselves immediately from such factories, docks, and communications centres."

He let that hang for a moment.

"We would wish to spare the Soviet people the total destruction that we can and will bring down upon them, so we make this one time offer to the Soviet leadership... and particularly Premier Stalin."

"Surrender now... unconditionally. Preserve your nation and your people instead of pursuing your personal agendas."

"I can assure you that if you do not now accept our terms, then you may expect a rain of ruin from the air, the like of which has never been seen on this earth."

"Behind these air attacks will follow sea and land forces in such numbers and with such power as you have not yet seen and cannot imagine, and they will bring with them the fighting skills of which you are already well aware."

He paused, the effort of the delivery making him momentarily light-headed.

"The clock is running... the sands are ebbing away... make the most of this time, for we will **not** falter in our resolve, and we will bring all the horrors of war to every hearth and home in the Soviet Union and beyond to her Allies."

"That is our message... that is our position."

"People of America and the world, good luck to you all, and I pray to God that we shall soon see an end to this latest round of madness."

He closed his eyes and prayed the briefest of prayers for his country.

'Dear God, bring an end to this insanity.'

"God bless America. Good night."

0108 hrs, Sunday, 16th March 1947, the Kremlin, Moscow, USSR.

The radio was switched off, creating a loaded silence into which only one man dared to venture.

"We attacked? We're the aggressors? The man's a fucking idiot!"

Stalin shouted at anyone in distance.

"They attacked us... they... attacked... us!"

Those privy to the finer details of Raduga could not wholly understand their leader's indignation, but nonetheless held their peace.

"Bastards! Fucking bastards! They'll pay for this, Comrades!"

Voznesensky spoke up, voicing their collective thoughts.

"I cannot believe that our agencies did not see this coming. How could such an enterprise go undetected?"

Beria bristled.

"There was nothing... no information, fact or suspected, Comrades. Neither us, nor the GRU, had the faintest sniff of this treachery. Indeed, with the death of the capitalist's high command, it would have been considered unlikely even if we knew something was planned."

"None the less... you'll check everything again. Find out if there's been an error and who's to blame for it, Comrade Beria."

"Of course, Comrade General Secretary."

"And order the woman back here immediately!"

Stalin turned his attention on the wider audience.

"So, the fool threatens us with his wonder weapons! We have our own, Comrades... and we'll use them to counter this treachery... this betrayal!"

Not everyone around the room was privy to the existence of the Raduga Project and its array of weapons, and a number of men shifted uncomfortably in their chairs, hoping that their leader would hold his tongue.

"The Red Army will be ordered to resist this betrayal with every means at its disposal, and we will initiate our own plans for the mass destruction of our enemies!"

0121 hrs, Sunday, 16th March 1947, Friedrich-Ebert-Strasse, temporary government building #1, Magdeburg, Germany.

They had listened to the words of the American President, and then those of the British Prime Minister that followed an hour later.

Immediately afterwards, a secret military briefing had commenced, detailing just how incredibly well matters had gone.

Two Colonels, one German, the other Austrian, laid out the staggering successes of Undenkbar, and how not only their own forces, but also those of Poland, Britain, France, and America were now pushing into territory previously held by the Soviets.

The plan had been given such a huge boost with the unexpected death of Eisenhower and the propelling of Patton into the top job.

The latter had been spoken of, a sort of unattainable yet cherished hope, the circumstances of it unimaginable until fate took a hand and placed Eisenhower on Strong's aircraft.

Such were the circumstances that had come together to put Undenkbar successfully in motion that those listening could not help but think their plans had been given help by God, and that such fortuitous events simply demonstrated that they were correct in both thought and deed.

Those without faith simply grasped that they had been handed success by an incredible amount of good fortune and luck.

The plans of the three countries, Germany, Austria, and Poland, had come to fruition and the Allies, enraged by the apparent Soviet aggression, and under the guiding hand of the aggressive George Patton, were already throwing themselves against the Red Army intent on revenge.

Von Vietinghoff's account of Patton's meeting with senior commanders only gave them greater hope that the enemy would be brought to heel in a final and terminal fashion.

The US President had already committed NATO to using the new bombs, unwittingly assuring the plotters that huge destruction would be wrought on their bitter enemies.

On the other side, it seemed relatively clear that the Soviets would respond to what they would see as naked aggression, despite their clearly weakened state, and fight back with their normal fury.

Stalin would not permit any less, and that would further ensure the destruction of the Communist state.

The cream on the whole matter was that there was no hint of suspicion, no awkward questions being aimed at them, the whole contrivance having been accepted at face value.

From the organised removal of Allied intelligence officers who appeared privy to the existence of Undenkbar, through fictitious reports of battles on the Polish and German frontlines, to the silent raids on rear line positions of all types, prioritising those with artillery round radar detection capability to help conceal the unfortunate but necessary bombardment of some of their allies to promote the idea of a Soviet attack.

All in all, an incredibly successful operation, to which, when finally alone, Speer, Renner, and Diels raised a glass of cognac.

"Gentlemen, to the success of Undenkbar."

Renner's toast didn't go far enough for Speer.

"That and more, Präsident Renner. I give you another toast."

He stood, encouraging the others to follow suit.

"I give you this toast, gentlemen. To the Fourth Reich!"

"The Fourth Reich!"

"Sieg Heil!"

0400 hrs, Sunday, 16th March 1947, Vienna, Austria.

"Ok Boys, Let's go!"

The artillery barrage was still pummelling the target area but the Rangers leapt from their positions, confident that the gunners knew their job and would advance the barrage according to schedule.

The 89th US Infantry Division had thrown itself against the enemy defences and found them wanting, almost unprepared for any direct action on behalf of the Allies.

Initially successful beyond their wildest dreams, the defence stiffened success morphed into bitter failure with two

410

battalions of the 355th Regiment mauled so badly as to be combat ineffective.

Fig # 228 - US Forces engaged at the Schönbrunn Palace.

US FORCES ENGAGED IN THE SCHONBRUNN PALACE GARDENS ON 16TH MARCH 1947

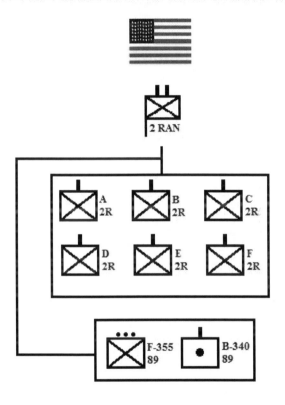

Which was why the 2nd Rangers had been thrown forward to thicken out the assault on the splendid building and grounds of the Schönbrunn Palace.

The planning was hasty, and it showed, but the men were confident in their skill at arms and charged forward, Able, Baker,

411

Charlie, and Fox companies leading a flat assault line, with Dog and Easy companies sat ready to reinforce any breakthrough.

Fig # 229 - Soviet Forces engaged at the Schönbrunn Palace.

SOVIET FORCES ENGAGED IN THE SCHONBRUNN PALACE GARDENS ON 16TH MARCH 1947.

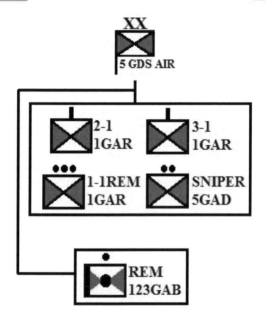

Starting in an east-west line that incorporated the ruined Gloriette, their destination was the magnificent and imposing one thousand, four hundred and forty-one room summer residence of the Hapsburg Emperor, the Schönbrunn Palace, a mere seven hundred and fifty metres to the north.

Able arrowed to the left flank, their own flank set against Maxingstrasse, intent upon storming the Tiergarten, whose residents, animal and human alike, had been subjected to a severe hammering from mortars for the previous hour.

412

The main garden area between Baker and Charlie and their target had absorbed fire from 105mm and 155mm guns of the 89th's divisional artillery, as had the now burning palace.

Fox Company had their right flank on Grünbergstrasse.

It seemed that the Soviet defenders had cornered the market on flares and the night became transformed as the palace garden areas were bathed in light, supplementing the illumination already provided by the burning Tiergarten and other structures.

Muzzle flashes added their own macabre light and the remaining snow contributed its reflective qualities, the whole bizarre combination transforming the night into a special sort of hell for attackers and defenders alike.

The Rangers had a number of infrared equipped weapons, none of which were useful in the strangely-illuminated environment, and battery packs were quickly dropped off to ease the burden of the designated soldiers.

On the left flank, men started going down under intense fire, and the attack stalled instantly.

The company commander organised his 60mm mortars and soon a smoky barrier was placed between his men and the Tirolerhaus, from where the deluge of machine-gun fire had originated.

Able were back up and rolling round the side of the smoke before the defending Russians knew they were moving again, and a desperate hand to hand fight ensued.

Meanwhile, Baker and Charlie took their own casualties as dug-in enemy started piling on the pressure.

On the right flank, Fox had the best of it, until a nest of heavy machines guns on the other side of Grünbergstrasse hit them hard and forced most of the company to ground.

The attack disintegrated into a leapfrogging affair, as the Rangers moved from cover to cover, sometimes simply to fall into a trench or shell hole for a moment of safety before starting up again, sometimes to fight at close quarters with an enemy intent on denying them the ground.

It quickly became reminiscent of the Great War, the whole garden area having been turned to a lunar landscape by both old and new ravages.

In thirty bloody minutes, Baker Company had almost reached Rustenallee and risked moving too far ahead of Charlie, who were still short of the first objective, held up by fierce resistance based around the Neptunbrunnen, a huge ornamental fountain that lay positioned at the head of the Great Parterre, the open route straight to the palace itself.

0431 hrs, Sunday, 16th March 1947, Rustenallee, the Schönbrunn Palace gardens, Vienna, Austria.

"Walter!"

The first sergeant scuttled across the hedge line, albeit with little identifiable as a hedge left by the ravages of war.

"Captain?"

"We're stalled until Charlie sort out the fountain. I'm gonna get on the horn to Captain Fairlawn, but I want you to get me an assault group ready to hit that in the flank a-sap. Three squads."

Barkmann pointed towards the offending enemy position, its knocked-about statues rising above the rubble and tree trunk positions that made it a difficult nut to crack.

"Yessir."

Ford experienced eye took in the position and he pointed to a group of shell holes.

"Start line there, Captain?"

Barkmann nodded, already working on the details of his conversation with Fairlawn.

Four minutes later, Lukas Barkmann dropped in beside his sergeant in the allotted position, a line of holes that ran along the route of the Schönbrunn TiergartenAllee, or at least where it used to be.

"Charlie's gonna pour fire on the target. Fairlawn's got up some bazookas to help some. Two minutes of direct fire and we go in…"

Something exploded off to their right and the waiting group were deluged in earth and snow.

"What the fuck's that?"

Ford spat the earth from his mouth.

"Sure's summat big, Captain."

"All the more reason to stay close to the commies."

Another huge shell landed, this time further back, adjacent to the already ruined Gloriette.

They both ignored the shattered something that arced through the cold night air.

US counter-battery teams worked the problem and the pair of Soviet 203mm howitzers only got off one more shot each before 'B' Battery, 340th Field Artillery Battalion, the designated counter-battery unit, put its 105mm shells on target, permanently silencing the two huge guns and most of their crews.

Fig # 230 - The Schönbrunn Palace Gardens, Vienna, Austria.

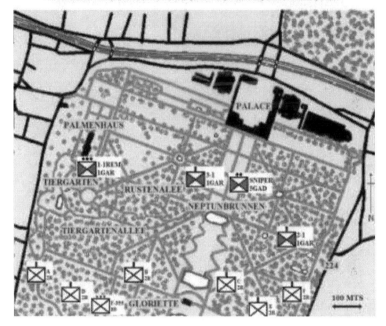

SCHONBRUNN PALACE AND GARDENS, VIENNA, AUSTRIA, 16TH MARCH, 1947

"Yeah, we go in. They'll confine their fire to the statues and all points east. Either radio or two red flares for we're in. Any questions?"

The last Russian shell down fell near the Rangers headquarters group and vapourised the liaison officer from the 355th Regiment, along with his men.

"I'm good to go, Captain."

In front of Barkmann's assault group, Charlie Company had started piling it on, the bazooka shells providing more visible effect than actual substance amongst the defenders hidden in the rubble and tree trunk bunkers.

The 60mm mortars put down more smoke in an attempt to mask the assault's left flank.

The order was given as soon as the smoke started to spread, and the three squads rose up as one.

415

A burst of fire, aimed speculatively by a defender, put one of the men running to Barkmann's left down hard, and instinctively the group spread out either side of the silent man.

Each had a grenade in hand and, on hearing the breathless order, sent it flying towards the fountain area.

The Rangers hit the cold earth and tensed themselves.

The sound of so many grenades exploding in such a small time was, in itself, impressive.

Closely on the heels of the echoing explosions came the screams of men in extremis, awful sounds that could have come straight from a horror film.

Barkmann, leading from the front, vaulted a small log barrier and realised he was heading towards two stunned men.

Somehow he adjusted himself in mid-air and planted a boot in the face of one dazed man, smashing his nose and lips, sending him cartwheeling sideways.

Rolling and coming to one knee, the Ranger captain put a short burst into the body of the other man, whose sightless eyes had not seen the threat.

A second burst stilled the man with the bloodied face.

Another ranger came over the barrier and was immediately flung backwards by a PPSh burst that creatively ripped him open from groin to shoulder.

In turn, the enemy SMG man felt momentary pain as first a bayonet and then two shots took him in the back between the shoulder blades.

Ford pulled his Garand clear and used the momentum to smash the butt into the face of the next man who scurried round the corner of the fountain. The metal butt plate took the unfortunate man in the throat and he dropped to the muddy ground where Ford left him to asphyxiate.

The dying man was leading a surge of Russians, as the local commander realised the new threat and sent men to reinforce his right flank.

The Garand M1E20 saved his life as the eighteen rounds left decimated the eight-man group, putting every one of them on the ground in varying states of distress... or forever silent in four cases.

Barkmann moved up against the stone wall and put a small burst down the scrape from which the men had emerged.

Ford had a new clip in and gestured two men forward.

Producing the flare pistol, Barkmann put two red flares into the air in short order, and Charlie Company responded by moving fire away to the right, with no fire directed to any point left of the centrepiece statue.

Above Barkmann's head, another head rose and its owner, intrigued by the flares that had just passed his nose, pulled out a pistol in order to shoot down into the Ranger's commander at close range.

A bullet from Irlam's Springfield sniper rifle dissuaded him, and the wounded man flew backwards into the faeces and watery slush beyond.

The covering party had been established to watch the left flank of the attackers, but Irlam had decided to take a hand in proceedings if he could.

Barkmann shouted to Ford as two more Rangers moved around the corner to back up the vanguard.

"Keep on here, Sergeant. I'm taking a squad around the wall this side. Watch out for friendlies, ok?"

"Yessir."

Barkmann dropped to one knee and waved down Carrera.

With sign language he conveyed his plans and the newly-promoted Sergeant organised his squad in short order.

They moved off, keeping tight to the stone wall, with two men hanging back, their Garands trained on the wall above the squad's heads, in case anyone displayed interest in their advance.

They made quick progress to the angle, where the lead man held out a hand, bringing the small party to a halt.

Four fingers indicated the number of enemy... and they were close at hand.

Carrera moved quickly up and took the bull by the horns.

The small position was isolated from its neighbours by a large fallen tree, under which a pathway had been created.

Detailing one of the BAR gunners to cover that, he checked that the two tail men were on the job and then readied his men, indicating that they should be silent.

In the log and sandbag position, four alert enemy soldiers served a 12.7mm DShK heavy machine-gun, and its muzzle was gently moving across the landscape, seeking out a target.

Alert... but looking the wrong way.

The five Rangers moved swiftly round the corner, keeping out of the line of fire of the BAR and, gathering pace, slammed into the defenders from the side.

Surprisingly, one man, an officer, reacted quickly enough to fire his pistol and Pfc Rigby stumbled as his leg was knocked out from underneath him.

417

A bayonet pinned the MG commander to the fallen tree and two rounds blasted the blade clear, ending his screams.

The other three Russians were clubbed and bayonetted to death quickly, but the damage had been done.

The BAR stuttered into life and bullets whizzed by, smashing into the face and shoulders that had emerged from the sunken pathway, sending the remaining parts bloodily back whence they had come.

Carrera quickly tossed a grenade down the same route and the resultant explosion took lives amongst the reacting enemy.

Realising the danger, Barkmann pulled the group back, and not before time as three grenades came over the top of the tree and landed amongst the fallen, causing the dead and stunned Soviet soldiers to suffer more indignities.

Behind them the sound of firing rose, and it became clear that Ford was in a serious gun battle.

Barkmann hesitated, undecided on whether to fall back, stay put, or advance.

His Ranger instincts took over, and he elected for a version of the latter.

Leaving the BAR and one man to cover them, he looked to the wall for a way out of the predicament.

Two men bridged a rifle between them and propelled Barkmann up on to the top of the wall.

He immediately felt very lonely and wished he had not been so bold, as fully twenty Soviet soldiers were assembling close by, ready for a rush against Ford's position.

He quickly tossed a grenade and dropped down behind the sandbags, letting rip with his Thompson in short controlled bursts.

The sandbags started to disintegrate as return fire came close.

"Get grenades over the wall now… ten yards!"

A few of his men responded and threw their deadly charges where he instructed.

The enemy soldiers scattered but still some shrapnel hit home, causing some serious injuries.

Two Rangers joined their commander and started to pick off the stranded Russians.

Both were knocked off the wall in the same burst of fire and fell upon their comrades below.

Carrera organised the remainder and another two men joined Barkmann on the wall.

Combined with a surge by Ford and his men, the Russians gave ground, but not before another of Barkmann's squad had gone down hard.

The retreating enemy stopped at another sandbagged defence line, roughly dead centre of the fountain's pool, and ruggedly decided to go no further.

As they dropped back, Barkmann, his mind now less hazy, acted swiftly and decisively.

"Follow me!"

He led the survivors of his squad across the top of the wall, staking their safety in speed of movement against the disorientation of the retreating defenders.

Below the wall, the covering BAR team understood instinctively and put down fire on the fallen tree trunk, stopping only when their commander descended the wall, dropped onto the large trunk, and started to sweep the enemy beyond with bursts of fire.

The squad followed suit, and they caught the enemy below by surprise.

Carrera jumped down first and was immediately thrown back up as a grenade exploded between his feet.

He hung from the fallen trunk like a shattered scarecrow and screamed his last few moments out before blood loss overtook him.

The grenade thrower turned to run but was put down by Carrera's vengeful men.

The Rangers jumped down and ran on, past dead and dying enemy, pausing only occasionally to put a bullet in a writhing body, or bayonet something that looked suspicious.

The BAR team moved up behind them, and occasionally added a bullet of their own to the mess of humanity.

They were joined by a full squad from Charlie Company, and soon Barkmann's attack had some real momentum.

The positions in front of the main statues of the fountain were more prepared for the Ranger's arrival, and more of Barkmann's men were hit, forcing the Americans to ground.

Behind them, the Charlie squad pressed forward, through and then beyond the Baker Company survivors, rushing into the barrels of the defenders.

"Fall back, for fuck's sake! Fall back!"

Half a dozen men were already down and the momentum was totally lost.

In a handful of seconds, the newly arrived squad had lost half its strength, and another man was killed as the survivors fell back.

"Stupid... fucking stupid!"

Barkmann raged at himself, but all could hear is words clearly.

The surviving defenders had repositioned another 12.7mm machine-gun and its heavy bullets were chewing away at the sandbags and tree trunks in which Barkmann and his men had taken refuge.

"Smoke grenades!"

He watched as those who had them brandished them.

"In their positions... I want them in their positions. We move right... fast and low, then hook back in the front. Ready!"

He yelled the order and the little missiles flew through the air, most landing close to the defensive line. Three landed the other side of it and gave the defenders next to them heart attacks before they realised what they were.

The Soviet officer in charge of the position yelled at his men and they fired everything they had down the line towards the American soldiers.

He even added a few of his last grenades for good measure, and imagined the enemy assault force being slaughtered in the storm of metal.

That same force smashed into the corner of his positions, on the edge of the smoke cloud, and started dealing out death and destruction in all directions.

Despite the close range, the Garands proved extremely effective, as the Rangers were far enough away to be able to pick off their enemy with roughly aimed shots, two per target, which normally resulted in a display of blood and pain, before moving on to find another victim.

The dispersing smoke did nothing to save the defenders, and more than one man received a double dose of lead from two or three Rangers at a time.

An SKS took some revenge, dropping two men before its owner's stomach came apart under the simultaneous impact of four .30-06 and a triplet set of Thompson bullets.

Barkmann pulled the trigger on an empty magazine and dived to his left as a bloodied figure let fly with an automatic weapon, one bullet neatly removing the helmet strap and stinging his ear.

One of the Rangers loomed over the man and sent two shots flying through his head.

The Russians, undernourished and tired, broke and ran, the retreating gaggle disappearing into the growing gloom and smoke.

Barkmann set his surviving men to watch their side of the wall and organised the survivors of Charlie's squad, plus the BAR team, with a view to seeing what was happening on the other side of the fountain.

He stopped in his tracks and picked up the weapon that had nearly claimed his life.

It had all the looks of the German assault rifle, but it wasn't, and Barkmann knew its appearance was important.

He stowed it away under a tree trunk and resumed his intended plan.

On the other side of the fountain, Ford and his men had been stopped dead between the centre of the pond and the wall where he and Barkmann had split up.

Neither side seemed to have any grenades left, which was a mercy and a problem, depending which way they looked at it.

The ground in between the two factions was less than five metres across, but it was covered with the detritus of war, and the remains of those who had been unlucky this day.

Ford wondered if the area had been a designated latrine, the smell of urine and faeces was so overpowering.

The two sides gathered themselves, but considered the occasional unaimed shot as enough effort for the moment.

The stalemate would be expensive to break for whichever side decided to try.

Ford considered the alternatives and found none suitable.

He needed more men, more grenades, more time...

A crack behind him made him whirl round, but the bullet went high over his head and claimed the life of one of the more inquisitive Russians.

Irlam, from his new perch on the wall, close to where Barkmann had first lain, was high enough to start picking off the defenders.

He drew fire, but in doing so, the defenders exposed enough of themselves for Ford's men to have a shot, and soon the defenders found that anything but hugging the ground was likely to prove fatal.

A BAR started up and caused havoc amongst the defence, as Barkmann and his men, perched amongst the statues, fired down into the defenceless men.

Hands started to go up, accompanied by the sound of weapons being discarded, and the demoralised soldiers rose to their feet.

Ford seized the moment and ordered his men to surge forward.

On the wall above, Lukas Barkmann gave the order and the guns fell silent. Other defenders, seeing the raised hands, started to surrender, and more of the new weapons were dropped to the floor.

Flares erupted into the night once more, and the shadows of Ranger and Red Army soldiers alike danced across the frozen mush of the pond.

Suddenly more machine-gun fire erupted, this time from Soviet positions closer to the Palace, and a storm of bullets ripped into bodies indiscriminately. Rangers and Russians were bowled over as the defenders of the palace were ordered to fire upon their surrendering comrades.

The casualties amongst the fountain's defenders were awful, and the majority of those struck died under two or more impacts.

Ford and four of his men went down bloodily, a single 12.7mm bullet ploughing its way through the NCO's shoulders from side to side.

Another bullet knocked Charlie's BAR gunner out of his hiding place, leaving his lower jaw clinging to the dorsal fin of the exquisitely craved but battle damaged horse-cum-mermaid behind which he had taken cover.

Barkmann's group tumbled off the statues, some backwards to drop the other side, near the BAR group, who were presently unengaged.

The Ranger officer and three others went forward, dropping quickly into the pond area and ducked behind anything that would stop a bullet.

He found Ford, struggling for breath, with each attempt bringing more bubbly blood to his lips.

"Shit, Walter. Rest easy now. Medic! Medic!"

There wasn't one, but it made Barkmann feel better yelling it, and probably Ford for hearing it.

One of the men put a dressing on Ford's right upper arm, where the exit wound was spilling blood in dangerous spurts.

"Look after him. Walter, I'm gonna get you outta here."

Barkmann looked at the options and cursed the fact that his radio was now on the other side of the wall.

"What the fuck!"

Something landed so close that the shock sent his helmet flying away and tossed one of his men skywards.

'Mortars... for fuck's sake... mortars...'

A moment of panic seized him, a cold and warm wave of fuzziness spread through his brain as his stomach turned to iced water.

'No... no... not now... not ever...'

He fought the nerves and indecision and won, albeit by the narrowest of margins.

'Gotta move.'

"Move back!"

He gestured towards the corner of the wall, in the direction of the rest of his company.

Ensuring that two men gathered up Ford, and that the other two badly wounded were looked after, Barkmann decided to stand and watch their backs.

The man alongside him grinned with madness in his eyes.

"Just you and me and Betty then, Captain."

Heliopolous patted the Winchester M-12 shotgun with undisguised love, the carbine on his back rejected for the pump-action's hitting power.

More mortar shells arrived, off target and nowhere near Barkmann or his retreating Rangers.

A rifle cracked, bringing a yelp of pain from closer to Barkmann than he cared.

Irlam had also stayed put and picked off an advancing Soviet soldier, part of a group pushed forward by officers eager to retake the fountain.

The sniper's rifle spoke again, ending the life of the leader of the counter-attack.

None the less, his men pushed forward as the mortar barrage walked southwards.

Irlam picked off another two before they identified where he was hiding and a DP started to pepper his position.

He dropped off the wall and jogged round to the statues to see if he could work from there.

Meanwhile, the Russians took advantage of the respite and surged.

A running man flew over some sandbags and Barkmann, by instinct alone, fired from the prone position, catching the man in mid-air and throwing him backwards, life extinct.

Screaming in her fear and anger, a woman NCO followed, her SKS sporting a bayonet aimed for the officer's belly.

A twelve gauge destroyed her chest and she followed her comrade backwards.

Two more soldiers charged forward and each time the sound of a shotgun being pumped was followed by a spread of shot that took a life.

More Russians, wiser this time, came at the position from more than one direction.

The Greek Ranger missed with his shot and could only jerk the butt into the face of his nearest enemy.

Heliopolous' blow collapsed an eye socket and the screaming man clawed at him in desperation.

A head butt added to the man's injury and he recoiled away, giving Heliopolous time to put his final shot into the soldier's face.

He discarded 'Betty' as he had no time to reload.

To his right, Barkmann wounded a bearded NCO before his Thompson jammed.

Two soldiers rushed him unseen and Heliopolous' warning saved him from injury as he rolled to one side, the rifle shots and bayonet thrusts missing him completely.

With his M1911 in his hand, he dropped both men before they could work the stiff bolts of their Mosins.

Heliopolous brought up his carbine only for it to be knocked from his hands by the impact of a bullet.

His hand was numb from the impact and the Ranger simply couldn't get it to work enough to free his pistol before his enemy was on top of him.

The Russian soldier pulled the trigger but nothing happened.

Screaming a curse, he plunged the weapon forward and the bayonet took Heliopolous in the upper thigh, protruding through the flesh at the back.

Screaming in pain, he lashed out at the man who instinctively ducked his head.

The feeling returned to Heliopolous' hand as he smashed a number of bones on the man's helmet.

The bayonet slid out and the merciless soldier slammed it hard and low into the Greek's body, where its progress was halted by the Ranger's belt buckle.

None the less, the impact was enough to double Heliopolous over, and the swinging butt knocked him to the ground unconscious.

Delaying the coup-de-grace, the soldier decided to cock his weapon again, which gave Barkmann enough time and opportunity to put bullets through his back and head, the latter of which blew the soldier's face across the pond.

The pistol had been emptied and the Ranger sensed he had no time to reload and dove towards the first weapon he could see.

With no time to make an error, he remembered what he had seen previously and pulled back on the charging handle and brought the large weapon up to horizontal.

He staggered as the recoil took him off-balance, unprepared as he was for what the weapon would offer.

He put four men and women down in short order, three of which moaned and writhed as blood seeped from numerous wounds.

Something fell against his leg and he saw a grenade waiting to spread its shrapnel in all directions.

He dived over a tree trunk, but the blast caught his legs and rolled him over.

A few pieces of metal and some bits from the pond floor struck his legs and ankles, but none sufficiently to stop him from scurrying away, should a second grenade follow.

The strange weapon had dropped from his hands and he moved to pick it up.

A scream made him realise he had lost the race, and he rolled away as another female soldier pulled the trigger on her SKS rifle.

She was out of ammunition.

In fact, many of the defenders were out of ammunition, as high expenditures and Allied air and artillery strikes took great toll on stocks.

Barkmann, winded by the evasion and fall, moved only slowly and the woman saw her moment and rushed forward, bayonet ready.

Her scream of triumph turned to one of sheer agony as her shoulder disappeared in the passage of a bullet from Irlam's Springfield.

The kinetic energy knocked her backwards and on to a tree trunk, the short but perfectly placed branch punched through her spine and exited her stomach, bringing untold agonies.

There were very few engaged in the awful fighting in and around the fountain that didn't hear her piteous cries.

Irlam made the decision not to end her grief, reasoning that it would affect her comrades more than his.

Barkmann had no such rational thoughts, as his mind started to come apart, the screams and squeals the final straw in his mental breakdown.

He came apart mentally, his own screams joining with, but not overriding those of the dying woman.

Irlam, his first thought that his leader was wounded, moved out from behind the statue of the half-naked female adjacent to Neptune himself.

A single bullet struck him in the throat and sent him backwards into the pile of dead Russian bodies below.

Within a minute, Irlam had bled to death.

In the Roman Ruin, Corporal Baschuk, once of the NKVD, but now of the 5th Guards Airborne Division's Sniper company, worked the precise action of his Kar98k and looked for more targets.

He smoothed his hand down the superbly efficient German rifle, muttering his normal congratulations to her.

'Ahh Elvira... zolotse Elvira.'

Named for his mother, long since dead of hunger during the siege of Leningrad, he worshipped the weapon, as once had another.

Although then Elvira went by another name.

'Irma.'

0703 hrs, Sunday, 16th March 1947, emergency casualty-clearing station, 76 Maxingstrasse, Vienna, Austria.

Lieutenant Colonel Williams, the 2nd Rangers commander, had finished reporting the failure of his battalion's attack and was now visiting the overflowing aid post.

Many of his men lay there, alongside the occasional doughboy from the 355th, or even a wounded Russian.

He found Ford recovering from emergency surgery, still unconscious but expected to survive.

Many more of his men were being made comfortable for their journey to whatever lay ahead after life was extinct.

Despite the doctor's warnings, he was still unprepared for the sight of Lukas Barkmann sat on a bed, crying silent tears through eyes that looked at something half a world away, rocking slowly in a spreading wet patch of his own making.

"Lukas... Lukas..."

There was no reaction.

"Lukas?"

426

He put his hand gently on Barkmann's shoulder and jumped as the reaction was swift and pronounced.

The scream penetrated his ears to the point of causing pain, and the young officer dived under the bed where he curled up in a ball and sobbed like a child.

"Oh fuck... Lukas... I... err... shit..."

Williams had no idea what to do so decided to say no more.

He turned on his heel and sought out the doctor to speak about his captain, before he resumed his journey around the beds of bloodied men.

The 2nd Rangers assault on the Schönbrunn Palace had failed to cover even half of the distance to its objective.

Casualties had been extreme, and only one of the reserve companies was considered anywhere near effective.

Able had taken heavy casualties trying to take the Tiergarten, and initially failed, partially due to a new weapon that gave the Soviet soldiers greater firepower.

Only the fact that the enemy seemed to grow low on ammunition allowed them to make a final push and secure the whole zoo area, although they could not push the resilient enemy out of either the old or new Palm Houses.

Baker was the most heavily engaged and damaged of the Rangers' companies, with only thirty-seven men left unaffected, physically or mentally.

Not one Baker Company man had crossed the Rustenallee.

Charlie Company had fared only slightly better, and did, in the end, restore the American position in the Neptune Fountain.

Captain Fairlawn, Charlie's commander, mostly lay alongside the sleeping Heliopolous; mostly because his legs still lay on the battlefield where they had been separated from his body by a burst of DShK fire.

Fox Company had lost least and advanced most, the advance elements reaching the public swimming pool and obelisk fountain before the precariousness of their advance halted them.

Reluctantly, Fox had pulled back as both flanks lay exposed.

Easy Company had walked right into the Soviet mortar barrage and suffered high casualties.

Williams decided that enough was enough and refused to commit Dog Company to the fool's errand that the attack had turned into.

Seventeen of the new weapons were sent back for intelligence analysts to examine, along with the initial debrief of a captured Soviet NCO.

Before the intelligence haul went back, William's G-2 officer examined everything and ok'd it for removal.

He picked up one of the new weapons and felt its balance, both liking and hating it at the same time. Liking for its solid and reliable feel, hating it because it was in the hands of his enemy.

He initialled the report and the weapons et al were taken away.

He accepted a cigarette from his friend.

"One things for sure, Al... we ain't heard the last of them things."

Gesualdo nodded as he drew in the smoke.

He'd seen the capability of these new... whatever they were... in action, and they were decidedly bad news.

"Yep. Reckon those bastards will be around for a while. What they called?"

The G-2 checked his notes.

"No name, the guy just called it an AK-47."

"Well, name or not, the fucking thing's bad news."

"Amen to that."

By the sword you did your work, and by the sword you die.

From 'Agamemnon' by Aeschylus

Chapter 194 - THE BLADES

0904 hrs, Monday, 17th March 1947, Colonel General Kaganovich's office, the Kremlin, Moscow, USSR.

"Sit... sit... mind the cables... you look terrible, Comrade."

"I feel terrible, Comrade General."

She picked her way over the power leads to the film projector.

"Was it a difficult journey back?"

"No. The Allies made it quite clear that all members of delegations would travel unhindered, provided that details of flights were rostered... although I admit, I half expected a squadron of Spitfires to descend upon us en route."

Kaganovich could understand that, given the Allies' treachery in launching an unprovoked attack... admittedly, he conceded to himself, before their own unprovoked attack on the Allies.

A fine point, but an important one, although the act of the enemy had justified Stalin's efforts to secure highly destructive weaponry and launch his own attack.

He poured tea from a superbly ornate samovar he had recently acquired and placed one before the woman.

"So, Tatiana, I'm intrigued as to why you've come to see me before presenting yourself and your report to the General Secretary..."

That Kaganovich was intrigued was obvious, although Nazarbayeva had no idea what exactly the very dangerous man was intrigued about.

"Officially, one of my men is flying in with a file to allow me to brief the GKO thoroughly... unofficially... I discovered something of great concern to me... and I decided that I'd come and speak to you first."

Inside, Kaganovich felt smug, but kept his face relatively blank, maintaining a modest enquiring look just to keep up appearances.

"Then speak... and speak freely, Tatiana... I'll do you no harm for speaking your mind to me... and rest assured there are no recording devices in the room."

Technically he was correct.

The recorders were in a separate room.

She launched into the presentation she had prepared in her room and on the flight back, revealing Pekunin's treachery, the use of code words, although she decided not to reveal what they were.

Kaganovich said nothing and simply listened, occasionally pursing his lips or shaking his head at her words.

The existence of a secret group plotting to overthrow the leadership brought a gasp, as much for the fact that he had secretly hoped she didn't know it, as much as for show.

The accusations of Stalin starting the war on lies, the approach to resume her former mentor's role as a go between... the knowledge of the submarine carrying anthrax...

'Who the fuck is Polkovnik Ramsey?'

The suspected existence of large Japanese submarines and equipment pertaining to their nuclear project...

The words spilled from Nazarbayeva's mouth.

In another room, next to two recorders manned by NKVD personnel loyal to Kaganovich, two important men sat listening, hooked on every word.

"So, what is that you ask of me, Comrade Nazarbayeva?"

"These traitors... how best to smoke them out?"

"You didn't give me the code phrases... deliberate on your part, of course."

"Yes, Comrade General."

The silence was awkward.

"Comrade General, let me be blunt. I suspect everyone, and if I told you the phrases..."

"I understand, Comrade Nazarbayeva. More tea?"

"Unless you have something stronger?"

"Ah, yes... of course."

Rumours of her drinking and other proclivities had long since reached his ears, rumours he had carefully ushered away from other receptive ears, namely those of his direct boss.

He opened his drawer and took out a small bottle of a home brewed walnut vodka, careful not to knock it against the Tokarev pistol he had set there earlier... just in case.

The Deputy Head of the NKVD poured two measures and slid one glass across the polished desktop.

"Na Zdorovie!"

430

"So, what do you intend to do, Comrade?"

"Clearly I need to flush these bastards out, but I've already tried, without luck... although I actually didn't know who I was trying to contact. I simply used the phrases that Pekunin gave me."

She considered speaking further and committed herself.

"VKG is important. He was listed by Pekunin. There were other names who rejected the idea... such as Molotov."

"Molotov was asked?"

Kaganovich's acting skills were excellent.

"Yes... so... who is VKG?"

"No idea, Comrade Nazarbayeva."

The listeners exchanged knowing looks.

Kaganovich poured another drink before asking the big question.

"What do you intend to do, Tatiana?"

"Nothing yet, Comrade. I must discover who they are. I hoped you could help me with that?"

"Possibly."

Nazarbayeva sat upright in an instant, the guarded comment sending a charge of electricity through her brain.

"You know about this... you know about all of this, don't you, Comrade General?"

"I know some of it, Tatiana."

"Who are these bastards... these traitors... these..."

He held up his hand and gestured her to sit down.

"Traitors? No. Patriots... men who love the Rodina... yes."

Her eyes narrowed as she digested the words and assigned them meaning.

"You're one of them, aren't you?"

"I love the Motherland as I love my own children, Comrade Nazarbayeva. As a patriot, I'm prepared to act against enemies of the Rodina, be they inside or out."

She downed the latest drink in one and stood again.

"I arrest you in the name of..."

"Sit down, you stupid woman... SIT!"

The door flew open and two guards, armed with state-of-the-art AK-47s, tumbled through the opening, alerted by the shouted word.

Kaganovich held out a calming hand.

"Thank you, Comrades, You may wait outside. A small disagreement, nothing more."

The two NKVD guards noted that the woman's hand was on her empty holster, as if to grab for its missing contents, but ceded the room under orders.

"Please... sit down, Tatiana."

She did so and accepted a refilled glass, her mind whirling with the enormity of the situation.

"Your old general... Pekunin... provided us with a way to get messages to the Allies regarding the potential for a change of leadership, one that he considered was the only way to save the Motherland from oblivion... and this was before the demonstration of atomic weapons by our enemies."

"But..."

"But just listen. What you have heard is quite true. We went to war on false accusations... false information deliberately enhanced by our leadership to whip up a frenzy across the country. The Allies never intended to attack us..."

"But..."

"Listen! They never intended to attack us... never."

He calmed down enough to continue in an even voice.

"We were sent to war by a leadership that simply wants more power and influence. All the dead, ours and theirs, are on the hands of men who care nothing for death... save their own!"

Nazarbayeva went to interrupt but hesitated, her mind in a turmoil.

"Your sons have been needlessly sacrificed on the paths of their ambition! You know I speak the truth, Tatiana."

He listed each in turn.

"Vladimir... sacrificed on a suicidal mission contrived for purposes of revenge and little more."

"Oleg... Oleg deliberately betrayed by your leaders to advance some sort of tryst with Franco... which never even got off the ground. They sat in front of you and confessed it... they confessed it!"

"Ilya assassinated by an agent of the NKVD... I've seen the reports on that one too... three sons, Tatiana, three sons..."

"You don't have to tell me what I've sacrificed for the Rodina, Comrade Polkovnik General!"

Kaganovich nodded and held out his hands by way of apology, the palms upwards, almost as if to advance and embrace the woman.

"Forgive me, Tatiana, but you've sacrificed too much... and not for the Rodina... no, for them. We all have. My son Gennady wounded and a prisoner in Italy... a cousin badly injured in pilot training, and two nephews lost in Germany... and my niece Mara... darling Mara...destroyed by napalm in the Moselle... and it's been for nothing."

"Not for nothing!"

"Yes, for nothing!"

Tatiana teetered on the edge of an abyss, almost for the first time seeing her personal losses as a totality, and alongside that, the dawn of appreciation that they really might have been sacrificed just for other's personal ambitions.

The prop that had been her understanding that her sons had died for the Motherland started to crumble before Kaganovich's eyes.

He understood the mental struggle that was going on in front of him.

"Tatiana, your sons died in the uniform of the Red Army, serving the Rodina, but under false pretences... circumstances that were contrived by the leadership... a leadership that has betrayed the trust placed in it... a leadership that must be replaced so that the Motherland can survive."

A tear rolled down her cheek as she looked up into his eyes.

"But Comrade Stalin is our leader... we owe him so much... so much..."

He offered his handkerchief.

"Comrade Stalin brought us through the Patriotic War but has since steered the Rodina down the paths of his own, and others, agendas. How many more mothers must mourn because of his... because of their personal agendas?"

"But the Allies have just attacked us!"

"Did they? Come on then. What signs did you see? What intelligence did you miss? You gave no warning to the GKO... did you fail?"

"Quite clearly I failed, Comrade General."

"As did I... but there were no signs... were there?"

"No... except..."

"Except?"

"The Germans... there was something going on with them... nothing solid... just rumours."

"Indeed... but that aside... our leadership intends to take us back to war again... a war that would have seen new terrors on both sides. I talk of atomic weapons and the biological and nerve agents we captured from the Germans or secured from the Japanese."

He stood and looked out of the large window.

"You know yourself, the submarine was carrying Anthrax. It was the plan to insert that into the drinking water in Northern

433

Germany. That plan was already in motion, Tatiana... a plan from which you were excluded."

A thought struck her like a thunderbolt.

"Raduga... the whole thing... running to take the war back to the Allies... before they attacked... if they attacked... it didn't matter if they attacked?"

"No, Tatiana... it didn't."

"Atomic... biological... nerve gas... everything?"

"Yes, and we both know it has been for some time... in fact... it never really stopped and was always offensive in nature, despite what you were told."

"They intended to take us back to war in any case? All that time... despite their words of appeasement... the ceding of territory... the casualties, millions of dead... regardless... come what may... German provocation... they wanted war again? Holy Mother."

"Yes, Holy Mother indeed. Now, we have the bomb... and they have the bomb... and we'll all annihilate each other unless this is ended."

"How?"

Kaganovich laughed softly.

"That's the question, Tatiana. There seems little way to do so without... well..."

"Removing them?"

"Removing... yes... in some way..."

"Killing them?"

"Yes. There would seem to be no other way."

In the other the room, the listeners held their breath.

"To save the Rodina, kill the General Secretary and sue for peace?"

"We just sued for peace, a peace that saw us retain Polish territory and other advantages. That peace has just been shattered by some means as yet unclear to us. Who can say if that it wasn't our doing? I certainly know that, no matter what, our leader intended to take us back to war once his pet project was fully functioning. So I cannot deny... you cannot deny that this latest attack actually wasn't actually orchestrated by our leadership?"

"There were no indications!"

"There were no indications of any attack... by them... or by us."

Nazarbayeva's mind was in a whirl as it was assaulted by new words and thoughts.

'You have a son and a husband in uniform still... will they too be killed in such a cause?'

434

Kaganovich sensed his moment.

"What else can we do, Tatiana? What would you have us do? ...What would you do?"

The verbal barrage overwhelmed her momentarily.

"To save the Rodina... the Motherland... you do what needs to be done."

She pushed her empty glass forward in expectation of a refill, and the NKVD general obliged.

"So, the question is, would you join any group that put the Motherland first, and looked to rid the Rodina of the present leadership?"

The question was huge and elicited no answer.

Kaganovich became very aware of the growing presence of the Tokarev automatic in his drawer.

"There must be another way, Comrade General."

"Perhaps there is. Let me know if you discover it, Comrade Nazarbayeva."

He returned the bottle to the drawer, and left it open enough to ensure that the pistol could be out in a moment.

"So, what will you do? Will you betray us? Me?"

"No, Comrade Kaganovich. I will not. What purpose would that serve? If things are as you say... as they seem... then we must protect the Rodina... but I find it hard to believe that the lust for personal glory and such has brought is to this. I'll think more on this, but I will not betray you, but neither will I be a party to violence against the General Secretary."

"Not betray us, you mean... it's not just me."

"No... VKG to name but one. Who is VKG?"

"He'll reveal himself in good time, I'm sure."

1000 hrs, Monday, 17th March 1947, Colonel General Kaganovich's office, the Kremlin, Moscow, USSR.

"So, do we kill her or do we hope she comes on board?"

Khrushchev shrugged in peasant fashion.

"If she doesn't see it our way, we have no choice."

VKG nodded but stayed silent.

He did not want Nazarbayeva's blood on his hands but, in real terms, they were already tainted with the blood of thousands so one more innocent made little difference.

"You know her better than we do. We take a risk every second we sit here, but she is central to our plans. With her we can achieve everything and seize power. Without her... well... we would need to rethink so much."

"And that's important, Comrades. It's not just a question of removing the bastards... they must be replaced by the right leadership... namely us."

VKG nodded and added his own comment.

"And we know that with Nazarbayeva's help we can achieve this."

Kaganovich conceded both statements.

"So, more pressure. Is it time?"

The two others pondered the question.

"Are we ready to go?"

Khrushchev's enquiry was aimed at the military man.

"No, but we can adapt and seize any moment. I can order the Moscow Military District to act whenever I need."

Kaganovich reminded them of his own objections.

"If we use her now, we may lose control over the situation. She is as likely to go off like a rocket as join us in carefully laid plans."

They understood his often-stated position.

"We must retain control over the situation... but we need her... she must be committed and controlled. The seeds have been sown today. She'll be watched, and any hint of betrayal will result in her instant removal... my men have specific orders on that. The stakes are high but we still have time... I think. "

"And you assure us she won't decide to betray us?"

He answered Khrushchev's question with a shake of his head.

"No... but I assure you that if she decides to do so, she'll die before she manages it."

VKG made his decision.

"Then we're agreed. We wait?"

In unison, they voiced their agreement.

"We wait."

Nazarbayeva completed her briefing for the GKO without mention of the going-on in Kaganovich's office, or of her contact with Ramsey.

Her need to tackle Stalin direct on matters relating to Raduga had long since taken second place to her professional needs to equip her leadership with the best information possible.

In concert with Beria, she repeated the intelligence view that there was no hint of any action on the part of the Allies, a rare agreement between them.

But, none the less, the Allies had attacked.

'Appeared to attack...'

Her hints at some issue with the Germans again received support from Beria, but were scoffed at by the General Secretary, who lambasted his Intelligence officers for their lack of ability.

Others had been removed, or worse, for lesser offences, Stalin reminded them both.

None the less, neither was relieved nor sanctioned, which in itself gave Nazarbayeva food for thought.

'Was it you, General Secretary, eh? Is that why you laugh at the German issues, eh? Is that why you only chastise us, eh? Because you know it was you?'

The presence of armed NKVD guards in the briefing room was a new occurrence, based upon a recommendation from Beria, who suspected there might be treachery afoot.

In honesty, Beria always suspected treachery, but Kaganovich had been quite insistent, so handpicked men were now permitted to attend such meetings, men with selectively deaf ears and alert eyes, ready for any sign of trouble.

One of them had been ready to gun Nazarbayeva down the moment she opened her mouth, but she had stayed true to her word.

However, she still had her own needs, again agitated into life by Stalin's behaviour, and the words tumbled from her lips.

"Comrade General Secretary. I have a question."

"By all means, Comrade."

"Raduga. Is it still running in any way?"

"No."

Stalin looked her straight in the eye with his best paternal and reassuring look.

"You know it was closed down. Research continues of course, but the operation is defunct. Now, I've an important meeting. Is that all?"

"Yes, thank you, Comrade General Secretary."

'Bastard!'

And in the moment, she changed.

'At last!'

Across the battlefield, the hammering rain reduced in intensity, allowing men to see a little further than the fifty yards or so that had been the case during the first two attacks.

Officer's and NCO's voices rose in unison, shouting the motto of the elite unit.

"Go for broke!"

The Nisei threw themselves forward for a third time, encouraged by the lessening fire from the Soviet positions.

The Soviet cavalrymen, without horses for as long as they could remember, stood their ground and died in their scores, fighting with shashkas in hand when ammunition ran out.

Occasionally one Cossack would get lucky and cut a Japanese-American down, but invariably they died where they stood, shot down safely from distance.

A knot of Cossacks formed around an officer and those with ammunition shot down attackers, causing the assault to peter out once more.

The major in charge pulled his men back and called in the air support that had now, finally, become available.

A number of Takeo's men would still be alive had the weather cleared in time, but it didn't, and he had lost comrades who had journeyed with him from Hawaii through Italy to the heart of the eastern border of Czechoslovakia.

Four USAAF Thunderbolts swept in from the west and deposited their HVAR rockets on the remaining enemy positions, as steered in by the Nisei's attached Forward Air Controller.

The man knew his trade, as did the American fliers, and a hole was blasted in the last line of defence.

For their part, the cavalrymen of 3rd Battalion, 22nd Guards Cavalry Regiment, showed great valour and tried to patch up their line as best they could, but the FAC played his trump card, and three A-25 Shrikes, recently configured for ground attack, flew in a staggered line formation and deposited gallons of napalm across the Soviet lines.

Chikara Takeo checked that the FAC had no more aircraft inbound and sprang to his feet.

"Let's go! Go for broke!"

His men followed suit and they swept forward into the oily smoke, dispatching a screaming burning soldier here and there.

Fig # 231 - US Forces engaged at Veľký Saris.

US FORCES COMMITTED TO BATTLE AT VELKY SARIS ON 18TH MARCH 1947.

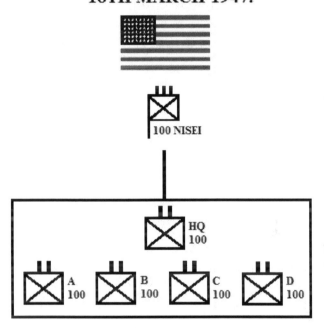

Instinct saved Takeo as he flung himself sideways, a hideously burned Cossack lunging out of the smoke with a smoking and broken rifle, its bayonet still efficient enough to catch in the trigger guard of his carbine and wrench it from his grasp.

The crazed man failed to disentangle his weapon before one of Takeo's men put three bullets into him, releasing him from his tortured world.

His saviour screamed and went down clutching his shoulder as a bullet came out of the smoke and smashed into the joint, wrecking it completely.

Without ceremony, Takeo grabbed the Garand and slipped a spare clip out of the crying soldier's pouch.

The attack was again losing momentum, more so because of the choking smoke and fumes than any stiff resistance on the part of the Cossacks.

The ground, churned by artillery and mortars, and already affected by heavy rain and the continuing thaw, was horrendous underfoot, clogging and sucking at the feet of the men struggling through it, which also the Nisei's advance.

Again, the surviving Cossacks rallied behind an officer and even launched a small counter-attack, which brought the FAC away from his radio and to the more earthly arts of self-defence.

He used his carbine to defend himself but, even so, desperate enemy made it to his position and hacked him to death, although neither of them lived for more than the briefest of heartbeats more.

As the smoke cleared, Takeo look out over a landscape the like of which he had never seen before.

The bodies were everywhere, and in the many and unusual positions of death that high explosive can create.

The cratered landscape was no more or less than he had expected, given the barrage that had been laid down before his attack.

It was the tree stumps that created the incredible feeling of some distant planet's surface, combined with the small fires that burned brightly, sometimes vegetation, often something that had once lived and breathed.

He produced his binoculars and scanned the ground, seeking out further opposition before he moved on to his final objective atop the daunting Height 570, topped with the ruins of the ancient Saris Castle.

There seemed to be nothing, at least, nothing alive to stand between him and his final yards of advance.

Not until just below the summit did his eyes detect anything that looked like a threat.

The rain started again and the cloudy sky again turned milky yellow and full of threat.

"Major! Major!"

Takeo turned to see his headquarters group close up.

"From Colonel Petersen... he expected you to be on the objective by now."

Takeo smiled widely.

"What did he actually say, Akio?"

"Err... you're to get your ass on that goddamned fucking hill pronto or you'll have a new job overseeing latrine details."

"That sounds about right."

He checked the hill again, carefully studying the route he had chosen.

"OK, we go with Able Company leading on the left there. Tell Captain Ishuri to wait for me. I'll be there to lead the attack."

Takeo suddenly remembered the Garand in his hands and helped himself to some of his radio operator's ammo as he talked.

"Contact Baker and Dog to provide covering fire on the top and right side. I want one platoon from each assigned to my headquarters as an additional reserve... straight away. Get the sniper section set up..."

He scanned the battlefield for a suitable area and immediately remembered one, a modest range of what were probably once farm buildings at the bottom of the slope, now virtually levelled by the battles that had rolled over them during the last few years.

"Get them set up there a-sap."

Akio Tanuga made swift notes.

"I'm off to prep Able... let them know I'm coming, Lieutenant. I'll deal with Charlie on my way. Get the others set up and let me know when we're all ready to roll. If Petersen calls, tell him I'm leading from the front."

Takeo ducked beneath a protruding branch and caught his sword's handle, halting his progress.

"Whoa Major."

Tanuga grabbed the handle and extracted it from the embrace of the fallen tree.

"Good to go, Major."

"Thanks."

Takeo sprinted across the muddy battlefield to where Charlie Company sat in close reserve, waiting for instructions.

1150 hrs Tuesday, 18th March 1947, Saris Castle, Height 570, Veľký Šariš, Czechoslovakia.

"Steady, comrades, steady now. Remember who you are!"

Those who had known the man during the Patriotic War would have been staggered at the change in him, from miscreant and troublemaker to a leader of men, men who would follow him to and through the gates of hell, which was about where they presently found themselves.

Captain Vasily Egonevich Kazakov had come a long way since he had killed his own officer in front of the Gurkha positions all those months previously.

22nd Guards Cavalry Regiment had seen a great deal of fighting and had paid for its experience in rivers of blood, so few of those left having been there at the start.

Such was the 22nd's reputation that it had been kept reinforced whilst other regiments in the Corps had been allowed to wither, often supplying the reinforcements that kept the 22nd alive.

Whether the 22nd was currently alive was a matter of opinion, so ravaged was it by the fury of the US assaults.

As normal, many casualties were caused by air and artillery strikes, but the horrendous weather had brought a respite from the former, one that had provided the experienced soldiers with opportunities to strengthen their positions and get ammunition forward.

Not enough on either count, as it proved, the expenditure of bullets far in excess of norms for far less return in the murky wet conditions.

Fig # 232 Soviet forces engaged at Vel'ký Saris.

SOVIET FORCES ENGAGED AT VELKY SARIS ON 18TH MARCH 1947

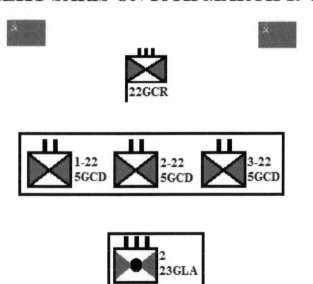

The removal of the only undamaged bridge over the Torysa River to their rear also contributed to the slowing trickle of ammunition that reached them.

3rd Battalion had been given the prize position, that of the hill, castle and adjoining slopes, a position that was presently stacked with their dead and wounded, and one that had shrunk considerably over the last eleven plus hours.

What was left of 3rd Battalion clung to the summit and ruins, Takeo's last attack having wiped out the remaining groups that had not been able to pull back up the slope.

"Comrade Kapitan! The Amerikanski are moving!"

Kazakov sprinted to the right side of his position to where one of his senior NCOs pointed down the slope.

At the same time, bullets and mortar rounds started to arrive, marking the start of Baker and Dog companies covering efforts.

"They're focussing on this side, away from the town."

"I think so too, Comrade Kapitan, Your orders?"

"Hold them back, Vassily. I'll bring more men over, and see what help our mortar comrades can provide for us."

Fig # 233 - Vel'ky Saris, Czechoslovakia.

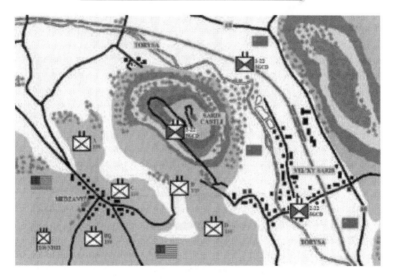

Kazakov could no longer contact the artillery support, his radios and operators long since departed, victims of accurate artillery.

443

In any case, it was of little import, given that French Typhoons had found the allocated support regiment on the move and scattered guns and prime movers to the winds with their rockets and cannon fire.

The Cossack captain moved quickly back, occasionally throwing a glance at the areas into which small arms fire was arriving, and was more often being rewarded with the sight of his men, well hidden and safe.

Here and there the sight of a newly-killed corpse was apparent, but for the most part there were few casualties to the blizzard of fire.

He ducked inside the castle ruins and found his team hard at work, new telephone cables installed but already made redundant by the last barrage.

"Get it sorted, Comrade Starshina!"

The man's protestations were cut short and the NCO signaller, newly arrived with 3rd Battalion and unaware of his commander's lack of good grace, returned to organising another wire-laying party.

"Ammunition parties?"

"Comrade Kapitan, I have sent more men back. Not one of the last two parties has returned. We have what we have."

The NKVD Lieutenant shrugged, which simple action riled the volatile Kazakov, but he stayed his hand. Now was not the time to get embroiled with the Chekist who, despite his youth and fanatical devotion to the 'fucking party', was actually quite an efficient officer.

None the less, the Cossack officer's words contained a certain barb.

"This is your responsibility, Comrade Leytenant. We need more ammunition or we'll be swatted off this fucking hill… and it'll be your name that tops my fucking report. Are we clear?"

"Yes, Comrade Kapitan."

Kazakov motioned to his second-in-command as he lit a cigarette.

"Boris, the Amerikanski are preparing for an attack on our right, using the hill to mask our support elements in the town. I'm going to need a response group. That's where you come in. Reform my reserve."

He leant out of one of the numerous holes, encouraging Boris Tarkovsky to look where he pointed.

"That's diversionary fire… I'm sure of it. I'm going to risk everything on that decision. I want two men in three withdrawn right now. No heavy weapons… leave the machine-guns behind… DPs only on that score. Form two platoons, ready to act as reserve, under your command. I want you position there," he pointed to an area covered with rubble and the shreds of vegetation, "Organised for defence to the north and northwest, but ready to move on my orders... or your own, of course."

He moved across the area with surprising speed and pushed the camouflage netting upwards.

"I want what's left organised in three equal groups. Send one to me immediately at Vassily's position, and have the other two organised similarly north and northeast."

Kazakov stopped for a moment, partially to draw down on his cigarette and partially to consider an important question.

He resolved it with a nod of his head in the direction of Junior Lieutenant Ryabkov.

"Young Klimenti has command of that. Any questions?"

"General orders. Comrade Kapitan?"

"Hold the hill... kill them all... any more questions?"

Kazakov slapped his friend on the shoulder.

"Good. Let's move. The bastards'll be upon us shortly."

He sprinted from the headquarters position content that he had done all he could do, but worried by the fact that his last magazine was already on his weapon.

At his waist was his Tokarev.

In his scabbard was his shashka.

At his side was a kukri that once belonged to a Gurkha soldier whom he had slain with the man's very own weapon...

...which, by Kazakov's reckoning, also made it his.

1201 hrs, Tuesday, 18th March 1947, base of Height 570, Medzany, Czechoslovakia.

Captain Ishuri cried.

Cried for his wife... his sons... his mother... his life.

Within seconds of rising from the ground to lead his men forward, a sniper's bullet had smashed its way through his stomach and shattered against his vertebra beyond, destroying both bone and delicate spinal cord in the process.

In truth, he cried more for the life he expected now to live, more than the possibility that it might now be ending.

The medic did what he could with the stomach wound, rolling his captain gently onto his back, and in the doing ensuring that the spinal cord was forever sundered, as sharp bone moved and completed the process of creating a paraplegic.

445

Takeo could spare Able Company's commander no time as he shouted the men forward up the increasing slope.

The shell holes and detritus of war proved both a godsend and an impediment, as the task of moving upwards was made more difficult, interspersed with moments when the attackers were safe within sheltered ground.

Naturally, the men started to enjoy these moments, and Takeo found the steam going out of his attack.

"Get moving! Don't stop! Don't stop!"

Here and there a man would go down and not rise. But the fire was surprising light, almost to the point where Takeo wondered if there was some trap in store.

He dropped into a small depression and extended his hand for the walkie-talkie.

As he started to speak, he realised he was kneeling in over a foot of water.

'Shit.'

"Kapuna-Seven-Six, Kapuna-Six-One, over."

"Kapuna-Six-One, Kapuna-Seven-Six receiving, over."

"Kapuna-Seven-Six. Shoot X-Ray now. I repeat, shoot X-Ray now, over."

"Kapuna-Six-one. On the way, over."

Takeo stuck his head up and decided to leapfrog to another hole before the mortars came down.

They dropped pretty much on the money and he decided not to issue any corrections.

"Kapuna-Seven-Six. Kapuna-Six-One, on the money. Two minute intervals, Acknowledge, over."

"Kapuna-Six-One, Kapuna-Seven-Six, two minute intervals, understood. Over."

Takeo tossed the walkie-talkie back to his corporal and decided on another hop forward.

Once every two minutes, the mortars would advance towards the summit by one hundred yards, and he needed to keep his men as tight as he dared to get the full benefit of his plan.

Again, he noticed that they were preferring cover to moving forward, so he took the decision to shout some more.

Emerging from his hole, he waved the Garand and hollered at any men he could see.

"C'mon you Buddaheads! Go for broke, One-Puka-Puka! Go for broke!"

446

One or two at first, and then the rest followed, driven upwards by a mixture of bravery, stupidity, peer pressure, and inspiration.

Above them, the sounds of growing resistance mingled with the crump of mortar shells, and men started to fall into the mud and puddles of height 570.

A head bobbed and Takeo acted instinctively, putting two shots close by and then rolling away as the enemy rifle grenade exploded.

He found a deep muddy puddle, and the cold water chilled him to the bone.

Takeo came up for air without his helmet, but decided against wasting time locating it.

He had missed his target, and the man rose again, this time dropping his grenade on the money and sending two of Takeo's men flying in a mist of blood and other fluids.

Medics started to be outnumbered by calls upon their skills.

The rifle grenade position was in advance of the Cossack line and needed to be taken out, as Takeo could see it was already firing into the flank of some of the lead groups.

He reached for his grenade but found it had gone, probably dislodged during the climb or his accidental bath.

"Grenade that fucking position! Now!"

Two men launched explosives at the Soviet strongpoint and both missed although shrapnel did its work by keeping heads down.

"Follow me!"

Takeo was up and running, his feet somehow finding traction in the mud, traction that was denied to his men.

He arrived at the enemy position by himself.

The man with the rifle grenade was just popping up again and received a kick in the face that stove in his temple with the sharpest of cracks.

Another man, nose down in a box of grenades, neither saw nor felt the bayonet that rammed into the side of his neck.

He was dead before Takeo blasted the bayonet free.

One of the riflemen whirled and got off a snap shot that knocked the Garand from his hands.

As the Cossack struggled with the bolt of his Mosin, Takeo simply threw himself forward in the hope of getting to the soldier before the rifle bolt slid home.

Head met head in a sickening crash and both men recoiled and dropped, unable to grasp the moment as each was as disoriented as the other.

447

Takeo's radioman struggled over the lip of the position and saw the dazed Cossack.

Five bullets later, the man's head and neck were minced meat, the frightened Nisei soldier taking no chances and letting rip with the reminder of his clip.

The charger pinged clear and he grabbed another clip, only to be thrown back as a burst of submachine-gun fire ripped across his chest.

The newly arrived Cossack turned to Takeo and pulled the trigger.

The PPd fired two bullets before it closed on an empty chamber, both of which sailed past well away from the recovering Major.

He grabbed behind his back, trying to reach his sword before he remembered his pistol.

The Russian dropped his useless weapon and extracted a Nagant revolver.

Takeo rolled away and came up holding a Soviet rifle.

He fired from the lying position and hit the man in the throat.

However, he had inadvertently pickled up the rifle grenade and, whilst the heavy impact destroyed much vital for the sustenance of life, it did not immediately kill the man.

More to Takeo's growing clarity of mind was the now primed grenade that bounced off flesh and landed eight feet from him.

"Fuck, fuck, fuck!"

He rolled over a dead body and flattened himself as best he could.

It was enough to protect him and the grenade exploded, doing damage only to the dead and silencing the man with the ruined throat.

Coming more to his senses, he grabbed the Garand from his dead signaller, took another two clips of ammunition.

On examination, he decided that neither piece of the walkie-talkie was now fit for purpose.

In the interim, the mortar barrage had moved on and Able Company were in danger of falling too far behind.

He rose again, this time less steadily and, despite the thumping headache, rallied his men with more exhortations.

"Keep going, men! Keep going! Get close to them! Go for broke! Go for broke!"

He pressed forward, only to slip sideways and splash into one of the deeper man-made pools on the top of the slope.

Takeo came up gasping for air, but with a clearer mind, the icy waters having done the job of a hundred aspirin.

Rising up again, he realised that he had lost yet another weapon.

Rejecting a search as an unnecessary delay, he pulled out his Colt 1911 and waved it in the air.

"Charge! Charge! Charge!"

A bullet tugged at his wrist, ripping away a flap of skin and severed his watchstrap; another opened up the crotch of his trousers.

"Charge! Go for broke!"

The line seemed to accelerate and come together as one entity and, despite the loss of more men, it crashed into the Soviet positions.

1211 hrs, Tuesday, 18th March 1947, Saris Castle, Height 570, Veľký Šariš, Czechoslovakia.

"Hold the bastards! Hold them, Brothers! Fucking hold them!"

Kazakov was set back from the line and in a position to see without the distraction of having to fight for his life.

'No good... no fucking good at all... Blyad!... Blyad!'

He turned around to where his men lay and turned back again, suddenly unsure from which group to summon more manpower.

After a moment's hesitation, he went with his gut and decided upon Tarkovsky and he waved his arms before pointing down a certain line, indicating where he wanted the first reserve group to arrive.

To Tarkovsky's credit, the counter-attack group was up and running in seconds and ploughed into the line right on time, and in precisely the place that Kazakov needed.

"Well done, Boris. Fucking well done, Brother!"

If all had been equal, the Cossack captain would have flung the rest of his men forward and pushed the Amerikanski all the way down the hill... but all things were not equal,

His men were tired.

There was little ammunition.

There were other threats.

His orders were to hold, not go 'gallivanting off around the countryside' as he put it to himself.

449

Plus, he wanted to preserve the lives of as many of his brother Cossacks as possible, and a counter-attack down the slope would only bring greater death and sacrifice with it.

He screamed in anger as he watched Tarkovsky go down under a barrage of rifle butts and kicks.

"Noooo!"

He drew breath and screamed louder.

"You fucking bastards!"

Turning to the rear again, he sent the other unit down the same line, seeing that Tarkovsky's men had lost heart as their leader died.

He also waved across to Ryabkov, using both hands to send the first unit down one line and then indicating a direction change.

Again, the cavalrymen showed their mettle and were moving quickly.

Amongst the enemy to his front, Kazakov saw the enemy officer.

He also realised that these Amerikanski were smaller men, none of them reaching the average height of his own Cossacks, and yet they fought with a ferocity he hadn't seen since the woods where he had come close to death at the hands of fellow warriors; Gurkhas.

This enemy officer was swinging a sword and firing a pistol, and was proving a rallying point for his men. Even as the first of his reinforcements arrived, the enemy started to noticeably gain the upper hand and a few of Kazakov's men started to run.

He needed to stop that immediately so strode purposefully down the slope, calling the retreating Cossacks to him.

They responded and he led them back into the fray. As he got to the top of the position, he quickly dispatched a wounded enemy with a single swipe of his shashka, taking the man's throat down to the spine beyond.

A second American company was almost on top of them.

"You, soldier!"

He summoned a panting man to his side.

"Back up the slope there and off to the left, Find the reserve platoon and bring them to the hill's edge... over there... see where I mean... that stand of trees there."

It was nothing more than a group of vertical sticks long since stripped of anything green, but it was enough for the soldier to understand.

"Yes, Comrade Kapitan."

"Right, brother. The battle and our lives depend on you. Go like the wind and get those men there immediately. Go!"

The man disappeared like a gazelle and Kazakov turned back to fighting the battle.

Again, his men seemed to have the ascendency and he ordered those on the flanks of the main resistance to concentrate on the newly arriving enemy.

The American officer was still standing, swinging his sword at all comers, and with success judging by the traces of blood on his blade.

Those who chose to try and shoot him received a bullet in return, and his position, at a junction in the rough trench scraped on the lip of the slope, served to protect him from most direct fire.

A bloodied NCO slid in beside Kazakov and it took a moment to identify Vassily

"Ah, Yesaul."

He used the Cossack rank as he always did when the two men had only ears for the other.

"You look like shit, Vassily."

Blood dripped from a number of places, some clear, other well hidden.

"I feel like shit, Ataman. May I have leave?"

"Later. For now, let's rid ourselves of this little thorn, eh? Any grenades left?"

"Fuck all, Ataman. Otherwise I'd have blown the little bastard up myself, He's a fighter for sure. These bastards are Japanese... can you believe it? They swapped sides pretty quickly, eh?"

"That's interesting. I've an idea."

He spoke quickly and with little enthusiasm, the sparkle of battle gone from his eyes, and those of his senior NCO.

Vassily Razin scuttled away, not feeling any of his wounds in particular, but generally feeling war weary and keen to rest.

By now, most of the defenders were back pouring fire into the attacking Charlie Company, often with recently liberated American weapons, which the cavalrymen found to their liking, particularly the Garand, although less so with the M1 Carbines.

As the last reserve platoon fired into the left flank of the Nisei attack, it faltered irrevocably, and started back down the slope with bullets kicking at men's heels.

A knot of attackers remained at the lip of the slope and, one by one, they were silenced.

Not one surrendered, not that putting hands in the air would have made a difference to the Cossack soldiers, for they fought their war by a different set of rules.

451

Kazakov, also now wounded in a manner he did not understand, limped to a position near the last few survivors, and watched as they were picked off, or fell to a bayonet or shashka.

Some of his own brothers succumbed and he felt a wave of anger sweep over him as an old comrade, who had once watered his horse on the Volga, was thrown backwards by the impact of heavy Garand rounds.

The rifleman was shot down from behind and crazed avengers took their time hacking away at the dead body.

The enemy officer had shot another of Kazakov's men before he went ahead with his plan.

Calling for a ceasefire, he hobbled forward, aware of the growing wet feeling in his boot.

He held his shashka in one hand, his Tokarev in the other and stood in front of the man's position, exposed and vulnerable but sensing his plan would work.

It was simple really.

The man was Japanese, and everyone knew how their soldiers had a samurai honour thing going; he'd seen evidence of it himself when serving on the Eastern border.

Kazakov would stand in silent challenge and, when the lunatic American came out, Razin would drop him to the ground.

However, Takeo did not play the game as the Cossacks intended and Razin showed his hand too early.

Kazakov screamed in despair as a bullet from the 1911 took the top of his senior NCO's head off and spread the contents across the ground behind him.

Appalled by the sight of the collapsed body, Kazakov found himself rooted to the spot and looking straight down the barrel of an automatic pistol. His own weapon was still pointed at the earth, and bringing it up for a shot would take more time than the bullet that would surely travel his way if he tried it.

The Japanese-American waved his gun, encouraging Kazakov to throw his pistol away, which he did without taking his eyes of the man in front of him.

The Colt 1911 followed suit and he cursed himself for not noticing that the enemy officer's weapon was locked open on an empty clip.

A scream brought him back from his annoyance, and he jerked into action as Takeo charged forward, katana raised to strike down.

Kazakov took a step back and dropped to one knee as his wounded leg squealed new objection.

452

"Banzai!"

The katana swept down towards the cossack's head, only to be met by metal inches from its target.

Takeo thought his blow would go home and found himself slightly off balance.

As he brought his blade round for another swipe his lower belly exploded in the most violent pain as a kukri was rammed hard through his flesh, jamming in his pelvis with the point exiting between the cheeks of his backside.

His mouth was still wide open in a scream of extreme pain when Kazakov's shashka swept across his shoulder and bit into the side of his neck, angling down into the body.

Both his blades remained lodged hard in the bones of his dying victim, so Kazakov reached for his small knife and shuffled on both knees to where the American had fallen.

The Nisei officer's screams continued as the whole of the hilltop was bathed in the most incredible sunlight, the clouds seemingly moving aside to allow the dying Takeo one final moment of life's beauty.

Kazakov howled in fury as he plunged the knife into Takeo's chest, continuing long after the man's life force had left his body, and with each thrust yelling at his enemy.

"Bastard!"

"Fucking bastard!"

Klimenti Ryabkov was the one who gently grabbed the arm and stopped the continued butchery of Takeo's body.

"Kapitan... stop now, Kapitan... he's dead... very dead... we must leave this place, Comrade Kapitan."

Kazakov looked at the young officer's face and returned to reality, immediately understanding the danger he had placed his men in.

"Where are the Amerikanski bastards?"

"They've all pulled back down the slope. Comrade Kapitan."

'Blyad! What have I fucking done?'

"Get everybody off the hill... off the fucking hill now!"

"But Comrade Kapit..."

"Now, Klimenti, for the love of the Motherla..."

The sound was there... the sound that had heralded death for so many of their brothers.

'Too late... I've killed us all... you're a fucking fool, Vasily! A fucking stupid fool!'

453

Ryabkov was screaming at anyone, trying to get the men to escape the killing ground.

Kazakov simply stood his ground and planted a foot on Takeo's corpse, wrenching his shashka free.

In anger and blind fury, he pointed it at the sky.

It would not reach his enemies, who approached at a uniform three hundred and seventy miles per hour, a mile between each vic of three aircraft, with fifteen aircraft in total.

"Bastards!"

The familiar large canisters tumbled down, two from each aircraft, causing panic amongst the running men below.

1232 hrs, Tuesday, 18th March 1947, base of Height 570, Medzany, Czechoslovakia.

Colonel Petersen gripped his binoculars as he watched the clearly crazy Soviet officer wave his sword at the approaching Mustangs.

The renewed sun and absence of wind and rain granted him the air support he needed to finish the job, and he had come forward to order his boys off the hill before too many were lost.

Had he had radio communications, Takeo and scores of his men would not now be lying in the open, red and ruptured.

His hands gripped the binoculars tightly as he spotted a wounded soldier writhing in agony just below the crest.

He was a Nisei.

'Oh Mother of God!'

There was nothing he could do, but he could not take his eyes away, as if to do so was almost dishonouring the man's impending ultimate sacrifice.

The first vic flew over and dropped on the far side of the hill.

He had seen this before, and understood that the aircraft would walk the napalm backwards, which made it easier for them to see their targets as each vic attacked in turn.

The hilltop was transformed into a burning sea in which the occasional swimmer could be seen, dying in extreme agony,

As the final group of three Mustangs drove in, he risked a quick glance at the Russian with the sword who stood resolutely waiting for death.

The final fireballs washed over both the sword-waving lunatic and the wounded Nisei.

An hour later, Petersen arrived on the top of the hill as the grisly work was already in progress, some of his men tasked with moving the blackened pygmy bodies into a pile ready for a multiple burial when the graves registration units arrived.

Charlie Company had earned the right to be first up the hill, and the tired Nisei had found no hint of resistance.

The napalm had dried out much of the surface and the firm footing allowed the company to move quickly and start forming decent defensive positions, in case of a Soviet counter-attack.

There was no chance of that, not that Petersen would have known, as orders to the 5th Guards Cavalry Division now confined them to the east bank of the Torysa River.

Four hours later, the 100th [Nisei] Infantry Battalion was relieved.

Few people realize that luck is created.

Robert Kiyosaki

Chapter 195 - THE BRIEFCASE

1503 hrs, Tuesday, 18th March 1947, the Kremlin, Moscow, USSR.

Stalin's attitude had changed, and not for the better.

Nazarbayeva shifted uncomfortably under the tirade of abuse that had now been going solidly for two minutes and, or so it seemed, without the General Secretary repeating any word of significance.

Beria smirked as the hated woman received a roasting over the GRU's failure to give any warning prior to the Allied attack, or to generate any significant intelligence after it.

He examined her body, her curves, as a man who has experienced the pleasures in sight can recall those he has experienced beneath.

His smile spread wide as he remembered the delicious penetrations of her bod...

"And you can wipe that smile off your fucking face too! The NKVD shagged the camel on this matter, or do I need to remind you again?"

Beria's pleasant thoughts came crashing down.

"Apologies, Comrade General Secretary. Whilst you were dealing with General Nazarbayeva, my mind had strayed to the subject of our retaliation."

Stalin's finger wagged between the two of them, like the weapon of an executioner selecting his victim.

"I was too light on the fucking pair of you before... I want fucking answers!"

Stalin nodded sharply.

"Right. I've heard what Comrade Marshal Beria had to say. So... your turn."

"Yes, Comrade General Secretary. I was in Camp Vár when the attacks took place, and all seemed perfectly calm and natural there."

Nazarbayeva's mind flicked to her discussion with Ramsey but she steered it back to the discussion in hand.

456

"I returned and ordered a complete review of the evidence of the last six months. That's quite a task as you can imagine, and that task is still underway, Comrade General Secretary. I ordered to look back from last Friday, as it's more likely that anything we missed would be nearer the attack date, given there would be more going on."

Beria had said pretty much the same thing so it drew no response from Stalin.

He simply sat there puffing on his pipe and giving nothing away.

"So far there's no clue as to any enemy attack... in fact... information we have received since the attack makes me feel that the Allies were caught by surprise."

Stalin laughed.

"That's what he said...," he selected the NKVD head with the stem of his pipe, "Which is obviously fucking ridiculous, as they fucking attacked us! Have you two been colluding to make me look a fucking fool? Eh?"

Beria had already had his mauling so kept quiet to allow the woman to take every ounce of hurt.

"No, Comrade General Secretary. If that was the conclusion that Comrade Marshal Beria came to, then he came to it separately, and I can only agree with his assessment."

To Stalin and Nazarbayeva, that was an endorsement of Beria's statement.

To Beria, it was a condescending agreement that he had arrived at the same conclusion as her.

'When this has died down, I'm going to finish you, bitch...'

Stalin selected Nazarbayeva with the stem of his pipe.

"Then tell me this, Comrade Nazarbayeva... how could the Allies fucking attack us and be taken by surprise at the same fucking time."

He slammed his hand down on the table and leapt to his feet, using the stem to switch between the two intelligence officers as he made each point in turn.

"How the fuck can they be taken by surprise when they attacked? Do you take me for a fool? Is this some fucking attempt to cover your own asses? Eh? Who fucked up here? More than just you, I suspect? GRU? NKVD? Both of you? Eh?"

Beria went to speak but got short shrift.

"I've heard what you have to say. You... Comrade Nazarbayeva... you're always full of theories. Tell me yours... and don't hold back... don't hold back at all."

Stalin hit the table so hard he clearly hurt himself and brought tears to his eyes.

"Tell me what has happened here, Comrade General, and make it fucking good. I've been kind to you... so very kind and accepting... but this cannot be allowed to stand... this sort of uselessness and ineptitude must... and will... be punished. Now fucking SPEAK!"

Stalin's spittle ran gently down her cheek and onto her top lip.

He neither apologised nor offered her one of the small cloth towels he used to wipe his desk down.

For her part, Nazarbayeva simply wiped her hand across the moisture and coughed to clear her throat.

"I'm totally convinced that the attack was not planned and instigated by the Allies as such. I believe it was instigated by Germany alone... possibly with the collusion of some of the Polish Army... and these are my reasons, Comrade General Secretary."

"Oh, spare me the fucking German option again eh?..."

"Comrade General Secretary, you asked me how it could happen, and I'm giving you an option that is not only feasible, but the only explanation that can presently be considered such."

"Then speak... but I warn you... no fairy tales, Comrade."

She spoke of Gehlen and De Walle, of Abwehr agents and associations with senior men.

She recalled Ramsey's words and finished by reciting them word for word.

When she finished her doubts washed over her, as it all seemed so weak... and yet, she sensed it was true.

Stalin's anger seemed to have dissipated none the less, and his voice returned to normal, steady and unhurried.

"Comrade General, that's a lot of words for so little real information."

Stalin sat down again and ravaged his hair with his fingertips, as if trying to press some buttons on the brain below.

"Find out for sure. I want you to find out beyond any doubt... do everything you can to find out how this whole fuck up started. Work together. You and Kaganovich are thick as thieves so I'm told. Is that a problem, Comrade Marshal?"

"Not at all, Comrade General Secretary."

Beria was secretly delighted that Stalin had immediately provided him with the means to side-step any blame should the cause not be discovered.

"But understand this..."

The finger switched between the GRU and NKVD officers, resembling a rifle at a firing squad, as the angry man surfaced for one final time.

"... I want results and no fucking excuses. You've both fucked up for the last time. No more, do you hear me, Comrades? No more!"

"Yes, Comrade General Secretary."

Their voices combined into one, and received a nod from Stalin.

"Good. Anything else? No, then I..."

Something made her speak... despite determining not to... she did it anyway.

"Yes, Comrade General Secretary."

"Go on, Comrade Nazarbayeva."

"I understand that you assured that Raduga is now defunct, except for research... but...I have found reference to a circulation group 9226. Is Raduga's research running in some way that requires the GRU to be excluded?"

"Did you not ask me this already, woman?"

"Yes, and I'm sorry, Comrade General Secretary. I just wanted to know if there was any possibility that it might have been resurrected... given the current circumstances."

"Ah... I understand... as I said, the research elements of Raduga proceed as was always intended, Comrade General."

He looked at Beria, seeking a show of support.

"From memory, I believe that 9226 is the reporting group for progress on technical matters relating to Atomic weapons."

"Yes, Comrade General Secretary. A Middle Machinery group... well mainly... NKVD are involved as we oversee the project security. I believe GRU is simply not part of this group."

"There you go then, Comrade Nazarbayeva. It's not a GRU concern. Now, let's concentrate on finding out how this fuck up started eh?"

Nazarbayeva took her leave, knowing that both Stalin and Beria had openly lied to her.

The die was cast.

1703 hrs, Tuesday, 18th March 1947, Imperial College, London, England.

"Thank you for seeing me at such short notice, Professor."

"Always a pleasure to entertain a member of our American forces, General. How may I be of assistance?"

459

"You spoke with Len Cheshire regarding some urgent matters that were for the attention of General Strong?"

"Yes, shocking business... poor old Kenneth... and Eisenhower too, of course... all of them... shocking business."

"Yes, I agree, Sir. However, life and the war go on, and I'm here because apparently you have vital information about the Soviet's war effort.

The two discussed the nature of the information, and Penny produced the original documents for examination.

"Where did this come from?"

"Haven't the foggiest, old chap, but it's the biggest nut in there."

Strong's filing required that each item was date stamped and initialled, which provided some information to help with the main problem.

"Where did it come from, Sir?"

"Again, I haven't got the slightest clue. All I know is that it tells me that the Soviets are further advanced than we suspected."

"May I please take this, Professor? It's vital for my investigation."

"Feel free, General. I have two copies of everything anyway."

"I wonder if you would be free tomorrow for lunch? There's someone who would like to meet up with you."

"Absolutely, free day tomorrow. Was going to do some desk work, but I can always make myself available for a nice lunch. Time?"

"There'll be a car for you at the main entrance at midday."

"Intriguing. Do tell me more."

"I won't be there, I'm afraid, professor. I have business elsewhere. You'll be meeting with General Groves and Colonel Pash, who're both extremely interested in what you have to say."

"I'll be there, General."

"Now, if you'll excuse me, I have so much to do. Thank you for your time, Professor."

They shook hands.

"My pleasure. Take care, General."

Back in his London office, Rossiter grabbed the telephone and sought a connection to NATO headquarters.

"General Rossiter's office, Major Cortez speaking."

"Jed, it's me. Drop everything. I want you to pull Strong's appointments diary for March 7th. Anything at all that's in there, down to the last detail... anything...I want to know. Also entry logs to the building for the same day. I'm in the London office and I'll be waiting by the phone."

"I'm on it, General."

"I'll be waiting, Jed."

By the time Rossiter had lowered the receiver into the rest, Jesus Cortez was on the move to Strong's outer office.

The phone rang and Rossiter snatched it up in an instant.

"Rossiter."

He listened intently, noting each name or meeting in turn, and mentally checked off each as being unlikely.

"Is that it?"

He laughed, remembering how Kenneth Strong liked his scotch, so a delivery of it was probably of little import.

"What was that? Say that last bit again?"

Rossiter's pencil flew across the paper, noting the information down with growing excitement.

"So, he cancels his car for 1930... and then again the rescheduled pick-up at 2030... and there's no rescheduling after that... so he either didn't leave or left by another means... plus... of all things flowers... so... an important visitor not on his list who deserved flowers as a last minute thing... a woman visitor... a special woman visitor..."

The silence was deafening.

"He wasn't having an affair was he?"

"Not a chance, Sir. Absolutely not a chance."

"OK, so who came to the headquarters... say from six onwards... females first."

Cortez checked down the list of entrants, starting at 1800.

"Three female for sure... there may be more, Sir. A WAAF section officer, Christine Mann ... one of Tedder's chicks I suspect. Daphne Hamilton-Hewitt, British Red Cross... and Madame Knocke, whoever the hell she is."

'Isn't that the ex-SS bastard's name... the one in the Legion?'

461

"Knocke... who did she see?"

"Not recorded, General."

The phone went uncomfortably quiet as Rossiter's disappointment oozed down the line.

"Santa Maria... here it is, General. Logged request from the office of General Strong... seeking a doctor to attend meeting room 12 to check a heavily pregnant female visitor."

"Bingo... that's her pregnant... that's why there's flowers. An unexpected pregnant guest. Wouldn't be anyone in uniform, so has to be her... Madame Knocke. Excellent work, Jed. Keep digging... anything you can come up with on Madame Knocke at all. Thank you and good night."

"Buenas noches, General."

Two telephone calls and a visit from a breathless clerk later, Rossiter had a new file to examine, the cover alone making seriously interesting reading.

'de Valois, **Now KNOCKE [1-4-47]**
Anne-Marie Claudette Armande,
Commandant,
Service de Documentation Extérieure et de Contre-
Espionnage *[SDECE]*
Codename - COQUELICOT
Bodyguard - assassin - analyst
DOB - 2-18-1919
Major Involvements
[a] *Attached SOE - Failed Assassination of*
FldMshl ROMMEL [Top Secret]
[b] *Soviet assault on Chateau Kœnigsbourg.*
[c] *Assassination of JOAN OF ARC [Top Secret]*
[d] *Assassination of MONTELIMAR [Top Secret]*
[e] *Suspected assassination of CASTLE [Top Secret]*
[f] *Suspected assassination of MOUNTAIN LION [Top*
Secret]
[g] *Assassination of TRISTRAN [Top Secret]*
[h] *Suspected assassination of MONUMENT [Top Secret]*
[j] *Suspected assassination of CALENDAR [Top secret]*
[k] *Part of mutiny within Legion Camerone -* [l]*GENERAL*
MOLYNEUX.

[a] *File linked Eur-Int-X-E-3048*
[b] *File linked Eur-F-Gen-292891-Koenigsbourg*
[c] *Files linked Eur-Int-X-E2-4444 / Eur-Int-X-E5-616*

462

d File linked Eur-Int-X-E1-38119
e Files linked Eur-Int-X-E2-4444/ Eur-Int-X-E4-307
f File linked Eur-Int-X-E2-4488
g Files linked Eur-X-E1-38188/ Eur-D-Mil-SS-13772
h Files linked Eur-X-E5-0017/ Spec-X-Most Secret-500
j File linked Eur-X-E5-0018/ Spec-X-Most Secret-500
k Files linked Eur-X-F-Gen-301104- Camerone Mutiny.
l File linked Eur-F-Nil-Leg- 2021.

Additions- Married Ernst-August Knocke m January 4th
1947

m File linked Eur-D-Mil-SS-19725

Category 1

'Jesus but she's one serious woman! Category one as well. Not one to get on the wrong side of.'

Rossiter consumed the file as quickly as he could whilst he waited for the car that would take him to Brize Norton.

When he got to the record of the events of March 13th he almost choked.

The pieces slotted into place.

What was reported as a possible robbery was anything but, and it was clear that the woman had been targeted by...

'...who?'

His mind dropped into a lower gear and accelerated forward, dragging information from its recesses and marrying bits and pieces together into an idea that almost overwhelmed him.

Before he stepped on his aircraft, Rossiter lodged an urgent call to the head of the SDECE.

"Ribiere."

"Bonjour, Henri."

"Bonjour, Sam. I take it this is not a social call eh?"

The gruff Frenchman was still recovering from a near-fatal car accident, but was at his desk as much as possible, and still as keen as ever to deal with the enemies of France.

"No, you're right, Henri. I can't say too much for now, but your secretary, Madame Coquelicot, I think there's an issue with her, and she needs more personal supervision. I'm not happy with her version of events."

Henri-Alexis Ribiere, hero of the Resistance, understood exactly what Rossiter was saying, especially as the Coquelicot file was still on his desk.

"Yes, I've looked at this matter only today. I'll do as you ask, of course. Will I see you soon?"

"This very evening, if you are free for dinner, Henri."

"But of course, mon ami. I shall make a reservation at a new establishment I've recently found… say, for eight?"

"I think that'll be just fine, Henri. I'll be coming into Orly. See you shortly."

The door opened and an RAF Flight Lieutenant stuck his head round.

"Apologies, General, but your flights been called again."

"Gotta go now, Henri. See ya later."

He replaced the handset and nodded at the RAF officer.

"Change of plan though."

"In what way, Sir?"

"Paris, not Frankfurt. We're flying to Paris."

"Well I'm afraid that won't be poss…"

"Oh yes it will be. Trust me, Flight Lieutenant."

Rossiter's plane touched down at Orly airfield and he was immediately whisked away by a car arranged by Ribiere.

Thirty minutes later the two senior men were sat in a quiet corner of 'Au pied du cochon' chewing over the possibility that Anne-Marie had been targeted for her meeting with Strong, which opened up concerns over the nature of the air crash that claimed the lives of so many senior men.

The two men discussed theories, and played Devil's Advocate with each other, but each time they came round to one unpalatable possibility.

Somehow, undeniably, the Germans were involved.

1109 hrs, Wednesday, 19th March, 1947, House of Madame Fleriot, La Vigie, Nogent L'Abbesse, near Reims, France.

Normally, a light aircraft touching down in the fields near the house would have drawn inquisitive eyes, but the Auster was expected, so the security group were relatively relaxed about its presence, or as relaxed as men who expected belligerent armed men to descend upon them at any moment can be.

Rossiter exchanged handshakes with the head of the SDECE guards and was escorted to the main house and formally ushered through to the conservatory, where he found Madame Fleriot and Anne-Marie enjoying tea.

In the garden, the two girls were playing with more SDECE agents, one of whom had sisters their age, and the other who was old enough to be their grandfather.

"Madame Fleriot, Madame Knocke, thank you for seeing me at such short notice."

"Our pleasure, Général Rossiter, Please, sit. Tea?"

"Thank you."

Jerome needed no bidding and provided the necessary refreshment in rapid time, before leaving quickly to watch the young agent in the kitchen produce his latest culinary masterpiece.

"So, how may I be of assistance, Général?"

"Thank you, May I say that I've heard of your narrow escape, and I hope that you are both well?"

The question was awkwardly put, given that both women carried the marks of their recent encounter quite openly.

Armande Fleriot, her arm in a sling and a dressing on the side of her head, looked her normal magnificent self, save for the addition of bandages, whereas the heavily pregnant Anne-Marie looked battered completely, although, Rossiter deduced, more by the demands of her pregnancy than recent events.

He reminded himself that both of these ladies had undertaken their previous trades in ways that would make grown men shiver.

The pregnant woman had her left ankle in plaster, her right thigh heavily bandaged, and matched Armande's sling with one of her own.

"We are well, thank you, Général."

There was no more to be said, so Rossiter plunged headfirst into the maelstrom.

"As you know, I've spoken with Henri Ribiere, and we both agree that this supposed robbery was a deliberate assassination attempt aimed at you, Madame."

Anne-Marie nodded but said nothing.

"You met with General Strong, did you not?"

"Yes."

"May I ask why?"

Ribiere had already told her to cooperate fully with Rossiter's questions, so the words flowed quickly.

"I was going through Georges de Walle's things and found some information that needed to be presented to General Strong as quickly as possible."

She waited as he took a sip of the superb Earl Grey.

"I spoke to him about the death of Georges, and how it was not what it appeared. I believed that the bomb was aimed at him, not the German legionnaires. The death of Gehlen was also not what it seemed. There are other links possibly connected to the two intelligence officer's deaths, which are German... suspicions. A place called Uspenka, Uranprojekt... VNIEF..."

"VNIIEF... the Soviet atomic weapons programme... apologies, please continue."

"I don't think I need to... do I, Général??"

Rossiter's face had been quite expressive.

"Actually, no. This fits with other information. I will tell you, and this is not to be discussed, especially with your husband... we received a file from the Soviets that makes certain allegations against the Germans. Officially it is viewed with deep mistrust, and seen as a tool for the spreading of discontent amongst the Allies."

He leant forward.

"Unofficially, it would appear to have some substance, and we now suspect German involvement in the deaths of Georges de Walle, Gehlen... and the loss of General Strong's aircraft."

Rossiter let that sink in whilst he finished his tea.

"Merde!"

Armande Fleriot spoke softly but the word carried all her surprise and fear with great eloquence.

"Madame Knocke, I need to know how you came by the information... Uspenka... U235?"

"It was a note sent to my husband by his dead cousin."

"Dead cousin?"

"Pardon. What I meant was a cousin who had been considered long dead. It was first sent to Ernst's godmother in the Mosel, and she forwarded it to him."

"Do you know how she came by it?"

"No idea. Ernst did intend to go and see her to discuss the matter, but the war overtook his intentions. To be honest... she was associated with the camp system. Ernst distanced himself from her once he knew that. You understand."

"Of course. May I ask the godmother's name and address?"

"Frau Hallmann... Annika Hallmann... Haserich in the Mosel... not far from Zell-Mosel ... it's a small place apparently."

466

"I'll find it. Thank you very much for your time, ladies. I hope your recoveries go well... and to you, Madame, I hope your child is well and healthy when he or she comes into this unsettled world."

He stood, followed by Armande. Anne-Marie could not, so simply offered her hand to the American officer.

"Enchanté, Général."

"It has been a pleasure, Madame Knocke."

"I'll walk you to the door, Général. I need to stretch my legs."

"Général, thank you for being candid with us."

"I made a judgement call, Madame. I was left in no doubt that I could trust you. You are both highly thought of by your seniors."

Armande dropped her head in courteous acknowledgement of the compliment.

"Two things. May I trouble you for a map, and then may I please make a call?"

"But of course, Général. This way."

She led him into the library and retrieved a 1938 Michelin map of the Mosel.

Rossiter had not expected anything less from the older woman.

Quickly checking the area, he moved to the phone and placed a call.

"General Rossiter's office, Major Cortez speaking."

"Jed, it's me. I'm still keeping this whole thing tight, so I'm off on my travels again. What facilities have we got near Haserich in the Moselle?"

"Give me a minute, General."

Rossiter could hear doors opening and shouts, and was able to imagine Cortez moving into the outer office and calling for maps and information.

It was a surprising short time before the Major was back on the telephone.

"Assuming you want to be able to land, you can do so between Haserich and nearby Blankenrath. Sloped but clear."

"No, I want a facility that I can get some men from."

"Trouble, sir?"

467

"Just being careful, Jed."

"OK, Sir. We have fuel and medical facilities at Zell, but nowhere to land... hang on... Kappel... there's a small dirt strip at Kappel... and a French military office in the centre of the village."

Sam Rossiter found Kappel and decided it was perfect.

"Excellent. I need you to get hold of the frogs... pardon me, our French Allies..." he shrugged apologetically to Armande Fleriot, "... and let them know I'm coming, and will need a vehicle and four of their men armed for bear."

"Anything else, Sir?"

The question was more about Cortez's need for information than enquiring as to Rossiter's needs.

"It'll have to keep, Jed. I'm off to Kappel straight away."

"Take care of yourself, General."

He gently replaced the ornate handset, only just noticing the enamel inlays in the carved handle.

Armande Fleriot broke his thought process.

"Anne-Marie did not ask, but I will. Will they come again?"

Rossiter considered his answers and quickly decided not to bother to hide the facts.

"Yes. We've more information now, but we're not advertising it. So, if it's true, they'll still think that the matter is containable. In which case, it's likely they might try again. You've a security team for that purpose, do you not?"

"Of course, but I just wanted to hear it from you. I suspected as much... as does Anne-Marie. We shall remain vigilant. Goodbye, Général."

"Madame Fleriot."

As the general made his way back to the waiting aircraft, habit made Armande extract the pistol from her shoulder sling and check it for the tenth time that day.

'We'll be ready next time, you German bastards!'

1638 hrs, Wednesday, 19th March 1947, Haserich, Mosel.

Rossiter and the French captain listened impassively to the explanation offered by the local police.

"This very morning, Herr General. We were summoned by our briefträger... err... postingman, Herr Pfluggman. He had some bread from his wife for Frau Hallmann and entered the house."

He noticed Rossiter's expression.

468

"They are acquaintances... and Frau Pfluggman is ... was friends with Frau Hallmann."

The body was carried out of the building by two ancient attendants and placed in the waiting truck.

The policeman ventured more information.

"He found her in the basement. Looks like two blows to the back of the head. First thought was that she could have fallen down the stairs and hit her head on the way down."

"But?"

"There are things here that are not as they seem, Herr General."

He beckoned them to follow him, not down into the basement, but into the barn attached to the property.

"Watch the mud there."

Rossiter picked his way past the puddled water from a leaking hosepipe.

"So... what am I looking at here, Herr Kunze?"

There was nothing in the barn except empty shelving... rack after rack of wooden surfaces that bore no load.

Areas of the barn were separated off, mainly those that contained muddy footprints.

"This barn has been stripped of its contents, and it's been done so very recently."

"How do you know that?"

"Look at the shelves, Herr General."

Rossiter did so, but didn't understand the point.

"Staub... err... pieces..."

He looked at the French officer for help and the man searched his memory.

"He means dust, mon Général."

Rossiter looked again and immediately saw the tell-tale dust marks on the leading edge and relatively dust-free shelf beyond.

They were all the same.

"What did they take?"

"That's the really interesting bit, Herr General. Please follow me."

They went off at a pace until they were back in the first floor kitchen, where a crestfallen and shocked looking Pfluggman was sat drinking coffee and smoking cigarettes.

"Herr Pfluggman, our postingman."

He motioned the two officers towards a pair of chairs and signalled one of his men to produce more coffee.

469

"Herr Pfluggman, please tell these men about the barn and what was kept inside of it."

The postman took a deep swig of his water to steady his frayed nerves and spoke in a troubled voice.

"No one was supposed to know about the files."

Rossiter's senses lit off yet again.

"What files, Herr Pfluggman... tell the General."

"Personnel files... details of German soldiers..."

Inspector Kunze understood the man's reluctance, but pressed him hard, wishing Rossiter to hear it from the horse's mouth.

"Tell him, Hans. Tell him what you know."

"Herr General, one day Frau Hallman was out and I went looking for her... I could not help myself but take a look. I never told her... she never knew I'd seen what they were."

Rossiter waited, holding his breath.

Kunze gripped Pfluggman's shoulder to encourage him to continue.

"Herr General... there were thousands of them... many, many thousands... all that I saw had cloth fronts, but I looked at most of the bookcases and they all contained files on personnel... SS personnel."

"What the... those shelves contained the personal files of SS personnel... thousands of SS personnel?"

"Jawohl, Herr General."

'What the fuck is going to be thrown up next?'

"Is there anything else you want to know, Herr General?"

Kunze posed the question purely because the American had dropped into stunned silence.

He rubbed his aching stomach to try and knock back the growing pain.

"Actually, yes, there is. Herr Pfluggman, I am hoping you recall delivering an unusual letter to Frau Hallmann. I am informed that it came to her via official channels?"

"A letter, you say?"

"Yes, possibly military by nature?"

"Ah, there was one thing. I remember it well. She had no idea who it was from, and certainly hadn't been expecting it. It originated from the US Army."

"How could you know that?"

Pfluggman shrugged the shrug of officials the world over.

"I give people letters, they open them, I then know where they come from... I've a memory for such things. It came from an APO address"

"Did she open the letter in front of you?"

"No, she didn't and in any case, it wasn't a letter."

"Go on."

"It was something like a briefcase."

Rossiter understood that he was onto something he really didn't understand and backtracked a little.

"So... you bring a briefcase to Frau Hallmann, sent from an American military postal address somewhere..."

"Eight-five-three."

"I'm sorry?"

"A.P.O. Eight-five-three."

"You sound very sure of that, Herr Pfluggman."

"The number lives with me day in, day out, Herr General. My son died on U-853, sunk off the American coast by your warships at the end of the war. Eight-five-three is a number I don't easily forget."

"I understand... and I'm sorry that you lost a son, Herr..."

"Two. My youngest was killed in this latest madness, Herr General. I have two sons and two daughters still alive... all in uniform... all serving new masters."

"Again, I'm very sorry to hear of your loss, Herr Pfluggman. I just need to understand this matter. Can you remember when it was that you delivered the briefcase to Frau Hallmann?"

Pfluggman smiled sadly.

"Yes... it would be...err... August 17th last year... I celebrated the birth of my twelfth grandchild, Annelise... my second granddaughter down in Blankenrath and the proceedings were a little boisterous. There was some damage... the Gendarmerie were called... misunderstanding... but some of us spent some time in the cells. Herr Inspektor Kunze'll be able to confirm, but I tell you now, I gave her the briefcase on Saturday the 17th of August."

"Thank you, Herr Pflugmman. Inspector Kunze, if you please?"

They walked out onto the landing.

"Inspector, I need to make a phone call straight away. I'll need you and your men to place this whole site under guard until I can have some people out here to sort through everything. My suspicion is that this is a matter of huge significance. I can say no more. I hope you understand?"

"But of course, Herr General. I did some time in the 4th Panzer Division's Feldgendarmerie and then the Abwehr before coming back to normal policing. I understand how things work."

Rossiter felt a chill go down his spine but managed to not show any outward reaction.

'A wolf in sheep's clothing?'

"Thank you, Inspector. Now, if I might use the phone?"

"General Rossit..."

"It's me, Jed. Just listen. I want a team in Haserich yesterday. There's something going on here I don't understand. Hallmann is dead... murdered."

Rossiter checked that no one was within hearing distance, but still lowered his voice.

"The police officer here is ex-Abwehr. I'd rather we had someone from our service sitting on top of this one."

Cortez understood that loud and clear.

"I need you to get APO list pronto, Jed."

"Got it right here, General."

Cortez leant back and plucked it off the shelf behind him."

"Eight-five-three... where is it?"

The sound of rustling pages indicated Cortez's search in progress.

"Err... Camp O'Reilly, Puerto Rico, General."

"What? You gotta be kidding me, Jed?"

"No, Sir, that's correc... wait... fuck... sorry, Sir... gimme a second..."

In about twenty, Cortez was back.

"There's a new version out. I must have filed the old one back in the hole. One moment, General... here we are... eight-five-three, you say?"

"That's the one, Jed."

"Well I'm damned... Sir... O'Reilly closed down and the APO was reassigned to an outfit in Innsbruck... it's a WAC unit... part of the AGC, General."

'Adjutant General's Corps?'

"Not processing personnel, but belongings."

'Bingo!'

"OK, Jed. Get the cavalry organised. You know where I'm going. I'll get in contact once I get there. Bye."

Rossiter took his leave of Inspector Kunze, leaving the French Captain and two of his men on site with very specific orders.

472

The Mercedes car leapt away from the site of Frau Hallman's murder, closely watched by two pairs of eyes.

Kunze, once of the Abwehr, always of the Abwehr, used the telephone still warm from Rossiter's grasp to call a friend who was still within the intelligence service.

The other pair of eyes watched on from a quiet house opposite, behind which were two nondescript Bussing-Nag lorries, once of the 2nd Panzer Division, and then of the Soviet 4476th Motorised Supply Battalion, and now in the possession of a group of men who served Betar and Irgun, Jewish resistance movements based in Europe and Palestine.

Avraham Hinzelberg made notes all through the American General's visit, and was especially interested when he spent time in the barn, from where the Jewish activists had taken the records of every SS member of the HIAG and stowed them in the two old but mechanically reliable trucks.

For some reason, Avraham glanced across at the hockey stick he had taken from Frau Hallmann's house.

The item he had used to kill her, still showing signs of clotted blood and matted hair where he had struck the SS bitch down.

'The Monster' Hallman had been on their kill list for some time, but she had been preserved because of what she kept in her charge, until such time as orders came from higher authority, and she was no longer necessary.

The murdered and abused inmates of Natzwiller-Struhof camp were suitably avenged when he smashed her head in with two rapid blows.

For now his orders were to observe and record: moving the intelligence haul would come later, when it was safe to do so.

Hinzelberg knew a man in Linz called Simon Wiesenthal.

He was a camp survivor who had endured Mauthausen-Gusen, and who had just set up offices in the Austrian city, wherein information was being collated on SS officers and men... and women... believed to have any association with the concentration camps.

Hinzelberg was of the opinion that there was no need to distinguish.

If a German bastard had worn the uniform then he was guilty as sin and therefore condemned already.

Which was the point of his mission, and where Wiesenthal differed from him.

Simon Wiesenthal wished to bring the guilty to justice.

473

Hinzelberg and his commanders wanted to bring justice to the guilty.

Swiftly and with maximum force.

And now he possessed the means to do the Lord's work.

"Barukh atah Ha-shem, Elokaynu, melekh ha-olam."

'Blessed art thou Lord, our God, King of the Universe, for you shall be revenged upon the scum of the earth.'

1203 hrs, Thursday, 20th March 1947, headquarters building, 75th Investigative Company, Alpenzoo, Innsbruck, Austria.

"No, Sir, General, Sir, we simply don't keep those records."

"Not at all?"

"We have records for US items of course, but not for those we occasionally send to foreign nationals."

Rossiter could feel his frustration building but understood that the woman simply couldn't help.

"So there's no way for me to get any further with this inquiry? There's nothing to help here at all."

"Look, General. Let me level with you. This job is pretty shitty, you know what I mean. We don't hang around long enough to get acquainted, let alone spend time recording stuff that isn't American. We even just send the Brit and Allied stuff off... no records... it's a shitty deal here."

Rossiter could imagine that sorting through personal effects belonging to God knew who would be a mentally sapping task.

"When was it you said, General?"

"August last year. Probably more towards the beginning and middle."

"That's a long time for this unit, General. Let me get Tabitha."

The female captain strode off with a purpose, allowing him to examine his surroundings.

He did not find the old zoo building fit for purpose, and yet over twenty women were arranged along long tables piled with effects, some of which were clean, some of which were contaminated with undesirable memories of their owners.

Anything from wallets to moneyboxes to civilian clothing was on display.

Rossiter realised that, unusually in his view, there was no chatter amongst the women, as each simply applied themselves to the job in hand, silently sorting through items in the hope of finding clues as to the identity of the loved one who should receive the dead soldier's mementoes.

"General Rossiter?"

"That's me."

He turned round to find himself face to face with quite the oldest woman he had ever seen in uniform.

The imposing NCO saluted smartly.

"Staff Sergeant Tabitha Hood reporting as ordered, Sir."

"Tabitha Hood? The Tabitha Hood of Kentucky?"

"Guess so, General, Sir."

He had heard of her before, but never seen a picture of the granddaughter of Confederate General Thomas Bell Hood, commander of Hood's Division in Longstreet's Corps at the Battle of Gettysburg.

Despite going onto other glories, Hood had never accepted the failure of General Lee to go round to the right of the Union line, and his granddaughter was a vocal champion of her grandfather's reputation and sharp critic of the acclaimed genius that was Robert E Lee.

Approaching fifty-five, Hood had no place in the army in Europe, and yet here she was, stood in front of Rossiter.

"Sergeant, I'm told you were here in August last?"

"Yes, Sir."

"I need you to try and remember if there was anything significant about that time? I'm thinking particularly of a briefcase that this unit processed and sent to a German woman... a Frau Hallmann in Haserich... in the Moselle?"

"Briefcase you say? That narrows it down a bit. Any date in mind, General?"

"I know it was delivered to its final destination on 17th August. Over that, I don't know diddly squat, Sergeant."

"I'm sure that I didn't process a briefcase. I get called in when it's slightly more delicate a task, shall we say..."

Her weird laugh aside, he understood what she meant.

"Tell you what though. Let me check the records for that date."

"The Captain said you didn't keep records for non-US disposals."

Hood looked at Rossiter with a sort of twinkle in her eye.

"She's an officer... what would she know? She's only been here a month. Mind you, General, in a sense she's actually right, but we do keep records of items we can't place, so that'll help give me a prompt."

475

Tabitha Anna-Bell Fraser Hood, humming something indistinct and yet strangely macabre, led off to a darker corner and rummaged in some files.

"Here we are. August 46... we're in luck... only a few thousand items..."

Her humour was wasted on Rossiter as he looked around him, the racks' contents materialising in the gloom. Unallocated personal effects bagged and tagged, ready for the day when some new information came to light.

"Your lucky day, General. I thought something twigged in the back of my mind. Here it is..."

She put the book down and focussed the weak lamp upon it.

"The briefcase was unallocated originally... came into us on or about 2nd August... why... ah... Rebecca Clifford... useless cow was young Becky... thought she owned the place like a five-star but couldn't hack it... I could tell you some stories about that silly bitch... anyway... item reviewed on the 9th August by O'Bannion... good girl she was... got pregnant though... evidence found... shipped 10th August."

"Nothing else, Sergeant Hood?"

"No directly, General, but it sits between some stuff that's still on our books."

Hood retrieved the log numbers.

"Let's investigate, shall we?"

Off she led again, returning to the humming of whatever it was she hummed to brighten her day and depress anyone within earshot.

It took less than five minutes to locate articles 20398 and 20400.

"A lighter."

She handed 20398 to Rossiter.

"And a damaged lapel badge."

She looked at it and cursed.

"Goddamnit. Sorry, Sir. I should have remembered this."

The badge changed hands and its nature was immediately apparent.

"Red Cross?"

"Yep, General. Grosslocken or summat like that. Some of our boys were on a training exercise and ran across the plane wreck. Red Cross inspection flight returning from somewhere on the enemy's side. Ran straight into the tallest piece of real estate around. No survivors. We got most of it away... the Red Cross wanted it all, but our colonel stuck by his guns and went by the book. Your briefcase came from the flight, no doubt about it, General."

"Do you know when this was, Sergeant?"

"End of July is all I can venture, General. We only record arrivals if the stuff stays. In this case, August 2nd, so allow for at least a day or two to get to us. Probably around the 28th."

"Thank you, Sergeant Hood, You've been extremely helpful. I'll let your officer know that on the way out."

"With respect, General, I wouldn't bother. I'm on the flight home tomorrow and she won't remember my name past Saturday morning anyway."

"On leave or permanent job stateside, Sergeant?"

"Medical discharge, General. I'm officially mad as a fucking hatter so I'm free of this man's army and back to stabbing old Lee in the front."

'That explains a lot.'

"Thank you again, Sergeant."

"My pleasure, General. Maybe I'll see you at one of my lectures stateside?"

"You know, maybe you will at that, Sergeant Hood."

He saluted her and went on his way, his steps worryingly in time with her renewed humming.

Innsbruck had its own intelligence facility, so Rossiter, once he had identified himself, was shown to a small room that boasted a chair, table, and telephone.

He let Cortez trot out his normal line in full before speaking.

"Right, I'm nearly there now. The briefcase that Hallmann got came from a Red Cross flight that crashed in Austria around the end of July. Unless they were particularly careless, that should narrow it down to one aircraft. I'm going to see what I can manage here, but get on it straight away and find out where that aircraft came from. OK?"

"OK, General. Haserich… seems there were a number of people inside the barn building. Different shoe marks throughout, all fresh. Early estimates are five at least. They actually missed one complete set of shelves, of over six hundred files."

"We've got them in our hands now I take it?"

"Actually no, Sir."

"Well, for fuck's sake, Jed, get on the horn and make sure we get it taken away for safekeeping. Do I have to think of everything? Jesus H Christ but that's basic shit right there. Goddamnit"

Cortez had let Rossiter vent off, deciding not to interrupt him whilst he was on a roll.

"General... the barn was secured and transport was organised for the following morning. A fire started and claimed everything in the building, and part of the main house too."

"A fire? A fire started... just like that?"

"Highly doubtful, of course, especially as the volunteer fire department found their equipment damaged and unusable."

"Deliberate... arson..."

"Apparently so. The local police spoke with the fire department chief. Everything points to deliberate."

"Fuck... Kunze... has to be Kunze..."

"No Sir, not in person at any rate. He's in Zell hospital with appendicitis... not him."

'Then who?'

"OK, Jed. Keep on it. I'm coming back to headquarters. Have everything ready for me at eighteen-hundred."

"Yes, Sir, General, Sir."

1239 hrs, Thursday, 20th March 1947, bridge over the Kästenbach, Reidenhausen, Mosel.

"You were successful, Hauptscharführer?"

"Yes, Brigadeführer. Any files left in the barn are destroyed. I know my business, Sir. Spread them out, kerosene, fire. But there is a problem, Brigadeführer."

"I destroyed what I found which, according to Obersturmfuhrer Krause's description, was a fraction of the total. They have already been moved, Brigadeführer!"

"Verdamnt!"

Pannitz stayed silent whilst his commander worked out his fury.

For his part, Otto Kumm pummelled the stone bridge with both fists.

"The Allies have them... we must fine them immediate... what?"

"No they don't, Brigadefuhrer. I spoke to one of my associates. He states categorically that the only vehicles that left the

478

scene from the moment the buildings caught fire were Feuerwehr, staff cars, and a civilian truck that was used solely to carry away Frau Hallmann's body. There were no documents taken."

Kumm digested the bombshell.

"So... whoever killed Frau Hellmann also took the documents."

It was not a question.

"Does your man have any ideas, Hauptscharführer?"

"He and another are making further enquiries right now, but there's an unconfirmed report, Brigadeführer. I'll know more soon."

"An old comrade from the Luftwaffe in Blankenrath... he swears he saw some Jews nosing around in the woods above Haserich."

"Jews?"

"Yes, Brigadeführer."

"Scheisse! We have to find them. If the Zionists have our comrade's records, none of them will be safe. Mobilise every man, Hauptscharführer. I'll get more men sent to you as soon as possible. Do whatever you must do, but find those fucking records!"

1744 hrs, Thursday, 20th March 1947, Allied Intelligence Special Operations Centre, die Hegerhaus, Horberg Masslau, Germany.

Rossiter's aircraft landed at the small grass strip at Kötschlitz, half a mile south of Horberg Masslau, and he immediately travelled north to the woods west of the village, wherein a special facility had been created, well away from prying eyes.

The base was centred around an old but well-appointed gamekeeper's house, die Hegerhaus, in whose grounds a joint Allied Intelligence Special Operations Unit had been created, comprising nondescript wooden buildings such as graced army camps the world over, their simplicity in this case hiding the true purpose of their occupants.

Men received instruction there, lived there, and occasionally died there, as the training was fierce and hard.

Given the security that surrounded the site, OSS, SOE, SDECE and others had decided to it was the perfect spot to set up a joint operation, in order to pool talent and information.

The Abwehr were not included, a deliberate decision made when the camp was set up, shortly after the arrival of Nazarbayeva's divisive documents.

Rossiter flopped into a seat in the dining room and stuffed the hamburgers down his neck in record time. Three mugs of coffee followed, as much for the caffeine as for the liquid intake, the effects of his prolonged mission round Europe starting to take effect.

Opposite him, Rear-Admiral Sir Roger Dalziel was still deciding on the best way to eat his American treat by the time that Sam Rossiter started into number two.

"Your man seems very keen to get started, Sam."

Rossiter followed Dalziel's eyes to where Cortez was hopping from foot to foot, clearly bursting with some important news.

"I gotta eat, Sir Roger. Kinda neglected myself the past day or so. I need coffee and food to deal with what's ahead here. I'm telling you… I know what he's got to say, and I sense this is a real biggie and we're gonna need our minds cleared and primed."

"The SDECE boys are ready to go. No one from SOE here that I'm aware of… leastways, not for the meeting."

That didn't surprise anyone, given that the meeting had been called only twenty minutes beforehand, the moment Rossiter got to a phone when he touched down and Cortez had dropped his bombshell.

A WAAF Flight Officer was sat across from the pair of senior men, but neither realised that she was an SOE officer, as her arrival only slightly predated that of Rossiter.

Alphonse Guiges, once of de Walle's staff, deferred to Denys Montabeau, another of de Walle's protégés, and the senior man rose to move into the small briefing room, ready for the eighteen-hundred start.

Christine Mann, once known as Krystal Liese Uhlmann-Schalberg, decided to follow instead of risking getting lost.

Rossiter finished the last of his burger and wiped his mouth.

"Damn, but I needed that."

Dalziel was not yet half way through his, and decided to give up the fight as the item didn't seem to be set up for use with cutlery.

"Shall we, Sam?"

"Yep. This is gonna blow your mind."

Back in NATO's Leipzig headquarters, what had become as strange was now decidedly perturbing, as Major von der Hartenstein-Gräbler of the Abwehr reported to his superiors.

Key members of the Allied Intelligence agencies simply were going missing for hours on end, something that was as worrying as it was unusual.

1800 hrs, Thursday, 20th March 1947, Allied Intelligence Special Operations Centre, die Hegerhaus, Horberg Masslau, Germany.

"OK, Major. Let's have it, from the beginning."

Cortez swung into his presentation, leaving out nothing, laying out the events in chronological order.

Rossiter had taken time to grab another coffee and sat savouring it as the others in the room were enlightened.

The two SDECE agents were agitated and vocal as the information on de Walle was revealed.

Also, the assassination attempt on Anne-Marie drew their real anger, both of them having worked with her when under the Deputy Head of Deux.

The briefing revealed the atomic aspirations of the Soviet Union, something that was now starker in their minds, since images and stories of the attacks on Japan had come to Europe.

Cortez started into matters surrounding the briefcase, and Rossiter focussed his mind, ready for the bombshell at the end.

The murder of Frau Hallmann and the subsequent arson aside, the trail of the briefcase was set out.

"Our British colleagues have a source in the Red Cross who was able to get the information to us very quickly."

Cortez flicked a switch and a swiftly drawn and coloured map of a part of the USSR came into being, projected against the white wall behind the excited Major.

"This is the Volga… Stalingrad would be about here, some fifty miles to the northwest," he pointed off the map, "of this," he put the wooden stick's tip on a built-up area, "The nearest town… Akhtubinsk."

He allowed them a moment to orient themselves.

"The Red Cross were visiting a large camp in the area… and flew back from this airfield here… a mile northeast of Akhtubinsk."

"The camp they were visiting is here," he circled a highlighted area between a village and the banks of the Volga.

Rossiter's eyes smiled in anticipation.

"This village is named Uspenka."

'Bingo!'

"That's it?"

"Yes, Sir, Admiral. That is the place."

"The prison camp is a sham?"

"No Sir, we actually think not. The Red Cross report from a subsequent visit detailed prisoner numbers, condition, facilities et cetera... it's kosher. We've only got one set of photographs and they were taken during the camp's construction. I believe we need proper interpretation of these photos, and more ordered a-sap, Admiral."

Dalziel knew just whom he would call on and he sought Rossiter's agreement, which was given without words.

The US Brigadier General had also immediately thought of Jenkins and her quiet sergeant.

Their attention had wandered for a moment, something that Cortez had spotted, so he patiently waited for them to refocus on the matter in hand.

"Here we have a tank training facility. We've information from our former association that it's a long-standing camp... in fact there's a possibility that some Allied officers visited in 1944... we're on that right now... but there was recently a sniff that it was upgraded as a battle-training camp for tankers and armored infantry."

The pointer covered the distance from the Nizhniy Baskunchak training camp to Uspenka.

"Around forty miles, which at first sight put it well out of the way but..."

The pointer returned to the middle ground.

"This is where many of the exercises take place, which would make Soviet tanks and armored infantry less than an hour's hard drive from the Camp... which, by the way, we know is called Camp 1001."

Cortez continued filling in details on what was known, more to the point, what wasn't known about Camp 1001 and the area surrounding it.

Rossiter leant across to Dalziel, who responded by coming closer.

"Red Cross have anything more on this, you reckon? Anything not in the report?"

"We can but ask, but we simply must not attract attention with our own attention. I'll get word to our man immediately... see what he can tell us. 1001 doesn't jump out at me, so I suspect it's not on the radar for anything in particular. I'll get my staff to look through the necessary and see what we can find. Suit you, Sam?"

By the end of the briefing, there were many theories about Camp 1001, all of which needed further investigation.

The following day, a deep penetration reconnaissance mission was devised, one that would conceal the precise point of investigation.

Target-Akhtubinsk.

The Russian town would be bombed, lives lost, both Soviet and Allied, planes shot down, buildings destroyed, all for the need to have one aircraft in the attack fly a course directly overhead of Camp 1001 and Uspenka, its precision cameras recording every single detail, despite the buzzing of enemy fighters around the box of bombers desperately fighting their way home.

1127 hrs, Friday, 21st March 1947, Camp Steel, on the Meer van Echternach, Luxembourg.

"Sir, order, most immediate."

Crisp was going over the figures given to him by Captain Bluebear, whose company had recently been on operational deployment and were pulled off the line shortly after the whole war kicked off again.

Whiskey Company were back there now and disengaging them was proving to be a major headache for Crisp and his staff.

He had only just flown back from Königsberg, where his units were allocated to the British. Each in turn rotating through their attachment to give them time in the line, and exposure to colder weather conditions.

He dropped the camp roster and picked up the new message.

"Oh shit. Thank you, Corporal."

The messenger departed as Crisp picked up the telephone.

"Con, get yourself over here right now. We got orders to move."

Marion Crisp chuckled.

"Yes... the whole shooting match. We're upping sticks."

He killed the connection and made another.

"Lieutenant Garrimore. I want all officers informed immediately. Orders Group at 1200 in lecture room three."

Garrimore's objection was silenced swiftly.

"I don't care if they're watching Steamboat Willie, just make that room available for twelve-hundred, Lieutenant. Thank you."

Again he made another connection.

483

"RSM, can you step into my office now please. Thank you."

Crisp had come to lean heavily on Ferdinand Sunday, the former Argyle and Sutherland highlander turned Royal Marine.

Only the night before, when he crashed into his pit exhausted by travel and meetings, he'd had a dream... no, a premonition... that he would need all his reliable men in the days to come.

That tingling chill revisited him as he waited for Sunday, and he was sure that it was an omen of bad things ahead.

1200 hrs, Friday, 21st March 1947, lecture room three, Camp Steel, on the Meer van Echternach, Luxembourg.

"Atten-shun!"

Sunday brought the assembly to their feet as Colonel Crisp and his 2IC, Major Constantine Galkin, strode purposefully into the packed room.

"At ease, boys. Light 'em if you got 'em."

He waited whilst the packets rustled and lighters flicked before continuing.

"Boys, we've just received orders. The whole unit is on the move..."

The voices started up, some in excitement, some in trepidation, all in enquiry.

Galkin stepped forward.

"As you were, gentlemen!"

The noise went as quickly as it came.

"Thank you, Major... now... we'll be flying outta Bitburg tomorrow morning. That means I want us ready to move at 0300, and I mean move everything that isn't nailed down... and half of what is."

The laughs were modest but unforced.

"Advance party will be led by Major Galkin. Order up is X-Ray, Yankee, and Zebra. My headquarters, except HQ platoon, will accompany Zebra. Between us we'll hand over the camp to the oncoming unit... we don't know who they are yet."

He added as almost an afterthought.

"Whiskey won't be in this move. No time to get 'em out so they're staying and we go light one company. That's the way it is, boys."

He stepped back and let Galkin take over and struck up a cigarette of his own.

484

"Ok boys, listen in. We leave nothing in stores or the armoury. Both loads'll accompany X-Ray to the field. Until we get a loading programme, that'll mean we'll have people on the ground with the kit until we all get away. RSM Sunday'll be responsible for security on both counts, and he'll support HQ platoon in keeping things tight."

The Lieutenant in charge of HQ Platoon smiled at the RSM, who glared back, leaving the young officer in no doubt who was in charge of who.

"All vehicles will be left at Bitburg, signed over to the base security force... that'll fall to Zebra to carry out."

Bluebear nodded his understanding.

"All company officers are responsible for ensuring we leave no trace regarding our nature or purpose. I want us outta here with no one the wiser as to us being an elite bunch... leave it like we were lesser mortals from the infantry."

"So we gotta crap in the sinks and hide the cutlery, Major?"

The laughter boomed out.

"Whatever floats your boat, Lieutenant Hässler!"

Crisp savoured the moment, enjoying the camaraderie of the elite soldiers.

"Any questions?"

The single question sprang from a dozen throats.

"Where we going, Sir?"

Crisp moved forward.

"Leipzig."

There was a gasp, partly of relief and partly of disappointment, and, as far as Crisp could make out, the latter held sway.

"And before you say any more, I know as much as you now do. But I tell you this, boys... we're moving closer to Indian country and I've a feeling we're going to be handed a beauty."

He had been right and the wave of excitement washed up over him as men smiled and slapped a comrade's shoulder.

"We've been training hard... winter... snow...RCLs... close combat... parachute... demolition... the whole kit and caboodle... so I don't doubt that Uncle Sam'll likely send us to the desert soon!"

He waited whilst they laughed at the standard army joke, stubbing out the remains of his cigarette with great care as he pulled his final words together.

"Ok now, boys. Listen in. Whatever we're going forward to do will be important. We're a special force, highly trained up to do

485

our masters bidding, so it ain't guarding supply dumps or bridges. It'll be in harm's way, that's for sure, and I want us fully geared up for whatever is thrown at us. Keep on top of your men. They're good men, but they are like coiled springs. Keep 'em exercised and mean, but watch them like hawks. I don't want anything happening along the way, particularly with the RAF boys at Bitburg."

He specifically mentioned Bitburg, referring obliquely to an altercation that took place between men in Zebra Company and members of the RAF Regiment stationed at the nearby base.

Whilst he had issued punishments to those concerned, he had also secretly celebrated the fact that eleven of his men had kicked ass against over twice their number.

"Right. I want your briefings ready for me at eighteen hundred hours in this room. Make sure your non-coms are up to speed. No one leaves the camp from this moment without my or Major Galkin's permission. Let's get to it, gentlemen."

"Atten-shun!"

Sunday called them to order.

Salutes were exchanged and the two senior men marched out of the room, leaving the excited officers to start hatching their plans.

1616 hrs, Sunday, 23rd March 1947, Allied Intelligence Special Operations Centre, die Hegerhaus, Horberg Masslau, Germany.

Rossiter had just finished receiving the latest information from Colonel Crisp, and he had to say that the man was everything he had heard him to be.

Not the brash airborne officer type that he had often met, but a quiet, unassuming man with a clear idea of how things were done, and an efficient manner and purpose when doing them.

But there was something else.

The man had the thousand yard stare common to men who had seen things that others would not believe, and experienced the very worst that war can provide, but there was also a something that Sam Rossiter had rarely seen in his service, a something that declared itself when he saw Crisp with his officers, with his NCOs, and with his men.

There was an admiration, a two-way thing going on, with the Colonel absolutely committed to his men, their welfare and well-being, and that being returned by men who clearly had faith in his ability, almost to the point of what seemed to Rossiter as a total blind obedience bordering on worship.

Despite the questions, Rossiter only told Crisp that they were preparing an intelligence folder on a possible target, a place that the paratrooper and his men might be dropped into to perform a number of vital tasks.

It was easy for Rossiter to stall Crisp, given that he had no idea what the mission would be, or indeed, whether there would even be one.

Much depended on the newly arrived team presently working on photo-recon evidence from the costly raid on Akhtubinsk.

Three Liberator aircraft had been lost from the RAF's 70 Squadron, and two from 1 Squadron RAF, who flew thoroughbred Spitfire XXIs, plus a single accidental loss amongst the Thunderbolts of 261 Squadron RAF.

When Rossiter heard the losses from the raid he had set in motion, he closed his eyes and prayed that it would be worth it.

Time would tell.

'Oh God... all those British boys lost... please let me be right... in heaven's name ple..."

He jumped out of his skin as his silent prayers were interrupted by Cortez's urgent knocking.

"Damn, but I nearly shit myself, Jed. I take it we've got something?"

Cortez was grinning from ear to ear and the excitement of the moment was clearly etched on his face.

"You betcha, General, Sir. She's summat else, like you said. The Admiral's all over her at the moment but she's pulled something outta the bag that you need to see right away."

Rossiter sprang from behind the desk and the two set off at slightly more than a canter, arriving at the entertainment hut, whose projector and blank walls were fully in use.

"Admiral."

"General. I think you'll be glad to hear that the mission has proven successful."

He moved to follow Dalziel to a map of the prison camp, one drawn in the same style as Jenkins had drawn of the IRA camp at Glenlara what seemed a lifetime ago.

Photographs, some from a single shot camera, some selected and lifted from cine film, were strewn around the large table, each with a label and some connected to points on the drawing by pins and cotton.

"What do you have for me, Flight Officer Jenkins?"

"Proof that you're right, Sir... or at least that the camp holds secrets."

487

"Show me."

The attack had been sent in as early as possible in the morning, and arrived at just after 0900 hrs. Part of the reasoning for this was to give the interpreters shadows to play with. The angle of the sun meant that shadows could reveal things that otherwise might be hidden.

As in many things, timing was everything, and the photos revealed groups of men clearly being herded by others, an extensive prison camp laid out neatly, with row after row of wooden huts surrounded by security fences, towers, and likely more.

The new imaging cameras were state of the art, and their pictures, aided by precision German lenses, were beyond anything that Rossiter or even Dalziel had ever seen.

"Here, Sir."

The projector threw up a picture that showed a close-up of the camp's northern edge.

"What am I looking at, Flight Officer?"

"This line here, Sir. It's wire, complete with towers and mines."

"Mines?"

"Most certainly. Because it's sandy and quite windy, you can clearly see the bumps where the wind has blown away the surface... here... here... here... he..."

"Yes, I get your point, thank you. It's a camp though. Wire is to be expected surely?"

He offered his comment without sarcasm, as he knew the woman was a magician in her field.

"Yes indeed, General. But the point is, it's here... here... and here... but it's not here... at least not inward facing like the camp system clearly is... or more exactly inward and outward. This area here is only facing outward."

He peered and sort of understood what Jenkins was driving at.

"All the way to the river... the wire faces outwards only. See here... the track marks... these lorries," she handed over a separate photo that showed vehicles arriving at the prison camp, "They don't stay in the camp... I'm sure of it... they go through the camp and into this area... with only outward facing security. On the riverside there are established posts... you can see them quite clearly here and here... all along the waterfront... I estimate no more than twenty yards apart... backed up by larger bunkers set back and higher up... here and along this line, General."

He looked and saw, although not with the same clarity and assurance that Jenkins clearly did.

The silent Flight Sergeant who was her constant assistant moved with controlled excitement and shoved a picture under Jenkins' nose.

In the way of specialists all the world over, Jenkins immediately ignored the senior ranks and moved away to a separate table.

Something resembling a pow-wow with her NCO and another bespectacled youth ensued, the latter speaking excitedly as he had clearly found something of great import.

Jenkins patted the man's back in delight and returned, holding the photograph.

"General. We have your answer. There's a lot more work to do, but I can definitely tell you that all's not what it seems here."

She laid the photograph on the projector slab and examined the larger display, smiling with insider knowledge.

"What am I looking at, Flight Officer?"

"Corporal Gentle has found something outside the camp… or rather, that appears outside the camp, but isn't."

She moved towards the image, her shadow cutting out part and focussing the two senior men's eyes on the section that was still brightly displayed.

"Here. This seems to be outside the camp, but it isn't. There's a fence, but it's not an ordinary one."

Dalziel got as close as he could but failed to spot the things that had caught gentle's eye.

"Here, Sir… that's a pack of wolves heading away… here are men… probably security… here is a dead wolf… and here's another… it's still smoking if you look closely."

"Electric fencing? What on earth for? That's a long way away from the camp."

"For this."

She highlighted a dark 'L' shape that was set inside the now clearly discernible electric fence.

"Shadow… that's a structure. It's square and probably something like thirty yards each side and approaching seven yards high."

"What the deuce?"

"And there's more, Sir."

She nodded to her NCO who took a photo from under Gentle's nose and brought it to his officer.

"Can I cut these, Flight?"

He nodded and even provided the scissors.

Jenkins laid the two halves side by side, one photo taken a few hours beforehand, the other back when the camp was being constructed.

There was absolutely no doubt whatsoever that the large building was totally new.

"There are others too. Here... if you look closely... the vegetation is seared around this hole. In the view of my team, that's a heat vent... an exhaust or similar."

A light went off in Dalziel's mind.

"It's underground, isn't it?"

"Yes, Sir. There's something underneath this camp. Everything I've seen so far points to it. The buildings have no worn paths between them. There is parking here, probably for the lorries that come into the camp, but the size of building is far in excess of the parking space. If I was a betting girl, I would say that's a lift. The building there is quite tall... maybe to provide room for the lifting gear et cetera..."

Rossiter spoke gently but firmly.

"I know what you can do from our last encounter, Flight officer. Can you produce a similar map of the whole area... with all the details for this place? And I mean all the details... and quickly?"

"Yes, Sir. Of course, this site is much larger than the previous one, but my team are on top of the problem already, as you see. Give us time and space and we'll give you everything you need, Sir."

"You've got it. Any time of day or night, my door is open. Get cracking Flight Officer. I want to know everything about 1001... what you calling it?

"Moria, Sir. Gentle found the first clues, so he got to name it."

Dalziel chuckled.

"Tolkien strikes again, eh?"

"Tolkien?"

"He's a writer, Sam. Wrote the Lord of the Rings... it's a fantasy novel. Moria's an underground kingdom."

"Never heard of him, but it'll do. Keep me informed, Jenkins. Well done to you and your team, and keep it up."

They exchanged brief salutes and Sam Rossiter hurried to his office to make a number of calls.

Having finished briefing Donovan, Rossiter rose to watch as the latest bunch of men arrived.

Had he had the time, he would have spent longer watching the two groups, new arrivals and old arrivals, eye each other with quiet suspicion.

He snorted.

'Old arrivals, my goddamned ass. Been here less than twenty four!'

None the less, the old understood that the new were different.

The new were not British, American... none of the Allied nations.

Even though their uniforms were now nondescript, the men bore all the hallmarks and arrogance of soldiers from another time.

SS.

Shandruk and his men had arrived.

He dragged himself away and quickly sought a line to the NATO headquarters.

"Hello? This is Brigadier General Rossiter. I need to see General Patton. Yes, it is urgent."

Rossiter controlled himself as best he could but his anger vented immediately.

"Well, I'm sure General Patton is a very busy man, but if I don't get to see him this evening, you're likely to be sat in a pile of rubble very shortly, Colonel. Now, I'm coming to see the commander and you better make sure his diary is cleared for me or I'll be finding you a nice assignment with a rifle company. Do I make myself clear, Colonel?"

The phone descended on the cradle with sufficient force that he felt the need to examine the set up for damage.

'Damnit, Sam... don't beat up on the hired help!'

He reproached himself immediately, and vowed to apologise to the man in person.

It wasn't his way, but a simple sign that the pressure was building... and he was still tired, so very tired.

He checked his watch.

'Damn... I'm late... one more call.'

This one was more complicated to route and it was some time before he heard a familiar voice in his ear.

491

"Odekirk."

"Ode! It's Sam here."

"Sam, be all that's wonderful. Thought you headed back to the war, Sir."

"I did. That's where I am right now. I need to speak to the man pronto. He there?"

"Yeah, but over the other side. I can put you though if you like?"

"Swell, but first I need to know something. Pardon me if I don't come straight out with it, but can you tell me, yes or no... did you finish up the lumberyard?"

"The lumberyard?"

"Yeah. Is it ready to use?"

"Shit... I mean... yeah. Yes it is."

"Keep that between you, me, and the boss for now, Ode. Now, can you get me through to the man?"

"I'm on it. See you soon I hope, Sam."

"Count on it, Ode."

Odekirk switched the phone through to another extension way over the other wide of the Glendale Factory.

Rossiter stifled a grin at the opening exchange between the two men.

"Ode, if this is about those fucking seats again I'll tie you out under the Arizona sun and guide hungry ants to your sweatier parts."

"Gimme a break, will yer? I've got Sam Rossiter on the phone for you... all the way from Europe."

"What's he want?"

"He swore me to secrecy, but he wanted to know if the lumberyard was finished. I told him yes."

"The hell he did? Ok, put him through, Ode."

The phone went silent before bursting into life.

"To what do I owe this pleasure, Sam?"

"Business, Howard... real business. Ode tells me the lumber yard is up and running."

It actually wasn't, but he wasn't about to say that.

"All but the last few nuts and bolts, Sam. Were you so impressed with it that you want another sit in the seat?"

"No, Howard. Your country needs to borrow it yesterday."

"What? You mean after all the shit I've taken, now... of all times... now?... you fucking want it now?"

"Calm down, old timer. It's not a war department thing, it's a 'me' thing. I'm keeping this as tight as I possibly can. The big

492

question is... is she ready or not... and I need to know right now, Howard?"

He swivelled in his chair and looked out through the glazed side of his office, examining as many inches of the 'lumberyard' as he could take in.

"Yeah... she's ready. Whatcha got in mind, Sam?"

Rossiter started his play.

"Howard, one of my officers presented himself at your main reception at oh-eight-hundred hours, with orders to remain there until summoned. Can you get him brought to your office immediately please?"

"Sure thing, Sam. A moment."

The receiver was muffled whilst the order was issued.

"I'm back and he's on his way."

"Remind me of the numbers of the lumberyard again will you?"

The details flowed easily, all indelibly carved into the memory of the man who had driven the project from start to finish.

A Marine Colonel was shown into the room and immediately produced an envelope marked for the man on the phone.

"Your man's just handed me an envelope. I take it you want me to read it now?"

"On the express understanding it goes back into his possession and you keep the contents strictly between you and your immediate team, Howard."

"You got it."

"And that means Ode better keep his mouth shut, unlike a moment ago."

"What can I say, Sam... he works for me."

Sam heard the rip of paper and a tuneless whistle as the contents were avidly consumed.

The whistling stopped abruptly.

"My God, Sam... are you fucking serious? I mean... really serious?"

Clearly, Brigadier General Rossiter was extremely serious.

"Forty-eight hours tops, Sam. I can have her moving in forty-eight hours tops. Where we going?"

"You're in?"

"Too right I'm in!"

"Landmark. It's a code word. Ask my officer for the second envelope and give him the word."

Sam listened intently as the exchange took place and another envelope disgorged its contents, this time a map.

493

"You're mad, aren't you? To hell with it. You only live once. Ok, I'm game. That the final destination?"

He smiled at the stony-faced Marine officer as Sam Rossiter laughed in his ear.

"Of course, I'm not that stupid. So there's fuelling facilities, everything we need there? Look, I'll send a few of my boys over there pronto. Make sure it's organised for everything we'll need. Plus, we'll need to stop on the way to top off. At least twice. You got that sort of clout."

He laughed at Rossiter's response.

"Yeah, well I guess we all know someone with that sort of clout. Fair point, Sam. Go on..."

He listened intently.

"I'll ring you as soon as I've selected them. No problem. Into Lisbon, you say?"

He made more notes.

"Military flight... Ok... send me the details as soon as you've organised it. Let me give my boys three hours to get ready. Nothing sooner than that, Sam."

He nodded, making another swift note.

"Final thing. What's the actual mission... yeah, yeah, yeah... I know, but don't give me that. Gimme a clue... think about the pool party... anything you can use?"

Rossiter thought quickly until he remembered the paper plane competition and which one lost by the biggest margin.

"The conversation with Jean. Out and back... remember?"

The clue was weak, but it was enough.

"Holy shit. How far... how many... shit, you can't say, can you... Ok, Sam. I'm on it."

Rossiter asked the question and Howard's face spilt from ear to ear.

"Me, of course. You don't think I'd let anyone else have her, do you?"

"Whoa there, Howard. They'll never allow that."

"**They'll** never know until I'm over the Atlantic... will they, Sam?"

Rossiter could see his friend drawing himself up to his full six foot four height.

"Not from my lips, Howard. I'll get back to you as soon as things are clearer, and with the details for your advance party.|"

As was his way, Howard replaced the receiver without another word and rushed from the office.

On his way to his normal thinking place, he encountered Joe Petrali, one of his dedicated team of engineers.

"You got anything planned for a week or two, Joe."

"No, Sir. Wife wants me to go up and see her nephew ride. Apparently he's a nail on for next season's National Board Track Championship."

Joe Petrali was a biker through and through, and was still holder of the bike speed record of 136.183 mph, set at Daytona Beach in 1937.

"I want you to be elsewhere... need you to be elsewhere. You up for a challenge, Joe?"

Not the thing to say to a biker head who had triumphed at every discipline his beloved bikes could throw at him.

"What sort of challenge, Sir?"

He followed his boss' eyes as the words tripped gently into his ears.

"That sort of challenge."

The Lumberyard...

Officially known as the Hughes H-4 Hercules, but more often called the Spruce Goose.

"What?"

"Keep it under yer hat, Joe. I need you to pick a couple of guys and go ahead of us... advance party. Need to know where they want us to go first's fit for our purpose."

"Where we going, Sir? San Diego? Cisco? Tijuana?"

The final destination was delivered with an American version of a Mexican lilt.

Howard grinned from ear to ear.

"Cyprus."

"Cypress?"

"No. Cyprus."

"Cyprus... like Mediterranean Cyprus?"

"Paphos to be exact."

"No way we get there, even with the fuel mods. Gotta be two stops easily."

"Fuelling we can do en route, but I need an advance party to check out the base. We'll need to service her. You confident on the revised range figures?"

"I'll run them again, but I know I'm right. With the modifications we can achieve four thousand for certain, maybe four-two with a little effort, but I'm promising only four with weight to specification A. Anything over that and it'll come down obviously."

"That'll be enough, Joe. Now... pick your crew, gather your stuff... enough for two weeks in the saddle, and get back here within two hours. Tell the good woman it's all my fault, ok?"

"Yes, Sir, Mr Hughes, Sir."

2000 hrs, Sunday, 23rd March 1947, NATO Headquarters, Leipzig, Germany.

"I hear you threatened my staff, General Rossiter."

"That I did, Sir. They were protective of your time, but I couldn't stand for that bullshit... not today, Sir."

Patton bent the riding crop between his hands.

"That bullshit keeps me sane so don't do it again. Clear? My boys work damned hard on keeping things on an even keel. Now, what's got you all hot and bothered, Sam?"

Patton continued to flex his crop as he listened to the story unfold, complete with the very latest assessments from Jenkins and her team of magicians.

There was no doubt whatsoever that there was a secret facility underneath Camp 1001, one that the Soviets were at great pains to hide.

It was also clear that, were it ever discovered, the act of bombing it would hold no guarantees, save for the inflicting of massive casualties on the Allied prisoners held in the camp above it.

"Shit. You absolutely sure of this, Sam?"

"We've tracked all across Europe following leads, and just got the big break. Everything comes together to point to this place as the facility we've been looking for, Sir."

Patton examined the map in greater detail.

"It's within range of our bombers but, as you say, a lot of our boys would die if we did... and without guarantees that we'd hit the right place... or even that we'd destroyed everything we need to destroy."

"There's an alternative that I'm looking at, Sir. I've set some pieces in motion, as we're clearly on a timed operation here. Nothing that can't be reversed, of course. The whole operation would need presidential approval."

"Presidential approval? You mean... of course that's what you mean. Right... gimme what you've got."

Rossiter made his pitch and Patton listened in silence as the assets were named, and their intended part revealed.

Group Steel.

SOE's Ukrainians.

496

The Spruce Goose.

Composite Group 663.

40th Transportstaffel, DRL.

There would be others, involved on the peripheries, but the actual plan involved units that Sam Rossiter had already slotted into his developing plan.

"Give me an alternative, Sam."

"There's none that I can see, General."

"You know some politician is gonna suggest we just bomb it, don't you?"

"I sure hope not, General."

"They will, but it won't happen. Not on my goddamned watch it won't!"

"Grab some coffee while I have another look at this."

Rossiter did so methodically and slowly, taking the time to bring himself down off the high he had worked himself to during the presentation.

He passed Patton a steaming mug and received a mumbled acknowledgement from the concentrating man.

"Cyprus... why Cyprus?"

"No great enemy network identified. The Kingdom of Iraq would be closer, but the presence of the Goose would draw attention, and we know that the NKVD and GRU have a lot of people on the ground. Better chance of containing the information on Cyprus. We fly the mission from there, confuse enemy monitoring with lots of aggressive flights in the area, and sneak the Goose in. although we may have to stage in the Kingdom for fuel if nothing else. We'll see how the planning goes on that score."

"OK, Sam. And 663... staged outta Shaibah? What's Shaibah, wherever the goddamned hell that is?"

"It's a modest unimportant airfield in the Kingdom, Sir. Not used for anything much but aircraft maintenance at the moment. Used to be a big training facility... BOAC stop over... all sorts. However, one of my staff pointed out that it's recently been extended to serve as an emergency strip for any B-29s that have technical difficulties. Seemed too good an opportunity to pass over."

"But the 29s have long legs, Sam. Why from Persia?"

"Easier route, Sir. We could fly in from Europe, but not from their present base, so I figured if we had to relocate then why not go the whole hog and get them in and out with least difficulty."

"Yep... I can see that... I like that. Seems like you're on top of things, Sam."

Rossiter acknowledged the compliment with a gentle nod.

497

"One last thing, Sam. If I'm gonna sell this to the President, I need to know a little more. You say we can get in and take their secrets, and also know what it is we're about to destroy. Maybe snatch a few scientists and the like. I can see that. We can stop the Soviets deploying a bomb… if they haven't already, of course. But what about the boys in the camp? A lot of them are gonna die."

"Yes, Sir, a lot of them are going to die, but we'll give them a fighting chance and, simply put, we can't afford not to. Like you said, the alternative is simply to bomb… and that'll mean we kill them all and have no idea what we've achieved at the same time. I see this as the only way… unless some genius can come up with a better solution in the time available, Sir."

Patton considered his General's words and made a decision.

"Right. I want that in a full briefing document that I can present to the President. I want it here, tomorrow morning… 0830, General. Give your presentation again to some other officers so they can come onside with the plan… the plan… what you have in mind? We need a name."

Rossiter hadn't given it a moment's thought and was caught on the hop, but his mind met the challenge.

"In… take everything… kill everything,,, out again, leave nothing but destruction in your wake… gotta be Viking, Sir."

Patton's unforced laugh sealed the deal.

"Viking it is, Sam. Now, get to it."

"Yes, Sir!"

"Oh and Sam… pretty soon we're gonna be all over these suckers. We're stepping up the pressure big time… all across the front. I don't want anything interfering with my ticker tape parade back home. Get on top of this shit and stay on top of this shit."

"I heard the buzz, Sir."

"It's gonna be a lot louder than that, General."

Across Allied Europe, a few officers pondered new orders, unspecific directions that implied a difficult operation ahead.

In airbases and barracks, men worked to put together a plan to fit the requirements issued by Brigadier General Rossiter.

Enquiries made with higher commands were passed on until they met the cascade coming down from Patton's headquarters.

Those who questioned Rossiter's authority were left in no doubt that the plan would require their full cooperation, or the NATO commander would take an unhealthy interest in their future career path.

Back in Horberg Masslau, the two disparate groups of soldiers came together to plan the operation that would probably kill them all.

They had questions, but they also had orders and both Shandruk and Crisp had no uncertainty that the mission, whatever it was, was as vital and important as they came.

When Brigadier General Rossiter returned to the camp the following evening, he briefed them on the precise nature of their mission, and the special tasks that would need to be performed.

Rossiter, with mission security as his prime concern, forbade the cascading of information to the troops.

Both Crisp and Shandruk railed against that, but the General was adamant.

The impasse was broken when the two officers conceded the point, with the proviso that, before the men left they would be told the true nature of the site and the equipment they were there to photograph, steal, or destroy.

As both Crisp and Shandruk put it, 'men who are about to risk everything deserve to know what they're gonna be dying for!'

It was the first real moment of unity between the two officers, and, as consummate leaders, they both decided to build on it, for the benefit of their men and the mission.

The release of atomic energy has not created a new problem. It has merely made more urgent the necessity of solving an existing one.

Albert Einstein

Chapter 196 - THE HUSBAND

0615 hrs, Tuesday, 25th March 1947, with the Polish Army, Lithuania.

To the second, the guns of the Polish Army fired together and sent a stream of high explosive washing over the Soviet front and second line positions.

The bombardment was organised with great precision, the Polish attack only part of the huge offensive that Patton had planned.

As usual, the counter-battery units waited on accurate information and took out a large number of the Red Army artillery that sought to hit back.

Patton's initial efforts to strike back had floundered, as much for the Allied lack of readiness as for the Soviet sternness in defence.

Only in the German and Polish zones had there been any recognisable success in terms of ground made, although the success in killing Soviet soldiers and destroying their means to fight was notable along the entire front line, particularly as the Allied air forces held sway over the battlefield, both by day and by night.

This time, George Patton had taken his time to set everything up properly, and his forces were attacking from the shores of the Baltic to the border with Yugoslavia to the south.

He knew what was coming to Europe, kept safely in the bowels of the USS Guam, and he knew that President Truman now had the will to use them, so George Patton was determined that he would remove the imperative and cover himself in glory at the same time.

The 1st Polish Armoured Division's lead units watched and waited as second hands clicked round to 0645, the time of the scheduled advance.

Fig # 234 - Seirijai, Lithuania.

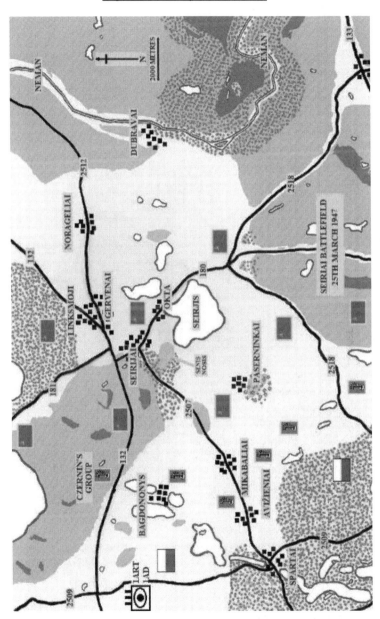

Their artillery would not stop, but it would advance slowly at a fixed rate, timed to move away from the advancing line of armoured vehicles, both tanks and APCs.

Fig # 235 - Polish Forces engaged at Seirijai, Lithuania.

UNITS OF THE POLISH ARMY ENGAGED AT SEIRIJAI ON 25TH MARCH 1947.

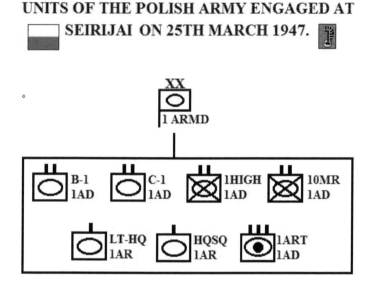

Leading the way were the reconnaissance troops of the 10th Mounted Rifles, their Coventry and Boarhound armoured cars surging from cover to cover ahead of the main advance, whose axis was on a broad front out of, and either side of, the ruins of Avižieniai, the main body of which was to roll over and through the villages of Mikabaliai and Paserninkai, before enveloping the waters of the Seirijis and forming a corridor all the way to the Neman River southeast of Dubravai, where the Corps' engineers would throw bridges across the obstacle, with a view to delivering part of an envelopment of the Soviet forces that would then become trapped in the Neman River bend, centred on the village of Vilkiautinis.

The southern element would repeat the Neman crossing at Druskininkai, where there were still viable crossing points, although more bridging assets were available, should they be required.

North of the main thrust was a secondary effort based around two squadrons of tanks from the 1st Armoured Regiment, supported by men of the 1st Highland Battalion, spearheaded by the

Light Tank Troop of the 1st Armoured Regiment's Headquarters Squadron.

Their mission was to strike down Route 132, straight through to the junctions with Routes 180 and 181, where they were to take and hold the pile of rubble that was once Seirijai and ensure no interference from the Soviet forces to the north and northwest.

In peacetime, Route 132 had wound its way through lush forest, a landscape that now only lived in the memory, as high explosive and napalm had converted the countryside into a barren wasteland, bereft of anything but Soviet fortifications and bunkers.

0700 hrs, Tuesday, 25th March 1947, Bagdononys, Lithuania.

The second hand clicked into place and Czernin's commander gave the order to advance.

He spoke in a normal voice and ordered his driver to move forward.

The path of their advance had already been agreed, partly from examination of the terrain through binoculars, and partly from looking for hours at the aerial photographs that had been used to form the full plan of attack.

The terrain itself made the whole affair perilous, with the undulations and folds capable of hiding many things that could kill their M24 Chaffee tank, and hiding in such a way as to spring the surprise presence of a killer enemy at the last possible second.

Ahead of the advancing Light Tank Troop and men from the Highland battalion, the artillery had done grim work amongst the Soviet defenders, but there were enough left to bring despair and death to the attacking force.

Czernin had spent months in hospital after his near-fatal encounter with a mine, and parts of him were still somewhere on the battlefield of Nottersdorf.

His old crew were no more, and he had welded his new men into a tight and efficient unit in the time since his return to the company some four months previously.

Czernin knew that their level of efficiency was about to be tested in the hardest school of all.

The tank was approaching the first of their listed special points; a place that could not be fully interpreted from photos and required further examination... and above all caution.

Czernin gave the order and dismounted, quickly scrabbling up the side of a muddy ridge to understand the area ahead, something that had been impossible to work out from the aerial pictures.

503

A quick look revealed a nasty surprise.

The Soviets had set an anti-tank gun into an artificial mound, one that pointed sideways across the battlefield, sited to take vehicles using Route 132 in the side.

It was protected by a group of infantry that were trying very hard to look like anything but a group of infantry, staying low and unmoving under camouflage.

Czernin spoke quickly into his walkie-talkie and the commander of the Highland battalion's mortar platoon acknowledged with the minimum of fuss.

Within a minute, mortars shells were dropping on the secret position, and the defending infantry lost interest in their charge and placed self-preservation at the head of their priorities.

The observing Polish NCO watched as two, then four ran back to another prepared position, one that offered more shelter and that was not under direct mortar strikes. There was red mixed with the brown mud and green grass in the positions they had just evacuated, testament to the accuracy of the mortar strike.

Czernin gave the ceasefire order and summoned forward one of the supporting halftracks, giving the Highland Battalion's men a quick directional steer over the rolling ground and down upon the anti-tank gun which could not traverse given its defensive set-up.

He watched as the halftrack started up the slope and almost screamed into the WT.

"Niebieskie-Bizon-trzy-dwa! Biały-Huzar-Dwa-Dwa! Stop! Stop! On foot... I said on foot... get out of the vehicle... get out of the veh..."

The other obliquely mounted gun position, set some four hundred metres back, put a shell through the front of the M5 halftrack, a solid shot that destroyed the engine and sent deadly pieces of metal flying in all directions.

The men inside needed no order and bailed out on the side opposite their nemesis and headed straight down the slope towards the mortared position.

One man fell as they ran but was quickly up and limping as the Highland soldiers charged into the AT position, following up three grenades that took much of the fight out of the gunners.

Czernin counted nine men, meaning that the halftrack, struck a second time and now burning, still held three young men from Poland.

The mistake was not his fault, but he felt a bitter taste in his mouth at not double-checking that the Highland officer had understood his words.

He would have no chance to pursue the matter further as the man in question was roasting within the roaring flames.

Czernin took another look and saw a further group of infantry sprinting down the slope to avenge their comrades, almost running into more mortar fire.

Now that the AT position had been silenced, the next Chaffee in line swept past his tank and breasted the rise before quickly dropping down again and out of sight of any waiting Soviet killers.

Having handed responsibility over to the next tank, Bazyli Czernin moved back to his own vehicle and climbed aboard.

A mug of coffee was thrust into his hand as he ordered the repositioning of his tank.

"Thanks, Jan."

His loader grunted and passed the thermos flask back into the front of the vehicle.

'No Russian artillery? No mortars? Strange...'

Ahead came a crack of a high velocity weapon and he stuck his head out of the cupola for a better view, immediately deciding that he needed to be back behind the metal as a white-hot shell screamed overhead.

Whilst he understood that his Chaffee wasn't the intended target, fast-moving metal has no friends and is wisely avoided.

Up front, the commander of the tank that had been the target shouted into his radio, providing contact information and a location.

Czernin's forehead wrinkled, as the stated enemy gun position failed to correspond with any recorded on his map, known, or suspected.

The mortars were busy again and accurately so, from the radio reports that filled his ears.

Instinct... something that cannot be underestimated on the battlefield... made him shout into his microphone.

"Driver, full right turn... top speed... head for the ruined building!"

The Katyusha rockets started to arrive as he moved out of the zone into which a company of the deadly rocket vehicles had fired.

The Soviet fire plan was quite simple.

They had understood that the dips would become gathering places for the assaulting troops, and their tube weapons had merely waited to give the attackers time to gather.

The Light Tank Company's commander was killed as two rockets bracketed his jeep and destroyed it, him, and his men.

The second in line Chaffee was flipped over, breaking seven of the ten limbs of the crewmen inside. As they struggled to escape, fire took hold and another five sons of Poland were soon gone.

Fig # 236 - Soviet forces engaged at Seirijai, Lithuania.

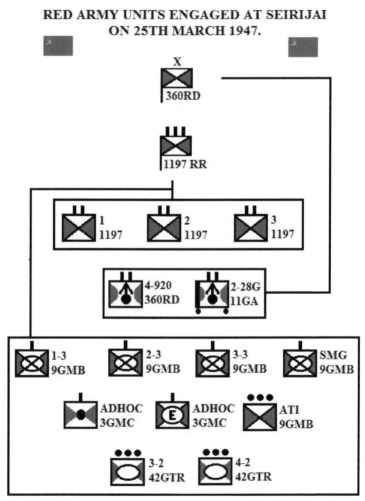

Major Pomorski, the commander of 'B' Squadron, 1st PAR, was thrown from his Dingo scout car as an explosion tossed the light vehicle off the road, tumbling like a toy car, over and over, before coming to rest on its wheels but decidedly out of the fight.

Pomorski, incredibly, just wiped the mud off his face and hailed down the lead tank, scrambling onto the engine and ordering the attack forward.

After few dips on the uneven ground, the valiant officer understood that he had not come away scot-free as his sprained ribs announced themselves with every bump on the road and painful breath.

Czernin's turn to lead came round quickly and the Chaffee leapt forward towards the small stream that marked his next point of reference,

The modest stream was swollen by rain and melt water, but only in width, not depth, which was just as well as the small culvert had long since succumbed to high explosive.

A bush spouted a smoky trail and Czernin's driver, without orders, jinked to the left, allowing the hollow-charge projectile to sail past the turret.

Even as the crew struggled to reload the RPG-1, the Chaffee's tracks ran over the bush that they had made their hiding place and snuffed out their lives.

Another projectile came their way and missed as the propellant gave out and the missile fell harmlessly to earth.

The hull machine-gunner helped the running men on their way with bursts from his .30cal weapon, without, as Czernin noted, managing even a single hit.

He ordered the gunner to rip up another bush that caught his eye but nothing emerged as a result so he felt safe to debus once more, having ordered the Chaffee to relocate, just in case the running Russians decided to stop long enough to tell someone where they were.

He slid up on wet mud and hid his head behind a pile of earth thrown up by a shell, barely exposing any part of himself, just in case the photos had been wrong.

They were absolutely correct, in that there were no enemy positions that he could see, although the incredibly detailed prints had failed to reveal his worst nightmare.

Mines.

Where shells had rent the soil, the tell-tale shapes of unexploded mines were everywhere, a mix of anti-personnel and the larger anti-tank mines being clearly on display.

'I fucking hate mines.'

He examined the ground ahead and reasoned that the path the enemy had run down was either clear or had no anti-personnel mines.

By studying the ground, Czernin could see that the muddy footprints clearly ran between two piles of stones, piles that were supposed to look natural but seemed decidedly contrived to his experienced eye.

He also understood that he would not order the next leapfrog move and expose his corporal to the risk.

Czernin quickly pegged two white squares out in the mud, roughly five yards apart, as markers that signified a safe point to cross the ridge.

Back in the tank, he reconnected his microphone and spoke rapidly to the next tank behind.

"Bially-Huzar-Dwa-Pięć, Biały-Huzar-Dwa-Dwa! Move up to my position only. Suspected minefield ahead. Understood, over?"

His corporal acknowledged and Czernin switched to the regimental net to broadcast his warning, rapidly reading the coordinates defining his assessment of the affected area.

His commanding officer replied with a promise and an order.

'Fuck.'

"Right, Dawid, move right."

The driver edged the vehicle past the destroyed bush to where Czernin reasoned the safe route through the mines started.

"Move between the markers I pegged out... when we go over the ridge, go quickly, but stop once we're below the sky line. I need to see the ground before the engineers arrive to sort out the mines. Stay alert, boys. Driver, advance."

The powerful engine carried the tank over the ridgeline and down again in the blink of an eye, and Dawid Scorupco swiftly applied the brakes, although the mud proved unequal to the task of stopping the Chaffee, and it slid inexorably down the rest of the slope.

The crack of an anti-personnel mine confirmed Czernin's suspicions... and fears...

... and then he saw something that had previously been hidden to him.

"Fuck it... gunner, gun vehicle, right four... high-ex... fire when on."

The turret whirred and the shout came back quickly.

"On... firing!"

The breech flew back and Jan Milosz rammed another shell home.

Czernin examined the enemy vehicle as best he could through the smoke and flame that marked its death.

Whatever it was, it was dead.

The six-wheeled scout car appeared to mount something nasty and threatening, a multi-barrelled weapon that had started to swing the moment Czernin had spotted it.

The BTR-152 had been caught out of position during the artillery attack and had no chance to relocate.

Its quad KPVT mount had not fired a shot before the HE shell had snuffed out the lives of all aboard and set the wreck on fire.

Exposing the barest minimum above his cupola, Czernin swept the area on all sides, seeking anything that could interfere with the efforts of the coming engineers.

There were no enemy positions that he could see or even suspect in sight, so he sent a confirmation message to his CO and elected to move forward on foot once more.

Careful to see what he might drop on, Czernin gingerly climbed down the side of the tank, checking the ground he would step on and further field for tripwires.

The single AP mine had detonated as the tracks slid over it, causing no damage.

He could feel the nerves build but determined that he had to press on.

The binoculars moved across the ground, seeking evidence of the presence of the deadly charges and, occasionally, he saw the prongs of an anti-personnel mine, but nothing else.

Down the route he intended to drive, there was nothing of note… no clue as to the presence of death hiding in the mud.

An explosion from the left drew his attention and he hunched low against the Chaffee automatically.

Another explosion followed in quick succession and he quickly realised that the weird sound that had been bothering his ears was a flail tank about its business, the mine-destroying tank's chains rotating and beating a path through the minefield.

More mines were set off and a mine explosion detached one of the chains, sending it flying towards a group of engineers, who wisely scattered in all directions.

Behind the flail tank, the tanks of 1st Regiment were ready to push up, once the light tank troop gave the all clear.

On the extreme left of the advance, one of the troop's Chaffees fireballed, struck by some sort of infantry anti-tank weapon.

The supporting infantry quickly deployed and put in an assault on the ridgeline position from where the smoke trail had emanated. One of the soldiers hit the ground hard, put down by an

SKS rifle, before his vengeful comrades overran and seized the position without consideration for the taking of prisoners.

There was more firing now as the northern side came under pressure, its exposed flank under fire from anti-tank guns hidden amongst the roots and fallen trunks of the once proud forest.

A Chaffee pulled in behind his own and the commander brought the .50cal round, ready to pour fire into anything ahead.

Czernin waved to his fellow NCO, climbed back on board against regulations, scaling the side of the vehicle for speed, and ordered his tank forward slowly.

More than one of the crew took a look at the sandbags that lined the floor of their vehicle, also imagining the extra sheet of steel that their vehicle had stand-off-welded to the underside of their vehicle, testament to Czernin's utter hatred of the mine.

Still they were not reassured, but they drove on anyway.

The occasional AP mine detonated, but it quickly became clear that there was nothing that would stop the light tank from crossing to the other side of the dip.

As his tank started to gain the far slope, Czernin ordered another halt and again debussed, stopping only to place two more zone markers out before he scuttled to the top of the rise and looked for what lay ahead.

His eyes were greeted with a charnel house of blood and bodies, the detritus of scores of men ground up by the Polish artillery bombardment.

Czernin couldn't imagine what had possessed the Soviets to move up, back or sideways under such an intense bombardment, but clearly something had flushed them out into the open and they had paid a heavy price.

Occasionally, something moved amongst the carnage, but such movement was rare, the vast majority of the butcher's work having been fatal by nature.

Looking behind him, he pumped his fist and the other Chaffee surged forward, following on through the safe corridor with no problems.

At just over eighteen tons, the Chaffee was outweighed by most AFVs on the modern battlefield, but its weight proved sufficient to cause further indignities to the dead and dying Russians that filled the dip.

Czernin winced more than once as a piteous scream was swiftly silenced by an unforgiving track.

Off to the right, the defenders that had bolted previously decided to move further back and broke cover, the old wooden pen having hidden them totally from sight.

The lead Chaffee's turret rotated leisurely and mowed them down, leaving one silent and two screaming for mothers they had little chance of seeing again.

Czernin returned to his tank and ordered a forward move, only to discover that the tank was 'playing up' and that Driver Scorupco needed to nurse the machine's steering.

The shouting in Czernin's ear almost deafened him, as the lead tank called for reinforcements.

Behind him, the vehicles waiting accelerated forward and swept past Czernin's lame duck, responding to the call to get forward and join in the shooting party.

The Soviet commander had panicked and ordered his anti-tank guns back to their second position for fear of them being overrun.

Whilst he was correct in that view, his timing ensured that the guns were being hitched up and unable to fire at the precise moment the lead Chaffee came over the brow of the hill.

It was a slaughter, and as more tanks joined in, Soviet gunners raised their hands in a futile gesture of surrender.

The Poles and the Russians had a long history of enmity, and more than one man present had lost a relative in the Katyn Woods, or the Soviet backstabbing attack of 1939.

Pomorski sensed an opportunity and ordered the assault to move forward immediately, keen to strike an enemy weakened and clearly badly commanded.

Leading the 1st's advance were Comets, and the first troop swept over the next ridge and disappeared from view.

The sharp crack of high-velocity tank weapons announced contact, and the radio messages drew more resources forward.

Czernin's Chaffee moved as quickly as it could across the ground in between and was up and over the ridge and, to none of their liking, quickly embroiled in a sharp tank versus tank action.

"Gunner, target tank, left three… quickly man!"

The Chaffee jinked as best as it could, the steering not responding properly, but enough to make aiming difficult, even with the stabilisation unit.

Czernin read the battlefield quickly.

"Driver, in behind that burning tank…the Comet straight ahead… there… quickly."

The Comet was lazily burning and could have exploded at any time, but he reasoned that its bulk would provide cover while he

511

tried to not get noticed; light tanks in a medium tank battle tend to have the life expectancy of a sick mayfly.

In reality, the smoke was a better concealer than the metal of the dead tank, although it made their eyes water and sting.

"On! Fire!"

The 75mm sent a shell down range and, at the close distances the battle was being fought at, penetrated the side of the T34.

But it did not kill it.

The tank was a M44 conversion with the 100mm weapon, which would put the shell in the front and out the back of their small tank without even noticing it had hit anything.

"Again! Under the turret! Hit it under the turret!"

The black smoke emerging from their target's engine compartment hindered his aim, but Czernin's gunner concentrated, taking the extra half-second to make sure he was on target.

The AP shell struck home directly on the turret ring and jammed the turret in place, its barrel pointing uselessly at the area behind the Chaffee.

"Any fucking chance, Bartek?"

The gunner simply gave an affirmative-sounding hum and sent another shell into the immobilised tank.

"Impressive!"

Czernin watched as the tank simply came apart in one violent explosion, catching men halfway out of hatches.

The front plate of the tank cartwheeled away, crashing into the side of one of the Polish Comets, causing those inside to evacuate their bowels in fright.

The turret went high into the air and dropped back onto the burning wreck, before dropping off the back and coming to rest with its barrel in the air.

Despite being outnumbered, the Comets were giving a good account of themselves, using standard AP in the main, conserving the new HESH, which were still not so readily available as to be used on anything but the big boys.

As one, the surviving T34s turned for the ridge behind them and all but one made it over and down the other side before the 1st Regiment could react.

Czernin listened to his new orders and consulted the map.

Pomorski had decided to combine the Light Tank Troop, the headquarters tank troop, and a handful of engineers and infantry, and send them off to the right to circumvent the positions ahead, a plan that had been discussed, should it become necessary.

The main weight of the tank squadron and Highland infantry struck straight down Route 132 and saw immediate results as the enemy started to melt away in front of them.

Czernin's troop led the way, using speed to circumvent the enemy's main force, only stopping occasionally to direct one of the Centurion's from the HQ troop onto a hidden target.

Five Centurion IIs backed up the light force, the idea being that they could establish themselves on an area of raised ground named the Old Man's Nose, which oversaw Routes 180 and 2507 and controlled them from the elevated position, with the Chaffees and infantry providing a security force to keep any would-be heroes at bay.

0729 hrs, Tuesday, 25th March 1947, 1197th Rifle Regiment's command post, Seirijai, Lithuania.

Lieutenant Colonel Zvorykin listened impassively as the details of the destruction of his forward units were laid bare.

His regiment, a regiment in name only, was being overrun by the damned Poles, and even his tank support was running from the field after receiving a sound drubbing.

The moment he understood the position, he had shouted for assistance from his superior, who had made all the right noises about sending support, coupled with threats should his unit give ground.

'We're long past that, you fucking moron!'

He thought it, so wanted to shout it down the telephone, but said nothing but the words expected of him as he started to organise a fighting withdrawal of his surviving units, bringing them back to a line on Routes 180 and 181, but centring the defence on Seirijai to protect the vital junction.

The division's temporary allocation to 10th Guards Army was clearly a poisoned chalice, not the attachment to an elite formation as it had seemed at first.

He imagined the Guards formation not worrying about his 'second-class' soldiers, and allowing them to bleed whilst they sorted their own affairs.

Zvorykin had lost all of his enthusiasm for war, and much of his faith in his fellow man since the heady days of Tostedtland and the drive into Northern Europe.

The arrival of one of the new BTR-152s drew his attention.

It slithered to a halt in a wave of mud and water, and out leapt a mud-splattered and bloodied officer of mechanised troops, who was clearly a man on a mission.

He returned the Captain's salute, keen to hear what the Guards officer had to say.

"Polkovnik Zvorykin?"

"I am."

"Kapitan Nazarbayev, 9th Guards. We've been trying to reach you but the radios…"

The jamming had been extremely successful, making telephone the only means of communication in Zvorykin's headquarters, when lines hadn't been cut by artillery or, in one instance, by the actions of his own tank support.

Zvorykin nodded and moved to the map table.

"Talk to me, Comrade Kapitan."

"Sir, my battalion is a mile or two behind me here…" he indicated the road to Linksmoji, "…on Route 132. We're to be your direct support to hold Seirijai. I've two platoons of tanks, a company of engineers, and a company of anti-tank guns under my command too. Your orders from Leytenant General Obukov are straightforward. You must hold here, which is why I am to place my men under your command."

Zvorykin nodded his understanding.

"A full battalion of men?"

"Yes, Comrade Polkovnik. Three full companies, my own headquarters, plus a submachine company, I've already instructed the SMG boys to deploy immediately to here. I considered them more suited for the defence of this place."

"Good… good… right… no time to lose."

The colonel looked over the positions and made his decision.

"I want your anti-tank units along here… what sort of guns?

"85mm D-44s, one platoon of 100mms, plus a tank-hunter group with the latest RPG-2."

"Excellent. Deploy the 100s east along Route 180… up to the lake. There are positions already created there… a number of my own guns have already been knocked out so there'll be plenty of room."

His pencil made the notations.

"Here, arrange your 85s… keep a platoon undeployed… around here… Gervėnai."

Yuri Nazarbayev made his own notes.

"I agree with the deployment of your SMG company… we'll strengthen the front and the right flank… here and … here."

Zvorykin thought for a moment.

"Tank hunter group into the town. One SMG platoon to be held in reserve... plus your own headquarters units... right here. I'll organise a field telephone to them."

He drew Nazarbayev down to the map with his gaze.

"I need to counter-attack here."

He used his pencil to circle the modest hillock that oversaw Routes 132, 180, 2512, and 2507.

'Senis Nosis.'

"It's a vital point... and whoever controls it holds the town and the whole area in the palm of their hand. Tanks and mechanised infantry assault displaced my own force... far too easily... there are only a few of the bastards up there and I want them shifted back off before they reinforce. I've some mortars for support, but my rocket barrage unit has been dispersed by enemy counter-battery fire. No contact with any artillery, I'm afraid to say, Comrade Kapitan. We hold here."

A jumble of names and numbers indicated Zvorykin's forward positions.

"The shitty Poles are also to the south, and my men are falling back there too."

Nazarbayev understood the Colonel's dilemma perfectly. The height in question was raised enough to dominate the routes in and out of Seirijai.

"I'll lead the attack myself, Comrade Polkovnik. One full company... plus a platoon of tanks and the engineers. I'll take a signals group to lay a line so we can communicate. What can you give me?"

"Three platoons of infantry... also I can add a machine-gun platoon."

"I'll attack with my boys first. I'll bring your men up later to hold the hill while I redeploy to form your mobile reserve. Satisfactory, Comrade Polkovnik?"

"Excellent, Comrade Kapitan... Nazarbayev, you say. Any relation to..."

"No, Comrade Polkovnik."

"Fine... it's now seven-thirty-six. Time of attack?"

Nazarbayev considered everything he had to do, and knew his men would carry out their orders swiftly.

"0815, Comrade Polkovnik?"

"Excellent."

Things became even better as the signals officer announced that contact had been re-established with both Katyusha units.

Czernin watched as the badly burned men were loaded onto one of the jeeps.

They were a pitiful sight and their cries of pain and suffering were almost too much to bear.

One moment the Centurion had been lazily picking off targets to the southeast, the next moment fire was licking out of the cupola as burning men pushed themselves out of the furnace and into the morning's light.

Whatever it was had been an accident; it certainly hadn't been enemy action.

One of the piteous casualties would know and be able to tell, unless it was the fault of the man who still remained in the burning tank, long since past help and meaningful rescue.

The remaining four tanks were conserving their ammunition, although a supply truck was rumoured to be on its way.

Czernin's Chaffees were concealed towards the rear of Old Man's Nose, ready to rush forward if needed.

Men of the Highland infantry were concealed, some in shell holes, others in former Soviet positions, near enough to watch over the Centurions in case the enemy grew bold and stalked them down.

The engineers took over the Soviet headquarters bunker that had cost them four men to overrun during the swift attack on the height.

The assault had seen Czernin's light tanks and the mounted engineers and infantry wash over the defensive positions at lightning speed, and the majority of the defenders retreated as fast as their legs could carry them.

It was only at the small headquarters that any real resistance was met, and the four dead engineers and disabled halftrack served as testament to the short but bitter fight.

The headquarters now also served as an aid post, where another four engineers were tended by an overworked medic.

Major Visnevski, the commander of the Highland Battalion's A Company, had accompanied his part-company and assumed command of the hill's defence.

Having organised evacuation for the wounded and resupply for all units, he called an orders group together to discuss defence of the vital height.

516

The engineer unit was represented by an aging sergeant, their officer amongst the wounded.

Fig # 237 - Old Man's Nose, Seirijai, Lithuania.

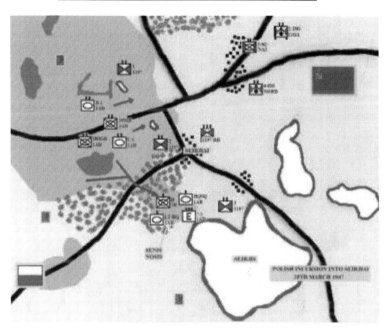

A captain commanded the tanks and Czernin was now senior amongst the light tank troop commanders present.

Visnevski used a hand drawn diagram of the hill to support the main map, part of which bore the blood of his orderly, who also lay close by, being tended by the solitary medic.

"The tanks are already arranged on the leading slope, with infantry in support... here... here... here... and here... the engineers are holding the area round the bunker here... you...," Czernin suddenly realised he was the focus of the Major's words, "I need your tanks moved to here and here... two in each place... ready to push forward and support the infantry if the enemy gets numbers forward. Your fifth tank will place itself... err... here, with my reserve infantry section. That'll be yourself, Sergeant Major. If there's a gap, you and the infantry will plug it... understood?"

"Yes, Sir."

517

"Good. I'm assured we'll get an artillery FOO here very soon. Until then we've the normal channels for artillery... and purple for any air assets that come our way. Any questions?"

"Ammunition, Sir?"

"Still on its way as previously stated. No further news. Experience tells me we need to conserve but if you've a target, put it down... tank or rifle... put the bastard down. Clear?"

They all agreed with that and mumbled their understanding.

"I'm not sure how long we'll be here, but it'll be at least until our forces have taken Seirijai and Okta. Figure midday at the earliest. Anything else?"

He waited a second or two before continuing.

"Excellent. Sergeant Major, make your moves as quickly as possible."

"Yes, Sir."

"Now, back to your units and the very best of luck, boys."

Eighteen minutes later, Major Sebastian Visnevski's head was parted from his shoulders by shrapnel from the second salvo of Katyusha rockets to descend upon the Old Man's Nose.

0815 hrs, Tuesday, 25th March 1947, 500 metres northeast of Senis Nosis, Seirijai, Lithuania.

"Advance! Speed, comrades! Speed!"

The BTR-152s and mixed tanks leapt forward as one, making good ground as the defenders of Senis Nosis recovered from the effects of two Katyusha strikes.

The BTR-mounted 12.7mm DShK blasted away above his head, and was quickly joined by the two flanking smaller SGMB machine-guns, the three weapons spitting a combined rate of up to 1600 rounds per minute in the direction of the hill.

The platoon of T34/100s took the right flank and scaled the secondary level without taking any fire of note.

Centrally, four T-54s made a dash straight for the crown of Senis Nosis.

On the left flank a single T34/85 nervously pushed forward behind Nazarbayev's advancing mechanised infantry.

He would have liked to put some smoke on the hill but that was denied him.

Not even the tanks possessed smoke.

'Not one fucking smoke shell between them!'

Still, the advance was rapid and without casualties so far.

The pleasurable thought was immediately driven from his head as the lead T-54 was engulfed in smoke and flame, the modern tank transformed from running vehicle to inferno in less than two seconds.

"Mudaks! Jink, Comrade, jink!"

One of his BTRS took a direct hit and his brain refused to acknowledge the evidence of pieces of his men being thrown metres into the air.

Bullets were pinging off the light armour of the armoured personnel carrier as the defenders of the hill brought machine-guns to bear.

Looking through his observation slit, Yuri Nazarbayev could see the flashes from the enemy's weapons.

There were a lot.

He made a decision that many would criticise after the battle.

"Teegr-Dva, Teegr-Dva, Teegr-Dva-Dva, Teegr-Dva-Tree, move around to the left... go around to the left, over."

He pointed in the direction he wished to go so his driver could steer away from the increasing volume of fire to their front.

The two motorised infantry companies responded immediately, and the centre and left of the assault moved obliquely left, leaving the T54s in the centre ground without infantry support.

Nazarbayev contacted their commander, ordering the tanks to provide support from cover.

On the right flank the attack went in as planned.

0820 hrs, Tuesday, 25th March 1947, Polish reserve position, Old Man's Nose, Seirijai, Lithuania.

"For fuck's sake, Sergeant Major. We're needed over there!"

"No."

The infantry CSM, of equal rank to Czernin but under his command, baulked at the recon NCO's lack of response to the threat posed on the left flank of the position.

By nothing more than luck, the Soviet attack had chosen a route that denied all but one of the Centurion's a shot, leaving only the left flank guard to take on the platoon of T34/100s.

"At least let me send my AT team over there, Sergeant Major!"

519

"No. there's a greater threat here. I already have two tanks that will bolster up over there… but the enemy has moved off to the right and disappeared under the ridge line there."

As he spoke, Czernin suddenly had a moment of clarity.

"Dupeks!"

He shot a quick glance at the map and dropped down from the tank beside the angry infantryman.

"I know what the bastards are doing. Look here."

A Centurion yielded to another hit and started to burn lazily, allowing the crew to get out and carry their wounded driver to safety.

"They're coming around the hill. Set up to cover our rear immediately! Send a runner to the engineers to inform them."

For all his annoyance with Czernin, the man was a professional and organised his men at high speed.

Czernin was back in his turret and calling orders to his crew when the Bren gun beside his tank started to rattle.

"They're here! Driver forward… and… right turn… hard right… drop in behind that wrecked lorry… gunner… numerous targets coming over the ridge… engage on sight… high ex."

His crew sorted, Czernin looked out of his hatch to take in as much of the battlefield as he could.

"Target…on…fire!"

His tank rocked back and the leading BTR slammed to a halt as an AP shell destroyed its engine, driver, and commander.

Czernin fingered his microphone.

"I said high-ex!"

"It's what was fucking in it!"

The loader's voice betrayed his fear so Czernin let it go, but determined to give Milosz a serious chewing out later.

In front of his eyes, the BTRs disgorged men who tumbled from the still-moving vehicles, although more died as his other tank put a shell on target.

The hull machine-gun joined in the defence and, in concert with the thump of Bren guns, bullets starting to claim casualties amongst the Soviet motorised troops.

"Target…on… fire!"

The shell struck home and removed the rear end of a turning BTR, treating the defenders to the weird sight of what appeared to be half a vehicle driving away down the hill.

It would have been comical enough for laughter if the bullets weren't raining down upon the Polish defenders.

An incredible storm of lead was coming back at them and Czernin kept his head down low to avoid losing it.

"Target... on... fire!"

The Chaffee rocked back on its suspension once more, but this time Bartek Otulski missed, and missed badly.

"Bartek, forget the fucking vehicles... take out some of these shitty machine-guns... direct HE."

"On it."

"Infantry surging left!"

The driver's warning made Czernin stick his head fractionally above the cupola.

The turret whipped round at full speed traverse and the coax stuttered, knocking two of the attackers down, and forcing the others to ground.

Czernin considered the .50cal on his pintel mount, but decided using it would be the last and most stupid thing he ever did.

"Traverse right... quickly... infantry group... shit! Bazooka!"

The turret traversed again and bullets spat, joined by the hull machine-gun, and the group of men were chewed up by fast moving lead.

None the less, something came their way and passed just by the side of the hull before exploding behind them.

"What the fuck is that?"

Czernin did not expect an answer; all he knew that it was deadly and had only just missed.

"Look out for those bloody things!"

His peripheral vision caught three smoke trails reach out to his companion tank and wipe it and its crew off the face of the earth.

"Four's gone... keep your eyes open for these bazookas... kill them straight away... don't wait for orders!"

He grabbed the thompson from its clips.

The sound of bullets striking the tank now resembled handfuls of hi-speed gravel, such was the volume of fire.

"Target... on... firing!"

The 75mm gun sent another HE shell into the enemy assault force.

A smoky trail reached out and Czernin instinctively ducked.

The explosion rocked the light tank and hot gases punched through the interior.

'Am I still alive?'

He decided he was, given the stench that rose from where Milosz's bowels had opened in terror.

"Report!"

The crew all called in, except Milosz who was screaming in pain, and it was Otulski who supplied the details of their lucky escape.

"It hit the fucking barrel!"

"What?"

"The fucking thing hit the barrel."

Czernin understood now why his loader was holding his face, and why the smell of the explosion and the hot gases were all-pervasive.

'Oh my god! You poor bastard!'

The stream of product from the explosion had come straight out of the breech and struck Milosz in the left side of the face as he leant over to get another shell.

From what Czernin could see, it had virtually melted the man's eyeball and burned from ear to nose down to the bone.

He had to be brutal in order for them to survive.

"Michal... tend to Jan... driver... reverse slowly!"

He pushed his head back out as the hull gunner did what he could, which was enough to silence the burned loader as an ampoule of morphine brought instant relief.

The turret machine-gun hammered out in defiance as the Chaffee backed away.

Czernin stuck his head out quickly and gave Scorupco steering instructions into a shell hole.

'Perfect.'

The hull machine-gun could still operate, but the hole covered the lower portion of the hull and the tracks.

The fire had died away and he considered the .50cal once more.

His second Chaffee exploded for a third and final time, the blast virtually ripping the small vehicle apart and almost blowing the fire out.

He hadn't known the Sergeant who commanded that well, but sadly knew that he had four children and a wife waiting in Edinburgh.

Unaware of what was going on in the general battle, Czernin tried contacting other tanks in his troop, without success.

He snatched up the thompson halfway through one attempt, and shot down two Soviet soldiers who materialised twenty yards from the left side of the tank.

The two men went down bloodily, both writhing and moaning in the mud.

"Commander out!"

He dropped off the side of the tank and drove home a fresh magazine as he moved towards the two men.

The RPD light machine-gun that one had carried he had seen before.

It was the tube weapon in the other's hands that had caught his eye more.

Quickly checking the area before he moved forward, he put a burst into each man before collecting their weapons, plus a bag containing more of the strange projectiles.

Bullets started to pluck at the earth around him as he moved back towards the Chaffee and he was forced into cover.

The tank's turret turned and sent a few bursts towards the enemy and the fire dropped away enough to encourage him into a second effort.

He rose and immediately dropped to the ground again, again fumbling for his thompson.

A pair of enemy soldiers, oblivious to his presence, dropped into a hole behind the Chaffee and prepared to fire one of the strange rockets at it.

The submachine-gun chattered and one man was thrown away by multiple impacts.

The other dropped out of sight, the 'bazooka' still in his possession.

Czernin made a quick decision and was up and running in an instant, thompson at the ready, his entire focus on getting to the enemy missile man before he raised his head to take the shot.

The Russian did raise his head to fire, but not with the brand new RPG-2 he had been holding, but with a Tokarev automatic pistol, and Czernin was the target.

The fifth bullet the Soviet soldier fired struck the submachine-gun, sending it from his grasp and painfully jarring his wrist.

Another clipped the side of his upper left arm enough to draw blood but not enough to stop his charge and impact into the Soviet guardsman.

His body hammered into the Russian and drove the shouting against the body of his comrade lying in the bottom of the hole.

Czernin felt bones give way and a groan of excruciating pain came from the man he had just inflicted massive injuries on.

Both lungs were pierced by broken ribs, and at least one of his thighbones had given way when folded hard around the SKS rifle the dead man still gripped in his hands.

Foamy blood immediately sprang from the dying man's mouth as he cried for his mother, but Czernin was in no mood for quarter.

He grabbed the discarded Tokarev and put two bullets into the man's chest at point blank range.

The dying man gurgled a few times more before falling silent.

Catching his breath, Czernin felt his own aches and pains surface, but grabbed the SKS and checked the vicinity for more tank hunter teams.

Yet more bullets came his way, and he quickly worked out that his tank was more exposed than he first imagined, as the firing came from close in, and on both sides of the Chaffee.

Breathing deeply, Czernin tried to get as much oxygen as possible into his lungs so he could make a quick sprint to the rear of the tank and use the squawk-box to warn them of their predicament.

He was up and running before he had completed the thought.

0828 hrs, Tuesday, 25th March 1947, Senis Nosis, Seirijai, Lithuania.

"For fuck's sake, kill the bastard!"

Nazarbayev was reloading at the precise moment the enemy tanker had sprinted from cover and watched impotently as the man had a charmed life in the storm of bullets his men fired at him.

His eyes took in the detail of the SKS in the enemy's hands.

'Palenkov gone for sure... and probably Huninin too.'

His plan had not gone well as the enemy were prepared for his rear attack.

'Mudaks!'

He had left his other two RPG teams to watch the rear of his assault, in case new enemies arrived on the field, but now he needed at least one here, as the enemy tank was proving to be a serious block on his advance.

A runner was dispatched to bring one up the slope whilst Nazarbayev quickly came up with a new plan with two of his senior NCOs.

524

It never got off the ground as a shout drew his attention back to the Chaffee, which was manoeuvring back slowly, its hull and co-axial MGs hammering away defiantly.

If nothing else, Nazarbayev was decisive.

"Give me the mine!"

Instantly, the German-made mine appeared and was thrust into his hand.

"Cover me if anyone interferes, Comrades!"

He levered himself upright was running like a greyhound before anyone could comment.

The Hafthohlladung weighed about three and a half kilos, a not inconsiderable weight to carry when stalking an enemy tank.

Somewhere off to his left rear, an enemy saw the threat he posed and tried to bring him down.

He accelerated more, although he thought it impossible to run faster as his heart and lungs seemed to want to burst from his chest with every leap and bound.

The tank loomed large in front of him and he made the last surge, failing to notice the bullet that ploughed across his left calf.

Inside the tank they heard the metal on metal sound as the magnets attached themselves.

Nazarbayev tugged on the ignitor as a bullet spat off the tank's side and clipped his temple.

Shaking the blood from his eyes, he pulled again and the charge was set.

He ran.

0833 hrs, Tuesday, 25th March 1947, Old Man's Nose, Seirijai, Lithuania.

Czernin sprang up and ran straight into the Soviet officer coming the other way.

They crashed into each other and collapsed at the rear of the still reversing tank.

Czernin's pain returned as his previous injuries manifested themselves and stole his breath.

Nazarbayev felt light headed, the Poles' chin having connected hard with his forehead, further opening the ricochet wound.

Both men were stunned by the shockwave as the Hafthohlladung detonated.

It was an unequal contest, the magnetic charge capable of penetrating nearly 140mm of armour, nearly four times the maximum thickness the Chaffee could muster.

525

The side armour surrendered with ease and the tank was flooded with the stream of hot gases and plasma.

Unseen by either man, Scorupco emerged from the driver's position, swathed in orange flame, only to fail in his efforts and succumb to his injuries, falling partially down the front of the tank where his torso hung from the hatch by burning legs.

Self-preservation became their prime concern, and both men ran as fast as they could, to put distance between them and the burning Chaffee.

Some of the Polish defenders saw simply another Soviet rush, and fired on the pair.

It was Czernin that took the first hits, leading because Nazarbayev was slowed by his calf wound.

Two bullets entered and exited his right forearm no more than four inches apart, knocking him slightly off-balance. Another round took him in the hip. The mud did the rest, and he disappeared into another shell hole.

Nazarbayev followed him as a bullet clipped his heel and spun him round in mid leap precisely as another round crashed into his left shoulder and took him totally off his feet.

The two men crashed to ground and rolled into each other, bringing further pain to Czernin and adding a dislocated little finger to Nazarbayev's woes.

Neither man had any great interest in fighting any more, as their energy drained along with their blood.

The Soviet officer eyed his enemy, but decided that there was no threat so did what most soldiers would do in such a situation.

He lit a cigarette.

Czernin felt the desire wash over him and, with his rough Russian, managed to get one of his own.

The two bleeding warriors lay in the mud gasping and smoking as the battle grew in ferocity all around them.

A grenade went off near the top of the hole, covering both with a wash of mud.

The tension broke as Czernin started to laugh at the vision in front of him, the red and brown figure looking comical to his eyes.

They both laughed the laugh of the 'slightly mad but getting decidedly madder', and the conversation started to flow as each man set aside thoughts of who might come into the hole first and concentrated on staying awake as the soporific effect of their wounds started to kick in.

They laughed at each other, grew angry with each other, shared each other's histories, and shared pictures of loved ones, and in Nazarbayev's case, lost ones.

As both men started to drift into unconsciousness, Nazarbayev found the energy to dispute the war in its entirety.

"Well we didn't start this latest fucking mess, Comrade!"

Czernin coughed his way through a rib-provoking bout caused by the second cigarette.

"I fucking know that, Kapitan."

Nazarbayev, slowly being carried away on a fuzzy white cloud of blood loss and exhaustion, managed to speak one last time.

"So who fucking did then, Starshina?"

Czernin coughed his way to the edge of unconsciousness as Nazarbayev made the journey first, although the last vestiges of his conscious mind caught Czernin's reply.

'... We did...'

1722 hrs, Tuesday, 25th March 1947, ad hoc medical facility, Seilunai, Lithuania.

Nazarbayev opened his eyes against his better judgement as his head pounded like there were blacksmiths at work in every corner.

'Mudaks!'

He rolled to one side and deposited everything he had in his stomach into a conveniently placed enamel bowl.

His stomach convulsions brought pain from every part of his body and he fell back exhausted and drained by his efforts.

His heart sank as he saw a Polish medical orderly walk past with an armful of bloody bandages.

'I'm a prisoner!'

"Welcome back to us, Comrade Kapitan."

He focussed on the man in front of him, a lieutenant of the Red Army medical corps.

"Leytenant? What is this place?"

"Temporary hospital, Comrade Kapitan. We'll have you away to clean sheets in Moscow soon enough."

"But the Pole?"

"He'll live. Comrade Kapitan. Just about, anyway. Not the first time he's seen the inside of a field hospital, but I think it'll be his last. No more soldiering for him."

"No... the Pole... the orderly?"

"Ah, you mean Jan… he was captured earlier. He's helping out here. Good man he is, Comrade Kapitan. Now, please drink."

The medical officer held out a cup of water for Nazarbayev to sip.

He did, and immediately hung himself over the side of the bed to bring it back up again.

"You must drink, Comrade Kapitan. It's very important. The sickness will go. Please?"

"The battle?"

"We won… or at least… we stopped them. Hard to think of it as winning, Comrade Kapitan."

"My men?"

"Mostly still in and around Seirijai, less those that are here… or no longer with us."

"How many?"

"Short answer is that I don't know, Comrade Kapitan. What I do know is that I haven't seen a butcher's yard like this since Berlin, and that's a fact. Now drink."

The effort of a third bout of vomiting drained him so much that he fell back into a deep sleep, assisted by opiates administered by one of the nurses, his mind conjuring up the faces of his men as he slept and recovered…

…Huninin…

…Zvorykin…

…Hubertus…

…Popov…

…Senis Nosis…

…Palenkov…

…Obdurov…

…We did…

1844 hrs, Tuesday, 25th March 1947, RAF Photo Interpretation Room, Bautzen Airfield, Germany.

"Yes… yes, I do see what you mean, Sperry."

The Squadron leader in charge of the section screwed up his eyes and counted the tanks… possible tanks, he corrected himself…

The track marks weren't there, but then they rarely were, even nowadays, so good were the Soviets at hiding things.

But they had not got it all right, which was why Ruby Sperry had called him over to look at the product of a Spitfire recon mission over Lithuania.

"Right ho, Sperry. I'll bump this up with my recommendation. I endorse your view that the Degimas woods contain the best part of a Soviet tank regiment. Well done, Sperry. Now go and get yourself a cuppa, take five minutes, and then start on the yield from the Poles' mosquito please."

Ruby Sperry enjoyed her tea and cigarette, knowing she had done her job well and that her efforts would soon see a complete tank regiment transformed into scrap.

There are things in Russia which are not as they seem.

Georgy Zhukov.

Chapter 197 - THE REVELATIONS

1130 hrs, Wednesday, 26th March 1947, Degimas Woods, Lithuania.

"There's no way… simply no way out at all."

"Damn. So we must sit tight… nothing more to it than that. Just hope that the bastards'll go away soon."

The partisan leadership nodded at the SAS officer's summary of choices available.

Licking their wounds in a well-established underground camp deep in the Degimas Woods, the partisans of the 'Shield of St Michael' were surprised and not a little unnerved to learn that a Soviet armoured regiment had also joined them under the deep canopy of leaves.

None the less, they were confident that they would not be discovered; the NKVD had swept the area three times previously without finding any clue as to their presence.

The entrance to their site was a natural hole, no more than two metres wide, hidden in between the trunks of five trees, leading to a single large cave in which the entire group could hide.

The entrance was covered over with a simple lattice of stout wood overlaid with earth and the normal detritus of the forest floor.

Even those who knew it was there often failed to see it until the cover was moved.

Water was in abundant supply, the small pool in the centre of the curved floor constantly fed from a nearby stream: fresh, cold, and plentiful.

It was food that they needed, as the last of their personal rations had been consumed the previous evening, the main supplies being some four kilometres away, guarded by a few of the less able partisans.

"Fuck it then. Set guards. Let's get some rest, eh?"

Bottomley looked at the two haggard faces in front of him.

"You two grab some kip first then. I'm good for now."

The two partisan leaders didn't bother complaining or remonstrating, and both were asleep within a minute.

Pyragius and Mikenas were awoken from their slumber by urgent hissing from the duty guards, and then other sounds rapidly became discernible.

"Air raid!"

Bottomley was organising the movement of people away from the cave entrance, quite wisely, seeing it as the only place where casualties were likely, although more than one of those present glanced earnestly at the stone roof and wondered... or prayed... or both.

The tremors started as bombs fell upon the woods, seeking out the Soviet tank regiment that had been identified as lurking under its green leaves.

Occasionally the odd piece of stone was dislodged and came tumbling down amongst the sheltering partisans, but nothing to cause them real consternation.

Above them, thirteen Lincoln I bombers of 57 Squadron RAF brought fourteen thousand pounds of bombs each to drop on the tank regiment.

The woods were smashed apart by high explosive, as were men, tanks, and all the supporting vehicles that went with half a Guards tank regiment.

Men were killed a dozen times over as their lifeless bodies were picked up and thrown in diverse directions, as dictated by the accurate arrival of five hundred and thousand pound bombs. Tanks weighing many tons were simply swatted aside by the sheer force of so much power.

252nd Guards Heavy Tank Regiment had never seen action, being a new force formed from men drawn from elite units and fleshed out with new recruits.

Part of the regiment was elsewhere and preserved from the destruction, similarly concealed in woods just over a kilometre away, north of Gudžiūnai.

The heavy IS-IIIs and IS-IVs were mostly wrecked beyond use or recovery, and not a single tank from thirty-three escaped damage or was still operational by the time that 57 Squadron turned for home.

The personnel suffered hideous casualties and no single tank or vehicle crew was intact when roll call was taken.

Of the support services, there was simply nothing left, save a few wide-eyed men and women whose total mental breakdown probably meant that their soldiering days were over.

As far as the eye could see, the trees had been stripped or felled, the remains of some decorated with the remains of men, or of vehicles.

One sight drew a number of eyes.

A Gaz tanker lorry had been picked up by the incredible forces and deposited in the middle of a stand of five trees, its tyres pointed to the skies, the fuel load leaking and feeding a raging fire underneath, one that consumed the very trees that held it proud of Mother Earth, where it sat like a kettle above a fire.

Beneath it, the burning fuel had flowed into the cave.

Those who died due to asphyxiation were spared a far crueller death.

The Shield of St. Michael was no more.

1617 hrs, Wednesday, 26th March 1947, Timi Woods Camp, Paphos, Cyprus.

To avoid the organised mayhem surrounding the presence of so many VIPs, Crisp had taken his leadership group off for a stroll on the beach and a private discussion in the cool shadows of the rocks.

They were well into a lively discussion when something distracted them.

"That sounds throaty."

The officers screwed up their eyes, trying to make out the origin of the deep throb that had started to worm its way into their senses.

"Definitely over there somewhere."

Hässler pointed in roughly the direction he figured, and many eyes strayed to check his guess.

Nothing.

Bluebear had his eyes closed from the moment he heard the approaching beast, concentrating in the way of his ancestors, absorbing every detail as he occasionally moved his head in fine adjustment.

Crisp shook his head.

"Nah... it's more over there, whatever it is."

Again they followed his lead but there was no reward, save an empty blue sky.

Bluebear opened his eyes and smiled.

"It is there."

532

"Nothing."

"Yes, Colonel…it is there."

Bluebear pointed at sea level and all eyes followed the motion.

And it was… whatever it was.

Coming in low, the aircraft was just visible in the haze.

It grew… and grew… and grew.

"What the fuck's that?"

There were no suggestions.

Hassler repeated himself.

"What the fuck **is** that?"

Crisp understood, although he couldn't offer an accurate response.

"That, gentlemen, is our ride. Guarantee it. Green paint and red paint, remember?"

The ferrets had discovered a large supply of military green paint, with some smaller cans of red, plus stencils.

"Now we know. Whatever that is, we'll be getting intimately acquainted with it, and it'll be painted green, that's for goddamned sure!"

They watched as the aircraft continued to grow larger and larger and finally as it lined up for its landing on the pond-like waters off Paphos air base.

The Spruce Goose touched down and taxied to the long jetty, upon which stood USMC Brigadier General Sam Rossiter of the OSS, Major General William Donovan, the head of OSS, Major General Sir Colin Gubbins, head of SOE, Rear Admiral Sir Roger Dalziel, BNI, and one other, to whom they all deferred.

Despite being fully briefed, the size of the aircraft still took all of them by surprise, even Sam Rossiter who had actually been inside it before.

Assisted by launches, the massive flying boat was manoeuvred into position and secured.

Still the party stood impassively on the jetty, the entourage waiting for some sort of signal or movement from the man who stood as still as a rock, his eyes taking in every detail of the massive aircraft.

Howard Hughes alighted and took a short but seemingly precarious walk along a small wooden walkway that had been made to precise specifications, specifications that proved to be about two foot short of ideal.

He noticed the welcome party, as if for the first time, and walked up extending his hand to grasp the one held out to him.

"Mr Hughes. Welcome. We meet again, Sir."

"Indeed we do, Prime Minister.

"An impressive beast I must say."

"Thank you, Prime Minister... and she'll be up to the job, whatever it is."

"I hope so, Howard, I really do hope so. Come... let us get you into some semblance of order before dinner. You go on ahead now. I'll be along directly."

They shook hands again and Hughes slipped in beside Rossiter at strode off at pace, keen to get the circulation back into his aching limbs.

Donovan edged closer to Churchill.

"I had no idea you'd met Mr Hughes before, Prime Minister."

"Just the once, General Donovan. Hearst Castle in San Simeon... 1929 it was... he was only a young man then, but still... he had the air of eccentricity... a hint of the 'devil may care' about him even then."

Donovan laughed.

"That'll come in very handy where he's going, Prime Minister."

"Alas, you are right. Let us hope he has luck in abundance too."

0900 hrs, Thursday, 27th March 1947, Paphos Airfield, Cyprus.

The silence was oppressive.

Rows of soldiers smartly at ease, arranged by company, their different uniforms now disappeared in favour of an identical bland battledress, no matter what the soldier's origin or unit.

By far the largest group on parade came from Group Steel, now known as the 1st Special Service Force, a name previously used by a joint US-Canadian commando force, the famous Devil's Brigade.

The reasoning behind employing the old name was simply that if it became known, then the Soviets would have heard of it before and be less likely to become overly inquisitive.

The Ukrainians of the SOE's Special Action Group was now officially part of the same unit, making up a fifth company, Victor, to add to Whiskey, X-Ray, Yankee, and Zebra companies of the original Steel group, the former having been transported in only two days beforehand.

Each of the original companies had one hundred and forty men, plus Crisp's headquarters added a further eighty-five.

With Shandruk's Ukrainian troopers, the old runway was home for seven hundred and nine men.

Ferdinand Sunday's voice rang out, bringing every man to a state of readiness for his parade orders.

"Parade... parade... atten-shun!"

As one the men responded, and the differences declared themselves immediately, the attention position for the Ukrainians being wholly different to those of the US soldiers.

The two jeeps drew up and the man that every eye concentrated upon stepped out at a lively pace and mounted the small dais.

Churchill nodded to the immaculate RSM.

"Parade... parade... stand at...ease!"

The feet shot out again and the men prepared for the expected pep-talk.

"Sergeant-Major... have the men gather round, if you please."

Sunday, taken aback for the merest of moments, saluted the British Prime Minister and brought himself back to the attention.

"Parade... parade... stand easy... gather round... at the double!"

The rigid ranks broke immediately and there was almost a race to be at the front of the group.

"Settle down now! Settle down, you bunch of bast... you lot!"

Churchill grinned.

"Thank you, Sergeant Major. Can you hear me at the back there, men?"

Those furthest back chorused their replies, even the Ukrainians who didn't understand what he had said and were just following the actions of others.

"Excellent... now, Gentlemen, I know that all of you are wondering what you are doing here on this lovely island. Well, I can answer your question directly, right now."

He sought eye contact with as many of his audience as possible, sharing a smile or a nod of encouragement with those he was about to order into battle.

"You will shortly be asked to undertake a mission... possibly the single most important mission in the history of warfare... a mission that will bring great dangers... great risks to you all."

That got their attention.

"Men, the mission will require travel to a place where the enemy is developing weapons similar to those dropped on Japan, the atomic weapons that ended the resistance of the Empire of Japan."

Immediately, most men grasped the singular importance of the mission.

"We simply cannot tolerate the enemy having these weapons, and we must remove and destroy them in their entirety. Our own use has been controlled, and designed to end conflict, whereas there can be little doubt, following their recent dastardly attack on our forces, that they would intend to employ them to cause the maximum possible damage to the Allied cause."

Some understood the necessary bullshit that Churchill had just presented.

"The communist foe has other weapons in its arsenal, and we have already experienced their dastardly employment on the battlefields of Europe. We will deal with that awfulness as best we can, and I can tell you that our navies have already successfully prevented a full scale biological attack on the European mainland."

"We have thus far been lucky, but the threat posed by their atomic programme cannot be underestimated, and it falls to you to be asked to risk everything to save lives in their countless thousands."

The cheering started from a few throats and soon spread to many.

Churchill set his jaw to prevent any emotion from making itself known, for he believed that many of the men stood in front of him on this warm morning would find eternal rest in the soil of Russia.

As the noise started to subside, he removed his hat and fiddled with the brim as he composed his next words carefully.

"Men, I am compelled to be as honest as I can be, for it is only right that you hear this from my lips, and know that I speak on behalf of President Truman as well."

A hush fell upon the assembly as the man's genuine honesty and passion was made apparent by the anguish on his face and in his words.

"This is not a question of 'you will go', but one of you being asked to volunteer. No man will be forced, required, ordered… anyone who undertakes this vital mission will have chosen to go of their own free will. There will be no stigma for those who choose to remain… but I ask you… no… I implore you all to think about this and decide to volunteer because you… as I do… believe it is the right thing to do."

"Soldiers of 1st Special Service Force, understand this. We believe… I believe earnestly that this is the way… the only way… to make you, your families, your loved ones, and those with whom you serve, safe for the future."

Already, minds turned to the possibility of stepping aside and leaving their peers to take the strain.

The answer was pretty universal.

'Not a chance.'

"But you must know... must surely understand... that the mission you will go on is difficult and hazardous... but you would not be asked to go were it not of vital importance to the future of the Allied nations... indeed, to the future of the world. I ask this of all of you that volunteer to rise to the challenges ahead and go forth to remove the enemy's threat... their super weapon... and face the difficulties ahead together with the man stood beside you. I cannot tell you that this will end the war... neither can I tell you that it will bring the end nearer. What I can tell you is that it will ensure that the end of the war comes without the world having been transformed into a wasteland, and will ensure that our cause will triumph in the end. Thank you, gentlemen, and may God go with you all!"

The roar went up from hundreds of throats as men, inspired by Churchill's rhetoric, committed themselves to the cause he championed.

Shandruk and Crisp had been stood in the second row back and, as if tied together like marionettes, they threw immaculate salutes towards the Prime Minister, and were immediately followed by the men under their command, a wave of arms offering the military honour to Churchill, who was clearly moved by the display.

He replaced his hat with studious care and return the salute briefly, before falling back on his famous V for Victory.

Sunday stood ramrod straight and barked his commands crisply.

"Parade... parade... fall... in!"

The men immediately rushed back to their previous position and arranged themselves in line.

Churchill, accompanied by Sam Rossiter, was introduced to Marion Crisp and Ostap Shandruk, the latter of which he had read about in files so secret that they would never ever see the light of day.

The two officers, with RSM Sunday bringing up the rear and throwing demonic looks at anyone who had a piece of uniform out of place, accompanied Churchill on an inspection of the troops, although none of the men carried any weapon save a sidearm.

The Prime Minister could not help himself but admire the immense presence of a Red Indian soldier the like of which he had rarely seen in all his days of military parades and demonstrations.

Such inspections were a common thing for Winston, but he could see that these men were special in every sense, even the ex-SS soldiers that he thought he should see in a different light for reasons he both understood and failed to comprehend.

He finished his inspection and shook the hands of all three men, much to Sunday's discomfort.

"So, Colonel Crisp, assuming you yourself will go, how many of these fine men will follow you into Ragnarök?"

"Sir?"

"Ah, my apologies. Ragnarök is a mythical series of events that culminate in a terrible battle. How many will volunteer for this enterprise, do you think?"

Crisp smiled with twinkling eyes and turned to Ferdinand Sunday.

"Let's ask them, Sir. Sergeant Major?"

Sunday nodded and came to full attention, before marching smartly around the assembly to take post at the front of the parade.

"Parade... parade, listen in! Parade... all those wishing to volunteer for the mission... on my command... one pace forward... parade..." he left his orders hanging whilst the customary translation was rapidly spoken for the Ukrainian contingent,"... Volunteers... by the left, one pace...march!"

Seven hundred and six pairs of feet took one smart pace forward and came back to attention with a crash of their right boot.

Churchill had his answer.

1300 hrs, Thursday, 27th March 1947, Timi Woods Camp, Paphos, Cyprus.

Churchill had left Cyprus at 1240 on the dot, having taken lunch with the leadership of the 1st SSF.

He had spent some considerable time handling the tomahawk and battle knife of Captain Charley Bluebear, and hearing of their history, both from olden times and more recently at Rottenberg.

Rossiter scheduled the first briefing on their mission for 1300 hrs, and the leadership, down to senior NCO level, were all present, as well as four men who were in pseudo military uniform, although clearly not military.

The part that Hughes, co-pilot Dave Grant, and the two flight engineers, Don Smith and Joe Petrali, would play required their presence and input.

538

Donovan made a statement introducing the four men, and then stepped aside to leave Rossiter as the main briefer...

'... or harbinger of doom...'

On a nod from the Marine general, the covers were pulled back on two maps, one showing a detailed area of Southern Russian, the other a painstakingly hand drawn map of a facility near Uspenka.

Rossiter left the men a few moments in which to absorb the information and to let off a little steam.

He looked Crisp directly in the eyes as the hubbub died away and understood that the paratrooper colonel immediately understood that he had been handed a real hot potato.

He would have not been surprised at Crisp's thoughts.

'Jesus H...the biggest bastard of a fucked up mission in the history of bastard fucked up missions!'

Rossiter spoke to the man in the front row of seats.

"You ready, Colonel?"

'How about fucking never?!'

"Good to go, Sir."

Crisp suddenly realised that Rossiter was referring to the new unit insignia he had passed to Crisp, ready to hand out prior to the briefing.

A positive measure that Rossiter hoped would help ease the pain of what was to come.

"Ok, listen in, Gentlemen."

Crisp produced the box that Rossiter had given him and held aloft a unit insignia.

Two U's superimposed on a yellow background, with red, white, and blue stripes as a border.

"This is our new badge. A U for the Ukraine... and one for the good old US of A... yellow for the land on which we will first fight, and with a red, white and blue border for the RSM and his boys."

They all laughed and then, as each man looked at Sunday's face, stopped laughing immediately.

"Take one and pass the box on. There are others to take back to your boys. All badges of rank and unit insignia to be sown on uniforms before reveille tomorrow morning."

Crisp passed the box to Shandruk who took his badge and moved the box on its rounds.

Crisp quickly moved over to Hughes and his crew, and handed over four badges, accompanied with handshakes, symbolising the inclusion of the civilians in the group.

For their part, the four men were clearly delighted by the gesture.

The Marine officer nodded to himself.

'That was well done, Colonel... very well done.'

"Let us begin."

Rossiter pointed at the map of Southern Russia.

"You'll fly from here to Talesh, where you will refuel, before flying north and into the Soviet Union."

He let that sink in for a moment.

"This is the great city of Stalingrad... here is the town of Akhtubinsk... the River Volga... village of Uspenka... and here, gentlemen, is the prize... Camp one thousand and one."

He moved across to the second display.

"This is... sorry, was... as far as we were concerned, a POW facility for Allied prisoners. It is that and more, boys. This schematic shows you the layout of that prison camp... we estimate enough accommodation for approaching two thousand prisoners. We're still trying to get recent figures from Red Cross sources."

The pointer swept over other points on the diagram.

"We also estimate that the guard force consists of a full guard battalion here... a mobile company based here... plus..."

He moved back to the main map.

"Here... right there's a Red Army training facility... tank training facility... probably at regimental strength."

The low groan escaped no one's ears.

"And there are two airfields... the complex here at Akhtubinsk and here...at Butyrki. This is a small strip that is also the main Stalingrad-Astrakhan highway and appears to have nothing stationed there, so it's assumed to be an emergency runway and little more."

Rossiter coughed.

"However, the main complex here is home to at least three squadrons of aircraft, most of which are fighters."

Crisp looked off to his right and saw that Shandruk's eyes were boring in to him, and he wasn't sure if they were angrier or more incredulous than his.

He gave the slightest of shrugs and turned back to Rossiter, who in turn was looking directly at him.

"Colonel Crisp, gentlemen, your mission is to liberate the prisoners in this camp and to take over the secret facility that lies beneath it, remove certain items of note... any scientists too...demolish whatever you cannot carry, and evacuate... all within one hour maximum."

The hubbub of voices was immediate as the enormity of the basic mission was laid bare.

"Bullshit!"

Crisp leapt to his feet and his eyes swept the room, although he had recognised the voice immediately.

"Whoever you are, you'll can that sort of talk, soldier."

Crisp resumed his seat and Rossiter resumed without further comment.

"That's the idea, and we have to put meat on the bones of it. There is so much that I don't know... can't tell you. There's nothing I won't tell you if I know it... I owe you all that much. I have dedicated and skilled people working all hours, trying to get more information, but for now, all I can tell you is this."

He moved back to the schematic of the camp and pointed at some unlabelled parts,

"We believe these are vents... entrances... for an underground complex that holds the Soviet atomic programme. We believe that they have been assisted greatly by equipment and expertise from Japan, and have made startling progress. We believe that this facility holds the greatest threat to our cause... and our freedom... and that's why we're sending you to destroy it."

"They have the bomb or are developing the bomb?"

"I cannot say for sure how advanced they are now, Colonel Crisp, but I can say as sure is eggs are eggs that this is where it's being developed and that we do know, from other sources, that they're much further along than we'd given them credit for."

"And you can't bomb it because of all our prisoners."

Crisp made it a statement, and Rossiter's unexpected reply made his jaw drop.

"On the contrary... we intend to bomb it."

There was what almost amounted to an outcry amongst the assembled soldiers.

"The planning done thus far gives us a window of one hour from the time the operation is initiated... that's one hour to liberate the camp and get as many of the prisoners out of harm's way as possible. We cannot allow more than that. There must be no opportunity for then to remove or salvage anything of value."

"So, let me get this right, General Rossiter.

Crisp strode to the front of the room and touched the map at each place as he made his points.

541

"We fly from here to... Talesh... and then onto Camp 1001... where we make an assault against a full battalion of infantry plus change... not far from a tank regiment's training facility, all under the umbrella of about three Soviet air squadrons. We liberate the entire camp and then go underground, where it's just possible we might find more enemy soldiers... find something, we know not what, grab it, kidnap a few men in white coats, set a few charges, police up the POWs and hightail it before you start dropping bombs all over the place... all in one hour."

Crisp's face was red with the effort of controlling himself.

"Look here, General... we volunteered for this mission but by God, no one can have imagined it was going to be anything like this. It's a suicide mission!"

Rossiter composed himself and turned to the rest of the room.

"This is not an easy mission... far from it... but it's not a suicide mission... we can plan this to make the timetable work. And that timetable is set in stone, make no mistake. The follow up bombers have an hour to get in for the attack, and even then it could be cutting it fine. Any longer than that and the Soviet air responses will be more than air force can handle."

"Colonel Crisp is rightly concerned, but we haven't yet started to iron out the issues and get our operational plan in place."

Disbelief was written large on every man's face, and Rossiter simply couldn't blame them for their doubts. It was a true monster of a mission.

"Let us plan the mission, gentlemen... get everything sorted as to the best of our abilities. Then, if it's impossible, we call your part off."

"Our part?"

"Yes, Major Shandruk... just our part. No matter what, the bombers will go in."

"But your men... sorry... our men... our prisoners... you intend to bomb anyway and kill them all?"

Rossiter had been prepared for this question, although he was as yet unprepared to order the mission itself, the idea of killing thousands of Allied soldiers caused so much turmoil, despite the necessity of closing 1001 down.

"That's the bottom line of it, Major Shandruk."

The sound that emanated from a dozen throats spoke of anguish, mixed with disgust, and not a little hatred.

"'Scuse me, General."

"Lieutenant?"

"So… if we go, we get one hour to get as many of our boys out of Dodge as possible… and then you bomb. If we don't go… you bomb the poor fuckers anyway?"

"Yes, Lieutenant, that's the size of it."

Hässler mouth worked but no sound came out. The reply was furnished by Bluebear.

"This is some fucked up mission!"

Those who knew him understood such words didn't ever trip from his mouth, but such was his incredulity. The noise level rose as men voiced their objections in simple soldierly terms.

Crisp took centre stage again, but he contented himself with eyeballing Bluebear and no more.

Holding his hands out, he called the room to order. The men fell into grudging silence.

"Gotta agree with Captain Bluebear… this is one fucked up mission for sure… but… we've yet to work on our plan so let's apply ourselves and see what we can come up with."

Turning to the diagram, he patted the prison camps lines as he spoke.

"I for one ain't gonna have the blood of these boys on my hands, so I'm going, come what may… just to give them the best chance of survival."

Rossiter nodded in agreement and also in thanks for the paratrooper's straightforward words.

"Right, let's get started now. General, what assets can we call on here?"

Relieved to be on firmer ground, Rossiter produced a list of transport and fighter aircraft that could be made available.

It was a start, although Crisp could already see that there was nowhere near enough room to bring back all the men and prisoners.

The group started to throw in suggestions.

Some were pie in the sky, whereas others had true merit.

It was Crisp who suggested taking weapons to arm the prisoners…

…Shandruk who suggested a way to open the camp up.

…Hughes who ventured an idea to get them closer.

…Galkin who swiftly formed an operation outline that pulled everything together.

…Rossiter who dropped the name of Oberst Trannel of the DRL into the pot, offering a vague solution to the tank regiment issue. Even though he hadn't even broached the matter with the German officer yet, as their European ally was under such heavy suspicion.

It was Bluebear that asked a question that changed everything, dragging an answer out of Rossiter, who revealed something he had wished not to reveal.

"What's safe distance for when the bombers come in, General?"

Many eyes looked at the map, assessing circles of increasing diameter.

"No closer than eight miles."

"Goddamned air force can't drop 'em more accurately than that!"

Galkin's comment brought on a modest wave of laughter, except for those who had grasped exactly what Rossiter's words implied.

Those who understood turned their eyes to Crisp whose mouth was twisted in anguish.

"Goddamnit, General! So we gotta go in, come what may!"

He turned to his men and spoke with total certainty.

"According to the debriefing documents I have studied, our atomic bombs damaged buildings and wounded people up to eight miles from the point of explosion. The air force are gonna put an atomic on the place. If we don't go in and get some of those poor bastards out… well, they're all gonna die."

"What happened to 'nothing you won't tell us', eh… General?"

Rossiter flushed at the accusation, more so because the bloody Greek Major was absolutely correct.

"I'm still not supposed to have told you. You must understand that such missions are classified beyond your wildest dreams. You cannot share that information with your men… you simply cannot!"

He grabbed the pointer off Crisp and moved next to the map of Southern Russia.

"The air attack will be in two waves. The first will be using earthquake bombs to open up the ground and destroy as much of the facility as possible. The second wave will drop an atomic device, destroying everything for a radius of four miles. Everything."

He passed the pointer back and moved forward into the group that had gathered closer.

"That's where we're at, boys. This site's crucial and has to go. We want to give our prisoners the best possible chance, and we can combine that with an intelligence grab… but we can't leave anything salvageable for the commies to continue with their research.

That will be the President's call, but don't mistake me. He **will** make that call."

The silence was laden with meaning, and heavy with unfavourable portents.

Crisp decided to grab the bull by the horns.

"To hell with it. We're gonna make this work, cos we're gonna do it or die trying. Move on, gentlemen."

And that ended the doubts and objections, at least those spoken... at least until the mess table called them before they returned to continue with their planning... and at least until they flopped into bed exhausted by their labours, leaving the bones of the initial plan partially covered with substance.

Over the coming days, more and more of the plan was developed, assisted greatly by a fantastic scale model created by the indomitable Jenkins and her staff, combining the certainties of the above ground with the possibilities of what lay below.

The engineer section, supplied with willing hands from the rifle companies, created a reflection of the model in real scale, using anything from tarpaulins, to wooden frames, all to provide the best possible training to their men.

The Spruce Goose lay at anchor close in shore and parties attended in relay to learn about boarding and disembarking, and also so that Hughes and his band of merry men could develop the loading plan to ensure the best weight distribution.

Priorities changed as more information arrived and further assets became available, or in the case of the Curtiss Commando transport aircraft, were transferred from the Pacific by direct order of President Truman in the face of resistance by none other than MacArthur himself.

A USAAF liaison officer made recommendations, and a further group of Air Force officers arrived, all to put together the distraction, escort, and extraction planning, which snowballed in size and complexity the more minds were set to solving the issues.

One man arrived to act as an observer and answer questions, as far as he could, specifically related to his unit's part in the mission.

Wing Commander Leonard Cheshire was rarely approached, often avoided, almost as if his unit was seen as the great relentless evil in the process.

Their part of the Viking mission, the ground attack and extraction, was given a name, one that Crisp suggested; a name that held great meaning for a number of those present.

Operation Kingsbury, named for a ship on the bottom of the Baltic, a ship in which many of his beloved troopers still lay unrecovered.

1154 hrs, Saturday, 29th March 1947, Karup Air Base, Denmark.

He recovered from his surprise and relaxed from his salute.

"General Donovan, Vice-Admiral, please."

Banner gestured the two senior men towards some functional seating.

"How may I be of service, Sir?"

Donovan cleared his throat and pressed ahead.

"At this moment in time, this is for your ears only. Wing Commander Cheshire has been briefed in on the mission as far as I am about to brief you."

He took the folder that Dalziel held out, a folder drenched in the signs of the highest secrecy.

Neither man knew that Rossiter had felt honour bound to be indiscrete with Crisp and his men and neither, pursuant to the marine's earnest request, would ever learn that the men of the 1st SSF knew nearly as much as they did already.

"The mission has been developed further. The overall mission is Operation Viking. The air mission that you will be flying is part of that. The insertion group goes under the name of Operation Kingsbury. I have included the basic brief on Kingsbury for you. You'll understand why. Admiral Dalziel's man'll be remaining with your unit as direct liaison and he'll bring further details to you as they become known. The contents of this folder will be known only to you, and you will keep it secure under lock and key at any time it is not in your immediate possession. Is that clear?"

"Yes, General."

Donovan accepted another copy from Sir Roger Dalziel, and the three read the information therein, two for the umpteenth time, one for the very first.

Both senior men knew that there would be a reaction, but not how bad it would be.

"You have gotta be fucking kidding, General?"

Donovan had been pre-warned about Banner's approach to such matters, but still felt his anger rise.

"That's the mission, Colonel... and if you don't want it I'll find someone who can handle it."

546

Banner's look conveyed every essence of contempt he could muster.

He took a deep breath and spoke much more calmly than he felt.

"General, it's not a question of want. It's a question of practicalities... in the first instance anyways."

As if by silent agreement, both men relaxed back into their chairs.

"Go on, Colonel."

"Sir, I've only two crews trained... actually training with the Jasper I have one, plus my own crew. I say training. We've still a long way to go before I can declare that delivery side combat ready. Plus just one aircraft converted to Jasper... SOP requires a stand-by bird at the very least... plus the forward air base, acclimatisation, specialist ground crew, the whol..."

"I understand that, Colonel. But this is all about window of opportunity and speed... and SOPs'll be going to hell in a handcart."

"That sort of shit gets folks killed, General."

Donovan understood what the man meant... and wholly agreed.

"The mission is critical, Colonel."

"They're all goddamned critical in one way or another, General. Ain't never been sent out on anything that wouldn't shorten the war or save countless lives."

Donovan chuckled inadvertently and the act removed much of the tension in the room, allowing Dalziel to speak.

"Colonel Banner, let me be frank. This site represents the enemy's atomic resources, as best as we can ascertain. We simply have to deprive them of the means to retaliate in kind. The mission as described offers us the best opportunity to prevent the deployment of Soviet weapons for years to come."

"With all due respect, Admiral... the mission as described is a FUBAR... a fuck up of monumental proportions... in my honest opinion, rushing something like this is only going to get men killed."

"There's no choice."

"There's always a choice, Admiral."

Donovan stood up and moved to the window, stopping the two others in their tracks.

He took in the airfield, the lumbering bombers... the men going about their normal duties... a scene of relative normality...

Donovan pulled himself back from his thoughts.

"Colonel, I can tell you that this mission's the most important operation with which I've been associated in my long career."

Banner understood that, if Donovan was being genuine and not blowing smoke up his ass, then that meant something.

The general turned back to the room.

"This mission will fly. Men will die, some by design, some because the mission is a FUBAR... but this mission will fly. Your outfit is in this because you've the skills and experience to deliver your ordnance on the target... and from what I've heard... the balls!"

He moved back to the table and picked up a folder, holding it like a preacher of old would hold the Bible to demonstrate a point.

"The British 9 Squadron will do their part because they have the skills, and yes, some of them will die."

Banner adjusted his position, feeling suddenly uncomfortable.

"Group Steel and Kingsbury... well... a lot of those boys are not coming home... but they're going anyway... all volunteers... and yes... they know your part in this before you say anything."

It was not the lie he supposed it to be.

Donovan dropped the folder on the table and waited for the sharp crack to die away before continuing.

"Colonel Banner, I know your reputation as a maverick, but I also know you... I've known men like you for my whole career... some real types in the old Rainbow Division I can tell you... hell, I was once like you myself!"

He leant forward with hands opened in concession.

"Look, son... this has to run as soon as we say run it... the President will give it the go-ahead and when he does... well... we just gotta do the best we can and there's an end to it. Save all the usual shit for the marines... it's a bitch of a mission... but it's our bitch and we'll do it the best we goddamned can."

"Of course we'll do our best, General."

The angry note in his vote died instantly away.

"How long do we have, Sir?"

Dalziel delivered the bad news.

"We suspect less than a week before the mission has to go ahead."

"A week?"

"Maybe an extra day of two... two weeks absolute tops... much depends on intelligence received, Colonel."

"Then there's no time to lose, Admiral."

There was little more to be said.

548

The senior officers left after exchanging salutes.

"Did we do the right thing, Bill?"

Donovan knew precisely what the newly appointed Chief of Military Intelligence for NATO meant.

"We'll tell them before they fly the mission, Sir Roger. Wiser heads reckon that letting them know everything now might take their minds off training and the mission."

"But will they do it... will he do it?"

"What, Banner? Sure, he'll do it. He'll hate it and curse us for the rest of his days, but he'll do it, once he's told, because it needs to be done."

"Hell of a job, Bill."

"It sure will be, Sir Roger."

"I actually meant telling him."

Donovan grimaced and put his hand on Dalziel's shoulder.

"I know you did, but one of us is going to have to. Hell, he might even work it out with the brief on Kingsbury that he's got."

The Admiral dropped into thoughtful silence.

'Will he work out what we intend to ask of him? Could he even imagine that we would ask such a thing of him?'

They walked wordlessly back towards their Avro Anson C19 VIP transport, whose crew had started pre-flight checks the moment the two officers moved in their direction.

Dalziel committed himself.

"I'll do it, Bill. I'll tell him. That's the sort of thing that he has to be told face to face by someone who can answer the inevitable questions. I'll tell him."

Donovan respected the Englishman's resolve without envying him the task.

They walked silently towards the waiting aircraft, although they shared the same thoughts.

'How do you tell a man he's going to drop a bomb that will probably kill thousands of our own?'

"Sir... there's something you need to come and look at."

Crisp, on his way for some chow, fell into step with Galkin and they headed towards the supply section.

"Some uniforms just came in... well... see for yourself, Colonel."

Galkin ceded the passage to Crisp, who strode into the old hangar that served as their stores.

His first instinct was to grab for his sidearm but he recognised one of the men in the uniform of a Soviet paratrooper and understood Galkin's problem.

"How many?"

"Eight hundred by docket. We ain't counted them in yet, Colonel. Something that you haven't told us?"

Crisp grinned.

"Something they haven't told any of us I think, Con. Guess we're going on this one wearing fancy dress, eh?"

Inside, Crisp was fuming, as this sort of foul up made him worry what else might have been missed.

"Well, fuck it anyway. Get 'em counted and signed for. Keep them safe and sound until I find out what the hell is going on. I'll find some unsuspecting officer to oversee sizing later."

For a moment he debated issuing a stern warning to the supply soldiers regarding loose mouths and dismissed it just as quickly.

They were supply soldiers and such a warning was pointless; everyone would know in twenty minutes.

Actually, in less.

Nine minutes later, Crisp was sat at the officer's dining table when Captain Timmins dropped down opposite him.

"Good afternoon, Comrade Colonel."

"Afternoon, Captain Cowboy."

The name had stuck to him, much like the remains of the putrefied cow he had landed in many months previously.

"I hear we're dressing up as Russians for the mission, Colonel?"

"Soldiers will always gossip, Cowboy."

"So it **is** true."

"I didn't say that, did I?"

"You didn't deny it either, Sir."

"No. I was too busy thinking about who was going to do a job for me. I need a responsible man to volunteer for a difficult mission. Any ideas?"

"None whatsoever, Colonel Sir... however I've an 'ornery old NCO who needs a run out."

"Let me guess... Master Sergeant Montgomery Hawkes the Third?"

"Wow! Guess that's why they made you a Colonel, eh Colonel?"

Everybody knew that Hawkes had a special place in Crisp's heart, not one that made the NCO off limits, but one that made Crisp vulnerable to army humour and pranks.

Timmins leant back to allow the plate of lamb and vegetables to be slid in front of him.

"Spassiba."

The orderly grinned.

"Away with you or it's the Siberian mines for you, corporal."

The man went way chuckling, at which point Crisp decided he had his man.

"Nope. They made me Colonel cos I can sniff out Captains who like to pick on poor old veterans like the elderly Hawkes, and poke fun at their commanding officer. Report to Major Galkin at the stores hangar after dinner... tell him you're there to record sizes... he'll understand."

Crisp's grin went from ear to ear.

Timmins took it in good heart and stowed away his lunch with gusto.

"Certainly, Comrade Colonel."

1200 hrs, Saturday, 29th March 1947, Camerone Division Headquarters, Staszow, Poland.

Knocke examined the hand written document for the third time, taking longer to read it than both previous times put together.

"Who else knows about this, Albrecht?"

"Myself, Celestin, and his man, the author of the report."

The artillery officer from Alma had been very thorough and very secretive, preparing his report by hand for St.Clair so as not to have an official trail.

"Capitaine Stefan Antal? One of yours?"

"Surprisingly one of yours apparently, mon Général. Karsjarger or something like that."

551

"Karstjäger… a Waffen Gebirgsjager division if I recall… anyway…"

Knocke passed the document back to Haefali with exercised care, the Swiss officer's arm only recently out of plaster and clearly still painful.

"That appears to be a preposterous suggestion."

Albrecht Haefali went to open his mouth in protest but Knocke continued his assessment.

"But he's thorough… states what he knows… what he suspects… provides evidence… I inclined to believe it. You?"

"Absolutely, mon General. I spoke at length with Celestin. He agrees. What we don't know is what to do now."

Knocke shook his head.

"Nothing."

"What?"

"We do nothing."

"Merde! Mon General, we've been handed evidence that proves beyond doubt that the fire we received on the night of March 15th came from our lines… German Army lines to be specific!"

"Yes, we do. We know simply because his unit was exercising at night, in the wrong location I might add, and escaped any attack by the Russian infiltration teams…"

He left that hanging as the two men understood the lie in the statement, and corrected himself.

"… by the infiltration teams. He's handed us tracking data, numbers, times, everything we need to prove that we were fired on by Allies… Germans… in my case, my own countrymen. This is proof that we've been taken back to another war, not by the Communists, but by a faction on our side… our side, hah!"

Haefali nodded but remained quiet.

"So, what would you have me do with this information, eh?"

Again, Haefali's mouth remained tightly closed.

"What would Celestin have me do? Eh? To whom do I go? We have a war going on all around us? Do I create a storm that causes us to come apart? The Allies fall out and then bang! We open the way for another wave from the East? Is that what I do?"

"Well no… I understand… I think."

"You think, Albrecht? It's simple, man. This cannot be allowed to come out as it will doom the Allied cause and hand Europe to the Communists… you can see that surely?"

"Yes… I see that clearly now, mon Général. So what do we actually do?"

"We hide it... keep it safe... fight on and win... and then, and only then, we make sure it gets into the right hands so that those responsible can be brought to justice."

"Want me to speak with Celestin?"

"No, I think I'll do that myself, thank you anyway, Albrecht. Is this the only copy?"

"No. I'm assured that Antal has one, plus this one. Two in total, mon Général."

"They must be preserved, but hidden from prying eyes, Albrecht. I'll take responsibility for this one. If you speak straight to Antal, tell him our thinking and ask for his silence... I'll deal with Celestin directly and let him know that you've spoken to the man. Understood?"

Haefali understood perfectly.

"Understand this, my friend. There'll be a reckoning for this... someone has provoked a renewal of the conflict and many men have died as a result. If this had been an accident, we'd have heard by now. No, this was a design... a deliberate organised act to bring horror to the world once more. There **will** be a reckoning!"

Haefali stood and accepted Knocke's hand, but the urgent knock on the door interrupted his words.

"Oberführer. Urgent orders from headquarters, Sir."

Knocke took the documents from the duty officer, signed for them and waited for the door to close.

"You might want to take a seat, Albrecht."

"Or pour a drink, mon Général?"

Knocke caught the signs on the map work, and words jumped off of the paper.

"Make it a large one."

"Attack orders, Sir?"

"Yes..."

He examined the map a little more closely.

"We'll be going to Tarnobrzeg and Sandomierz... on the Vistula."

"On the Vistula?"

"We're to cross it... but there's no intact bridges."

"Feh!"

Knocke rummaged for a sheet he knew would be there.

"We'll have extra resources allocated... regular German Army units on our left flank... assault engineers... boats... even a paratroop drop to help out."

"Feh!"

"Your boys'll have one hell of a time, Albrecht."

553

"Any more good news?"

"Scheisse!"

Knocke almost spat the words.

"This is wrong... just wrong... fucking intelligence!"

Haefali waited.

"They list our opposition as no more than a rifle division plus support. And yet their own update sheet from yesterday quotes that rifle division plus unidentified armoured units, possibly a Guards Motorised unit. Bescheissen staff planners! Forget the drink. Albrecht. Back to your unit now, but via Celestin please... I don't have time now, but I want him to understand. Just ask him to do nothing, and look after Antal. I'll speak to him later in greater depth. On your way out, ask my staff to arrange a senior officer's meeting for 1800 here, please... briefing and orders. We've to attend General Lavalle tomorrow morning and I want something in place when we see him."

"À vos ordres, mon Général!"

"Mudaks! High command cannot be serious!"

Polanów was thirty-five kilometres distant from where Knocke was sat, but the problems were the same.

Artem'yev, recently returned to full health and adorned with Major General's stars, commanded the recently formed 116th Guards Motorised Rifle Division, an independent formation full of experienced men, from some of Makarenko's old 100th Guards troopers, the ones who had been left behind, through to wounded men whose units had either been disbanded or destroyed whilst they were recuperating.

His Chief of Staff remained stony faced.

Artem'yev had changed by all accounts, although Barashnikev had only heard of him by reputation before being sent to the new division.

That the Major General had seen more action than most was a given, and a fact attested to by the plethora of medals on his tunic, the two Hero awards standing particularly proud.

But he had become a gruff and unhappy man since his old unit had been destroyed in the field as he recovered from his many wounds.

His bad humour was not helped by the outline orders that his eyes were consuming.

Barashnikev poured the man some tea and waited patiently, hoping that the tuts and gasps would stop and transform into tangible military terms.

"Thank you."

Artem'yev put the paperwork down and lifted the mug to his lips, taking a decent swig of the warm sweet tea to which he had become accustomed since his stomach injury.

"Well, Misha, someone has come up with a fucking nightmare, I can tell you!"

Mikhail Barashnikev nearly choked on his drink as his commander used the diminutive of his name for the first time ever.

'Signs of a recovery?'

"By St Basil's balls but this is a shitty thing."

Artem'yev shoved the paperwork across the table top where Barashnikev had to act quickly to stop it hitting the damp earth floor.

As he looked through it, his commander summarised.

"We've to mount an impressive attack... and fail... fall back... draw the enemy on and into a trap to be sprung by our comrades of the 3rd Guards Tank Army. Simple really... Yob tvoyu mat!"

The plan looked simple on paper but any one with half a brain could see that the risks were immense, and that the 116th would be making itself incredibly vulnerable.

'Which is the fucking point, I suppose... bastards...'

"Comrade General, this won't work."

Artem'yev pointed at the paperwork and laughed.

"No... that shit won't... but what we devise will... or our men'll pay for it."

He stood and stretched his aching back... his painful stomach... his tight thigh... his almost seized shoulder... all products of battle.

"Right, Misha. A working lunch I think. Irlov!"

The sacking was drawn aside and a child's face appeared.

"Comrade General?"

"We'll take lunch here, now. What have you found for us, Comrade Yefreytor?"

"Sausage, pickled egg, and fine fresh bread, Comrade General."

"Excellent. You'll make Serzhant yet, young Irlov!"

The boy disappeared as Artem'yev finished the last of his tea.

"Right, clear the table, Misha. Let's see what we can come up with that doesn't lose me my division."

1203 hrs, Sunday, 30th March 1947, Lieutenant General Kaganovich's Dacha, Moscow, USSR.

"Only the very finest, Tatiana."

She could not help but agree, the caviar and toasted bread easily sliding down, aided by an exquisite Georgian Mtsvani wine.

There were other items, such as she hadn't seen in wartime, and in quantities undreamt of since the morning the Nazi tanks crossed the border in 1941.

Kaganovich had already briefed her that there were others, important others, who would arrive later.

Which begged a question.

"So, Comrade General… I assume you have me here early for a good reason, not just my company?"

Kaganovich inclined the glass in acknowledgement.

"Indeed, Tatiana, indeed. I believe the time has come to fully enlighten you, which will be a painful journey for you, I'm afraid."

"Enlighten? What is there that I don't know already? You have my support. What more do you need?"

"Your commitment."

She drained her glass and refilled it before speaking.

"You have my support, Comrade General."

"And yet, despite what has been wrought upon your family… upon you personally… the lies and deceptions practised by those in authority… you're not yet fully with us, are you, Tatiana?"

"My sons? You mean my sons?"

The wine glass was emptied in the blink of an eye.

"My sons died for the Motherland… "

They both knew the lie spilled too easily from her lips.

"No, Tatiana… they didn't… you know they didn't so why do you persist in lying to yourself?"

She took a deep draught from the refilled glass and became a vulnerable mother for just a moment.

"Perhaps it is easier for me to cope that way?"

"Perhaps it is."

"Yes, perhaps it is… You've told me that my son Vladimir was lost due to anger against Makarenko… or the needs of the state, with the sacrifice of Ilya and Oleg in the dirty machine of espionage…

but they died in uniform... for the Motherland... that is my solace, Comrade General."

"And you, Tatiana? What of yourself? What you have become as a result of their actions?"

"What I have become?"

"Yes... I have eyes and ears, Tatiana. You know what I talk of."

"Ah... the drink... yes, I know... it helps me..."

"Not just the drink."

"What?"

"Yuri... the other men... you have been transformed by the actions of others."

"No... no... by my own actions. Mine... mine alone..."

"No."

"What's happened is my fault. I blame myself."

"No, Tatiana."

"No?"

Kaganovich leant over and placed a tender hand on her arm.

"Oh no, Tatiana. I've some things to show you. It'll be hard for you... but I think you must understand what's brought you to this dark place in your life."

She finished her glass and set it down without thought for more.

Kaganovich produced the full files he had either copied or stolen from Beria's own records and had beefed up a little here and there, just to add a little more weight to his effort to bring the woman fully into the plan.

She had heard it before... at least in the main... but a file was something she understood. It had a weight all of its own.

She read.

Read of the Chateau... of her son Oleg and his proclivities, encouraged by Beria, who then traded his life on a whim that might bring Franco onside, but was never really expected to.

In Beria's own handwriting, the evidence of his hatred for her making his decision easier.

The death of her beloved Ilya at the hands of the English traitor lauded by both Stalin and the bespectacled devil, again Beria's note outlining the celebration the news brought.

"Bastards."

Kaganovich had bided his time.

"There is more..."

557

He handed over an army document that included an order from a senior NKVD general, effectively ordering Yuri's unit to be placed in the most dangerous positions on the battlefield. Pretending to be an order designed to afford him the maximum number of opportunities to win the coveted Hero Award, it screamed at her from the pages as just another attempt by Beria, or even Stalin, to inflict more hurt upon Nazarbayeva's family.

A report from NKVD General Gustenov reported success in passing on the order, and confirmed that no suspicion was apparent as to the reasons behind it.

"Bastards... the fucking bastards... "

Much of what Nazarbayeva had clung to over the last months started to peel away as she understood that her boys had not died for anything but the hate that a man in power bore her, and Stalin's indifference to her suffering and pain.

"Bastards!"

"There is more."

As she looked at Kaganovich, a tear spilled from her left eye.

He knew he had her.

"Please come with me, Tatiana."

She accompanied him to one of the bedrooms, which had been cleared of everything except two chairs and a projector.

She sat down and Kaganovich started the machine rolling.

As soon as the oil lamps came into view she knew what she was about to watch.

The tears rolled down her face as she struggled to maintain control, not against anguish, but against the overwhelming feeling of anger.

She watched as she was defiled by Beria and his colonels, absorbing each bestial act with a harder clench of her teeth and driving her nails into the palms of her hand to distract herself with pain.

The soundtrack provided more horrors, more awfulness...

"I'm sorry, Tatiana..."

She looked at him and his heart chilled in an instant.

Her look was one that he had never seen before but that, somehow, he wholly understood.

She had changed and was no longer the woman she had been when she arrived at the dacha; vulnerable, weak, worn down by her excesses...

Now she was simply a woman who understood what she had been subjected to...

…and what she would do to revenge herself upon those responsible.

Stranov came into the film and subjected her to sexual violation in every way possible.

"I've seen enough, Comrade General."

Nazarbayeva stood and briskly walked out.

Kaganovich switched off the projector and turned to follow, walking straight into the muzzle of Nazarbayeva's automatic.

"What part do you have in this?"

His hands above his shoulders instinctively, Kaganovich felt real fear, for the woman's eyes were cold in her fury.

"None."

"And you have this film how?"

"One of my men found it and brought it to me."

"When?"

"Recently."

"Don't lie. When?"

"A couple of months back, Tati…"

"And you choose to show me now? To give me those documents now! You show me the fucking film now? You're playing me, Comrade General… playing me for your own ends!"

He knew he had no option but to be truthful, for her eyes made it plain that the gun was not just an ornament in the present situation.

"At first, I simply didn't know what to do. And then, when you came into our secret world, it seemed… well… it seemed that if you were told at the right time, you'd be more committed to our cause."

"So, you admit that you intend to use me for your own purposes then?"

"Not like that, Tatiana, it's simply not like that… Mudaks!... yes… it is … but for the right reasons, woman… you must see that?"

"Why the fuck would I see that, Comrade General?"

The pistol drew closer to his face as her rage increased, which did nothing for the watery feeling in Kaganovich's bowels.

"Because we need you so badly. You're the key, the one who can unlock everything so we can take control of the Motherland and save her from these fucking monsters… these men who play with our lives like chessmen on a board."

"I'm the key? How can I be the key, Kaganovich? Do you take me for a fool?"

"He takes you for what you are, Tatiana Nazarbayeva. Now drop the gun."

The new voice carried authority and weight, whoever it was behind her, and she had no doubt that another weapon, possibly more, were trained upon her.

None the less, the Tokarev remained steady, aimed at Kaganovich's nose, unwavering, unshaking, as if frozen in the ice that gripped her heart.

"I tell you now, Comrade General. I trusted you, yes, even a Chekist such as you can earn my trust. If you have deliberately deceived me... if you have any part in this whole affair... my sons... the dacha... I'll kill you. Count on it."

Through the fear that clogged his arteries and veins, and caused his heart to race and lungs to claw at the air, Kaganovich understood something.

As did the man holding the Walther PPK towards Nazarbayeva's back.

'We have her!'

The Tokarev dropped slowly away and Kaganovich drew a deep breath and commenced, as he was convinced, the bonus extra years of his life, for her eyes had shouted at him, preparing him for death at her hands.

The use of his legs was almost lost with the strain of the moment and he staggered away to the nearest seat, using furniture to gain the wooden chair before he dropped into it, drained by the experience.

Khrushchev kept his pistol on the woman, even as she relaxed her posture and slipped the pistol back into its holster.

Behind him, Gorbachev, Gurundov, and Laberova holstered their own weapons and moved into the room, carefully keeping out of Khrushchev's line of fire and away from the woman.

Nazarbayeva's eyes bored into those of Khrushchev and he had a small taste of that which had reduced Kaganovich's legs to jelly.

He reminded himself that this woman was a combat soldier and decided to act more calmly than he was used to.

Khrushchev holstered his weapon.

"Come, Tatiana Sergievna, let us eat. We've much to discuss... and, on a personal note, I'm sorry for the loss of your sons and for... well... you know."

Tatiana did not bother to ask if those present had all seen the film. She cared not any more, for her mind was focussed on other matters.

A car drew up outside, the gravel track announcing its presence.

Gorbachev read her thoughts.

"We were in the dacha next door and walked over, Comrade Nazarbayeva. You couldn't have heard us."

She nodded and reached for a carafe of water, pouring herself a large glass to silently toast her new resolve.

Doors slammed as whoever it was alighted their vehicle. The doorway filled with a man in uniform, a man she instantly recognised.

'VKG! Of course... so simple now...'

"Greetings Comrades! And to you Leytenant General Nazarbayeva."

The man smiled and walked forward and extended his hand.

"I hear there is nothing like Christmas in Krakow, Tatiana."

She took his hand in hers and shook it firmly.

"Except perhaps May Day in Moscow, Comrade Marshal Zhukov."

'VKG... the Victor of Khalkin-Gol...'

He broke the contact and hugged her tight, kissing her on both cheeks, and then moved around his fellow conspirators.

Kaganovich, now nearly recovered, encouraged everyone to take food, which they did, and the conversation, punctuated with the sounds of men consuming a hearty lunch, turned to family and general matters, a precursor to their later more serious discussion.

Laberova stood motionless at the door, and was joined by her twin sister, bearing one of the new AK-47s and looking decidedly menacing.

Security firmly in place, those in the dacha turned from food to talk of revolution.

Nazarbayeva listened and absorbed everything, not as before, to relay to those in authority, but now to understand, all the better to seek a suitable revenge for her and her family, and to rid the Rodina of the vermin who drove her towards destruction.

When talk turned to the moment when power would be wrung from Stalin's grasp, attention seemed to focus on her.

"Comrades, just come out with it. I'm fully committed to this process. Tell me what you want me to do."

They told her, at least the barebones of how they imagined her part playing out.

Silence descended and they held their collective breath.

Nazarbayeva smiled.

"For my sons… for the Motherland… I'll do it."

Hearts skipped a beat and then the hugs started as the final piece in their puzzle fell into place.

In the face of huge pressure by the conspirators, Nazarbayeva allowed herself a small sip of wine to seal the agreement.

"Comrades, if I may ask please?"

Khrushchev, clearly the main man in the organisation, gestured for the others to quieten down.

"When will we act, Comrades?"

The Governor of the Ukraine rubbed his chin in thought.

"That has yet to be decided, Comrade, but perhaps we should look to it now?"

He turned around.

"When can we be ready?"

Zhukov was the key to the timetable and confidently gave his opinion.

"Within the week. I say we utilise our pre-planning and go for it next Saturday, at the earliest."

"Pre-planning, Comrade Marshal?"

Khrushchev spoke up, annoyingly for the army officer, dealing with Nazarbayeva's question.

"We make sure that we have 'meetings' organised, open, innocent meetings that ensure we are where we need to be at certain key times so that we can act if the circumstances are right."

Zhukov interrupted.

"I have rethought this… in two Saturdays we have a full convergence at three o'clock, do we not?"

Kaganovich looked around the room, taking in the shrugs and nods from those assembled.

"Then we are agreed, Comrades? Three o'clock in the afternoon of April 14th, we end this abomination and protect the Motherland."

"Yes!"

So now they all knew the timescale, and how long they had until victory or death at the hands of NKVD butchers.

Kaganovich, Zhukov, and Khrushchev exchanged more furtive looks, for they knew something else as well.

Lo, there do I see my Father...
Lo, there do I see my Mother...
And my Sisters, and my Brothers...
Lo, there do I see the line
Of my people back to the beginning...
They do bid me to take my place among them
In the Halls of Valhalla,
Where the Brave...
may live...
forever.

The 13th Warrior.

Brothers will fight and kill each other,
Sisters' children will defile kinship.
It is harsh in the world,
Whoredom rife,
An axe age, a sword age
Shields are riven,
A wind age, a wolf age
Before the world goes headlong.
No man will have mercy on another.

Vǫluspǫ, The Poetic Edda.

CHAPTER 198 - RAGNARØKKR

1124 hrs, Sunday, 30th March 1947, NATO Headquarters, Leipzig, Germany.

"Any more questions, Gentlemen?"

The final presentation had taken Patton less than fifteen minutes.

The questions from his senior men, and those seconded from Norway and Persia, had taken just over an hour.

"Good. We hit them, and we hit them goddamned hard... and we don't stop hitting them until they raise their hands... and then only maybe."

George Patton chuckled at his own humour, in concert with most of the officers present.

"The bombs'll be dropped... I can't tell you where and why... but they will be dropped... but they may not be enough."

He turned to the huge map and put his hands on his hips like a dictator examining his empire, the markings of the immense coordinated attack loud and clear for all to see.

"We'll hit the bastards everywhere... no respite... no stopping... won't know what's hit 'em."

Turning back round, Patton leant on the table.

"We know we'll lose men, but I want as much done now as we can. What we don't do now will fall to the generations to come, cos communism is a resilient enemy."

There were mumbles of agreement from pretty much every mouth.

"When they give up, I want our front line as close to Moscow as it can be... because we, you and I, won't have another chance like this... and if, sometime in the future, we and the Commies come to blows once more, we won't have the advantages that we have now."

He came erect and set his jaw.

"So, when we attack... in Norway... in Iran... in Siberia...and in Europe... give the bastards hell and don't let up... keep attacking... push them back... and back... and back... otherwise it'll be your grandkids that gotta pay the price of our failure."

The Allies intended to end the war, one way or another....

...commencing at 0500 hrs on the morning of Tuesday, 1st April 1947.

2351 hrs, Sunday, 30th March 1947, headquarters of 1st GMRD, Polanów, Poland.

The commanders remained ramrod straight as Colonel General of Armoured Troops Pavel Rybalko delivered the final orders personally.

Rybalko was a brilliant armoured warfare specialist and his reputation ensured that 3rd Guards Tank Army got the very best men and equipment available.

That best was well represented by the units dedicated to the task of destroying the hated SS legionnaires, a grouping of quality formations temporarily known as Special Combat Group Rybalko.

Its contents were the very finest that Mother Russia could now field.

His own soldiers were from 91st Tank Battalion, soon to be awarded Guards status, and tankers and infantrymen from the 6th

Guards Tank Corps, whose trail of honour ran through most important and bloody battles that the Red Army had fought since Kursk.

Fig # 238 - Soviet forces, Koprzywianka River, Poland.

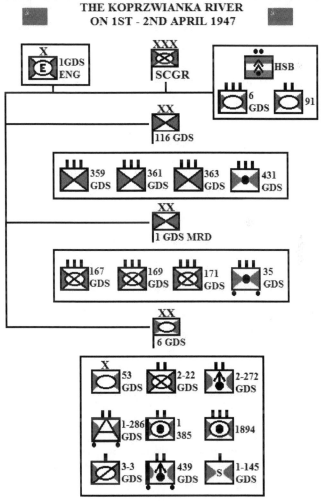

His other units were elite in name and in reputation.

Deniken and his superbly equipped 1st Guards Mechanised Rifle Division.

Chekov and the experienced and steadfast men and women of the 1st Guards Mechanised Assault Engineer Brigade.

Artem'yev and his veteran soldiers of the 116th Guards Rifle Division.

The Hungarian Major Sárközi, whose appearance amongst the elite group had been the subject of unspoken contempt until his soldiers had demonstrated what they could do with their deadly weapons of war.

The youngest and perhaps least experienced of them all, Major Stelmakh, commander of the newly reformed and re-equipped 6th Guards Independent Breakthrough Tank Regiment, not yet a full-size formation but still packing a terrible punch for its size.

The leadership of his units sported more decorations than an assembly of Soviet Marshals and politicians, and, Rybalko thought with no little smugness, his commanders wore honours earned upon the field of battle, not at some party seminar.

Only the Hungarian Sárközi lacked the Hero Award, but he wore his country's own highest award, the Gold Medal for Bravery.

'If courage alone were enough, these men would take me to the beaches of France by themselves!'

He spoke with renewed pride.

"Comrades, the eyes of the Rodina are upon us... upon you! In the years to come, when victories are spoken of in every corner of our lands, it will be this battle... this battle... that is spoken of with greatest reverence. You're all old soldiers here... you need no words to drive you on to victory. Just look after yourselves, use the lives of your soldiers wisely, and victory will be ours!"

"Urrah!"

The operation would commence with Artem'yev's attack at 0200 hrs on Tuesday morning.

2351 hrs, Sunday, 30th March 1947, headquarters, Legion Corps D'Assaut, Grzybów, Poland.

"Then that's all we need, gentlemen."

Knocke and Lavalle relaxed noticeably, the final results of aerial reconnaissance factored into their planning.

The Guards Motorised unit was a problem, but it seemed small in size and not located on the planned route of advance.

Those strange vehicles with the small cylinders on were likely flamethrowers, and would need watching, but were not considered a big problem because of their low numbers.

However, the new enemy heavy tanks, although relatively few in number, required careful thought, some movement of resources, and additional taskings for their air cover.

Their presence had previously been unsuspected and they would prove to be a problem unless the air support could neutralize them early in the battle.

The task given to the Corps D'Assaut had been great, but if the Gods of War played things fair and square then they would achieve their aims and broach the Vistula defences by securing two major crossing points at Tarnobrzeg and Sandomierz, the latter of which still had an operating and decently-sized bridge, contrary to the original intelligence estimate.

Camerone would take the lead, with Alma relegated to support and flank duties, with the 1er Infanterie tasked to make a diversionary attack south of the main assault, and slightly earlier, in order to try and lure any response forces away from the Vistula opposite Camerone, and other units moving along the Vistula keeping pace with Uhlmann's lead group.

Once Sandomierz had fallen then Alma would concentrate upon Tarnobrzeg, with the Legion corps' reserve troops in support.

Undoubtedly Lavalle had relied heavily on his senior commanders, from the tried and trusted tankers such as Uhlmann to the mud pounding infantrymen like St.Clair.

He felt confident that the Corps would do its job, but less confident about the cost.

"Gentlemen, our work is done. I'll inform you of any late changes as soon as I can, but failing a second ice age or biblical visitation, we go at 0500 on the 1st. Any further questions?"

There were none.

"Good luck to you all. I've every confidence in you. Dismissed."

Lavalle watched as they filed out, the combination of French/American uniform and German Knight's Cross and other decorations still difficult to fully grasp, no matter how many times he met his senior commanders.

By prior arrangement, Knocke and St.Clair remained behind.

The three relaxed into seats next to the fire, deliberately away from the table that carried the paperwork of their hopes and fears.

Speaking directly to the flames, Lavalle opened his heart.

"We've all the information we need to make an effective plan… we've made an effective plan… and yet…"

Knocke snorted in amusement, albeit amusement tinged with the anticipation of battle and the horrors it inevitably held.

"We've done the best we can with what we have, Christophe. Camerone can do the job and if we run into difficulties, then Celestin will come and help us out. The river crossing will be hard, but if the paratroopers do their job properly, Sandomierz will fall. It's Tarnobrzeg that worries me more, but we've put plenty of Alma's infantry nearby just in case we need to force passage with more weight."

He inclined his glass to the commander of Alma, who returned the gesture and sampled a sip of the superb Armagnac.

"God knows but we have the men and the equipment to do the job," Lavalle continued, "But I can't help feeling that we've missed something."

Ernst-August Knocke drained the last of his glass and stood.

"Well, we have planned for everything we know about, and anything we suspect. No sense in worrying about the unknown. It'll either bite us in the collective arse tomorrow or amount to nothing at all. Either way, with your permission, General, I'll return to my unit. I need to iron out a few small things and get some sleep before we attack."

The three shook hands without formal ceremony and went their separate ways.

Had they but known it, they were about to lead their men into the gates of hell, and one of the three of them would remain forever in the blood-soaked soil of Southeastern Poland.

0007 hrs, Monday 31st March 1947, Volga River jetty, Camp 1001, Uspenka, USSR.

"Congratulate your men, Comrade Polkovnik. Very professional display. Clearly you've practised this task heavily to achieve such perfection."

Skryabin tried to appear modest as Colonel General Serov lavished praise upon the slick operation that had unfolded in front of his eyes.

Major Durets remained silent, inside fuming that his efforts were being creamed off by his superior. Durets conducted all training for the guard force, from perimeter and rapid response, down to the

568

present task of escort and transfer of inventory items to the Volga River flotilla's camouflaged barges and boats.

For Skryabin, the whole idea of training was a waste of his time, time which was better spent in a perfumed salon in Akhtubinsk in pursuit of pleasures of the flesh, or in the company of senior officers, where he could use his skills to display himself like the proud peacock he was.

Stealing Durets' kudos was natural to him, and he basked in the praise of the senior NKVD general.

"Thirsty work, Comrade Polkovnik General. May I offer you a drink in my quarters?"

"Thank you but no, Comrade Polkovnik. I intend to keep these two beauties close by at all times. I'll leave with the minesweeper directly."

He turned to Durets who stiffened immediately.

"Comrade Mayor Durets. I'll make sure your part in this is well known. Excellent work."

He saluted and Durets understood, even in the reduced light in the bunker entrance, that the look on the general's face spoke of his understanding... that Serov was no fool and knew just who had brought the NKVD guard detachment to peak performance.

"Thank you, Comrade Polkovnik General. We all serve the Rodina as best we can."

Serov laughed and, away from Skryabin's view, winked conspiratorially.

"I wish it were so, Comrade Mayor."

He turned to Skryabin and received a tremendous salute.

"I'll also mention your part in my report, Comrade Polkovnik."

Skryabin was too pleased with himself to fully grasp the hidden meaning.

Serov moved away quickly, followed by his small entourage.

Within minutes, the small minesweeper pulled away with Serov and the scientists on board, leading the way for the barges carrying Obiekts 901 and 902... destination Stakhanovo.

Three hours later, Kaganovich was woken from his sleep with the news that two of the Soviet Union's atomic weapons were on their way to war.

Events started to gather momentum, seemingly developing a life of their own, inexorably bringing together plans and intentions, hopes and fears, risks and actions, on both sides of the divide, all unknowingly started to focus on a point in time some days ahead.

569

Saturday the 14th...
Har Meghiddohn.

0300 hrs, Tuesday, 1st April 1947, Bukowa, Poland.

The rain was constant and extremely heavy which probably contributed to the successes of 116th Guards Infantry Division.

"Alarm! Alarm!"

The shout was taken up by many throats and weapons came to life instantly,

Flares shot into the sky above the waiting vehicles of the Camerone's assault force, highlighting both them and the swarm of Soviet infantry that were already nearly upon them.

Commandant Durand, newly appointed commander of the 1er/1er RdM, was woken from his catnap by the combination of shouts and shots, and immediately understood what was happening before his eyes.

Alongside him the .50cal of the command halftrack burst into life as one of his men started hacking away at the human waves that threatened to wash over them.

He snatched at the radio and got off a quick report, ignoring the sudden spurt of blood that lashed his face as a running legionnaire took a bullet in the head as he passed the vehicle.

His radio message spread throughout Camerone and Alma, but not quick enough for some units, who found themselves moving from peace and quiet to close combat in the blink of an eye.

Artem'yev's men had achieved complete surprise.

Lavalle listened to Knocke's words, the telephone adequately conveying the strain that the sneak enemy attack had placed on both man and plan.

"And what do you intend, Général Knocke?"

He listened as he fumbled for a cigarette, understanding the words and trying to fix them to his mental map of the battleground.

"Yes... yes... I agree... we may have an opportunity here... yes, liaise with him direct, with my authority... of course... no... I'll inform our German Allies...Jurkowice you say?"

Now he needed a map, although he was sure he understood.

"Moment."

570

He moved round the large desk, inadvertently dragging the telephone box off the polished surface.

Fig # 239 - Allied forces, KOPRZYWIANKA River, Poland.

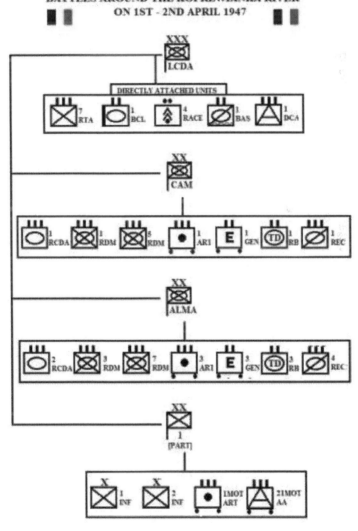

FORCES OF THE LEGION CORPS D'ASSAUT AND SUPPORTING UNITS ENGAGED IN COMBAT DURING THE BATTLES AROUND THE KOPRZWIANKA RIVER ON 1ST - 2ND APRIL 1947

It clattered to the floor and Lavalle feared he had lost the connection.

"Ernst?"

He breathed a sigh of relief and turned the map the right way round.

"Thank God. Yes... Włostów... no further.... I agree... I'll ask them to have a response force positioned there as soon as possible... yes, Route 77... yes, of course, and any artillery support... I don't know how the rain will affect that. I've yet to contact air... let's hope not, Général."

He pondered the question for the moment.

"Unless we have good reason, I say use this opportunity. The attack order stands until I rescind it, Général Knocke... no... use any resources you need to deal with this incursion in the first instance... we will adapt... yes indeed, no plan survives first contact... bravo!"

Lavalle smiled.

'So typical of the man. What a soldier!'

"And to you Général Knocke. Stay safe."

He replaced the receiver, having committed his forces to use the enemy's attack to his advantage, to overcome it, and continue their own drive on the Vistula.

Suddenly, Lavalle felt the weight lifted, the suspicion that had troubled him previously had declared itself and was now addressed, and the enemy's attack would now be used against him, as his soldiers were now out in the open, not in prepared positions from which they would need winkling at greater cost.

All in all, despite initial losses amongst his forward assault units, not a bad exchange.

0219 hrs, Tuesday. 1st April 1947, headquarters, 116th Guards Rifle Division, Koprzywnica, Poland.

"No, Comrade Mayor, withdraw now... that's an order."

Artem'yev pointed to the situation map, drawing Deniken's eyes to where the Major in question sought to press home his attack.

"No, Mayor. You're the only one having successes. We've run into a prepared enemy. Call off your attack and withdraw to your start position... now, Sokolov...now!"

Żyznów had almost fallen before the assault of one of Artem'yev's battalions and the keen commander had wanted to press on and occupy the village.

In fairness, Artem'yev conceded, the man does not know the full picture.

Satisfied with the response, he tossed the handset back to his radio operator and turned back to Deniken.

"Without a doubt, Comrade General, we've run into forces that were preparing to assault us. My casualties are bad but the plan's running, young Sokolov aside."

Fig # 240 - The battleground, Koprzywianka River, Poland.

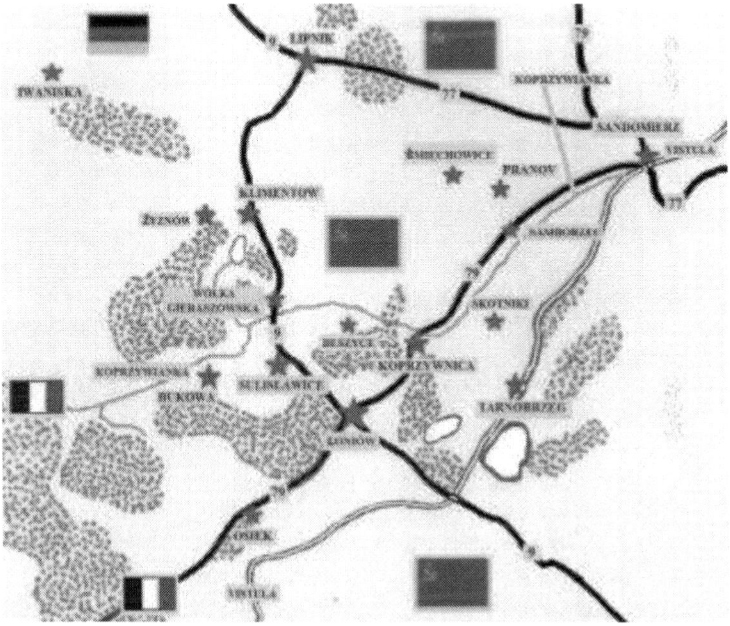

He waved his hand in the direction of the radio.

Deniken studied the map in silence.

Artem'yev took a long swig from a water bottle and joined him.

"I think we have a problem in that our timings are going to be totally fucked up, Comrade General... but... our plan to draw them on is going to work because they already intended to come."

Deniken nodded and accepted the water bottle and slaked his own mounting thirst.

'Nerves?'

Artem'yev read his thoughts.

573

"I always get thirsty in combat myself, Comrade General."

"New one to me, Comrade Polkovnik. Perhaps the weight of command, eh?"

The infantryman accepted the water bottle back with a smile.

"Yes, Comrade… they will come on… but they won't be as vulnerable as we hoped. They'll be prepared for an advance, so things'll be more difficult. None the less, the opportunity to destroy the SS bastards is here and we'll seize upon it. Your assessment of our new timetable?"

Artem'yev looked at the distances involved and made a swift calculation.

"The SS of old would be up my arse in an instant… these bastards have the same reputation… they'll take what they see as an opportunity and come on hard and fast… I'll be back on the Klimontów line within the hour… units will filter in bit by bit but it will be established by 0330, no later."

Deniken made his notes as the older man spoke.

"Here the trick will be not to retreat in such a way as to make them suspect anything… but fast enough to preserve my boys… I'm thinking 0430 to be back on the Śmiechowice to Samborzec defensive line."

Nearby artillery hammered into the ground, dropping a few specks of earth across the maps.

The two grinned at each other.

"Like the SS bastards of old."

"We beat them once. We'll do it again, Comrade General."

Deniken slapped his comrade on the shoulder.

"We will indeed… but only if we get this right. 0430 it is… I'll hold you to that, Comrade. Keep them interested… keep them coming on… and at 0430, I'll unleash the very devil upon them."

They shook hands and Deniken rushed out into the darkness to make it back to his own headquarters before daylight brought the enemy's aircraft buzzing round.

As his staff car leapt away, the night sky was riven by yet more enemy artillery as Camerone reacted to the 116th's attack with its own advance.

Involuntarily he shivered, although both the morning and rain were warm enough.

'Like the SS bastards of old… a hard day ahead…'

He shivered again, for he suspected that the Devil would accommodate both sides this day.

Knocke examined the map and was cautiously pleased.

He wasn't quite sure where the caution came from, for his main assault element was driving the enemy before them, not allowing them to settle into any defensive positions.

But the caution was there, an almost instinctive thing that made him examine the battlefield further afield.

Two of his three assault groups were now engaged, with only Haefali's 3^e Group as yet unblooded.

Uhlmann's 1er Group was leading the way towards Koprzywnica, with Haefali's men tucked in behind, ready for their phase to start.

Emmercy's 2^e Group were already investing Klimontów on the left flank, although the retreating Red Army were less inclined to give ground in that area than to the south, where larger inroads were being made.

The DRH forces, drawn from the Grossdeutschland Division, were advancing into the enemy lines and were well advanced down Route 74.

A battlegroup had already occupied the key position at Włostów, and would soon be in possession of the key junction at Lipnik, which meant that Route 77 would become available for Emmercy, once he had overcome resistance in Klimontów.

Up against the Vistula, the assault elements of Alma were moving steadily forward, maintaining pace with Uhlmann's advance in order to keep the Camerone legionnaires' left flank secure.

Everything was going well.

And yet...

'I'll move up now... get Truffaux up with the divisional reserves... Route 9... just south of Wólka Gieraszowska... yes... yes, that'll do... but into a defensive posture I think...'

He wished the Corps' reserves were closer up but that was beyond his capabilities.

'What's the problem here?'

Knocke senses were alive with the scent of danger.

Morning would hopefully bring aerial reconnaissance information that would make the smell go away, but for now he pondered the map and the continuing reports, seeking the thing that troubled him.

Lavalle had his own suspicions and decided to do something outside the plan.

Only a small adjustment but once it was done he would feel easier.

"Colonel… Knocke will need some support I think so order Général Renat-Challes to move the Corps' reserve units forward now. I want them at Sulisławice immediately… on and around the junction of Floriańska with Route 9. Also inform Général Knocke of my actions."

The new CoS questioned him with a quiet look.

"Yes, Maurice, I know. It's far forward but I want it done. And remind Général St.Clair that I want Alma sticking to Camerone's right flank like glue."

The man moved away to get Lavalle's words transformed into action.

Somehow he felt easier for the call, and recalled the words of one of his instructors at St Cyr.

'Small decisions can sometimes affect great enterprises.'

Not that he knew it, but between them Lavalle and Knocke had just saved their Corps from annihilation.

0321 hrs, Tuesday, 1st April 1947, two kilometres northeast of Koprzywnica, Poland.

The artillery fire was provided a constant 'strobe effect' of lighting for the Legion's forces to advance.

Although not all were going forward.

Uhlmann's tank was pulled over under a stand of trees as his driver checked the problem that was dogging the engine performance.

Whilst the regimental commander was delighted with most aspects of his Schwarzpanther, even though it was not one of the turbine versions that the DRH was equipping with, he was less than enamoured with its reliability, something his crew sweated over often.

The old problems with overheating and engine fires had been solved in peacetime, but the new beast suffered from electrical issues and often transmission problems, the latter of which often meant a tank lost until it was recovered, or at least in the workshops for a long time.

"Wiring loom, Obersturmbannführer."

The driver dropped back into his hatch and the engine turned over first time.

Uhlmann ordered the tank back into line and joined the column just behind the tank belonging to his senior NCO and friend, once a Sturmscharführer of the SS Wiking Division.

Braun recognised his commander's tank by its markings and waved respectfully to the indistinct figure in the cupola.

Ahead of them, the recon element, 1er/1er REC, had just lost one of their few antelope, the match of SDKFZ 251 hull and Puma turret falling foul of an enemy anti-tank gun.

Uhlmann listened as reports flooded in and orders were given, the lead elements of his advance deploying swiftly to isolate the problem and permit the advance to continue.

A handful of Soviet dead caught his eye, the obvious signs of clothing disruption betraying the looting of their corpses by others ahead in line.

They were prime men, who apart from the obvious evidence of traumatic death, looked fit and well fed.

'Fit... well fed...'

The radio overrode his thoughts with calls to arms, as ahead the battle grew fiercer.

'They've decided to stick then... now why is that... Samborzec?...'

He dropped into the turret and examined his map, seeing the notations that might or might not refer to possible defensive works on a line centring on Samborzec, and running northwest to southeast.

'Let's make that definite then... they are defensive positions... right... I'll move the RdM units to...'

"What the fuck did he just say?"

His attention transferred from map to headset in an instant.

The desperate commander of the 3^e RdM, Alma's lead unit, called for help once more.

'At Skotniki... tanks... merde... on our flank... there should be no tanks...'

Reports assailed his ears as the night sky started to flare up badly on his right flank, precisely where Alma ran into something unexpected.

Taking a few moments to examine the tactical position, Uhlmann debated two courses of action and elected for positive action on both fronts.

He ordered the advance to continue, but switched Braun's oversized tank platoon, part of 1er/1er RdM, and the 1st AT company to move towards the flank of the obstacle that presented to Alma, seeking to relieve the pressure that seemed to be bearing down on his sister division.

Exactly as Colonel General Rybalko had hoped.

As Uhlmann's forces split their focus, the Soviet retreat turned into a counter-attack of monumental proportions.

Two factors proved vital.

Firstly, the lead units of the DRH's Grossdeutschland had not secured the main road junction at Lipnik, as the leaders of the Corps D'Assaut had been informed, which meant that the left flank was not only insecure, but in an extremely precarious position.

Secondly, Ernst-August Knocke had positioned both himself and his reserve force at Sulisławice, a small backwater soon to enter into the annals of Legion history.

All along the front, flares and star shells brought day light to the battlefield as men died in their scores.

Fig # 241 - Legion Corps D'Assaut radio call signs.

RADIO CALL SIGNS FOR UNITS OF THE LEGION CORPS D'ASSAUT					
CAMERONE		ALMA		SUPPORTING UNITS	
DHQ	ANTON	DHQ	KLINGE	4 RACE	ZEBRA
1 RCDA	BERTA	2 RCDA	BÄR	7 RTA	WOLF
1 RDM	LEOPARD	3 RDM	MAUS	1 BCL	REH
5 RDM	GELBKOPF	7 RDM	ROTKOPF	1 BAS	WAL
1 ART	SCHNEKE	3 ART	ELEFANT	1 DCA	FUCHS
1 GEN	LAMA	3 GEN	PINGUIN	1 INF	CIDRE
1 RB	HUND	3 RB	KÄTZCHEN	2 INF	CASSIS
1 REC	FISCH	4 REC	PFERD	1 MOT ART	KIR
AIR LIAISON	ADLER	AIR LIAISON	ORKAN	21 MOT AA	CHARTREUSE

0331 hrs, Tuesday. 1st April 1947, Route 79, three kilometres northeast of Koprzywnica, Poland.

"All received and understood, Anton-two. Berta-six out."

Uhlmann had an aversion to retreating, something men of his breed shared, but he was also wise enough to understand that, no matter how good his men or equipment were, there were times when the enemy would have their day.

The situation had clarified itself very quickly, as Alma's lead units found themselves entwined in prepared defensive positions and tanks, all of which meant that his flank support had been temporarily lost.

The relocation of Braun's small battlegroup, actually Durand's battlegroup, as the 1er's battalion commander had joined the small force and taken personal command, was still ongoing, but Alma's reports of counterattacks made by flame-throwing engineers and medium tanks meant that the attempt to turn the Soviet's own flank was dead before it started.

That, and the order he had just received from Anton-two, Colonel D'Estlain, the acting CoS for Camerone, which halted his force's advance and required a realignment to remain butted-up to Alma's under pressure forces.

'Realignment equals retreat in my fucking book... but the Oberführer knows what he's doing.'

"Berta, Berta, Leopard-zero, over!"

"Leopard-zero, Berta receiving, over."

"Berta, Leopard-zero. Heavily engaged by tanks, infantry, and rockets, five hundred metres west of Skotniki. Four vehicles and three personnel carriers destroyed. Unable to advance. Over."

From memory, Uhlmann could place Skotniki and worked out that Durand must have crossed the river.

He made an instant decision.

"Leopard-zero, Berta. Withdraw immediately to the river line and hold. Understood? Over."

"Berta, Leopard-zero, Understood. Unable to contact Dora units, over."

A momentary chill pierced Uhlmann's heart.

"Leopard-zero, Berta. Understood. Wait out."

He switched to his regimental frequency.

"Dora-one-one, Dora-one-one, Berta, receiving, over."

"Berta, Dora-one-one, receiving, over."

Uhlmann's relieved exhalation of breath carried into the airwaves as he transmitted the retreat order and advised Brain of the loss of communications with Durand,

"Berta, order understood... tank to front, left three, two hundred, fire when on!"

The close encounter played out over the radio net as Braun forgot to stop broadcasting.

"Good shot, hard kill... driver... back up slowly... shit."

The radio went dead for the briefest of moments, long enough to make Uhlmann's heart skip a beat or three.

"Berta, Dora-one-one. Apologies...Recruit's disease. Order understood and executing. Dora-one-one out."

Braun switched to his platoon net and ordered the surviving five tanks back to the river line, where the enemy tide would be more easily halted.

He also confirmed the orders with the AT company commander, who reluctantly started to give ground, leaving behind three of his Schwarzjagdpanthers.

Back in the main attack area, Uhlmann, operating well to the left flank of his force, ordered his Schwarzpanther in behind a well-tended square bush, almost perfectly Panther-sized, so he could update his map and make sure his orders were correct.

The ground was lower and the vehicle nestled into a small depression... 'that's perfect'...and the engine immediately died.

The driver disappeared to resolve the matter, accompanied by the loader whose speciality had once been bicycles.

As Uhlmann spread the map on the top of the turret and covered himself with a zeltbahn to hide the pen light, the other crew took the opportunity to refresh themselves and smoke.

0334 hrs, Tuesday. 1st April 1947, Route 79, four kilometres northeast of Koprzywnica, Poland.

"Are you sure?"

"Absolutely, Comrade Mayor."

Kalinov, drenched with rain, reseated himself, having been allowed to get out of the tank for a call of nature, during which he had seen movement in the semi-darkness of the night battle.

His tank, an IS-III, was concealed along with the rest of the 6th Guards Independent Breakthrough Tank Regiment, a greatly reduced formation in terms of size, but one that packed a considerable punch.

"We'll remember him if he stays but we're under fire discipline so just line him up, Oleg."

Ferensky, the gunner, whispered with his loader and brought the 122mm gun to bear on the square hedge that Kalinov described.

The 6th had stayed silent as a considerable enemy force had passed under its guns, all part of the plan that intended to do the enemy units the maximum amount of harm.

The debate on ammunition reached Stelmakh's ears.

"What's the problem, Comrades?"

"Comrade Mayor, we've HEAT loaded but I recommend we switch to solid shot."

Stelmakh understood Kalinov's concern, although his gunner was confident that the hedge would not prematurely detonate the HEAT shell.

Stelmakh was inclined to change but consulted his gunner anyway.

"Oleg, can we be certain?"

"Well... I s'pose not, Comrade Mayor. The AP would certainly go through but I've fired through bushes with HEAT before without problems so..."

"No chances then... load AP, Comrades. We take no chances tonight."

There was no further discussion and Kalinov began the task of changing rounds, made more delicate an operation because of the two-part ammunition.

The task had been completed and another round of cigarettes had been consumed before Stelmakh's radio crackled into life.

"Chorniy-odin, Chorniy-odin, Zimniy Dvorets... execute, execute, execute, over."

'Shit... here we go!'

"All units Chorniy, all units Chorniy, plan one, repeat, advance plan one...commence attack, repeat, commence attack... out."

Stelmakh switched his focus to his gunner.

"Are you on that target, Oleg?"

"Yes, Comrade Mayor."

"Fire!"

"Firing!"

The 122mm breech leapt back as the massive gun sent a solid shot down range, aimed at the square hedge behind which the loader had claimed to see an enemy Panther tank.

0340 hrs, Tuesday, 1st April 1947, Route 79, three kilometres northeast of Koprzywnica, Poland.

Serzhant Oleg Ferensky was a superb gunner, with years of experience.

His aim was perfect but still flawed, as he did not know that the Panther was sat lower because of the scrape in the ground in which it had descended.

As a result, the heavy shell missed the tank and screamed over the top of the turret.

None the less, it did good work.

The 1[er] RCDA was decapitated...

... as was Rolf Uhlmann.

"Berta, Berta, this is Anton, come in, over."

For the eighth time, the radio waves remained silent.

Knocke held himself in check, willing the commander of his tank regiment to come back online, but sensing that another comrade had been lost to the dogs of war.

"Enough. Try the second in command again."

"Berta-two, Berta-two, Anton, over."

The silence held unmistakable portents of doom.

Knocke looked at the situation map and calmly thought through the whole action, taking in each change

He looked back to the signallers as the radio continued to crackle with reports of heavy fighting.

The action all focussed upon the area in which Uhlmann's assault force was engaged, and in the Alma zone, where units of the other division should have been providing a link between Camerone and the Vistula.

Knocke ordered Haefali's force to Koprzywnica but no further, something that drew D'Estlain back to the table once he had passed the order.

"Why no further, mon Général? Surely Haefali's presence would help stiffen Uhlmann's force?"

"I think we've moved well beyond that point now, Alphonse. This isn't an accident... we've walked into a strong enemy force here... they've concealed themselves... everything makes me think this is a trap and I'm going to get us out of this before we think about how to go forward again."

The radio brought forward more urgent voices, and both senior men stopped their discussion to listen in.

"Merde!"

D'Estlain moved towards the radio group to make certain he was hearing what he thought he was hearing, whilst Knocke took advantage of the moment to pour a glass of water.

Being away from the radios meant he heard more in some strange way, as his CoS was focussed on reports from Haefali.

Knocke's attention was on a report from their running mate in the DRH, the Grossdeutschland Division.

He sprang across the room and put his hand on the radio operator's shoulder.

"Confirm that report immediately."

The report was repeated and Knocke saw the death of his division laid bare in the words.

He was back at the map in the blink of an eye, accompanied by D'Estlain.

"Alphonse, we have a problem... a big problem. Grossdeutschland have reported a strong enemy thrust battered to a halt roughly half a kilometre from Włostów... here!"

"Mon Dieu!"

The point of the enemy advance was well beyond the key junction at Lipnik.

"No time to lose. Urgently request Leroy-Bessette to send his 1er Brigade to the area here... I want them to link with Grossdeutschland here and with Emmercy here. I'll sort that out with General Lavalle but make sure Leroy-Bessette gets his men moving quickly. Emmercy's units to hold in place, and orient for defence to the north, northeast, and east. Haefali is to orient..."

"Sir, Haefali's report had him under artillery fire with an enemy force approaching from the north and northwest."

"What?"

"He's here... at Koprzywnica... I believe he's got enemy moving down Route 758... here... and the north... this way."

"Verdammt normal! The bastards have flanked us already!"

Knocke's loud expression of emotion was enough to guarantee that anyone who hadn't grasped the seriousness of the situation was now fully aware.

"Right... I'll ask General Lavalle to deploy the rest of Alma along the line at ŁONIÓW... we'll use Route 9 as our backstop

583

line. Meanwhile, get Uhlmann's force back to Haefali and defend Koprzywnica until otherwise ordered. I need more information from there and I need it now."

There was an obvious problem that hadn't yet been addressed.

"I want the recon force in 7ᵉ RTA to check out the area here," he pointed to a circle that included Postronna and Zbigniewice.

"I want to know if there's anything of substance sat in there."

D'Estlain finished his notes.

"Shall we prepare to move back, mon Général?"

Knocke shook his head.

"No. I need to be close to this and, as things stand... and for all I know... enemy forces could be on their way here right now... and if so we're all the division has between it and destruction. We'll stay here, Alphonse."

A signal NCO interrupted their discussion.

"Sorry, mon Général, but Général Lavalle's on the telephone and insists on speaking to you immediately."

Knocke accepted the interruption with a nod.

"Alphonse, get our men moving quickly now."

"Oui, mon Général."

"Knocke."

He listened intently as Lavalle apprised him of the problems with Grossdeutschland's failure to push forward, and then requested the release of the 1ᵉʳ Division's infantry to protect the gap between the DRH division and Emmercy's group.

He was more than surprised when it was not given to him, as Leroy-Bessette's men had other fish to fry and Lavalle had an alternative organised already.

'Iwaniska?'

Consulting the map, he found the small village and measured the distance to the position he wanted the covering force to be, judging that it would be there quicker than the French infantry, although in smaller numbers.

The DRH's 101 Korps' commander, the parent unit for the Grossdeutschland Division, had allocated a powerful mobile force to plug the potential gap, mainly out of contrition for his premier unit's failure.

An all-arms Kampfgruppe was already en route from Iwaniska, which addressed part of Knocke's problems.

He felt his orders would address most of the other issues, but above all, Camerone was exposed and short of information on enemy deployments and numbers.

The DRH paratroopers had, quite rightly, been called back, as their operation would have simply resulted in their total destruction.

0457 hrs, Tuesday, 1st April 1947, five hundred metres south of Wólka Gieraszowska, Poland.

Uhlmann's death had been confirmed.

A matter of fact message had arrived stating that the commander of the 1er RCDA had fallen, sent by its highest remaining rank and, by default, commander of the regiment.

The man was an ex-Hauptsturmführer from Hohenstaufen and a steady, if unspectacular commander.

It was not until after the battle that Knocke found out how Uhlmann had lost his last battle, and how the old soldier's headless body had been brought back in a badly damaged Panther with only two living crewmembers.

The loss of experienced longstanding comrades like Uhlmann was keenly felt, not the least by Braun, who understood the silent radio for what it was, and who cried inside and out as he slugged it out with his tank on the banks of the Koprzywianka.

His tears were as silent as his rage, but he fought his tank like a demon and nothing with a Red Star on could live within range of his guns.

For now, the right flank of the assault group was secure.

Not that it mattered any more.

Knocke had already decided that Uhlmann's group, he couldn't think of it in other terms yet, would have to be pulled all the way back, given the increasing pressure upon Haefali's lines to the north and northwest, and the inroads being made into the main positions on Route 79.

No matter what he had tried, Camerone was being pushed back and better he pull back in an organised fashion than be beaten back in chaos.

The order went out to perform a fighting withdrawal all the way to Route 9, down the main routes leading to safety and the hastily prepared defensive line.

Haefali assumed command of the two combined forces and started one of the most difficult of military operations; a fighting withdrawal under pressure from a superior enemy whilst maintaining a constant and impenetrable defensive line.

For the most part the action was brilliantly conducted, except at Beszyce, where superior Soviet firepower blasted a way through the legionnaires and opened the way to the junction of Floriańska and Route 9…. at Sulisławice.

0458 hrs, Tuesday. 1st April 1947, Koprzywnica, Poland.

"Speed it up, Comrades. We must get back in the fight. Come on! Come on!"

Grabbing the offered propellant charge, Stelmakh hefted it and raised it up to the waiting hands of his gunner, Ferensky.

The IS-III had exhausted its supply of shells and managed to rendezvous with the supply train in the recently occupied Polish town.

"Dawai! Dawai!"

Unlike many officers, certainly regimental commanders, Stelmakh was sweating and grunting with his men, undertaking the heavy task of replenishing the tank's twenty-eight heavy shells and grabbing as much machine-gun ammunition as possible.

Stelmakh himself had expended every 12.7mm bullet from his roof-mounted weapon, and the tank had pulled into the replenishment point with one 122mm HE shell and seventeen 7.62mm to her name.

Over as quickly as it had begun, the tank was rearmed, and Stepanov moved her to the bowsers to top off the greedy tanks with as much fuel as he could cram aboard.

All told, the 6th Guards had come off extremely lightly so far, especially given the high-tempo of the fighting so far.

Two of the IS-IVs and one IS-VII had been lost, the latter to an enemy artillery shell that caused the heavy tank to come apart in spectacular fashion.

Even adding in the loss of the other IS-III and another IS-IV to mechanical failure, Stelmakh was still in command of a powerful mixed force of thirteen heavy tanks and an SMG company.

Following a change of orders, the 6th moved off down the Floriańska towards the breach in the Legion line.

0520 hrs, Tuesday. 1st April 1947, west of Kamieniec. Poland.

Chekov was inspired by the news that his 2nd Battalion had opened up a portion of the enemy's line, permitting the uncommitted units of 91st Tank Battalion to flood through and into the disorganised legion interior.

On his right flank, the 116th Guards Division's 359th Guards Rifle Regiment, temporarily under his direct command following its organised retreat, held firm against efforts from two directions, where they held a small bridge over the Koprzywnica just under three hundred metres away from the main escape route of the furthest advanced enemy group.

He had ordered forward the rest of his brigade's anti-tank weapons, as well as the Hungarian Mace group, intent on making the road a killing zone.

To his front, his men were now moving through the area hammered by the Katyusha of 272nd Guards Mortar regiment and, according to reports, the enemy soldiers had been slaughtered in their droves as they tried to withdraw.

Indeed, St.Clair's 3ᵉ RdM had suffered nearly 30% casualties since it started its advance and was short of everything a soldier needs in battle... save courage.

His joy turned to anger as new reports from the advance spoke of burning T34s and a fanatical resistance that started to eat up his two lead battalions; the 2nd and 3rd.

Chekov ordered his old but effective OT-34s to relocate and mentally dared the enemy soldiers to stand before their awful weapons.

Flamethrowers had the capacity to deprive even the bravest of souls of any will to fight.

The leadership of his Third Battalion had already changed twice during the battle, and the latest report placed the unit in the hands of the one-eyed woman; namely Viktoriya Vladimira Fedorensky-Batavska.

She had once been a staff officer within the Main Administration for Military Engineers, and served with great distinction during the battles in and around Stalingrad, firstly on the cutters and launches that plied their desperate trade back and forth across the icy water, and subsequently as a frontline soldier alongside Rotmistrov's guardsmen on the Mamayev Kurgan and in the rubble of the Red October factory, in which place she left behind her right eye, two fingers from her left hand, and a considerable portion of her left buttock.

Behind her back she was known as 'Pirat'; to her face she was simply Captain Batavska, and she was greatly feared.

Not the least of which reasons was because she was wholly mad.

None the less, Chekov ordered her to continue to push forward, promising reinforcements to maintain her advance towards her first objective; cutting Route 758 northwest of Tarnobrzeg.

He was confident she would do it, and returned his attention to the anti-tank gun position that was increasingly becoming a hornet's nest.

"Lev!"

His second in command was quickly by his side.

"I'm going forward to assess the river bridge defence. I'll take a platoon of the SMG company with me for security. Keep pressing forward here and here. Comrade General Rybalko'll be placing more troops under our command shortly. Use them as you see fit, but keep the rest of our headquarters units, and the reserve company of the 91st Tanks uncommitted, just in case I need them at the bridge."

Lev Kharsen nodded his understanding and made a quick assessment.

"I see no problems except here," he pointed to the stiffening resistance that had already cost the 91st Tanks a number of vehicles.

"Yes... I've sent the heavy flamethrowers forward now that they've topped up. That should fuck the bastards right off."

"That ought to do it, Comrade Polkovnik, although they'll be vulnerable if the 91st aren't up to the mark."

"Understood."

It was a small problem, in that they had been given no opportunity to understand their new running mates, and vice versa, but thus far the tankers seemed to be doing their job.

"Keep the boys at it, Lev. I'll be back as soon as I've made my assessment."

He slapped his man on the shoulder and moved away, nodding to the waiting Iska who had assembled the necessary men as soon as he heard his commander's words.

Four vehicles stood waiting, two each of captured US halftracks and BTR-152s, and the group raced away towards the increasing sounds of fighting on the Koprzywnica, some two kilometres away.

As the machines bumped down the scarcely identifiable track, Chekov accepted a cigarette from his senior NCO.

"So, that's a platoon is it?"

"You know me, Comrade Polkovnik... never been able to count."

"Only bottles and cigarettes anyway."

"No problems on that score, Comrade Polkovnik. Anyway, there's safety in numbers and we can't have you getting your uniform dirty, now can we?"

"Cheeky bastard NCOs can be reassigned, Comrade Praporschik!"

They shared a laugh, and left some things unsaid, as the rain stopped and the first strands of dawn declared themselves in the lightening sky.

0530 hrs, Tuesday, 1st April 1947, the Koprzywianka Bridge, four hundred metres southeast of Sośniczany, Poland.

Wary of attracting unnecessary attention, Chekov and his men dismounted at a road junction and jogged the rest of the way forward, where they found Sárközi putting the final touches to his unit's deployment.

He and the 359th Guards' battalion commander quickly filled the Colonel in on deployments and Chekov was very soon satisfied that the men knew their trade.

Across a front of roughly eight hundred metres, the position bristled with anti-tank guns and dug-in infantry, with the MACE launchers more concentrated around the bridge, in case the enemy developed any more ideas of crossing the watercourse.

As Chekov scanned the positions through his binoculars, he was the first to sense a movement in the receding shadows, his suspicions quickly confirmed by observers in the forward infantry positions.

Veteran instincts took over and men threw themselves into cover just as a rapid mortar strike washed over the part of the defensive area directly opposite the Legion infantry attack.

The strained silence of waiting was punctuated by mortar shells bursting and the screams of wounded men, and then destroyed totally as the defensive line erupted with machine-gun and rifle fire.

On the heights on the other side of Route 79, which ran between the two positions, larger weapons started bringing the Soviet force under fire, attracting a reply from some of the anti-tank guns.

The battle started to escalate as both sides added artillery to the inventory, and within minutes the whole area was bathed in explosions, smoke, and high-speed metal.

Just off to one side from Chekov's position, an 85mm D-44 anti-tank gun added parts of itself to the storm of steel as a Legion artillery shell struck home.

Chekov gripped his binoculars tightly as he watched brave men rush forward to pull some wounded men clear of the position and into relative safety.

Some were cut down by mortar shrapnel, but the three wounded men were dragged into the trenches in record time.

Runners arrived from all parts of the infantry battalion's front, the absence of proper communications equipment a surprise to Chekov.

He ducked down below the sandbags.

"Where's your communications, Comrade Mayor?"

"We have one radio only, Comrade Polkovnik. We had to leave much of it behind and our signals vehicle was destroyed by enemy artillery."

Chekov nodded and beckoned Iska forward.

"Get the field telephone equipment out of our headquarters vehicle... all of it... turn it over to the infantry commander. He has need of it."

Iska nodded and moved away, tapping two men on the shoulders as he went.

The three waited for the next set of landings before setting off to retrieve the equipment.

"Comrade Mayor, my men are getting you some telephones and cable... should help you control your battalion better."

The weary man grinned, a cigarette hanging from the corner of a bloody mouth.

"Thank you, Comrade Polkovnik. We were too good at retreating and... well... we'll get it all back shortly."

Another runner arrived and reported to the Major, who clutched his wounded side as he rose up and followed the line down which the NCO pointed.

He slapped the man on the back in gratitude and issued him with orders before sending him back out into the man-made storm.

"Comrade Mayor Sárközi, your time has come I think!"

The Hungarian moved quickly to the infantryman's side and followed the sweep of the man's binoculars with his own.

Chekov joined them and they immediately understood why the infantry attack was in progress.

"Infantry's nothing but a distraction attack," Sárközi said to no one in particular.

"My guns'll engage this new enemy when you do, until then we'll keep on at the bastards on the hills across the road... make it look like we haven't seen them."

590

The two laid their plans seemingly oblivious to the presence of the more senior man.

Not that Chekov cared, for the two clearly knew their trade.

Sárközi scurried away to prepare his ambush and the infantry major, one of remnants of Makarenko's paratrooper division long disbanded to bolster the 116th Division, sent runners out into the growing dawn.

0539 hrs, Tuesday, 1st April 1947, Route 79, five hundred metres east of Sośniczany, Poland.

The $2^e/1^{er}$ Genie led the way with their combination of lorries and halftracks, closely followed by the handful of tanks from the headquarters of 1er RDCA, including their dead commander's vehicle and its grisly cargo.

Sárközi instructed his crews not to engage the softer vehicles, not that they needed such instruction, but he reasoned that such orders were better safe than sorry.

Judging that there were enough hard targets in range, he used the Hungarian's radio system to allocate targets to each launcher.

Patiently waiting to ensure the best chances of success, he remained focussed on the moving tanks, not on the growing exchange across the river.

'Steady... steady... now.'

"Fire!"

Eight MACE rockets were on their way in the blink of an eye and he watched in awe, still capable of being fascinated by the fiery trails that spelt doom for the enemy encased in their steel targets.

Six hit, and all but two of them were transformed into fiery wreckage in an instant.

The engineer's anti-tank guns opened up and the Legion engineer company took some serious knocks, even though they were moving in and out of cover in their bid to escape the decreasing pocket.

Officers called in contact reports, some calm and collected, others clearly panicking, as the prospect of encirclement and annihilation reared its ugly head.

Seven more rockets were released, causing the Hungarian officer to seek out the eighth launcher and quickly finding it on its side and surrounded by inert forms.

The MACE launchers were now all mounted on GAZ jeeps for swiftness of redeployment, and his crews needed no orders to get them moving to alternate positions.

591

Once they were relocated, their crews swiftly reamed the launchers with more rockets, ready to take on whatever else might come down the road.

Of the RDCA's headquarters, only two vehicles had escaped unscathed, the rest, tanks and personnel carriers, lay smashed and broken on Route 79.

Less than 30% of the Legion engineer company escaped out of gun range, and even then, Soviet mortars pursued them off the battlefield.

The rest of Uhlmann's assault group was cornered and unable to move back.

0546 hrs, Tuesday. 1st April 1947, Szewce, Poland.

"Fire!"

The 88mm gun rocked back hard on its mount and sent a killing shot down the road, one that took the turret clean off one of the pursuing T34s.

"Good kill!"

Even though he only had half an eye on the battle, Braun was impressed with the gunner's skill, and not for the first time this day.

The sounds of distress on the radio were growing, and he left his crew to fight the immediate battle while he consulted his map.

From garbled cries for help, calm reports, and a veteran's intuition, Braun constructed an understanding of the situation.

'Hurensohn!'

His mind was made up in an instant and the radio crackled as he made contact with the AT commander.

The Captain thought Braun mad but went no further, other than to agree to the plan and wish him luck.

Durand went further, and dispatched two halftracks to accompany Braun on the crazy mission.

The five Schwarzpanthers and two M5 halftracks turned off Route 79 and charged straight towards the small bridge to the southeast, catching the defenders off-guard.

Expecting the Legionnaires to simply follow Route 79, the company of 116th Guardsmen and their AT support were swiftly overrun, and Braun led his small force on the first part of the four-kilometre drive to save the trapped force at Sośniczany.

0546 hrs, Tuesday, 1st April 1946, Route 79, Poland.

It was a surprise to everyone, Soviet and Legionnaire alike, that the first aircraft to appear over the battlefield bore a Red Star.

A ground attack unit of the Red Air Force arrived as directed by Rybalko's air commander, and attacked the Allied forces becoming bottled-up between Sośniczany and Szewce.

A mixture of cluster bombs and high explosive tumbled out of the sky and inflicted casualties upon the relatively helpless men below.

Relatively, as one of the Ilyushins was chopped from the sky by a Legion M-17 quad AA mount.

Returning for a second run, the ground attack aircraft exacted revenge for their lost comrades by destroying the surviving AA weapon before quitting the field as USAAF F-82 twin Mustangs hunted them down.

The long-range interceptors were not best suited for low-level operations, but still put three of the Soviet aircraft into the ground and chased the remaining Ilyushins away.

Elsewhere, men of Deniken's 169th Guards Rifle Regiment were visited by Skyraiders who brought their normal recipe of death to the battlefield: rockets, bullets, and napalm.

Further north, above the German battlefield, Soviet Yak-15 turbojets clashed with DRL Me-262s at higher altitude as, underneath them, the ground attack aircraft fought yet more desperate battles between themselves, and with the enemy AA defences.

Durand was bringing up the rear of the assault force, performing a brilliant fighting withdrawal, but finding his units becoming concentrated and vulnerable.

Once the aircraft had plied their trade, Soviet artillery again took up the baton, and casualties mounted once more.

Alma could not yet mount any relief back up Route 79, as enemy flame throwing tanks and infantry were penetrating their lines and causing considerable problems, but two battalions and tank support were being prepared for an attempt in the near future.

Efforts to push to the northwest had failed, so everything depended on the Alma relief attempt or on Braun and his hare-brained scheme.

Braun, knowing the time was vital, did not stop to immolate a Soviet supply column he found at Skotniki; he simply drove straight over the top of as much as he could, squashing carts, men, and horses, and firing as he went.

His luck held as he also crashed through a few small engineer-infantry units without loss.

'Wir kommen, Kameraden, Wir kommen!'

Even as Braun's as hoc group smashed into another reserve engineer platoon sat waiting to be called forward, Alma's under pressure front cracked, and St.Clair could only divert his relief force to try and patch up the hole, leaving the trapped assault force on their own again.

The lead elements of the Legion Corps D'Assaut reserve had arrived and were already shaking out into position with the 4ᵉ RACE, the X7 anti-tank rocket troops, moved straight into the front defensive line, whilst the hotch-potch of heavy tanks belonging to the 1ᵉʳ BCL and two companies of the 7ᵉ RTA occupied areas to the north of the position, the former within sight of the divisional command position.

Inside it, the reports were flowing thick and fast and one in particular caused great consternation, although Knocke received the news with stoicism, at least outwardly.

On the Russian Front particularly, he had been in some tight spots, but this was rapidly becoming the worst he had ever encountered, and it still had the capacity to get a lot worse.

The full failure of Grossdeutschland had become apparent when Emmercy's force came under heavy attack from the north and northeast, assaulted by a superior-sized enemy group of the latest T-54 tanks and motorised infantry.

Only a fanatical and costly stand by two companies, one of the AT battalion and one of the engineer, had stopped the Soviets from splitting Emmercy in half and leaving the road to the south open.

The Grossdeutschland Kampfgruppe had also done its part by driving into the enemy's right flank, calling away some assets to deal with the danger just in the nick of time.

Replete with markings, both current and historical, the situation map reflected the chaos of the battlefield, and needed close inspection to fully understand.

By the latest reports, the breach in Haefali's line was being closed just as Knocke examined the possibilities of the incursion, noting with no surprise that the thrusts through Haefali and Emmercy both potentially would have arrived at the ground upon which he was standing, something he had instinctively understood, and the reason why he had placed all that he possessed at Sulisławice.

The latest reports were wrong and the situation was more critical than Knocke could have imagined.

The absence of communication from the recon elements of the 7e RTA was worrying, and no amount of effort by the signallers could raise anyone from the unit. The air support commander urgently requested a recon flight to cover the area, but the air space over the battlefield was incredibly hostile and any photo mission would need escorts, escorts that were presently tasked elsewhere.

Emmercy's group was already split in two and the Frenchman was presently lying unconscious in his battle headquarters surrounded by men with hands on heads, waiting to know their fate at the hands of their captors.

Haefali's attempt to close the gap had failed, but an air attack by, of all things, French-manned Thunderbolts, had struck the Legion lines instead of its intended target, ensuring that the force intent on restoring the line suffered casualties and disruption before it moved, and allowing the enemy to move through relatively unhindered.

On Route 9, T-54s and APCs of the 1st GMRD gathered themselves and drove towards their primary objective.

The breakthrough at Beszyce was complete and elements of the 171st Guards Rifle Regiment and the 6th GIBTR were moving forward unchallenged towards their new objective.

Knocke's imagined convergence would be a reality in the shortest of times, not that he yet knew it.

Sulisławice.

0600 hrs, Tuesday, 1st April 1947, the Soviet positions on the Koprzywianka River near Route 79, Poland.

"The SS bastards're up to no fucking good, Comrade Colonel"

Chekov was inclined to agree but was too busy to do anything but grunt at the infantryman's comment.

"Can't see a damn thing except the guns on the heights there."

Legion artillery had put down a smoke screen at one stage, seemingly to mask a surge down Route 79, but it had come to naught, a sharp downpour making a nonsense of the artillerymen's efforts.

Across the way, the enemy guns still sent shells across the divide, but it was almost like both sides were holding their collective breath for what came next.

The trouble was that Chekov had no idea what was next, and he didn't like it one little bit.

He had no capacity to advance, at least not at this point, although to the south, his forces were progressing remarkably well against the enemy's efforts. The air force report of a mixed force heading at full tilt towards his penetration point was unwelcome, if not a surprise.

'Chinese whispers' had denied him knowledge of the situation in and around Skotniki, where his understanding of the casualties caused by enemy fire suggested enemy artillery, not the presence of enemy tanks in his rear, as the reporters had tried to convey before their lives were extinguished.

The enemy artillery and mortars ceased as if by magic, leaving the battlefield suddenly silent, except for a strange whining sound to his back.

The first Chekov knew of Braun's arrival in his rear was the explosion of one of his vehicle back at the road junction, followed by the briefest of exchanges of fire as the men he had left there were overcome by something… a something that caused a sensation of fear to turn his stomach to water.

Tank engines, the source of the whining that had first distracted him, grew in volume and a number of enemy armoured vehicles burst into view.

Braun had caught his enemy napping and he was determined to punish them.

"Dora-one-one, all Dora, pop red smoke now, repeat… pop red smoke now and spread out… line abreast… kill everything but keep moving… we'll swing back if necessary. Out."

The Schwarzpanthers, surrounded by a haze of red, poured 88mm fire into anything they could see, and machine-guns added to the killing frenzy.

Across the river, the trapped forces of Uhlmann's ill-fated assault force started to travel south, conscious that their period of freedom of movement was probably limited.

596

Fig # 242 - Braun's manoeuvre, the Koprzywianka River, Poland.

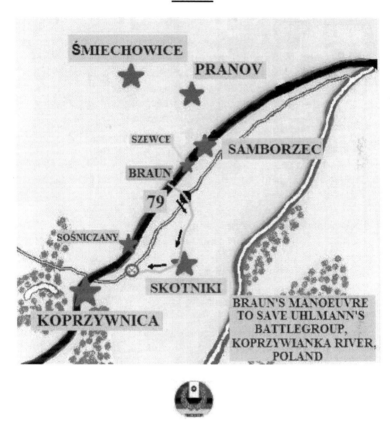

ŚMIECHOWICE

PRANOV

SZEWCE

SAMBORZEC

BRAUN

79

SOŚNICZANY

SKOTNIKI

BRAUN'S MANOEUVRE
TO SAVE UHLMANN'S
BATTLEGROUP,
KOPRZYWIANKA RIVER,
POLAND

KOPRZYWNICA

Back in the Camerone headquarters, a modest izba on the southeastern outskirts of Sulisławice, Knocke received Durand's radio message, reporting news of the ongoing attempt to relive the assault group, with visible relief.

Some engineer ATGs engaged the moving mass successfully, but brought retribution upon themselves as Braun's attack meant the Legion gunners on the heights could operate more freely and concentrate their fire, carefully avoiding the red smoke and anything immersed in it.

"Driver, alarm! Right quarter turn!"

The reactions of the tank driver saved their lives as the MACE clipped the nearside edge of the front glacis and bounced away, exploding above an engineer squad's trench and destroying the four men within.

"Gunner, gun, target to front, one hundred metres, low, straight ahead!"

The bow gunner pulled his trigger and sent a stream of bullets into whatever it was.

Men fell away from it and then disappeared as an 88mm shell easily smashed the GAZ and launcher.

The tank next to Braun's blossomed into an orange and red plume as one of the Hungarian gunners evened the score.

"Scheisse! Driver, keep manoeuvring, gunners engage on sight."

He propelled himself up through the cupola and found his eyes reacting to the growing light and increasing amount of acrid smoke.

Grabbing the MG-34 mount, he scanned the area and immediately found a target.

Cocking the weapon, he raked a group of soldiers who seemed to have ideas involving anti-tank grenades, ideas they lost interest in quickly, preferring self-preservation.

A bullet pinged off the side of the cupola and clipped his right elbow, bringing a squeal of pain.

Traversing the weapon, he put a burst into the sandbagged area from where the shots had come and was rewarded with a red mist.

He chose another target as one of the support halftracks dropped into the position, disgorging men in search of prey.

Chekov pulled himself out from underneath the dying Sárközi, the man's blood filling his eyes, nostrils, and mouth.

Braun's burst had destroyed the Hungarian's physical features and opened his chest, from which the last vestiges of his life's blood was pouring.

Aware of the sound of an approaching engine, he wiped his eyes and grabbed for the SKS rifle, at the same time throwing himself to one side as a heavy vehicle dropped down into the position and smashed through a number of his soldiers.

The first legionnaire who dropped off the side got two shots and went down screaming.

The next got similar.

598

Iska rose groggily to his feet, having been side swiped by the fender of the halftrack, holding his shattered ribs as best he could with a broken wrist.

"Untermensch!"

A German legionnaire rammed the butt of his ST45 into Iska's jaw and drove the bone backwards.

Iska died instantly, his neck broken and his brain penetrated by shattered bone.

Chekov screamed in anger and pulled the trigger, completely missing the killer and doing no more than attracting his attention.

Perhaps it was the uniform of a senior officer that made the difference, but the legionnaire did not shoot Chekov down.

Instead he rushed forward and cannoned into the engineer colonel, smashing him to the floor by body weight alone.

Winded and disoriented, Chekov was manhandled and found himself in the back of the halftrack with the two legion soldiers he had shot, before someone thought it wiser to knock him out.

The halftrack reversed back out of the hole and moved across the area in search of further threats.

The bulk of the assault force had moved past the choke point, but still Durand hesitated to send the green star flares of success into the sky.

Leaving some of the AT company to cover Braun's battle with their SP guns, he ordered the anti-tank guns on the heights to prepare to move back.

In the Soviet positions, the loss of commanders had been deeply felt, and most of those capable of rational thought plumbed for remaining in cover, rather than actively interfering in the withdrawal of Camerone's prime attack group.

But not all.

The Schwarzpanther rocked as the shell slammed into its flank, causing its shot to fly harmlessly away.

Braun, shaken by the hit but still focussed, estimated that the anti-tank gun was too far away to run down before it got another shot off, so he grabbed the MG-34 again and did what he could.

His driver performed the standard manoeuvre and presented an angled target to the enemy's firing point and hit the throttle, the idea being to increase the chances of a defection by angling all surfaces, as well as making the tank harder to hit.

However, the latter worked both ways, and both the turret coax and Braun's MG went far wide of the mark.

The next enemy shell missed the rear of the tank by the smallest of margins and Braun, having counted the time it took the enemy to reload, made the decision.

"Driver, left turn, run it down, full speed, man!"

The turbine engine brought the tank up to its full speed and the race between crews began, with only one winner, for whom life was the prize.

The hull MG stammered and made a difference, the AT gun's commander spinning away as bullets virtually severed his left arm at the shoulder.

Starshina Ivan Balyan, holder of the Hero of the Soviet Union award for his bravery whilst fighting the Legion in the Alsace, fired off his Tokarev in futile resistance before Braun smashed the life from him with another burst.

Within a second the crew's nerve broke and they scattered, not quick enough for the aimer, who was struck by the trails of the gun as the Legion tank smashed into the D-44 gun and propelled nearly two tons of metal in the direction of the fleeing man.

His screams were increased as the weight of the Schwarzpanther pushed down on the weapon, crushing him across the waist and almost cutting him in two.

Braun and his gunners took out the remaining crew with controlled bursts as ammunition ran low.

Behind them and to the extreme right of Braun's attack, one of his platoon's tank took a MACE hit on the front sprocket.

The track simply shattered and the heavy sprocket flew in all directions.

Braun watched impotently as the turret swung to engage the MACE, all the time yelling for the men to get out of the vehicle.

The Hungarian gunner made no mistake and the heavy rocket struck the nearside perfectly, just behind the driver's position.

After a moment, one man emerged, clutching the ruins of an arm, his uniform smoking and smouldering.

A heat haze started to embrace the destroyed tank as its contents began to burn.

The wounded man rolled off the turret and onto the engine deck, where he was picked off by one of the Hungarian guard troops.

The body lay on the grilles and was ravaged and consumed by the fire that engulfed the battle tank.

The anonymous ex-SS panzer soldier was the last casualty of the relief attempt, as two green star flares rose high and signalled the successful extrication of the assault force.

Braun charged his surviving vehicles over the bridge, all the time keeping heads down behind him, using up the last of his MG ammunition to remind any braver Soviet soldiers of their decided fragility.

Durand communicated the success to Knocke, who immediately ordered the whole group back to new positions along Route 9.

"A brilliant piece of work it seems, mon Général!"

Knocke could not deny D'Estlain's observation that the swift counter-attack into the rear of the enemy force had been a superb piece of soldiering, and he would certainly ensure that whoever had commanded received the recognition he deserved.

But for now, even though his situation appeared easier, there was still much to concern him.

The lack of contact with Emmercy was his prime concern, but the DRH Kampfgruppe reported being in contact with Legion units in and around Klimontów, and fighting in progress in the village itself.

Whilst the Grossdeutschland reports were right in most respects, they were wrong in that the fighting in Klimontów was not resistance as such, simply mopping up by Soviet units keen to open the route completely.

Elsewhere, Haefali was struggling to maintain a complete front as he withdrew.

Lavalle had insisted that the Camerone headquarters be relocated to Bukowa and not remain in the front line, which order Knocke tactfully refused, stating his reasons for remaining, at least until Haefali's force was re-established on the Route 9 defensive line.

Accepting the Camerone commander's reasoning, Lavalle set about getting more of the chattels of war on line and ready for use.

The 1er Division's 1er Brigade had encountered enemy forces on the fringe of the Alma area and was unable to progress, especially as it was further impeded by more enemy air attacks.

The new plan, direct from 1er French Army Headquarters, was to use the situation to their advantage, continue to 'feign' disarray and withdrawal in the Camerone area, whilst encircling the attacking enemy force, using Alma and the 1er Division in the south, running adjacent to the Vistula, and uncommitted units of the DRH's 101st Korps in the north, namely the 116th Panzer Division and 3rd Fallschirmjager Division, forming pincers to encircle the encirclers.

When Knocke had been apprised of the plan he bit back his acid observation on feigned disarray.

But, he felt, with the new plan, and reinforcements arriving to his north and south, the worst was now over.

Alas for Camerone, the worst was yet to come.

Stelmakh received the breathless man's report as he sucked heavily on a captured cigarette.

"I saw them myself, Comrade Mayor. They went into the village and drove out to the northwest. I swear I can see no one left in it, which means…"

Stelmakh interrupted.

"Which means the road to Sulisławice is free and ours for the taking."

"Yes, Comrade Mayor."

"Excellent work, Comrade Mladshy Leytenant. We'll talk more of this after the battle, but for now get your men ready to move quickly. Once my Comrade driver has finished his tinkerings, we'll move out as one and strike straight through Skwirzowa and attack Sulisławice before the bastards can get settled. You've done well. Keep it up."

The happy young officer saluted and went to get his platoon of the SMG company ready to do his commander's bidding.

Meanwhile, Stelmakh turned his attention back to the man on the rear of 'Krasny Suka', who was sat looking at him, feigned disdain on his face.

"Tinkerings is it, Comrade Mayor?"

Stelmakh slapped the man's foot and passed the half-smoked cigarette upwards.

"A slip of the tongue, Comrade Driver. This is no time for your word games anyway, Stepanov, so what progress have you made?"

"Tinkerings complete, Comrade Mayor. Fuel filter was blocked, same as with the other two."

The delay in advance had been because two of the IS-IV had experienced engine failures, both of which had been quickly traced to contaminated fuel.

"So, we can advance?"

"I was thinking more of a leisurely drive back to Lublin... or maybe Moscow, Comrade Mayor."

"Excellent idea... we'll go via the village ahead. Now get yourself ready, you sad bastard."

Stelmakh mounted the tank as Stepanov moved across the turret and dropped into his driving position, ready to take 'Krasny Suka' back into battle.

Arranging the headset for comfort, he broadcast to the waiting regiment.

He called each units commander in turn, checking that there were no problems and that each was ready to play his part.

When it was over, he double-checked.

"Chorniy-odin, Chorniy-odin, any unit not ready to move immediately, report now, over."

There was silence.

"Chorniy-odin, all units Chorniy... advance!"

The 6th moved forward towards the undefended village and to Sulisławice beyond.

Two minutes beforehand, heading south on Route 9, T-54s and mechanised infantry of the 1st Guards Mechanised Rifle Division had disturbed the horizon and swept down off the heights, heading for their objective at full speed.

0611 hrs, Tuesday, 1st April 1947, Sulisławice, Poland.

Knocke was taking a breath of fresh air, one that he immediately contaminated with cigarette smoke, leaving D'Estlain to look after things whilst the early morning sun helped clear his mind.

Hässelbach had slipped a steaming hot mug of coffee into his hand and moved away without a word, sensing his leader needed some space.

603

Alternating between the wonderful fresh coffee and his rich tobacco, Knocke felt a calm descend, one that momentarily expelled his feelings of unrest and foreboding.

The leading edge of the heights to the north moved as he casually observed it, small black dots dancing on it like ants.

With the mug to his lips, Knocke screwed up his eyes, needing to know what caused the strange apparition, whilst inside he sensed he understood things only too well.

Shouts rose from those posted on watch and his worst fears became a reality.

"Alarm! Alarm! Alarm!"

Knocke's decision to arrange his reserve in a defensive posture was proved correct, although it had been arranged more with a defence against the east than the north.

None the less, the extra units from the Corps reserve were positioned with the north in mind, and they were already coming to readiness to deal with the large force that was pouring down the slope around Wólka Gieraszowska.

The whole valley area between the enemy and his own position was reasonably clear of obstruction, save for a few rises and dips, the occasional knot of trees and bushes, and the ever-present Koprzywianka River.

More shouts alerted him to the arrival of another Soviet force on the field, this time coming at them from the east.

Knocke rushed back into the headquarters to do whatever he could do stave off the disaster that appeared to be about to visit itself upon the whole Legion corps.

"Oh, for fuck's sake!"

Köster said it out loud but they were all thinking it.

He dropped easily into the turret and equipped himself with his radio microphone, all the time assessing the force that was increasing before his eyes.

Lohengrin had been idling, so was warmed up and ready to move.

The radio crackled into life as the 1er BCL's commander issued his orders.

Fig # 243 - 1er Bataillon Chars Léger at Sulisławice.

▮▮	1er Bataillon Chars Léger at Sulisławice	◢
HQ	1 x Tiger II, 1 x Wirbelwind, 2 x Wolf	
1e Comp	5 x M-26 Pershing, 1 x M-24 Chafee	
2e Comp	2 x Centurion, 2 x IS-II, 1 x ISU-122	
3e Comp	1 x Tiger II, 1 x Tiger I, 4 x ARL-44	
	Plus support group [workshops, fuel, supply]	

"All units Fuchs, all units Fuchs, Fuchs-zero calling. All units action enemy to north, repeat north. Prevent them from crossing the river. Do not advance, repeat, do not advance. Remain on the height. All units Fuchs-three to pull back and move west, repeat, move west... two hundred metres west of Nietuja. Fuchs-one acknowledge..."

Each company commander in turn repeated his orders, ending with the Third Company, whose experienced tankers were already backing up to use the main road to circle up to their new position.

It was immediately clear that an enemy force was heading due west across the edge of the heights, and it was this group that Third Company were tasked to engage.

'Kompagnie in name only.'

Köster thought that the odds were against them because of their reduced numbers.

Soviet artillery started to fall in and around Sulisławice in an effort to pin down the defence.

To the east, the defending legionnaires suffered the downpour, waiting for their enemy to get closer... waiting for the order to fire.

The crews in the Felix and Jaguar [fr] tanks of 4e Compagnie 1er RCDA observed the steel monsters of the enemy heavy tank regiment grind slowly forward, knowing that they were virtually impervious to anything they could hit them with.

The 17pdr equipped Felix tanks had precious few of the new HESH rounds, which proved universally capable, but the Jaguar [fr] relied solely upon its old HEAT shell, or the newest HVAT round that had yet to prove itself against the latest heavy tanks of the Red Army.

605

Even though only a platoon, the six launchers of the 4^e RACE, with their deadly 'Red Riding Hood' missiles, were the Legion's best hope against the leviathans of the 6th Guards Tanks.

The Legion infantry were arranged in their companies on the outskirts of Sulisławice, save the 3^e/3^e/5^e RdM positioned towards the rear of the village, instantly ready to man its vehicles and respond to any call.

For the moment, the infantry understood that the battle was simply one to endure, not participate in, at least until the enemy armour came in range of their AT weapons, and then it would be a different and bloody matter.

The incoming fire hit home and the IS-III rocked but continued inexorably forward, its 'pike' nose taking two hits and deflecting both shells away.

None the less, and despite his competence and undoubted bravery, the age-old problem affected Stelmakh and he felt the warmth spread down his inner thigh.

He didn't even worry about it now and neither did his crew. It was simply a reaction that he couldn't control, and they knew that he was a tried and tested warrior that they would follow to the ends of the earth if need be.

That didn't stop the soldiers having their fun.

"Excellent work, Comrade Mayor. The risk of fire is greatly reduced."

"Concentrate on your job, Comrade whatever-your-name-is!"

They had long since worked out that Kalinov was not who he represented himself to be, but the man was part of them now, so it simply didn't matter.

He was an excellent loader, so it was acceptable that he would tell them in time.

In the driving position, Stepanov was assessing the ground as they advanced and keeping an eye open for the tell-tale flash of enemy fire.

He smoothly moved one way and then jerked the other, making no regular movements that might allow an enemy gunner to understand his direction.

Another enemy shell streaked past the turret and buried itself in a small hillock beyond 'Krasny Suka'.

Stelmakh risked a look out of the cupola and saw that none of his tanks were yet stopped, something he celebrated in silence.

However, the right flank was behind and he flicked his microphone to send.

"Chorniy-pyat, Chorniy-pyat, Chorniy-odin, faster, faster, Comrade... you're falling behind... bring it up to the line. Chorniy-odin, out."

With some satisfaction he watched the extra puffs of black smoke mark the efforts of the five remaining vehicles in his depleted third company, a mix of IS-IVs and IS-IVm46, the latter's superior engine making the acceleration easier than the three older IS-IVs who suffered with the inferior powertrain.

As he watched a wave of heat washed over his face as an enemy artillery shell exploded dangerously close.

He dropped into the turret, running his hands over his face and shoulders just to check that he hadn't been hit, so close had the shell landed.

More arrived, shells of a calibre that would kill any of his tanks were they lucky enough to hit, which left him with a dilemma.

He had intended to move and identify targets before taking up cover and engaging on relatively equal terms, his big 122mm and the 130mm guns of the IS-VIIs more than capable of killing any enemy tank on the field.

But now, safety would probably lie closer to the enemy, which removed some of his advantage and could reasonably expose him to the attentions of enemy infantry with AT weapons.

Instinctively he sought relief in the topography of the battlefield, and elected to move to the left, bringing his force further south.

An urgent message from his headquarters advising that the smoke support would be lost after the new three salvoes made his decision all the more wise.

As Stelmakh ordered his regiment to change the axis of their advance, the presence of the friendly northern force became apparent, making his switch all the more reasonable and actually tactically advantageous.

Or at least so it seemed, for as his closeness might inhibit the artillery, it also brought the X-7 Rotkäppchen missiles of the 4^e RACE into play.

And the X-7, not that he knew what it was, was more than capable of killing any of his tanks, as he was about to find out.

Fig # 245 - Sulisławice, Poland.

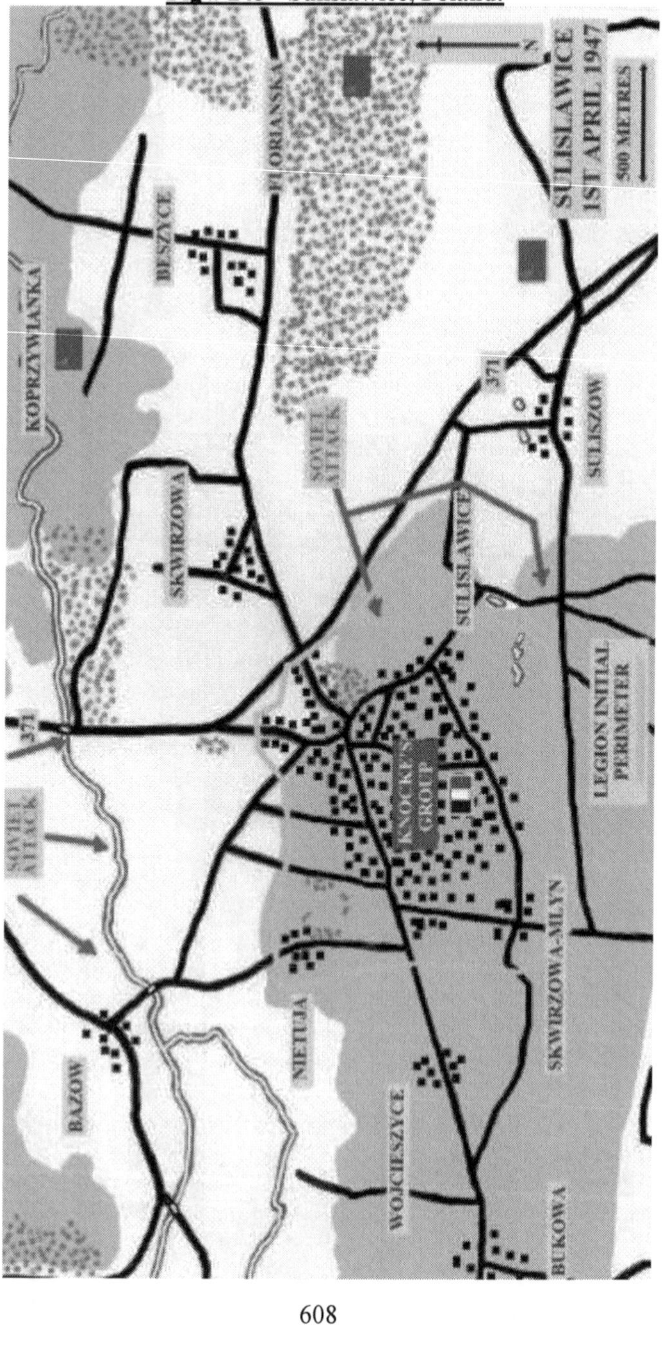

Once the fire order was given, 4ᵉ RACE's gunners released their X-7s and tracked the deadly little missiles as they swept downrange towards the advancing enemy tanks, their job made slightly easier by the size of the leviathans.

With a range of roughly a thousand metres, the flight time to target was just a fraction over four seconds, which was why a competent and highly trained rocket gunner was only produced by many weeks of teaching and, first and foremost, considered an extremely valuable asset.

Peters was the best of the best, and to observers, his four seconds of flying time always seemed to be stretched well beyond comprehension.

He even had time to understand that another X-7 was headed for his target and the wit to understand that a gentle change could bring him a fresh victim without loss of hit probability.

His missile struck home just after the one he had spotted and both target vehicles were enveloped in explosions as the hollow-charge warheads detonated.

X-7s were deadly weapons, capable of defeating armour in excess of 200mm thickness.

The missile that hit the other tank penetrated the 160mm thick hull armour and killed the tank and crew in the blink of an eye, assisted by the explosion of the propellant charge that the tank's loader was handling at the time.

The turret rose into the air and came back down on the rear of the still moving IS-IV.

Peters' rocket struck the turret of his target and, although it did not destroy the tank, the main gun was rendered useless unless it could find a target in the sky, jammed into a raised position by scarred metal.

From their safe position behind the ridgeline, Peters' support crew were already rearming the launcher with another Rotkäppchen missile.

At the start of the battle there were only six for each launcher, and they were the very last available until the French or German industries decided that more production was worth the effort.

The 'powers that be' had tried to convince the procurers of the importance of the weapon, but always met with resistance based

609

around other effective alternatives and the time and cost of training operatives.

Just in case the 4^e RACE got seriously in harm's way, it had been issued with a large number of panzerfausts, a few captured Soviet rocket grenades, and a pair of the new US M20 bazookas; the so-called Super Bazooka.

That the Legion had the weapon before many of the US forces was only down to the successful scavenging by her forage parties, much to the puzzlement of a number of quartermasters up and down the Allied front, whose inventories came up short no matter how many times they counted.

However, yet again, ammunition was short for both rocket weapon systems.

One advantage of the Rotkäppchen launcher system was that it was generally deployed out of the line of sight, and so the need to relocate was less than normal.

Peters decided to fire from the same position himself, safe in the knowledge that the smoke trail of the first rocket would not identify his hiding place.

He guided his X-7 into the tank he had previously damaged.

The tank came to a lazy halt and belched smoke as her crew abandoned her.

This time he elected to move.

The IS tanks might not be able to see him or fire at the launcher, but they had mortars and artillery who could do a good job trying to locate him regardless.

No mortar fire came initially, and the enemy artillery response fell more to their front; a mistake, he thought.

'Scheisse! Smoke!'

The IS force commander had asked for smoke to mask his tanks, an extremely successful counter to the X-7 troops, because even if it didn't fully obscure a target, the smoke could simply make for a difficult perspective, something that was vital to the wire-controlled missile when guided by eyes nearly a kilometre away.

Some gunners still fired, but there was only one tangible result from their expenditure, so the RACE commander called for a ceasefire, and relocated his men further back.

Peters had a last look at the enemy and decided that they might be changing the axis of their advance.

The arrival of enemy mortar shells prevented him from confirming his suspicions and he ran as fast as his legs could manage and his equipment would allow him.

The Felixes and Jaguars of 4^e/1er RCDA were still engaging, but not yet employing their limited HESH, as per an order issued by the unit commander... an order not wholly agreed with.

None the less, the Legion tankers were disciplined, and engaged the enemy heavy tanks with APDS and HEAT.

Back with the RACE, Peters and his nearest comrades received orders to relocate, orders that were either brilliant in conception, or incredibly stupid, depending on how well the IS tanks were supported.

The Kätzchen were brought forward and the small force loaded up.

The three small fully-tracked APCs sped off to relocate on the flank of the advancing enemy tank force to ambush them from the side, something that would require speed of reaction, skill, and above all, luck.

Peters clung to the MG-42 mount as he tried to see the enemy's movements and, with the occasional glimpse, understood that they were switching from a straight advance and were already angling towards the area he had just vacated.

His map was less than helpful, one of a number of inferior quality ones made available to the rear line units when stocks of the better ones ran out, but he found a long thin stand of trees that would provide him with enough cover to position and shoot.

Another bonus of the X-7 system was its swiftness to deploy in trained hands.

The three Kätzchen bounced along the muddy track and swept into the rear of the stand of trees, still possessing most of their foliage, unlike the majority of woods in the area.

The gunners pulled their launchers clear and were already dragging them forward before Peters could even get his FuG 510 set and its associated paraphernalia clear of the locker.

He ran forward through the light undergrowth and found his own crew establishing the launcher in a prime position.

Hooking up, he moved forward and found a perfect observation point, an almost table-like affair where a fallen trunk lay against a severed tree, providing a seat for him and a place to put his control system, whilst providing excellent physical cover for both him and his kit.

Concentrating on the battlefield, he quickly realised that he could now see less than when in the position he had vacated.

None the less, he knew they were coming, so he patiently held his fire.

Two of the crewmen had returned to the Kätzchen and dismantled the rearmost MG-42, and both were now positioned to provide fire support, should enemy infantry arrive to play a part.

The ex-SS troopers could hardly bear to breathe as they waited...

...and waited...

0618 hrs, Tuesday, 1st April 1947, northern defensive line, Sulisławice, Poland.

3ᵉ/1ᵉʳ DCA screamed through Nietuja and shook out into a firing line just short of the ridge opposite the enemy force that was no longer heading west, but had turned and was driving at speed towards the river itself.

Köster's mind recalled another battle, where Soviet tanks had crossed bridges secretly laid under the water, and his heart was in his mouth as the leading T54s approached the river, and then he exhaled in relief as they stopped short of the water and assumed positions that might provide them some sort of shelter from any incoming fire.

Köster's tanks had been sent further west to broaden the front and provide an ability to interrupt any enemy movement westwards along the modest track that ran from Wólka Gieraszowska to Bazów and all points west.

The other units of the 1ᵉʳ BCL were engaging the main body of the advancing T-54s, trying to hit out at the two flanks in an effort to herd them into a concentrated bunch, something the Soviets would need to do to cross the obstacle of the river, but something that Knocke ordered early on, in order to make his artillery fire even more effective.

For some reasons, the T-54s and their accompanying APCs did not play by the rules, and remained on a relatively broad front and less of a target for the Legion artillery.

The reason suddenly became clear to any of the observing Legion officers and tank commanders, and target priorities shifted quickly.

The engineer tanks were spotted too late for the Legion to perform any credible active interference.

The Soviet artillery relocated their smoke barrage from the east side of Sulisławice to the northern approaches, and only a handful of shots were fired at the new arrivals before the slope nearest to the Legion tankers was covered with chemical smoke, successfully masking much of the assault force.

Immediately that happened, the Soviet bridging engineers already at the river went to work putting something in place that might stand a chance of supporting their light vehicles.

There was no chance that the brave men could erect anything capable of supporting one of the battle tanks, but the bridge layers that screamed down the slope at their highest possible speed could.

Their crews were free of any illusions, understanding that the smoke was all that stood between them and the concentrated fire of the defensive force.

On the extreme right flank of the attack group, the left as Köster looked, a Soviet tank 'flashed' and swung lazily, before stopping with a uselessly flapping broken track.

Given that the Legion artillery had not been firing at the spot, and that Third Company had yet to open fire, he rightly concluded that it was a mine, a possibility that might give Third an advantage if the enemy decided to spread even further to the west.

A radio order penetrated his concentration, as the Third's commander gave the command to engage.

He knew Jarome was on a target so simply passed the order on.

Lohengrin jumped as the 88mm sent a solid shot across the river and crashing into a stationary T-54.

The AP40 shell enjoyed an advantage of angle, having been fired from the ridge looking down, which meant it was able to carve through the T-54's armour.

Despite the Tiger gun's venerability, it was still a potent weapon on the modern battlefield, although Lohengrin's vertical armour plates made her more vulnerable than the more modern vehicles.

The T-54s below had their own successes and each of the BCL's units had lost vehicles already.

Perversely, Third had been the last to engage but had already lost two of its ARL-44s, one to a dislodged turret following a direct hit, the other to its transmission overheating and the catastrophic failure that resulted.

The design was seriously flawed, and unpopular with the ex-SS Panzertruppen, who were used to better, but it had been pressed into service and its 90mm gun was more than capable of successfully taking on most Soviet tanks.

It was also surprisingly accurate, more so than the 75mm and 88mm weapons to which most were more used.

It was one of the ARLs that killed the first bridge-laying tank, assisted by another shower that helped beat down the smoke.

Zilinski cursed his luck.

The commander of the 7th Guards Special Tank Brigade, the man who replaced Arkady Yarishlov following his hideous wounding at Naugard, watched as the smoke started to dissipate and his forces took increased casualties.

"Mudaks!"

Unlike Yarishlov, Zilinski chose to ride into battle in an APC rather than a tank, and he had taken a position on the heights opposite the Legion lines from where he could better observe the unfolding events.

He was normally a cautious leader, but Deniken had been on the radio, haranguing him for any delays and ordering him to press and press hard.

The opportunity to destroy the hated SS bastards of the Legion was not to be missed, so Zilinski committed his men to a suicidal task, simply to protect his bridge layers.

He spoke rapidly into his radio, addressing the whole reinforced tank battalion, the support unit, and then one specific company.

Returning to his binoculars, he observed the tanks putting down smoke directly on the enemy positions and then the company he had ordered over the bridge moving to concentrate for the attack.

Simply put, he was prepared to sacrifice some of his men to get the bridges in place, not trusting solely to the smoke from his tanks and mortars, having decided to hand the enemy the maximum amount to think about at one time.

"Blyad!"

His lead tank came apart as something unforgiving hammered into it.

As dispassionately as he could, he watched as three of the vehicle's crew ran around like human torches until they fell, either consumed by the fire they carried with them or shot down by their comrades.

Another tank died as he wiped his hand across his face, but this time the men aboard escaped without apparent injury.

614

The furthest forward T-54 nosed onto the modest bridge and accelerated across, the desperation of her crew apparent even from that distance.

Another followed but fell victim to a hit as it turned off the road, its track rolling out behind it as the driver coaxed the wounded vehicle towards the illusion of safety represented by an old building.

The enemy gunners turned on the wounded tank and simply blew it apart.

Yet another of his tanks had died before it reached the small stone structure, but the remainder were moving forward, bravely attempting to do their commander's bidding.

Another paid the price, but Zilinski missed its death as he watched the first of the transportable bridges drop into place, the IS-II chassis bridging vehicle backing away to permit the first of his tanks to cross up river of the bridge.

"Yes! Yes! We've done it… my men've done it! Kapitan! Report to Comrade General Deniken… tell him we've bridged the river west of Route 9 in…" he quickly checked and added the bridges still being deployed, "… five places. Now, man!"

The remainder of his tank battalion acted as they had already been ordered, and the company and platoon commanders sent their tanks across the river.

Their own smoke screen was of little use, and each unit in turn felt the weight of the defence as casualties mounted.

Their accompanying infantry had started to cross beforehand, relatively unmolested by the tankers of 1er BCL.

Not that they hadn't been seen; it was simply that they were to be left to the watching legionnaires from a company of Truffaux's 3^e/5^e RdM, and the tirailleurs of the 7^e RTA.

Truffaux had positioned his command group behind his third company, so it was he who gave the order to start slaughtering the advancing infantry.

The legionnaires and tirailleurs lashed out with their machine-guns, a mix of MG-34s, 42s, M2s, and a surprising number of BARs.

The heavier weapons concentrated their fire on the temporary crossing points and inflatables, whereas the lighter weapons, including a number of the latest ST-45s carried by the 7^e RTA soldiers, flayed the men already across the river and working their way up the slope.

Legion mortars opened up, adding to the misery of the under-pressure infantry, although some were quickly silenced by the appearance of a pair of Shturmoviks, who deposited their cluster bombs in the middle of Sulisławice, killing and wounding many of the mortar men and destroying nearly two-thirds of the mortar ammunition.

FW-190s of the DRL's 23rd [Lehr] Jagdstaffel swept across the battlefield in hot pursuit of the pair of Shturmoviks and chopped one from the sky over Rozki, where it plunged into a group of Polish buildings, killing many of the cowering civilians.

The other escaped as La-9s swept in to protect the last surviving ground attack aircraft.

The Focke-Wulfs turned away, their ammunition and fuel already depleted by previous encounters in an air space increasingly and unusually Soviet in ownership.

To add to their woes, the DRL staffel had turned over the airspace above a large portion of the 1st Battalion, 286th Guards AA Regiment and their ZSU-20-4 vehicles.

The relatively slow moving FWs were at a perfect height for the SPAA mounts, and three were felled in the first volley of shots.

The gunners switched to other targets, some of which were already showing the outward signs of damage. Gunners homed in on the damaged aircraft, following smoke trails, and three more DRL aircraft were hacked from the battle's airspace, but also added in one of the pursuing Lavochkins, whose proximity overrode the gunners' natural caution when firing into an airspace containing friend and foe.

Three of the AA guns triangulated and blew the tail off the La-9 before gun controllers realised the error.

Too late for the experienced pilot, veteran of the early days of the Patriotic War.

His thoroughbred aircraft simply span into the Polish soil below and exploded, leaving very little to be salvaged when the battle moved on.

In front of the burning Lavochkin, the remaining FWs drove hard for the safety of their own lines, knowing that they couldn't out-climb the Soviet fighters, but intent on springing a trap of their own.

Their leader took them on a rapid turn to starboard, which the pursuers mirrored.

Behind the Soviet fighters, a group of USAAF Shooting Stars remained high above the battlefield, unaware of the low-flying Lavochkins and providing top cover for a gaggle of Tigercats on an

S&D mission, one of only two squadrons that were not based in the Pacific or Persia, on their way to a ground attack mission of their own.

However, the Tigercats spotted the juicy target and, on the orders of the mission commander, the rear group jettisoned their bombs and turned to engage the unsuspecting La-9s.

The heavy twin-engine USAAF fighter-bombers carried a heavy punch, with four 20mm and four .50cal heavy machine-guns.

Three Soviet fighters fell in the first pass, and the inexperienced pilots panicked and scattered, despite their still superior numbers.

Not a single shot was fired back at the Tigercats as they chased the disorganised Soviet regiment in all directions, and the skies over the Koprzywianka River suddenly cleared of all aircraft.

Deniken consulted with Lisov and ordered part of the 171st to change its axis of movement, in order to try and break through behind Koprzywnica and at the same time bring force to bear on the south and southeast sides of the Sulisławice defences, defences that were far stronger than had been anticipated, making the overall plan fall a little behind schedule.

Having communicated with Rybalko, ostensibly to seek permission for the change, Deniken decided to shift his battle headquarters closer to the front, and within minutes the group was mobile towards the sound of the guns.

0628 hrs, Tuesday, 1st April 1947, Sulisławice, Poland.

Peters' small group ran for their lives, leaving one lazily burning Kätzchen behind, with one of the launchers and four of their comrades.

All in all, the 4ᵉ RACE and 4ᵉ/1ᵉʳ RCDA's Panthers and Felix tanks had knocked out seven of the big tanks and at least double that number of the newly arrived SPAT and tanks of the 6th Guards Tank Corps.

The X-7 gunners had not done as well as they would have hoped, more than one control wire snagging on the numerous bushes that covered the battlefield, and the huge IS-VIIs that had been their targets were seemingly impervious to direct hits, unless from the side, which was how the two that were burning had died, victims of Peters' redeployment onto the left flank of Stelmakh's force.

Stelmakh himself had risked all by attacking the ambush group head-on, and more than one shot hit the IS-III as it presented opportunities of a side shot to some of the tanks on the height.

It was his 122mm that had turned the Kätzchen into so much burning scrap, along with its highly trained crew and two valuable Rotkäppchen missiles.

6th GIBTR had made it into the lee of the slope and that immediately resulted in a great lessening of incoming fire.

They moved forward cautiously, their surviving SMG soldiers, always conscious of the threat of enemy anti-tank soldiers, shooting enthusiastically into all sorts of bushes and possible hiding places on the principle of 'better safe than sorry'.

Waiting for them were the SPs of the headquarters and 3ᵉ/1ᵉʳ Régiment Blindé, commanded by the unflappable Jorgensen.

The reports from the northern sector were worrying in the extreme.

The size of the enemy force was rapidly approaching the point that Knocke feared his lines would be overrun, no matter how well his men fought... and they were fighting magnificently by all accounts.

A number of the bridges were now down, although the precise numbers were not clear. But enough tanks and APCs had crossed the water to make them less of a priority target.

In the Legion tanks, gunners and loaders sweated profusely as they worked their weapons hard, all in an effort to stem the mounting tide.

The ARL-44s had all gone.

The IS-IIs had gone.

Two of the Pershings had gone and another was unable to fire, even if it could find a replacement gunner and loader

The Tiger II in the headquarters had gone... along with the unit's commander.

Lieutenant Albrecht von und zu Mecklenburg found himself in charge of the unit, with his battalion commander and company commander both dead, and the second in command on his way to the aid post, knocked unconscious and bloodied by Soviet mortars.

At first, he had resented being given command of the British tank, but quickly understood that his veteran crew found the vehicle more than up to the task of killing the enemy and, more importantly to all of them, very good at keeping them alive.

The Centurion once known as Lady Godiva had taken three hits and shrugged them off without any overt sign of damage or effect, other than to fray the nerves of those inside her steel walls.

The 20pdr cannon fired a range of telling projectiles and he had not yet needed to use the few HESH in his stock, the APDS round more than sufficient to defeat the T-54s on front of him.

Unlike the 17pdr, which had required men like Patterson to create special shells, the 20pdr came equipped with its own lethal canister shell, and Mecklenburg was keen to see its effects on the approaching Soviet infantry.

He had spent the earlier war serving on the Italian Front in an aufklarungs unit, where he had once seen a 234/3 armoured car smash down a British infantry attack single-handed, with the use of the 75mm L/24's canister round, a singularly deadly shot containing nine hundred and sixty steel balls. The 20pdr canister was apparently much worse, and he relished the opportunity to flay the hated untermensch with it.

There was a problem with his gun's stabiliser, a lovely advantage when it worked, but as he was engaging from cover in the main, the loss was not too keenly felt.

All in all he loved his new tank and, despite his relative lack of experience, controlled his portion of the battlefield with ease.

"Target tank, left two, seven hundred, engage."

"On. Firing!"

The 20pdr shell streaked down towards the T-54 and found luck on its side.

The enemy tank dipped its nose into a small hole and opened up its vulnerable roof plates to the incoming shell.

In a flash of sparks and molten metal, the APDS ate straight through the modest top armour and exited through the floor, having travelled through some of the underfloor ammunition and the loader's right foot.

The man barely had time to scream before the propellant charges surrendered to the energy of the passing shell and exploded.

Pieces of tank flew in all directions, causing havoc with nearby infantry.

Still the 7th Guards Tanks pressed forward for, even though they continued to suffer, the fire was steadily lessening as, bit by bit, their persecutors grew fewer in number.

On the Legion's left flank, Lohengrin was holding her own but Köster understood it was only a matter of time.

"Scheisse! Target tank, left eight, six hundred, fire when on!"

He had missed the approach completely, and his mind was already working back over things to establish how the enemy could have got so close without being observed.

"Firing!"

Jarome hit, but the shell angled off into the sky, the angling of the thick turret armour saving the vehicle and crew.

"Make sure of the bastard, Hans… we're gonna have to move shortly! Driver, stand by!"

Jarome concentrated by some sense made him hold his fire.

Köster dropped his head down into the fighting compartment to see what was going on just as the breech leapt back and the gunner's fire warning reached his ears.

The enemy tank had stopped to fire and Jarome seized the moment, slotting a solid shot into the join between turret and hull immediately underneath the main gun.

Whatever it did inside was anyone's guess, but the driver pushed himself up and out of vehicle and staggered away before collapsing onto the damp grass.

Köster decided that now was the time.

"Driver, reverse and back left… move!"

Two more tanks came out of a defile, clearly how the first had come so close without being observed.

One put a shell on target, a fantastic shot from the moving tank, and the 100mm shell banged into the turret front but the angle saved them and it ricocheted off.

As the Tiger I reversed, Köster called the gunner in on the new targets and had a grandstand view as the lead tank ran straight over the survivor of their last kill.

Köster grimaced as he fancied he heard the man's scream, but concentrated on looking backwards and correcting Meier's reversing angle slightly.

"And halt. Forward and right… behind that wall."

The driver changed gears with ease and Lohengrin was back behind some cover in an instant.

"Are you on, Hans?"

"And waiting…"

"Fire!"

"Firing!"

Again the 88mm hit its target and swiped straight down the nearside running gear, making a huge mess of tracks and wheels alike.

"What the fuck?"

"Report."

"No way I aimed there… that hit must have done something."

"Can you fix it, Hans?"

"Maybe… but no time, Rudi. I'll have to judge it."

An inaccurate gun was all that Köster needed, especially in the gutter fight around him.

"You have the tank, Hans. Commander out!"

He grabbed the MP-40 and pushed himself up and out in the blink of an eye.

Köster dropped behind the turret, rolled across the engine gratings and off the rear, careful not to burn himself on the hot exhausts.

As he scuttled down the offside, half-crawling, half-kneeling, the 88mm cracked again and he knew the gunner had scored a kill, the secondary explosion and fireball both noticeable, even in the growing sound of the battle.

From a position just in front of his tank, he could see the new scar on the turret front, and it ran through the area where the gunner's sight lay.

'Verdammt!'

He retraced his steps to the rear of the Tiger and pulled himself back onto the vehicle engine deck.

A shell casing flew out of the loader's hatch in the rear of the turret, followed by a blackened face.

"Hans reckons we've gotta go as soon as you're in, Hauptscharführer!"

"Ok!"

A quick look revealed the reason for the move and he dropped back inside the turret and ordered Meier to reverse once more.

The positions on the right were almost overrun and Lohengrin was out on a limb.

The tirailleurs of the 7ᵉ had put down scores of the advancing infantry, but still they came, driven on by anything from courage to fear of the consequences of failure.

Around them came the surviving T-54s, firing as they came.

The Soviet barrage arrived on cue, held back until the final moment for its fullest effect.

Zilinski knew he had one shot with the hidden unit and expected no more as, as recent history showed, surviving the battle was the priority for the rocket barrage troops, rather than actually firing the a second salvo.

Katyusha units had learned to relocate to avoid the counter-battery fire and roving ground attack aircraft.

The Katyusha rockets arrived along the ridgeline and the northern edge of Sulisławice and brought death and destruction at a critical time.

More of the 3ᵉ's precious tanks were destroyed or immobilised, and the tirailleurs suffered horrendous casualties.

Zilinski had gambled and succeeded.

Some of the 7ᵉ RTA gave way and ran, leaving the surviving tanks exposed and with precious little support.

Here and there, a few braver men stayed close and kept the enemy anti-tank hunters at bay, but the Soviets, armed with a mixture of LANs and RPGs started to score hits.

Von Mecklenburg dithered for a moment, caught between no retreat and understanding his predicament.

"All Fuchs, all Fuchs. Pull back to the edge of the village. Repeat, leave the ridgeline and fall back to the village. Ende."

He gave his own driver the order to reverse and the Centurion moved back smoothly.

Exposing himself as little as possible, he observed a pitiful few vehicles moving back as per his orders.

The last Wolf used its superior speed to roar backwards and away from the advancing terrors, passing the retreating Wirbelwind, the quadruple AA tank having not yet fired a shot.

A single M26, smoking like a factory chimney, reversed away from the ridgeline, both crew and observer unsure if the damaged tank would make it.

Both Centurions were still runners and seemed to be the most reluctant to move, still remaining just short of the ridgeline.

The last vehicle he could see clearly was the ISU-122, still alive, still fighting, stopping to fire and dropping back alternately, the heavy machine-gun on its roof belting out at any infantry that threatened.

A sharp crack to his rear startled Von Mecklenburg and he turned wide-eyed.

The liberated M-24 light tank had now joined the fray, helping to keep the enemy away from the Soviet SP gun's path of retreat.

He turned to the left and tried to make out anything of note over in the nearby village of Nietuja.

He thought he saw something but lead spattered off the Centurion's flank and forced him to duck low.

'Seven... is that fucking all... just seven?'

In the fiery ruins of Nietuja, the last two tanks of Third Company were hidden in the smoke and so evaded his gaze, but thanked their lucky stars for the cover as they slipped back as Soviet tank hunting teams swarmed over the ridge.

Von Mecklenburg spotted the surge of enemy infantry off to the left of the ISU.

Now was his chance.

"Load canister. Gunner target right four... anti-tank troops... take them out."

The shell slid home and von Mecklenburg settled himself to observe.

'Fucking slavs!'

"On!"

"Fire!"

The 20pdr spat out a stream of solid steel balls which engulfed the nine men stalking the ISU.

The Soviet anti-tank teams simply flew apart, the high-speed impact and power of so much metal simply destroying any semblance of their human forms and scattering pieces and fluids in a wide arc.

"Fucking hell!"

"Donnerwetter!"

"There's more to the left... another shot!"

The Soviets decided that discretion was necessary and melted away into the ground before the metal storm arrived.

None the less, the ground was churned up in places, and turned red with the products of dying men.

Von Mecklenburg was seriously impressed, but could not enjoy the moment.

"Achtung! APDS. Target tank, left six, three hundred, fire when on!"

The turret swung easily and the gunner's warning and weapon discharge became one.

The 20pdr's APDS shell punched through the T-54's armour like the proverbial hot knife through butter but failed to hit

623

anything of note and the enemy tank moved on, angling itself and setting up a shot.

"Driver, back le…"

The huge double sound robbed him of his senses, so loud was the shock of the 100mm shell's passage, angling off the glacis plate before smashing into the very top of the gun mantlet and deflecting upwards.

His gunner remained on target and another APDS struck the target, this time with even less effect than before.

Von Mecklenburg shook his head to try and regain some of his senses and felt the blood run down his face and splatter on his hands.

He hadn't even realised he had hit his head, so badly had his senses been affected.

His lips moved but he could hear nothing, and wasn't sure that he was even making sense.

None the less, the tank stopped as he had commanded, and the enemy's shell streaked past the turret by the narrowest of margins.

His ordered ammunition change had also been heard, and the gunner put a HESH shell on target.

Externally, the shell left a mark to show its point of impact.

Internally, spalded metal reduced the turret crew to nothing more than offal.

The T-54 was as dead as they came.

Speaking without hearing, von Mecklenburg ordered the Centurion further back and into the building line, taking advantage of a lull as the Soviet thrust temporarily ran out of steam, and the Guards' officers prepared their men for the final attack.

Deniken's force from the 171st Regiment struck hard into Haefali's men, forcing them backwards.

The legionnaires rallied and counterattacked, retaking a portion of the Floriańska road.

Harangued by Deniken, the 171st's leader led his men forward from the front in a second surge, assisted by men from Artem'yev's 361st Guards Rifle Regiment and a company of tanks from 53rd Guards Tank Brigade.

By accident, not design, the focus of the attack struck the join between Haefali's 1st and 2nd Battalion, battalions in name only, having been reduced by the heavy fighting to keep open an escape route for the Uhlmann attack force.

Haefali's group split in two and the attacking Soviets pushed hard and opened the gap, moving left and right but also pushing forward until they encountered a scratch force of recon troopers and engineers at Rozdole, and the semblance of a Legion defence line formed again.

None the less, as Haefali's report to Knocke indicated, it was only a matter of time until the Soviet numbers proved decisive.

In the confusion of the battle, Knocke did all he could to stave off disaster, and his urgent request to St.Clair got reserve units of the Alma moving to protect Route 79, the escape route from Koprzywnica.

It was Knocke's last act as a divisional commander before circumstances returned him to another side of his role; that of combat soldier.

From the north, the Soviets swept over the ridgeline in greater numbers and smashed into the waiting tirailleurs and legionnaires.

From the east came the remainder of the 171st Regiment, supported by more men of the 116th Division and tanks from the 6th Guards Tank Corps, released by Rybalko to ensure success and the capture of Route 9.

From the southeast came the remnants of the 6th GIBTR.

All were focussed on the modest village of Sulisławice and control of its heights and roads.

"Alarm!"

Knocke looked up from the map table as the shout was taken up by others around his headquarters building.

Firing commenced close at hand, although the sounds of battle had generally been increasing as the fight grew closer.

Maillard, the man who had once struck Knocke with his weapon at the behest of Molyneux, dashed in breathlessly, gasping in air to deliver a report.

"Deep breaths, Captaine."

"Apologies, mon General. The Russians have broken through in the east. They are less than a hundred metres from this building. You must evacuate yourself immediate, Sir."

Knocke nodded and shrugged.

"I think the time for evacuation is well past, Capitaine. We must stand and not move back. The whole division is relying on us."

He grabbed Maillard's shoulder as he seemed to flag.

"One more effort, Capitaine. We've beaten them before and we'll beat them again."

Knocke looked around the headquarters and realised that every eye was upon him.

"Time to earn our pay, Kameraden."

He beckoned D'Estlain to one side.

"Still nothing from Emmercy?"

"Nothing at all, mon Général. Given the enemy's present moves I suspect he is beyond help or contact."

"Yes, you're probably right, Alphonse, but keep trying. I'll contact Lavalle immediately. You speak to St.Clair. Tell him of our predicament and that we're relinquishing control to him until this mess is sorted, Make sure all Camerone units understand the situation. Make sure you speak to Durand and Haefali directly."

"Oui, mon Général."

"Then I want you and a skeleton staff to get out of here. Head towards Bukowa and keep on going until you find friendly units. If you can re-establish control then all well and good, but I need you out of here as soon as possible... just in case."

D'Estlain opened his mouth to argue but Knocke stopped him with the simple measure of offering a salute.

His protest was strangled at birth and he could only start obeying his commander's instructions.

Knocke noticed Hässelbach and Lutz stood in the doorway, each carrying sufficient hardware and ammunition to conquer a small country.

Quite clearly, they were a self-appointed bodyguard and Knocke was secretly pleased to see them so well prepared.

He pored further over the map to see if there was more that he could do and decided on one last radio message.

Durand signed off and returned the handset to his radio operator.

The remaining leadership of the Uhlmann group had gathered in woods just south of Cegielnia, and the strain was writ large on their faces.

They had heard Knocke's final instructions to them and understood that if Sulisławice fell then they would not escape their present predicament... unless they moved fast now and to hell with all caution.

Knocke had not given them false hope, and had admitted that the likelihood of a successful defence of Sulisławice was not high, but that it would be held for as long as humanly possible.

He had not ordered them to do anything as such, but had given them alternatives, depending on their tactical situation.

Above all, they were to save as much of the group as possible, and work with Haefali to extricate the Camerone from its disastrous predicament.

He had quickly set out the options as he saw them and placed the decision in their hands.

The call had ended in a rushed fashion as some threat caused Knocke to cut short his messages.

Durand looked at the map, gripping the small table in his vice-like grip, an outward display of his anger and concern.

"Ideas, mes amis?"

Jung, somehow separated from his unit in Haefali's group, spoke nervously, unused to such invitations.

"The shortest route seems to be back to Alma but..."

"...but if Loniów has fallen, we'll have the lot opposite up our arses in an instant."

Braun had a way with words.

Durand laughed.

"All our options will end up in a fight, but I agree with Major Braun."

He used the French rank, even though it sometimes brought confusion.

"We could cut due east and use the river as a secure flank... a longer journey and still fraught with danger, although we can find refuge with the bulk of Alma."

No one fancied that option.

"Join up with Haefali, leapfrog back across country rather than the roads, and smash our way through Loniów?"

"There's another way... another option... one I think we have to take."

Artillery started dropping to their rear, almost as if to affect their thinking.

"Well, Uncle Joe's boys are trying to reduce our options."

Durand's comment had the desired effect and the group laughed lightly.

"What's your other way?"

Durand accepted a cigarette from Braun and listened as the senior NCO spoke.

"The one route we've rejected. The Oberführer told us there was no chance of escaping to the west as he's about to be overrun, only south or southeast. But there's the issue. The Russians also know that, so west... that's where we can go and achieve some surprise surely?"

Durand married the words to the map.

"But here's a Soviet infantry regiment by all repor..."

They ducked low as a shell whipped in close by and dropped earth and stones amongst them.

"A full regiment with tank support and all the rest of it."

"So we go above them, Commandant."

"The Floriańska?"

"Yes, Sir...why not? They won't be expecting it... it allows us to move tight with Haefali. Yes, we'll have exposed flanks but we'll have exposed flanks whichever way we go, and this way we serve a higher purpose... Sulisławice... we'll save Sulisławice!"

The men stiffened, for they knew what Braun meant to say, but held back from voicing.

'Knocke... we'll save Knocke!'

Durand clapped his hands to break the moment.

"Let me speak to Colonel Haefali... but I like it."

Aircraft of the DRL flew away from the target area, satisfied that they had put their ordnance bang on target.

In that they were wholly correct.

The furthest advance of Rybalko's northern force had been stopped dead in its tracks, in some cases quite literally, as the panzers of Kampfgruppe Schemmerring, derived mainly from the 116th Panzer Division, smashed the lead elements in and around the village of Ujazd.

From there, they and the Grossdeutschland group had rolled much of the enemy back, leaving a few pockets of resistance to be mopped up later.

At Kamieniec and the river line of the Koprzywianka River that ran through it, elements of the 167th Guards Rifle Regiment and its tank support from 7th Special Guards Tank Brigade stood and stopped the German advance.

Neither mortars nor artillery could shift the defenders and the urgency of the situation with the Legion Corps meant that there was no time for finesse.

As he was about to send his men forward, Schemmerring received welcome news and delayed his attack.

DRL aircraft from two units swept over the battlefield, followed by a squadron from the USAAF.

The lead unit was the 11th Schlachtstaffel, the last unit in the DRL to operate the Hs-129-B3 ground attack aircraft that had graced the Luftwaffe in WW2.

The new leadership of the Luftwaffe had decided that such a powerful weapon could not be allowed to fade away, so production of a version with new power plants, an improved recoil mount, and a more streamlined gun pod had been authorised and commenced, despite the fact that testing of the prototype had only just got underway

Their powerful 75mm Bordkanone ripped the T-54s apart like tin cans, and the first pass the DRL flyers left eight in various stages of disrepair.

Each Hs-129 was equipped with a magazine-fed main weapon that could fire twelve rounds simply by a press of a firing button.

The payoff was an aircraft that was slow and cumbersome to fly, which was why the Hs-129s never went anywhere without friends.

The Red Air Force tried to interfere, but the DRL had FW-190s and Spitfires flying overhead, and no interceptors ever looked like getting through.

The Henschels made further passes, losing one of their number to ground machine-gun fire, but exacting a huge price on the tanks and vehicles of the defenders.

After them came Thunderbolts, who firing their rocket ordnance in the village, deliberately avoiding the two bridges that spanned the river.

They then turned and bore in again, and each aircraft in turn dropped two M29 cluster bombs, which held ninety 4lbs fragmentation charges each.

Finally came the USAAF, a full squadron of the improved Skyraiders laden with everything in the inventory.

5" FFAR rockets streaked down and smashed the infantry positions on the riverbanks.

By now the Soviet soldiers understood the pattern of attack and Guards' soldiers who had stood the rigours of the Eastern Front started to flee from their positions, knowing what was to come.

Running down the river line, the squadron of USAAF attack aircraft laid napalm along the defensive lines, taking the lives of those who had broken ranks as well as those who had stoically remained.

Men ran like burning torches, screaming, squealing, adding to the horrific scene that greeted Schemmerring as he observed the strikes.

The situation was now changed and he ordered a modest part of his force to attack the defences at Kamieniec, sensing that the enemy was spent and needed only the smallest of pushes to run from the field, preferring to concentrate most of his force for the push to break through to the surviving legionnaires of Emmercy's group, surrounded at Pokrzywianka and a couple of other places further east.

Part of the Grossdeutschland battlegroup pressed ahead and crashed straight into the fires and destruction that was Kamieniec and showed that Schemmerring was wholly correct, for the surviving Russians fell back in disarray before them.

His main force, the remainder of the GD group plus his own 116th Division Kampfgruppe, turned to the southeast and pressed down Route 758, pushing the stunned Soviet guardsmen before them.

The headquarters of the Legion Corps D'Assaut was a hive of activity; some of it well focused and direct, some of it the work of men who were clearly rattled by the worsening situation.

Lavalle took a minute to himself with a cigarette and coffee, observing the map as it was updated, and no amount of reappraisal could make it look anything other than a disaster of monumental proportions.

Either the Legion had been tremendously unlucky and simply attacked into an unknown major Soviet assault, or it had walked into a well-concealed trap.

Whichever it was would be decided by men other than he, who would have time to consider everything in their enquiries.

Time was not a luxury he had.

'What else can I do? What els…'
"What was that, Maurice? What did he say?"
Delacroix smiled as he replied.

"Good news, mon Général! Our comrades in the German Army have driven back the Soviet incursion northwest of Klimontów. They report good progress and anticipate relieving Colonel Emmercy within the hour."

"No… no … not that… what did Haefali say?"

Delacroix turned back to the radios and refocussed on the one man who was recording the words of the third assault group's commander.

The operator finished writing, acknowledged receipt, and handed the paper to an NCO who handed it on to the Legion's CoS.

He skim read it and moved to the map, reading its subtle lines and colours as he translated the words into the battle situation.

"Mon Dieu! He can't be serious, Sir?"

Lavalle read the report and laughed aloud, albeit briefly.

"He's deadly serious, Maurice. Absolutely deadly serious. Now, let's get Alma prepped up for this… maybe… no… definitely get the part-brigade from 1st Division moved up to Route 9. No sense in keeping them back in reserve now. We need to distract as much as possible if this is going to work. Get onto air… we need as much as they can give us. We also need to tell our DRH comrades. Merde… he's either brilliant or suicidal… and I can't decide which. Now, if you please, Maurice. No time to lose!"

Delacroix sped away to do his commander's bidding as Lavalle headed for the telephone to report to the Army Commander.

After some questioning, he escaped his leader's wrath and incredulity, and returned to the map table.

Lavalle relaxed as much as he could, and the moment of lessened tension gave him a clarity he had lacked in the previous moments.

He nodded to himself and smoked another cigarette as he wondered why he hadn't understood in the first instance.

Delacroix disturbed his thoughts.

"All communications sent and acknowledged, mon Général. You look like you're happy. Something the Général said?"

"Hardly, Maurice. He said if that doesn't work you're being transferred to the Camel Corps."

The comment hit the spot and his CoS guffawed loudly.

"I'll take you with me, mon Général. But why the smile? Have I missed something, Sir?"

"We both did, Maurice… we both did."

631

The colonel waited expectantly, casting his eye over the map to find signs of Lavalle's revelation.

A finger was tapping on convergence of two routes.

Route 9 and Floriańska.

Sulisławice.

Delacroix didn't understand.

And then he did, and simply nodded.

'Knocke'.

0654 hrs, Tuesday. 1st April 1947, Sulisławice, Poland.

They were still holding against all comers or, as Knocke thought to himself, the Russians were simply not trying as hard.

The hastily-dug trenches had proven invaluable as the remnants of the group clung to the rear end of Sulisławice and the small hamlet of Skwirzowa-Młyn to the south.

They had resisted everything the enemy had thrown at them, and exacted a terrible price from the attacking Guards, but not without cost to themselves.

Knocke's bodyguard was now down to one man, with Lutz seriously wounded and near death in the aid post, his stomach perforated by a burst of PPSh fire.

Amongst the dead was Colonel Renat-Challes, cut down by a mortar splinter as he organised the eastern defences.

Commandant Truffaux was there too, killed up close and personal when his position was overrun and he refused to leave a wounded officer behind.

A counter-attack by his men recovered his shattered body before the position was lost once more.

Companies were now platoons, and units were led by sergeants and corporals.

There was no man now who was safe and away from direct fighting.

Nearly every legionnaire was in the front line, for they were surrounded and there was no place to hide.

The sounds of fighting to the northwest grew louder, but the ring around them remained.

Solid and impenetrable.

Zilinski, coordinating the attack, winced as the orderly handled his ankle.

He had mounted a ruined wall to better observe the enemy positions and it had collapsed, snapping his ankle and tearing flesh from his calf.

He had ordered the bone bound as tight as possible so that he could manage to move around in some way.

The pain was immense and he had slugged a couple of glasses of vodka before the doctor had slipped him something outside of army issue to help ease his suffering.

His mind was now relaxed, almost emptied of the stresses of battle, unless he focussed hard on the problems he faced.

Which were twofold.

Firstly, the ex-SS and their lackeys fought every bit as hard as they had done in the Patriotic War.

He hadn't fought them in the new war until this point.

Now he knew that the rumours were true, and they were still the hardest men the Allies could field.

Secondly, his commander, the ill-humoured Major General Deniken was on his back, threatening and cajoling him to complete his mission and secure the roads in and around Sulisławice.

His units, such as Deniken insisted that he should be attacking and winning with, were great on paper.

But his battalions had shrunk to companies and his command structure was ravaged.

As always, the enemy killed the leadership whenever the opportunity arose, and they had given the Legion bastards plenty of opportunities.

Leaving his mortars and artillery to put shells into the enemy defensive perimeter, Zilinski had earlier met with the commanders of 53rd Guards Tanks, and the 361st, 167th, and 171st Guards Rifle Regiments, in order to plan one last coordinated attack.

0700 hrs, Tuesday. 1st April 1947, Sulisławice, Poland.

"Urrah! Urrah!"

"Alarm! Alarm!"

Shouts came from men on all sides, as the Guards rose up and charged once more, the tanks moved forward, and men stood to their weapons for the final defence.

Again, it was the tirailleurs of the 7ᵉ RTA, battered and reduced to a shadow of their former strength, that suffered the focus of Zilinski's attack, his 167th Regiment augmented by his own headquarters troops and those of the 53rd Guards Tank Brigade, mainly consisting of two companies of SMG troops.

Elsewhere, a wave of attacks went in, providing pressure on all points of the enemy defence.

The light tanks and armoured cars of 3rd Guards Motorcycle Battalion had cut the road west, and they now demonstrated against the rear of the Legion position, although more carefully than before now that they understood that enemy anti-tank troops were there in numbers.

They actually were not as numerous as the motorcycle troops thought, but Peters' men had plenty of weapons and the will to use them profligately, as the ruined T-70s and 80s indicated, the last of which had fallen to a shot from an enemy Tiger I tank that arrived in the nick of time.

Zilinski's attack plan simply required the motorcycle unit to remind the defence of its presence, not expose itself to greater harm, an order followed with great enthusiasm.

The Legion perimeter buckled but held, the tirailleurs pinned in place by the bastions provided by the survivors of the 1er BCL.

The Centurions were both still operational, although von Mecklenburg's fellow commander had been killed during the last attack.

His position was taken by the commander of the overheated ARL-44, his vehicle having seized up and stubbornly refusing to move.

1er BCL was down to five running tanks.

Two Centurions, the Tiger II, a Wolf, and Lohengrin.

The M-24 and one M-26 Pershing were still fighting, but neither could not move.

The ISU-122 had succumbed to enemy RPGs and grenades, and the Wirbelwind had died spectacularly when an 82mm mortar bomb had dropped into its open turret.

The initial explosion had been impressive enough, but the subsequent fireworks were remarkable as its mass of 20mm ammunition exploded like a children's party display.

Elsewhere, nine Panthers of various types clung to the ruins.

Jorgensen's tank-destroyers had survived well, losing solely two Jagdpanthers and, as always, the Einhorn remained supreme with seven kills to its name.

The surviving Legion mortars were down to a handful of rounds and already the crews' thoughts turned to the moment when they would have to pick up their weapons and become infantrymen.

For now they waited, sights almost on minimums, waiting for the order to fire their last few rounds at the point of most concern.

They had very little time to wait as the positions of 2^e Compagnie of 3^e/5^e RdM were overrun by a wave of screaming guardsmen from Artem'yev's 361st Regiment.

Mortar shells started to land amongst the second echelon of the 361st's men, which gave the survivors and two platoons of the reserve 1er Compagnie to counter-attack, supported by a pair of Jaguars.

They nearly succeeded but the mortar shells ran out and the Soviet reserves surged forward in time to stop the Legionnaires in their tracks.

Leaving one platoon to bolster the front positions, Lieutenant Tüpper, the de facto commander of 1er Compagnie, recovered his men and got them resupplied and readied the reserve unit for the next call to action.

His force was swelled by the arrival of men from the werkstatt and supply units, under the command of the ever-cheerful Commandant Walter Fiedler.

They had little time to sort out the niceties as the tirailleurs buckled under a surge of tanks and infantry.

With only one Jaguar [fr] as support, Fiedler led off his group and two section of Tüpper's men to restore the line.

En route, Fiedler met Knocke, who was doing the rounds of his men, keeping up morale and learning as much as he could about the situation.

"Look after yourself, Walter!"

"Have no fear, Oberführer. I'll survive to keep your rust buckets going!"

He dashed off into the battle ahead, followed by his men.

Knocke moved on again, surrounded by the military police, led by Maillard, and protected by the bodies of Hässelbach and Ett, who had replaced the unfortunate Lutz.

Despite Knocke's annoyance with their close presence, the two made sure they kept as tight to him as they possibly could.

Soviet mortar rounds started to rain down again, and two of the MPs went down hard as shrapnel ripped into their bodies.

One man would never rise again, but the other still lived, so a soldier was detailed to carry him back to the aid post for treatment.

The party moved on once more.

Ahead, a sharp crack indicated that a large gun was in operation.

The party moved cautiously until they could observe the position.

A Pak 44, served by a single man, was resisting a pair of enemy tanks and their infantry support.

Around the huge anti-tank gun there were Legion infantry in the rubble, their weapons pouring bullets towards the advancing Soviets, seemingly without effect.

"Leave it to me, mon General! Gallet! Blanc! You two, with me!"

Maillard sprang up and, with the two men in close attendance, sprinted towards the Pak 44 and its lone gunner.

Gallet had once served in artillery, so Maillard assigned him to load and to direct himself and Blanc as to what to do.

The German legionnaire gunner appeared completely mad and laughed his way through the brief conversation as to who would do what.

"Put it up the pipe and I'll send it to our cousins, kettenhund!"

He grabbed Maillard's shoulder and tapped the breech of the huge gun.

"Just keep your turnip out of the way of that or you'll need a new one. Kapische?"

"Oui."

"Right... let's kill the bastards!"

A shell burst behind the gun, fired by one of the T34s hiding in the ruins.

Blanc screamed as a piece of his ear was slashed by a brick fragment.

It was messy and painful, and made the man curse constantly as he moved back and forward from the crates containing the huge shells to the waiting hands of Gallet.

"Right, kettenhund! Watch out!"

The breech flew back as the shell leapt towards its target.

"Fuck and abhorrence. Again... faster now!"

Wagner was no longer sane in the real sense, the butchering of his crew, his old comrades, having unhinged his mind.

"Loaded!"

"Good, good, kettenhund... we'll make a gunner of you yet... watch out!"

Again the Pak spat a shell at the Soviet force.

Maillard wrinkled up his nose in disgust as the heavy shell moved through the space occupied by a Soviet soldier, leaving nothing more than a pair of legs before it raced on and penetrated the T34's hull.

"Ha! Ha! Ha! Trick shot... more!"

Another shell went home as the barrel rotated to line up with the other tank.

Bullet struck the gun's armoured plate as a Maxim was got to work from the first floor of what had once been a tailor's shop.

"You cheeky bastards!"

Rather than killing the tank, Wagner chose to engage the machine-gun.

The 128mm cracked again and the shot smashed into the position adjacent to the Maxim team.

The Soviet machine-gun and its servants ceased to be a problem.

"Blessed Christmas to you and yours, you bastards... fuck with me, will you?"

He turned around and found Maillard still waiting with an open breech.

"Kettenhund, kettenhund, wherefore art my fucking shell, kettenhund?"

Wagner pulled out his Walther pistol and started firing over the top of the gun shield.

'Totally fucking mad!'

Maillard was not the only one thinking it, as Knocke and his men were observing everything.

Content that the position would hold for now, the Camerone commander and his small contingent moved on.

"I see the aerials, Hauptsturmfuhrer. No shot."

Jorgensen hummed his acknowledgement and considered relocating, but immediately rejected the idea.

All around him were men of the 5ᵉ RdM and he didn't want any accidents.

Besides, whatever it was would have to move forward sooner or later.

His Schwarzjagdpanther was perfectly positioned, another reason he was loathe to move out.

637

It covered the main road that rose from the valley below, and there were already two tanks lazily burning to demonstrate the superiority of his position.

They had both been easy kills, upgunned T34/100s that had offered no resistance to the brutal power of his 128mm.

But he knew that the Soviet heavy tanks were beneath the ridgeline, and that they would prove a more difficult nut to crack, his efforts so far having brought only one kill, and that was shooting down with the height advantage.

Normally SP guns were at a disadvantage in such circumstances, but the ruins of Sulisławice channelled the enemy down excellent lines of fire, and the odds seemed to be in their favour... for now.

"It's moving, Hauptsturmfuhrer. Heading left."

'So it is.'

Jorgensen pictured the tactical situation and understood that the enemy vehicle had made a bad choice.

A very bad choice.

The IS-IV, for that was what it was, moved away from the road that Jorgensen covered, seeking an alternate on the right flank of the 6th GIBTR.

It chose a modest alleyway that just about accommodated the large tank's bulk.

Nosing carefully forward, its accompanying infantry moved through the ruins on either side, seeking lurking AT soldiers, or looking further forward to find other threats.

The leading scouts simply missed the lurking killer until it was too late, although the IS-IV's commander blurted out a warning as his instincts lit off.

"Blyad! Reverse, comrades! Reverse!"

The 'pile of rubble' fired and the 128mm shell simply opened up the IS-IV like it was a child's plaything, sending metal and burning fuel in all directions, often with fatal results for the accompanying infantry.

Putting another shot into the area, this time a HE shell, the Einhorn slowly backed out of its position and relocated, ready for another attempt.

Knocke observed the second shot and decided not to be near to the potent tank destroyer in case it attracted artillery or mortars in retaliation.

Moving away from the slowly manoeuvring Einhorn, he and his party found themselves close by a Jagdpanther and its accompanying Legionnaires.

The MPs spread out as Knocke, Hässelbach, and Ett climbed over some rubble and dropped down into a position crammed with exhausted legionnaires.

"Stillgestanden!"

"No, no... as you were, Kameraden."

The soldiers relaxed as Knocke approached the NCO in charge, who was giving the evil eye to the young inexperienced soldier who had called them to attention.

The sergeant did not salute; veterans simply didn't attract that sort of attention to themselves or senior ranks.

"Oberführer, Oberscharführer Sperl and seven men... now commanding 8th Zug, 3rd Kompagnie, 3rd Battalion, 5th Regiment. On tank protection duties. Two men dead and three wounded removed to the aid post, including Zugführer, Lieutenant Malfoix."

"Relax, Oberscharfuhrer."

Sperl did so quite openly, and flopped back onto the damaged chair that had been his resting place before the commanding officer arrived.

Knocke made great play of checking out the position, and looking out into the area beyond, but was really appreciating the men and their capacity to endure.

His assessment was worrying.

Returning to Sperl, he settled himself on some rubble and extracted his cigarettes.

All eyes focussed on the pack.

"Are you all out?"

"Think we smoked the last of poor Willi's cigarettes over an hour ago. Our billet burned out and we got through what we had quite quickly, Oberführer."

"Here... have these."

Knocke turned over the pack and also pulled a full one out of his trouser pocket.

"Danke, Oberführer, danke!"

Hässelbach interpreted his leader's eye contact, and moved forward, liberating his other 'water' bottle, proffering it to the exhausted NCO.

"Here, kamerad... but take it easy... it's potent stuff."

"Danke, kamerad."

Sperl took a slug and thought he was about to cough his intestines up through his throat."

"Fucking hell but that's savage stuff, kamerad. What's that so I know to avoid it in future?"

"Potato peelings and pork…mixed and fermented… local speciality so I'm told… that's why the Poles are all fucking mad!"

The outburst encouraged laughter from tired men, and the bottle did the rounds, with each man adding his own unfavourable comments on the contents.

Knocke refused the drink when it arrived in his hands.

"No, I think I'll pass this time."

He stood and the men around him automatically braced, despite his hand gently waving them to remain as they were.

"You're doing a great job, boys. We've just got to hold for a little while longer and the rest of the Corps will be up and relieve us. Just keep at it and don't let the bastards knock you out of here. Look after yourselves and see you after the war!"

The men semi-cheered and semi-laughed as he clambered back out, pausing only to turn and issue the normal words between soldiers.

"Hals- und beinbruch, Kameraden!"

Pausing to exchange greetings and get an update from Jorgensen through the Schwarzjagdpanthers squawk box, the party moved on until they were back where they started, on the west side of the defence.

Knocke dismissed the MPs to get some rest, and went to investigate the positions occupied by the specialist rocket troops of 4^e RACE.

"Achtung!"

The experienced troopers did not stand or salute, but braced themselves, ready for orders or whatever else might come their way.

Again Knocke waved the men to relax and stopped the NCO reporting with a quick gesture.

He reached to his tunic pocket and then stopped himself.

"I find myself without, Hässelbach."

A packet magically appeared and flew across the small space to Knocke.

He lit two, and passed one to the waiting NCO.

"Danke, Oberführer."

The pack headed around the group and returned to Hässelbach in a much lighter state.

"Peters, isn't it?"

The man nodded wearily.

"I've heard many good things about you and your wonder rockets."

"Thank you, Oberführer. We've only got two left now, and just the one launcher."

They smoked as Peters went on to detail the state and responsibilities of his unit, his flow interrupted twice by the burst of nearby mortar shells.

"Well, we'll make sure we find some more. If they're to be had, we'll get them, Peters."

Knocke stopped to cough as more dust fell from the rickety ceiling.

"Thank you, Oberführer. For now, we'll use what we have to hand."

The man keeping watch fired a controlled burst with his ST-45.

He spat and spoke to no one in particular.

"Think that was their breakfast arriving. Lucky bastards."

'Scheisse... the men haven't eaten... how could I forget?'

Knocke stood up and dusted himself off.

"I'll see what rations I can get sent round, Peters. Meanwhile, keep your men here and hold them back. This is the lightest point of our defence... at least from what I can see. I'll send some extra men to bolster this side... and I hope they'll come bearing some hot food."

He squeezed the NCO's arm in a comradely fashion and took leave of the group with nods and waves of his hand.

Knocke headed back to the building that housed what was left of his headquarters, only to find most of it smashed flat to rubble and matchwood.

He exchanged silent looks with Hässelbach and Ett.

Across the road was the building in which the reserve had their contact point, and he liaised with Tüpper, who now sported a bloody bandage round his head.

"Happened when the artillery hit us, Oberführer. Flattened your headquarters... everyone was out by then thankfully. I lost three men... good men."

"So is the reserve reformed?"

"I've two platoons to my name, Oberführer. One regular, one ersatzgruppe, pulled together from anything including mortar men and tank crew. My tanks are all back out in the front line, but I've commandeered the old beast outside, just to give me some clout if needed."

Tüpper pointed out of the window to where the two platoons were positioned, either side of the tank that he had forcibly seconded from the 1e DCA.

Despite the circumstances, Knocke found himself amused and even happy at the sight.

"I'll go and speak with your troops, Lieutenant. Do we have a field kitchen or are the cooks in your ersatz platoon too?"

"Both, Oberführer. The kitchen is set up over on the right there... behind that lump of metal... where the ersatzgruppe is placed. Quartermaster Niveau was reluctant to abandon his equipment, so he relocated the lot... ladle in one hand, rifle in the other. He's making soup apparently."

"Excellent. I'll visit him directly. I'll be using some of the ersatz platoon to distribute the food as soon as it's ready. I also need you to leaven off eight men to reinforce the rocket troopers over to the wes..."

A runner broke into their conversation and, having been unable to decide whom to report to, spoke to both officers at the same time.

"Sirs, Capitaine Jorgensen reports that the enemy are gathering to his front. He requests infantry reinforcements immediately, and any ammunition that can be spared, especially grenades."

"I'll leave that with you, Lieutenant."

Knocke saluted and left the position, heading towards the silent metal beast up the road.

0750 hrs, Tuesday, 1st April 1947, headquarters of Special Combat Group Rybalko, Zawichost, Poland.

Despite all his planning...

Despite the use of the very best the Motherland could supply...

Despite the valour of the soldiers and airmen...

Despite all the advantages, both contrived or brought on by Mother Nature herself...

Despite everything... the whole plan was behind schedule.

Not only that, but things were developing in spite of him, partially because of the fluid situation, and partially because of the enemy's resistance and movement.

Rybalko was furious, and his humour did not improve as more and more reports arrived at his headquarters.

To the north his forces had blunted themselves on a German panzer division and both sides were hammered to a halt.

To the south, the French Alma Division had conceded ground but now stuck to a defensive line on Route 9 like it was nailed in place.

His 1st Guards Engineer had bled dry trying to shift the Legion bastards out... and to cap it all, Chekov, their commander, was missing, possibly killed.

'...*probably killed...good man too...* '

Centrally, his forces had done extremely well and virtually surrounded one of the French Legion formations in and around Klimontów, and another force that had backed up behind it, and to its left.

His encircling strike had reached Route 9 and all but closed the enemy's escape route at Łoniów... all but, but not quite.

Expecting a major attempt to escape down that route, Rybalko had oriented his forces in two directions but, as yet, no attempt to break out had materialised.

Instead, there were confused reports of strong forces pushing up to the south of Łoniów, and some extra troops appearing in the area of the enemy's Alma Legion Division.

Added to that the increasing southern focus of the nearby units of the German Army and things were less than satisfactory.

And then there was the junction at Sulisławice.

"What's happening at Sulisławice, Comrade?"

Major-General Ziberov was a humourless man who, despite advice from men in important positions, still sported a small moustache resembling that of the deceased German dictator.

He shook his head in exasperation.

"Comrade Polkovnik General, the reports were of heavy fighting but no progress. Last communication with Polkovnik Zilinski indicated a short respite whilst he resupplied and concentrated his forces. His final attack will begin at 0820... some hours after we should have been through the village and beyond."

"He has enough forces at his disposal. Tell him I expect his report of victory before 0900. And what's this?"

He selected an area of the map around Byszówka.

"When we split the Legion unit at Klimontów, it would seem that these troops to the east did not all surrender."

The reports had been slightly exaggerated, in that his forces had taken a few dozen wounded men prisoner, including the force's commanding officer, and the importance grew as it passed further up the chain of command.

In reality, a good portion of Emmercy's group had survived intact, admittedly on the wrong side of the Soviet thrust, but had established itself defensively in and around Byszówka, where it now sat astride Route 9, limiting any moves to back up the 7th Guards Special Tanks that had previously used it to head south.

"What are we doing about it, Ivan?"

"General Artem'yev is personally leading a special group from his division to overcome the obstacle and open Route 9 up again."

"Excellent, excellent... and this?"

"We're unsure at the moment, Comrade Polkovnik General. Some garbled reports of a small attack... possibly coming from Koprzywnica... they've just come in but I'm having them questioned right now. Possibly stragglers from the enemy forces we've bottled up in Koprzywnica... possibly a diversion to make us think they're moving back down the Floriańska... nothing more than that."

Rybalko frowned and scratched his bald head, seeking out the place that was itching.

It was in his brain and beyond physical contact.

"Tell me your thinking, Ivan. Why would they not come down the Floriańska?"

"A longer route... poorer road really, especially after the artillery and mortars have done their work. Long exposed flanks... it's not the sensible option... plus we see enemy forces massing here... south of Łoniów, and extra units bolstering the Alma Division between Łoniów and the Vistula. There's no support available in the direction of Sulisławice... except for the small force that Zilinski can't seem to shift."

The reasoning made sense.

The Red Air Force had paid heavily acquiring the information about forces behind the enemy's lines, but it was accurate and up to date.

And yet...

'And yet these bastards are capable of anything...'

The itch went and Rybalko went into overdrive.

"Order our units here to prepare for attacks to their front from the newly arrived 'relief' force. Ivan... the forces here must still be prepared to resist a breakout but..."

Rybalko paused and thought it through one final time.

'... but of course they fucking would!'

"Order our forces on the Floriańska... and here... and here... to reorient themselves to oppose an attack out of the pocket... towards Sulisławice. Tell Deniken... this is him here, yes?"

The forward HQ of the 1st Guards Mechanised had moved up but the writing was unintelligible, hastily scrawled by a young officer under increasing pressure.

"Yes, that's HQ 1 GMRD, Comrade General."

"Good. I want him and his reserve force sat astride the Floriańska now. He commands and nothing... but nothing... escapes this trap."

"And Zilinski, Comrade General?"

"Tell him enough that he's aware of the possibility, but keep him focussed on Sulisławice... and 0900 stands... more need now than ever to get the fucking place in our hands. Questions?"

There were none and Ziberov was quickly away to get things organised.

Rybalko took a sip of his sweet tea and summoned his air liaison officer.

"Comrade Polkovnik, I want you to relay the following to the Frontal Aviation commander... as a priority."

Even as Rybalko passed on his needs, the men of the trapped Legion assault groups smashed into part of the 171st Guards Rifle Regiment just east of Beszyce.

The breakthrough to Sulisławice had begun in earnest.

0752 hrs, Tuesday, 1st April 1947, Sulisławice, Poland.

"Stillgestanden!"

The bow gunner was new to the tank crew, so had no idea what he was about to witness.

All he knew was that the divisional commander had just walked up to the tank and he was the only man who wasn't snoring.

Knocke would have let the men sleep, but it was too late now.

Köster looked like a man from another planet, a man who had just been woken from the deepest of deep sleeps, which was indeed wholly accurate.

Meier looked only slightly more focussed.

The other two men, Hans Jarome and whoever it was, looked like they had been smoking something wholly unauthorised, their eyes no more awake than the boots on their feet.

"At ease, kameraden... at ease."

He moved forward, nodding at the alert crewman who was so in awe that he forgot to report to the senior officer.

"Rudi... Klaus... Hans..."

Knocke held out his hand and all three men took it in turn as they started to wake up quickly, as one does when confronted by senior ranks in unexpected places.

"Relax now."

645

Knocke nodded to the two new members and took a seat on a convenient fruit box as Hässelbach made himself comfortable on a piece of brickwork.

"How are we doing, kameraden? Alles klar?"

Rudi Köster gave a brief but full resume of their fighting state and running condition.

"How are the bolts now, Klaus? Still holding?"

"Yes indeed, Oberführer. No problems at all. Good quality... and I got hold of a spare set... just in case."

Knocke returned the grin.

"But of course you did."

Köster had his cigarettes out and they did the rounds.

"Coffee for our guests, Linus."

The sentry, shocked at the informality, even though he had heard how these men had fought alongside Knocke at Brumath, busied himself with producing six mugs of steaming coffee from the saucepan that sat above a modest fire to the rear of the Tiger's bulk.

He passed the drinks round and realised he had miscalculated, so went without himself.

"A hard fight, kameraden."

"Yes... yes it is, Oberführer. We've lost a lot of old comrades today."

Knocke raised his coffee mug.

"To our old comrades."

They echoed the sentiment and drank in silence.

Knocke's thoughts were dark indeed.

'More old comrades than you know, my friends.'

"And who are your new comrades?"

"This one's the quiet type, Oberführer. Farber... Gunther Farber."

The general and private exchanged nods.

"And this one is Linus Wildenauer... apparently he trained as a vet but wanted to fight, so here he is, in our steel horse."

The crew laughed and Knocke assumed it was a well-rehearsed private joke, which it was.

Again, he exchanged nods with the new man, and then beckoned them all to sit.

"So, of course you understand the shitty situation we're in. Well, so does General Lavalle, and he's put together a relief to pull us out of this mess. In the meantime, we hold and that's that."

There was no reply needed.

"You're my only mobile reserve, so expect to get called early, and to go all over the plateau. How you off for fuel, Klaus?"

"All topped off, Oberführer, but I doubt there'll be another load. Once the Panthers have drained it down, I suspect it'll all be gone."

Which was in line with what Knocke had heard earlier.

"I hear they've got some of the big boys out there, Oberführer. Stalin tanks, all shapes and varieties."

"Seen one myself to the east side, but Jorgensen and the Panzerjager are there and dealing with them quite nicely."

"There's no more ammunition for our gun, Oberführer, so I'm running with a half-load, but we've stashed as much machine-gun ammunition as we can on Lohengrin, just in case we can't get back to here to rearm again."

"He's after promotion, Oberführer. Trying to be efficient but it was Jarome's and my idea. We run the tank. He's just a glory-hunting figurehead."

Knocke smiled but stayed silent, not wishing to steal Köster's moment.

"In which case, with your permission, Oberführer, I'm excused duties and off to have a fish in the river. You can put this one in charge. His mouth will bore the enemy to death and we'll have final victory assured."

Jarome guffawed loudly and slapped Meier on the shoulder.

"That's you all fucked up then, driver Meier. Am I relieved too, Oberführer?"

Knocke would have normally have played the game, but he simply didn't have the right frame of mind for it.

"Unfortunately... today I cannot spare any of you..."

He punched Köster on the forearm in a soft and playful fashion.

"... even the glory-hunting figureheads."

They all shared a laugh at that, even Köster himself.

Knocke stood, bring all of them to their feet.

"Well, I thought I'd come round and see how you all were. Take care, kameraden. There'll be more battles to come. Hals- und beinbruch!"

They took their leave of each other, but Knocke still dwelt at the side of the old Tiger, in which he had fought as a tank commander one bloody day at Brumath all those months ago.

He touched his hand to the cold steel and smiled.

Hässelbach coughed by way of reminder, and the legend that was Knocke simply slapped the legend that was Lohengrin before moving on to another group of soldiers.

647

The Katyusha strike arrived.

Accurate and deadly, the rockets plunged down amongst the defenders of the crucial junction and maimed and claimed men's lives all over the village.

Ett was struck down by shrapnel in the legs and was carried away to the aid post, still protesting his ability to fight.

Amongst those killed was Maillard, not by a rocket strike, but as a result of a secondary explosion at one of the small ammunition points.

Knocke had ordered such points established at the beginning of the battle, in order to minimise losses should a shell strike one, as occurred when the Katyusha rocket plunged into the small brick outhouse.

A piece of brick struck Maillard in the temple and he fell instantly, never regaining consciousness.

As the last rocket descended, the cries went up from around the perimeter, as Russians rose to charge, and legionnaires and tirailleurs braced themselves to fight for their lives.

Nearest to the 4ᵉ RACE positions, Knocke heard the tell-tale fizz of an X-7 being fired and was immediately drawn to the position, knowing that the missile would not have been expended on a light tank or an armoured car.

The 6th GIBTR had shifted round after its failures on the ridgeline, and now advanced on better ground towards the thin line of defenders, minus another IS-IV, struck down by the unerring aim of Peters, the miracle worker.

The imbalance of forces was obvious, and Knocke's brain shouted out for a solution.

"Hässelbach!"

The NCO arrived before his name had echoed away.

"Double back to Lieutenant Tüpper and tell him I need thirty of his men here, right now, with AT weapons! Plus, get Lohengrin mobile and tell Köster he'll be up against Stalin tanks."

Hässelbach was leaping away as Knocke turned back to his front and sought a place he could sit down and have a quiet moment to himself whilst he waited for the reserve force to arrive.

An old chair met his gaze, missing one leg but still carefully usable, and he settled himself down to gather his thoughts and steel himself for what he was sure was to come…

… and jerked awake.

'Mein Gott! What have I done!'

Unbelievably, he had fallen asleep.

He cursed himself in a silent and unforgiving scream of rage, knowing he had let every man in his command down by his actions.

Knocke sat up and then struggled to stand as he was neatly positioned between two pieces of brickwork.

Finally struggling upright but feeling decidedly wobbly on his feet, Knocke looked around to see if anyone had noticed his indiscretion…and immediately ducked in self-preservation.

Three Soviet soldiers were almost through the front line and on top of his position, having slipped through between the ruins unseen by Peters' force.

"Alarm!"

Least he thought he shouted a warning.

He couldn't hear anything.

The MP-40 was slung around his shoulder as it had been since he had decided to remain fighting with his men rather than escape, and now it refused to come round and act in preservation of his life.

The strap had caught on his holster and no amount of pulling would allow the sub machine-gun to come free.

The three Russians had already risen up, determined to silence the single enemy who had spotted them, hopefully before anyone else noticed the struggle.

That intent saved Knocke's life, as they declined to use their weapons in order to maintain a tenuous grip on secrecy.

Feeling a momentary panic, the old soldier forced himself into a second's calm and he grabbed for his holster, which, with the MP-40s strap around it, denied him access to his automatic.

Other choices were denied him as the first man was nearly upon him. SKS rifle held out in front of him with bayonet aimed directly at Knocke's chest.

Fate took a hand, or rather moved something, as the man pressed down on a piece of rubble causing another part to shift.

He lost his footing and crashed headfirst into another unforgiving piece of masonry.

The SKS flew at Knocke like a missile and struck his thigh, before falling just to one side.

The blow stung and water formed in his eyes, but the gift of a gun was too much to ignore and he swept the unfamiliar weapon up in his hands and turned to meet his new assailant.

The two Soviet motorcycle troopers arrived together and crashed into Knocke with no attempt to bayonet or club him; simply to put him down with brute force.

They succeeded, and the trio of bodies slammed into sharp and solid masonry.

One of the Russians gasped as a rib gave way, but the other landed sympathetically, only grazing his cheek and knuckles.

Knocke felt his ankle twist, and the blow in the small of his back brought on an instant stabbing pain that made him catch his breath.

He rolled instinctively and heard the butt of the enemy soldier's weapon hit the rubble with force.

"Alarm! Alarm!"

He shouted as best he could, but the exertions of rolling around to avoid the rifle butt robbed him of much of his power. At least he could now hear himself shout, albeit breathlessly.

He stopped rolling, held in place by the strap of the MP-40, which was stuck under an immovable piece of wall.

"Scheisse!"

The Russian fell directly on top of him and his lifeblood flowed across Knocke's face and into his eyes and mouth.

He felt his neck muscles protest as his chin was forced upwards at an odd angle.

"Get that piece of shit off him!"

The words came from someone else, the someone who had put two bullets through the back of the Russian's head and saved Knocke's life.

Daylight was restored as the carcass was dragged off him and willing hands dragged Knocke to his feet.

Walter Riedler, now a much-decorated sergeant and recently returned from an NCO's course in France, commanded the group of men sent back by Tüpper.

It was he who had downed the man preparing to kill his commander.

The irony of that was not wasted on Knocke, even in his dishevelled and exhausted state, for it was the young soldier Riedler who had once saved the life of his long gone friend, Von Arnesen, a lifetime ago.

"Thank you, Sergent Riedler... thank you."

The wounded Russian grunted then gurgled as one of the ex-SS soldiers kicked him hard in the throat, and the man struggled for air as the swelling shut off his airway.

He died without attracting any further attention.

"You were very lucky, Oberführer... really very lucky."

"Yes, I can see that, Sergent. Good shot, I think."

"I meant the mortar shell, Oberführer. Was really close. We thought you were dead."

"Mortar shell?"

"Yes. I saw you relaxing so waited for my men to catch up and then boom... mortar shell... must have landed a few feet away from you... sent the chair right over that way. You went up and came back down. Then after a few seconds you got up and the Russians arrived. Couldn't shoot for fear of hitting you. Then you were down, he was up."

Knocke hadn't fallen asleep, which was actually and strangely more of a relief than the fact that he had hadn't been killed.

"Thank you again, Sergent. We'll talk after the battle, but for now, get your men over to Peters and make sure you hold."

Riedler nodded and waved his men forward, the whole group rattling past at the double.

"And watch out for infiltrators. There may be more of them!"

The last man raised his hand in acknowledgement and the reinforcement group moved out of sight.

He felt hands tugging at his MP-40 and sling, as Hässelbach worked to free both weapons from the leather's grasp.

He hadn't even realised that his 'bodyguard' was there.

"You were luck, Oberführer."

"So I'm told, Hässelbach."

"Must be your lucky day, Oberführer."

"Somehow I doubt that!"

He hoped he would be alive when sunset visited itself upon the Polish village, just to see the truth of it.

"Ready?"

"When you are, Comrade Mayor."

The motorcycle unit's attack had stalled, mainly because the tanks had failed to get up and support.

Two of Stelmakh's tanks were hit, one of them flaming like a Bunsen burner, the second smoking lazily, but both equally dead, although the second had disgorged three shocked and wounded men who found safety with the infantry.

651

Now it was his decision to lead, as his last few tank commanders seemed reluctant to try again.

"Load HE."

The metallic clang as shell entered breach and the weapon was prepared were set against a strained silence, as they all knew that 'Krasny Suka' was about to take the biggest of risks.

"Driver... advance!"

Stepanov slipped the IS-III into a low gear and edged the tank forward, eyes wide open and ready to respond instantly to any threat or command.

The main gun swung in the direction of their advance as Ferensky tensed like a coiled spring.

Head poking out through the cupola, Stelmakh felt himself start to react and then, much to his surprise, not, despite the fear that gripped him and wrestled with his innards.

Kalinov simply hummed, denied any input from the outside world, save the sounds of battle that started to rise once more.

Around the IS-III, the motorcycle troopers and two platoons of men from the 22nd Guards Motorised Rifle Brigade pushed forward, carefully moving from cover to cover, screening the tank as they advanced.

A few bullets spanged off the tank's plates, one close enough to make Stelmakh jump with fright, the spark stinging his cheek until the heat died away.

The DShK had been set ready so that all Stelmakh needed to do was rise up and aim, although to do so would risk exposing himself to enemy fire.

The turret coaxial stuttered and Stelmakh watched as tracer bullets ate away at partially demolished wooden structure, from which two men emerged running as if the devil was on their heels.

The turret rotated slightly and walked bullets into the hindmost man, who fell like a rag doll.

The crew understood that there was no time for ceremony and Stelmakh had ordered that any target should be engaged without orders.

His eyes swept the area ahead, to the side, and occasionally in the air above, just in case the dreaded enemy ground attack aircraft came calling.

He missed seeing the muzzle and only caught the discharge of the weapon, before the hull front disappeared in a violent explosion.

"Yob tvoyu mat!"

Stepanov's voice had gained almost an octave, but he was intact, if not scared shitless.

"Where is he?"

Ferensky had not seen the flight of the Panzerschreck, neither had he seen the point of origin.

Stelmakh instinctively knew he had no time to tell him and propelled himself up through the turret.

The DShK hammered briefly before jamming.

"Mudaks!

He pulled the cocking handle to free the stoppage... hoping to free the stoppage... and pulled the trigger again.

Nothing.

He looked at the Legion anti-tank soldier, and saw only sightless eyes, and beyond another body, that of his loader who had also been caught by the short burst.

Both men were dead by his hand and 'Krasny Suka' lived to fight on.

"Driver, halt."

Stepanov needed no further encouragement, his hands trembling on the steering controls, the anti-tank rocket having hit just to the left of his position.

Checking that the infantry were moving up either side, Stelmakh pushed himself further out of the turret and unjammed the weapon.

He ducked instinctively as a small firefight developed off to the right, the supporting infantry getting up close and personal with a group of Legionnaires.

A flurry of grenades was followed by a sharp assault, and the position was taken at the cost of three men from both sides.

The assault moved on.

"It's not good, Rolf."

The bloodied man was panting, having narrowly escaped a Soviet frontal assault with his life.

"I lost three men back there. We're massively outnumbered... the schreck team didn't get the tank either, so he's going to be coming round that corner soon enough."

"What is it?"

"It's a Three for sure. Bastard thing machine-gunned Willi and Franz. They hit it, but you know… they're a fucking bitch them things."

"Yeah. Right. You have to hold the line there."

Peters indicated the building that the survivors of the recent attack were huddled in.

"Need you to keep the bastards off my back. I've got one Rotkäppchen left but this isn't the time. We'll try the Soviet fausts from the flank… just keep the infantry off my fucking back, Klaus!"

"I'll need more men, Rolf."

Peters had few men left that weren't already tied up, just two sections from the new arrivals.

"OK, take six men from the two reserve sections, three from each. Just hold them, Klaus… hold them."

The man moved quickly off to get the extra men.

Peters moved over to the weapons point, where he selected two of the Soviet panzerfaust copies, one for him and one for his companion.

"Right then, Patrice, just like I showed you in training and we'll kill the bastard. Follow me and keep low."

The Belgian legionnaire, one of the few non-Germans in the 4ᵉ RACE, took the Lans from Peters' hand without comment.

The two moved off to find a good position from which to get a side shot at what was about to come around the corner.

The 122mm belched flame as an HE shell was sent on its way to obliterate a machine post that was giving the infantry a hard time.

Alongside the heavy tank, two armoured cars were also pushing up, the commanders emboldened by the progress being made.

Armed with machine-guns, the BA-64s helped sweep the area, concentrating on any points that could harbour an anti-tank weapon.

"Driver, advance, take the right hand turn ahead when I say."

Stepanov, slightly calmer now after his near-death experience, mumbled a reply.

The IS-III moved forward slowly.

A scruffy infantry officer emerged from a building and waved the tank down.

"Driver, halt."

Stelmakh stood up and leant over the cupola.

"Comrade Mayor. Kapitan Holmin, 22nd Guards. We've taken all the buildings on this side of the street, so you're clear to the junction. We've not progressed further... there's a solid nest of the bastards in the first house around the corner this side... yellow and green shutters... can't miss it... any chance you can sort them out with a shell or two?"

"What's ahead of us when we come round the corner, Comrade?"

"Ruins mainly, a couple of intact buildings... I've a pair of DPs set up to watch for anything that sticks its head up."

"What about my left flank when I'm round the corner?"

"That's the motorcycle boys' job. Haven't seen them so maybe they're hung up."

"Risky for me, Comrade."

The infantryman could understand the problem.

Fighting a tank in a built-up area in an environment rich with heavily armed and competent infantry was no fun for anyone, least of all the men in the steel boxes.

"Understood, Comrade Mayor. I'll push a group of my men over the road before you turn. Orders to watch out for you. Good enough, Comrade Mayor?"

"Good enough, Comrade. We'll move up on your signal. Good luck."

The man moved away at a speed that defied description.

Stelmakh briefed his men.

"A section of enemy just slipped across the road, Sergent."

Peters had been checking the anti-tank weapon and completely missed the foray.

"How many?"

"Six... I think, Sergent."

That complicated matters, as Peters had selected an ambush spot that now appeared to be right in the way of the advancing group.

"Keep your weapon handy and get rid of the Lans tube as soon as you've fired it. We may need to defend ourselves against those bastards before we can relocate."

"Yes, Sergent."

"And wait for my signal before you fire, Patrice."

"Yes, Sergent."

A growing engine sound marked the closeness of the enemy tank and both men settled into the firing position, ready to send the deadly Lans warheads to deal with the threat.

"Keep your head down, man!"

In his keenness, and in his fear, Patrice Evreaux had risen up too far.

He dropped quickly, cursing himself for his foolishness.

"Sorry, Sergent."

"Minimum exposure... remember... small target... check the area behind... slow breathing... steady trigger finger... remember your training, Patrice."

"Sorry... yes, Sergent."

The approaching tank engine stopped abruptly.

"Really? Call yourself a driver?"

"I didn't stall it. The fucking thing just stopped."

"Restart the engine."

The starter motor turned over but the V-12 diesel stubbornly refused to fire up.

"You're fucking shitting me... get it started, Onufriy!"

Despite the perfect tone of the starter motor, there was no throaty roar in reply.

Nothing.

"Right. Let's get this sorted. Commander and driver out!"

The two BA-64 commanders were confused.

Having expected the IS-III to lead the charge, they now found themselves positioned either side of a lame duck.

With either too much courage, or insufficient wisdom, they pressed ahead.

The lead armoured car reached the bend and tentatively nosed around it before slipping across the road and in behind a pile of rubble where six guardsmen had secreted themselves.

The infantry leader spoke briefly with the BA-64's commander, gesticulating up the road and agreeing a plan.

Within seconds, the machine-gun on the armoured car was working, spraying bullets all over the place, but concentrating where they had seen an enemy soldier with a panzerfaust.

The second vehicle joined in as it rounded the bend.

Evreaux span away screaming as two bullets smashed into his shoulder and neck.

"Verdammt!"

Peters ducked as brick particles bit into his face.

The armoured cars were on the very edge of his range, and he was there for the enemy tank, but he had no choice.

Peters edged off to one side to give himself a chance and glanced carefully through gap in the rubble.

The bullets struck all around the hole as the second armoured car rounded the bend and opened fire.

He moved over to the other side and got the same result, although he glimpsed the enemy infantry group moving in the buildings closer to him.

He looked at the damaged staircase more closely, having previously rejected the idea.

Before he thought it through, Peters grabbed the second Lans and was moving up the rickety construction in a crouching crawl cum run.

'Perfect'.

He settled his breathing and calculated his aiming point.

The missile sped away and impacted directly on the bottom edge of the driver's hatch.

The armoured car kept moving forward and impacted with a pile of rubble, which impact rolled the vehicle onto its side.

Smoke and flame started to rise immediately and no one got out.

Before the enemy could recover, Peters had the second Lans up and aimed.

The BA-64 slipped into reverse and the missile struck the road in front of it.

But the fates were not kind to the Russian crew.

The warhead skipped off the roadway and smashed into the lower front, destroying the vehicle just as well as a direct hit.

The brave commander pulled his wounded driver clear as the vehicle started to lazily burn.

'Now to get the fuck out of here!'

A grenade sailed into the downstairs area and exploded.

There was a low rumble and the stairs collapsed.

"Scheisse!"

The floor shifted and he almost lost his grip, but it held and he recovered his ST-44.

The enemy infantry group was one building away and he decided to return the favour.

A fragmentation grenade brought shouts of consternation from the building and then screams as its metal fragments found refuge in soft flesh.

He raised himself up for a quick look and fear froze him in place.

"Firing!"

The IS-III's gun sent an HE shell at the target and the explosion sent pieces of brick, wood, and something softer in all directions.

The tank's blocked fuel filter had been fixed and Stepanov exonerated, at least in his own eyes.

On rounding the bend, Stelmakh and Ferensky had spotted the enemy AT position, and witnessed the infantry's difficulties.

Pushing the burning BA-64 out of the way, 'Krasny Suka' had taken an angled position and targeted the ruined building.

As the last pieces of rubble bounced away, the small infantry group rose up and charged forward, simultaneously with a surge from the main group to Stelmakh's right side.

"Driver, advance."

The IS-III moved slowly forward, remaining slightly behind the infantrymen.

"Driver, halt. Gunner, target, building, right two, green and yellow shutters, fire when on."

The turret traversed slightly and the gun flew backwards as Ferensky put lead on target.

It only needed one shell and the whole structure imploded.

The infantrymen rose up and charged the still collapsing rubble, confident the enemy defenders were in no state to resist.

They were wrong, and two of their number fell as a burst of automatic fire came from one relatively intact corner.

Vengeful men closed in on the firer and a brief struggle ensued before he was beaten down and killed.

"Driver, advance."

Stepanov accelerated forward, moving quicker than before as the infantry gained distance.

Inside, Kalinov served the weapon and struggled with the new shell as the vehicle bumped over the masonry and obstructions, and he alone was spared the sight that froze the blood in the others' veins.

"Holy Mother!"

"Fire!"

The 88mm shell covered the one hundred and fifty metres in the blink of an eye and hammered into the hull adjacent to the track guard.

The IS-III returned fire and also hit its target, but the Tiger had been angled perfectly and the HE shell flew off the front glacis leaving a silver reminder of its passage.

Even when it found refuge in the side of a shop, the dud shell failed to explode.

Lohengrin's own shell had not penetrated the thick angled armour, but had destroyed much of the nearside front track and wheel assembly.

Köster went for a second shot.

"Hit him again! Driver, standby to reverse!"

The Tiger commander was counting on the legendary slow reload speed and his driver's skill to avoid a second hit on his tank.

He was right on both counts.

Jarome spent an extra half a second with his aim and put his AP shell into the gap between the mantlet and the hull top.

The Tiger jerked back immediately and out of sight, denying the enemy tank the opportunity to return the shot.

Not that it could.

The Tiger's shell had wrought great damage without actually knocking out the IS-III.

The blow on the mantlet had sent a shockwave through the whole gun mount, which disrupted the optical system and, much to Ferensky's discomfort, gave him a depressed fracture of the orbit where he had been pressed firmly up against the gun sight.

"Blyad… that fucking hurts… I think the gun's fucked, Comrade Mayor."

"Check it... fuck, you alright, Oleg?"

"It hurts but I can see."

"Lev?"

Kalinov held up his hand, examining it himself for the first time.

The dislocated fingers and torn webbing were apparent, both to him and to Stelmakh.

Numerous electrical items had felt the shock and smoke wafted gently through the interior. Even the fume extractor added more smoke than it removed as its out-of-line motor protested.

"Onufriy?"

The smoke caught in Stelmakh's throat and he spluttered his words.

"Onu...friy?"

'The intercom must be out.'

Stelmakh leant forward and shouted into the front of the tank.

"Onufriy! Stepanov, you fucking goat shagger!"

After deflecting downwards, the shell had penetrated the driver's hatch and stuck fast, with six inches protruding into the space below.

The gap between the hatch and Stepanov's head was two inches.

Stelmakh knew his tank was crippled and ordered his crew to evacuate.

Leaning forward, he pushed himself forward to get as close to his driver as he could.

It was dark, all the lights having shorted out.

Grabbing the torch, he flicked the switch and immediately vomited.

The 88mm shell protruded through the hatch and into Stepanov's head.

He had been killed instantly.

Stelmakh wiped his mouth and slipped out of the turret down to the front of the tank, knowing he was exposing himself, but not prepared to abandon a man who he considered a friend as well as a comrade.

The hatch would not shift and he knew he would not yet be able to recover the dead man.

Returning to the tank. Stelmakh resolved to man the machine-gun until such times as efforts could successfully be made to extract the corpse and get the tank back in the fight.

"We didn't kill the bastard."

Köster could only agree with Jarome's statement.

"No room for us to manoeuvre worth the name. The Oberführer told us to stick here, so here we stick."

"Bastard'll be waiting for us if we poke our snout back round."

Dripping with sarcasm, Meier's voice entered the conversation.

"Well thank you, Ober-fucking-Gruppen-fucking-führer-Jarome, our resident tactical genius."

"That'll do, kameraden."

Köster smiled in spite of himself.

"We'll try the next street up. See if we can flank them. If that's alright with you, Herr Feldmarschal Meier."

The crew laughed in response to the goad, which Meier seized upon instantly.

"I approve of your plan, Sturmscharführer. You'll make a decent tank commander yet."

"Arschloch! Now, left turn... that's the arm with your watch on... up to the next junction."

The Tiger moved off, but was waved down by a hurrying senior NCO.

Köster stuck his head out of the turret.

"What gives, Hässelbach?"

He scaled the front of the tank and spoke in gasps, having run to find the Tiger commander.

"We need your tank... quickly... the bastards've broken through... northeast corner... the Oberführer's leading our last reserves... I'll direct you... but we must hurry!"

"Hang on tight then. Driver, forward!"

"Yes! Yes! We have the shits now!"

Zilinski punched his fist into his hand as his forces surged forward noticeably.

The pressure had mounted and Zilinski seized the opportunity and sent in the last of his reserve, the full company of

661

rifleman and four tanks enough to overcome the struggling legionnaires and sunder the line.

The key had been the huge anti-tank gun that dominated the vital approach, although the Panthers that had protected its flanks were now all destroyed and it would have inevitably followed them into hades as his infantry approached it from the flanks.

One of the surviving T34m46/100s had finally put a shell right on target, and the attackers had been rewarded with the vision of the gun and its crew cartwheeling in all directions and coming apart before their eyes.

Shouting at anyone in range, Zilinski was overcome with joy and rage in equal measure.

Joy because they had finally broken the SS bastards, and rage because of the cost of it all.

"Inform Comrade General Deniken that we've broken the defence."

"Yes, Comrade Polkovnik."

The radio sparked into action, relaying the good news, news that spread across the Soviet units.

They had been discussing the enemy prisoners before Zilinski's headquarters had come on the radio to announce impending victory.

Deniken greeted the report with his now usual bad-humour.

"And about fucking time too. He's used up half my fucking division and he celebrates like it's fucking May Day in Moscow!"

He accepted the tea that was thrust into his hand and turned back, mug in one hand, binoculars in the other, seeking out the problem to his front.

"So where did the bastards go?"

Ivan Lisov, the 1st GMRD's 2IC, had no answers.

Sometime beforehand, a small mixed group of enemy vehicles had come into view and an exchange of shots had taken place, one that left a Legion halftrack knocked out on the Floriańska.

The enemy group had dropped back out of sight and nothing more had been seen of them since.

A few mortar shells had been sent in their general direction, but went unrewarded by any evidence of secondary explosions.

Shortly after the encounter, a small detachment had been sent out to reconnoitre, but had not yet reported any contact.

"It could still be their main force, Comrade Mayor General."

"True, Lisov... very true... but there's heavy contact at Skrzypaczowice. They wouldn't be so stupid as to try and break out both ways... and Route 79 makes more sense... distance... and the presence of the relieving force."

Lisov finished his own tea and sought a refill before airing his thoughts.

"Unless Skrzypaczowice is a diversion... and they're coming this way with their full force, Comrade Mayor General?"

"Why? Why would they do that? It's a longer, more difficult route... and they have to know that we're all over Sulisławice by now surely?"

They lapsed into silence, considering the situation, racking their brains for more information.

Deniken had a moment of clarity.

"That's why they're coming this way."

"What?"

"Because of Sulisławice... that's why they're coming this way, Lisov."

Deniken lit a cigarette before explaining.

"Because it's the least likely thing to do... because Sulisławice is important to them... it's a rescue mission as much as an escape from our trap!"

"Rescue what? Rescue who? Sulisławice is ours all but a few bricks."

The radio sprang into life before Deniken could say another word, and the message immediately showed him to be correct.

"The bastards've caught us with our cocks out! "

Deniken pulled the map closer.

"They've cut through the tracks... Beszyce... the bastards... bastards...right... move our reserve to here... form a line and make sure they stop the swine right there."

He drew a pencil line across the road to the east of Skwirzowa, from the heights, south to a modest rise adjacent to the Floriańska.

"Stop them there, Lunin."

"Yes, Comrade Mayor General..." Lunin looked over at the forlorn group of French soldiers, presided over by a dusty and bloody senior officer, "... and them... have you decided?"

Deniken looked across and read the hate in Emmercy's eyes.

663

"We've no place... no time for them, Comrade. Are we clear?"

"Gelbkopf-two-one, Gelbkopf-one, don't stop... whatever you do... keep going, out."

Haefali's second battalion had crashed into the Soviet lines at Beszyce and taken the defenders by surprise, greatly assisted by the subterfuge of leading with a captured T34m46/100.

Behind it came the surviving Jaguars of 3ᵉ/1ᵉʳ RCDA, and behind them the majority of the combined forces of Haefali's and Uhlmann's assault groups.

Elsewhere, on the road to Łoniów, a small force under Durand and Braun, was making noisy demonstrations against the Soviet blocking units, desperately trying to seem a lot more powerful than they were.

The legion artillery and mortars helped in creating that illusion, an illusion that successfully hid the true axis of their advance and fooled men like Deniken and Lunin until the last moments.

The lead elements smashed through the Soviet line and the rest of the joint force poured through, opening up the gap.

Haefali's command group moved up, positioned in the middle of the swarm of Legion vehicles.

"Gelbkopf-one, Fisch-three-one, over..."

The recon force commander, now in charge of the combined remnants of both 1st and 3rd companies of the reconnaissance battalion and 3rd company of the engineers, sounded calm and business-like.

"Fisch-three-one, Gelbkopf-one, go ahead, over."

"Gelbkopf-one, Fisch-three-one, conditions favourable, request permission to execute Plan one, over."

'Yes! Our ploy's worked!'

"Fisch-three-one, Gelbkopf-one, execute plan one. Out!"

There was actually only one plan, and the gap opened up by the infantry and tanks was quickly filled with the fast-moving vehicles and light tanks of the 1ᵉʳ REC and the 1ᵉʳ Genie.

'Don't stop... whatever you do... keep going!'

A mixed group of AFVs from the RDCA and Blindé were to follow on with all speed.

'Don't stop... whatever you do, men... keep going!'

Haefali was jubilant but still understood there was so much more that needed to go right for their operation to be a success.

'Now... it depends on...'

The radio burst into life once more, both making his heart race and calming his nerves in the same instant.

It was the Air liaison officer.

"Gelbkopf-one, Gelbkopf-one, Adler, over."

He acknowledged and waited for the all-important words.

"Gelbkopf-one, Gelbkopf-one, Adler... waiting, over."

'Yes! Now for Braun and Durand...'

"Adler, Adler, Gelbkopf-one, execute, over."

Haefali hardly heard the response as his plans came together.

He could imagine the lined-up aircraft streaming down upon the Soviet forces on the road to Łoniów, hammering the enemy troops, all to provide breathing space for the diversionary force to disengage and return to the main body for the march on Sulisławice.

Soviet resistance to his front was growing, so he applied himself to the business of defeating the force to his front and keeping the Floriańska open.

0848 hrs, Tuesday, 1st April 1947, the hell that was Sulisławice, Poland.

The warning message from Lunin to Zilinski did not arrive.

The radio, operator, and half of Zilinski's headquarters group had been obliterated by an 88mm shell, one of a number that were fired into the Soviet incursion by the redeployed 'Lohengrin'.

In truth, Köster had made a huge error and overrun his own positions, ending up inside a cordon of angry Russians, but he fought his way out, and in the process removed the commander of the encircling Soviet forces.

Zilinski had not expected to see an enemy soldier, let alone five encased in a battle tank a few metres away from his position.

Stunned by the bursting shell, he simply walked like a zombie into a stream of bullets from Wildenauer.

Further back, the Russian Guards Lieutenant-Colonel who was left in charge was battered and shell-shocked.

Uniform smoking and covered with blood, not all his own, the officer struggled to control his twitching hands as he listened to the requests for orders.

Unable to think clearly, he simply ordered a full out frontal assault all around the Legion positions.

Lohengrin's machine-guns stuttered and swept the area in front of the tank, claiming victims with every burst.

The guardsmen were like ants swarming over larger prey, intent on submersing the Tiger in a sea of bodies.

They nearly succeeded, and one man got an RPG shot in, one that hit the large pannier on the rear of the turret and destroyed most of their reserve MG ammunition.

The final reserves were committed, led by Knocke himself, and the Soviet thrust was beaten back.

And then they came again.

0853 hrs, Tuesday. 1st April 1947, the hell that was Sulisławice, Poland.

"Alarm! Here they come again!"

There were less of them now, but they had recovered weapons and ammunition from the wounded and the dead of both sides, so the defensive fire from the shrinking perimeter was still heavy, as the attacking Guards soldiers found out.

Knocke had reformed a small reserve and it sat in the middle of an area that was no more than three hundred and fifty metres wide in any direction.

The enemy surge was immense, almost as if the devil himself were behind the Russian soldiers, whipping them forward with promises of unspeakable horrors should they fail again.

The Legion lines recoiled as the surge bought the enemy the first line.

A second effort mainly fell away in the face of withering fire, but not on the eastern side, where infantry got in close and killed two of the last Panzerjager, leaving solely the Einhorn as a runner.

"Go, Köster, go!"

Knocke waved his hand to the east as a runner gasped out his report on the crisis point.

Looking around him, and listening to the details of the situation, Knocke decided that he could not hold his reserve back.

He clapped the exhausted runner on the upper arm.

"Right. Take a breather here. When you're ready, return to your unit. Klar?"

"Oui, mon Général. Merci… bon chance."

Knocke waved his arm and led the reserve off to the eastern side.

The roar of Lohengrin's 88mm drew them off to the main road.

Hässelbach still insisted on staying close to his leader, making sure he walked in front at all times.

It was his warning that saved them.

"Cover!"

The veteran soldiers disappeared from view in an instant as the source of Hässelbach's warning drove past.

An IS-VII, not that they knew what it was exactly, rattled past, its crew seeking a position from which to outflank the two Legion vehicles.

"Kameraden, let's go tank-hunting!"

The three men with the AT weapons found themselves the focus of attention, and were up and following Knocke and Hässelbach round the bend, as the others provided security for the stalking teams.

Four Soviet soldiers were jogging up the road in the wake of the huge tank, and they were surprised to find enemy soldiers where they thought there were none.

One went to bring his AK-47 up, but a burst of fire smashed him to the ground.

For a moment there was hesitation, but the remaining three soldiers threw down their weapons and raised their hands.

"Scheisse... no time for this... sorry."

An old NCO shot all three down and moved his group on in support of Knocke and the AT soldiers.

With Hässelbach in the lead again, the group moved quickly through a half-collapsed restaurant and almost ran into the back of the IS-VII, the idling engine unheard above the noise of battle.

Overhead, a long line of Allied aircraft flew on their way to somewhere else, intent on creating excitement for Soviet soldiers throughout the river valley.

The closeness of the tank created its own unique problems.

There were no easy shots that wouldn't risk the AT soldiers too.

The tank's huge gun fired, dislodging bricks and dust within the rickety structure, some of which fell on the men, some of which fell on the tank.

The turret turned slightly and stopped, the sound of the electrical traverse turning more intense as it struggled against a problem.

Unknown to the crew or the AT stalkers, a joist had perched itself on the hull front, vertically held in place by the old restaurant's sign mount and the IS-VII's towing cable, providing an obstacle that prevented the main gun traversing.

The turret hatch opened and a head poked out cautiously, seeking the problem, finding it, and deciding on a solution.

Knocke grabbed Hässelbach and dragged him forward as he started to run.

"Leg up!"

The NCO grasped his leader's intent but didn't get his posture right and Knocke's first effort failed.

Hässelbach meshed his hands, providing a step for Knocke's left foot, and he propelled himself up onto the back of the tank.

The head started to turn, recognising the scrabbling sound for what it was, but too late.

Knocke shot him in the face at point blank range.

The wounded man fell back into the tank screaming, followed by the muzzle of an MP-40.

The magazine discharged twenty-five rounds in the blink of an eye, and they flew around the interior of the heavy tank like wasps, wasps whose sting was deadlier than any insect.

"Grenade!"

Knocke had none so he called for one to be thrown up.

Catching the phosphorous grenade that one of the AT soldiers threw up, he warned the men around him.

"Keep clear, kameraden!"

As he pulled the pin, the men moved away at high-speed, not wishing to get caught in any blast.

Knocke dropped the grenade into the tank and dismounted, heading towards Hässelbach's knot of soldiers.

The grenade ignited with a modest plop and smoke immediately started to pour from its open turret hatch.

There were also screams from wounded men.

"Move on, kameraden!"

The screams continued briefly but ceased abruptly as the fire took hold.

Although the IS-VII burned fiercely, it did not explode, but the fire still spread to the old restaurant and adjoining houses, transforming the structures into raging fires.

Ahead, machine-guns stammered, and they quickly stumbled across Lohengrin and a knot of legionnaires under intense pressure.

Taking up positions on the flank, Knocke and his men started to pick off the Soviet attackers, careful not to fire towards their own.

A group of his men moved round further to the left, led by the NCO who had executed the Russian prisoners.

Establishing an MG-42, they ripped shreds off the men gathering for a flank move against the position, putting a platoon size force to flight.

The men closer to the knot of legionnaires pressed harder, knowing safety lay closer to their foe.

The superior numbers started to tell and soon the fighting was up against Lohengrin herself.

Knocke called his men about him and surged forward.

With careful bursts, he swept a few men away from his chosen path, and the rest crashed into the sides of the attacking Russians, firing as they went, stabbing and slashing as they came into close contact.

The repulsed Soviet platoon made a second effort to advance, but the MG-42 kept them at bay.

Barrel changed in the blink of an eye, it swept the road and small square any time there was a target to shoot at.

The opportunities grew less and less as courage deserted the Soviet soldiers.

Around Lohengrin, the fight was savage and without mercy.

Men clawed at each other's throats when weapons failed or were lost.

The stench of blood, urine, and faeces was overpowering, as men descended into the depths of their bestial natures in order to fulfil life's most important mission; that of surviving, come what may.

Hässelbach shrieked as a burly Russian bit a huge chunk out of his ear, the man screaming with animal passion as he spat the savaged flesh in his opponent's face.

Stimulated by pain, he grabbed the Russian's head and pulled it down, planting his forehead on the top of the man's nose at speed.

Both men were howling with the pain of their injuries as a body cannoned into them, forcing them apart.

They both kicked out at the new arrival, not knowing if he was friend or foe.

Another legionnaire confronted the big Russian and slashed a spade at his neck, severing the jugular in one swipe.

Hässelbach looked around for Knocke and saw him stood at the back of the Tiger tank, pistol in hand, picking off selected targets here and there as they threatened one of his men, or tried to climb on Lohengrin.

"Watch out!"

He shouted uselessly as Knocke fumbled for a fresh magazine just as a Russian charged around the rear of the stationary tank.

The man fired his rifle and the blow knocked Knocke's leg out from underneath him, even though the bullet simply transited his muscle without hitting anything of consequence.

Working the bolt, the Guardsman struggled with locking the lever down.

With Knocke on the ground, Hässelbach took the shot and the rifleman was thrown backwards by the impact of bullets.

The Tiger's engine revved, a pre-arranged sign it was preparing to move and anyone around should beware.

Knocke struggled out of the way as Lohengrin slipped backwards, coughing as the acrid exhaust fumes affected his breathing and sight.

The turret traversed and a shell flattened a building from which a DP had just started firing.

Testing his right leg, Knocke grimaced as pain shot up and down the limb.

Running his hands up and down, he found more stickiness around the calf and pulled out a wood splinter that he hadn't even felt.

When he'd fallen, his leg had crashed into a baulk of timber, and there were two more such pieces embedded in his flesh.

"Let me help you, Oberführer."

Grabbing the extended hand, Knocke pulled himself upright and put weight on the damaged leg.

"That aches a bit, I'll bet, Oberführer. Let's get you bandaged up."

The two hobbled over to a small public bench that had become the focus of medical activity.

There was no time for either of them, as the two medical orderlies did all they could to save men who were dying.

"I lost my weapon... not sure where."

"I'll find you a replacement as soon as we're fixed up, Oberführer."

Knocke recognised a man whose head was swathed in bandages.

"Felix! Good to see you. How are you?"

"I'll live, Oberführer, I may have problems wearing glasses, mind you. Bastards had my nose off."

In truth it was his own driver who had braked hard, causing Jorgensen to lurch forward and smash his face into the cupola just as

670

he was getting out. His nose had been virtually ripped off by the impact. The driver was amongst the hideously wounded men around him, and would not survive to see the following dawn.

"Cigarette?"

"Danke, Oberführer."

Three more hands appeared from out of the group of battered men, and rich smoke enveloped the smokers, bringing its own kind of calm and relaxation, despite the sounds of renewed fighting close at hand.

"Well, kameraden... I think Moscow may be beyond us for a day or two."

The laughs were punctuated with sounds of pain and coughing, as men's wounds protested at the movement caused by their amusement.

"Apologies, kameraden. Just thought you should know the situation."

Deniken knew they had failed.

They had been denied victory, not by the damned SS, but by the enemy's air force.

Admittedly, his forces had been split by the bold thrust towards Sulisławice, and he had lost heavily in the same village itself, but the main damage had been done on the road to Łoniów, and throughout the second echelon of the attack, where the fighter-bombers had ranged across the land, having gained air dominance, firing their damned rockets and dropping their damned bombs without check.

'And the firebombs... always the firebombs!'

His senior commanders were all dead or wounded; the same went for Artem'yev's regiments.

There was no information available on the 1st Guards Engineers, or on 6th Guards Tanks Corps, but for sure they would have suffered.

He had established contact with the commander of the 91st Tank Battalion, but the man was no wiser than he on such matters.

Contact with Rybalko had been lost nearly an hour previously, and much had happened in that time.

He decided that he would reform his line either side of the Floriańska and then move up towards Sulisławice, maintaining a broad front, although the military power to project himself up the

671

planned route had long been spent in the valley of the Koprzywianka River.

"Comrade Lisov... we'll move up behind the second battalion. Get everything ready."

"But Comrade Mayor General, there's still a question of..."

"I need to move up now. I need to see what's happening. Now. Get us ready to move."

Lisov's objection died in his throat and he turned to get the small staff organised and back on the road.

Six minutes later, the command group was on the Floriańska, heading towards Sulisławice.

"Attack in line, watch your spacing. Dive, dive, dive."

The four Thunderbolts of the French 13^e Escadron, once the RAF's 345 Squadron, dived upon the rich pickings on the valley floor beneath them.

Around the supply point established at Krysin, the Soviet AA gunners were wide-awake and put up a furious barrage.

The lead aircraft staggered under the impact of cannon shells and turned away to port, streaming smoke and sparks.

His wingman followed him, acting on the shouted instructions of his section leader.

The two flew northwards at an increasingly slower speed as the Capitaine nursed his ruined aircraft back to friendly air space.

Behind them the two remaining Thunderbolts put their RP-3 rockets into the soft-skinned vehicles in and around the small junction, creating chaos and destruction with the 1st GMRD's logistical column.

"Don't take your rockets home, Canard-trois."

"I'm staying with you, leader."

"I'm getting rid now. Find a target. I'll fly straight and level, don't mess about and just do it, Pierre."

"Roger, leader."

Canard-trois lost height slowly and Pierre Haufranche sought a suitable target.

A burst of AA fire attracted his attention, and he focussed his mind on the target ahead.

Blobs of glowing metal rushed past his cockpit as the desperate gunners tried to stave off his attack.

The blobs shifted slightly and started chewing into the metal fuselage, and two hit the boss of the propeller, causing the whole assembly to shake and rattle, and begin tearing itself apart.

Further shells opened up the wing tanks and bathed the whole aircraft in fire.

Haufranche opened the canopy and propelled himself out into space as the Thunderbolt started to disintegrate in mid-air.

His commander watched in fury as the glowing shape detached from the burning aircraft and deployed a parachute that was quickly engulfed in flames.

Mercifully, the journey to the earth was short and Haufranche's pain was terminated on impact.

Screaming at no one in particular, the French section leader elected to put his aircraft into a dive and put all his focus into the display in front of him, ignoring the flak that streamed up at him once more.

The engine ran super-hot but he still powered into his dive, intent on extracting revenge for his cousin.

The flak struck his aircraft again, but he was not to be turned, and the RP-3s leapt from their rails.

His aircraft was hit again.

Canard leader turned but found a lack of response.

Pulling back on the stick, the Thunderbolt tried to overcome the damage caused by the hits and the airflow through the numerous holes, and only just failed.

The wingtip clipped a lorry and Canard leader flipped over and cartwheeled end over end across the Floriańska highway.

"That's fine shooting, Lisov. I'll decorate the gunner and commander of those guns."

"The other one's coming in, Comrade Mayor General. Heading for the AA guns themselves it looks like."

Deniken grunted.

"Move!"

The BTR moved forward at increased speed, intent on pulling ahead of the SPAAs and their personal fight with the diving plane.

"He's fired... not at us!"

Lisov's words were superfluous as it was obvious that the rockets were aimed at the guns.

"They got him!"

"Bastard!"

The rockets struck amongst the SPAA vehicles, sending two into fireballs.

The enemy aircraft was low and turning, too low and too slow...

"Watch out!"

Deniken shouted uselessly at the supply lorry as the Thunderbolt streaked in and the wing hit the cab.

Deniken and Lisov could only watch as the spiral of metal and flames ate up the ground between them, inexorably spinning itself into a whirlwind of death.

What was left of the Thunderbolt collided with a BTR-152 of the 1st Guards Mechanised Rifle Division's headquarters, containing both the divisional commander and his 2IC.

There were no survivors.

0915 hrs, Tuesday, 1st April 1947, Sulisławice, Poland.

The Soviet forces had pulled back to the edge of the village, licking their wounds and trying to get organised, and the tired legionnaires and tirailleurs found time to catch their breath, if only for a moment.

A shot had come from no one knew where, but its effect had been catastrophic, and the old Legion NCO had flown backwards, dead before he hit the wall behind.

His MG-42 team decided on self-preservation and ducked down behind the brickwork.

"Sniper!"

Around the small square, men headed for cover and prayed that they were not in the sights of the deadly rifleman.

Others on the edges had crashed through ruined doors and windows and escaped the line of fire.

They started to work through the ruins in search of the deadly rifleman.

Another shot brought more suffering as a tirailleur officer fell without a sound as the back of his head flew off, spraying his men with the contents of his skull.

One younger soldier screamed and rose up to run, but was immediately knocked back by another bullet.

He whimpered his way through the last painful seconds of his life.

The sniper, there were actually three of them, settled into a new firing position, one that offered a better angle on the small square.

Left behind to both worry the defenders and provide advance warning of any aggressive moves, the tired enemy legionnaires initially proved easy meat.

The Mosin rifle kicked into his shoulder for a third time and he was rewarded with a spray of red as his target fell from sight.

To Orsov's left, another shot rang out, then two more in quick order, clearly from Palininski, whose weapon of choice was a prime SVT-40 automatic rifle with a ten round magazine, a surprising choice as it was far heavier than the Mosin, and Yelena Palininski was such a slight girl.

A figure moved and he fired instinctively.

'Missed!'

He risked another shot at the disappearing soldier and, although the man made cover, Orsov knew he had hit him.

'Time to move.'

He tensed, knowing his life was forfeit, and that the barely detectable sound was a footfall close behind him.

"If I was one of those SS bastards, you'd be well fucked, Comrade Orsov."

Orlov let out a huge breath of relief.

"I'm moving so don't get in my way, Comrade Serzhant."

The other man had been transiting the derelict shop and hadn't known Orlov was there until he fired.

"No problem. I'm off to the old church, Leonid. Better to see what the fuckers are up to."

A bullet pinged off the brickwork near David Uranovski, the sergeant commanding the sniper team attached to 167th Guards Rifle Regiment.

The two men hugged the floorboards and wormed their way towards the rear of the building.

A solid sound announced the arrival of a grenade, which skittered along the floor and dropped next to Uranovski.

He pulled it into his arms and under his chest… and tensed.

The HG337r as it was known in the Wehrmacht, was a Soviet RGD-33 grenade from stocks likely captured in 1942-43, and this one bore a fragmentation jacket, which increased its deadly radius and killing power.

Uranovski's arms, chest, and head disintegrated in the blast, and the remnants of his body were thrown back across the floor.

Pieces of the grenade, eleven in all, struck Orlov and robbed him of his sight and ability to move.

He screamed in pain, until he screamed no more, a burst from a tirailleur's ST-45 terminating his suffering.

Relieved to have erased the snipers for only a few men lost, the legionnaires missed something vital, possibly in their tiredness, possibly in their haste to be away from the awfulness of the damage to both enemy soldiers.

Neither man used an SVT-40.

"Snipers are down, Oberführer. Two of them. The tirailleurs sorted the bastards out."

"Excellent work. That mustn't happen again. We mu…"

The bullet arrived before the sound and hit Jorgensen in the back of neck before exiting his upper chest and finding more soft flesh beyond.

A second bullet struck Hässelbach, even as he was reacting to the spray of blood from the Blindé's commander.

A third bullet passed through the air between him and the falling Knocke, finding nothing but the road beyond.

Two more bullets were fired.

Another burst through Hässelbach's arm as he bent over to stop Knocke from landing hard.

The final shot from Yelena Palininski's weapon went far over the group, but still took a life, striking down a legionnaire beyond.

Shouts rang out all around the square and men again scuttled for cover.

Five shots in just over three seconds, and she had seen three hits, possibly a fourth.

The weapon had jammed and she dropped into cover to free it.

In the square, all was chaos.

Jorgensen was clearly dead, his glazed eyes carrying indignation, surprise, and pain in equal measure.

Hässelbach's strength seeped from him as his wounds leaked blood, but he pushed himself across the ground to his commander's side.

Knocke was sat on the ground, his face grey and ashen, with his hands on his stomach, almost on the verge of unconsciousness.

The sound of his pain invaded every ear, as the old soldier squealed in agony.

"Sani! Sani!"

He pressed Knocke's hands to the stomach wound.

The screaming stopped as Knocke started to lose consciousness.

"Press here, Oberführer… wake up, man… stay awake, for fuck's sake!"

Fiedler dropped to his knees next to his stricken leader and ripped away at a shirt he had grabbed from somewhere on his path.

The pain returned and Knocke started to scream hideously, the high-pitched sound causing ears to crackle, so loud and piercing was it.

Fiedler fashioned a bandage and added his voice to that of Hässelbach.

"Sani! Sani!"

Bending Knocke slightly to one side, Fiedler pushed the bandage around his back and into Hässelbach's waiting hand.

It emerged soaked in blood.

He ran his hand round to the small of Knocke's back and discovered a huge exit wound.

"Oh fuck! Sani!"

Knocke fell silent again.

Fiedler made a pack of more of the shirt and pushed it hard against the large wound.

Knocke moaned at the pressure and coughed up a little blood.

"Oberführer… lie still now… we'll soon have you back on your feet… but just lie still for now, eh?"

Knocke laughed and coughed some more, bringing another surge of blood from his lips.

"You always were a bad liar, Otto."

Hässelbach could not bring himself to say more.

The sani arrived and started working, although he was low on anything that a medical orderly could normally be expected to carry.

"He needs a doctor, Obersturmführer... this is bad... very very bad..."

There was no doctor and hadn't been since the Soviet artillery killed both men some hours beforehand.

Hässelbach looked away from the desperate medic, and saw that a crowd had gathered round the desperately wounded Knocke.

Through a gap, he saw Köster in his turret, aware that something important was happening and keen to get a look at whatever it was.

The sight triggered a memory deep in Hässelbach's mind.

"Linus! Köster! Get your gunner Linus here now! All of you... find medical supplies... in vehicles... on enemy soldiers... anything you can...move!"

Despite the occasion sound of battle or the explosion of a shell, his voice carried loud enough for all to hear, and carried with it urgency and authority and was acted on immediately.

Linus Wildenauer arrived in company with Köster.

"You were a vet... close enough to a doctor... do something, Wildenauer."

The young man's mouth was wide open and he stood frozen.

"Do something!"

Knocke's coughing and moans of pain broke Wildenauer out of his trance and he dropped to the ground, searching his mind for information.

A hand grabbed Hässelbach's tunic in a vice-like grip and pulled him down closer to the wounded man's level.

"Otto... Otto..."

"Yes, Oberführer?"

"You know what to tell my wife... Greta and Magda... quick and painless. Tell my girls... tell them I love them... and Anne-Marie... just tell her I love her and our new child so very muc..."

A clot of blood shot from Knocke's mouth.

Men started to arrive holding out pieces of medical kit, from scissors to one ampoule of pain-relieving morphine.

It was immediately administered and Knocke passed into merciful darkness.

Palininski got off two more shots, both at close range, as she tried to stop the hunters overwhelming her.

She failed and went down under a flurry of kicks and punches.

The clothes were ripped from her and the legionnaires took their pleasures, more by way of revenge than for personal satisfaction.

After being abused in every way devised by man, the battered but still conscious naked girl was hung by her neck from a protruding floor joist.

She kicked for some time before the noose and the prodding bayonets claimed her life.

The Soviet cordon was broken in two places.

Firstly by the arrival of forces dispatched by Lavalle, the 1er BAS soldiers, dismounted from their amphibians, supported by the rest of the 7e RTA, slammed into the positions of the Guards motorcycle troops and the remnants of the 6th GIBTR.

Shortly afterwards, Haefali's advance units broke into the rear of the dead Zilinski's force and started taking prisoners, Soviet morale seemingly broken by the bitter fighting.

News of Knocke's injuries spread like wildfire, and the rumour machine had him marked down as dead to slightly winded, and all points in between.

The truth was that, despite the attentions of Linus Wildenauer and of the captured Soviet medical officer, Knocke was gravely wounded and not expected to survive.

In real terms, the battle on the Koprzywianka River did not end until around 1500 hrs on 2nd April, when the final disengagement took place, although there were four more multi-aircraft missions launched by Armée de L'Air, the DRL, and USAAF units, and two by the Red Air Force.

The Soviet's bill was severe, with both the 1st GMRD and 116th GRD fielding less than 30% of the manpower they had started the battle with, although wounded and stragglers would bring that number up to about half over the next few days.

Both had lost their commanders; Deniken to an air attack and Artem'yev to severe concussion from a close artillery strike.

6th GIBTR had three running tanks, one of which was 'Krasny Suka'. Stelmakh was one of only four officers left unwounded.

Sárközi's MACE unit was annihilated, although the price it had extracted from the tanks of the 1er RCDA was extremely high.

1st GMAEB was at roughly 65% strength, but its commander, Chekov, could not be found, despite the efforts of his men.

Similarly, 91st Tank Battalion was around 65%, although disabled vehicles and crews were found across the battlefield over the next few days.

6th Guards Tank Corps had taken a beating from air attack in the main, losing significant portions of its artillery and mortars to ground attack aircraft and counter-battery fire. Its 53rd Guards Tank Brigade lost heavily at Sulisławice and around Route 9, and the 2nd Battalion, 22nd Motorised Rifle Brigade suffered the highest losses of any fielded unit, with solely 27 men left unwounded at roll call the following day, although a number had surrendered to the legionnaires in Sulisławice. It was the captured medical officer from 2nd/22nd who worked alongside Wildenauer long into the night and early morning, saving lives and easing the suffering of those who would pass anyway.

The Red Air Force lost one hundred and one badly needed aircraft over the battlefields of southeast Poland, although only thirty-nine pilots and crew were killed

On the Allied side, the air losses were less, but only moderately so, given the numerical and technical superiority they had enjoyed, as the increased AA presence marked down many ground attack aircraft.

Sixty-seven Allied aircraft were lost, and forty-nine took their pilots with them, a staggeringly high rate that was brought on by the predominantly low-level nature of the attacks.

Losses in the DRH were modest by comparison to the rest of the Allied ground force, with Grossdeutschland suffering the greatest at just under 10% of their committed force dead, wounded and missing, with the 116th Panzer close behind at 8%.

The 1er Division's infantry brigades were both damaged but took over the line duties from the two hammered Legion Divisions.

Alma was badly mauled, and 3e RdM and 7e RdM were down to 55% and 60% effectives respectively.

The rest of the division mirrored those losses, with the exception of the 3e Genie and 2e Blindé, who had both been extremely lucky, and suffered only a handful of casualties between them.

The corps troops of the LCDA were savaged beyond repair, save for the relieving force of 1er BAS and the rest of 7e RTA, the latter of which had lost two battalions in all but name, so high had the onus been on the North African infantry.

Only three of the 1er BCL's tanks were salvaged from the battlefield, and only one of those, the immortal 'Lohengrin', left the bloodied field under her own power.

Camerone was virtually destroyed as an effective unit, both by casualties and by the mortal wounding of her commander and Legion talisman.

Haefali and Braun had extracted an important number of men and machines, but they were, in both cases, commanding forces spent and in need of recovery.

Emmercy's force was smashed apart, a small portion taken prisoner, a larger segment scattered to the winds to the northwest of Klimontów and now intermingled with units of the 116th Panzer.

Haefali found himself in charge of recovering the remnants of Camerone and extracting it from the line before the exhausted men totally ceased to function.

In human terms, the battle had cost the Legion some of its finest.

Emmercy's body was found with many of his men, executed beside the Floriańska highway near Skwirzowa.

The body of Uhlmann was carried from the field on the rear of a Jaguar, his headless corpse wrapped in a tarpaulin and covered with the flag of the Legion.

Truffaux, Jung, Jorgensen, and Peters had all fallen at Sulisławice.

Found amongst the dead of a vicious hand to hand fight around the K44 Pak was Wagner, the mad gunner.

In the final moments of victory, Sergent-chef Yitzhak Rubenstein, who had once helped Haefali and Knocke lay to rest the slaughtered Soviet paratroopers at the Chateau du Haut-Kœnigsbourg, sharing the Kaddish with the two officers, was struck down by machine-gun fire.

In the perverse way that war often deals out its fates, he was killed in combat with men who were once members of the 100th Guards Division, the division from which the men he had honoured were drawn and who now filled out the ranks of Artem'yev's 116th.

Alma lost its commander, when St.Clair was flayed by shrapnel from groin to chest, and carried from his burning staff car by survivors from his headquarters group, whilst yet others shook their fists impotently at the Armée de L'Air Thunderbolts that had dropped bombs on their own.

The other wounded included Renat-Challes, Hässelbach, and Fiedler, although all of them were expected to recover.

Across the whole Corps, the losses were felt intensely, and with a very real grief for so many comrades lost and maimed.

But no loss, no death, no wounding, was more keenly felt or more widely mourned that that of Knocke.

At 0302 hrs, Wildenauer took his leave as Lohengrin prepared to move back behind the lines.

He clambered into the tank and his crewmates looked at him with a newfound respect, and with hope in their eyes.

"So... how is he, Linus? Good news, I hope?"

He knew that the senior men in the Tiger's crew had a special relationship with Knocke, so he considered lying.

But, in the end, he chose the truth.

"He won't last the night."

It does not matter how slowly you go as long as you do not stop.

Confucius

CHAPTER 199 - THE PLOTTERS

2211 hrs, Friday, 4th April 1947, House of Madame Fleriot, La Vigie, Nogent L'Abbesse, near Reims, France.

Commandant Vincennes had taken the call and driven straight away to bring the awful news in person, using the drive as an opportunity to compose himself and work out how best to deliver his news.

Jerome answered the door, demonstratively indignant that anyone could possibly call to disturb the household at this ungodly hour.

In fairness, the old man quickly sensed the nature of the visit and treated the French officer with equanimity, helping him off with his sodden raincoat and leading him to take a seat in the lounge before heading off to rouse Madame Knocke.

By the time he had reached the stairs, he had decided to wake Madame Fleriot first, given his suspicions.

Armande Fleriot's eyes flicked awake as soon as he knocked lightly on her door, and her eyes strayed to the weapon that had been ever-present by her bedside since the attempted assassination of her family.

After hearing Jerome's fears, she quietly dressed and went to wake Anne-Marie.

"Ah, Commandant Vincennes, so lovely to see you again, although your timing is less than impeccable."

"Madame Fleriot, at your service."

"Please sit... Jerome is bringing coffee and Anne-Marie will be down in a moment."

She leant forward and spoke in a softer voice but somehow with a harder tone.

"Commandant, I assume this is not a social call. You will know she is pregnant. Gently if you please..."

The door opened and Anne-Marie Knocke walked in with the urgent pace of someone who needs to know the answers to the myriad of questions bouncing around inside her head.

"Commandant Vincennes."

"Enchanté, Madame Knocke."

She took her seat adjacent to Armande, battling her emotions and the growing sense of fear that chilled her to the very bones.

Vincennes looked uncomfortable and hesitated, trying to find the right moment and recall his chosen words.

Jerome entered with coffee at the moment that Armande Fleriot provoked matters.

"Commandant, we both understand that this is not a social visit and that you come bearing news... clearly urgent news. I pray you, speak of it now and torture us no longer."

"Of course... I regret, Madame Knocke, that my news is for you... and it is bad news indeed."

Anne-Marie remained sat bolt upright despite the imminent collapse she felt was about to wash over her.

"I've received word from the front. It is with the deepest regret that I must inform you that you husband, Général Ernst Knocke, was wounded... it's feared mortally. My news is old, I admit. I'm told that your husband was struck down on Monday, during the great attack, and was not expected to survive the night. I have received no more and I came as soon as I was ordered to. Madame, I am truly sorry... and France will grieve with you... Madame? Madame?"

Anne-Marie clutched her distended form, as if holding her man close, the awful words churning around in her mind.

Madame Fleriot spoke in her stead.

"So, Commandant, you come here to tell us that he may be dead... or may not be dead... are you a fucking cretin?"

Even Jerome stopped in mid-motion.

Never before had Armande Fleriot spoken a harsh word in his company, let alone such language, and to a guest and officer of the French Army.

"Madame, I am told what I am told... and I was told to get here as soon as possible."

Vincennes was cringing inside.

Jerome was shocked.

Fleriot was red-faced and angry.

Anne-Marie was drained of colour and silent.

But then, as things started to declare themselves, it became obvious that Anne-Marie Knocke was in shock-induced labour.

2301 hrs, Friday, 4th April 1947, GRU West Headquarters, Brest Litovsk, USSR.

"Come in."

The door opened and in walked one of the more recent additions to Nazarbayeva's staff.

"Comrade Leytenant. Are you duty officer?"

Nazarbayeva already knew the answer to the question, but asked it anyway.

"No, Comrade General. I was just finishing up my report on the French Army activities. I wondered if you wished to see it before you returned to your quarters?"

Nazarbayeva put down the report she was already reading in favour of the one offered up by Hana Rikardova.

"Precis it for me, Comrade Leytenant. Please sit."

"The French First Army has suffered heavy losses amongst it elite soldiers and appears to be all but spent already. Since the battles on Tuesday, they have made next to no advances, and only on two occasions have they made attempts that had any possibility of achieving any reasonable tactical success... both defeated by our forces. Of greatest note is the destruction of their Legion Corps, the one that has done us so much harm over recent months. Whilst Rybalko's own force was badly damaged in the actions on Tuesday and Wednesday this week, it's beyond doubt that he has crippled the Legion Corps and it's now out of the line."

"Excellent... and we have hard figures on their casualties and equipment losses?"

"Yes, Comrade Leytenant General, as much of it was left on the field we occupied... and there's more to reinforce my assessment that the Legion Corps is now to be considered as... err... virtually destroyed."

Nazarbayeva poured two glasses of water and pushed one across to the clearly dry-throated young officer.

"Thank you... we've killed much of their experienced leadership... the ex-SS soldiers... confirmed as dead are Knocke and Uhlmann, the driving forces behind the Camerone unit. I believe they won't recover from it, Comrade Leytenant General."

"Good... excellent in fact. I'll read the full report as soon as I get an opportunity. I'll be flying to Moscow tomorrow... that should give me an opportunity."

The tone in Nazarbayeva's voice would normally have been interpreted as the end of the conversation, but Rikardova made no attempt to move.

"Yes, Comrade Leytenant General. I wondered if I might accompany you on your visit?"

The silence was complete as the two women locked eyes.

Nazarbayeva considered a number of responses until deciding on a lighter approach.

"And why would I consider your request, Comrade Leytenant?"

"Because there is nothing like Mayday in Moscow, except..."

"Except perhaps Christmas in Krakow?"

"Yes indeed, Comrade Leytenant General."

Silence returned, and neither seemed to wish to break the moment, although the atmosphere was filled with tension.

Eventually, Nazarbayeva spoke.

"I'm listening."

"I'm here to give you a message, Comrade General. A delegation from the Allies arrives in Moscow tomorrow and you must meet with one of their number... a Colonel Ramsey. He has information that is vit..."

"Who do you work for?"

"For you, Comrad..."

"Don't be so fucking stupid. Where do your loyalties lie, eh?"

"My loyalties lie with the Motherland, Comrade. I assure you th..."

"So who do you work for within the Motherland?"

"Comrade Khrushchev had me placed here to be of service... and to handle certain delicate tasks."

"Did he now? So your allegiance is to him, not to the Motherland?"

"They're one and the same, Comrade General."

"So who are you really, Leytenant?"

"I am who I am. Hana Georgievna Rikardova of the GRU, but I'm also a member of a small and very secret section within the Communist Party apparatus. As is Comrade Khrushchev... and he's directed me to be here to watch over you and help where I can."

Had she been asked that same question by Menzies or Gubbins, she would have replied that she was Hanna Richards of MI-6 and committed to King and Country.

When she had been asked it by Gehlen, she was Annadell Reichart of the Abwehr and a committed member of the National Socialist Party of Germany.

Rikardova was a lot more than she seemed.

She also possessed orders to terminate Nazarbayeva if her loyalty to the new cause seemed about to wane.

But for now, she was in Nazarbayeva's office with instructions from Khrushchev, and she relayed them quietly, making sure that her commander understood each perfectly.

At 1000 hrs the next day, the aircraft carrying Nazarbayeva and Rikardova took off for Vnukovo airfield.

Some two hours later, an RAF Skymaster landed at Vnukovo, having departed from Sweden some hours earlier, and followed an agreed safe air route, shepherded all the way by impressive numbers of Soviet fighter aircraft.

The C-54 landed on Russian soil without incident and the Allied delegation was whisked off to Moscow, ready for meetings with the Soviet hierarchy.

1754 hrs, Saturday, 5th April 1947, the Kremlin, Moscow. USSR.

Nazarbayeva accepted the report from one of the Moscow GRU officers and read it with increasing concern.

Almost oblivious to the process, she walked through security.

The metal detector screamed out its warning, as it always did whenever Nazarbayeva entered the protected area of the Kremlin.

"I regret, Comrade Leytenant General. If you will."

The NKVD officer frisked the GRU general thoroughly, a little too thoroughly for Nazarbayeva's liking as he dwelt on her chest pockets and thighs.

He even checked her holster, although he had been watching as she had removed her pistol and placed it in the bag set aside for her personal but restricted items.

"It's my foot brace… it's always my foot brace."

"I regret, Comrade Leytenant General, but I have my orders. If you please?"

With practised ease she slipped off her left boot and flicked it up into the hands of the inspecting officer.

He slipped his hand in and felt the warm metal.

"I regret, Comrade Leytenant General."

He placed the boot down and stepped back to allow her to slide it back on, which she did with her normal skill.

An Air Force colonel set the machine off and he received a far less courteous examination.

"Your meeting with the General Secretary is scheduled for seven, is it not?"

"Yes, Comrade General."

"Excellent, then we have time now. May I offer you a drink?"

Kaganovich motioned towards a small table replete with various spirits.

"Thank you, but no. Just water please."

He had heard of the change in the woman's habits but had to check for himself.

The reports on her licentious behaviour had also dried up.

"Clearly there's something on your mind. That folder by any chance?"

"Yes, Comrade Polkovnik General. I just received it. GRU South sent it on to me, but I think the significance has not yet been understood."

He poured her a water, and himself a Chivas Regal.

"Go on."

"They've received many reports from their agents on the ground regarding increased Allied air presence."

Kaganovich was in a playful mood.

"I'm never sure if the camel lovers can tell a Spitfire from a Seagull."

She passed across the cover sheet with its summary of the increase in air power in the region.

"They report more heavy bombers and more fighters, and you'll see they seem to be able to at least count engines. As I said, Comrade General, I've only just got this but at first sight, it seems like they're reporting American B-29s and British Lancasters... the fighters could be anything of course... except the twin hulls... most likely the Mustang upgrade... long range escort... very long range."

"Your thoughts, Tatiana?"

688

"Clearly they intend to expand their air operations out of Persia. I think I'd be looking at our facilities within range of their bases... with the intention of improving our defences, Comrade Polkovnik General."

Inside, Kaganovich was debating whether or not to reveal the report that had arrived with Beria the previous day, but he elected to keep it secret for the moment, solely for his own purposes.

Nazarbayeva continued, oblivious to Kaganovich's internal debate.

"The atomic research facility is clearly in range, but there's no indication that its location and purpose have been detected."

Kaganovich knew better and reversed his decision, immediately seeing the advantage.

"The Allies have performed an overflight of the facility on the Volga."

"The atomic research facility?"

"Yes, Comrade General. But it would appear that they tried to hide it within a bombing mission."

"How do we know this?"

"Red Air Force reports from an engaging interceptor pilot. He recognised the aircraft as a photoreconnaissance craft... apparently by the artwork on it... a naked woman by all accounts. Anyway, he had previously engaged it without success on three occasions."

Nazarbayeva nodded her understanding and yet...

"But how could he know it was photographing Camp 1001?"

Kaganovich read the section again to remind himself of the facts.

"The attacking force was heading for Stalingrad, but they split into five distinct groups, each covered by fighter regiments. He engaged the group that flew directly over Camp 1001, despite the fact that it was protected by the largest number of fighters... the group contained the naked woman aircraft, which turned back after it had just passed Akhtubinsk, streaming smoke and accompanied by six fighters... all of its own accord."

She frowned.

He read more.

"The pilot could not engage the aircraft... and has stated that, in fact, no one engaged it... and yet it turned back, seemingly damaged."

"So you think they know what's there, Comrade Polkovnik General?"

"Decidedly likely. They've overflown the area before. NKVD's Southern Office was very thorough and included the previous definite and possible overflights...there are six in all. Two by photographic aircraft for certain, and four that could have been bombing missions against Akhtubinsk and Stalingrad, possibly contrived to overfly to conceal the purpose... and five of them have been flown since the beginning of March."

"What? And you learn of this now?"

"Yes. Bear in mind that as far as most in NKVD South are concerned, Camp 1001 is simply Camp 1001, and any mission to photograph it wouldn't normally draw a special report. Secrecy comes with complications sometimes, as we both know. It's only come to my attention now because of a request for information issued by Air Commander South, based on the intelligence he received on curious air operations being conducted in Persia."

That there were NKVD agents entrenched in all areas of Southern Command did not need saying.

She sipped at her drink and considered the problem.

"So, I assume you've decided on a course of action, Comrade Polkovnik General?"

"Yes. I intend to report what I suspect to Comrade Beria and give my recommendations."

"May I ask what they might be, Comrade General?"

"Yes, Tatiana. I consider it wise to relocate the hardware and processes at Camp 100. I intend to recommend that to the GKO shortly."

"Hardware?"

"Most of our weapons are there."

"Weapons?"

"Our atomic weapons... most of them are there."

"Most?"

"Some have already left for air bases."

"Mother of God. We have weapons already? We're deploying them already? You feed me information in drips, Comrade Polkovnik General!"

"Yes... I'm sorry... I told you the Japanese assistance made us advance... we have weaponised the material."

"So we have atomic weapons... and they plan to use them? Are they mad? Our enemy's more advanced than us, surely? If we use such weapons, then they will most certainly use them on us. There will be no end... chemical, biological, atomic... we'll transform this world and nothing will ever be the same!"

"Yes, Tatiana, that's our fear... I mean... the fear of those of us who can see this future if we do not stop this now... although an asset within their own programme has the Allies with no more than six devices... which I believe our leadership thinks we can easily endure... and our capacity to strike back is, in many ways, superior."

"Easily endure... easily endure?"

'Are they fucking totally mad?'

Nazarbayeva saw untold horrors in her mind, her vivid imagination throwing up images of a ravaged world in which nothing was the same, and everything was destroyed.

"What do you suggest, Comrade Polkovnik General?"

"Nothing at the moment, but I'll talk to the others immediately..."

"But I have to tell the leadership of this..."

Kaganovich had played his hand well.

"Yes... yes you must...I'll speak to the others whilst you are apprising the GKO... I'll contact you later."

There was no opportunity to discuss the instructions she had received from Khrushchev.

1934 hrs, Saturday, 5th April 1947, the Kremlin, Moscow, USSR.

She had delivered her normal briefing to the GKO and then sought a further session for Stalin's ears only.

Of course, that meant Stalin and Beria.

Beria shifted uncomfortably as she delivered her information hot from Kaganovich's office, whereas the dictator listened impassively.

"Thank you, Comrade Leytenant General."

She was surprised at the control shown by both men, given her knowledge of what Camp 1001 represented.

It was Beria that spoke up first, although his keenness to understand how the bitch had got hold of NKVD information was immediately dampened by the certainty that it was Kaganovich.

He would find out later from those who watched his deputy like a hawk.

"So, the Southern Command has caught wind of some sort of secret operation being run out of Persia... we've increased numbers of enemy aircraft in the area... and we've evidence of overflights to sensitive facilities of great importance to the Motherland."

"Yes, Comrade Marshal."

691

"Moving our research facility is no small thing, and yet you would still recommend moving it, Comrade General?"

"Yes, Comrade General Secretary, I would."

"Thank you for your briefing, Comrade General Nazarbayeva. I will speak to the Ministry shortly. Thank you."

The two men said no more, their silence a way of terminating the meeting, leaving Nazarbayev to salute and leave the meeting room.

They waited in silence until the door closed.

Stalin spoke first.

"How long?"

"I've no idea... but the break in production would impact greatly... and transporting everything would need time to arrange."

"But if she's right?"

Beria took a moment to think about it.

"If she's right, then we risk losing everything... equipment... material... expertise... everything, Comrade General Secretary."

"We've no choice then, Lavrentiy."

"I agree, Comrade General Secretary."

"Forty-eight hours?"

"According to the emergency planning, the facility can be stripped down in thirty-six hours, but there will be complications due to the haste..."

"Thirty-six it is then... no more... I have an idea..."

'An idea? Mudaks! I'll mark it in my fucking diary!'

Stalin continued, oblivious to his henchman's thoughts.

"An accident."

"Accident?"

"If the Allies know it's there, then an accident would allay their concerns, will it not?"

"Ah, yes... I see, Comrade General Secretary... I see exactly what you mean... especially if we accompany it with some extra dressing..."

Stalin smiled.

It was not pleasant, but then it wasn't meant to be.

"Yes... yes... "

Stalin started to sketch out the barebones of his idea on paper, whilst Beria was already well ahead of him in his mind.

"Comrade General Secretary... perhaps I might suggest broadening the plan a little."

It took the head of the NKVD less than two minutes to explain what his distorted mind had just devised.

"The Ukraine, Lavrentiy?"

"What have we got to lose, Comrade General Secretary?"

"Why not throw in the fucking Balts too then?"

Beria shrugged.

"Why not? Why stop there, Comrade General Secretary?"

Beria reeled off a few more names.

It took Stalin less than twenty seconds to agree.

A total of less than three minutes to arrive at a monstrous decision... less than three minutes that condemned a million people to death.

The messenger had caught up with Nazarbayeva just before she entered her car, just in time to deflect her to the Grand Park, where Kaganovich was taking a constitutional.

"Comrade Polkovnik General. You wanted to speak with me?"

"Indeed I do, Comrade Nazarbayeva. Your meeting went well?"

She passed on her version of events, which pretty much tallied with his own, except for the part where the three of them had been alone.

Kaganovich listened intently, factoring in the decisions already made by the others.

Nazarbayeva finished up with a bombshell.

"I did not hear what they said when I left the room, but I felt... think... no, sensed that I may have started a process."

"Female intuition, Comrade Nazarbayeva?"

"You may call it that... but I felt it as very real."

Kaganovich hung back from derision and instead relied on respecting the woman's instincts and basic intelligence.

"I'll bear that in mind and you may well be right. We want you to do something for the Motherland... something that'll be difficult to understand, I expect... but the Rodina will profit from it."

Nazarbayeva stumbled on a stone as she gave Kaganovich her full attention.

"You know the line I won't cross, Comrade Polkovnik General."

"Yes... I do... we do. I understand that Comrade Khrushchev's ears gave you a request?"

Nazarbayeva's eyes narrowed.

"Yes, she did, Comrade General."

"And did you bring it?"

Her gripped instinctively tightened on her briefcase.

"Yes."

"Good... then here is what you must do."

She listened.

She stopped in her tracks.

She said no... and no again...

Kaganovich explained the decision fully, understanding her knee-jerk reaction to such an action... as she put it 'betrayal', but he showed her how, in reality, it served the Motherland, however unsavoury it might appear.

When they parted, he returned to report that Nazarbayeva was committed to her part in their desperate plan.

At 2011 hrs on Saturday, 5th April 1947, the Knockes were delivered of a son.

Whether the newborn Jürgen Georges Knocke had a living father was still unknown.

The end is nigh...

List of Figures within Endgame.

Author's note on the Auschwitz section.

When I first decided to take on the particular section dealing with the ex-SS and their time at Auschwitz, I understood that it would have to be done in such a way as to properly represent the matters I wished to raise.

I also knew that whatever I wrote, some would find it distasteful or even derogatory. As you can see, that did not stop me from trying to write about the issues.

When I first stood in the middle of Auschwitz-II Birkenau some years ago, I was amazed to feel nothing in the place. I wrote at the time that it was as if the whole area had surrendered every essence of its being, every last measure of emotion, and that it had seemed to have been left with nothing whatsoever, a vacuum into which you could bring every part of your imagination.

Truly, I have never been in such an empty place in my life, and I have been to other dark places such as Malmedy, Wormhoudt, Natzwiller-Struthof, Mauthausen, and Nordhausen.

To tackle the enormity of such a place is decidedly beyond my skills as a writer, but I so wanted to try to impart that feeling to the reader.

I chose to do so in a different way, by incorporating it in a story where the ex-SS come to a place synonymous with themselves and the victims of the regime they both represented and fought for.

Anyone with the slightest knowledge on the subject, and certainly myself, knows enough about the SS to know that the force contained some of the vilest beings ever to darken the planet, individuals who should have been exterminated long before they got into a position from where they could impact other's lives so terribly.

I also know that many of them were through and through Nazis, or whatever that represented for them at the time. We now apply the label of 'Nazi' in a different way, in many ways making it synonymous with the camps, and I am directly aware that some of those who joined the party had absolutely no idea of what it would finally come to represent, and what its full and horrible agenda was.

In other words, what they joined was not what it became, and their continued membership of it, given the likely consequences of trying to leave, is something we can probably all understand but not necessarily condone.

My point on the enormity just being too much to contemplate is quite valid. For quite some time, even the Allies refused to believe the stories of mass killings and genocide that slowly started to emerge, considering them beyond possible.

697

How wrong they were.

The defence of 'just obeying orders' holds no water for me. I never ever followed an order I considered incorrect or wrong, although in my career they were rarely life-changing orders, and then also rarely was my life involved.

However, I did want to expose that 'defence' for what I consider it to be; a weak man's solution.

But I also wanted to bring to mind the alternative.

It is my fondest hope that, were I positioned as Bach was in the book, or thousands of others during the war itself, then I would have had the moral courage and conviction to place what is right and my code of honour above my own well-being, and that I would have refused to enact orders that brought about such suffering and death.

But, in honesty, I am in the closing years of my life, and such decisions are made more cheaply than when in the flower of youth or of recently acquired manhood.

I, like most people, have absolutely no idea what I would have done had I been so placed.

Hopefully, this chapter will promote that debate within the reader, although you will find no certain answers; of that I'm sure.

What I set out to achieve was firstly to put over some idea of the awfulness of Auschwitz and Birkenau.

Secondly, I wanted to highlight that the common impression of the SS, that being that all were guilty of the crimes of the camps. Absolutely, all were guilty by association, by wearing the uniform, but many members of the Waffen-SS, and I make the distinction Waffen-SS, were not aware of the horrors conducted by the regime for which they fought so bravely.

To some, that makes me an SS apologist. I do not see it that way; I might be wrong but I don't think so. I would certainly consider myself one who is armed with enough information to know that the SS contained both good and bad men, and also that I possess enough impartiality to understand and represent that view openly.

As I said at the beginning of this series, it is my view that there are no bad peoples, just some bad people.

Thirdly, I wanted to challenge the reader to consider the subject of moral duty, orders, and self-preservation.

Whatever you take away from this, and whether or not you now see me as an SS apologist or simply a poor writer, I would ask that you understand my real hopes and purpose in writing the chapter.

That it should never ever happen again.

Thank you.]

698

Legion Tank conversions and types.

ALLIGATOR
Stug III chassis with extended fighting compartment. Armed with the 75mm KwK 42 L/70.

AARDVARK
Panzer IV chassis with Achilles turret installed – limited number. Armed with 17pdr.

WOLF
Panther chassis with Panzer IV turret installed. Armed with the 75mm KwK 40 L/48.

ANTILOPE
Standard SDKFZ 251 with additional plate and armoured roof, and a Puma turret installed. Armed with the 50mm KwK 39/1 L/60.

HUNDCHEN
Standard SDKFZ 251 with strengthening for gun mount. Armed with the 128mm Pak 44 L/55, taken from damaged AT weapon mounts or unserviceable Nashorne SP guns.

DRAGON
Standard SDKFZ 251 with roof installed and strengthening. Armed with recycled Maultier mounts and 4-6 Wurfrahmen.

PANTHER II
Upgraded Panther in line with plans conceived during previous war. Armed with either the 75mm KwK 42 L/100 or 88mm KwK 43 L/71, depending on turret and tube availability. Limited numbers produced, consuming redundant stocks of Tiger II parts.

EINHORN
Jagdpanther variant with extended fighting compartment. Armed with the 128mm Pak 44 L/55.

HYENA
Panther hull with M4A376mm turret added.

FELIX
French produced Panther hybrid. Armed with the 17pdr and equipped with French-produced Maybachs. None used operationally [French-

engined versions remained as training vehicles] until German produced Maybachs were available. Limited production but was surprisingly successful.

JAGUAR
Latest version of the Panther F with improved drive train and infrared optics as standard. Armed with the 88mm KwK 43 L/71. Initially produced in France, German industry quickly followed suit, and the Jaguar became the preferred tank to fill out the new Panzer Divisions. French produced Jaguars had the official designation Jaguar (fr).

SCHWARZPANTHER
Initially produced without the gas turbine engine, the tank carried an 88mm, MG-42 hull mount, and spaced armour.

SCHWARZJAGDPANTHER
No wartime-produced versions carried the gas turbine engine. Armed with a 128mm gun, MG-42 hull mount, and twin auto gun turret on roof on later versions.

Glossary

AK-47	Soviet automatic rifle. 7.62mm normally fitted with a 30 round magazine
Arado-234	German twin-engine jet bomber
ARL-44	French tank produced post WW2 utilising many parts from old designs and armed with a 17pdr gun.
Auergesellschaft	German company that was connected with numerous military projects, such as the German Atomic programme.
Bearcat, Grumman F8F	US single-engine heavy fighter developed late in WW2
Belzec	Nazi extermination camp in occupied Poland.
Beriev Be-4	Soviet twin-engine flying boat.
BOAC	British Overseas Airways Corporation.
Bordkanone 75mm	Aircraft mounted development of the 75mm Pak 40 anti-tank gun.
BTR-152	Soviet 6x6 armoured personnel carrier, capable of carrying 18 infantry and 2 crew.
Bundesheer	Army of the Austrian Republic
BV-141	Luftwaffe single-engine reconnaissance aircraft known for its strange asymmetrical design.
C-118 Liftmaster	US four-engine transport aircraft, known as the DC-6 in civilian service.
Chikushō	Japanese - literally, oh shit!
Chivas Regal	A blended Speyside whisky.
Çibuk [chibouk]	Turkish long-stemmed pipe.
CNFC	Çanakkale Naval Fortified Command
CoS	Chief of Staff
CZ-27	Czechoslovakian 7.65mm semi-automatic pistol with an 8 round magazine.

D-44 anti-tank gun	Soviet divisional artillery weapon of 85mm used in an AT role.
Diamond T M-19	US heavy tank transporter and trailer combination.
EF-131 trident	Luftwaffe six-engine jet bomber developed post-war by the Soviets.
Electric Eel	US early version of a towed sonar array, consisting of a trailed cable with sound sensors installed at regular intervals.
Enshinbunriki	Japanese... literal translation is centrifuges
Ersatzgruppe	German... literal translation replacement group
FECOM	Far East Command
FFAR	Folding fin aerial rocket, an air-to-ground- explosive rocket.
Fido acoustic torpedoes	Mark 24 mine, an air-deployed anti-submarine homing torpedo that entered service in 1943.
Flitters	Irish colloquialism - in tatters.
FuG 510	German missile guidance system, FuG 510/238 "Düsseldorf/Detmold" used a joystick to command the deployed device through trailing wires [i.e. wire-guided].
Futatabi	Japanese - literally, again, once more.
Gatos	USN class of mass-produced submarines, the GATO class.
Gertrude	Sound powered underwater phone for communications between submarines developed in 1945.
Guam, USS	CB-2, an Alaska class large cruiser, some times considered a battle-cruiser.
Har Meghiddohn	Hebrew... literally Mountain of Megiddo. We more commonly know it as Armageddon.

Hedgehog	Anti-submarine spigot launcher with 24 charges set to fire ahead of a submarine and explode on contact.
Hornet, De Havilland.	British twin-engine fighter developed from the Mosquito and armed with 4 x 20mm Hispano cannon.
Hs-129-B3, Henschel.	Luftwaffe twin-engine ground attack aircraft armed with a 75mm cannon that could destroy any tank then in service. The aircraft itself was slower and less responsive than previous versions.
I-250, Mikoyan-Gurevich [MiG-13]	Soviet single motor jet fighter aircraft, a project that was eventually cancelled.
IS-IVm46	Soviet heavy tank with a 130mm main gun, new gearbox, upgraded suspension, and twin all-new engines.
IS-VII	Soviet heavy tank of 68 tons, armed with a 130mm gun.
Izba	Traditional Russian country dwelling.
Jimmy	Colloquial name for the Number One on an RN vessel.
Junkers-287	Incomplete Luftwaffe forward swept wing bomber with four jet engines, called Trident in Soviet service.
Kätzchen [Gepanzerter Mannschaftstransportwagen Kätzchen]	German infantry transport and prime mover based on Panther and Tiger II components.
Kettenhund	German... literally 'chained dog', the derisory term for Military Policemen in the German Army, who wore a metal gorget.
Kfz 71, Krupp	German army command version of the Kfz 70, 6x6 lorry.
KKE	The Communist Party of Greece.
Kripos	German... Kriminalpolizei... Criminal Police... criminal investigation department of the police.

La-9, Lavochkin.	Soviet single-engine propeller-driven fighter produced after the end of WW2.
Lancaster MR-3	Coastal Command conversion of the Lancaster Bomber [Maritime Reconnaissance v3].
Lans	Soviet copy of the Panzerfaust.
Le Boudin	The Foreign Legion's slow marching song. A Boudin is literally a blood sausage or black pudding.
Leitstrahl	German guidance system using a radio beam, used in conjunction with the V-2 and other advanced projects.
Lewisite	Organoarsenic compound used in weapons as a vesicant [blister agent] and lung irritant developed in the US, where it became known as 'the Dew of Death'.
M-17	US development of the M-16 Quad .50cal AAA mount developed from the M5 halftrack and sent to the USSR in numbers as part of lend lease.
M20 bazooka	US 88.9mm rocket launcher.
M-29 Chamberlain	Red Gambit's designation for the production model of the T-29 heavy tank.
M-30 Hancock	Red Gambit's designation for the production model of the T-30 heavy tank.
M-40 GMC	155mm SP Howitzer on an altered M4 chassis.
M-41 HMC 'Gorilla'	155mm SP Howitzer on a lengthened M24 chassis.
M-46 Pershing II	Red Gambit's designation for the M-46 Patton. Clearly as Patton survives in RG, using his name was impossible.
Majdanek	Nazi concentration camp on the outskirts of Lublin, Poland.

Mongoto	Japanese - literally, the Things.
MP-40	German 9mm sub-machine gun with 32 round magazine.
Mustang, F-82 Twin	US conjoined Mustangs on a twin hull configuration, each with a single engine. Pilot's positions retained in both cockpits, but one could be replaced by a radar set and operator, at which time pilot was in the left side.
Odalik	An odalik or odalisque is a Turkish female attendant, often used to refer to women who pander to men's needs, up to and including as a concubine.
Operation Cougar	Projected US invasion of Eastern Russia from Chinese bases.
Operation Kingsbury	Part of Operation Viking, covering the ground assault and extraction undertaken by 1st SSF and its support elements.
Operation Niji	Japanese Operation to transfer atomic secrets, scientists, and machinery from Japan to Soviet control, sailing huge submarines halfway round the world to the Black Sea.
Operation Raduga	Soviet Operation to employ a range of destructive weapons, from Atomic bombs, dirty bombs, biological and nerve agents against Allied targets in Europe and beyond.
Operation Tiger	Projected US invasion of Siberia.
Operation Viking	Overall Allied operation for the negation of the VNIIEG facility at Uspenka.
Oruspu!	Turkish colloquialism - bitch or whore.
Osoaviakhim Project	Soviet project that brought many specialists and associated equipment from military related projects under their umbrella, mainly gleaned from occupied territories.

Owl, Curtiss O-52	US single-engine observation aircraft,
Pak 44, 128mm Pak 44.	German 128mm anti-tank gun of high penetrative performance but low manoeuvrability.
Panzer VII	German heavy tank development not realised in WW2, equipped with either a 105mm or 88mm weapon.
Pizdets/Peezdets	Ukrainian - extremely uncouth word :-)
Porton Down	During WW2 it was the centre of British research on chemical and biological weapons.
Raki	Turkish anise drink.
ROE	Rules of engagement.
S&D	Unspecific mission that sent aircraft into a given area with orders to take out anything and everything they found. Literally, Search and Destroy.
SD	German security service, full name Sicherheitsdienst der Reichsführer-SS.
Seiran, Aichi M6A Seiran	Japanese single-engine seaplane designed to be sub launched, created for the mission to bomb the Panama Canal and Western seaboard of the USA.
SGMB	Soviet SG-43 medium machine-gun fitted with special mountings for use in vehicles.
Sheptat'	Soviet copy of the Gertrude underwater communications system.
Shooting Star, Lockheed P-80.	US single turbojet fighter that came into operational testing at the end of WW2.
Shrike A-25, Curtiss	USAAF version of the Curtiss SB2C Helldiver, a single-engine dive-bomber.
SOP	Slang - standard operational procedure

Squid launchers	British anti-submarine mortar with three barrels. Highly effective sub killer.
ST-45	German assault rifle designation that was produced by the French through CEAM, as the CEAMm46.
T34m46/100	Soviet production vehicle of a T34m44 with a modified interior and extended turret rear, incorporating the 100mm gun.
T-70	Soviet light tank armed with a 47mm or MG as main armament, crew of 2.
Tabun	Nerve agent that fatally interferes with the nervous system.
Theresienstadt	Nazi concentration camp established in Terezin, Czechoslovakia.
Thunderjet, Republic F-84.	US single turbo jet engine fighter-bomber.
Tigercat, F7F Grumman	US twin-engine heavy fighter that served mainly with the USN and USMC. It packed a powerful punch with 4 x 20mm Cannon and 4 x .50cal machine guns.
TR-1	The Lyulka TR-1 was the USSR's first home produced jet engine.
Tupolev 4, Tu-4	Soviet reverse engineered copy of the B-29 heavy bomber.
Uranprojekt	Nazi Germany's nuclear weapons project.
V-2	Germany's long-range ballistic missile, also known as the A-4.
Vosper MTB	British motor torpedo boat.
Yak-15	Soviet single turbojet fighter with a reversed engineered German Jumo jet engine.
Zeltbahn	German triangular poncho that could be combined with three others to make a tent for four men.
ZSU-20-4	[RG only] Soviet mobile 20mm Quad AA gun mounted on a truck chassis.

Bibliography

Rosignoli, Guido
The Allied Forces in Italy 1943-45
ISBN 0-7153-92123

Kleinfeld & Tambs, Gerald R & Lewis A
Hitler's Spanish Legion - The Blue Division in Russia
ISBN 0-9767380-8-2

Delaforce, Patrick
The Black Bull - From Normandy to the Baltic with the 11th
Armoured Division
ISBN 0-75370-350-5

Taprell-Dorling, H
Ribbons and Medals
SBN 0-540-07120-X

Pettibone, Charles D
The Organisation and Order of Battle of Militaries in World
War II
Volume V - Book B, Union of Soviet Socialist Republics
ISBN 978-1-4269-0281-9

Pettibone, Charles D
The Organisation and Order of Battle of Militaries in World
War II
Volume V - Book A, Union of Soviet Socialist Republics
ISBN 978-1-4269-2551-0

Pettibone, Charles D
The Organisation and Order of Battle of Militaries in World
War II
Volume VI - Italy and France, Including the Neutral
Countries of San Marino, Vatican City [Holy See], Andorra,
and Monaco
ISBN 978-1-4269-4633-2

Pettibone, Charles D
The Organisation and Order of Battle of Militaries in World
War II
Volume II - The British Commonwealth
ISBN 978-1-4120-8567-5

Chamberlain & Doyle, Peter & Hilary L
Encyclopaedia of German Tanks in World War Two
ISBN 0-85368-202-X

Chamberlain & Ellis, Peter & Chris
British and American Tanks of World War Two
ISBN 0-85368-033-7

Dollinger, Hans
The Decline and fall of Nazi Germany and Imperial Japan
ISBN 0-517-013134

Zaloga & Grandsen, Steven J & James
Soviet Tanks and Combat Vehicles of World War Two
ISBN 0-85368-606-8

Hogg, Ian V
The Encyclopaedia of Infantry Weapons of World War II
ISBN 0-85368-281-X

Hogg, Ian V
British & American Artillery of World War 2
ISBN 0-85368-242-9

Hogg, Ian V
German Artillery of World War Two
ISBN 0-88254-311-3

Bellis, Malcolm A
Divisions of the British Army 1939-45
ISBN 0-9512126-0-5

Bellis, Malcolm A
Brigades of the British Army 1939-45
ISBN 0-9512126-1-3

Rottman, Gordon L
FUBAR, Soldier Slang of World War II
ISBN 978-1-84908-137-5

Schneider, Wolfgang
Tigers in Combat 1
ISBN 978-0-81173-171-3

Stanton, Shelby L.
Order of Battle – U.S. Army World War II.
ISBN 0-89141-195-X

Forczyk, Robert
Georgy Zhukov
ISBN 978-1-84908-556-4

Kopenhagen, Wilfried
Armoured Trains of the Soviet Union 1917 - 1945
ISBN 978-0887409172

Korpalski, Edward
Das Fuhrerhauptquartier [FHQu], Wolfschanze im bild.
ISBN 83-902108-0-0

Nebolsin, Igor
Translated by Stuart Britton.
Stalin's Favourite - The Combat History of the 2nd Guards
Tank Army from Kursk to Berlin. Volume 1: January 1943-
June 1944.
ISBN 978-1-909982-15-4

Poirier, Robert G., Conner, Albert Z.
The Red Army order of Battle in the Great Patriotic War.
ISBN 0-89141-237-9

Read the beginning of the final book in the Red Gambit series now.

I am Alpha and Omega, the beginning and the end, the first and the last.

The Book of Revelation - 22:13

CHAPTER 200 - THE CONVERGENCE

1424 hrs, Sunday 8th April 1947, Moscow City Zoo, Moscow, USSR.

It was a zoo in two halves, split down the middle, like a divide between the old and new sections, by the Bolshaya Gruzinskaya, a major Moscow thoroughfare.

The Allied contingent had the opportunity to look around and relax as best they could, albeit under the close attention and watchful eyes of a blizzard of uniformed and non-uniformed intelligence officers.

On the road itself, street sellers peddled their wares, from souvenirs to hot food, the latter attracting the attention of a number of the hungrier members of the group.

With a savoury pastry in one hand and a hot sweet tea in the other, Ramsey could only just manage with his briefcase tucked up under his arm.

Helpfully, his closest observer offered to carry the case but her offer was declined and instead Ramsey offered up the tea and took a firm grip on his case.

It was to be expected, but it didn't stop the NKVD minder trying.

As was his way, Ramsey started to create a problem with his artificial legs, something he did to allow him to separate from the group on occasion, when other more clandestine duties called.

His personal minders remained close at hand, two men and two women, whilst the rest of the group, headed up by the irrepressible Horrocks, completed their journey across the Bolshaya Gruzinskaya and onto the newest section of the City Zoo.

Ramsey was ushered to a green painted bench.

He sat down heavily and made a great show of rubbing his thighs.

One of the Allied group decided to stay with him and keep the British officer company.

"Playing up, John?"

"Too bloody right, Miguel. Very sore for some reason."

He continued to rub them as he and the US intelligence officer went through their pre-arranged routine.

"I need to sort the bloody strapping out."

Lieutenant Colonel Miguel de la Santos USMC looked around, seemingly in search of something, but already knowing just where to look.

He pointed dramatically.

"There's a head, John. That'll do, won't it?"

"Just the job, Miguel. Excuse me, Mayor... I need the toilet..."

He pointed to emphasise his words.

The impassive GRU officer simply nodded and moved aside to let Ramsey stand.

Ramsey offered Santos his briefcase for safekeeping.

It was an exquisite touch, designed to disarm the overseers.

Moving in apparent discomfort, Ramsey made his way across to the toilet and placed a few coins in the dish overseen by a fierce looking old woman who tended the Spartan facility, and whose words of thanks sounded more like a diesel engine starting up on a cold morning.

The GRU Major stopped Ramsey from entering and sent in his number two, who turfed out the two men he found inside before checking the facility, emerging to simply nod at his commander.

Ramsey was allowed to enter.

The cubicle's false wall swung open.

"Polkovnik... we meet in the strangest of places."

"General... that we do."

"It was necessary, I'm afraid, and thank you. No briefcase?"

"No... I don't need one."

"But..."

He reached down and unclipped his left leg.

Unscrewing the lower calf, he revealed a large cavity that could take a good size roll of A4-sized paper... similar to a large report file such as was handed over to him.

"What do I have here, General?"

"Vital information that you need to get to your commanders immediately. I vouch fully for its authenticity... and given what it is, you'll need to impress upon them that it is authentic and requires that they act immediately."

"I will tell them, general."

"I came here myself for that reason, and also to explain why... they'll ask you why, Polkovnik."

It was all too cryptic for Ramsey's tastes but he had to accept matters as they were.

"Go on, General."

"Because we don't wish this conflict to escalate to something that can no longer be stopped. There'll shortly be a change in the Motherland's leadership, and when it happens, you'll know that we, the new leadership, are serious people who will do what's necessary to protect our Motherland."

Ramsey had just been handed a momentous piece of intelligence and was momentarily thrown.

Gathering himself quickly, he reattached his leg.

"I will deliver that message, General."

"Good... now we must hurry or our people'll start to wonder what you are doing. Good luck, Comrade Polkovnik Ramsey."

"And to you, General Nazarbayeva."

0348 hrs, Tuesday, 10th April 1947, forty kilometres south of Clark's Harbour, Nova Scotia.

"... And ... mark. Down periscope... take us down to 120."

Kalinin kept his voice low, as did all submariners in time of stress, as if a passing fish might overhear.

Their express orders had been to avoid any sort of contact on their journey across the Atlantic, and that had been successfully done, although passing up big and vulnerable targets was foreign to all, but clearly necessary to preserve the secrecy of the mission.

However, now, as the group of submarines neared the coast of the United States, it was proving more difficult to remain hidden, as the waters grew heavy with the hulls of warships and merchantmen.

The 'mark' had recorded the angle of the enemy vessel and Kalinin leant on the map table with the navigator, examining the plot.

"Target, range five thousand, Comrade Leytenant."

The officer made a mark and together they apprised the tactical situation.

"Come to port... 247 degrees, Comrade Kapitan?"

"Agreed... Starshy Leytenant..."

His first officer was quickly at the table.

"Come to port, steer 247... keep us at this depth until our friend is off the hydrophone then back to normal. Understood?"

"Understood, Comrade Kapitan."

"Advise the others by Sheptat immediately."

He referred to the 'Gertrude' underwater communications system that had been stolen from the Americans.

The number one set about discharging his orders, leaving Kalinin a moment to look at the greater picture.

By now, Nobukiyo and his the rest of his group, 'Soviet Vozmezdiye' and I-1, would be nearing the final staging point before they closed in to their firing position off Block Island.

'... if they're on time and if there's been no problems... '

Kalinin's attack group consisted of 'Soviet Initsiativa', I-402, and I-14, and the three of them, having rendezvoused off Newfoundland, were now moving gradually southwest, keen not to arrive in the heavily traversed waters ahead of schedule.

Their luck had not been overly tested during their voyage across the Atlantic, but it had certainly been given a full workout once they had arrived within range of land, with aircraft and naval patrol ships plaguing their every hour.

Once, I-1 had been subjected to an attack by a Canadian Liberator, but it had come to nothing.

The RCAF crew's after-action report was challenged and it was suggested that they had dropped on a pod of whales.

None the less, not to know of the reprieve, the whole submarine group had taken a detour back out towards deep water, one that had used up valuable fuel, although I-353 still trailed the main force by some two hundred miles, ready to provide resources if needed.

Not that the Japanese boats would need them.

They had no plans to return home.

Kalinin handed over command to his first officer and returned to his quarters where, before he grabbed a few hours' sleep, he again reminded himself of the geography of his own target.

He dropped off to sleep and dreamt...

...of Jamaica...

...of Chelsea...

715

...of Charles...
...and of Harvard...

1130 hrs, Thursday, 12th April 1947, Timi Woods Camp, Paphos, Cyprus.

Crisp accepted the salutes of his leadership and watched as they sprinted away to get their men aboard the waiting aircraft.

He still had trouble thinking of it as an aircraft, so vast was the Spruce Goose that it promised to defy the very idea that gravity would ever relinquish its grip upon the airframe and permit it to rise into the air.

But, he reminded himself, fly it did.

The vast interior was soon to be crammed with his soldiers. It was already accommodating weapons, ammunition, food, and medical supplies, but the weights had all been calculated and the incredible aircraft gobbled up everything without batting a proverbial eye.

As he observed the loading of his soldiers, he caught sight of Hughes and his band of civilians, dressed in the same uniforms as his soldiers, gesticulating wildly as they argued over weight distribution, fuel consumption, and the plethora of things that seemed to exercise and amuse them on a regular basis.

They had dismissed the warnings about being captured and the likely outcome of having their identities discovered.

Their issue of the uniforms was greeted with boyish howls, almost as if a dressing up party was in the offing.

That the uniforms belonged to the Red Army would be enough to ensure that anyone captured wearing them would be shot, but they were simply essential to the plan to storm Camp 1001, otherwise Crisp would not be wearing one himself.

Crisp relaxed and decided on a cigarette before he took up his place on the Spruce Goose.

He sampled the calming smoke and revisited the minutiae of the plan.

Part of his force had gone on ahead, shoehorned into a number of Curtiss Commandos, their part in the operation to be discharged in a separate place, but just as vital as the main force's job in many ways.

716

Shandruk's force had also already departed, their part in the operation due to commence prior to the arrival of the main force.

The Ukrainian's role was vital, and could well mean the difference between success and failure in the ground plan.

Undoubtedly, the air plan would succeed, but in succeeding could well mean disaster for Crisp, his men, and those already on the ground.

On other bases, both on airfields or on slipways, aircraft with special roles to play were undoubtedly already being prepared.

The coordination required was incredible, and the original plan developed by Sam Rossiter and his team had been amplified and improved time after time.

Jenkins' fantastic model had proved to be invaluable in planning the operation, although the complicated structure had now been dismantled and its constituent parts spread around so as to provide no clues as to its purpose.

Rossiter arrived on cue, to wish Crisp luck and shake his hand one more time.

"Can you do it, Colonel?"

"General... I can tell you this. We're ready and able, trained, and up for the mission. If it can be done, it'll be done... and if it can't be done... well I guess the Air Force'll have to carry the ball."

Rossiter extended his right hand and grasped that of Crisp.

"The very best of luck to you and your men, Colonel Crisp."

"Thank you, Sir."

They saluted as RSM Sunday marched towards them, his bearing as perfect as if he were commanding a review on Horse Guards Parade.

"Sah! Mister Hughes reports that he's ready to take off. All men are aboard. All supplies aboard and secured."

"Thank you, Sergeant Major."

Ten minutes later, the green-painted Spruce Goose, decorated with the markings of an aircraft of Soviet naval aviation, rose slowly from the waters of the Mediterranean, destination Tabruz, on the Caspian Sea.

1207 hrs, Thursday, 12th April 1947, 7th Mechanised Cooperation Training School, Verkhiny Baskunchak, USSR.

The atmosphere was always relaxed, but today it was more so as the final exercises were almost complete, and the unit under training had performed superbly, the joint product of excellent leadership by the experienced commanders and of great teaching by the men in the room.

They had just briefed Colonel Bortanov on the exercise he was expected to undertake the following day, and had let him go to prepare his plans, along with the staff of 218th Tank Brigade.

Accompanying him was Lieutenant Colonel Tob of the 115th Naval Infantry Brigade, also training with Bortanov's unit prior to being attached to a newly forming Tank Corps, to be based around the 218th.

It was important for the successful final exercise that the staff of 7th Mechanised Cooperation Training School had no exposure to the home force's planning, as they were to participate as the enemy force.

In just a few weeks, Yarishlov had forged his experienced officers into a solid unit, and 218th Tanks was the second unit to pass out of the three-week training programme far better prepared than when they entered.

As overall commander, Yarishlov had men under him to oversee the various disciplines required for the advanced battle tactics and manoeuvre course that was his to design and deliver.

Colonel Nikolay Zorin, once commander of the veteran 39th Guards Tank Brigade, was his tank commander.

Although they had never served together during either war, Yarishlov held Zorin in high esteem.

He was still thoroughly competent and innovative tank leader, despite the serious wounds he had suffered at Hamburg in the early days of August 1945.

Which was also another reason why Zorin held a special place in his heart; he had fought against his friend John Ramsey, and the pair of them often shared a vodka whilst Yarishlov listened to the stories of the incredible British resistance around the Rathaus and canals of the old Hanseatic League city.

Zorin and Kriks had become thick as thieves as a result, as had Colonel Bailianov and Yarishlov's senior NCO, partially because of previous experiences together in and around Tostedt in August '45, and partially because Bailianov and Kriks had a shared passion for chess, and were well matched in ability.

Bailianov's role with the training establishment was to command the infantry and anti-tank forces that opposed the units under training, a job in which he constantly outdid himself, much to the exasperation of Zorin and the tank training staff, although good-humouredly so.

He had learned his craft under one of the very best infantry commanders in the Red Army, namely T.N. Artem'yev, and he was rapidly approaching his mentor's quality.

Last of Yarishlov's unit commanders was Major Harazan, an engineer by trade and inclination, and a veteran of hard fighting against the SS Legion in the Alsace, where he was wounded.

Subsequently he fought with Chuikov's Alpine Front, where he sustained another wound, one serious enough that it removed him permanently from front line duties, although many observers failed to realise that he had only one leg, so spritely was he on the prosthetic limb that replaced his lower left leg.

The comradeship Yarishlov felt for his men greatly helped him overcome his daily personal struggle with pain and the after-effects of his horrendous injuries.

"Right... that's the guests sent on their way with their briefing. Any changes to the normal planning?"

Harazan raised his hand, as he always did, ever conscious of his lower rank and status amongst his fellow officers, and therefore always striving to achieve better and better results.

"Comrade General, I believe that we may profit from advancing our minefields. I've noticed that the units tend to deploy into battle formation around here."

He leant over a detailed model table that covered all of the tank training grounds, from Bataevka on the Astrakhan-Akhtubinsk highway, across to the main base at Baskunchak, a distance of some thirty-five kilometres, running north to south a mean distance of forty-two kilometres.

The Verkhiny Baskunchak facility was, at just under one thousand five hundred square kilometres, the second largest mock battlefield in the whole of the USSR.

Yarishlov examined the idea and found himself flanked by his two colonels.

"I understand your suggestion, Comrade... but wouldn't that make getting around them easier?"

"Only if they know they're there, Comrade General. In the last six sessions run with this general scenario, this is the place where they shake out from march order to battle order... without fail."

Yarishlov looked at the men either side of him for input.

Both were clearly mulling over the issue.

Zorin spoke first.

"And if they shake out beforehand... and detect the minefields and go around them?"

"Hold on."

Everyone focussed on Bailianov.

"If we advance the fields to this point, as young Harazan suggests... but we do so carelessly... so they can be seen... where would you deploy your tanks, Nikolay?"

Yarishlov had the answer already, but Zorin carefully considered his response.

"I'd be round the sides of it... both sides probably... with a view to a two-pronged assault... actually that would work better for me overall, so it's a non-starter I think."

Yarishlov laughed.

"I'm thinking that Edward Georgievich has something rather nasty up his sleeve. Tell him."

Bailianov took the wooden blocks representing his rocket and gun anti-tank troops and moved them forward, following them up with a few of his infantry groups.

Zorin swore.

"Fucking hell. Remind me never to fight you for real. That's a bitch."

"Isn't it just? By moving up the mines... and moving up the AT screen, we disorganise them quicker and further out, take them in this more favourable ground, and be back to our normal first line of defence long before they're back in condition to advance."

Both Bailianov and Harazan beamed, until Zorin threw his bucket of water on the idea.

"They'll cry foul of course. It's in advance of the agreed combat line, Comrades."

Their pink-skinned commander had a glint in his eye that no-one had noticed, not even Harazan, who taken his idea to his commander before the meeting.

Yarishlov had willingly participated in the little subterfuge to bolster the younger man's self-worth issues.

"There was an alteration to the written brief that our adversaries took with them. Did you not notice? And with your legendary attention to the smallest of matters too…"

Both colonels grabbed their copies and turned to the relevant page.

Bailianov laughed and dropped his copy on the table.

"So, you two hashed this up between you, eh?"

"Not at all. I played a small part, of course, but it was young Harazan's idea from the start."

"Remind me never to piss off my commander, Edward. What a bastard!"

Zorin got a curt nod by way of reply, Bailianov's rumble of laughter making him unable to speak effectively.

Yarishlov had altered the map work relative to the upcoming mock battle. It now reflected a different 'end of march' line, one that fitted in with Harazan's plans.

"Well, if nothing else, it'll teach the pair of them attention to detail!"

They all laughed, except Kriks, who adopted a face displaying mick anger and severity.

"Fucking officers picking on the poor front line soldiery again. Lying, deceitful lot! Just to make yourselves look good. I'm disgusted by the lot of you and I'll complain to Comrade Stalin first chance I get. He'll sort you out!"

"Now, now, you peasant. Calm yourself or the first chance you get will be when you get off the transport to Siberia."

The officers dissolved into laughter at Harazan's retort, as did Kriks, once he got over the shock of being harangued by the boy of the group.

"Fuck it. What do I care? Least we're all out of harm's way and the war's a million miles away. I need a drink."

He pulled out his flask and passed it round the cheerful group.

Whilst the war wasn't a million miles away, it was a long way off, but none of them realised that the war was coming to them, and that by the end of the following day, more of them would be dead than remained alive.